He saw many other things he'd have sketched if he'd had energy left over from medicine. He'd begun as an art student in Edinburgh, in rebellion from the Cole medical tradition, dreaming only of being a painter, for which the family had thought him touched. In his third year at the University of Edinburgh he was told he had artistic talent, but not enough. He was too literal. He lacked the vital imagination, the misty vision. 'You have the flame but lack the heat,' his professor of portraiture had told him, not unkindly but too plainly. He was crushed, until two things happened. In the dusty archives of the university library he came across an anatomical drawing. It was very old, perhaps pre-Leonardo, a nude male figure that appeared cut away to reveal the organs and blood vessels. It was entitled 'The Second Transparent Man' and with a wonderful shock he saw it had been drawn by one of his ancestors, whose signature was legible, 'Robert Jeffrey Cole, after the fashion of Robert Jeremy Cole.' It was evidence that at least several of his ancestors had been artists as well as medical men. And two days later he wandered into an operating theatre and saw William Fergusson, a genius who performed surgery with absolute certainty at lightning speed to minimize the patient's shock from the agonizing pain. For the first time, Rob J. understood the long line of Cole doctors, because the certainty came to him that the most glorious canvas could never be as precious as a single human life. In that moment, medicine claimed him.

This book is dedicated with love to Lorraine Gordon,
Irving Cooper, Cis and Ed Plotkin, Charlie Ritz, and
the lovely memory of Isa Ritz.

Also by Noah Gordon:

THE PHYSICIAN
CHOICES
THE LAST JEW
THE RABBI
THE DEATH COMMITTEE
THE JERUSALEM DIAMOND

SHAMAN
NOAH GORDON

sphere

SPHERE

First published in Great Britain in 1992
by Little, Brown and Company
This edition published by Warner Books in 1993
Reprinted 1993, 1994 (twice), 1996, 1997, 1998, 2001
Reprinted by Time Warner Paperbacks in 2002
Reprinted 2003, 2004
Reprinted by Time Warner Books in 2005
Reprinted by Sphere in 2006
Reprinted 2007, 2009 (twice), 2010, 2011, 2012, 2013, 2014

A CIP catalogue record for this book
is available from the British Library.

ISBN 978-0-7515-0082-0

Printed and bound in Great Britain by
Clays Ltd, St Ives plc

Papers used by Sphere are from well-managed forests
and other responsible sources.

MIX
Paper from
responsible sources
FSC® C104740
www.fsc.org

Sphere
An imprint of
Little, Brown Book Group
100 Victoria Embankment
London EC4Y 0DY

An Hachette UK Company
www.hachette.co.uk

www.littlebrown.co.uk

I
COMING HOME
April 22, 1864

1
Jiggety-Jig

The *Spirit of Des Moines* had sent signals ahead as it approached the Cincinnati depot in the coolness of dawn, detected by Shaman first as a delicate trembling barely perceived in the wooden station platform, then a pronounced shivering that he felt clearly, then a shaking. All at once the monster was there with its perfume of hot oiled metal and steam, charging toward him through the gloomy grey half-light, brass fittings gleaming in the black-dragon body, mighty piston-arms moving, the pale smoke cloud belching skyward like the spout of a whale and then drifting and trailing in dissolving tatters as the locomotive slid to a halt.

Inside the third car only a few of the hard wooden seats were empty, and he settled himself on one of them as the train shuddered and resumed its progress. Trains were still a novelty, but they involved travelling with too many people. He liked to ride a horse alone, lost in thought. The long car was crammed with soldiers, drummers, farmers, and assorted females with and without small children. The crying of the children didn't bother him at all, of course; but the car was redolent with a combination of stink–stale stockings, soiled nappies, poor digestions, sweaty and unwashed flesh, and the fug of cigars and pipes. The window seemed designed to be a challenge, but he was

3

large and strong and finally succeeded in raising it, an act that quickly proved an error. Three cars ahead, the tall stack of the locomotive cast forth, in addition to smoke, a mixture of soot, live and dead cinders, and ash, swept backward by the speed of the train, some of it finding its way through the open window. Soon an ember had set Shaman's new coat to smoking. Coughing and muttering in exasperation, he slammed the window closed and beat his coat until the spark was dead.

Across the aisle, a woman glanced at him and smiled. She was about ten years older than he, dressed fashionably but sensibly for travelling in a grey wool dress with a hoopless skirt trimmed in blue linen to highlight her blonde hair. Their eyes met for a moment before her glance returned to the tatting shuttle in her lap. Shaman was content to turn away from her; mourning wasn't a period in which to savour the games between men and women.

He had brought an important new book to read, but each time he tried to become engrossed in it, his thoughts returned to Pa.

The conductor had worked his way down the aisle behind him, and Shaman's first knowledge of his presence was when the man's hand touched his shoulder. Startled, he looked up into a florid face. The conductor's moustache ended in two waxed points and he had a greying ginger beard that Shaman liked because it left his mouth clearly visible. 'Must be deef!' the man said jovially, 'I've asked you three times for your ticket, sir.'

Shaman smiled at him, at ease because this was a situation he had met again and again, all his life. 'Yes. I *am* deaf,' he said, and handed the ticket over.

He watched the prairie unroll outside his window, but it wasn't something to keep his attention. There was a sameness to the terrain and, besides, a train flashed past things so fast they barely had time to register on his consciousness before they were gone. The best way to travel was on foot or on horseback; if you came to a place and you were hungry or had to piss, you could just turn in and

4

satisfy yourself. When the train came to that kind of place, it vanished in an instant blur. The book he had brought was *Hospital Sketches*, by a Massachusetts woman named Alcott who had been nursing the wounded since the beginning of the war, and whose picture of the agony and terrible conditions in army hospitals was creating a stir in medical circles. Reading it made things worse, because it caused him to imagine the suffering that might be facing his brother Bigger, who was missing in action as a Confederate scout. If, indeed, he reflected, Bigger wasn't among the nameless dead. That kind of thinking led him directly back to Pa over a road of choking grief, and he began looking about him desperately.

Near the front of the car, a skinny little boy started to vomit, and his mother, sitting white-faced among piles of bundles and three other small children, leapt to hold his forehead in order to keep him from soiling their belongings. When Shaman reached her, she had already started the unpleasant cleaning up.

'Maybe I can help him? I'm a doctor.'

'No money to pay thee.'

He waved it aside. The boy was sweating after the paroxysm of nausea but was cool to the touch. His glands weren't swollen and his eyes seemed bright enough.

She was Mrs Jonathan Sperber, she said in answer to his questions. From Lima, Ohio. Going to join her husband, homesteading with other Quakers in Springdale, fifty miles west of Davenport. The patient was Lester, eight years old. Wan, but with colour returning, he didn't appear to be gravely ill.

'What's he been eating?'

From a greasy flour sack her reluctant hands took a homemade sausage. It was green, and his nose confirmed what his eyes told him. Jesus.

'Uh . . . did you feed this to all of them?'

She nodded, and he looked at her other young ones with respect for their digestions.

'Well, you can't feed it to them anymore. It's gone way too high.'

5

Her mouth became a straight line. 'Not so high. It's well-salted; we've eaten worse. If it's that bad, the others would be sick and so would I.'

He knew enough about homesteaders of whatever religious persuasion to hear what she was really saying: the sausage was all there was; they ate spoiled sausage or nothing. He nodded and walked back to his own seat. His food was in a cornucopia twisted from sheets of the Cincinnati *Commercial*, three thick sandwiches of lean beef on dark German bread, a strawberry-jam tart, and two apples that he juggled for a few moments to make the children laugh. When he gave the food to Mrs Sperber, she opened her mouth as though to protest, but then she closed it. A homesteader's wife needs a healthy dose of realism. 'We are obliged to thee, friend,' she said.

Across the aisle, the blonde woman watched, but Shaman was trying the book again when the conductor came back. 'Say, I know you, it just come to me. Doc Cole's boy, from over to Holden's Crossing. Right?'

'Right.' Shaman understood it was his deafness that had identified him.

'You don't recall me. Frank Fletcher? Used to grow corn out there on the Hooppole road? Your daddy took care of the seven of us for more'n six years, till I sold out and joined the railroad and we moved into East Moline. I member sometimes when you was just a shadder you'd come with him, behind him on the horse, holdin' on for dear life.'

House calls had been the only way his father could spend time with his boys, and they had loved making house calls with him. 'I do recall you now,' he told Fletcher. 'And your place. White frame house, red barn with a tin roof. The original sod house you used for storage.'

'That was it, all right. Sometimes you came with him, sometimes your brother, what's his name?'

Bigger. 'Alex. My brother Alex.'

'Yeah. Where's he at now?'

'Army.' Not saying which one.

'Course he is. You studyin' to be a minister?' the conductor said, eyeing the black suit that twenty-four hours earlier had hung on a rack in Seligman's Store in Cincinnati.

'No, I'm a doctor too.'

'Lordy. Hardly seem old enough.'

He felt his lips tighten, because his age was harder to deal with than the deafness. 'I'm old enough. Been working in a hospital in Ohio. Mr Fletcher . . . my father died on Thursday.'

His smile faded so slowly, so completely, there was no mistaking the power of his sadness. 'Oh. We losin' all the best ones, ain't we? The war?'

'He was home at the time. The telegraph message said typhoid.'

The conductor shook his head. 'Will you kindly tell your momma the prayers of a whole lot of folks are with her?'

Shaman thanked him and said she'd appreciate that. '. . . Will vendors be getting on the train at any of the stations up ahead?'

'No. Everybody brings food on.' The trainman looked at him worriedly. 'You won't have a chance to buy the least thing until you change trains in Kankakee. Lord's sake, didn't they tell you that when you bought your ticket?'

'Oh, sure, I'm fine. I was just curious.'

The conductor touched the brim of his cap and went away. Presently the woman across the aisle stretched to reach the luggage rack and take down a good-sized oak splint basket, showing an attractive line from bosom to thigh, and Shaman went across the aisle and took it down for her.

She smiled at him. 'You must share mine,' she said firmly. 'As you can see, I've enough for any army!' He disagreed, but allowed perhaps she had enough for a platoon. Soon he was eating baked chicken, pumpkin bannock, potato pie. Mr Fletcher, coming back with a battered ham sandwich he had begged someplace for Shaman, grinned and declared that Dr Cole was better at foraging than the Army of the Potomac, and left again with the avowed intention of eating the sandwich himself.

Shaman ate more than he talked, shamed and astonished by his hunger in the face of grief. She talked more than she

7

ate. Her name was Martha McDonald. Her husband, Lyman, was sales agent in Rock Island for the American Farm Implements Co. She expressed regrets at Shaman's loss. When she served him, their knees brushed, a pleasant intimacy. He had long since learned that many women reacted to his deafness by being either repelled or aroused. Perhaps those in the latter group were stimulated by the prolonged eye contact; his eyes never left their faces while they spoke, a necessity caused by the fact that he had to read their lips.

He had no illusions about his looks. But if he wasn't handsome, he was large without being clumsy, he exuded the energy of young maleness and excellent health, and his regular features and the piercing blue eyes that had come to him from his father at least made him attractive. At any rate, none of this mattered where Mrs McDonald was concerned. He made it a rule – as inviolable as the necessity to scrub his hands before and after surgery – never to become involved with a married woman. As soon as he could manage it without adding insult to rejection, he thanked her for a fine lunch and moved himself back across the aisle.

He whiled away most of the afternoon with his book. Louisa Alcott wrote of operations done without agents to deaden the pain of the cutting, of men dying of poisoned wounds in hospitals reeking of filth and corruption. Death and suffering never ceased to make him sad, but needless pain and unnecessary death made him mad as hell. Late in the afternoon Mr Fletcher came by and announced that the train was travelling at forty-five miles per hour, three times the speed of a running horse, and without tiring! A telegraph message had told Shaman of his father's death the morning after it happened. He wonderingly considered that the world was hurtling into an era of swift transport and swifter communication, of new hospitals and methods of treatment, of surgery without torture. Tiring of grand thoughts, he covertly undressed Martha McDonald with his eyes and spent a pleasant, cowardly half-hour imagining a medical examination that progressed to seduction, the safest, most harmless violation of his Hippocratic oath.

The diversion didn't last. Pa! The closer he came to home, the more difficult it was to contemplate reality. Tears prickled behind his eyelids. Twenty-one-year-old physicians shouldn't cry in public. Pa . . . Night fell blackly, hours before they changed trains at Kankakee. Finally, and too soon, scarcely eleven hours after they had left Cincinnati, Mr Fletcher announced the station as 'Ro-o-ock I-I-I-Sla-a-and!'

The depot was an oasis of light. As he left the train, Shaman saw Alden at once, waiting for him under one of the gas lamps. The hired man patted his arm, giving him a sad smile and a familiar greeting. 'Home again, home again, jiggety-jig.'

'Hello, Alden.' They lingered for a moment under the light, in order to talk. 'How is she?' Shaman asked.

'Well, you know. Shit. Hasn't really struck her yet. She hasn't had much of a chance to be alone, with all the churchfolk, and the Reverend Blackmer right there in the house with her all day.'

Shaman nodded. His mother's inflexible piety was a trial to them all, but if the First Baptist Church could help them through this, he was grateful.

Alden had guessed correctly that Shaman would carry only one bag, allowing him to bring the trap, which had good springs, instead of the buckboard, which had none. The horse was Boss, a grey gelding his father had liked a lot; Shaman rubbed his nose before getting up into the seat. Once they were under way, conversation became impossible, for in the darkness he couldn't see Alden's face. Alden smelled the same, of hay and tobacco and raw wool and whisky. They crossed the Rocky River on the wooden bridge and then followed the road northeast at a trot. He couldn't see the land on either side, but he knew every tree and rock. In some places the road was hard to use because the snow was almost gone and the melt had turned it to mud. After driving for an hour, Alden reined up to breathe the horse where he always did, and he and Shaman got down and pissed on Hans Buckman's wet lower pasture and then walked a few minutes to get the kinks out. Soon they were crossing the narrow bridge over their own river, and the scariest part for Shaman came when the house and the barn loomed into view. Up to now it hadn't been unusual, Alden picking him up in Rock Island and driving him home, but when they arrived, Pa wouldn't be there. Not ever again.

Shaman didn't go right into the house. He helped Alden unhitch and followed him into the barn, lighting the oil lantern so they could talk. Alden reached into the hay and pulled out a bottle that was still about one-third full, but Shaman shook his head.

'You become Temperance up there in Ohio?'

'No.' It was complicated. He was a poor drinker, like all Coles, but, more important, a long time ago his father had explained to him that alcohol drove away the Gift. 'Just don't use it very much.'

'Yeh, you're like him. But tonight, you should.'

'Don't want her to smell it on me. I've got enough trouble with her without fighting about that. But leave it, will you? I'll come and get it on my way to privy, after she's gone to bed.'

Alden nodded. 'You be a little patient with her,' he said hesitantly. 'I know she can be hard, but . . .' He froze in astonishment as Shaman came and put his arms around him. That wasn't part of their relationship; men didn't hug men. The hired man patted Shaman's shoulder self-consciously. In only a moment Shaman had mercy on him and blew out the lantern and went through the dark yard to the kitchen, where, all others departed, his mother was waiting.

2
The Inheritance

Next morning, although the level of brown liquid in Alden's bottle had gone down only a couple of inches, Shaman's head throbbed. He had slept poorly; the old rope mattress hadn't been tightened and reknotted for years. He cut his chin shaving. At midmorning, none of those things mattered. His father had been buried quickly because he'd died of typhoid, but the service had been postponed until Shaman's return. The small First Baptist Church was jammed with three generations of patients who had been delivered by his father, treated for diseases, gunshot wounds, stabbings, groin rash, broken bones, and who only knew what else. The Reverend Lucian Blackmer delivered the eulogy – warmly enough to forestall the animosity of those in attendance, yet not so warmly that anyone might get the notion it was all right to die as Dr Robert Judson Cole had done, without having had the good sense to join the one true church. Shaman's mother several times had expressed her gratitude that, out of respect for her, Mr Blackmer had allowed her husband to be interred in the church burying ground.

All afternoon the Cole house was filled with people, most of them bringing dishes of roasts, forcemeats, puddings and pies, so much food the occasion took on an almost festive quality. Even Shaman found himself nibbling on slices of cold baked heart, his favourite meat. It had been Makwa-ikwa who had taught him to fancy it; he had thought it an Indian delicacy, like boiled dog or squirrel cooked with the innards, and it had been a happy discovery that many of his white neighbours also cooked the heart after butchering a cow or killing a deer. He was helping himself to another slice when he looked up to see Lillian Geiger crossing the room purposefully towards his mother. She was older and more worn, but she was still attractive; it was from her mother that Rachel had inherited her looks. Lillian had on her best black satin dress, with a black linen overdress and a folded white shawl, the little silver Star of David swinging against her fine bosom on its chain. He noticed she was careful whom she greeted; there were some who might reluctantly give polite greetings to a Jewess, but never to a Copperhead. Lillian was cousin to Judah Benjamin, the Confederate secretary of state, and her husband, Jay, had departed for his native South Carolina at the beginning of the war and joined the Army of the Confederacy with two of his three brothers.

By the time Lillian made her way to Shaman, her smile was strained. 'Aunt Lillian,' he said. She wasn't his aunt at all, but the Geigers and the Coles had been like kinfolk when he was growing up, and this was the way he'd always addressed her. Her eyes softened. 'Hello, Rob J.' she said, in the old, tender way; no one else called him that – it was what they called his father – but Lillian seldom had called him Shaman. She kissed him on the cheek and didn't bother to say she was sorry.

From what she heard from Jason, she said, which was rare, because his letters had to come across the lines, her husband was healthy and didn't seem to be in danger. An apothecary, he had been made steward of a small military hospital in Georgia when he had joined up, and now was commandant of a larger hospital on the banks of the James River in Virginia. His last letter, she said, contained the news that his brother, Joseph Reuben Geiger, a pharmacist like the other males in his family, but one who had turned cavalryman, had been killed in the fighting under Stuart.

12

Shaman nodded soberly, also not voicing the regrets people had come to take for granted.

And how were her children?

'Fine as fine. The boys have grown so, Jay won't know them! They eat like tigers.'

'And Rachel?'

'She lost her husband, Joe Regensberg, last June. He died of typhoid fever, like your father.'

'Oh,' he said heavily. 'I heard typhoid fever was common in Chicago last summer. Is she all right?'

'Oh, yes. Rachel is very well, as are her children. She has a son and a daughter.' Lillian hesitated. 'She is seeing another man, a cousin of Joe's. Their engagement will be announced after her year of mourning has been completed.'

Ah. Surprising it should still matter so, twist in so deeply. 'And how do you enjoy being a grandmother?'

'I like it very much,' she said, and, separating herself from him, passed on into quiet conversation with Mrs Pratt, whose land adjoined the Geiger place.

Towards evening, Shaman heaped a plate with food and took it up to Alden Kimball's stuffy little cabin that always smelled of wood smoke. The hired man sat on the bunk in his underwear, drinking from a jug. His feet were clean, he had bathed in honour of the funeral service. His other woollen undersuit, more grey than white, was hung to dry in the middle of the cabin, suspended by a cord tied between a nail in a beam and a stick placed between the shoulders.

Shaman shook his head when offered the jug. He sat in the single wooden chair and watched Alden eat. 'Been up to me, I'd have buried Pa on our own land, overlooking the river.'

Alden shook his head. 'She wouldn't of stood for it. Be too close to the Injun woman's grave. Before she was . . . killed,' he said carefully, 'folks talked enough about them two. Your ma was somethin' awful jealous.'

Shaman was itching to ask questions about Makwa and his mother and father, but it didn't feel right to gossip about his parents with Alden. Instead he waved goodbye and

13

made his departure. It was dusk when he walked down to the river, to the ruins of Makwa-ikwa's *hedonoso-te*. One end of the longhouse was intact, but the other end was fallen in, the logs and branches rotting, a certain home for snakes and rodents.

'I'm back,' he said.

He could feel Makwa's presence. She had been dead a long time; what he felt for her now was regret that paled against his sorrow over his father. He wanted comfort, but all he felt was her terrible anger, so certainly that the hair rose on the back of his neck. Not far away was her grave, unmarked but carefully tended, the grass cut, the border transplanted with wild yellow day lilies that had been taken from a nearby patch along the riverbank. The green shoots were already spiking through the wet earth. He knew it must have been his father who had taken care of the grave, and he knelt and pulled a couple of weeds from among the flowers.

It was almost dark. He fancied he could feel Makwa trying to tell him something. It had happened before, and he always half-believed that was why he could feel her rage, because she couldn't tell him who had killed her. He wanted to ask her what he should do next, with Pa gone. The wind made ripples on the water. He could see the first pale stars, and he shivered. There was a lot of winter's cold left, he thought as he went back to the house.

Next day he knew he should hang around the house in case there were laggard visitors, but he found he couldn't. He put on working clothes and spent the morning dipping sheep with Alden. There were new lambs and he castrated the males among them, Alden claiming the prairie oysters to fry with eggs for his dinner.

In the afternoon, bathed and again wearing the black suit, Shaman sat in the parlour with his mother. 'Best go through your father's things and decide who's to have what,' she said.

Even with her blonde hair mostly grey, his mother was one of the most interesting women he had ever seen, with

14

her beautiful long nose and sensitive mouth. Whatever it was that always got in their way was still there, but she could sense his reluctance. 'It has to be done sooner or later, Robert,' she said.

She was getting ready to bring empty dishes and plates to the church, where they would be picked up by visitors who had brought food to the funeral, and he offered to take them over for her. But she wanted to visit with Reverend Blackmer. 'You come too,' she said, but he shook his head, knowing it would entail a long session of listening to why he should allow himself to receive the Holy Spirit. Continually, the literalness of his mother's belief in heaven and in hell astonished him. Remembering her past arguments with his father, he knew she must be suffering special anguish now, because it had always tortured her that her husband, having refused baptism, wouldn't be waiting for her in paradise.

She held up her hand and pointed to the open window. 'Somebody comin' on a horse.'

She listened for a while and gave him a bitter grin. 'Woman asked Alden if the doctor's here, says her husband's hurt over to their place. Alden told her the doctor died. "Young doctor?" she asks. Alden says, "Oh, him, no, he's here."'

Shaman thought it was funny too. Already she'd gone straight to where Rob J.'s medical bag waited in its customary place by the door, and she handed it to her son. 'Take the wagon, it's all hitched up. I'll go to church later.'

The woman was Liddy Geacher. She and her husband, Henry, had bought the Buchanan place while Shaman was away. He knew the way well, it was only a few miles. Geacher had fallen from the haymow. They found him still lying where he'd landed, breathing in shallow, painful gasps. He groaned when they tried to undress him, so Shaman cut away his clothing, careful to separate the seams so Mrs Geacher could sew the garments together again. There was no blood, just nasty bruising and a puffed-up left ankle. From the bag Shaman took his father's stethoscope.

'Come here, please. I want you to tell me what you hear,' he said to the woman, and fitted the pieces into her ears. Mrs Geacher's eyes widened when he placed the bell to her husband's chest. He let her listen for a good long time, holding the bell in his left hand while he felt the man's pulse with the fingertips of his right hand.

'Thump-thump-thump-thump-thump!' she whispered.

Shaman smiled. Henry Geacher's pulse was fast, and who could blame him. 'What else you hear? Take your time.'

She listened at length.

'No soft crackling, like someone was crumpling dry straw?'

She shook her head. 'Thump-thump-thump.'

Good. No broken rib had pierced a lung. He relieved her of the stethoscope and then went over every inch of Geacher's surface with his hands. With no hearing, he had to be more careful and observant with every one of his other senses than most doctors. When he held the man's hands, he nodded in satisfaction at what the Gift told him. Geacher had been lucky, landing on enough old hay to make the difference. He'd banged up his ribs, but Shaman couldn't find any sign of a bad fracture. He thought the fifth through the eighth ribs probably were cracked, and possibly the ninth. When he bound the ribs, Geacher breathed easier. Shaman strapped up the ankle and then took a bottle of his father's painkiller from the bag, mostly alcohol with a little morphia and a few herbs. 'He's going to hurt. Two teaspoonfuls every hour.'

A dollar for the house call, fifty cents for the dressings, fifty cents for the medicine. But only part of the job was done. The Geachers' nearest neighbours were the Reismans, a ten-minute ride away. Shaman went there and talked to Tod Reisman and his son Dave, who agreed they could pitch in and keep the Geacher farm going a week or so, till Henry was back on his feet.

He drove Boss slowly on the way home, savouring spring. The black earth was still too wet to plough. That morning in the Cole pastures he'd seen that the low flowers were arriving, bird's-foot violet, orange puccoon, pink prairie

16

phlox, and in a few weeks the plains would be alive with taller colour at its brightest. With pleasure, he breathed in the familiar heavy sweetness of manured fields.

When he got home, the house was empty and the egg basket was missing from its hook, which meant his mother was in the henhouse. He didn't seek her out. He examined the medical bag before replacing it by the door, as though he were seeing it for the first time. The leather was worn, but it was good cowhide and would last and last. Inside, the instruments, dressings, and medications were as his father's own hands had arranged them, neat, in order, ready for anything.

Shaman went to the study and began a methodical inspection of his father's belongings, rummaging through desk drawers, opening the leather chest, separating things into three categories: for his mother, first choice of all small objects that might hold emotional value; for Bigger, the half dozen sweaters Sarah Cole had knitted from their own wool to keep the doctor warm on cold night calls, their father's fishing and hunting equipment, and a treasure new enough so Shaman saw it for the first time, a Colt .44-caliber Texas Navy revolver with black-walnut grips and a nine-inch rifled barrel. The gun was a surprise and shock. Even though his pacifist father had agreed, finally, to treat Union troops, it was always with the clear understanding that he was a noncombatant who wouldn't bear arms; why, then, had he purchased this obviously expensive weapon?

The medical books, the microscope, the medical bag, the pharmacy of herbs and drugs, would go to Shaman. In the chest under the microscope case was a collection of books, a number of volumes of stitched ledger paper.

When Shaman looked through them, he saw that they were his father's lifetime journal.

The volume he picked at random had been written in 1842. Leafing through it, Shaman found a rich, haphazard collection of medical notes, pharmacology, and intimate thoughts. The journal was sprinkled with sketches – faces, anatomical drawings, a full-length nude drawing of a woman; she was, he realized, his mother. He studied the

17

younger face and stared fascinated at forbidden flesh, aware that beneath the unmistakably pregnant belly there had been a foetus that would become himself. He opened another volume that had been written earlier, when Robert Judson Cole was a young man in Boston, fresh off the boat from Scotland. It too contained a female nude, this time with a face unknown to Shaman, the features indistinct but the vulva drawn in clinical detail, and he found himself reading of a sexual affair his father had had with a woman in his boardinghouse.

As he read the entire account, he grew younger. The years fell away, his body regressed, the earth reversed its spinning and the fragile mysteries and torments of youth were restored. He was a boy again, reading forbidden books in this library, looking for words and pictures that would reveal every one of the secret, base, perhaps thoroughly wonderful things men did with women. He stood and trembled, listening lest his father should emerge through the door and find him there.

Then he felt the vibration of the back door being firmly closed as his mother came in with her eggs, and he forced himself to close the book and replace it in the chest.

At supper he told his mother he had begun to go through his father's belongings and would carry an empty box down from the attic in order to pack away the things that would go to his brother.

Between them hung the unspoken question of whether Alex was alive to return and use them, but then Sarah made up her mind to nod. 'Good,' she said, obviously relieved that he was getting to the task.

That night, sleepless, he told himself reading the journals would make him a voyeur, an intruder into his parents' lives, perhaps even into their bedroom, and that he must burn the books. But logic told him his father had written them to record the essence of his life, and now Shaman lay in the sagging bed and wondered what the truth had been about how Makwa-ikwa had lived and died, and worried lest truth might contain grievous dangers.

Finally he got up and lighted the lamp, carrying it down

18

the hall stealthily so as not to awaken her.

He trimmed the smoking wick and turned the flame up as high as it would go. That produced a light barely adequate for reading. The study was uncomfortably cold, this time of night. But Shaman took the first book and started to read, and presently he was unaware of the illumination or the temperature, as he began to learn more than he had ever wanted to know about his father and about himself.

II
FRESH CANVAS,
NEW PAINTING
March 11, 1839

3
The Immigrant

Rob J. Cole first saw the New World on a foggy spring day as the packet *Cormorant* – a clumsy ship with three squat masts and a mizzen sail, but the pride of the Black Ball Line – was sucked into a commodious harbour by the incoming tide and dropped its hook in the choppy swells. East Boston wasn't much, a couple of rows of ill-built wooden houses, but from one of the piers, for three pence, he took a little steamboat ferry that threaded its way through an impressive array of shipping, across the harbour to the main waterfront, a sprawl of tenements and shops smelling reassuringly of rotting fish, bilges, and tarred rope, like any Scots port.

He was tall and broad, larger than most. When he walked the crooked cobblestoned streets away from the water, it was hard going because the voyage had made him bone-weary. On his left shoulder he bore his heavy trunk, while under his right arm, as if he carried a woman by the waist, was a very large stringed instrument. He absorbed America through his pores. Narrow streets, scarcely allowing room for wagons and carriages. Most buildings of wood or constructed of very red brick. Shops well-supplied with goods, flaunting colourful signs with gilded letters. He tried not to ogle the females entering and leaving the shops, although he had an almost drunken urge to smell a woman.

He peeked into a hotel, the American House, but was

intimidated by chandeliers and Turkish carpets, knowing its rates were too high. In an eating house on Union Street he had a bowl of fish soup and asked two waiters to recommend a boarding house that was clean and cheap.

'Make up your mind, lad, it'll either be one or the other,' one of them said. But the other waiter shook his head and sent him to Mrs Burton's on Spring Lane.

The one available room had been built as servant's quarters and shared the attic with the rooms of the hired man and the maid. It was tiny, up three flights of stairs to a cubby under the eaves, certain to be hot in the summer and cold in the winter. There was a narrow bed, a little table with a cracked washbowl, and a white chamber pot covered by a linen towel embroidered with blue flowers. Breakfasts – porridge, biscuits, one hen's egg – came with the room for a dollar and fifty cents a week, Louise Burton told him. She was a sallow widow in her sixties, with a direct stare. 'What is that object?'

'It's called a viola da gamba.'

'You earn your living as a musician?'

'I play for my pleasure. I earn my living as a doctor.'

She nodded doubtfully. She demanded payment in advance and told him of an ordinary off Beacon Street where he could get his dinners for another dollar a week.

He fell into the bed as soon as she was gone. All that afternoon and evening and night he slept, dreamless save that somehow he still felt the pitch and toss of the vessel, but in the morning he awakened young again. When he went down to attack his breakfast, he sat next to another boarder, Stanley Finch, who worked in a hatter's shop on Summer Street. From Finch he learned two facts of prime interest: water could be heated and poured into a tin tub by the porter, Lem Raskin, at a charge of twenty-five cents; and Boston had three hospitals, the Massachusetts General, the Lying-In, and the Eye and Ear Infirmary. After breakfast he soaked blissfully in a bath, scrubbing only when the water cooled, and then laboured to make his clothing as presentable as possible. When he came down the stairs, the maid was on her hands and knees washing the landing. Her bare

24

arms were freckled, and her gluteal roundnesses quivered with the vigour of her scrubbing. A sullen tabby's face looked up at him as he passed, and he saw that beneath her cap her red hair was the colour that pleased him least, the shade of wet carrots.

At the Massachusetts General Hospital he waited half the morning and then was interviewed by Dr Walter Channing, who wasted no time in telling him the hospital needed no additional physicians. The experience was quickly repeated at the other two hospitals. At the Lying-In, a young doctor named David Humphreys Storer shook his head sympathetically. 'Harvard Medical School turns out doctors every year who have to stand in line for staff appointments, Dr Cole. The truth is, a newcomer has little chance.'

Rob J. knew what Dr Storer wasn't saying: some of the local graduates had the help of family prestige and connections, just as in Edinburgh he had enjoyed the advantage of being one of the medical Coles.

'I would try another city, perhaps Providence or New Haven,' Dr Storer said, and Rob J. muttered his thanks and took his leave. But a moment later, Storer came hurrying after him. 'There is a remote possibility,' he said. 'You must talk with Dr Walter Aldrich.'

The physician's office was in his home, a well-kept white frame house on the south side of the meadowlike green they called the Common. It was visiting hours, and Rob J. waited a long time. Dr Aldrich proved to be portly, with a full grey beard that failed to hide a mouth like a slash. He listened as Rob J. spoke, interrupting now and again with a question. 'University Hospital in Edinburgh? Under the surgeon William Fergusson? Why would you leave an assistantship like that?'

'I'd have been transported to Australia if I hadn't fled.' He was aware his only hope was in the truth. 'I wrote a pamphlet that led to an industrial riot against the English crown, which for years has been bleeding Scotland. There was fighting, and people were killed.'

'Plainly spoken,' Dr Aldrich said, nodding. 'A man must struggle for his country's welfare. My father and my

25

grandfather each fought the English.' He regarded Rob J. quizzically. 'There is an opening. With a charity that sends physicians to visit the city's indigent.'

It sounded like a grubby, inauspicious job; Dr Aldrich said most visiting physicians were paid fifty dollars a year and were happy to receive the experience, and Rob asked himself what a doctor from Edinburgh could learn about medicine in a provincial slum.

'If you'll join the Boston Dispensary, I'll arrange for you to assist evenings as docent in the anatomy laboratory of the Tremont Medical School. That will bring you another two hundred and fifty dollars a year.'

'I doubt I can exist on three hundred dollars, sir. I have almost no funds.'

'I have nothing else to offer. Actually, the annual income would be three hundred and fifty dollars. The work is in District Eight, for which the dispensary's board of governors recently voted to pay the visiting physician one hundred dollars instead of fifty.'

'Why does District Eight pay twice as much as other areas?'

Now it was Dr Aldrich who chose candour. 'It is where the Irish live,' he said in a tone as thin and bloodless as his lips.

Next morning Rob J. climbed creaking stairs at 109 Washington Street and entered the cramped apothecary's shop that was the Boston Dispensary's only office. It was already crowded with physicians awaiting their daily assignments. Charles K. Wilson, the manager, was brusquely efficient when Rob's turn came. 'So. New doctor for District Eight, is it? Well, the neighbourhood's been unattended. These await you,' he said, hanging over a wad of slips, each bearing a name and address.

Wilson explained the rules and described the Eighth district. Broad Street ran between the ocean docks and the looming bulk of Fort Hill. When the city was new, the neighbourhood was formed by merchants who built large residences in order to be near their warehouses and

26

waterfront businesses. In time, they moved on to other, finer streets, and the houses were occupied by working-class Yankees, then in turn by poorer native tenants as the structures were subdivided; and finally by the Irish immigrants who came pouring from the holds of ships. By then the huge houses were run-down and in disrepair, subdivided and subrented at unfair weekly rates. Warehouses were converted into hives of tiny rooms without a single source of light or air, and living space was so scarce that beside and behind every existing structure there had risen ugly, leaning shacks. The result was a vicious slum in which as many as twelve people lived in a single room – wives, husbands, brothers, sisters, and children, sometimes all sleeping in the same bed.

Following Wilson's directions, he found District Eight. The stink of Broad Street, the miasma given off by too few toilets used by too many people, was the smell of poverty, the same in every city in the world. Something within him, tired of being a stranger, welcomed the Irish faces because they shared his Celticness. His first ticket was made out to Patrick Geoghegan of Half Moon Place; the address might as well have been on the sun, for almost immediately he became lost in the maze of alleys and unsigned private ways that ran off Broad Street. Finally he gave a dirty-faced boy a penny to lead him into a tiny crowded court. Inquiries sent him to an upper storey of a neighbouring house, where he made his way through rooms inhabited by two other families to reach the tiny quarters of the Geoghegans. A woman sat and searched a child's scalp by candlelight.

'Patrick Geoghegan?'

Rob J. had to repeat the name before he won a hoarse whisper. 'Me Da . . . dead these five days, of brain fever.'

It was what the people of Scotland, too, called any high fever that preceded death. 'I'm sorry for your trouble, madam,' he said quietly, but she didn't even look up.

Downstairs he stood and gazed. He knew every country had streets like this, reserved for the existence of injustice so crushing it creates its own sights and sounds and odours: a whey-faced child seated on a stoop gnawing a bare bacon

27

rind like a dog with a bone; three unmatched shoes worn beyond all repair, adorning the littered dirt lane; a drunken male voice making a hymn of a maudlin song about the green hills of a fled land; curses shouted as passionately as prayers; the smell of boiled cabbage dampened by the stink, everywhere, of overflowed drains and many kinds of dirt. He was familiar with the poor neighbourhoods of Edinburgh and Paisley, and with the stone row-houses of a dozen towns where adults and children left home before daybreak, plodding to the cotton factories and woollen mills, not to drag themselves home until well after night had fallen again, pedestrians only of the dark. The irony of his situation struck him: he had fled Scotland because he'd fought the forces that formed slums such as this, and now in a new country his nose was being rubbed in it.

His next ticket was for Martin O'Hara of Humphrey Place, a shed-and-shanty area cut into the slope of Fort Hill and reached by means of a fifty-foot wooden stairway so steep as to be virtually a ladder. Alongside the stairway was a wooden open gutter down which the raw wastes of Humphrey Place oozed and flowed, dropping to add to the troubles of Half Moon Place. Despite the misery of his surroundings, he climbed quickly, becoming acquainted with his practice.

It was exhausting work, yet at the end of the afternoon he could look forward only to a meagre, worried meal and an evening at his second job. Neither job would provide him with money for a month, and the funds he had left wouldn't pay for many dinners.

The dissection laboratory and classroom of the Tremont Medical School was a single large room over Thomas Metcalfe's apothecary shop at 35 Tremont Place. It was run by a group of Harvard-trained professors who, disturbed by the rambling medical education offered by their alma mater, had designed a controlled three-year programme of courses they believed would make better doctors.

The professor of pathology under whom he would work as dissection docent proved to be a short, bandy-legged man about ten years older than himself. His nod was perfunctory. 'I am Holmes. Are you an experienced docent, Dr Cole?'

'No. I've never been a docent. But I'm experienced at surgery and dissection.'

Professor Holmes' cool nod said: We shall see. He outlined briefly the preparations to be completed before his lecture. Except for a few details, it was a routine with which Rob J. was familiar. He and Fergusson had done autopsies every morning before going on rounds, for research and for the practice that enabled them to maintain their speed when operating on the living. Now he removed the sheet from the skinny cadaver of a youth, then donned a long grey dissection apron and laid out the instruments as the class began to arrive.

There were only seven medical students. Dr Holmes stood at a lectern to one side of the dissection table. 'When I studied anatomy in Paris,' he began, 'any student could buy a whole body for only fifty sous at a place that sold them each day at high noon. But today cadavers for study are in short supply. This one, a boy of sixteen who died this morning of a congestion of the lungs, comes to us from the State Board of Charities. You will do no dissecting this evening. At a future class the body will be divided among you, two of you getting an arm for study, two a leg, the rest of you sharing the trunk.'

As Dr Holmes described what the docent was doing, Rob J. opened the boy's chest and began to remove the organs and weigh them, announcing each weight in a clear voice so the professor could record it. After that, his duties consisted of pointing to various sites in the body to illustrate something the professor was saying. Holmes had a halting delivery and a high voice, but Rob J. quickly saw that the students considered his lectures a treat. He wasn't afraid of salty language. Illustrating how the arm moves, he delivered a ferocious uppercut at the air. While explaining the mechanics of the leg, he did a high kick, and to show how the hips worked, a belly dance. The students ate it up. At the end of the lecture they crowded around Dr Holmes with questions. As the professor answered them, he watched his new docent place the cadaver and the anatomical specimens in the pickling tank, wash down the table, and then wash and dry the instruments and put them away. Rob J. was scrubbing his own hands and arms when the last student left.

'You were quite adequate.'

Why not, he wanted to say, since it was a job a bright student could have done? Instead, he found himself asking meekly if advance payment was possible.

'I'm told you work for the dispensary. I worked for the dispensary myself once. Goddamned hard work and guaranteed penury, but instructional.' Holmes took two five-dollar notes from his purse. 'Is the first half-month's salary sufficient?'

Rob J. tried to keep the relief from his voice as he assured Dr Holmes it was. They turned down the lamps together, saying goodnight at the bottom of the stairs and going separate ways. He was giddily conscious of the notes in his pocket. As he passed Allen's Bakery, a man was removing trays of pastries from the window, closing for the night, and Rob J. went in and bought two blackberry tarts, a celebration.

He intended to eat them in his room, but in the house on Spring Street the maid was still up, finishing the dishwashing, and he turned into the kitchen and held out the pastries. 'One is yours, if you help me steal some milk.'

She smiled. 'Needn't whisper. She's asleep.' She pointed toward Mrs Burton's room on the second floor. 'Nothin' wakes her once she sleeps.' She dried her hands and fetched the milk can and two clean cups. They both enjoyed the conspiracy of the theft. Her name was Margaret Holland, she told him; everyone called her Meg. When they finished their treat, a milky trace remained in the corner of her full mouth, and he reached across the table and with a steady surgeon's fingertip obliterated the evidence.

4

The Anatomy Lesson

Almost at once he saw the terrible flaw in the system used by the dispensary. The names on the tickets he was given each morning didn't belong to the sickest people in the Fort Hill neighbourhood. The health-care plan was unfair and undemocratic; treatment tickets were divided among the wealthy donors to the charity, who passed them out to whomever they pleased, most of the time to their own servants as rewards. Frequently Rob J. had to search out a tenement to care for someone with a minor complaint, while just down the hall an unemployed pauper lay dying of medical neglect. The oath he'd taken when he had become a physician forbade him to leave the desperately ill patient untreated, yet if he was to keep his job, he had to turn in a large number of tickets and report that he had treated the patients whose names were on them.

One evening at the medical school he discussed the problem with Dr Holmes. 'When I was with the dispensary I collected treatment tickets from my family's friends who donated money,' the professor said. 'I'll collect tickets from them again, and give them to you.'

Rob J. was grateful, but his spirits didn't rise. He knew he wouldn't be able to collect enough blank treatment tickets to care for all the needy patients in District Eight. That would require an army of physicians.

The brightest part of his day often happened when he returned to Spring Street late in the evening and spent a few minutes eating contraband leftovers with Meg Holland. He fell into the habit of bringing her small bribes, a pocketful of roasted chestnuts, a piece of maple sugar, some yellow pippins. The Irish girl told him the gossip of the house: how Mr Stanley Finch, second floor front, bragged – bragged! – he'd got a girl in the family way in Gardner and run off; how Mrs Burton could be unpredictably very nice or a holy bitch; how the hired man, Lemuel Raskin, who had the room adjoining Rob J.'s had a powerful thirst.

When Rob had been there a week, she mentioned ever so casually that whenever Lem was given half a pint of brandy he swallowed it all at once and thereupon couldn't be awakened.

Rob J. made Lemuel a gift of brandy the following evening.

It was hard to wait, and more than once he told himself he was a fool, that the girl had just been prattling. The old house had a variety of night-time noises, random squeaking of boards, Lem's gutteral snoring, mysterious poppings in the wood siding. Finally there was the smallest sound at the door, really only the suggestion of a knock, and when he opened it, Margaret Holland slipped into his cubby carrying the faint odours of womanhood and dishwater, and whispered it would be a cool night and held out her excuse, a threadbare extra blanket.

Barely three weeks after the dissection of the youth's cadaver, the Tremont Medical School was sent another bonanza, the body of a young woman who had died in prison of puerperal fever after birthing a child. That evening Dr Holmes was held up at the Massachusetts General and Dr David Storer of the Lying-In served as professor. Prior to Rob J.'s dissection, Dr Storer insisted upon giving the docent's hands the closest of inspections. 'No hangnails or breaks in the skin?'

'No, sir,' he said a bit resentfully, unable to see a reason for the interest in his hands.

32

When the anatomy lesson was over, Storer told the class to move to the other side of the room, where he would demonstrate how to conduct internal examinations of patients who were pregnant or had female problems. 'You may find the modest New England woman will shy away from such examination or even forbid it,' he said. 'Yet it's your responsibility to gain her confidence in order to help her.'

Dr Storer was accompanied by a heavy woman in an advanced stage of pregnancy, perhaps a prostitute hired for the demonstration. Professor Holmes arrived while Rob J. was cleaning the dissection area and setting it in order. When he finished, he started to join the students who were examining the woman, but an agitated Dr Holmes suddenly barred his way. 'No, no!' the professor said. 'You must scrub yourself and leave here. At once, Dr Cole! Go to the Essex Tavern and wait there while I gather together some notes and papers.'

Rob did so, mystified and annoyed. The tavern was just around the corner from the school. He ordered ale because he was nervous, although it occurred to him that perhaps he was being fired as docent and shouldn't spend the money. He had time to finish only half a glass before a second-year student named Harry Loomis appeared bearing two notebooks and several reprints of medical articles.

'The poet sent these.'

'Who?'

'Don't you know? He's Boston's laureate. When Dickens visited America, it was Oliver Wendell Holmes who was asked to write lines welcoming him. But you needn't worry, he's a better doctor than he is a poet. Capital lecturer, isn't he?' Loomis cheerfully signalled for a glass of ale of his own. 'Although a bit dotty about washing one's hands. Thinks dirt causes infection in wounds!'

Loomis also had brought a note scrawled on the back of an overdue laudanum bill from the drug house of Weeks & Potter: *Dr Cole, read these before returning to the Tremont Med Schl tomorrow night. Without fail, pls. Sinc yrs, Holmes.*

He began to read almost as soon as he got back to his room at Mrs Burton's, at first somewhat resentfully, and then with growing interest. The facts had been told by Holmes in a paper published in the *New England Quarterly Journal of Medicine* and abstracted in the *American Journal of the Medical Sciences*. At first they were familiar to Rob J. because they precisely paralleled what he knew was happening in Scotland – a large percentage of pregnant women sickening with extremely high temperatures that quickly led to a condition of general infection and then to death.

But Dr Holmes' paper related that a Newton, Massachusetts, physician named Whitney, assisted by two medical students, had undertaken a post-mortem examination of a woman who had died of puerperal fever. Dr Whitney had had a hangnail on one finger, and one of the medical students had a small raw scar from a burn on his hand. Neither man had felt that his injury was more than an unimportant nuisance, but within a few days, the doctor's arm began to tingle. Halfway up his arm was a red spot the size of a pea, from which a fine red line extended to the hangnail. The arm rapidly swelled to twice its normal size, and he developed a very high fever and had uncontrollable vomiting. Meanwhile, the student with the burned hand also became febrile; within a few days his condition deteriorated rapidly. He turned purple, his belly became very swollen, and finally he died. Dr Whitney came very close to death, but slowly improved and eventually recovered. The second medical student, who had had no cuts or sores on his hands when they had done the autopsy, developed no serious symptoms.

The case was reported, and Boston doctors discussed the apparent connection between open sores and infection with puerperal fever, but gained few insights. However, several months later, a physician in the town of Lynn examined a case of puerperal fever while he had open sores on his hands, and within a few days he was dead of massive infection. At a meeting of the Boston Society for Medical Improvement, an interesting question had been raised. What if the dead doctor had not had any sores on his hands?

Even if he hadn't become infected, wouldn't he have carried the infectious material around with him, spreading disaster whenever he happened to touch another patient's wounds or sores, or the raw womb of a new mother?

Oliver Wendell Holmes hadn't been able to get the question out of his mind. For weeks he had researched the subject, visiting libraries, consulting his own records, and begging case histories from doctors who had obstetric practices. Like a man working an intricate picture puzzle, he brought together a conclusive collection of evidence that covered a century of medical practice on two continents. The cases had appeared sporadically and unnoticed in the medical literature. It was only when they were sought out and brought together that they buttressed one another and made a startling and horrifying argument: puerperal fever was caused by doctors, nurses, midwives, and hospital attendants who, after touching a contagious patient, went on to examine uncontaminated women and doomed them to a feverish death.

Puerperal fever was a pestilence caused by the medical profession, Holmes wrote. Once a doctor realized this, it must be considered a crime – murder – for him to infect a woman.

Rob read the papers twice and then lay there stunned.

He yearned to be able to scoff, but Holmes' case histories and statistics weren't vulnerable to anyone with an open mind. How could this runty New World doctor know more than Sir William Fergusson? On occasion Rob had helped Sir William perform autopsies on patients who had died of puerperal fever. Subsequently they had examined pregnant women. And now he forced himself to remember the women who had died following the examinations.

It seemed that, after all, these provincials had things to teach him about the art and science of medicine.

He got up to trim the lamp so he could read the material still another time, but there was a scratching at the door and Margaret Holland slipped into the room. She was shy about taking off her clothes, but there was no place to go for privacy in the small room, and anyway, he was already undressing too. She folded her things and removed her crucifix. Her body was plump but muscular. Rob kneaded the indentations her whalebone stays had left in her flesh and was progressing to more rousing caresses when he stopped, struck by a sudden terrifying thought.

Leaving her in the bed, he got up and splashed water into the washbowl. While the girl stared as though he had taken leave of his senses, he soaped and scrubbed his hands. Again. Again. And again. Then he dried them and returned to the bed and resumed their love play. Soon, despite herself, Margaret Holland began to giggle.

'You are the strangest young gentleman I have ever met,' she whispered into his ear.

36

5
The God-Cursed District

At night when he returned to his room he was so tired that he was able to play the viola da gamba only infrequently. His bowing was rusty but the music was a balm, unfortunately denied him because Lem Raskin soon hammered on the wall to tell him to be quiet. He couldn't afford to feed Lem whisky in order to provide for music as well as sex, so music suffered. A journal in the medical-school library recommended that following intercourse a woman who didn't wish to become a mother should douche with an infusion of alum and white-oak bark, but he was certain Meggy couldn't be depended upon to douche regularly. Harry Loomis took it very seriously when Rob J. sought his advice, sending him to a neat grey house on the south side of Cornhill. Mrs Cynthis Worth was white-haired and matronly. She smiled and nodded at Harry's name. 'I give good price to medical folk.'

Her product was made from the intestinal cecum of sheep, a natural cavity of gut, open at one end and thus admirably suited for conversion by Mrs Worth. She was as prideful about holding up her wares as if she managed a fish market and they were sea creatures with eyes bejeweled in freshness. Rob J. drew a breath when he heard their price, but Mrs Worth was unperturbed. 'The labour is considerable,' she said. She described how the ceca had to be soaked for hours in water; turned inside out; macerated again in a weak alkaline solution that was changed every twelve hours; scraped carefully until they were free of mucous membrane, leaving the peritoneal and muscular coats exposed to a vapour of burning brimstone; washed in soap and water; blown up and dried; cut on the open ends to lengths of eight inches; and furnished with red or blue ribbons so they could be tied shut, offering protection. Most gentlemen purchased by threes, she said, as they were cheapest that way.

Rob J. bought one. He expressed no colour preference, but the ribbon was blue.

'With care, one may serve you.' She explained that it could be used again and again if washed after each use, blown up and powdered. When Rob left with his purchase, she bade him a cheerful good day and asked to be recommended to his colleagues and patients.

Meggy hated the sheath. She was more appreciative of a gift Harry Loomis gave to Rob, telling him to have a wonderful time. It was a bottle containing a colourless liquid, nitrous oxide, called laughing gas by the medical students and young doctors who had taken to using it for entertainment. Rob poured some into a rag and he and Meggy sniffed it before making love. The experience was an unqualified success – never had their bodies seemed droller or the physical act more comically absurd.

Beyond the pleasures of the bed there was nothing between them. When the act was slow, there was a little tenderness, and when it was furiously physical there was more desperation than passion. When they spoke, she tended either to gossip about the boarding house, which bored him, or to reminisce about the old country, which he avoided because memory caused him pain. There was no contact between their minds or souls. The chemical hilarity they shared a single time through the use of nitrous oxide was never approached again, for their sexual gaiety had been noisy; though the drunken Lem had been oblivious, they knew they had been lucky to go undetected. They laughed together only once more, when Meggy peevishly

38

observed that the sheath must have come from a ram, and christened it Old Horny. He was troubled by the extent that he was using her. Observing that her petticoat was exceedingly darned, he bought her a new one, a guilt offering. It pleased her tremendously, and he sketched her in his journal reclining on his narrow bed, a plump girl with a smiling cat's face.

He saw many other things he'd have sketched if he'd had energy left over from medicine. He'd begun as an art student in Edinburgh, in rebellion from the Cole medical tradition, dreaming only of being a painter, for which the family had thought him touched. In his third year at the University of Edinburgh he was told he had artistic talent, but not enough. He was too literal. He lacked the vital imagination, the misty vision. 'You have the flame but lack the heat,' his professor of portraiture had told him, not unkindly but too plainly. He was crushed, until two things happened. In the dusty archives of the university library he came across an anatomical drawing. It was very old, perhaps pre-Leonardo, a nude male figure that appeared cut away to reveal the organs and blood vessels. It was entitled 'The Second Transparent Man' and with a wonderful shock he saw it had been drawn by one of his ancestors, whose signature was legible, 'Robert Jeffrey Cole, after the fashion of Robert Jeremy Cole.' It was evidence that at least several of his ancestors had been artists as well as medical men. And two days later he wandered into an operating theatre and saw William Fergusson, a genius who performed surgery with absolute certainty at lightning speed to minimize the patient's shock from the agonizing pain. For the first time, Rob J. understood the long line of Cole doctors, because the certainty came to him that the most glorious canvas could never be as precious as a single human life. In that moment, medicine claimed him.

From the start of his training he had what his Uncle Ranald, who was in general practice near Glasgow, called 'the Cole gift' – the ability to tell, by holding a patient's hands, whether he or she would live or die. It was a diagnostic sixth sense, part instinct, intuition, part input from inherited sensors no one could identify or understand, but it worked so long as it wasn't blunted by the overuse of alcohol. For a physician it was a true gift, but now, transplanted to a distant land, it was one that ground Rob J.'s spirit, because District Eight had more than its share of people who were dying.

The God-cursed district, as he had come to think of it, dominated his existence. The Irish had arrived with the greatest expectations. In the old country a labourer's daily wage was sixpence, when there was work. In Boston there was less unemployment and workers earned more, but they were worked fifteen hours a day, seven days a week. They paid high rents for their slums, they paid more for their food, and here there was no little garden, no tiny patch for growing mealy bog apples, no cow for milk, no pig for bacon. The district haunted him with its poverty and filth and its needs that should have paralyzed him but instead stimulated him to work like a tumblebug attempting to move a mountain of sheep shit. Sundays should have been his to use as a brief time of recovery from the numbing work of the terrible week. Sunday mornings, even Meg got a few hours off to allow her to go to mass. But each Sunday found Rob J. back in the district, freed from the necessity of conforming to the schedule dictated by the appointment slips, able to donate hours that were his, hours he didn't have to steal. It took him no time at all to establish a real if mostly unpaid, Sunday practice, for everywhere he looked there was illness, injury, disease. Word spread very quickly of the physician who was able and willing to converse in the Erse, the ancient Gaelic language shared by the Scots and the Irish. When they heard him uttering the sounds of their old home, even the bitterest and foulest-tempered brightened and beamed. *Beannacht De ort, dochtuir oig* – Bless you, young doctor! – they called after him in the streets. One person told another about the lad of a doctor who 'had the tongue,' and soon he was speaking the Erse every day. But if he was adored on Fort Hill, he was less than popular in the office of the Boston Dispensary, for all manner of unexpected patients began to appear there with prescriptions from Dr Robert J. Cole for medications and crutches and even for food prescribed to treat malnourishment.

'What is happening? What? They are not on the list of those referred by donors for treatment,' Mr Wilson complained.

'They're the ones in District Eight who need our help most.'

'Nevertheless. The tail must not be allowed to wag the dog. If you are to remain with the dispensary, Dr Cole, you must obey its rules,' Mr Wilson told him severely.

One of the Sunday patients was Peter Finn of Half Moon Place, who suffered a tear in the calf of his right leg when a crate fell from a wagon while he was picking up half a day's wages on the wharves. The laceration, bandaged with a dirty rag, was swollen and painful by the time he showed it to the doctor. Rob washed and sewed together the ragged lips of flesh, but corruption began at once, and the very next day he was forced to remove the stitches and place a drain in the wound. The infection proceeded at a terrifying rate, and within a few days the Gift told him that if he was to save Peter Finn's life, the leg must be taken.

It was on a Tuesday, and the matter couldn't be put off until Sunday, so he was back to stealing time from the dispensary. Not only was he forced to use one of the previous blank treatment slips given him by Holmes, he had to give his own scarce and hard-earned money to Rose Finn so she could go to a tenement saloon for the jug of poteen that was as necessary to the operation as the knife.

Joseph Finn, Peter's brother, and Michael Bodie, his brother-in-law, reluctantly agreed to assist. Rob J. waited until Peter was stuporous with morphia-laced whisky and laid out on the kitchen table like a sacrifice. But at the first cut of the scalpel the longshoreman's eyes bugged in disbelief, the cords in his neck stood out, and his great scream was an accusation that made Joseph Finn turn pale and Bodie stand useless and trembling. Rob had strapped the offending leg to the table, but with Peter thrashing and

41

bellowing like an agonized beast, he shouted to the two men, 'Hold him! Hold him down, now!'

He cut as he had been taught by Fergusson, truly and swiftly. The cries ceased as he sliced through flesh and muscle, but the grinding of the man's teeth was more terrible than screams. When he severed the femoral artery the bright blood leapt, and he tried to take Bodie's hand and show him how to stem the arterial fountain. But the brother-in-law lurched away.

'Come back. Oh, you son of a bitch.'

But Bodie was running down the stairs, weeping. Rob tried to work as if he had six hands. His own size and strength enabled him to help Joseph pin the thrashing Peter to the table, while at the same time he somehow found the dexterity to pinch off the slippery end of the artery, damming the blood. But when he let go to reach for his saw, the haemorrhaging began anew.

'Show me what to do.' Rose Finn had slipped next to him. Her face was the colour of flour paste but she was able to grasp the artery end and control the bleeding. Rob J. sawed through the bone, made a few quick cuts, and the leg dropped free. By this time, Peter Finn's eyes were glassy with shock and his only sound was raw, ragged breathing.

Rob carried away the leg, wrapped in a threadbare stained towel, to be studied later in the dissection room. He was dull with fatigue, more from his awareness of Peter Finn's martyrdom than because of the exertion of the amputation. He could do nothing about his bloodied clothes, but at a public tap on Broad Street he washed the blood from his hands and arms before going on to his next patient, a woman of twenty-two he knew to be dying of the consumption.

When they were at home in their own neighbourhoods, the Irish lived miserably. Outside their own neighbourhoods, they were calumnized. Rob J. saw posters in the streets: 'All Catholics and all persons who favour the Catholic Church are vile impostors, liars, villains, and cowardly cut-throats. A TRUE AMERICAN.'

42

Once a week he attended a medical lecture in the second-floor amphitheatre at the Athenaeum, in its sprawling quarters that had been made by joining two mansions on Pearl Street. Sometimes after the talk he sat in the library and read the Boston *Evening Transcript*, which reflected the hatred that twisted the society. Distinguished clergymen like Reverend Lyman Beecher, minister of the Hanover Street Congregational Church, wrote article after article about the 'whoredom of Babylon' and the 'foul beast of Roman Catholicism.' Political parties glorified the native-born and wrote of 'dirty, ignorant Irish and German immigrants'.

When he read the national news to learn about America, he saw that it was an acquisitive country, grabbing land with both hands. Recently it had annexed Texas, acquired the Oregon Territory through a treaty with Great Britain, and gone to war with Mexico over California and the southwestern portion of the American continent. The frontier was the Mississippi River, dividing civilization from the wilderness into which the Plains Indians had been pushed. Rob J. was fascinated with Indians, having devoured James Fenimore Cooper's novels throughout his boyhood. He read whatever material the Athenaeum had on Indians, then turned to the poetry of Oliver Wendell Holmes. He liked it, especially the portrait of the tough old survivor in *The Last Leaf*, but Harry Loomis was right, Holmes was a better doctor than he was a poet. He was a superlative doctor.

Harry and Rob took to ending their long days with a glass of ale at the Essex, and often Holmes joined them. It was evident that Harry was the professor's favorite student, and Rob found it hard not to envy him. The Loomis family was well-connected; when the time came, Harry would receive the proper hospital appointments to ensure him a satisfying medical career in Boston. One evening over their drink, Holmes remarked that while doing some library work he had come upon reference to both Cole's Goiter and Cole's Malignant Cholera. His curiosity whetted, he had searched the literature and found ample evidence of the Cole family's

43

contributions to medicine, including Cole's Gout, and Cole's and Palmer's Syndrome, a malady in which edema was accompanied by heavy sweats and stertorous respirations. 'Furthermore,' he said, 'I found that more than a dozen Coles have been professors of medicine in either Edinburgh or Glasgow. All kinfolk of yours?'

Rob J. grinned, embarrassed but pleased. 'All kinfolk. But most of the Coles down through the centuries have been simple country physicians in the lowland hills, like my father.' He said nothing about the Cole Gift; it wasn't something one discussed with other doctors, who would think him either unhinged or a liar.

'Is your father there still?' Holmes asked.

'No, no. Killed by runaway horses when I was twelve.'

'Ah.' That was the moment when Holmes, despite the relatively small difference in their ages, determined to fill a father's role in gaining Rob admission to the charmed circle of Boston families through an advantageous marriage.

Soon after that, twice Rob accepted invitations to the Holmes house on Montgomery Street, where he glimpsed a lifestyle similar to the one that once he had thought possible for himself in Edinburgh. On the first occasion, Amelia, the professor's vivacious, matchmaking wife, introduced him to Paula Storrow, whose family was old and rich but who was a lumpish and painfully stupid woman. But at the second dinner his partner was Lydia Parkman. She was too slender and lacked any sign of breasts, but beneath her smooth walnut-brown hair her face and eyes radiated a wry and mischievous humour, and they spent the evening engaged in a teasing but far-ranging conversation. She knew some things about Indians, but they talked mostly about music, for she played the harpsichord.

That night, when Rob came back to the house on Spring Street, he sat on his bed beneath the eaves and contemplated what it might be like to spend his life in Boston, colleague as well as friend to Harry Loomis and Oliver Wendell Holmes, married to a hostess who presided over a witty table.

44

Presently there was the small knock he had come to know. Meg Holland let herself into his room. She wasn't too thin, he noted as he smiled a greeting and began to unbutton his shirt. But for once Meggy sat on the edge of the bed without moving.

When she spoke, it was in a hoarse whisper, her tone even more than her words striking deep into his spirit. Her voice had a tight, dead quality, like the sound of dried leaves pushed by a breeze across hard, cold ground.

'Caught,' she said.

6

Dreams

'Right and proper,' she told him.

He couldn't find the words to say to her. She'd been experienced when she came to him, he cautioned himself. How did he know the child was his? *I always wore the sheath*, he protested silently. But in fairness he knew he'd worn nothing the first few times, and again on the night when they'd tried the laughing gas.

He was conditioned by his training never to countenance abortion, and he was sensitive enough now to resist suggesting it, aware that her religion was the strongest part of her.

Finally he told her he would stand by her. He wasn't Stanley Finch.

She didn't appear tremendously buoyed by the declaration. He forced himself to take her into his arms and hold her. He wanted to be tender and comforting. It was the worst possible moment to perceive that her feline face within a few years would be decidedly bovine. Not the face of his dreams.

'You're a Protestant.' It wasn't a question, for she knew the answer.

'I was so raised.'

She was a plucky woman. Her eyes filled for the first time only when he told her he was uncertain about the

46

existence of God.

'You charmer, you scoundrel! Lydia Parkman was favourably impressed by your company,' Holmes told him next evening at the medical school, and beamed when Rob J. said he thought her an extremely pleasant woman. Holmes mentioned casually that Stephen Parkman, her father, was a Superior Court judge and an overseer of Harvard College. The family had begun as dealers in dried fish, eventually had become flour merchants, and now controlled the widespread and lucrative trade of barrelled grocery staples.

'When do you intend to see her again?' Holmes asked.

'Soon, of that you can be certain,' Rob J. said guiltily, unable to allow himself to think of it.

Holmes' ideas about medical hygiene had revolutionized the practice of medicine for Rob. Holmes told him two stories that buttressed his theories. One concerned scrofula, a tubercular disease of the lymphatic glands and joints; in medieval Europe it was believed that scrofula could be cured by the touch of royal hands. The other tale dealt with the ancient superstitious practice of washing and bandaging soldiers' wounds and then applying ointment – terrible unguents containing such ingredients as decaying flesh, human blood, and moss from the skull of an executed man – to the weapon that had inflicted the hurt. Both methods were successful and famous, Holmes said, because inadvertently they provided for the patient's cleanliness. In the first case, the scrofulous patients were washed completely and carefully lest the royal 'healers' should be offended when it came time to touch them. In the second case, the weapon was smeared with foul stuff but the wounds of the soldiers, washed and then left alone, had a chance to heal without infection. The magic 'secret ingredient' was hygiene.

It was difficult to maintain clinical cleanliness in District Eight. Rob J. took to carrying towels and brown soap in his bag and washed his hands and instruments many times a day, but the conditions of poverty combined to make the district a place in which it was easy to sicken and die.

He tried to fill his life and his mind with the daily medical

47

struggle, but as he dwelt long and hard on his predicament, he wondered if he was bent on his own destruction. He had thrown away career and roots in Scotland by his involvement in politics, and now in America he had compounded his ruination by entangling himself in a disastrous pregnancy. Margaret Holland was facing the situation practically; she asked him questions about his means. Far from filling her with dismay, his annual income of $350 seemed comfortable to her. She asked about his people.

'My father is dead. My mother was failing badly when I left Scotland, and I'm certain that by now ... I have one brother, Herbert. He manages the family holding in Kilmarnock, raises sheep. He owns the property.'

She nodded. 'I've a brother, Timothy, lives in Belfast. He's a member of Young Ireland, always in trouble.' Her own mother was dead; there was a father and four brothers in Ireland, but a fifth brother, Samuel, lived in the Fort Hill area of Boston. She asked timidly if she shouldn't tell her brother about Rob and ask Samuel to keep his eyes open for rooms for them, perhaps near his own flat.

'Not yet. Still early days,' he said, and then touched her cheek to reassure her.

The idea of living in the district horrified him. Yet he knew if he remained a doctor to the immigrant poor, only in some such warren could he maintain life for himself, a wife, and a child. Next morning he regarded the district with fear as well as rage, and despair grew in him that matched the hopelessness he saw everywhere in the mean streets and alleyways.

He began to sleep restlessly at night, disturbed by nightmares. Two dreams recurred again and again. On a bad night, he had them both. When he couldn't sleep, he lay in the dark and went over the events in detail again and again, so that finally he couldn't tell whether he was asleep or awake.

Early morning. Grey weather, but with an optimistic sun. He stands among several thousand men outside the Carron Iron Works, where large-calibre ships' guns are made for the English navy. It

48

begins well. A man atop a crate is reading the broadside Rob J. had written anonymously to bring men to the demonstration: 'Friends and Countrymen. Roused from the state in which we have been held for so many years, we are compelled, by the extremity of our positions and the contempt heaped upon our petitions, to assert our rights at the hazard of our lives.' The man's voice is high and cracks at times to reveal his fright. He is cheered when he is done. Three pipers play, the assembled men singing lustily, at first hymns and then more spirited stuff, ending with 'Scots Wha' Hae Wi' Wallace Bled'. The authorities have seen Rob's broadside and have made preparations. There are armed policemen, militia, the First Battalion of the Rifle Brigade, and well-trained cavalry soldiers of the Seventh Hussars and the Tenth Hussars, veterans of European wars. The soldiers wear gorgeous uniforms. The high polished boots of the hussars gleam like rich dark mirrors. The troops are younger than the policemen but their faces contain an identical hard contempt. The trouble starts when Rob's friend Andrew Gerould of Lanark makes a speech about the destruction of farms and the inability of labouring men to live on the mite given for work that enriches England and makes Scotland ever poorer. As Andrew's voice grows in heat, the men start to roar their anger and to shout, 'Liberty or death!' The dragoons edge their horses forward, pushing the demonstrators from the fence surrounding the iron works. Someone hurls a rock. It strikes a hussar, who drops from his saddle. Immediately the other horsemen draw swords with a rattle, and a shower of stones fells other soldiers, spattering blood on blue, crimson, and gold uniforms. The militia begins to fire into the crowd. The cavalrymen are hacking. Men scream and weep. Rob is hemmed in. He can't flee on his own. He can only allow himself to be swept beyond the vengeance of the soldiers, fighting to keep his feet, knowing that if he stumbles he will be trampled by the terror of the running mob.

The second dream was worse.

Amidst a large assemblage again. As many as had been at the iron works, but this time men and women standing before eight gallow trees raised at Stirling Castle, the crowd contained by militia formed up all around the square. A minister, Dr Edward Bruce of Renfrew, sits and reads silently. Opposite him sits a man in black. Rob J. recognizes him before he takes refuge behind a black mask;

49

he is Bruce Something-or-other, an impoverished medical student who is earning fifteen pounds as executioner. Dr Bruce leads the people in the 130th Psalm: 'Out of the depths have I cried unto thee, O Lord.' Each of the condemned is given the customary glass of wine and then led onto the platform, where eight coffins wait. Six prisoners choose not to speak. A man named Hardie looks out over the sea of faces and says in a muffled voice, 'I die a martyr to the cause of justice.' Andrew Gerould speaks clearly. He appears weary and older than his twenty-three years. 'My friends, I hope none of you has been hurt. After this is done, please go quietly to your homes and read your Bibles.' Caps are placed over their heads. Two of them call farewell as the nooses are fixed. Andrew says nothing more. At a signal it is done, and five die without struggle. Three kick for a time. Andrew's New Testatment falls from his nerveless fingers into the silent crowd. After they are cut down, the executioner chops through each neck with an axe, one by one, and holds up the terrifying object by the hair, saying every time as the law prescribes: 'This is the head of a traitor!'

Sometimes when Rob J. escaped from the dream he lay in the narrow bed under the eaves, touching his limbs and trembling with relief that he was alive. Staring up into the darkness, he wondered how many people no longer were living because he had written the broadside. How many destinies had been changed, how many lives were ended because he had projected his beliefs onto so many people? The accepted morality said that principles were worth fighting for, dying for. Yet when everything else was taken into account, was not life the single most precious possession a human being owned? And as a doctor wasn't he committed to protect and preserve life above all? He swore to himself and to Aesculapius, the father of healing, that he would never again cause a human being to die because of a difference in beliefs, never again even strike another person in anger, and for the thousandth time he marvelled at what a hard way it had been for Bruce Something-or-other to have earned fifteen pounds.

7
The Colour of the Painting

'It is not your money that you spend!' Mr Wilson told him sourly one morning as he handed over a sheaf of appointment slips. 'It is money given to the dispensary by leading citizens. The charity's funds are not to be wasted at the whim of a doctor in our employ.'

'I've never wasted the charity's money. I've never treated or prescribed for any patient who wasn't genuinely ill and badly in need of our help. Your system is bad. It sometimes has me treating somebody with a strained muscle while others die for lack of treatment.'

'You exceed yourself, sir.' Wilson's eyes and voice were calm, but his hand holding the slips trembled. 'Do you understand that in future you must limit your visits to the names on the slips I assign to you each morning?'

Rob desperately desired to tell Mr Wilson what he understood, and what Mr Wilson might best do with his appointment slips. But in view of the complications in his life, he didn't dare. Instead, he forced himself to nod and to turn away. Stuffing the sheaf of slips into his pocket, he made his way into the district.

That evening, everything changed. Margaret Holland came to his room and sat on the edge of his bed, her place for announcements.

'I'm bleedin'.'

He forced himself to think first as a doctor. 'Are you haemorrhaging, losing a great deal of blood?'

She shook her head. 'At first, a little heavier than usual. Then, like my regular bleedin'. Almost done now.'

'When did it begin?'

'Four days past.'

'Four days!' Why had she waited four days to tell him? She didn't look at him. She sat absolutely still, as if steeling herself against his fury, and he realized she'd spent the four days struggling with herself. 'Came close to not telling me at all, didn't you.'

She didn't answer, but he understood. Despite his being strange, a hand-washing Protestant, he had been an opportunity for her eventually to escape the prison of her poverty. Having been forced to peer into that prison at close range, it was a wonder to him that she'd been able to tell him the truth at all, so that instead of anger at her delay, what he felt was admiration, overwhelming gratitude. He went to her, lifted her to her feet, and kissed her reddened eyes. Then he put his arms about her and held her, patting her gently from time to time, as if comforting a frightened child.

Next morning he wandered, light-headed, at times his knees weak with relief. Men and women smiled at his greeting. It was a new world, with a brighter sun and more benevolent air to breathe.

He took care of his patients with his usual attentiveness, but in between each case his mind was racing. Finally he sat on a wooden stoop on Broad Street and contemplated the past, the present, and his future.

For the second time he had escaped a terrible fate. He felt he had received a warning that his existence must be carefully, more respectfully, used.

He thought of his life as a large painting in progress. Whatever happened to him, the finished picture would be of medicine, but he sensed that if he stayed in Boston the painting would be rendered in shades of grey.

Amelia Holmes could arrange what she called 'a brilliant match' for him, but having escaped an unloving impoverished marriage, he had no desire to cold-bloodedly seek out an unloving rich one or to allow himself to be sold on Boston society's marriage market, medical meat at so much per pound.

He wanted his life to be painted with the strongest colours he could find.

When he was through with his work that afternoon, he went to the Athenaeum and reread the books that had so captured his interest. Long before he finished them, he knew where he wanted to go and what he wanted to do.

That night as Rob lay in his bed, there was a familiar small signal at the door. He stared up at the darkness without moving. The scratching knock sounded a second time, and then a third.

For several reasons he wanted to go to the door and open it. But he lay without moving, frozen into a moment as bad as any of those in the nightmares, and eventually Margaret Holland went away.

It took him more than a month to make his preparations and resign from the Boston Dispensary. In lieu of a farewell party, on a brutally cold December evening, he, Holmes, and Harry Loomis dissected the body of a Negro slave named Della. She had laboured all her life and the body had remarkable musculature. Harry had demonstrated a genuine interest and talent in anatomy and would replace Rob J. as docent at the medical school. Holmes lectured as they cut, showing them that the fimbriated end of the Fallopian tube was 'like the fringe of a poor woman's shawl'. Every organ and muscle reminded one of them of a story, a poem, an anatomical pun, or a scatological joke. It was serious scientific work, they were meticulous about every detail, yet while they worked they roared with laughter and good feeling. Following the dissection they repaired to the Essex Tavern and drank mulled wine until closing. Rob promised to stay in touch with both Holmes and Harry when he arrived at a permanent destination, and to call on both of them with problems if the need should arise. They parted in such fellowship that Rob was regretful about his decision.

In the morning he walked to Washington Street and bought some roasted chestnuts, bringing them back to the house on Spring Street in a twist of paper torn from the Boston *Transcript*. He stole into Meggy Holland's room and left them under the pillow of her bed.

Shortly after noon he climbed aboard a railroad car, which presently was pulled out of the train yards by a steam locomotive. The conductor who collected his ticket looked askance at his luggage, for he had declined to put either his viola da gamba or his box into the baggage car. In addition to his surgical instruments and clothing, the trunk contained Old Horny and half a dozen bars of strong brown soap, the same kind Holmes used. So though he had little cash, he was leaving Boston far wealthier than when he had arrived.

It was four days before Christmas. The train glided past houses in which wreaths decorated doors and Yule trees could be glimpsed through windows along the track. Soon the city was left behind. Despite a lightly falling snow, in less than three hours they made Worcester, the terminus of the Boston Railroad. Passengers had to transfer to the Western Railroad, and in the new train Rob sat next to a portly man who promptly offered him a flask.

'No, thank you kindly,' he said, but accepted conversation to take the sting from the refusal. The man was a drummer of wrought nails – clasp, clinch, double-headed, countersunk, diamond, and rose, in sizes ranging from tiny needle nails to huge boat spikes – and showed Rob his samples, a good way to while away the miles.

'Travelling west! Travelling west!' the salesman said. 'You too?'

Rob J. nodded. 'How far do you go?'

'Just about the end of the state! Pittsfield. You, sir?'

It gave him an inordinate amount of satisfaction to answer, so much pleasure that he grinned and had to restrain from shouting for all to hear, as the words played their own music and shed a fine romantic light in every corner of the rocking railroad car.

'Indian country,' he said.

8
Music

He progressed through Massachusetts and New York via a series of short railroads connected by stagecoach lines. It was hard travelling in the winter. At times a stage had to wait while as many as a dozen oxen dragged ploughs to clear drifts or packed down the snow with great wooden rollers. Inns and taverns were expensive. He was in the forest of the Allegheny Plateau in Pennsylvania when he ran out of money and deemed himself lucky to find work in Jacob Starr's timber camp, doctoring lumberjacks. When there was an accident, it was likely to be serious, but in between there was little for him to do, and he sought out labour, joining the crews in hewing down white pines and hemlocks that had lived more than two hundred and fifty years. Usually he manned one end of a 'misery whip', or two-man saw. His body hardened and thickened. Most camps didn't have a doctor, and the lumberjacks knew how valuable he was to them, and protected him as he worked at their dangerous trade. They taught him to soak his bleeding palms in brine till they toughened. In the evenings he juggled in the bunkhouse to keep his calloused fingers dexterous for surgery, and he played his viola da gamba for them, alternating accompaniments of their raunchy bellowed songs with selections by J. S. Bach and Marais, to which they listened raptly.

All winter they stockpiled huge logs on the banks of a stream. On the back of every single-bitted axe head in camp, raised in steel, was a large five-pointed star. Each time a tree was felled and trimmed, the men reversed their axes and slammed the embossed star into the fresh-cut butt, marking it as a Starr log. When the spring melt came, the stream rose eight feet, carrying the logs to the Clarion River. Huge log rafts were assembled, and on them were built bunkhouses, cookhouses, and supply shacks. Rob rode the rafts downriver like a prince, a slow, dreamlike journey interrupted only when the logs jammed and piled up, to be unsnarled by the skilled, patient boom-men. He saw all manner of birds and animals, drifting down the serpentine Clarion until it joined the Allegheny, and riding the logs down the Allegheny all the way to Pittsburgh.

In Pittsburgh he said goodbye to Starr and his lumberjacks. In a saloon he was hired as physician to a track-laying crew of the Washington & Ohio Railroad, a line seeking to compete with the state's two busy canals. With a work crew he was taken into Ohio, to the beginning of a great openness bisected by two shining rails. Rob was given living quarters with the bosses aboard four railroad cars. Springtime on the great plain was beautiful, but the world of the W & ORR was ugly. The track layers, graders, and teamsters were immigrant Irish and Germans whose lives were regarded as a cheap commodity. Rob's responsibility was to ensure that the last ounces of their strength were available for laying track. He welcomed the pay, but the job was doomed from the start, for the superintendant, a dark-visaged man named Cotting, was a piece of nastiness who wouldn't spend money on food. The railroad employed hunters who killed plenty of wild meat, and there was a chicory drink that passed for coffee. But save at the table shared by Cotting, Rob, and the managers, there were no greens, no cabbage, no carrots, no potatoes, nothing to supply ascorbic acid except, as a very rare treat, a pot of beans. The men had scurvy. Though anaemic, they had no appetites. Their joints were sore, their gums bled, their teeth were falling out, and their injuries wouldn't heal. They were literally being murdered by malnutrition and heavy work. Finally, Rob J. broke into the locked supply car with a crowbar and passed out crates of cabbages and potatoes until the bosses' own foodstuffs were gone. Fortunately, Cotting didn't know his young physician had taken a vow of non-violence. Rob's size and condition and the cold contempt in his eyes made the superintendent decide it was easier to pay him off and be rid of him than to fight him.

He'd earned barely enough money from the railroad to buy a slow old mare, a used twelve-gauge muzzle-loading rifle and a light little goose gun with which to hunt smaller game, needles and thread, a fishline and hooks, a rusty iron frying pan, and a hunting knife. He named the horse Monica Grenville, in honour of a beautiful older woman, his mother's friend, whom for years he had dreamed of riding during the fevered fantasies of his adolescence. Monica Grenville the horse allowed him to work his way west on his own terms. He shot game easily after discovering that the rifle pulled to the right, and caught fish if there was opportunity, and he earned money or goods wherever he came to people who needed a doctor.

The size of the country stunned him, mountain and valley and plain. After a few weeks he became convinced he could go on as long as he lived, riding Monica Grenville ploddingly and eternally in the direction of the setting sun.

He ran out of pharmaceuticals. It was hard enough performing surgery without the aid of the few inadequate palliatives that were available, but he had neither laudanum nor morphine nor any other drug and had to rely on his swiftness as a surgeon and whatever rotgut whisky he was able to buy as he went along. Fergusson had taught him a few helpful tricks that he remembered. Lacking tincture of nicotine, given by mouth as a muscle relaxant to slacken the anal sphincter during an operation for fistula, he bought the strongest cigars he could find and inserted one into the patient's rectum until the nicotine was absorbed from the tobacco and relaxation took place. Once in Titusville, Ohio, an elderly citizen happened upon him overseeing a patient who was bent over a wagon shaft, the cigar protruding.

'Do you have a match, sir?' Rob J. asked him.

Later, at the general store, he heard the old man tell his friends solemnly, 'You would never believe how they was smokin 'em.'

In a tavern in Zanesville, he saw his first Indian, a crushing disappointment. In contrast to James Fenimore Coopers splendid savages, the man was a soft-fleshed, sullen drunkard with snot on his face, a pitiful creature taking abuse while begging drinks.

'Delaware, I guess,' the saloonkeeper said when Rob asked him the Indian's tribe. 'Miami, mebbe. Or Shawnee.' He shrugged contemptuously. 'Who cares? The mizzable bastards is all a same to me.'

A few days later, in Columbus, Rob discovered a stout black-bearded young Jew named Jason Maxwell Geiger, an apothecary with a well-stocked pharmacy.

'You have laudanum? You have tincture of nicotine? Potassium iodide?' No matter what he requested, Geiger answered with a smile and a nod, and Rob wandered happily among the jars and retorts. Prices were lower than he would have feared, for Geiger's father and brothers were manufacturers of pharmaceuticals in Charleston, and he explained that whatever he couldn't make himself, he was able to order from his family at favourable terms. So Rob J. put in a good supply. It was when the pharmacist helped carry his purchases to the horse that Geiger saw the wrapped bulk of the musical instrument and turned at once to his visitor. 'Surely it's a viol?'

'Viola da gamba,' Rob said, and saw something new enter the man's eyes, not exactly cupidity, but a wistful yearning so powerful as to be unmistakable. 'Would you care to see it?'

'You must bring it into the house, show it to my wife,' Geiger said eagerly. He led the way to the dwelling behind the apothecary shop. Inside, Lillian Geiger held a dish towel across her bodice as they were introduced, but not before Rob J. had noticed the stains from her leaking breasts. In a cradle slept their two-month-old daughter, Rachel. The house smelled of Mrs Geiger's milk and fresh-baked *hallah*. The dark parlour contained a horsehair sofa and chair and a square piano. The woman slipped into the bedroom and changed her dress while Rob J. unwrapped the viol; then she and her husband examined the instrument, running their fingers over the seven strings and ten frets as if they were stroking a newly recovered family icon. She showed him her piano, with its carefully oiled dark walnut wood. 'Made by Alpheus Babcock of Philadelphia,' she said. Jason Geiger brought another instrument to light from behind the piano. 'It was made by a brewer of beer named Isaac Schwartz who lives in Richmond, Virginia. It's just a fiddle, not good enough to be called a violin. Someday I hope to own a violin.' But in a moment, when they were tuning up, Geiger drew sweet sounds.

They regarded one another warily lest they prove to be muscially incompatible.

'What?' Geiger asked him, giving the visitor the courtesy.

'Bach? Do you know this prelude from *The Well-Tempered Clavier*? It's from Book II, I forget the number.' He played them the opening, and at once Lillian Geiger joined in and, nodding, so did her husband. *The twelfth*, Lillian mouthed. Rob J. cared nothing about identifying the piece, for this kind of playing was not to entertain lumberjacks. It was at once apparent that the man and woman were accomplished and accustomed to accompanying one another, and he was certain he'd make an ass of himself. Wherever their music progressed, his followed tardily and jerkily. His fingers, instead of flowing along the musical path, seemed to make spastic leaps, like salmon fighting their way up a falls. But halfway through the prelude he forgot his fear, for the habits of many long years of playing overcame the clumsiness caused by lack of practice. Soon he was able to observe that Geiger played with his eyes closed, while his wife wore on her face a look of glazed pleasure that was at the same time sharing and intensely private.

The satisfaction was almost like pain. He hadn't realized how much he had missed music. When they finished they sat and grinned at one another. Geiger hurried out to put a Closed sign on the door of his shop, Lillian went to check on her child and to place a roast in the oven, Rob unsaddled

59

and fed poor patient Monica. When they came back, it turned out the Geigers knew nothing by Marin Marais, while Rob J. had memorized none of the works of that Polish fellow, Chopin. But they all three knew Beethoven's sonatas. All afternoon they constructed for themselves a shimmering, special place. By the time the wailing of the hungry infant interrupted their play, they were drunk with the heady beauty of their own sounds.

The pharmacist wouldn't hear of his leaving. The evening meal was pink lamb tasting faintly of rosemary and garlic and roasted with little carrots and new potatoes, and a blueberry compote. 'You will sleep in our guest room,' Geiger said.

Drawn toward them, Rob asked Geiger about opportunities for physicians in the area.

'Lots of people hereabouts, Columbus being state capital, and a number of doctors already are here to take care of 'em. It's a good place for a pharmacy, but we're going to be leaving Columbus ourselves when our baby is old enough to survive the trip. I want to be a farmer as well as an apothecary, and I want land to leave to my children. Farmland in Ohio is just too damned high. I've been making a study of places where I can buy fertile land I can afford.'

He had maps, which he opened on his table. 'Illinois,' he said, and pointed out to Rob J. the part of the state that his investigations had indicated the most desirable, a section between the Rocky River and the Mississippi. 'A good supply of water. Beautiful woods lining the rivers. And the rest of it is prairie, black earth that's never felt a plough.'

Rob J. studied the maps. 'Maybe I ought to go there myself,' he said finally. 'See if I like it.'

Geiger beamed. They spent a long time hunched over the maps, marking the best route, arguing good-naturedly. After Rob went to bed, Jay Geiger stayed up late and by candlelight copied the music of a Chopin mazurka. They played it next morning after breakfast. Then the two men consulted the marked map one more time. Rob J. agreed that if Illinois proved to be as good as Geiger believed, he would settle there and write at once to his new friend, telling him to bring his family to the western frontier.

9
Two Parcels

Illinois was interesting right from the start. Rob entered the state in late summer, when the tough green stuff of the prairie was dried and bleached from too many long days in the sun. At Danville he watched men boiling down the water from saline springs in big black kettles, and when he left, he carried with him a packet of very pure salt. The prairie was rolling and, in places, adorned with low hills. The state was blessed with sweet water. Rob came to only a few lakes but saw a number of marshes feeding streams that merged into rivers. He learned that when people in Illinois spoke of the land between the rivers they most likely meant the southern tip of the state that lay between the Mississippi and the Ohio. It had deep, rich alluvial soils from both great rivers. Folks called the region Egypt, because they thought it was as fertile as the fabled soil of the great Nile delta. On Jay Geiger's map Rob J. saw that there were a number of 'little Egypts' between rivers in Illinois. Somehow, during his brief encounter with Geiger the man had earned his respect, and he kept on travelling toward the region Jay had told him was the likeliest one for settlement.

It took him two weeks to work his way across Illinois. On the fourteenth day the trail he was on entered a fringe of woods, offering blessed coolness and the smell of moist growing things. Following the narrow track, he heard the sound of a lot of water, and presently he emerged on the eastern bank of a good-sized river that he guessed to be the Rocky.

It was dry season but the current was strong, and the great rocks that gave the river its name created white water. Riding Monica along the bank, he was trying to pick out a place that appeared fordable when he came to a deeper, slower section. Between two huge tree trunks on the opposite banks, a thick rope cable was suspended. An iron triangle and a piece of steel were hung from a branch next to a sign that read:

HOLDEN'S CROSSING

Ring for Ferry

He clanged the triangle vigorously and, it seemed to him, for a long time before he saw a man leisurely making his way down the far bank, where the raft was moored. Two stout vertical posts on the raft ended in great iron rings through which passed the suspended hawser, allowing the raft to slide along the rope as it was poled across the river. By the time the raft was mid-river, the current had pulled the rope downstream, so that the man moved the raft over an arc instead of making a straight crossing. In the middle, the dark oily waters were too deep to pole, and the man pulled the raft along slowly by hauling on the rope cable. The ferryman was singing, and baritone lyrics carried clearly to Rob J.

> One day I was walkin, I heerd a complainin',
> An' saw a old woman the picture of gloom.
> She gazed at the mud on her doorstep ('twas rainin')
> An this was her song as she wielded her broom.
>
> Oh, life is a toil and love is a trouble,
> Beauty'll fade an riches'll flee,
> Pleasures they dwindle an prices they double,
> An nothin is as I would wish it to be. . . .

There were many verses, and long before they ended, the

62

rafter was able to start poling again. As the raft drew closer, Rob could see a muscular man, perhaps in his thirties. He was a head shorter than Rob and looked very much a native of the land, with heavy boots on his feet, brown linsey-woolsey trousers that were too heavy for the weather, a blue cotton shirt with a heavy collar, and a sweat-stained leather hat with a wide brim. He had a mane of black hair he wore long, and a full black beard, and prominent cheekbones balanced on either side of a thin curved nose that might have given cruelty to his face except for his blue eyes, which were cheerful and welcoming. As the distance between them closed, Rob felt the wariness, the expectation of affectation, that resulted from seeing a perfectly beautiful woman or a too-handsome man. But there appeared to be little affectation in the ferryman.

'Howdy,' he called. One final shove on the pole sent the raft grinding into the sandy bank. He held out his hand. 'Nicholas Holden, at your service.'

Rob shook his hand and identified himself. Holden had taken a dark, moist plug from his shirt pocket and cut himself a chaw with his knife. He held it out to Rob J., who shook his head. 'How much to ride across?'

'Three cents for you. Ten cents, the horse.'

Rob paid as requested, thirteen cents in advance. He tethered Monica to rings set in the floor of the raft for that purpose. Holden gave him a second pole, and the two of them grunted as they put their backs to it.

'Looking to settle in these parts?'

'Might be,' Rob said cautiously.

'Not a farrier, by chance?' Holden had the bluest eyes Rob had ever seen on a man, saved from femininity by a piercing glance that made him appear secretly amused. 'Damn,' he said, but seemed unsurprised at Rob's headshake. 'Sure would like to find me a good blacksmith. Farmer, are you?'

He perked up visibly when Rob told him he was a doctor. 'Thrice welcome, and welcome again! We need a doctor in the township of Holden's Crossing. Any doctor can ride this ferry for free,' he said, and paused in his poling long enough to count three cents solemnly back into Rob's palm.

63

Rob looked at the coins. 'What about the other ten cents?'

'Shit, I don't suppose the horse is a doctor too?' When he grinned, he was likeable enough to make you think he was ugly.

He had a tiny cabin of square-off logs chinked with white clay, near a garden and a spring and set on a rise overlooking the river. 'Just in time for dinner,' he said, and soon they were eating a fragrant stew in which Rob identified turnip and cabbage and onion but was puzzled by the meat. 'Got me an old hare and a young prairie chicken this morning, and they're both in there,' Holden said.

Over refilled wooden bowls they told enough about themselves to make things comfortable. Holden was a country lawyer from the state of Connecticut. He had big plans.

'How come they named the town after you?'

'*They* didn't. I did,' he said affably. 'I got here first and set up the ferry. Whenever someone comes to settle, I tell them the name of the town. Nobody's argued yet.'

In Rob's opinion, Holden's log house wasn't the equal to a snug Scots cottage. It was dark and stuffy. The bed, too close to the smoky fireplace, was covered with soot. Holden told him cheerfully that the only good thing about the place was the homesite; within a year, he said, the cabin would be razed and a fine house built in its place. 'Yessir, big plans.' He told Rob J. of the things that would soon come – an inn, a general store, eventually a bank. He was frank about his desire to sell Rob on settling in Holden's Crossing.

'How many families live here now?' Rob J. asked, and smiled ruefully at the answer. 'A doctor can't make a living taking care of only sixteen families.'

'Well, course not. But homesteaders are going to be coming in here more eager than a man on a cunt. And those sixteen families live within the township. Beyond the town line, there's no doctor between here and Rock Island, and there's lots of farms scattered through the plains. You'd just have to get yourself a better horse and be willing to travel a bit to make a house call.'

Rob remembered how frustrated he had felt because he had been unable to practice good medicine in the teeming population of District Eight. But this was the other side of the coin. He told Nick Holden he would sleep on it.

He slept that night in the cabin, wrapped in a quilt on the floor, while in the bed Nick Holden snored. But that was a no hardship to someone who had spent the winter in a bunkhouse with nineteen farting, hawking lumberjacks. In the morning Holden cooked breakfast but left Rob to clean the dishes and frypan, saying he had something to tend to and would be back.

It was a clear, fresh day. Already the sun was hot, and Rob unwrapped the viola and sat on a shaded rock in the clearing between the rear of the cabin and the tree line of the woods. Next to him on the rock he spread the copy of Chopin's mazurka that Jay Geiger had transcribed for him, and painstakingly he began to play.

For perhaps half an hour he worked on the theme and the melody until it began to be music. Glancing up from the page, he looked into the woods and saw two Indians on horseback watching him from just beyond the edge of the clearing.

He was alarmed, because they restored his confidence in James Fenimore Cooper, being hollow-cheeked men with bare chests that looked hard and lean, shiny with some kind of oil. The one closer to Rob wore buckskin pants and had a great hooked nose. His shaved head was divided by a gaudy scalplock of stiff, coarse animal hair. He carried a rifle. His companion was a big man, as tall as Rob J. but bulkier. He had long black hair held back by a leather headband, and wore a breechclout and leather leggings. He carried a bow and Rob J. could clearly see a quiver of arrows hanging from his horse's neck, like a drawing in one of the books on Indians in the Boston Athenaeum.

He didn't know if there were others in the woods behind them. If their intent was hostile, he was lost, because the viola da gamba is a poor weapon of choice. It occurred to him to resume playing, and he placed the bow back onto the strings and began, but not with the Chopin; he didn't want

65

to look away from them to gaze at the score. Without thinking about it, he played a seventeenth-century piece he knew well, *Cara La Vita Mia*, by Oratio Bassani. He played it all the way through, and then halfway through again. Finally he stopped, because he couldn't sit and play music forever.

Behind him he heard something and half-turned quickly to see a red squirrel skittering off. When he turned back, he was both vastly relieved and enormously regretful because the two Indians were gone. For a moment he could hear their horses moving off; then the only sound was the soughing of the wind in the leaves of the trees.

Nick Holden tried not to show how upset he was when he returned and was told. He made a quick inspection tour, but said nothing seemed to be missing.

'The Indians hereabouts were Sauks. They were driven across the Mississippi into Iowa nine or ten years back, with fighting that folks have come to call Black Hawk's War. A few years ago, all the Sauks who were still alive were moved onto a reservation in Kansas. Last month we heard that about forty braves with their women and children had lit out from the reservation. They were rumoured to be heading toward Illinois. I doubt that even they are stupid enough to give us any trouble, that small a bunch. I think they're just hoping we'll leave them alone.'

Rob nodded. 'If they'd wanted to give me trouble, they could have done it easily enough.'

Nick was eager to change the subject away from anything that might cast Holden's Crossing in a poor light. He had spent the morning looking at four parcels of land, he said. He wanted to show them, and at his urging Rob saddled up the mare.

It was government property. As they rode, Nick explained that the land had been platted by federal surveyors into parcels of eighty acres. Private property was selling at eight dollars an acre or more, but government land was priced at $1.25 an acre, an eighty-acre section for one hundred dollars. One-twentieth of the purchase price had to be put down at once to hold the land, and twenty-five percent had to be paid within forty days, the remainder being due in three equal instalments at the end of two, three, and four years from the date of entry. Nick said it was the best homesteading land anybody was going to find, and when they came to the land, Rob believed him. The parcels ran along almost a mile of the river, offering a deep fringe of riverbank forest that contained several pure springs and timber for building. Beyond the woods lay the fertile promise of the unploughed plain.

'Here's my advice,' Holden said. 'I wouldn't look on this land as four eighty-acre parcels, but as two hundred and sixty-acre pieces. Just now, the government is letting new settlers buy as much as two sections, and that's what I'd do, were I you.'

Rob J. grimaced and shook his head. 'It's nice land. But I just don't have the necessary fifty dollars.'

Nick Holden looked at him thoughtfully. 'My future is tied up in this might-be town. If I can attract settlers, I'll own the general store, I'll own the mill, I'll own the inn. Settlers flock to a place where there's a doctor. To me, it's money in the sock to have you living in Holden's Crossing. Banks are lending money at two-and-one-half-percent interest per annum. I'll let you have the fifty dollars as a loan at one and one-half percent, to be paid back within eight years.'

Rob J. looked around, drew a breath. It was *nice* land. The place felt so right to him that he had to struggle to control his voice as he accepted the offer. Nick shook his hand warmly and brushed off his gratitude: 'Just good business.' They rode slowly over the property. The southernmost double parcel was bottomland, virtually flat. The northern section was rolling, with several rises that could almost be described as small hills.

'I'd take the southern pieces,' Holden said. 'The soil's better, and easier to plough.'

But Rob J. already had made up his mind to buy the northern section. 'I'll keep most of it in grass and raise sheep, that's the kind of agriculture I understand. But I already know somebody anxious to be a dirt farmer, and maybe he'll want the southern pieces.'

When he told Holden about Jason Geiger, the lawyer grinned with pleasure. 'A pharmacy in Holden's Crossing? Wouldn't that be icing on the cake? Well, I'll put a deposit on the southern section to reserve it in Geiger's name. If he doesn't want it, it won't be hard to turn over land this good.'

The following morning the two men rode into Rock Island, and when they left the United States Land Office, Rob. J. was a landowner and a debtor.

In the afternoon he rode back to his property alone. He tethered the mare and explored the woods and the prairie on foot, studying and planning. As in a dream, he walked along the river, throwing stones into the water, unable to believe all this was his. In Scotland, land was enormously difficult to come by. His family's sheep holding in Kilmarnock had been handed down for many centuries, generation to generation.

That evening he wrote a letter to Jason Geiger describing the one hundred and sixty acres that had been reserved next to his own property, and he asked Geiger to let him know as soon as possible whether he wanted to assume permanent possession of the land. He also asked Jason to ship him an ample supply of sulphur, because Nick reluctantly had told him that in the spring there were always outbreaks of what folks called the Illinois mange, and the strong administration of sulphur was the only thing that seemed to work against it.

10
The Raising

Word got around at once about a doctor's presence. Three days after Rob J. arrived in Holden's Crossing he was summoned sixteen miles to his first patient, and after that he never stopped working. Unlike the settlers of southern and central Illinois, most of whom came from southern states, the farmers settling in northern Illinois came from New York and New England, more every month, by foot, horseback, or prairie schooner, sometimes driving a cow, a few hogs, some sheep. His practice would cover a huge territory – prairie rolling between great rivers, criss-crossed by small streams, broken by wooded groves, and marred by deep, muddy sloughs. If patients came to him, he charged seventy-five cents per consultation. If he made a home call, he charged a dollar, and if it was at night, $1.50. His working day consisted mostly of time in the saddle, because the homesteads were so far apart in this strange countryside. Sometimes by nightfall he was so travel-weary all he could do was fall onto the floor and into deep sleep.

He told Holden he'd be able to pay something toward his debt at the end of the month, but Nick smiled and shook his head. 'Don't hurry. In fact, I think I'd better lend you a little more. Winters are hard and you're going to need a stronger animal than that horse you ride. And with all your doctoring, you don't have time to raise yourself a cabin before snowfall. Best let me look around for someone who can build one for you, for pay.'

Nick found a cabin builder named Alden Kimball, a whipcord-thin tireless man with yellowed teeth from constantly smoking a stinking corncob. He had grown up on a farm in Hubbardton, Vermont, and more recently was a reprobate Mormon from the town of Nauvoo, Illinois, where folks were known as Latter-Day Saints and men were rumoured to have as many wives as they wanted. When Rob J. met him, Kimball said he'd had a disagreement with the church elders and just lit out. Rob J. wasn't inclined to question him too closely. It was enough for him that Kimball used an axe and an adze as if they were part of his body. He felled and trimmed logs and worked them flat on two sides where they lay, and one day Rob rented an ox from a farmer named Grueber. Rob somehow knew that Grueber wouldn't have trusted his valuable ox to him if Kimball hadn't been along. The fallen saint patiently insisted that the ox bend to his will, and together the two men and the beast in a single day snaked the shaped logs to the building site Rob had chosen on the riverbank. As Kimball joined the foundation logs with wooden pegs, Rob saw that the single great log that would support the north wall had a bad crook in it about a third of the way down its length, and he called it to Alden's attention.

'Be all right,' Kimball said, and Rob went away and let him work.

Visiting the site a couple of days later, Rob saw that the walls of the cabin had risen. Alden had chinked the logs with clay dug from a place in the riverbank, and was whitewashing the clay strips. On the north side, all the logs had a crookedness that almost exactly matched the foundation log, giving the entire wall a slight bend. It must have taken Alden a lot of time to search out logs with exactly the right defect, and, indeed, two of the logs had had to be worked with the adze to make them conform.

It was Alden who told him about a quarter horse Grueber had for sale. When Rob J. confessed he didn't know much about horseflesh, Kimball shrugged. 'Four-year-old, still puttin' on height and bone. Sound, nothin' wrong with her.'

So Rob bought the quarter-horse mare. She was what Grueber called a blood bay, more red than brown, with black legs, mane, and tail, and black spots like freckles all over her forehead, fifteen hands high, with a serviceable body and an intelligent look in her eyes. Because the freckles reminded him of the girl he'd known in Boston, he called her Margaret Holland. Meg for short.

He could see that Alden had an eye for animals, and one morning he asked if Kimball would care to stay on as hired man after the cabin was finished, and work the farm.

'Well . . . what kind of farm?'

'Sheep.'

Alden made a face. 'Know naught about sheep. Always worked with milch cows.'

'I grew up with sheep,' Rob said. 'Not much to watching them. Sheep tend to flock up, they can be handled easily on the open prairie by one man and a dog. As for the other chores, castrating and shearing and the like, I could show you.'

Alden appeared to consider, but he was just being polite. 'Truth to tell, don't care much for sheep. No,' he said finally. 'Thank you kindly, but suppose not.' Perhaps to change the subject, he asked Rob what he intended to do with his old horse. Monica Grenville had carried him west, but she was an exhausted mount. 'Don't figger to get much for her if you sell without bringin' her back to condition. Plenty of grass on the prairie, but you'd have to buy hay for winter feed.'

That problem was solved a few days later, when a farmer who was short of cash paid for a birthing with a wagonload of hay. After consultation, Alden agreed to extend the cabin roof out over the southern wall, supporting the corners with poles to create an open barn for the two horses. A few days after it was finished, Nick stopped by to look it over. He grinned at the attached animal shelter and avoided Alden Kimball's eyes. 'Makes for kind of a queer-looking cabin, you have to admit.' And he lifted his eyebrows at the cabin's north end. 'The damn wall is crooked.'

Rob J. rubbed his fingertips admiringly over the bend in

the logs. 'No, it was built that way on purpose, that's the way we like it. That's what makes it different from other cabins you're likely to see.'

Alden worked in silence for about an hour after Nick left; then he stopped hammering pegs and walked over to where Rob was scurrying Meg's coat. He knocked the dottle out of his pipe against his boot heel. 'Guess I'm able to learn to handle sheep,' he said.

11
The Recluse

For his starter herd, Rob J. decided to get mostly Spanish merinos, because their fine wool would make a valuable crop, and to cross-breed them with a long-wool English breed, as his family had done in Scotland. He told Alden he wouldn't buy the animals until spring, to save the expense and effort required to keep them during winter. In the meantime, Alden laboured at stockpiling fenceposts, building two lean-to barns, and putting up a cabin in the woods for himself. Fortunately, the hired man was capable of working unsupervised, because Rob J. was occupied. Those who lived nearby had got along without a doctor, and he spent his first few months trying to correct the effects of neglect and home remedies. He saw patients with gout and cancer and dropsy and scrofula, and too many children with worms, and people of all ages with consumption. He grew tired of pulling rotten teeth. He felt the same way about pulling teeth as he did about amputating limbs, hating to take away something he was never going to be able to put back.

'Wait until spring, that's when everybody around here comes down with some kind of fever. You'll make your fortune,' Nick Holden told him cheerfully. His calls took him onto remote, almost nonexistent trails. Nick offered the loan of a revolver until he could buy one. 'Travel is dangerous,

73

there are bandits like land pirates, and now those damned hostiles.'

'Hostiles?'

'Indians.'

'Has anyone else seen them?'

Nick scowled. They had been sighted several times, he said, but admitted against his will that they had molested no one. 'So far,' he added darkly.

Rob J. bought no handgun, nor did he wear Nick's. He felt secure on the new horse. She had great endurance, and he enjoyed the surefooted way she could scramble up and down steep riverbanks and ford swift streams. He taught her to accept being mounted from either side, and she learned to trot to him when he whistled. Quarter horses were used for herding cattle, and she had already been taught by Grueber to start, stop, and turn instantly, responding to the slightest shift of Rob's weight or a small movement of the reins.

One day in October he was summoned to the farm of Gustav Schroeder, who had got two fingers of his left hand crushed between heavy rocks. On the way, Rob became lost, and he stopped to ask directions at a sorry-looking shack that stood next to well-tended fields. The door opened just a crack but he was assailed by the worst of odours, stinks of old body wastes, rotten air, putrefaction. A face peered out and he saw red swollen eyes, dank, dirt-plastered witch's hair. 'Go away!' a hoarse female voice commanded. Something the size of a small dog scuttled in the room beyond the door. Not a child in there? The door slammed like a blow.

The groomed fields proved to be Schroeder's. When Rob reached the farmhouse he had to amputate the farmer's little finger and the top joint of the third finger, agony for the patient. When he was through, he asked Schroeder's wife about the woman in the shack, and Alma Schroeder looked a little ashamed.

'That is only poor Sarah,' she told him.

74

12
The Big Indian

Nights grew chill and crystal clear, with enormous stars, then for weeks in a row the sky lowered. The snow arrived, lovely and terrible, before November was old, then the wind came and carved the deep white covering, piling it into drifts that challenged but never stopped the mare. It was seeing how the quarter horse responded to the snow, with so much heart, that made Rob J. really begin to love her.

The bitter cold across the plains stayed that way through December and most of January. Making his way home one dawn after a night of sitting up in a smoky sod house with five children, three of whom had bad croup, he came upon two Indians in miserable trouble. He recognized at once the men who had listened to him playing the viola outside Nick Holden's cabin. The carcasses of three snowshoe hares attested that they had been hunting. One of their ponies had foundered, snapping a foreleg at the fetlock and pinning its rider, the Sauk with the great hooked nose. His companion, the huge Indian, had killed the horse at once and slit its belly, and then had managed to drag the injured man free of the carcass and place him within the horse's steaming cavity to keep him from freezing.

'I'm a doctor, maybe I can help.'

They understood no English, but the big Indian made no attempt to stop him from examining the injured man. As soon as he groped beneath the tattered fur clothing it was apparent that the hunter had suffered a posterior dislocation of the right hip and was in agony. The sciatic nerve had been damaged, because his foot hung loose, and when Rob pulled off his skin shoe and pricked him with a knife point, he was unable to move his toes. The guarding muscles had become as intractable as wood because of pain and the freezing cold, and there was no way to set the hip then and there.

To Rob J.'s annoyance, the large Indian mounted his horse and abandoned them, riding across the prairie toward the tree line, perhaps for help. Rob was wearing a moth-eaten sheepskin coat, won at poker from a lumberjack the previous winter, and he took it off and covered the patient, then opened his saddlebag and took out rag bandages that he used to tie the Indian's legs together to immobilize the unseated hip. Presently the large Indian returned dragging two trimmed tree limbs, stout but flexible poles. Tying them on each side of his horse as shafts, he connected them with some of his skin garments until he had a trailing litter. Onto this they lashed the injured man, who must have suffered terribly as he was trailed, though the snow gave him a smoother ride than if there had been bare ground.

A light sleet began to fall as Rob J. rode behind the travois. They travelled along the edge of the forest that bordered the river. Finally the Indian turned his horse into a break between the trees and they rode into the camp of the Sauks.

Conical skin *tipis* – there would prove to be seventeen when Rob J. had a chance to count – had been set up among the trees, where they were protected from the wind. The Sauks were warmly dressed. Everywhere was evidence of the reservation, for they wore the castoff clothing of whites as well as animal skins and furs, and old army ammunition boxes could be seen in several of the tents. They had plenty of dead wood for fires, and grey wisps rose from the smokeholes of the *tipis*. But the eagerness with which hands reached for the three skinny snowshoe hares wasn't lost on Rob J., nor was the pinched look in all the faces he saw, for

76

he had witnessed starving people before.

The injured man was carried into one of the *tipis*, and Rob followed along. 'Does anyone speak English?'

'I have your language.' The age was hard to determine, for the speaker wore the same shapeless bundle of fur garments as anyone else, with the head covered by a hood of sewn grey squirrel pelts, but the voice was a woman's.

'I know how to fix this fellow. I'm a doctor. Do you know what a doctor is?'

'I know.' Her brown eyes regarded him calmly beneath the fur folds. She spoke briefly in their own language, and the others in the tent waited, watching him.

Rob J. took a few sticks from their woodpile and built up the fire. When he freed the man from his clothing, he saw that the hip was internally rotated. He raised the Indian's knees until they were fully flexed, and then, working through the woman, he made certain that strong hands firmly held the man pinned down. Crouching, he got his right shoulder just beneath the knee of the injured side. Then he drove up with all his might, and the snap was audible as the ball found its way back into the socket of the joint.

The Indian lay as though dead. Through it all, he had scarcely grunted, and Rob J. felt that a swallow of whisky and laudanum was in order for him. But both medicinals were in his saddlebag, and before he could get them, the woman had poured water into a gourd and mixed it with powder from a small deerskin bag, and then had given it to the injured man, who drank it eagerly. She placed a hand on each of the man's hips and looked into his eyes and half-sang something in their tongue. Watching her and listening, Rob J. felt the hair lift on the back of his neck. He realized she was their doctor. Or maybe some kind of priest.

In that moment the sleepless night and the snow-struggle of the past twenty-four hours caught up with him, and in a fog of fatigue he moved out of the dimly lit *tipi* into the crowd of snow-dusted Sauks waiting outside. A rheumy-eyed old man touched him wonderingly. '*Cawso wabeskiou!*' he said, and others took it up: '*Cawso wabeskiou, Cawso wabeskiou.'*

The doctor-priest left the *tipi*. As the hood swung away from her face, he saw she wasn't old. 'What are they saying?'

'They call you a white shaman,' she said.

The medicine woman told him that, for reasons that were at once obvious to him, the injured man's name was Waucauche, Eagle Nose. The large Indian's name was Pyawanegawa, Comes Singing. As Rob J. travelled toward his own cabin, he met Comes Singing and two other Sauks, who must have ridden back to the horse carcass as soon as Eagle Nose was brought in, in order to reach the meat before the wolves. They had cut up the dead pony and were bringing the meat back on two packhorses. They passed him in single file without seeming to glance at him once, as if they were riding past a tree.

After he arrived home, Rob J. wrote in his journal and attempted to draw a picture of the woman from memory, but try as he might, all that came was a kind of generic Indian face, sexless and tight with hunger. He needed sleep, but he wasn't tempted by his straw mattress. He knew Gus Schroeder had extra dried ears to sell, and Alden had mentioned that Paul Gruever had a little extra grain put by for a cash crop. He rode Meg and led Monica, and that afternoon he went back to the Sauk camp and dropped off two sacks of corn and one of swedes and one of wheat.

The medicine woman didn't thank him. She just looked at the sacks of food and rapped out some orders, and eager hands hustled them inside the *tipis*, out of the cold and the wet. The wind flapped open her hood. She really was a redskin: her face was a ruddy, mordant rouge-brown. Her nose had a prominent bump on the bridge, and almost negroid nostrils. Her brown eyes were swimmingly large and her gaze was direct. When he asked her name, she said it was Makwa-ikwa.

'What does that mean in English?'

'The Bear Woman,' she said.

78

13
Through the Cold Time

The stubs of Gus Schroeder's amputated fingers healed without infection.

Rob J. visited the farmer perhaps too often, for he was intrigued by the woman in the cabin on the Schroeder place. Alma Schroeder at first was close-mouthed, but as soon as she was convinced that Rob J. wanted to help, she became maternally voluble about the younger woman. Twenty-two years old, Sarah was a widow, having come to Illinois from Virginia five years before with her young husband, Alexander Bledsoe. For two springs Bledsoe had broken the stubborn deep-rooted sod, struggling with a plough and a yoke of oxen to make his fields as large as possible before the summer prairie grass sent spears higher than the top of his head. In May of his second year in the west he came down with the Illinois mange, followed by the fever that killed him.

'That next spring she tries to plough and plant, all by herself,' Alma said. 'She gets in a *kleine* crop, breaks a little more sod, but she just can't do it. Just can't farm. That summer we come from Ohio, Gus and me. We make, what you call it? A rangement? She turns her fields over to Gustav, we keep her in cornmeal, garden sass. Wood for the fire.'

'How old is the child?'

'Two year,' Alma Schroeder said levelly. 'She never said, but we think Will Mosby was the father. Will and Frank Mosby, brothers, used to live downriver. When we moved here, Will Mosby was spending lots of time with her. We were glad. Out here, a woman needs a man.' Alma sighed with contempt. 'Them brothers. No good, no good. Frank Mosby is hiding from the law. Will was killed in a saloon fight, just before the baby come. Couple months later, Sarah gets sick.'

'She doesn't have much luck.'

'No luck. She's bad sick, says she's dyin' of cancer. Gets pains in her stomach, hurts so bad she can't . . . you know . . . hold the water.'

'Has she lost control of her bowels too?'

Alma Schroeder coloured. Talk of a baby born out of wedlock was merely observation of life's vagaries, but she wasn't accustomed to discussing bodily functions with any man but Gus, not even a doctor.

'No. Just the water . . . She wants me to take the boy when she goes. We're already feedin' five . . .' She looked at him fiercely. 'You got medicine to give her for the hurtin'?'

Someone with cancer had a choice of whisky or opium. There was nothing she could take and still look after her child. But when he left the Schroeders', he stopped by her cabin, closed up and lifeless-looking. 'Mrs Bledsoe,' he called. He rapped on the door.

'I'm Rob J. Cole. I'm a doctor.' He knocked again.

'Go. Go way. Go way.'

By the end of winter his own cabin took on a feeling of home. Wherever he went he acquired homely things – an iron pot, two tin drinking cups, a coloured bottle, an earthen bowl, wooden spoons. Some he bought. Some he accepted in payment, like the pair of old but serviceable patchwork quilts; he hung one on the north wall to cut down the draughts and used the other to comfort the bed Alden Kimball made for him. Alden also made him a three-legged stool and a low bench for in front of the hearth, and just before the snows carne Kimball had rolled into the cabin a three-foot section of sycamore tree and set it on its end. He nailed a few lengths of board to it and Rob spread an old wool blanket over the planks. At this table he sat kinglike on the best piece of furniture in the house, a chair with a seat of plaited hickory bark, taking his meals or reading his books and journals before bedtime by the uncertain light of a rag burning in a dish of melted lard. The fireplace made of river stones and clay kept the small cabin warm. Over it, his rifles rested on pegs, and from the rafters he had hung bunches of herbs, braids of onions and garlic, threads of dried apple slices, and a hard sausage and a smoke-blackened ham. In a corner he accumulated tools – a hoe, an axe, a grubber, a wooden fork, all made with differing degrees of workmanship.

Occasionally he played the viola da gamba. Most of the time he was too tired to make music all by himself. On March 2 a letter from Jay Geiger and a supply of sulphur came to the stage office in Rock Island. Geiger wrote that Rob J.'s description of the land in Holden's Crossing was more than he and his wife had hoped for. He had sent Nick Holden a draft of money to cover the deposit on the property and he would take over future payments to the government land office. Unfortunately, the Geigers didn't plan to come to Illinois for some time; Lillian was pregnant again, 'an unexpected occurrence which, though it fills us with joy, will delay our departure from this place'. They would wait until their second child was born and was old enough to survive the jolting ride over the prairie.

Rob J. read the letter with mixed feelings. He was delighted that Jay trusted his recommendation about the land and someday would be his neighbour. Yet he despaired because that day wasn't in sight. He would have given a lot to be able to sit with Jason and Lillian and make music that comforted him and transported his soul. The prairie was a huge, silent prison, and most of the time he was alone in it.

He told himself he should look for a likely dog.

By midwinter the Sauks were lean and hungry again. Gus Schroeder wondered aloud why Rob J. wanted to buy two more sacks of corn, but didn't press the matter when Rob offered no explanation. The Indians accepted the additional gift of corn from him silently and without visible emotion, as before. He brought Makwa-ikwa a pound of coffee and took to spending time by her fire. She eked out the coffee with so much parched wild root that it was different from any coffee he'd ever had. They drank it black; it wasn't good but it was hot and somehow Indian-tasting. Gradually they learned about one another. She had had four years of schooling in a mission for Indian children near Fort Crawford. She could read a little and had heard of Scotland, but when he assumed she was a Christian, she set him right. Her people worshipped Se-wanna – their top god – and other *manitous*, and she told them how to do it, in the old ways. He saw she was as much a priestess as anything, which helped her be an effective healer. She knew all about the botanical medicines of that place, and bunches of dried herbs hung from her tent poles. Several times he watched her treat Sauks, beginning by squatting at the sick Indian's side and softly playing a drum made from a pottery jar filled two-thirds with water and with a thin cured skin stretched over its mouth. She rubbed the drumhead with a curved stick. The result was a low pitched thunder that eventually had a soporific effect. After a while, she put both her hands on the body part that needed healing and talked to the sick person in their tongue. He saw her ease a young man's sprung back that way, and an old woman's tortured bones.

'How do your hands make the pain go away?'

But she shook her head. 'I can't 'splain.'

Rob J. took the old woman's hands in his. Despite the fact that her pain had gone, he felt the ebbing of her forces. He told Makwa-ikwa the woman had only a few days to live. When he returned to the Sauk camp five days later, she was dead.

'How did you know?' Makwa-ikwa asked.

'Death that's coming . . . some people in my family can feel it. A kind of gift. I can't explain.'

So each took the other on faith. He found her tremendously interesting, completely different from anyone he had known. Even then, physical awareness was a presence between them. Mostly they sat by her small fire in the *tipi* and drank coffee or talked. One day he tried to tell her what Scotland was like and was unable to determine how much she comprehended, but she listened and now and then asked a question about wild animals or crops. She explained to him the tribal structure of the Sauks, and now it was her turn to be patient, for he found it complicated. The Sauk Nation was divided into twelve groups similar to Scottish clans, only instead of McDonald and Bruce and Stewart they had these names: *Namawuck*, Sturgeon; *Muc-kissou*, Bald Eagle; *Pucca-hummowuck*, Ringed Perch; *Macco Pennyack*, Bear Potato; *Kiche Cumme*, Great Lake; *Payshake-issewuck*, Deer; *Pesshe-peshewuck*, Panther; *Waymeco-uck*, Thunder; *Muck-wuck*, Bear; *Me-seco*, Black Bass; *Aha-wuck*, Swan; and *Muhwha-wuck*, Wolf. The clans lived together with no competition, but every Sauk male belonged to one of two highly competitive Halves, the *Keeso-qui*, Long Hairs, or the *Osh-cush*, Brave Men. Each first man-child was declared a member of his father's Half at birth; each second boy became a member of the other Half, and so forth, alternating so that the two Halves were represented more or less equally within each family and within each clan. They competed in games, in hunting, in making children, in counting coup and other deeds of bravery – in every aspect of their lives. The savage competition kept the Sauks strong and coura-geous, but there were no blood feuds between Halves. It struck Rob J. that it was a more sensible system than the one with which he was familiar, more civilized, for thousands of Scots had died at the hands of rival clansmen during many centuries of savage internecine strife.

Because of the short rations and a queasiness toward trusting the Indians' food preparation, at first he avoided sharing Makwa-ikwa's meals. Then, on several occasions when the hunters were successful, he ate her cooking and found it palatable. He saw that they ate more stews than roasts and, given a choice, would take red meat or fowl over fish. She told him about dog feasts, religious meals because the *manitous* esteemed canine flesh. She explained that the more the dog was valued as a pet, the better the sacrifice at a dog feast and the stronger the medicine. He couldn't hide his revulsion. 'You don't find it strange to eat a pet dog?'

'Not so strange as to eat blood and body of Christ.'

He was a normal young man, and sometimes, even though they were bundled against the cold by many layers of clothing and furs, he became painfully horny. If their fingers touched as she handed him coffee, he felt a glandular shock. Once he took her cold square hands in his and was shaken by the vitality he felt surging in her. He examined her short fingers, the roughened red-brown skin, the pink calluses in her palms. He asked if she would come sometime to his cabin, to visit. She looked at him silently and reclaimed her hands. She didn't say she wouldn't visit his cabin, but she never came.

During mud season Rob J. rode out to the Indian village, avoiding the sloughs that had sprung up everywhere as the spongelike prairie was unable to absorb all the bounty of the melted snows. He found the Sauks breaking their winter camp and followed them six miles to an open site where the Indians were replacing their snug winter *tipis* by building *hedonoso-tes*, longhouses of interwoven branches through which the mild breezes of summer would blow. There was a good reason for moving camps; the Sauks knew nothing about sanitation, and the winter camp stank of their shit. Surviving the harsh winter and moving to the summer camp obviously had lifted the Indians' spirits, and everywhere Rob J. looked he saw young men wrestling, racing, or playing at a game he had never witnessed before. It utilized stout wooden staffs with leather webbed bags at one end, and a buckskin-covered wooden ball. While running at full speed, a player hurled the ball out of his netted stick and another player caught it deftly in his net. By passing it to one another they moved the ball considerable distances. The play was fast and very rough. When a player carried the ball, the other players felt free to try to dislodge it from his net by lashing out with their sticks, often landing wicked blows on their opponents' bodies or limbs, with contenders

84

tripping and crashing. Noting the fascination with which Rob was following the action, one of the four Indian players beckoned and handed over his stick.

The others grinned and quickly made him part of the game, which seemed to him to be more mayhem than sport. He was larger than most of the other players, more muscular. At the first opportunity, the man with the ball flicked his wrist and sent the hard sphere hurtling toward Rob. He stabbed at it ineffectually and had to run to claim it, only to find himself in the midst of a wildcat fight, a clashing of long sticks that mostly seemed to land on his flesh. The long passing baffled him. Full of rueful appreciation of skills he didn't possess, he soon handed the stick back to its owner.

While he ate stewed rabbit in Makwa-ikwa's longhouse, the medicine woman told him quietly that the Sauks wished him to do them a service. All through the hard winter they had taken pelts in their traps. Now they had two bales of prime mink, fox, beaver, and muskrat. They wanted to trade the furs for seed to plant their first summer's crop.

It surprised Rob J., because he hadn't thought of Indians as farmers.

'If we brought the furs to a white trader ourselves, we would be cheated,' Makwa-ikwa told him. She said it without rancour, the way she would tell him any other fact.

So one morning he and Alden Kimball led two packhorses laden with fur pelts, and another horse without a pack, all the way to Rock Island. Rob J. traded hard with the storekeeper there and in exchange for the furs came away with five sacks of seed corn – a sack of small early corn, two sacks of a larger, flinty, hard-kernelled corn for hominy, and two sacks of a large-eared soft-kernelled meal corn – and three sacks each of bean, pumpkin, and squash seeds. In addition, he received three United States twenty dollar gold pieces to give the Sauks a small emergency fund for other things they might need to buy from the whites. Alden was full of admiration for his employer's shrewdness, believing Rob J. had arranged the complicated trading deal for his own profit.

That night they stayed in Rock Island. In a saloon Rob

nursed two glasses of ale and listened to the bragging reminiscences of old Indian fighters. 'This whole place belonged to either the Sauk or the Fox,' said the rheumy-eyed barman. 'The Sauk called themselves the Osaukie and the Fox called themselves Mesquakies. Together they had everything between the Mississippi on the west, Lake Michigan on the east, the Wisconsin on the north, and the Illinois River on the south – fifty million damned acres of the best farmland! Their biggest village was Sauk-e-nuk, a regular town with streets and a square. Eleven thousand Sauks lived there, farming two thousand five hundred acres between the Rock River and the Mississippi. Well, it didn't take us very long to stampede them red bastards and put that good land to use!'

The stories were anecdotes of bloody fights with Black Hawk and his warriors, in which the Indians always were demonic, the whites always brave and noble. They were tales related by veterans of the Great Crusades, mostly transparent lies, dreams of what might have been if those telling them had been better men. Rob J. recognized that most white men didn't see what he did when he looked at Indians. The others talked as if the Sauks were wild animals who had been righteously hunted down until they had fled, leaving the countryside safer for human folk. Rob had been searching all his life for the spiritual freedom he recognized in the Sauks. It was what he had been seeking when he wrote the handbill in Scotland, what he'd thought he had watched die when Andrew Gerould had been hanged. Now he had discovered it in a bunch of ragtag red-skinned exotics. He was not romanticizing; he recognized the squalor of the Sauk camp, the backwardness of their culture in a world that had passed them by. But nursing his mug of drink, trying to pretend interest in the alcoholic stories of disembowelments, of scalpings, of looting and rapine, he knew that Makwa-ikwa and her Sauks were the best thing that had happened to him in this place.

14
Ball-and-Stick

Rob J. came upon Sarah Bledsoe and her child the way one surprises wild creatures in rare moments of ease. He'd seen birds drowsing in the sun with just rapt contentment after dusting themselves and preening. The woman and her son were sitting on the ground outside her cabin, their eyes closed. She'd done no preening. Her long blonde hair was dull and snarled, and the wrinkled dress that covered her skinny body was filthy. Her skin was puffy and her drawn white face reflected her illness. The little boy, who was asleep, had fair hair like his mother's, equally matted.

When Sarah opened her blue eyes and looked into Rob's, everything rushed into her face – surprise, fear, dismay, and anger – and without a word she swept up her son and bounded into the house. He went up to the cabin entrance. He'd come to hate his periodic attempts to talk to her through this slab of wood.

'Mrs Bledsoe, please. I want to help you,' he called, but her only answer was a grunt of effort and the sound of the heavy bar falling across the door.

The Indians didn't bust the sod with ploughs, the way white homesteaders would. Instead, they looked for thin places in the grass cover and poked through to the soil, dropping seeds into the drills left by their sharpened planting sticks.

They covered the toughest areas of grass with brush piles that would cause the sod to rot out in a year, so there would be more planting area in which to sow their seeds the following spring.

When Rob J. visited the Sauks' summer camp, the corn planting was done and celebration was in the air. Makwa-ikwa told him that after planting came the Crane Dance, their most joyous festival. Its first event was a great ball-and-stick game in which every male participated. There was no need to recruit teams, it was Half against Half. The Long Hairs had half a dozen fewer men than the Brave Men. It was the big Indian called Comes Singing who brought about Rob's undoing, for while he stood and talked with Makwa-ikwa, Comes Singing came and spoke with her.

'He invites you to run at the ball-and-stick with the Long Hairs,' she said in English, turning to Rob.

'Ah, well.' He grinned at them foolishly. It was the last thing he wanted to do, recalling the Indians' skill and his own clumsiness. The words of refusal were on his tongue, but the man and woman watched him with a special interest, and he sensed that the invitation had significance he didn't understand. So instead of waving the summons off, which a sensible man would have done, he thanked them politely and told them he'd be pleased to run with the Long Hairs.

In her precise schoolgirl English – so curious to hear – she explained that the contest would start in the summer village. The winning Half would be the one that put the ball into a small cave in the opposite riverbank, about six miles downstream.

'Six miles!' He was further astonished to learn that there were no sidelines. Makwa-ikwa managed to convey to him that anyone who ran off to the side in order to avoid his opponents would not be highly regarded.

To Rob it was a foreign contest, an alien game, a manifestation of a savage culture. So why was he doing this? He asked himself the question dozens of times that night, for he slept in Comes Singing's *hedonoso-te* because the game would start soon after dawn. The longhouse was about fifty feet long and twenty feet wide, constructed of woven branches covered on the outside by sheets of elm bark. There were no windows, and the doorways at each end were hung with buffalo robes, but the loose construction provided plenty of air. It had eight compartments, four on either side of a central corridor. Comes Singing and his wife, Moon, slept in one, Moon's elderly parents slept in another, and another was occupied by their two children. The other compartments were storerooms, in one of which Rob J. spent a restless night, studying the stars through the smoke hole in the roof and listening to sighs, bad dreams, windbreaking and, on several occasions, what could only have been the sounds of vigorous and enthusiastic copulation, although his host never sang a note or even hummed.

In the morning, after breakfasting on boiled white-flint hominy in which he tasted lumps of ash and mercifully didn't recognize other things, Rob J. submitted to an unlikely honour. Not all the Long Hairs had long hair; the way the teams would be differentiated was in their paint. Long Hairs wore black paint, a mixture of animal grease and charcoal. Brave Men smeared themselves with a white clay. All over the camp, males dipped their fingers into the paint bowls and decorated their skins. Comes Singing applied black streaks to his own features, chest, and arms. Then he proffered the paint to Rob.

Why not? he asked himself giddily, scooping out the black dye with two fingers like a man eating pease porridge without a spoon. It felt gritty as he drew it on his forehead and across his cheeks. He dropped his shirt to the ground, a nervous male butterfly shedding its chrysalis, and streaked his torso. Comes Singing stared at his heavy Scots brogues and disappeared, coming back with a pair of light deerskin shoes similar to those worn by all the Sauks, but though Rob tried on several pairs, he had a great foot, even larger than Comes Singing's. They laughed together at the size, and the big Indian abandoned the cause and left him shod in his heavy boots.

Comes Singing handed him a net-stick whose hickory handle was as stout as a cudgel, and motioned for him to follow. The competing forces assembled in an open square around which the longhouses were built. Makwa-ikwa made a pronouncement in their tongue, doubtless a benediction, and then, before Rob J. knew what had happened, she drew back her hand and flung the ball, which swam toward the waiting warriors in a lazy parabola that ended in the savage clashing of sticks and wild cries and grunts of pain. To Rob's disappointment, the Brave Men gained the ball, which was carried off in the net of a long-legged breech-clad youth, hardly more than a boy, but with the muscular legs of an adult runner. He was quick off the mark, and the pack followed behind like dogs after a hare. It was clearly a time for the sprinters, for the ball was passed several times on the dead run and soon was far ahead of Rob.

Comes Singing had remained by his side. Several times they gained on the swiftest men as combat was joined, slowing the forward movement. Comes Singing grunted in satisfaction as the ball was snared in the net of a Long Hair, but he didn't appear surprised when it was recaptured by the Brave Men a few minutes later. As the pack coursed along the tree line that followed the river, the big Indian gestured for Rob to follow him, and the two of them turned off from the route the others had taken and moved across the open prairie, their pounding feet sending the heavy dew flying from the young grass, so it looked as though a swarm of silver insects sought to eat their heels.

Where was he being led? And could he trust this Indian? It was too late to worry himself with such questions, for he had already invested his faith. He concentrated his energy on keeping up with Comes Singing, who moved well for so large a person. Soon he saw Comes Singing's purpose: they were running headlong in a straight line that might make it possible to intercept the others on the longer route along the river trail. By the time he and Comes Singing were able to stop running, Rob J.'s feet were leaden, he was gulping for breath, and there was a stitch in his side. But they got to the bend in the river before the pack.

Indeed, the pack had been left behind by front-runners.

As Rob and Comes Singing waited in a grove of hickories and oak, sucking as much air as possible into their lungs, three white-painted runners loped into sight. The leading Sauk didn't have the ball; he carried his empty net-stick loosely as he ran, as if it were a spear. His feet were bare, and for clothing he wore only a pair of ragged trousers that had started life as white man's brown homespun pants. He was smaller than either of the two men in the trees but muscular and made even more fierce-looking by the fact that his left ear had been torn off a long time ago, a trauma that had left that side of his head knotted with scar tissue. Rob J. tensed, but Comes Singing touched his arm, restraining him, and they let the scout runner pass. Not far behind, the ball was carried in the net of the youthful Brave Man who had snagged it when Makwa-ikwa had thrown it into play. Next to him ran a short, burly Sauk in cut-down trousers that once had been issued by the US cavalry, blue with a broad dirty-yellow stripe on each side.

Comes Singing pointed to Rob and then at the youth, and Rob nodded: the boy was his responsibility. He knew they had to strike before surprise was lost, because if this Brave Man ran away, he and Comes Singing wouldn't catch him.

So they struck like thunder and lightning, and now Rob J. saw one of the purposes of the leather thongs tied about his arms, for as quickly as a good shepherd would have upended a ram and bound his legs, Comes Singing flung the guard runner to the ground and trussed his wrists and ankles. And none too soon, for the scout runner had turned back. Rob was slower in binding the young Sauk, so Comes Singing went out alone to face the one-eared man. The Brave Man used his net-stick as a club, but Comes Singing eluded the blow almost disdainfully. He was half again the other man's size, and fiercer, and he grappled him to the ground and tied him almost before Rob J. was finished with his own prisoner.

Comes Singing picked up the ball and dropped it into Rob's net. Without a word or glance at the three bound Sauks, Comes Singing ran off. Holding the ball in the net as if it were a bomb with a lighted fuse, Rob J. plunged down the trail after him.

They'd gone unchallenged when Comes Singing stopped him and indicated they had reached the place where they would cross the reiver. Another use of the thongs was demonstrated when Comes Singing tied Rob's net-stick to his belt, leaving his hands free for swimming. Comes Singing tied his own stick to his loincloth and kicked off his deerskin shoes, abandoning them. Rob J. knew his feet were too tender to allow him to run without his boots, so he joined them by their laces and hung them around his neck. That left him with the ball, and he tucked it down the front of his trousers.

Comes Singing grinned and held up three fingers.

Though it didn't represent the soul of wit, yet it broke Rob's tension, and he threw back his head and laughed – a mistake, for the water that carried away the sound gave back cries of pursuit as their location was discovered, and they lost no time in entering the cold river.

They kept pace, although Rob used the European's breast stroke and Comes Singing propelled himself by moving his hands the way animals swim. Rob was enjoying himself mightily; he didn't feel like a noble savage, exactly, but it would take very little to convince himself he was Leather-stocking. When they reached the far shore, Comes Singing grunted at him impatiently while he pulled on his boots. The heads of their pursuers could be seen bobbing on the river like so many apples in a tub. When finally Rob was ready and the ball was back in his net, the foremost of the swimmers was almost across.

As soon as they ran, Come Singing's pointing finger showed him the mouth of the small cave that was their goal, and the dark opening pulled him forward. An exultant cry in the Erse rose to his tongue, but it was premature. Half a dozen Sauks burst onto the trail between them and the mouth of the cave; although the water had obliterated much of their paint, traces of white clay remained. Almost at once a pair of Long Hairs followed the Brave Men out of the woods and attacked. In the fifteenth-century, one of Rob's ancestors, Brian Cullen, had single-handedly held off an entire war party of the McLaughlins by whirling his great Scots sword in a whistling circle of death. With two less lethal circles that were nonetheless intimidating, the two Long Hairs now held three of their opponents at bay by whirling their sticks. This left three Brave Men free to try to get the ball. Comes Singing neatly parried a bludgeon swing with his own net-stick and then disposed of his opponent with the well-placed sole of his bare foot.

'That's it, in the arse, kick his murderous arse,' Rob J. bellowed, forgetting none could understand his words. An Indian came at him as if hemp-crazed. Rob sidestepped and, as the man's bare toes hove into range, stamped down a heavy brogan. A few running paces beyond his groaning victim, and he was close enough to the cave even for his limited skills. With a snap of his wrists the ball was on its journey. Never mind that instead of a hard, clean shot it bounced its way into the dim interior. The important thing was, they saw it enter.

He threw his stick into the air and screamed, 'Victore-e-e! To the Black Clan!'

He heard rather than felt the blow as the net-stick swung by the man behind him connected with his head. It was a crisp, solid sound, similar to one he'd learned to recognize in the lumber camp, the thunk made by a double-ditted axe coming into contact with a solid oak log. To his amazement, the ground seemed to open. He fell into a deep hole that brought on the darkness and ended everything, turning him off like a stopped clock.

15
A Present from Stone Dog

He knew nothing of being toted back to their camp like a sack of grain. When he opened his eyes it was dark of night. He smelled bruised grass. Roasted meat, perhaps fat squirrel. The smoke of the fire. The femaleness of Makwa-ikwa, who leaned over him and watched him with young-ancient eyes. He didn't know the question she was asking, aware only of a terrible pain in his head. The smell of the meat nauseated. Apparently she anticipated it, for she was holding his head over a wooden bucket and enabling him to vomit.

When he was finished, and weak and gasping, she gave him a potion to drink, something cool and green and bitter. He thought he detected mint, but there was a stronger and less agreeable taste. He tried to turn his head in refusal, but she held him firmly and forced him to swallow as if he were a child. He was annoyed with her, angry. But soon after, he slept. From time to time he awakened and she force-fed him the bitter green liquid. And in this way, sleeping, semiconscious, or suckling at Mother Nature's odd-tasting teat, he passed almost two days.

On the third morning the lump on his head was down and the headache was gone. She agreed he was getting better but dosed him just as heavily, and he slept again.

All around him, the festival of the Crane Dance continued.

Sometimes there were the mutterings of her water drum and of voices singing in their strange and guttural language, and the near and far-off noises of games and races, the shouts of the Indian spectators. Late in the day he opened his eyes in the dimness of the longhouse and saw Makwa-ikwa changing her costume. He focused on her womanly breasts, puzzling to him because there was enough light to reveal what appeared to be welts and scars forming strange symbols, runelike markings that ran from her chest wall to the aureoles of both nipples.

Although he didn't move and made no sound, somehow she sensed his wakefulness. For a moment as she stood before him, their eyes met. Then she faced away from him, turned her back. Not, he felt, to hide the dark, tangled triangle so much as to protect from him the mysterious symbols on the priestly bosom. Sacred breasts, he told himself wonderingly. There was nothing sacred about her hips and buttocks. She was large-boned but he wondered why she was called Bear Woman, for in her face and suppleness she was more like a powerful cat. He couldn't guess her age. He was afflicted by a sudden vision of taking her from behind while grasping in each hand a thick braid of greased black hair, like riding a sensual human horse. He contemplated with amazement the fact that he was planning to be the lover of a red-skinned female savage more wonderful than any James Fenimore Cooper had been able to imagine, and became aware of a vigorous physical response. Priapism could be an ominous sign, but he knew the manifestation was caused by this woman and not by an injury, and therefore presaged his recovery.

He lay quietly and watched as she put on a fringed garment of deerskin. From her right shoulder she hung a strap composed of four strands of coloured thongs, ending in a leather pouch painted with symbolic figures and a circlet of large bright feathers from birds unfamiliar to Rob, the pouch and circlet falling on her left hip.

In a moment she had slipped outside. Soon, as he lay there, he heard her voice rising and falling, certainly in prayer.

Heugh! Heugh! Heugh! they answered her in unison, and

she sang some more. He didn't have the slightest idea what she was saying to their god, but her voice gave him chills and he listened hard, peering up through the smoke hole of her lodge at stars like chunks of ice that somehow she had set on fire.

That night he waited impatiently for sounds of the Crane Dance to end. He dozed, awoke to listen, fretted, waited some more, until the sounds were done, the voices dwindled and fallen silent, the festivities over. Finally he was alerted by the sound of someone entering the longhouse, of the rustling of clothing removed and dropped. A body settled beside him with a sigh, hands reached out and found him, his hands discovered flesh. All was accomplished in silence save for indrawn breaths, an amused grunt, a hiss. He needed to do little. If he wanted to prolong pleasure, he could not, for he had been too long celibate. She was experienced and deft, he was urgent and quick, and afterwards, disappointed.

. . . Like biting into wonderful fruit to find it not what he had hoped.

Taking inventory in the dark, it now seemed to him that the breasts drooped more than he remembered, and under his fingers their walls were smooth and scarless. Crawling to the fire, Rob J. took a stick and waved the glowing end to cause it to burn.

When he crept back to the mat with the torch, he sighed.

The broad flat face that smiled up at him was in no way unpleasant, only he had never seen the woman before.

In the morning, when Makwa-ikwa returned to her longhouse, she wore again her customary shapeless costume of faded homespun. Clearly the Crane Dance festival finally was over. While she prepared the hominy to break their fast, he was sullen. He told her she must never send a woman to him again, and she nodded in a bland, non-committal way she doubtless had learned as a girl when the Christian teachers had talked to her severely.

The female she had sent him was named Smoke Woman, she said. As she cooked, she told him without emotion that she herself couldn't lie with a man, for to do so would be to lose her medicine.

Bloody aborigine nonsense, he thought in despair. Yet obviously she believed it.

But he considered it as they ate, her harsh Sauk coffee tasting more bitter than ever to him. In fairness, he acknowledged how quickly he would shun her if slipping his penis into her would mean an end to his doctoring.

He was forced to admire the way she had handled the situation, making certain the fires of his ardour had been banked before telling him simply and honestly where things stood. She was a most unusual woman, he told himself, not for the first time.

That afternoon, Sauks crowded into her *hedonoso-te*. Comes Singing spoke briefly, addressing the other Indians instead of Rob, but Makwa-ikwa translated.

'*I'neni'wa*. He is a man,' the big Indian said. He said that *Cawso wabeskiou*, the White Shaman, ever more would be a Sauk and a Long Hair. For all their days all Sauks would be the brothers and sisters of *Cawso wabeskiou*.

The Brave Man who had hit him on the head after the ball-and-stick game had been won was pushed forward, grinning and shuffling. He was a man named Stone Dog. Sauks didn't know about apologies, but they knew about reparations. Stone Dog gave him a leather pouch similar to the one Makwa-ikwa sometimes wore, only decorated with wood-pig quills instead of feathers.

Makwa-ikwa said it was to hold his medicine bundle, the collection of sacred personal articles called a *Mee-shome*, never to he shown to anyone, from which every Sauk draws strength and power. To allow him to wear the pouch, she gave him a gift of four dyed sinews – a brown, an orange, a blue, and a black – fastening them to the pouch like a strap so he could wear it from his shoulder. The cords were called *Izze* cloths, she said. 'Wherever you wear them, bullets can't hurt you, and your presence will help the crops and cure the sick.'

He was moved, yet embarrassed. 'I am happy to be a

97

brother to the Sauks.'

He had always had a hard time expressing appreciation. When his Uncle Ranald had spent fifty pounds to buy him the post of dresser at University Hospital so he could gain surgical experience while a medical student, he had scarcely been able to utter thanks. Now he didn't do better. Fortunately, the Sauk were not given to displays of gratitude either, or to farewells, and nobody made anything of it when he went out and saddled his horse and rode away.

Back at his own cabin, at first he made a game of selecting objects for his sacred medicine bundle. Several weeks before, he had found a tiny animal skull, white and clean and mysterious, on the floor of the woods. He thought it was a skunk's, it seemed the right size. All right, but what else? The finger of a birth-strangled child? Eye of newt, toe of frog, wool of bat, tongue of dog? Suddenly he wanted to assemble his medicine bundle with great seriousness. What were the objects of his essence, the clues to his soul, the *Mee-shome* wherein Robert Judson Cole derived his power?

He placed in the pouch the prize heirloom of the Cole family, the blue steel surgeon's knife that the Coles called Rob J.'s scalpel and that always went to the oldest son who became a physician.

What else could be drawn from his early life? It wasn't possible to put the cold air of the Highlands in a bag. Or the warm security of family. He wished he owned a likeness of his father, whose features he had long forgotten. His mother had given him a Bible when they had said goodbye, and for that reason he treasured it, but it wouldn't go into his *Mee-shome*. He knew he wouldn't see his mother again; perhaps she was already dead. It occurred to him to try to put her likeness to paper while it was still familiar. When he tried, a sketch came easily except for her nose, then it took anguished hours of failure until finally he had her right, and he rolled up the paper and tied it and placed it in the pouch.

He added the score that Jay Geiger had transcribed so he would be able to play Chopin on the viola da gamba.

A bar of strong brown soap went in, symbol of what Oliver Wendell Holmes had taught him about cleanliness and surgery. That started him thinking along new lines, and after some reflection he removed everything from the pouch but the scalpel and the soap. Then he added rags and dressings, an assortment of drugs and medicinals, and the surgical instruments he needed when he made house calls.

When he was done, the pouch was a medicine bag that carried the supplies and tools of his art and craft. Therefore it was the medicine bundle that gave him his powers, and he was extremely happy with the gift the blow to his hard head had won from the White Paint named Stone Dog.

16
The Doe Hunters

It was an important event when he bought his sheep because the blatting was the last detail needed to make him know he was at home. At first he worked the merinos with Alden, but it was apparent that Kimball was as capable with sheep as with other animals, and soon Alden was docking tails, castrating male lambs, and watching out for scab all by himself, as though he'd been a shepherd for years. It was well Rob wasn't needed on the farm, because as word spread about the presence of a good doctor, patients summoned him to ride greater distances. Soon, he knew, he'd have to limit the area of his practice, because Nick Holden's dream was working, and new families kept arriving in Holden's Crossing. Nick rode over one morning to inspect the flock and pronounce it odoriferous, and stayed 'to let you in on something promising. A grist mill.'

One of the new arrivals was a German named Pfersick, a miller from New Jersey. Pfersick knew where he could buy milling equipment, but he had no capital. 'Nine hundred dollars should do it. I'll put up six hundred for fifty percent of the stock. You put up three hundred for twenty-five percent – I'll advance what you need – and we'll give Pfersick twenty-five percent for running the business.'

Rob had paid back less than half the money he owed Nick, and he hated debt. 'You're putting out all the money, why not just take seventy-five percent?'

'I want to feather your nest until it's so soft and rich you won't be tempted to fly. You're as much a commodity to a town as water.'

Rob J. knew it was true. When he and Alden had gone to Rock Island to buy sheep, they'd seen a handbill Nick had distributed, describing the many advantages of settling in Holden's Crossing, among which the clinical presence of Dr Cole had been prominent. He couldn't see that going into the grist mill business would compromise his position as a physician, and in the end he nodded.

'Partners!' Nick said.

They shook hands on the deal. Rob refused a huge celebratory cigar – using stogies to administer nicotine anally had dampened his appetite for tobacco. When Nick lit up, Rob said he looked the perfect banker.

'That'll come sooner than you expect, and you'll be among the first to know.' Nick blew smoke at the sky in satisfaction. 'I'm going doe hunting in Rock Island this weekend. Care to join me?'

'What's there – in Rock Island?'

'People of the female persuasion. What do you say, old man?'

'I stay away from brothels.'

'I'm talkin' about choice private goods.'

'Sure. I'll join you,' Rob J. said. He had tried to speak casually, but doubtless something in his voice revealed he didn't treat such matters lightly, because Nick Holden grinned.

The Stephenson House reflected the personality of a Mississippi River town where nineteen hundred steamboats docked annually and where rafts of logs a third of a mile long often floated past. Whenever rivermen and lumberjacks had money, the hotel was noisy and sometimes violent. Nick Holden had made arrangements that were both expensive and private, a two-bedroom suite separated by a sitting-dining room. The women were cousins, both named Dawber, pleased by the fact that their patrons were professional men. Nick's was Lettie, Rob's was Virginia. They were small and pert, like sparrows, but they shared an arch manner that set Rob's teeth on edge. Lettie was a widow. Virginia told him she'd never married, but that night when he became familiar with her body, he saw she'd borne children.

Next morning when the four of them met at breakfast, the women whispered together and giggled. Virginia must have told Lettie about the sheath Rob called Old Horny, and Lettie must have told Nick, because as they rode homeward, Nick mentioned it and laughed. 'Why bother with those blamed things?'

'Well, disease,' Rob said mildly. 'And to ward off fatherhood.'

'Spoils the pleasure.'

Had it been all that pleasurable? He acknowledged that his body and spirit had been eased, and when Nick said he had enjoyed the companionship, Rob said so had he, and agreed that they must go doe hunting again.

The next time he rode past the Schroeders' place he saw Gus in a meadow wielding a scythe despite the amputated fingers, and they exchanged salutes. He was tempted to go right on past the Bledsoe cabin, because the woman had made it clear she considered him an intruder and the thought of her put him out of sorts. But at the last moment he turned the horse into the clearing and dismounted.

At the cabin he held his hand back before his knuckles could strike the door, because he could plainly hear from within the wailing of the child and hoarse adult screams. Bad sounds. When he tried the door, he found it unlocked. Inside, the smell was like a blow and the light was dim, but he could see Sarah Bledsoe on the floor. Next to her the baby sat, his wet face screwed up in terror so great at this final blow, the sight of a huge stranger, that no sound came from his open mouth. Rob J. wanted to pick up the child and comfort him, but as the woman screamed again he knew his attention must go to her.

He knelt and touched her cheek. Cold sweat. 'What is it,

Madam?'

'The cancer. Ah.'

'Where does it hurt, Mrs Bledsoe?'

Her hands, long fingers spread, went like white spiders to her lower abdomen on both sides of her pelvis.

'A sharp or a dull pain?'

'Stabbing! Piercing! Sir. It's . . . terrible!'

He feared her urine spilled from her through a fistula caused by childbirth; if so, there was nothing he could do for her.

She closed her eyes, for the evidence of her constant incontinence was in his nose and lungs with every breath.

'I must examine you.'

Doubtless she'd have objected, but when she opened her mouth it was to cry out in fresh pain. She was stiff with tension but tractable as he moulded her into a semiprone position on her left side and chest, her right knee and thigh drawn up. He could see that there was no fistula.

He had in his bag a small container of fresh white lard that he used as lubricant. 'You must allow yourself no distress. I'm a physician,' he told her, but she wept more from humiliation than discomfort as the middle finger of his left hand slid into her vagina while his right hand palpated her abdomen. He tried to make the tip of his finger an eye; at first it could see nothing as he moved and probed, but as it came close to the pubic bone he found something.

And then another.

Gently, he withdrew and gave her a rag to wipe herself, and went out to the brook to wash his hands.

In order to talk to her, he led her blinking into the harsh sunshine outside, and seated her on a stump with the cosseted child in her arms.

'You don't have cancer.' He wished it could stop there. 'You suffer from bladder-stone.'

'I shan't die?'

He was held to truth. 'With cancer you'd have little chance. With bladder-stone, there's decent chance.' He explained to her about the growth of mineral stones in the bladder, caused perhaps by unchanging diet and prolonged diarrhoea.

'Yes. I had diarrhoea for a long time after his birth. Is there a medicine?'

'No. No medicine to dissolve the stones. The little stones sometimes pass from your body with the urine, and often they have sharp edges that can tear tissue. I believe that's why you've experienced bloody urine. But you have two large stones. Too large to pass.'

'Then will you cut me? For God's sake?' she said unsteadily.

'No.' He hesitated, deciding how much she had to know. Part of the Hippocratic Oath he had taken said *I will not cut a person who is suffering from a stone.* Some butchers ignored the oath and cut anyway, slicing deep into the perineum between the anus and the vulva or scrotum to open the bladder and get at the stones, leaving a few victims who eventually recovered, and many who died of peritonitis, and others who were maimed for life because an intestine or bladder muscle had been severed. 'I'd go into the bladder with a surgical instrument through the urethra, the narrow canal through which you pass water. The instrument is called a lithotrite. It has two little steel pincers, like jaws, with which to remove or crush the stones.'

'Would there be pain?'

'Yes, mostly when I inserted the lithotrite and removed it. But the pain would be less than what you now suffer. If the procedure should succeed, you could be totally cured.' It was difficult admitting the greatest danger was that his skill might prove inadequate. 'If, in trying to grasp the stone in the jaws of the lithotrite I were to pinch the bladder and break it, or if I should tear the peritoneum, likely you would die of infection.' Studying her drawn face, he saw flashes of a younger prettier woman. 'You must decide if I am to try.'

In her agitation she held the baby too tightly and the boy began to cry again. Because of that, it took Rob J. a moment to realise what the word was that she had whispered.

Please.

He knew he'd need help while he performed the lithocenosis. Remembering the rigidity of her body during examination, he felt instinctively that his assistant should be a woman, and when he left Sarah Bledsoe he rode straight to the nearby farmhouse and had a talk with Alma Schroeder.

'Oh, I cannot, no never!' Poor Alma blanched. Her consternation was made worse by her genuine feeling for Sarah. '*Gott im Himmel!* Oh, Dr Cole, please, I cannot.'

When he saw it was so, he assured her it didn't diminish her. Some just couldn't stand to see surgery. 'It's all right, Alma. I'll find someone else.'

Riding away, he tried to think of a female in the district who might assist him, but he rejected the few possibilities, one by one. He had had enough of weeping; what he required was an intelligent woman with strong arms, a woman with a spirit that would allow her to remain steadfast in the face of suffering.

Halfway home, he turned the horse and rode in the direction of the Indian village.

17
Daughter of the *Mide'wiwin*

When Makwa allowed herself to think on it, she remembered a time when only a few of the people had white man's clothing, when a ragged shirt or a torn dress was strong medicine because everyone wore buckskin cured and worked and chewed soft, or animal furs. When she was a child in Sauk-e-nuk she was called Nishwri Kekawi, Two Skies, then – at first there were too few white people, *mookamonik*, to affect their lives. There was an army garrison on the island, established after officials in St Louis got some Mesquakies and Sauks drunk and coerced them into signing a paper whose contents they couldn't read sober. Two Skies' father was Ashtibugwa-gupichee, Green Buffalo. He told Two Skies and her older sister, Meci-ikwawa, Tall Woman, that when the Army post was rebuilt, the Long Knives destroyed the People's best berry bushes. Green Buffalo was of the Bear *gens*, a proper birth for leadership, but he had no desire to be a chief or a medicine man. Despite his sacred name (he was named after the *manitou*) he was a simple man, respected because he got good yields from his fields. When he was young he fought the Iowas and counted coup. He wasn't like some, always boasting, but when her uncle Winnawa, Short Horn, died, Two Skies learned about her father. Short Horn was the first Sauk she knew who drank himself to death on the poison the *mookamon* called Ohio whisky and the People called pepper water. Sauks buried their dead, unlike some tribes who simply raised a body into the crotch of a tree. When they lowered Short Horn into ground, her father had struck the grave's edge with his *pucca-maw*, wielding the battle club savagely. 'I have killed three men in war, and I give their spirits to my brother who lies here, to serve him as slaves in the other world,' he said, and that was how Two Skies learned her father was a warrior.

Her father was mild, a worker. First he and her mother, Matapya, Union-of-Rivers, farmed two fields of corn, pumpkins, and squash, but when the Council saw he was a good farmer they gave him two more fields. The trouble began in Two Skies' tenth year, when a *mookamon* named Hawkins came and built a cabin in the field next to one her father had in corn. The field Hawkins settled on had been abandoned after its farmer, Wegu-wa, Shawnee Dancer, had died, and the Council hadn't got round to reassigning the land. Hawkins brought in horses and cows. The crop fields were separated only by brush fences and hedgerows, and his horses got into Green Buffalo's field and ate his corn. Green Buffalo caught the horses and brought them to Hawkins, but next morning the animals were back in his cornfield. He complained, but the Council didn't know what to do, because five other white families had come and settled on Rock Island too, on land that had been farmed by Sauks for more than one hundred years.

Green Buffalo resorted to tethering Hawkins' livestock on his own land instead of returning them, and at once he was visited by the Rock Island trader, a white named George Davenport. Davenport had been the first white to live among them, and the People trusted him. He told Green Buffalo to give the horses back to Hawkins or the Long Knives would imprison him, and Green Buffalo did as his friend Davenport advised.

The autumn of 1831 the Sauks went to their winter camp in Missouri, as they did each year. When they came back to Sauk-e-nuk in the spring, they found that additional white families had come and homesteaded on Sauk fields, breaking down fences and burning longhouses. Now the Council no longer could avoid action, and it consulted with Davenport and Felix St Vrain, the Indian agent, and Major John Bliss, the leader of the soldiers in the fort. The meetings dragged on, and in the meantime the Council assigned other fields to the tribesmen whose land had been usurped.

A short, stocky Pennsylvania Dutchman named Joshua Vandruff had appropriated the field of a Sauk named Makataime-shekiakiak, Black Hawk. Vandruff began selling whisky to the Indians from the *hedonoso-te* Black Hawk and his sons had built with their own hands. Black Hawk wasn't a chief, but for most of his sixty-three years he'd fought against Osage, Cherokee, Chippewa, and Kaskaskia. When war between the whites had broken out in 1812, he'd gathered a force of fighting Sauks and offered their services to the Americans, only to be rebuffed. Insulted, he had extended the same offer to the English, who treated him with respect and gained his services throughout the war, giving him weapons, ammunition, medals, and the red coat that marked a soldier.

Now, as he neared old age, Black Hawk watched whisky being sold from his home. Worse, he witnessed the corruption of his tribe by alcohol. Vandruff and his friend B. F. Pike got Indians drunk and cheated them out of furs, horses, guns, and traps. Black Hawk went to Vandruff and Pike and asked them to stop selling whisky to Sauks. When he was ignored, he returned with half a dozen warriors who rolled all the casks from the longhouse, staved them in, and poured the whisky into the ground.

Vandruff at once packed his saddlebags with provisions for a long journey and rode to Bellville, home of John Reynolds, governor of Illinois. He swore in a deposition to the governor that the Sauk Indians were on a rampage that had resulted in a stabbing and much damage to white homesteads. He gave Governor Reynolds a second petition signed by B. F. Pike that said 'the Indians pasture their horses in our wheatfields, shoot our cows and cattle, and threaten to burn our homes over our heads if we do not leave.'

Reynolds was newly elected and had promised the voters that Illinois was safe for settlers. A governor who was a successful Indian fighter might dream of the presidency. 'By Jesus, sir,' he told Vandruff emotionally, 'you're asking the right man for justice.'

Seven hundred horse soldiers came and camped below Sauk-e-nuk, their presence causing excitement and unease. At the same time, a steamship belching smoke chugged up the Rocky River. The ship grounded on some of the rocks that gave the river its name, but the *mookamonik* freed it and soon it was anchored, its single cannon pointed directly at the village. The war chief of the whites, General Edmund P. Gaines, called a parley with the Sauks. Seated behind a table were the general, the Indian agent St Vrain, and the trader Davenport, who interpreted. Perhaps twenty prominent Sauks came.

General Gaines said the treaty of 1803 that had set up the fort on Rock Island also had given the Great Father in Washington all the Sauk lands east of the Mississippi – fifty million acres. He told the stunned and puzzled Indians that they had received annuities, and now the Great Father in Washington wanted his children to leave Sauk-e-nuk and go to live on the other side of *Masesibowi*, the large river. Their Father in Washington would give them a gift of corn to see them through the winter.

Chief of the Sauks was Keokuk, who knew that the Americans were too many. When Davenport gave him the words of the white war chief, a great fist squeezed Keokuk's heart. Though the others looked at him to answer, he was silent. But a man rose to his feet, who had learned enough language while fighting for the British, so he spoke for himself. 'We never sold our country. We never received any annuities from our American Father. We will hold our village.'

General Gaines saw an Indian, almost old, without a chief's headdress. In stained buckskins. Hollow-cheeked, with a high, bony forehead. More grey than black in the roached scalp lock that split his shaven skull. An insulting beak of a big nose leaping out between wide-set eyes. A sullen mouth above a dimpled lover's chin that didn't belong in that axe of a face.

Gaines sighed, and looked questioningly at Davenport.

'Name of Black Hawk.'

'What is he?' the general asked Davenport, but Black Hawk answered.

'I am a Sauk. My fathers were Sauks, great men. I wish to remain where their bones are and be buried with them. Why should I leave their fields?'

He and the general gazed at one another, stone on steel.

'I came here not to beg nor to hire you to leave your village. My business is to remove you,' Gaines said mildly. 'Peaceably, if I can. Forcibly, if I must. I now give you two days to remove. If you don't cross the Mississippi by that time, I will force you away.'

The People talked together, staring at the ship's cannon pointed at them. The soldiers who rode by in small groups, yipping and hollering, were well-fed and well-armed, with plenty of ammunition. The Sauks had old rifles, few bullets, no reserve of food.

Keokuk sent a runner to summon Wabokieshiek, White Cloud, a medicine man who lived among the Winnebago. White Cloud was the son of a Winnebago father and a Sauk mother. He was tall and fat, with long grey hair and, a rarity among Indians, a scraggly black mustache. He was a great shaman, tending to the spiritual and medical needs of the Winnebago, the Sauks, and the Mesquakies. All three tribes knew him as the Prophet, but White Cloud had no comforting prophecy to offer Keokuk. He said the militia was a superior force and Gaines wouldn't listen to reason. Their friend Davenport the trader met with the chief and the shaman and urged them to do as they were ordered and abandon the land before the dispute became bloody trouble.

So on the second night of the two days the People had been granted, they left Sauk-e-nuk like animals that were driven away, and they went across *Masesibowi* into the land of their enemies, the Iowa.

That winter Two Skies lost her belief that the world was safe. The corn delivered by the Indian agent to the new village west of *Masesibowi* was of poor quality and not nearly enough to keep hunger away. The People couldn't hunt or trap enough meat, for many had bartered their guns and traps for Vandruff's whisky. They mourned the loss of the crops left in their fields. The mealy corn. The rich, nourishing pumpkins, the huge sweet squashes. One night five women recrossed the river and went to their old fields and picked some frozen ears of the corn they had planted themselves the previous spring. They were discovered by white homesteaders and severely beaten.

A few nights later, Black Hawk led a few men on horseback back to Rock Island. They filled sacks with corn from the fields and broke into a storehouse, taking squashes and pumpkins. Through the terrible winter, a debate raged. Keokuk, the chief, argued that Black Hawk's action would bring the white armies. The new village wasn't Sauk-e-nuk, but it could be a good place to live, he argued, and the presence of *mookamonik* across the river meant a market for the furs of Sauk trappers.

Black Hawk said whiteskins would push the Sauks as far as possible and then destroy them. The only choice was to fight. The only hope for all red men was to forget tribal enmities and join together from Canada to Mexico, with the help of the English Father, against the greater enemy, the American.

The Sauks argued at length. By spring most of the People had decided to stay with Keokuk west of the wide river. Only three hundred and sixty-eight men and their families linked their fate with Black Hawk. Among them was Green Buffalo.

Canoes were laden. Black Hawk, the Prophet, and Neosho, a Sauk medicine man, set out in the lead canoe, then the others pushed off, paddling hard against the mighty current of *Masesibowi*. Black Hawk wanted no destruction or killing unless his force was attacked. As they moved downstream, when they approached a *mookamon* settlement he ordered

111

his people to beat their drums and sing. With women, children, and the old, he had nearly thirteen hundred voices, and settlers fled the terrible sound. In a few settlements they collected food, but they had many mouths to feed and no time to hunt or fish.

Black Hawk had sent runners to Canada to ask the British for help, and to a dozen tribes. The messengers brought back bad news. It wasn't surprising that old enemies like the Sioux and Chippewa and Osage wouldn't join with the Sauks against the whiteskins, but neither would their brother nation the Mesquakies, or any other friendly nation. Worse, their British Father sent the Sauks only words of encouragement and wishes for good fortune in war.

Remembering the cannon on warships, Black Hawk took his people off the river, beaching their canoes on the eastern bank from which they had been exiled. Since each scrap of food was precious, everyone became a bearer, even squaws who were big with child, like Union-of-Rivers. They skirted Rock Island and went up the Rocky River to meet with Potawatomi from whom they hoped to lease land on which to grow a corn crop. It was from the Potawatomi that Black Hawk heard that the Father in Washington had sold the Sauk territory to white investors. The townsite of Sauk-e-nuk and nearly all their fields had been bought by George Davenport, the trader who, pretending he was their friend, had urged them to abandon the land.

Black Hawk ordered a dog feast, for he knew the People needed the help of the *manitous*. The Prophet oversaw the strangling of the dogs, the cleansing and purification of the meat. While it was stewing, Black Hawk set his medicine bags before his men. 'Braves and warriors,' he said, 'Sauk-e-nuk is no more. Our lands are stolen. White-skinned soldiers have burned our *hedonoso-tes*. They have torn down the fences of our fields. They have ploughed up our Place of the Dead and planted corn among our sacred bones. These are the medicine bags of our father, Muk-ataquet, who was the beginning of the Sauk nation. They were handed down to the great war chief of our nation, Na-namakee, who was at war with all the nations of the lakes and all the nations

112

of the plains, and was never disgraced. I expect you all to protect them.'

The warriors ate the sacred flesh and were given courage and strength. It was necessary, for Black Hawk knew the Long Knives would be moving against them. Perhaps it was the *manitous* who allowed Union-of-Rivers to drop her baby at this encampment rather than along the trail. It was a man-child and did as much for the warriors' spirits as the dog feast, because Green Buffalo names his son Wato-kimita, He-Who-Owns-Land.

Spurred by public hysteria over rumours that Black Hawk and the Sauks were on the warpath, Governor Reynolds of Illinois called for one thousand mounted volunteers. More than twice that number of would-be Indian fighters came forward, and one thousand nine hundred and thirty-five untrained men were mustered into military service. They were assembled at Beardstown, merged with three hundred and forty-two regular militiamen, and quickly formed into four regiments and two battalions of scouts. Samuel Whiteside of St. Clair County was declared a brigadier general and placed in command.

Reports from settlers indicated where Black Hawk was, and Whiteside moved his brigade out. It had been an unusually wet spring and they had to swim even the smaller creeks, while ordinary sloughs became bayous through which they floundered. It took them five days of hard travel through trailless country to reach Oquawka, where supplies should have been waiting. But the army had blundered; there were no supplies, and the men long since had eaten what they had carried in their saddlebags. Undisciplined and cantakerous, they berated their officers like the civilians they actually were, demanding that they be fed. Whiteside sent a dispatch to General Henry Atkinson at Fort Armstrong, and at once Atkinson ordered the steamer *Chieftain* downstream with a cargo of food. Whiteside sent the two battalions of regular militia forward, while for almost a week the main body of volunteers filled their bellies and rested.

They never lost the awareness that they were in a strange and ominous environment. On a mild May morning the bulk of the force, some sixteen hundred mounted men, burned Prophetstown, White Cloud's deserted village. Having done so, they were inexplicably nervous and gradually became convinced that avenging Indians were behind every hill. Soon nervousness became fear, and terror produced a rout. Abandoning equipment, weapons, supplies, and ammunition, they fled for their lives before a nonexistent enemy, crashing through grasslands, brush, and forest, not stopping until, singly and in small groups, they made their shamefaced way into the settlement of Dixon, ten miles from the place where they had started to run.

The first actual contact took place not long after. Black Hawk and about forty braves were on their way to meet with some Potawatomi from whom they were trying to rent a cornfield. They had made camp on the banks of the Rock River when a runner told them a large force of Long Knives was moving in their direction. At once Black Hawk fixed a white flag to a pole and sent three unarmed Sauks to carry it to the whites and request a meeting between Black Hawk and their commander. Behind them he sent five Sauks on horseback to function as observers.

The troops were inexperienced Indian fighters, terrified at the sight of Sauks. They quickly seized the three men with the truce flag and made them prisoners, and then set out after the five observers, two of whom were overtaken and killed. The other three made it back to their camp, pursued by the militia. When the white soldiers arrived, they were attacked by about thirty-five braves led by a coldly furious Black Hawk, who was willing to die a good death to avenge the whiteskins' treachery. The soldiers in the vanguard of the cavalry had no idea that the Indians didn't have a vast army of warriors behind them. They took one glance at the charging Sauks and turned their ponies and fled.

Nothing is so infectious as panic in battle, and within minutes all was chaos within the militia. In the confusion, two of the three Sauks who had been captured with the flag of truce escaped. The third was shot and killed. The two hundred and seventy-five armed and mounted militiamen were gripped by terror and fled as hysterically as had the main body of volunteers, but this time their peril wasn't imaginary. Black Hawk's few dozen warriors stampeded them, harried the stragglers, and came away with eleven scalps. Some of the two hundred and sixty-four retreating whites didn't stop their withdrawal until they reached their homes, but most of the soldiers finally straggled into the town of Dixon.

For the rest of her life the girl who was then called Two Skies would remember the joy following the battle. A child felt the hope. News of the victory sped through the red-skinned world, and at once ninety-two Winnebago came to join them. Black Hawk strode about wearing a ruffled white shirt, a leather-bound law book under his arm – both found in a saddlebag abandoned by a fleeing officer. His oratory waxed. They had shown that the *mookamonik* could be defeated, he said, and now the other tribes would send warriors to form the alliance that was his dream.

But the days passed, and no other warriors came. Food dwindled and hunting was bad. Finally Black Hawk sent the Winnebago in one direction and he led the People in another. Against his orders, the Winnebago struck unprotected white homesteads and took scalps, including that of St Vrain, the Indian agent. Two days in a row the sky turned green-black and the *manitou* Shagwa shook air and earth. Wabokieshiek warned Black Hawk never to travel without sending scouts deep ahead, and Two Skies' father muttered heavily that it didn't take a prophet to know bad things were going to happen.

Governor Reynolds was furious. His shame over what had happened to his militia was shared by the populace of every border state. The depredations of the Winnebago were magnified and blamed on Black Hawk. Fresh volunteers poured in, drawn by a rumour that a bounty set by the Illinois legislature in 1814 was still in force – fifty dollars to be paid for every male Indian killed or every squaw or red-

115

skinned child captured. Reynolds had no trouble swearing in three thousand more men. Two thousand nervous soldiers already were camped in forts along the Mississippi, under the command of General Henry Atkinson, Colonel Zachary Taylor second in command. Two companies of infantry were moved into Illinois from Baton Rouge, Louisiana, and an army of one thousand regular soldiers was transferred from eastern posts under the command of General Winfield Scott. These troops were afflicted with cholera while steamboats carried them across the Great Lakes, but even without them, an enormous force, hungry for racial revenge and restored honour, had been set into motion.

For the girl Two Skies the world became small. Always it had seemed enormous during the leisurely journey between the Sauks' winter camp in Missouri and their summer village on the Rocky River. But now wherever her people turned there were white scouts and there was firing and screaming before they could break away. They took a few scalps and lost a few braves. They were fortunate not to encounter a main body of white-skinned troops. Black Hawk feinted and twisted in his tracks, laying false trails in an attempt to elude the soldiers, but most of his followers were women and children, and it was hard to conceal the movements of so many.

They quickly became fewer. Old people died, and some children. Two Skies' infant brother grew small-faced and large-eyed. Their mother's milk didn't dry up, but the flow slackened and turned thin, so there was never enough to satisfy the child. Two Skies carried her brother most of the time.

Very soon, Black Hawk stopped speaking about driving away the whiteskins. Now he talked of escaping into the far north from which the Sauks had come hundreds of years before. But as the moons passed, many of his followers didn't have enough faith to stay with him. Lodge by lodge left the Sauk party, slipping off by themselves. Small groups probably wouldn't survive, but most had made up their minds that the *manitous* weren't with Black Hawk.

116

Green Buffalo remained faithful, despite the fact that four moons after they had left Keokuk's Sauks, Black Hawk's party had dwindled to a few hundred people trying to keep alive by eating roots and tree bark. They returned to *Masesibowi*, as always taking comfort from the great river. The steamboat *Warrior* came upon most of the Sauks in the shallows at the mouth of the Óuisconsin River, trying to catch fish. As the boat moved toward them, Black Hawk saw the six-pound gun on the bow and knew they could fight no longer. His men waved a white flag, but the boat drew near and a Winnebago mercenary on the deck shouted in their language, *'Run and hide, the whites are going to shoot!'*

They had started to splash shoreward, screaming, when the cannon let go canister point-blank, followed by a heavy fire of musketry. Twenty-three Sauks were killed. The others made it into the woods, some of them dragging or carrying the wounded.

That night they talked among themselves. Black Hawk and the Prophet decided to go to the country of the Chippewa to see if they could live there. Three lodges of people said they would go with them, but the others, including Green Buffalo, had no faith that the Chippewa would give the Sauks cornfields when other tribes wouldn't, and they determined to rejoin Keokuk's Sauks. In the morning they said goodbye to the few who were going to the Chippewa, and they started south, toward home.

The steamboat *Warrior* tracked the Indians by following the flocks of carrion crows and vultures downstream. Wherever the Sauks went now, the dead were simply abandoned. Some were old people and children, some were those wounded in the previous attack. When the boat stopped to examine bodies, always the ears and the scalps were taken. It didn't matter if the patch of dark hair came from a child or the red ear was a woman's; they would be proudly carried back to small towns as evidence that their owners were Indian fighters.

Those Sauks still alive left *Masesibowi* and moved inland, only to meet the army's Winnebago hirelings. Behind the Winnebago, lines of soldiers fixed the bayonets that led the

Indians to call them Long Knives. As the whites charged, a
hoarse animal cry rose from them, deeper than a war whoop
but just as savage. They were so many, so intent on killing
in order to regain something they believed they had lost.
The Sauks could do nothing but fall back, firing. When they
reached *Masesibowi* again they tried to fight but were quickly
driven into the river. Two Skies was standing next to her
mother in waist-deep water when a lead ball tore through
Union-of-Rivers' lower jaw. She dropped into the water
face down. Two Skies had to turn her mother onto her back
while holding the infant He-Who-Owns-Land. She managed to do so only with the greatest difficulty; then she
understood that Union-of-Rivers was dead. She couldn't see
her father or her sister. The world was gunfire and screams,
and when the Sauks waded through the water to a little
willow island, she went with them.

They tried to make a stand on the island, huddling behind
rocks and fallen logs. But on the river, moving out of the
mist like a great ghost, the steamboat soon had the small
island under crossfire from its cannon. Some of the women
ran into the river and tried to swim its expanse. Two Skies
didn't know that the army had hired Sioux to wait on the
far bank and kill any who managed to cross, and finally she
slipped into the water, clamping her teeth into the soft loose
skin at the back of the baby's neck, leaving her hands free
to swim. Her teeth bit into the infant's flesh and she could
taste her brother's blood, and the muscles in her own neck
and shoulders became agonized by the strain of keeping the
little head above the water. She tired quickly and knew if
she continued, she and the infant would drown. The current
of the river swept them downstream, away from the fire,
and she turned back toward land, swimming like a fox or a
squirrel moving young. When she had achieved the shore,
she lay next to the screaming baby, trying not to see his
ruined neck.

Soon she picked up He-Who-Owns-Land and carried him
away from the sound of firing. A woman sat on the
riverbank, and as they approached, Two Skies saw it was
her sister. Tall Woman was covered with blood but she told

118

Two Skies it wasn't hers, a soldier had been raping her when a bullet hit him in the side. She had managed to get out from under his bloody body; he had lifted a hand and asked for help in his language, and she had taken a rock and killed him.

She managed to tell her story but didn't comprehend when Two Skies told her of their mother's death. The sound of screams and firing seemed closer. Two Skies carried her brother and led her sister deep into riverside brush, and the three of them huddled. Tall Woman didn't speak, but He-Who-Owns-Land never stopped his high-pitched bawling, and Two Skies was afraid soldiers would hear him and come. She opened her dress and lifted his mouth to her undeveloped breast. The little nipple grew under the dry tugging of his lips and she held the baby close.

As hours passed, the firing grew less frequent and the tumult died. Afternoon shadows were long when she heard the approaching steps of a patrol, and the baby started to cry again. She thought of strangling He-Who-Owns-Land so she and Tall woman might live. Instead, she did nothing but wait, and in a few minutes a skinny white boy poked his musket into the brush and then dragged them out.

On the way to the steamboat, wherever they looked they saw familiar dead without ears or scalps. On the deck, the Long Knives assembled thirty-nine women and children. Everyone else had been killed. The baby was still crying, and a Winnebago looked at the emaciated infant with the torn neck. 'Little rat,' he said scornfully, but a redheaded soldier with two yellow stripes on his blue sleeve mixed sugar and water in a whisky bottle and stuck a rag into it. He pulled the baby from Two Skies' arms and gave him the sugar teat to suck, and he walked away with a pleased face, carrying her brother. Two Skies tried to follow, but the Winnebago came and struck her across the head with his hand until her ears rang. The boat moved away from the mouth of the Bad Axe, through the floating Sauk bodies. It carried them forty miles downriver to Prairie du Chien. At Prairie du Chien she and Tall Woman and three other Sauk girls, Smoke Woman, Moon, and Yellow Bird, were taken off the steamboat and placed in a wagon. Moon was younger than Two Skies. The other two were older, but not as old as Tall Woman. She didn't know what became of the rest of the Sauk prisoners, and she never saw He-Who-Owns-Land again.

The wagon came to an army post they later learned to call Fort Crawford but didn't turn in, taking the young Sauk females three miles beyond the fort to a white farmhouse surrounded by outbuildings and fences. Two Skies could see ploughed and planted fields, and several kinds of grazing animals, and fowl. Inside the house she could scarcely draw a breath because the air was foreign with harsh soap and polishing wax, a smell of *mookamonik* sanctity she loathed for the rest of her life. At the Evangelical School for Indian Girls, she had to endure it for four years.

The school was run by Reverend Edvard Bronsun and Miss Eva, a middle-aged brother and sister. Nine years before, under the sponsorship of the Missionary Society of New York City, they had set forth to enter the wilderness and bring the heathen Indian to Jesus. They had started their school with two Winnebago girls, one of them feeble-minded. Perversely, Indian females had resisted their repeated invitations to come and work the Bronsuns' fields, tend their stock, whitewash and paint their buildings, and do their housework. It was only through the cooperation of law authorities and the military that their enrollment grew until, with the arrival of the Sauks, they had twenty-one sullen but obedient pupils tending one of the best-kept farms in their area.

Mr Edvard, tall and spare, with a freckled balding scalp, instructed the girls in agriculture and religion, while Miss Eva, corpulent and icy-eyed, taught how whiteskins expected floors to be scrubbed and furniture and woodwork to be polished. The pupils' studies consisted of housework and unceasing heavy farm labour, learning to speak English, unlearning their native languages and culture, and praying to unfamiliar gods. Miss Eva, always smiling coldly,

120

punished for infractions such as sloth or insolence or the use of an Indian word, utilizing supple switches cut from the farm's greengage plum tree.

The other pupils were Winnebago, Chippewa, Illinois, Kickapoo, Iroquois, and Potawatomi. All regarded the newcomers with hostility, but the Sauks didn't fear them; arriving together, they were a tribal majority, although the system of the place sought to nullify this advantage. The first thing each new girl lost was her Indian name. The Bronsuns' considered only six biblical names worthy of inspiring piety in a convert: Rachel, Ruth, Mary, Martha, Sarah and Anna. Since this limited choice meant that several girls shared the same name, to avoid confusion they also gave each pupil a numeral that became available only when its owner left the school. Thus, Moon became Ruth Three; Tall Woman, Mary Four; Yellow Bird, Rachel Two; and Smoke Woman, Martha Three. Two Skies was Sarah Two.

It wasn't hard to adjust. The first English words they learned were 'please' and 'thank you'. At meals, all foods and drinks were identified once, in English. From then on, those who didn't ask for them in English went hungry. The Sauk girls learned English quickly. The two daily meals were hominy and cornbread and hashed root vegetables. Meat, served rarely, was fatback or small game. Children who had experienced starvation always ate hungrily. Despite the hard work, they put flesh on their bones. The dullness disappeared from Tall Woman's eyes, but of the five Sauks she was most likely to forget herself and speak in the language of the People, and so she was beaten most often. In their second month as the school, Miss Eva heard Tall Woman whispering in the Sauk tongue and whipped her severely while Mr Edvard watched. That night Mr Edvard came into the dark attic dormitory and whispered that he had salve to spread on Mary Four's back to remove the pain. He led Tall Woman out of the dormitory.

Next day, Mr Edvard gave Tall Woman a bag of cornbread that she shared with the other Sauks. After that, he often came to the dormitory at night for Tall Woman, and the Sauk girls grew accustomed to the extra food.

121

Within four months Tall Woman began to be sick in the mornings, and she and Two Skies knew even before it showed in her belly that she was with child.

A few weeks later Mr Edvard hitched the horse to the buggy and Miss Eva took Tall Woman in the buggy with her and drove away. When she came back alone, she told Two Skies her sister was blessed. Miss Eva said from now on Mary Four would work on a fine Christian farm on the other side of Fort Crawford. Two Skies never saw Tall Woman again.

Whenever Two Skies was sure they were alone, she spoke to the other Sauks in their own tongue. Picking potato bugs, she told them stories Union-of-Rivers had told her. Weeding beets, she sang the songs of the Sauks. Chopping wood, she spoke to them of Sauk-e-nuk and of the winter camp, reminding them of the dances and festivals, and of kinsman dead and alive. If they didn't answer in their own language, she threatened to beat them worse than Miss Eva did. Although two of the girls were older and larger than she, none challenged her, and they kept their old language.

When they had been there almost three years, a Sioux girl came as a new pupil. Wing Flapper was older than Tall Woman. She was of the band of Wabashaw, and at night she taunted the Sauks with stories of how her father and her brothers had waited on the far bank of *Masesibowi* and had killed and scalped every one of their Sauk enemies who had made it across the river during the massacre at the mouth of the Bad Axe. Wing Flapper was given Tall Woman's name, Mary Five. From the start, Mr Edvard fancied her. Two Skies dreamed of killing her, but Wing Flapper's presence proved fortunate, for within a few months she too was pregnant; perhaps Mary was a begetting name.

Two Skies watched Wing Flapper's belly grow, and planned and prepared. Miss Eva drove Wing Flapper away in the buggy on a hot, still summer's day. Mr Edvard was one person, he couldn't watch everyone. As soon as the woman was gone, Two Skies dropped the hoe she'd been wielding in the beet field and crept out of sight behind the barn. She piled fat pine kindling against the dry timbers and ignited them with the sulphur matches she'd stolen and set aside for this moment. By the time the fire was noticed, the bar was well ablaze. Mr Edvard ran in from the potato field like a crazy man, shouting and pop-eyed, and directed the girls to set up a bucket brigade.

Two Skies stayed cool amid the general excitement. She gathered up Moon, Yellow Bird, and Smoke Woman. As an afterthought she took one of Miss Eva's plum switches and used it to move the farm's great porker out of the deep black mud of the sty. She drove the pig into Miss Eva's scrubbed and polished pious-smelling house and closed the door. Then she led the others into the woods and away from that *mookamon* place.

They avoided roads, staying in the woods until they reached the river. An oak log was snagged on the bank, and the four girls pushed it free. The warm waters contained the bones and ghosts of their loved ones and embraced the girls as they held on to the log and let *Masesibowi* carry them southward.

They left the river when it began to grow dark. That night they slept hungry in the woods. In the morning, picking berries in a riverside patch, they found a hidden Sioux canoe and stole it at once, hoping it belonged to a kinsman of Wing Flapper. It was midafternoon when they rounded a bend and came upon Prophetstown. On the bank, a red man was cleaning fish. When they saw he was a Mesquakie they laughed in relief and sent the canoe arrowing toward him.

As soon as he was able after the war, White Cloud had returned to Prophetstown. The white-skinned soldiers had burned his longhouse along with the others, but he built another *hedonoso-te*. When word was spread that the shaman had returned, families came as before from several tribes and raised lodges nearby so they could live their lives close to him. Other disciples arrived from time to time, but now he looked with special interest at the four small girls who had escaped the whites and blundered their way to him. For days he scrutinized them while they rested and fed in his lodge, noting the way three of them looked to the fourth for guidance in all things. He questioned them separately and at length, and each of them told him of Two Skies.

Always, Two Skies. He began to watch her with growing hope.

Finally he caught two ponies from his string and told Two Skies to come with him. She rode behind his horse for most of a day, until the ground began to rise. All mountains are sacred, but in flat country even a hill is a holy place; on the wooded hilltop he led her into a clearing musky with the smell of bears, where the bones of animals were scattered, and ashes of dead fires.

When they dismounted, Wabokieshiek took the blanket from his shoulders and told her to disrobe and lie on it. Two Skies dared not refuse, though she was certain the old shaman meant to use her sexually. But when Wabokieshiek touched her, it wasn't as a lover. He examined her until he was satisfied she was intact.

As the sun lowered, they went into the nearby woods and he set three snares. Then he built a fire in the clearing and sat by it, chanting while she lay on the ground and slept.

When she woke, he had collected a rabbit from one of the snares and was slitting the belly. Two Skies was hungry but he made no move to cook the rabbit; instead, he fingered the viscera and studied them at greater length than he had examined the body of the girl. When he had finished, he grunted in satisfaction and looked at her warily and with wonder.

After he and Black Hawk had heard about the massacre of their people at the Bad Axe River, their spirits had sickened. They had wanted no more Sauks to die under their leadership, so they had given themselves up to the Indian agent at Prairie du Chien. At Fort Crawford they had been turned over to a young army lieutenant named Jefferson Davis, who had taken his prisoners down *Masesibowi* to St. Louis. All winter they were confined in Jefferson Barracks, suffering the humiliation of the ball and chain. In the spring, to show the whiteskins how completely their army had vanquished the People, the Great Father in

124

Washington ordered the two prisoners brought to American cities. They saw railroads for the first time and travelled on them to Washington, New York, Albany, and Detroit. Everywhere, crowds like buffalo herds came to gape at the curiosities, the defeated 'Indian chiefs.'

White Cloud had seen enormous settlements, magnificent buildings, terrifying machines. Endless Americans. When he had been allowed to return to Prophetstown, he contemplated bitter truth: the *mookamonik* could never be driven from Sauk lands. Red people would be pushed and pushed, always away from the best farming and hunting. Those who were his children, the Sauks and the Mesquakies and the Winnebago, needed to become accustomed to a cruel world dominated by white men. The problem no longer was to drive the whites away. Now the shaman pondered how his people could change in order to survive, and yet retain their *manitous*, keep their medicine. He was old and soon would die, and he began to look for someone to whom he could pass on what he was, a vessel into which he could pour the soul of the Algonquian tribes, but he had found no one. Until this female.

All this he explained to Two Skies as he sat in the sacred place on the hill, stirring the favourable auguries in the carcass of the rabbit, which was beginning to stink. When he was finished, he asked if she would allow him to teach her to be a medicine woman.

Two Skies was a child, but she knew enough to be frightened. There was much she couldn't comprehend, but she understood what was important.

'I will try,' she whispered to the Prophet.

White Cloud sent Moon, Yellow Bird, and Smoke Woman to live with Keokuk's Sauks, but Two Skies stayed in Prophetstown, living in Wabokieshiek's lodge like a favoured daughter. He showed her leaves and roots and bark and told her which of them could lift the spirit out of the body and allow it to converse with *manitous*, which could dye deerskins and which make war paints, which should be dried and which steeped, which should be steamed and

125

which used as poultice, which should be scraped with upward strokes and which scraped with downward strokes, which could open the bowels and which close them, which could break fever and which dull pain, which could cure and which could kill.

Two Skies listened to him. At the end of four seasons, when the Prophet tested her, he was pleased. He said he had guided her through the first Tent of Wisdom.

Before she had been taken through the second Tent of Wisdom, her womanhood came upon her for the first time. One of White Cloud's nieces showed her how to care for herself, and each month she went to stay in the women's lodge while her vagina bled. The Prophet explained that she mustn't conduct a ceremony or treat illness or injury before attending the sweat lodge to purify herself after her monthly flow.

Over the next four years she learned how to summon the *manitous* with songs and drums, how to slaughter dogs in several ceremonial methods and cook them for a dog feast, how to teach the singers and hummers to take part in the sacred dances. She learned to read the future in the organs of a slain animal. She learned the power of illusion – to suck illness from the body and spit it out of her mouth as a small stone, so a victim could touch it and see that it had been banished. When the *manitous* couldn't be persuaded to allow someone to live, she learned how to chant the spirit of the dying on to the next world.

There were seven Tents of Wisdom. In the fifth, the Prophet taught her to control her own body do she could come to understand how to control the bodies of others. She learned to conquer thirst and to go long periods without food. Often he led her great distances on horseback and returned to Prophetstown alone with the two horses, leaving her to make her way back afoot. Gradually he taught her to master pain by sending her mind to a far-off small place so deep within herself that pain couldn't reach her.

Late that summer he took her back to the sacred clearing on the hilltop. They made fire and courted the *manitous* with song, and again they set snares. This time they caught a skinny brown rabbit, and when they opened the belly and read the organs, Two Skies recognized that the signs were favourable.

As dusk approached, White Cloud told her to remove her dress and shoes. When she was naked, with his British knife he slashed double slits on each of her shoulders, then carefully cut her to fashion scraps of skin like the epaulettes worn by white army officers. He passed a rope through these bloody slits and knotted a loop, and he threw the rope over a tree branch and hauled her up until she hung just off the ground, suspended by her own bleeding flesh.

With thin oak sticks whose ends had been made white-hot in the fire, into the sides of both of her breasts he burned the signs of the People's ghosts and the symbols of the *manitous*.

Darkness came while she was still trying to free herself. For half the night Two Skies thrashed, until finally the skin strap on her left shoulder tore. Soon the flesh on her right shoulder parted and she dropped to the ground. With her mind in the small distant place to escape the pain, perhaps she slept.

When the weak light of morning came, she was awake to hear the snuffling as a bear entered the far side of the clearing. It didn't scent her, for it moved in the same direction as the morning breeze, and it shambled with such slowness she could note its snowy muzzle and the fact that it was a sow. A second bear followed, all black, a young male eager to mate despite the sow's warning growl. Two Skies could see his great rigid *coska*, surrounded by stiff grey guard hairs, as he clambered to get behind the female and mount her. The sow snarled and whirled, snapping repeatedly, and the male fled. For a moment the female moved after him, then came upon the rabbit carcass and took it between her jaws and went away.

Finally, in great pain, Two Skies rose to her feet. The Prophet had taken her clothes. She saw no bear tracks in the hard-packed dirt of the clearing, but in the fine ash of the dead fire was a single clear track of a fox. A fox could have come in the night and taken the rabbit; perhaps she had dreamed the bears, or they had been *manitous*.

All that day she travelled. Once she heard horses and hid in the brush until two Sioux youths rode by. It was still light when she entered Prophetstown accompanied by ghosts, her naked body covered with blood and dirt. Three men halted their talking as she approached, and a woman stopped grinding corn. For the first time, she saw fear on faces that looked at her.

The Prophet himself wanted her. Tending her ruined shoulders and the burns, he asked if she had dreamed. When she told him of the bears, his eyes gleamed. 'The strongest sign!' he murmured. He told her it meant that as long as she didn't lie with a man, the *manitous* would stay close to her.

While she pondered that, he told her she would never be Two Skies again, any more than she would ever be Sarah Two. That night in Prophetstown she became Maka-ikwa, the Bear Woman.

Again the Great Father in Washington had lied to the Sauks. The army had promised Keokuk's Sauks that they could live forever in the land of the Iowa beyond *Masesibowi's* west bank, but white settlers had quickly begun to spill into that land. A white town was established across the river from Rock Island. It was named Davenport, honouring the trader who had advised the Sauks to abandon the bones of their ancestors and leave Sauk-e-nuk, and then had bought their land from the government for his own enrichment.

Now the army told Keokuk's Sauks they owed a large debt of American money and must sell their new lands in Iowa territory and move to a reservation the United States had set up for them a long ride to the southwest, in the territory of the Kansas.

The Prophet told the Bear Woman that so long as she lived, she must never accept as true the word of a white.

That year Yellow Bird was bitten by a snake and half her body welled and filled with water before she died. Moon had found a husband, a Sauk named Comes Singing, and

128

already she had borne children. Smoke Woman didn't marry. She slept with so many men, and so happily, that people smiled when they said her name. Sometimes Makwa-ikwa was stirred by sexual longing, but she learned to control desire like any other pain. The lack of children was a regret. She remembered how she had hidden with One-Who-Owns-Land during the massacre at Bad Axe, how her baby brother's tugging lips had felt at her nipple. But she was reconciled; already she had lived too closely with the *manitous* to question their decision that she could never be a mother. She was content to become a medicine woman.

The final two Tents of Wisdom dealt with blighting magic, how to make a healthy person sick by casting spells, how to summon and direct ill fortune. Makwa-ikwa became familiar with small imps of wickedness called *watawinonas*, with ghosts and witches, and with Panguk, the Spirit of Death. These spirits weren't accosted until the final Tents because a medicine woman had to attain self-mastery before summoning them, lest she join the *watawinonas* in their evil. Dark magic was the heaviest responsibility. The *watawinonas* robbed Makwa-ikwa of her ability to smile. She became wan. Her flesh melted until her bones seemed large, and sometimes her monthly bleeding didn't come. She saw that the *watawinonas* also were drinking the life from Wabo-kieshiek's body, for he became frailer and smaller, but he promised her he would not yet die.

At the end of two more years the Prophet brought her through the final Tent. If it had been in former days, that would have called for the summoning of far-flung Sauk bands, races and games, the smoking of calumets, and a secret meeting of the *Mide'wiwin*, the medicine society of the Algonquian tribes. But former days were gone. Everywhere, red people were scattered and harassed. The best the Prophet could do was provide three other old men as judges, Lost Knife of the Mesquakies, Barren Horse of the Ojibwa, and Little Big Snake of the Menomini. The women of Prophetstown made Makwa-ikwa a dress and shoes of white doeskin, and she wore her *Izze* cloths, and anklets and bracelets that rattled when she moved. She used the throttle-stick to kill two dogs and supervised the cleaning and cooking of the meat. After the feast, she and the old men sat all night by the fire.

When they questioned her, she answered with respect but forthrightly, as an equal. She brought forth the sounds of supplication from the water drum while she chanted, summoning the *manitous* and pacifying ghosts. The old men revealed to her the special secrets of the *Mide'wiwin* while retaining their own secrets, as she would retain her own from now on. By morning she had become a shaman.

Once that would have made her a person of great power. But now Wabokieshiek helped her assembled the herbs she wouldn't be able to find where she was going. Along with her drums and medicine bundle the herbs were packed on a brindle mule that she led. She said good bye to the Prophet for the last time and then rode his other gift, a grey pony, to the territory of the Kansas, where the Sauk now lived.

The reservation was on flatter land even than the Illinois plains.

Dry.

There was just enough water to drink, but it had to be toted a distance. This time the whites had given the Sauks land that was fertile enough to grow anything. The seeds they planted sprouted strongly in the spring, but before summer was more than a few days old, everything withered and died. The wind blew dust through which the sun burned as a round red eye.

So they ate the white man's food the soldiers brought them. Spoiled beef, stinking pig fat, old vegetables. Crumbs from the paleskins' feast.

There were no *hedonoso-tes*. The People lived in shacks made from green lumber that cupped and shrank, leaving cracks wide enough for winter snow to drift through. Twice a year a nervous little Indian agent came with soldiers and left a row of goods on the prairie: cheap mirrors, glass beads, a cracked and broken harness with bells on it, old clothing, maggoty meat. At first all the Sauks gleaned the pile, until somebody asked the agent why he brought these things and he said they were a payment for the Sauk land confiscated by the government. After that, only the weakest and most scorned ever took anything. The pile grew in size every six months, to rot in weather.

They had heard of Makwa-ikwa. When she arrived, they received her with respect, but they were no longer sufficiently a tribe to need a shaman. The most spirited of them had gone with Black Hawk and had been killed by whites or died of starvation or drowned in *Masesibowi* or been murdered by the Sioux, but there were those on the reservation who had the strong hearts of Sauks of old. Their courage was constantly tested in fights with the tribes who were native to the region, because the supply of game was dwindling and the Commanche, the Kiowa, the Cheyenne, and the Osage resented the hunting competition of the eastern tribes moved by the Americans. The whites made it hard for the Sauks to defend themselves, for they saw to it that there was plenty of bad whisky, and in return took most of the furs that were trapped. In increasing numbers the Sauks spent their days sick with alcohol.

Makwa-ikwa lived on the reservation a little more than a year. That spring, a small herd of buffalo wandered across the prairie. Moon's husband, Comes Singing, rode out with other hunters and killed meat. Makwa-ikwa declared a Buffalo Dance and instructed the hummers and singers. People danced in the old way, and in some of their eyes she saw a light she hadn't seen in a long time, a light that filled her with joy.

Others felt it. After the Buffalo Dance, Comes Singing sought her out and said some of the People wanted to leave the reservation and live as their fathers had lived. They asked if their shaman would go with them.

She asked Comes Singing where they would go.

'Home,' he said.

So the youngest and strongest departed the reservation, and she with them. By autumn they were in country that gladdened their spirits and made their hearts sore at the same time. It was hard to avoid the white man as they

131

travelled; they made wide circuits around settlements. Hunting was poor. Winter caught them ill-prepared. Wabokieshiek had died that summer, and Prophetstown was deserted. She couldn't go to white people for help, remembering what the Prophet had taught her about never placing her faith in a whiteskin.

But when she had prayed, the *manitous* had sent survival in the form of help from the white doctor called Cole, and despite the Prophet's ghost, she had come to feel he could be trusted.

So when he rode into the Sauk camp and told her that now he needed her help to perform his medicine, without hesitation she was able to agree to go with him.

18
Stones

Rob J. tried to explain to Makwa-ikwa what a bladder calculus was, but he couldn't tell if she believed that Sarah Bledsoe's illness really was caused by stones in her bladder. Makwa-ikwa asked him if he would suck out the stones, and as they talked it became apparent that she expected to witness a sleight-of-hand humbug, a kind of juggling trick to make his patient believe he had removed the source of her trouble. He explained several times that the stones were real, that they existed painfully in the woman's bladder, and that he would go inside Sarah's body with an instrument and remove them.

Her puzzlement continued when they got to his cabin and he used strong brown soap and water to wash down the table Alden had made for him, on which he would operate. They called for Sarah Bledsoe together, in the buckboard. The little boy, Alex, had been left with Alma Schroeder, and his mother was waiting for the doctor, her eyes large in her pinched white face. On the return trip Makwa-ikwa was silent and Sarah Bledsoe nearly dumb with terror. He tried to ease the situation with small talk but had little success.

When they reached his cabin, Makwa-ikwa leapt lightly from the buckboard. She helped the white girl down from the high seat with a gentleness that surprised him, and she spoke for the first time. 'Once I was called Sarah Two,' she told Sarah Bledsoe, only Rob J. thought she said 'Sarah too.'

Sarah wasn't an accomplished drinker. She coughed when she tried to swallow the three fingers of sourmash whisky he gave her, and she gagged on the additional inch or so he added to her mug for good measure. He wanted her subdued and dulled to pain but able to cooperate. While they waited for the whisky to work, he set up candles around the table and lighted them despite the heat of the summer, for the daylight in the cabin was dim. When they undressed Sarah, he saw that her body was red from scrubbing. Her wasted buttocks were small as a child's, and her blue-skinned thighs looked almost concave in their thinness. She grimaced as he inserted a catheter and filled her bladder with water. He showed Makwa-ikwa how he wanted her knees held, then he greased the lithotrite with clean lard, taking care not to get any on the little jaws that would have to grasp the stones. The woman gasped as he slid the instrument into her urethra.

'I know it hurts, Sarah. It's painful as it goes in, but . . . There. Now it will be better.'

She was accustomed to far worse pain, and the groaning dwindled, but he was apprehensive. It had been several years since he had probed for stones, and then under the careful eyes of a man who undoubtedly was one of the best surgeons in the world. The day before, he had spent hours practising with the lithotrite, picking up raisins and pebbles, picking up nuts and cracking their shells, practising with the objects in a small tub of water, with his eyes closed. But it was quite another thing to poke around within the fragile bladder of a living being, aware that to thrust carelessly or to close the jaws on a wrinkle of tissue rather than on a stone might result in a tear that would bring terrible infection and painful death.

Since his eyes could do him no good, he closed them now, and moved the lithotrite slowly and delicately, his whole being fused into one nerve that functioned at the end of the instrument. It touched something. He opened his eyes and studied the woman's groin and lower abdomen, wishing he could see through flesh.

Makwa-ikwa was watching his hands, studying his face, missing nothing. He brushed at a buzzing fly and then ignored everything but the patient and the task and the lithotrite in his hand. The stone . . . Lord, he could tell at once that it was large! Perhaps the size of his thumb, he estimated as he manoeuvered and manipulated the lithotrite ever so slowly and carefully.

To determine if the stone would move, he tightened the jaws of the lithotrite onto it, but when he put the slightest backward pressure on the instrument the woman on the table opened her mouth and screamed.

'I have the biggest stone, Sarah,' he said calmly. 'It's too large to come out in one piece, so I'll try to break it.' Even as he spoke, his fingers were moving to the handle of the screw at the end of the lithotrite. It was as though each turn of the screw tightened the tension within him as well, because if the stone wouldn't break, the woman's prospects were dismal. But blessedly as he continued to turn the handle there was a dull crunching, the sound of someone grinding a shard of pottery beneath his heel.

He broke it into three segments. Although he worked with great care, when he removed the first piece he hurt her. Makwa-ikwa wet a cloth and wiped Sarah's sweaty face. Rob reached down and unclenched her left hand, peeling the fingers back like petals, and dropped the piece of the stone into her white palm. It was an ugly calculus, brown and black. The middle piece was smooth and egg-shaped, but the other two were irregular, with little needle points and sharp edges. When she held all three in her hand, he inserted a catheter and rinsed the bladder, and she voided a lot of the crystals that had broken from the stone when he had crushed it.

She was exhausted. 'That's enough,' he decided. 'There's another stone in your bladder, but it's small and should be easy to remove. We'll take it from you another day.'

In less than an hour she had begun to glow with the fever that followed quickly after almost every surgery. They force-fed her liquids, including Makwa-ikwa's efficient willow-

135

bark tea. Next morning she was still slightly febrile but they were able to take her back to her own cabin. He knew she was sore and torn up but she made the jolting trip without complaint. The fever wasn't gone from her eyes but there was another light there, and he was able to recognize it as hope.

A few days later, when Nick Holden invited him to go off on another doe hunt, Rob J. agreed warily. This time they caught a boat upstream to the town of Dexter, where the two LaSalle sisters were waiting at the tavern. Although Nick had described them with roguish masculine hyperbole, Rob J. recognized at once that they were tired whores. Nick chose the younger, more attractive Polly, leaving for Rob an aging woman with bitter eyes and an upper lip on which caked rice powder couldn't hide the dark mustache – Lydia. Lydia was openly resentful of Rob J.'s emphasis on soap and water and his use of Old Horny, but she carried out her part of the transaction with professional dispatch. That night he lay next to her in the room that contained the faint olfactory ghosts of past paid passions and wondered what he was doing there. From the next room there were angry voices, a slap, a woman's hoarse shouting, ugly but unmistakable thuds.

'Jesus.' Rob J. knocked his fist against the thin wall. 'Nick. Everything all right in there?'

'Dandy. Damm it, Cole. You just get yourself some sleep now. Or whatever. You hear?' Holden called back, his voice thick with whisky and annoyance.

Next morning at breakfast Polly had a red swelling on the left side of her face. Nick must have paid her very well for her beating, because her voice was pleasant enough when they said good bye.

On the boat going home, the incident couldn't be evaded. Nick placed his hand on Rob's arm. 'Sometimes a woman likes a bit of the rough stuff, don't you know it, ol' buck? Practically begs for it, to get her juices flowing.'

Rob regarded him silently, aware that this was his last doe hunt. In a moment Nick took his hand from Rob's arm and began telling him about the upcoming election. He had decided to run for state office, to stand for the legislature from their district. He knew it would be helpful, he explained earnestly, if Doc Cole would urge folks to vote for his good friend whenever he made a house call.

19
A Change

Two weeks after ridding her of the large stone, Rob J. was ready to remove the smaller calculus from Sarah's bladder, but she had become reluctant. The first few days after the removal of the stone, she had passed more small crystals with her urine, sometimes accompanied by pain. Ever since the last bits of crushed stone had left her bladder, she had been symptom-free. For the first time since the onset of her illness she didn't have crippling pain, and the absence of the spasms had allowed her to regain control of her body.

'You still have a stone in your bladder,' he reminded her. 'I don't want it removed. It doesn't hurt.' She looked at him defiantly but then dropped her eyes. 'I'm more afraid now than I was the first time.'

He noted that already she was looking better. Her face was still drawn with the suffering of a long affliction, but she had gained enough weight to make inroads against the gauntness. 'That big stone we removed was once a little stone. They grow, Sarah,' he said gently.

So she agreed. Again Makwa-ikwa sat with her while he removed the small calculus – about one-fourth the size of the other stone – from her bladder. There was a minimum of discomfort, and when he was through, a sense of triumph.

But this time when the postoperative fever arrived, her

138

body became fiery. He recognized impending disaster early and cursed himself for having given her the wrong advice. Before nightfall her foreboding had been justified; perversely, the easier procedure to remove the smaller stone had resulted in a massive infection. Makwa-ikwa and he took turns sitting next to her bed for four nights and five days, while inside her body a battle raged. Holding her hands in his, Rob could feel the waning of her vitality. Now and again Makwa-ikwa seemed to stare at something that wasn't there and chanted quietly in her own language. She told Rob she was asking Panguk, the death god, to pass this woman by. There was little else they could do for Sarah except to bathe her with wet cloths, support her while they held cups of liquid to her mouth and urged her to drink, and dress her cracked lips with grease. For a time she continued to fail, but on the fifth morning – was it Panguk, or her own spirit, or perhaps all the willow tea? – she began to sweat. Her nightshirts became sodden almost as quickly as they could be changed. By midmorning she had fallen into a deep and relieved sleep, and that afternoon when he touched her forehead it felt almost cool, a temperature that nearly matched his own.

Makwa-ikwa's expression didn't change much, but Rob J. was beginning to know her, and he believed she was pleased by his suggestion, even if at first she didn't take it seriously.

'Work with you. All the time?'

He nodded. It made sense. He'd seen that she knew how to look after a patient and didn't hesitate to do as he asked. He told her it could be a good arrangement for each of them. 'You can learn some of my kind of medicine. And you have so many things to teach me about the plants and herbs. What they cure. How to use them.'

They discussed it first in the buckboard after bringing Sarah home. He didn't press the idea on her. He just kept quiet and allowed her to think about it.

A few days later he stopped by the Sauk camp and they talked again over a bowl of rabbit stew. The thing she liked least about the offer was his insistence that she had to live close by his cabin, so he could fetch her quickly in times of emergency.

'I have to be with my people.'

He had pondered about the Sauk band. 'Sooner or later some white man will file with the government for every piece of land you folks might want to use for a village or a winter camp. There's going to be no place for you to go except back to that reservation you ran away from.' What they must do, he said, was learn to live in the world as it had become. 'I need help on my farm, Alden Kimball can't do it all. I could use a couple like Moon and Comes Singing. You could build cabins on my land. I'd pay the three of you in United States money, as well as found from the farm. If it works out, maybe other farms would have jobs for Sauks. And if you earned money and saved, sooner or later you'd have enough to buy your own land according to white man's custom and law, and nobody could ever order you from it.'

She looked at him.

'I know it offends you to have to buy back your own land. White men have lied to you, cheated you. And killed a whole lot of you. But red men have lied to one another. Stolen from one another. And the different bands have always killed one another, you've told me that. Colour of skin doesn't matter, all kinds of people are sonsabitches. But not everybody in the world is a sonofabitch.'

Two days later she and Moon and Comes Singing, along with Moon's two children, rode onto his land. They built a *hedonoso-te* with two smoke holes, a single longhouse that the shaman would share with the Sauk family, large enough to accommodate the third child who already swelled Moon's belly. They raised the lodge on the riverband, a quarter of a mile downstream from Rob J.'s cabin. Nearby they built a sweat lodge and a women's lodge to be used during menstruation.

Alden Kimball walked around with wounded eyes. 'There's white men out there looking for work,' he told Rob J. stonily. '*White men*. Never occurred to you I might not want to work with damn Indians?'

'No,' Rob said, 'it never did. Seems to me if you'd come across a good white worker you'd have told me to hire him long since. I've got to know these people. They're really good people. Now, I know you can quit on me, Alden, because anybody'd be a fool not to grab you if you were available. I'd hate to have that happen, because you're the best man I'm ever going to find to run this farm. So I hope you'll stay.'

Alden stared at him, confusion in his eyes, pleased by the praise but smarting because of the clear message. Finally he turned away and began to load fenceposts onto the buckboard.

What tipped the scales was the fact that Comes Singing's prodigious size and strength, coupled with his agreeable disposition, made him a wonderful hired hand. Moon had learned to cook for white people as a girl in the Christian school. For single men living alone it was a treat to have hot biscuits and pies and tasty food. Within a week it was obvious that although Alden remained aloof and would never acknowledge surrender, the Sauks had become part of the farm.

Rob J. experienced a similar small rebellion among his patients. Over a cup of cider Nick Holden warned him, 'Some of the settlers have started calling you Injun Cole. They say you're an Indian lover. They say you must have some Sauk blood yourself.'

Rob J. smiled, in love with the notion. 'Tell you what. If anybody complains to you about the doctor, just hand them one of those fancy handbills you're so fond of passing around. The ones that tell how fortunate the township is to have a physician of Dr Cole's training and education. Next time they're bleeding or sickly, I doubt many of them will object to my alleged ancestry. Or the colour of my assistant's hands.'

When he rode out to Sarah's cabin to see how she was recuperating, he noted that the path leading from the trail to her door had been edged, smoothed, and swept. New

141

beds of woodland plantings softened the outer contours of the little house. Inside, all the walls were whitewashed, and the only smells were of strong soap and the pleasant scents of lavender, and pennyroyal, sage, and cicely hung from the rafters.

'Alma Schroeder gave the herbs to me,' Sarah said. 'It's too late to plant a garden this season, but next year I'll have my own.' She showed him the garden patch, part of which she had already cleared of weeds and brambles.

The change in the woman was more astounding than the transformation of the place. She had begun to do her own cooking every day, she said, instead of depending on occasional hot dishes carried over by the generous Alma. A regular diet and improved nutrition already had replaced her wan boniness with a graceful femininity. She bent to pick a few green onions that had volunteered in the garden tangle, and he studied the pink nape of her neck. Soon it would be hidden, for her hair was growing back like a yellow pelt.

A small blond animal, her little boy scuttled behind her. He too was clean, though Rob took note of Sarah's chagrin as she tried to brush clay stains from her son's knees.

'You can't keep a boy from getting messy,' he told her cheerfully. The child looked at him with wild and fearful eyes. Rob always carried a few boiled sweets in his bag to help him make friends with little patients, and now he took one and unwrapped it. It took him almost half an hour of quiet talking before he could edge close enough to little Alex to hold out the sweet. When the small hand finally took the candy, he heard Sarah's released breath and looked up to see her watching his face. She had wonderful eyes, full of life.

'I've made a venison pie, if you want to share our dinner.'

It was on his lips to refuse, but the two faces were turned to him, the little boy sucking in bliss on the candy, the mother serious and expectant. The faces seemed to be asking him questions he couldn't understand.

'I do love venison pie,' he said.

20
Sarah's Suitors

It made good medical sense for Rob J. to stop and see Sarah
Bledsoe several times in the next week while returning from
house calls, for each time he could do so by going out of his
way only a little, and as her physician he had to make
certain her recovery was smooth. Indeed, it was a wonderful
recovery. There was little to discuss about her health, except
to observe that her skin tone had changed from a deadly
white to a pink-peach that was most becoming and that her
eyes glowed with alertness and an interesting intelligence.
One afternoon she gave him tea and cornbread. The
following week he stopped by her cabin three times, and
twice he accepted her invitation to stay for meals. She was
a better cook than Moon; he couldn't get enough of her
cooking, which she said was Virginian. He was aware that
her resources were meagre, so he took to bringing a few
things, a sack of potatoes, a small ham. One morning a
settler who was short of cash gave him four fat, freshly shot
grouse in partial payment, and he rode to the Bledsoe cabin
with the birds hanging from his saddle.

When he got there he found Sarah and Alex seated on the
ground near the garden, which was being double-dug by a
perspiring shirtless hulk of a man with the bulging muscles
and tanned skin of one who earns his living out-of-doors.
Sarah introduced Samuel Merriam, a farmer from Hooppole.

Merriam had come from Hooppole with a cartful of pig dung, half of which already had been dug into the garden. 'Finest stuff in the world for growing things,' he told Rob J. cheerfully.

Next to the princely gift of a wagonload of pig shit, applied, Rob's little birds were a meagre present, but he gave them to her anyhow, and she seemed genuinely grateful. He made a polite refusal to her invitation that he might join Samual Merriam as her dinner guest, and instead dropped in on Alma Schroeder, who waxed enthusiastic about what he had accomplished in curing Sarah. 'Already it's a suitor down there, isn't it?' she said, beaming. Merriam had lost his wife the previous autumn to the fever and needed another woman without delay to take care of his five children and help with the pigs. 'A good chance for Sarah,' she said sagely. 'Although, women so scarce on the frontier, she'll have lotsa chances.'

On Rob's way home, he drifted by the Bledsoe cabin again. He rode up to her and sat in the saddle looking at her. This time her smile was puzzled, and he could see Merriam pause at his work in the garden and stare speculatively. Until Rob opened his mouth, he had no idea what he wanted to tell her.

'You yourself must do as much of the work as possible,' he said severely, 'because the exercise is necessary to your full recovery.' Then he tipped his hat and rode crankily home.

Three days later, when next he stopped at the cabin, there was no sign of a suitor. Sarah was struggling to separate a big old rhubarb root into sections for replanting, and finally he solved her problem by chopping it apart with her axe. Together they dug the holes in the loam and planted the roots and covered them with the warm soil, a chore that pleased him and earned him a share of her dinner of red-flannel hash washed down with cool spring water.

Afterwards, while Alex napped in the shade of a tree, they sat on the riverbank and tended her trotline, and he spoke to her of Scotland and she told him she wished there was a church nearby, so her son could be taught to have faith. 'Often now I think of God,' she said. 'When I believed I was dying and Alex would be left alone, I prayed, and He sent you.' Not without trepidation, he confessed to her that he didn't believe in the existence of God. 'I think gods are the inventions of men and that it has always been so,' he said. He could see the shock in her eyes and feared he had sent her into a life of piety on a piggery. But she abandoned talk of religion and spoke of her early life in Virginia, where her parents owned a farm. Her large eyes were such a dark blue as to be almost purple; they didn't sentimentalize, but in them he saw the love for that easier, warmer time. 'Horses!' she said, smiling. 'I grew up loving horses.'

It allowed him to invite her to ride out with him next day to visit an old man who was dying of consumption, and she made no attempt to hide the eagerness with which she agreed. Next morning, on Margaret Holland and leading Monica Grenville, he called for her. They left Alex with Alma Schroeder, who fairly beamed with delight at the fact that Sarah was 'riding out' with the doctor.

It was a good day for a ride, not too hot for a change, and they allowed the horses to walk, taking their time. She had packed bread and cheese in her saddlebag, and they had a picnic in the shade of a live oak. In the sick man's house she stayed in the background, listening to the rattling breathing, watching Rob J. hold the patient's hands. He waited until water warmed at the fireplace and then bathed the skinny limbs and administered a dulling draught, teaspoon by teaspoon, so sleep would make the waiting merciful. Sarah overheard him telling the stolid son and the daughter-in-law that the old man would die within hours. When they left she was moved and spoke little. To try to regain the easiness they had shared earlier, he suggested they switch horses on the way back, because she was a fine horsewoman and could handle Margaret Holland without trouble. She enjoyed riding the friskier mount. 'Both the mares are named after women you have known?' she asked, and he acknowledged it was so.

She nodded thoughtfully. Despite his effort, they were

145

quieter on the way home.

Two days later, when he went to her cabin, there was yet another man, a tall, cadaverously thin pedlar named Timothy Mead, who regarded the world out of mournful brown eyes and spoke respectfully when introduced to the doctor. Mead left her a gift of four colours of thread.

Rob J. took a thorn out of Alex's bare foot and noted that summer was coming to an end and the boy didn't have proper shoes. He took a tracing of the feet and next time he was in Rock Island stopped at the shoemaker's and ordered a pair of child's boots, taking great pleasure in the errand. The following week, when he delivered the small footwear, he saw that the gesture flustered Sarah. Still, she was a puzzle to him; he couldn't tell if she was gratified or annoyed.

The morning after Nick Holden was elected to the legislature he rode into the clearing by Rob's cabin. In two days' time he would travel to Springfield to make laws that would help the growth of Holden's Crossing. Holden spat contemplatively and turned the conversation to the common knowledge that the doctor was riding out with the Widow Bledsoe. 'Ah. There are things you should know, old buck.'

Rob looked at him.

'Well, the child, her son. You're aware he's a wood's colt? Born almost two years after her husband's death.'

Rob stood. 'Good bye, Nick. You have a good trip to Springfield.'

There was no mistaking his tone, and Holden clambered to his feet. 'I'm just trying to say it's not necessary for a man –' he began, but what he saw in Rob J.'s face made him swallow the words, and in a moment he swung into his saddle, said a discomfited farewell, and rode away.

Rob J. saw such a puzzling mixture of things in her face: pleasure at seeing him and being in his company, tenderness when she would allow it, but also at times a kind of terror. The evening came when he kissed her. At first her open mouth was soft and glad and she pressed against him,

146

but then the moment went bad. She twisted away. To hell, he told himself, she didn't care for him, and that was that. But he forced himself to ask her gently what was the matter.

'How can you be attracted to me? Haven't you seen me wretched, in a beastly condition? You have . . . smelled my filth,' she said, her face aflame.

'Sarah,' he said. He looked into her eyes. 'When you were ill, I was your doctor. Since then, I've come to see you as a woman of charm and intelligence, with whom it gives me great pleasure to exchange thoughts and share my dreams. I've come to desire you in every way. You're all I think about. I love you.'

Their only physical contact was her hands in his. Her grip tightened, but she didn't speak.

'Perhaps you could learn to love me?'

'*Learn?* However could I not love you?' she asked wildly. 'You, who handed me back my life, as if you were God!'

'No, damn you, I'm an ordinary man! And that's how I need to be –'

Now they were kissing. It went on and on, and it wasn't enough. It was Sarah who prevented what might easily have followed, pushing him roughly, turning away and arranging her clothing.

'Marry me, Sarah.'

When she didn't answer, he spoke again. 'You weren't meant to slop hogs all day on a pig farm or to stumble about the countryside with a pedlar's pack on your back.'

'What is it I was meant for, then?' she asked in a low, bitter voice.

'Why, to be a doctor's wife. It's very plain,' he said gravely.

She didn't have to pretend to be serious. 'There are those who will rush to tell you about Alex, about his lineage, so I want to tell you about him myself.'

'I want to be Alex's father. I'm concerned about him today, and tomorrow. I don't need to know about yesterday. I've had terrible yesterdays too. Marry me, Sarah.'

Her eyes filled, but she had yet another side to reveal to him. She faced him calmly. 'They say the Indian woman

147

lives with you. You must send her away.'

'"*They say.*" And "*There are those who will tell you.*" Well, I will tell you something, Sarah Bledsoe. If you marry me, you must learn to tell *them* to go to hell.' He took a deep breath. 'Makwa-ikwa is a good and hardworking woman. She lives in her own house on my land. To send her away would be an injustice to her and to me, and I won't do it. It would be the worst way for you and me to begin a life together.

'You must take my word that there is no reason for jealousy,' he said. He held her hands tightly and wouldn't let her go. 'Any other conditions?'

'Yes,' she said hotly. 'You must change the names of your mares. They're named for women you have ridden, is that not so?'

He started to smile, but there was real anger in her eyes. 'One of them. The other was an older beauty I knew as a boy, a friend of my mother's. I ached for her, but she thought of me as a child.'

She didn't ask which horse was named for which woman. 'It's a cruel and nasty male joke. You're not a cruel and nasty man, and you must change the mares' names.'

'You'll rename them yourself,' he said at once.

'And you must promise, no matter what may happen between us in the future, never to name a horse for me.'

'I so vow. Of course,' he couldn't resist noting, 'I intend to order a pig from Samuel Merriam, and . . .'

Fortunately, he was still holding her hands, and he didn't let go of them until she was returning his kiss in a very good way. When they stopped, he saw she was weeping.

'What?' he said, burdened by the uneasy intimation that being married to this woman would not be easy.

Her wet eyes glowed. 'Letters posted by coach will be a terrible expense,' she said. 'But finally I can send positive word to my brother and sister in Virginia.'

21
The Great Awakening

It was easier to decide on marriage than to find a clergyman. Because of this, some couples along the frontier never bothered about formal vows, but Sarah refused 'to be married without being married'. She had the ability to speak plainly. 'I've known what it means to bear and raise a fatherless child, and it will never happen to me again,' she said.

He understood. Yet autumn had arrived, and he knew that once the snows locked the prairie it might be many months before an itinerant preacher or circuit-riding minister would make his way to Holden's Crossing. The answer to their problem appeared one day in a handbill he read at the general store, advertising a week-long revival meeting. 'It's called the Great Awakening and will be held at Belding Creek township. We have to go, Sarah, because there will be no shortage of clergymen there.'

When he insisted they bring Alex with them, Sarah agreed eagerly. They took the buckboard. It was a trip of a day and a morning over a passable, if stony, road. The first night they stopped in the barn of a hospitable farmer, spreading their blankets on the fragrant new hay in the loft. Next morning, Rob J. spent half an hour castrating the farmer's two bulls and removing a growth from the flank of a cow, to pay for their lodging; despite the delay, they arrived

149

at Belding Creek before noon. It was another new community, only five years older than Holden's Crossing but already much larger. As they drove into town, Sarah's eyes widened and she sat close to Rob and held Alex's hand, for she was unaccustomed to the sight of so many people. The Great Awakening was held on the prairie next to a shady willow grove. It had attracted people from throughout the region; everywhere, tents had been pitched for protection against the midday sun and the autumn wind, and there were wagons of all types, and tethered horses and oxen. Entrepreneurs serviced the crowds, and the three travellers from Holden's Crossing drove past open fires over which vendors were cooking things that gave off mouth-watering smells – venison stew, river-fish chowder, roast pork, sweetcorn, broiled hare. When Rob J. tied the horse to a bush – she who had been called Margaret Holland, now renamed Vicky, short for Queen Victoria ('You have never ridden the young queen?' Sarah asked) – they were eager for dinner, but there was no need to spend money on vended food. Alma Schroeder had supplied the little party with a hamper so large that the wedding feast could have lasted a week, and they dined on cold chicken and apple dumplings.

They ate quickly, caught up in the excitement, staring at the crowds, listening to the cries and the babble. Then, each holding one of the little boy's hands, they walked slowly about the meeting. It was really two revival meetings in one, for there was nonstop religious warfare, competitive preaching by Methodists and Baptists. For a time they listened to a Baptist minister in a clearing within the grove. His name was Charles Prentiss Willard, and he shouted and howled, making Sarah shiver. He warned that God was writing their names in his book, who should have everlasting life and who should have everlasting death. What would win a sinner everlasting death, he said, was immoral and unchristian conduct, such as fornicating, shooting a fellow Christian, fighting and using bad language, drinking whisky, or bringing illegitimate spawn into the world.

Rob J. looked grim and Sarah was trembly and pale as they went out onto the prairie to hear the Methodist, a man named Arthur Johnson. He wasn't nearly so powerful a speaker as Mr Willard, but he said salvation was possible for everybody who did good deeds and confessed their sins and asked God's forgiveness, and Sarah nodded when Rob J. asked if she didn't think Mr Johnson could do the marrying. Mr Johnson looked pleased when Rob approached him after the preaching. He wanted to marry them before the entire open meeting, but neither Rob J. nor Sarah wanted to become part of the entertainment. When Rob gave him three dollars, the preacher agreed to follow them outside town, and he arranged them under a tree on the bank of the Mississippi River, with the little boy seated on the ground and looking on, and a placid fat woman Mr Johnson introduced only as Sister Jane to serve as witness.

'I've a ring,' Rob J. said, digging it out of his pocket, and Sarah's eyes widened, because he hadn't mentioned his mother's wedding band. Sarah's long fingers were slim and the ring was loose. Her yellow hair was tied back with a dark blue ribbon Alma Schroeder had given her, and she took the ribbon off and shook her hair until it fell loose around her face. She said she'd wear the ring on the ribbon around her neck until they could get it sized. She held Rob's hand tightly as Mr Johnson led them through the vows with the ease of long practice. Rob J. repeated the words in a voice whose huskiness surprised him. Sarah's voice trembled, and she looked slightly disbelieving, as if she couldn't credit that this actually was happening. After the ceremony, they were still kissing when Mr Johnson began trying to convince them to return to the revival, because it was at the evening meeting that the most souls came forward to be saved.

But they thanked him and said good bye, turning Vicky in the direction of home. The little boy was soon cranky and whining, but Sarah sang lively songs and told stories, and several times when Rob J. stopped the horse she took Alex down from the buckboard and ran and jumped with him, playing games.

They shared an early supper of Alma's beef-and-kidney pies and pound cake with a sugary frosting, washed down

151

with brook water, and then had a sober discussion regarding the kind of accommodations to seek for that night. There was an inn a few hours away, and the prospect obviously pleased Sarah, who never had had the money to stay at a hostelry. But when Rob J. mentioned bedbugs and the general uncleanliness of such establishments, she quickly agreed with his suggestion that they stop at the same barn in which they had slept on the previous night.

They reached it at dusk and, receiving ready permission from the farmer, climbed up into the warm darkness of the loft almost with the welcome feeling of returning home.

Worn out by his exertions and the lack of a nap, Alex fell at once into a sound sleep, and when he was covered they spread a blanket nearby and reached for one another before they were fully undressed. He liked it that she didn't pretend to innocence and that their hunger for one another was honest and knowledgeable. They made thrashing and noisy love and then waited for some sign that they had awakened Alex, but the little boy slept on.

He finished undressing her and wanted to see. It had grown black in the barn, but they crawled together to the little door through which the hay was hoisted into the loft. When he opened the door, the three-quarter moon threw a rectangle of light in which they examined one another at length. In the moonlight he studied gilded shoulders and arms, burnished breasts, a crotch-mound like the silver nest of a small bird, and pale, ghostly buttocks. He would have made love in the light, but the air was seasonable and she feared the farmer's eyes, so they closed the door. This time they were slow and very tender, and just at the moment of the best ripe undamming he cried to her exultantly, 'This will make our bairn. *This!*' and the sleeping little boy was awakened by his mother's rattling groans and began to cry.

They lay with Alex cuddled between them, Rob's hand stroking her lightly, brushing away bits of chaff, memorizing.

'You mustn't die,' she whispered.

'Neither of us, not for a very long time.'

"A bairn is a child?'

152

'Yes.'

'You believe we've already begun a child?'

'. . . Maybe.'

Presently he heard her swallow. 'Perhaps, to make certain, we should keep on trying?'

As her husband and as her physician, he thought it a sensible notion. On his hands and knees he crawled in the blackness across the fragrant hay, following the ripe glimmer of his wife's pale flanks away from their sleeping son.

III
HOLDEN'S CROSSING
November 14, 1841

22
Cursing and Blessings

From mid-November the air was bitter. Heavy snows came early, and Queen Victoria floundered through high drifts. When Rob J. was out in the worst weather, sometimes he called the mare Margaret and her short ears pricked up at her old name. Both horse and driver knew their ultimate goals. She struggled toward heated water and a bag full of oats, while the man hurried to return to his cabin of warmth and light that came more from the woman and child than from the hearth and oil lamps. If Sarah hadn't conceived during the wedding trip, it was soon after. Wrenching morning sickness didn't quench their ardour. They waited itchily for the little boy to sleep and then clapped together, bodies almost as quickly as mouths, with an eagerness that remained constant, but as her pregnancy progressed he became a cautious and wooing lover. Once a month he took pencil and notebook and sketched her naked next to the comfort of the fire, a record of the development of the gravid female that was no less scientific because of the emotions that found their way into the drawings. He made architectural renderings too; they agreed on a house with three bedchambers, a large kitchen, and a sitting room. He drew construction plans to scale so Alden could hire two carpenters and begin the house after spring planting.

Sarah resented Makwa-ikwa's sharing a part of her

husband's world that was closed to her. As warming days turned the prairie first into a quagmire and then a delicate green carpet, she told Rob that when the seasonal fevers came, she'd go with him to nurse the sick. But by the end of April her body was ponderous. Tortured by jealousy as well as pregnancy, she stayed home and fretted while the Indian woman rode out with the doctor, to return hours – sometimes days – later. Sodden with fatigue, Rob J. would eat, bathe when possible, steal a few hours of sleep, and then collect Makwa and ride out again.

By June, Sarah's last month of pregnancy, the fever epidemic had eased sufficiently for Rob to leave Makwa at home. One morning while he rode through heavy rains to tend a farmer's woman who was dying in agony, back in his own cabin his wife came to term. Makwa placed the biting stick between Sarah's jaws and tied a rope to the door and gave her a knotted end to pull on.

It was hours before Rob J. lost his struggle with gangrenous erysipelas – as he would report in a letter to Oliver Wendell Holmes, the fatal illness was the result of a neglected cut in the farm woman's finger, made while she chunked seed potatoes – but when he got home, his child still hadn't been born. His wife's eyes were wild. 'It's splitting my body, make it stop, you bastard,' she snarled as he came through the door.

Hostage now to Holmes' training, he scrubbed his hands until they were raw before approaching her. After he had examined her, Makwa followed him away from the bed. 'Baby's comin' slow,' she said.

'Baby's coming feet first.'

Her eyes clouded, but she nodded and returned to Sarah.

The labour went on. In the middle of the night he forced himself to take Sarah's hands, fearful of their message. 'What?' she said thickly.

He could feel her vital force, diminished but reassuring. He murmured of love, but she hurt too much to acknowledge words or kisses.

On and on. Grunting and screaming. He couldn't resist praying unsatisfactorily, frightening himself by not being

158

able to bargain, feeling both arrogant and a hypocrite. *If I'm wrong and you do exist, please punish me some other way than by harming this woman. Or this child struggling to escape,* he added hastily. Towards dawn, little red extremities appeared, big feet for an infant, the proper number of toes. Rob whispered encouragement, told the reluctant baby all of life is a struggle. Legs emerged inch by inch, thrilling him by kicking.

The sweet little prick of a man-child. Hands, the proper number of fingers. A nicely developed baby, but the shoulders stuck and he had to cut Sarah, more pain. The small face was pressed into the wall of the vagina. Worried that the boy would suffocate in maternal flesh, he worked two fingers inside her and held the canal way away until the indignant little face slid into the topsy-turvy world and at once issued a thin cry.

With trembling hands he tied and cut the cord and stitched his sobbing wife. By the time he rubbed her belly to contract the uterus, Makwa had cleansed and swaddled the infant and set him on his mother's breast. It had been twenty-three hours of hard labour; for a long time she slept as though dead. When she opened her eyes, he held her hand tightly. 'Good job.'

'He's the size of a buffalo. About the size Alex was,' she said hoarsely. When Rob J. weighed him, the scale said eight pounds, eleven ounces. 'Good bairn?' she asked, studying Rob's face, and grimaced when he said it was a hell of a bairn. 'Cursing.'

He put his lips to her ear. 'You 'member what you called me yesterday?' he whispered.

'What?'

'Bastard.'

'I *never!*' she said, shocked and angry, and wouldn't speak to him for almost an hour.

Robert Jefferson Cole, they named him. In the Cole family the firstborn male always was a Robert, with a middle name that began with J. Rob thought the third American president had been a genius, and Sarah considered the 'Jefferson' a link with Virginia. She had fretted that Alex would be jealous, but all the older child demonstrated was fascination. He was never more than a step or two from his brother, always watching. From the start he made it clear the other two could tend the baby, feed it, change its nappies, play with it, offer it kisses and homage. But the baby was his to watch over.

In most respects, 1842 was a good year for the little family. To help build the house, Alden hired Otto Pfersick, the miller, and a homesteader from New York State named Mort London. London was a fine, experienced carpenter. Pfersick was only adequate at working wood, but he knew masonry, and the three men spent days selecting the best stones from the river and skidding them up to the house site with oxen. The foundation, chimney, and fireplaces turned out to be handsome. They worked slowly, aware they were building for permanence in a country of cabins, and by the time autumn arrived, when Pfersick had to make flour full-time and the other two men had to farm, the house was framed and closed in.

But it was a long way from finished, so Sarah was sitting in front of the cabin, snapping the ends from a potful of green beans, when the covered wagon lumbered up their track behind two tired-looking horses. She regarded the portly man in the driver's seat, noting homely features and the road dust on his dark hair and beard.

'Might this be Dr Cole's place, ma'am?'

'Might be and is, but he's on a call. Is the patient injured or sick?'

'Isn't any patient, thank the Lord. We're friends of the doctor's, moving into the township.'

From the back of the wagon a woman now looked out. Sarah saw a limp bonnet framing a white, anxious face. 'You're not . . . Might you be the Geigers?'

'Might be and are.' The man's eyes were handsome, and a good strong smile seemed to add a foot to his height.

'Oh, you are *so* welcome, neighbours! You get down from that wagon this instant.' Flurried, she spilled her beans when she rose from the bench. There were three children in the back of the wagon. The Geiger baby, identified as Herman, was asleep, but Rachel, who was almost four, and two-year-old David were crying as they were lifted down, and at once Sarah's baby decided to add his yowling to the chorus.

Sarah noted that Mrs Geiger was four inches taller than her husband, and not even the fatigue of a long, hard journey could disguise the fineness of her features. A Virginia girl recognized quality. It was of an exotic strain Sarah never had seen before, but at once she began to think anxiously about preparing and serving a dinner that wouldn't shame her. Then she saw that Lillian had begun to cry, and her own interminable time in just such a wagon returned to her with a rush, and she put her arms around the other woman and found to her astonishment that she was crying too, while Geiger stood in consternation amid weeping women and children. Finally Lillian drew back from her, muttering in embarrassment that her entire family was terribly in need of a safe creek for scrubbing.

'Now, that is something we can solve at once,' Sarah said, feeling powerful.

When Rob J. came home he found them still with wet heads from the river baths. After the handshakes and back-pounding, he had a chance to see his farm afresh through the newcomers' eyes. Jay and Lillian were awed by the Indians and impressed by Alden's abilities. Jay agreed eagerly when Rob suggested they saddle Vicky and Bess and ride to inspect the Geiger holding. When they returned in time for a fine dinner, Geiger's eyes blazed with happiness as he tried to describe to his wife the qualities of the land Rob J. had obtained for them.

'You'll see, just wait until you see it!' he told her. After eating, he went to his wagon and returned with his violin. They couldn't bring his wife's Babcock piano, he said, but they had paid to have it stored in a safe, dry place and hoped someday to send for it. 'Have you learned the Chopin?' he asked, and in answer Rob J. gripped the viola da gamba with his knees and drew the first rich notes of the mazurka. The music he and Jay had made in Ohio was more glorious

161

because Lillian's piano had been part of it, but the violin and the viola blended ecstatically. When Sarah finished her chores, she came and listened. She observed that as the men played, Mrs Geiger's fingers moved at times, as if she were touching keys. She wanted to take Lillian's hand and make things better for her with words and promises, but instead she sat next to her on the floor while the music rose and fell and offered all of them hope and comfort.

The Geigers camped next to a spring on their own land while Jason felled trees for a cabin. They were as determined not to impose on the Coles as Sarah and Rob were to show them hospitality. The families visited back and forth. As they were sitting around the Geigers' campfire on a frosty night, wolves began to howl out on the prairie, and Jay drew from his violin a similarly long, quavering howl. It was answered, and for a time the unseen animals and the human spoke across the darkness, until Jason noticed that his wife was trembling with more than the cold, and he threw another log on the fire and put his fiddle away.

Geiger wasn't a proficient carpenter. Completion of the Cole house was delayed again, for as soon as Alden could manage to take time from the farm, he began to raise the Geiger cabin. In a few days he was joined by Otto Pfersick and Mort London. The three of them built a snug cabin quickly and attached a shed, a pharmacy to house the boxes of herbs and medicinals that had taken up most of the room in Jay's wagon. Jay nailed to the doorway a little tin tube containing a parchment lettered with a portion of Deuteronomy, a custom of the Jews, he said, and the Geigers moved in on the eighteenth of November, a few days before hard cold drifted down from Canada.

Jason and Rob J. cut a path through the woods between the Cole houses site and the Geiger cabin. It quickly became known as the Long Path, to differentiate it from the path Rob J. had already cut between the house and the river, which became the Short Path.

The builders transferred their efforts to the Cole house. With the entire winter to finish its interior, they burned scrap lumber in the fireplace to keep warm and worked in high spirits, fashioning mouldings and wainscoting of quarter oak and lavishing hours on the mixing of skim-milk paint to just the proper shades to please Sarah. The buffalo slough near the house site had frozen, and Alden sometimes stopped working wood long enough to strap skates to his boots and show them skills remembered from his Vermont boyhood. Rob J. had skated every winter in Scotland and would have borrowed Alden's skates, but they were much too small for his large feet.

The first fine snow fell three weeks before Christmas. The wind blew what looked like smoke, and the minute particles seemed to burn when they touched human skin. Then the real, heavier flakes fell to muffle the world with white, and it stayed that way. With growing excitement, Sarah planned her Christmas menu, discussing surefire Virginia recipes with Lillian. Now she discovered differences between themselves and the Geigers, for Lillian didn't share in her excitement over the coming holiday. In fact, Sarah was amazed to learn that her new neighbours didn't celebrate the birth of Christ, choosing instead to queerly commemorate some ancient and outlandish Holy Land battle by lighting tapers and cooking potato pancakes! Still, they gave the Coles holiday gifts, plum preserves they had carted all the way from Ohio, and warm stockings Lillian had knitted for everyone. The Coles' gift to the Geigers was a heavy black iron spider, a frying pan on three legs that Rob had bought in the general store at Rock Island.

They begged the Geigers to join them for Christmas dinner, and in the end they came, although Lillian Geiger ate no meat outside her own home. Sarah served cream-of-onion soup, channel catfish with mushroom sauce, roast goose with giblet gravy, potato balls, English plum pudding made from Lillian's preserves, crackers, cheese, and coffee. Sarah gave her family woollen sweaters. Rob gave her a lap robe of fox fur so lustrous it caused her to catch her breath and brought exclamations of appreciation from everyone. He gave Alden a new pipe and a box of tobacco, and the hired man surprised him with sharp-bladed ice skates made

163

in the farm's own smithy – and large enough for his feet! 'Snow's coverin the ice now, but you'll enjoy these next year,' Alden said, grinning.

After the guests had left, Makwa-ikwa knocked on the door and left rabbitskin mittens, a pair for Sarah, a pair for Rob, a pair for Alex. She was gone before they could invite her in.

'She's a strange one,' Sarah said thoughtfully. 'We should have given her something too.'

'I took care of it,' Rob said, and told his wife he'd given Makwa a spider like the one they gave to the Geigers.

'You don't mean to tell me you gave that Indian an expensive store-bought gift?' When he didn't reply, her voice became tight. 'You must think a whole lot of that woman!'

Rob looked at her. 'I do,' he said thinly.

In the night the temperature rose, and rain fell instead of snow. Toward morning, a soaking wet Freddy Grueber came banging on their door, a weeping fifteen-year-old. The ox that was Hans Grueber's prize possession had kicked over an oil lamp and their barn had gone up despite the rain. 'Never seen nothin like it, Christ, we just couldn't put it out. Managed to save the stock, exceptin' the mule. But my pa's burnt bad, his arm and his neck and both legs. You gotta come, Doc!' The boy had ridden fourteen miles in the weather and Sarah tried to give him food and drink, but he shook his head and rode for home at once.

She packed a basket with leftovers from the feast, while Rob J. gathered the clean rags and salves he would need and then went to the longhouse to fetch Makwa-ikwa. In a few minutes Sarah was watching them disappear into the rainy murkiness, Rob on Vicky, with his hood pulled over his head, his large body hunched over in the saddle against the wet wind. The Indian woman was wrapped in a blanket and riding Bess. On my horse, and going off with my husband, Sarah told herself, and then decided to bake bread because she'd never be able to return to sleep.

All day she waited for their return. When nightfall came, she sat late by the fire, listening to the rain and watching the dinner she had kept warm for him turn into something he wouldn't want to eat. When she went to bed she lay without sleeping, telling herself that if they were holed up in a *tipi* or a cave, some warm nest, it was her fault for driving him away with her jealousy.

In the morning she was seated at the table, torturing herself with her imagination, when Lillian Geiger came calling, missing town life and driven by loneliness to come through the wet. Sarah had dark circles under her eyes and looked her worst, but she greeted Lillian and chatted brightly before bursting into tears in the middle of a discussion of flower seeds. In a moment, with Lillian's arms about her, to her consternation she was pouring out her worst fears. 'Until he came, my life was so bad. Now it is so good. If I should lose him . . .

'Sarah,' Lillian said gently. 'No one can know what goes on in another's marriage, of course, but . . . You say yourself that your fears may be groundless. I'm certain they are. Rob J. doesn't seem to be the kind of man who would practise deceit.'

Sarah allowed the other woman to comfort and dissuade her. By the time Lillian left for home, the emotional storm was over.

Rob J. came home at midday.

'How is Hans Grueber?' she asked.

'Ah, terrible burns,' he said wearily. 'Bad pain. I hope he'll be all right. I left Makwa there to nurse him.'

'That's good,' she said.

While he slept through the afternoon and evening, the rain ceased and the temperature plunged. He awoke in the middle of the night and dressed in order to go outside and slip and slide to the outhouse, because the rain-soaked snow had frozen to the consistency of marble. After he had relieved his kidneys and returned to bed, he couldn't sleep. He had hoped to return to the Gruebers' in the morning, but now he suspected that his horse's hooves wouldn't find

165

a purchase in the icy surface that covered the ground. He dressed again in the dark and let himself out of the house, and he discovered that his fears were correct. When he stomped on the snow as strongly as he was able, his boot couldn't break through the hard white surface.

In the barn he found the skates Alden had made for him and strapped them on. The track leading to the house had frozen roughly because of use, and made for difficult going, but at the end of the track was open prairie, and the windswept surface of the hardened snow was smooth as glass. He skated down gleaming moonpath, at first tentatively and then with longer and freer strokes as confidence returned, venturing far out into flatness like a vast arctic sea, hearing only the hissing of his blades and the sound of his laboured breathing.

Finally, winded, he drew up and examined the strange world of the frozen prairie at night. Quite close and alarmingly loud, a wolf sounded its quavering banshee call, and the hairs lifted on the back of Rob J.'s head. If he were to fall, perhaps to break a leg, winter-starved predators would gather within minutes, he knew. The wolf howled again, or perhaps it was another; there was in the wail everything Rob didn't want, it was a call composed of loneliness and hunger and inhumanity, and at once he began to move towards home, skating more carefully and more tentatively than he had done before, but fleeing as though pursued.

When he returned to the cabin he checked to see that neither Alex nor the baby had kicked off his covers. They were sleeping sweetly. When he got into bed his wife turned and thawed his frigid face with her breasts. She made a small purring and moaning, a sound of love and contrition, taking him into a welcoming tangle of arms and legs. The doctor was weatherbound; Grueber would be all right without him so long as Makwa was there, he thought, and gave himself to warmth of mouth and flesh and soul, to familiar pastime more mysterious than moonlight, more pleasurable even than flying over ice with no wolves.

23
Transformations

If Robert Jefferson Cole had been born in northern Britain, at birth he would have been called Rob J., and Robert Judson Cole would have become Big Rob, or just plain Rob without the initial. To Coles in Scotland, the J was retained by a first son only until he himself became the father of a first son, when it was passed on gracefully and without question. It wasn't in Rob J.'s mind to disturb a family practice of centuries, but this was a new country for Coles, and those he loved weren't mindful of hundreds of years of family tradition. Much as he tried to explain to them, they never turned the new son into Rob J. To Alex, at first the small brother was Baby. To Alden, he was the Boy. It was Makwa-ikwa who gave him the name that became part of him. One morning the child, a crawler then, and just beginning to mouth words, sat on the dirt floor of her *hedonoso-te* with two of the three children of Moon and Comes Singing. The children were Anemoha, Little Dog, who was three, and Cisaw-ikwa, Bird Woman, who was a year younger. They were playing with corncob dolls, but the little white boy crept away from them. In the dim light that fell through the smoke holes he saw the medicine woman's water drum and, dropping his hand on it, produced a sound that caused every head in the longhouse to raise.

The boy crawled away from the sound, but not back to

the other children. Instead, like a man on an inspection, he went to her store of herbs and stopped gravely before each pile, examining them with deep interest.

Makwa-ikwa smiled. 'You are *ubenu migegee-ieh*, a little shaman,' she said.

Thereafter, Shaman was what she called him, and others quickly took up the name because somehow it seemed to fit and he answered to it at once. There were exceptions. Alex liked to call him Brother, and Alex was Bigger to him, because from the start their mother spoke to them of one another as Baby Brother and Bigger Brother. Only Lillian Geiger tried to call the child Rob J., because Lillian had heard what her friend had said about his family's custom, and Lillian was a great believer in family and in tradition. But even Lillian forgot and called the boy Shaman at times, and Rob J. Cole (the man) quickly gave up the struggle and retained his initial. Initialled or not, he knew that out of his hearing, certain of his patients called him Injun Cole and some called him 'that fuckin' Sauk-lovin' sawbones.' But broadminded or bigots, they all knew him for a good doctor. When he was summoned he was content to go to them whether they loved him or not.

Where once Holden's Crossing had been only a description in Nick Holden's printed broadsides, now there was a Main Street of stores and houses, known to one and all as the Village. It boasted the Town Offices; Haskins' General Store: Notions, Groceries, Farm Implements & Dry Goods; N. B. Reimer's Feeds & Seeds; the Holden's Crossing Institution for Savings and Mortgage Company; a boarding-house run by Mrs Anna Wiley, who also served meals to the public; the shop of Jason Geiger, Apothecary; Nelson's Saloon (it was to have been an inn in Nick's early plans for the town, but because of the presence of Mrs Wiley's boardinghouse, it never became anything more than a low-ceilinged room with a long bar); and the stables and smithy of Paul Williams, General Farrier. From her frame house in the Village, Roberta Williams, wife of the blacksmith, did custom sewing and dressmaking. For several years, Harold

Ames, an insurance man over in Rock Island, came to the Holden's Crossing general store every Wednesday afternoon to transact business. But as the government land parcels began to be all taken up, and as some of the would-be farmers failed and began to sell their prairie holdings to newcomers, the need for a realty office became obvious and Carroll Wilkenson came and set up as a real-estate man and insurance agent. Charlie Andréson – who, a few years later, also became the president of the bank – was elected mayor of the town in the first election and every one thereafter, for years. Andréson was generally liked, though there was nobody who didn't understand that he was the chosen mayor of Nick Holden and at all times was in Nick's watch pocket. The same went for the sheriff. It hadn't taken Mort London more than a single year to discover he wasn't a farmer. There wasn't enough joinery work around to give him a steady living, because homesteaders did their own carpentry whenever it was possible. So when Nick offered to back him in a run for sheriff, Mort agreed eagerly. He was a placid man who minded his own business, which mostly was keeping the drunks quiet in Nelson's. It mattered to Rob J. who was the sheriff. Every doctor in the county was a deputy coroner, and the sheriff decided who would conduct the autopsy when a death occurred as a result of a crime or an accident. Oftentimes an autopsy was the only way a country doctor could do the dissecting that made it possible to keep surgical skills honed. Rob J. always adhered to scientific standards as rigorous as Edinburgh's when he did a postmortem, and he weighed all vital organs and kept his own records. Fortunately, he always had gotten on well with Mort London, and he did a lot of autopsies.

Nick Holden had been returned to the state legislature three terms in a row. At times some of the citizens of the town became annoyed at his air of proprietorship, reminding one another that he might own most of the bank, and part of the mill and the general store and that saloon, and Lord alone knew how many acres, but by God he didn't own them and he didn't own *their* land! But generally they watched with pride and astonishment as he operated like a real politician down there in Springfield, drinking bourbon whisky with the Tennessee-born governor and serving on legislative committees and pulling strings so fast and so skilfully that all they could do was spit and grin and shake their heads.

Nick had two ambitions, held openly. 'I want to bring the railroad to Holden's Crossing, so mebbe someday this town will become a city,' he told Rob J. one morning, enjoying a kingly cigar on the porch bench at Haskins' store. 'And I sorely want to be elected to the United States Congress. I'm not gonna get us a railroad staying down there in Springfield.'

They hadn't pretended real warmth since Nick had tried to talk him out of marrying Sarah, but they both were friendly whenever they met. Now Rob regarded him doubtfully. 'Getting into the US House of Representatives will be hard, Nick. You'll need votes from the much larger congressional district, not just from around here. And there's old Singleton.' The incumbent congressman, Samuel Turner Singleton, known throughout Rock Island County as 'our own Sammil', was firmly entrenched.

'Sammil Singleton *is* old. And soon he's gonna die or retire. When that time comes, I'll make everyone in the district see that a vote for me is a vote for prosperity.' Nick grinned at him. 'I've done all right by you, haven't I, Doctor?'

He had to admit it was so. He was a stockholder in both the grain mill and the bank. Nick also had controlled the financing of the general store and the saloon but hadn't invited Rob J. to participate in those businesses. Rob understood: his roots were sunk deeply in Holden's Crossing now, and Nick never wasted blandishments when they weren't necessary.

The presence of Jay Geiger's pharmacy and the steady flow of settlers into the region soon attracted another physician to Holden's Crossing. Dr Thomas Beckermann was a sallow middle-aged man with bad breath and red eyes. Lately of Albany, New York, he settled in a small frame house in the

170

Village, hard by the apothecary shop. He wasn't a medical-school graduate, and he was vague when discussing the details of his apprenticeship, which he said had been taken with a Dr Cantwell in Concord, New Hampshire. At first Rob J. viewed his coming with appreciation. There were enough patients for two doctors who weren't greedy, and the presence of another medical man should have meant a sharing of the long, difficult house calls that often took him far into the prairie. But Beckermann was a poor doctor and a steady, heavy drinker, and the community quickly observed both facts. So Rob J. continued to ride too far and treat too many.

This became unmanageable only in the springtime, when the annual epidemics struck, with fevers along the rivers, the Illinois mange on the prairie farms, and communicable illnesses everywhere. Sarah had nurtured the picture of herself at her husband's side, administering to the afflicted, and the spring after her younger son's birth she waged a strong campaign to be allowed to ride out with Rob J. and help him. Her timing was bad. That year, the troubling diseases were milk fever and measles, and by the time she began to pester him, he already had very sick people, a few of them dying, and he couldn't pay her sufficient attention. So Sarah watched Makwa-ikwa ride out with him all through another spring, and her inner torment returned.

By midsummer the epidemics had quieted and Rob resumed the more routine pattern of his days. One evening, after he and Jay Geiger had restored themselves with Mozart's Duet in G for violin and viola, Jay raised the sensitive question of Sarah's unhappiness. By now they were comfortable best friends, yet Rob was taken aback that Geiger should presume to enter a world he had considered so inviolably private.

'How do you come to know of Sarah's feelings?'

'She talks to Lillian. Lillian talks to me,' Jay said, and struggled with a moment of abashed silence. 'I hope you understand. I speak out of . . . genuine affection . . . for you both.'

'I do. And along with your affectionate concern, do you

171

have . . . advice?'

'For your wife's sake, you have to get rid of the Indian woman.'

'There's nothing but friendship between us,' he said, failing to control his resentment.

'It doesn't matter. Her presence is the source of Sarah's unhappiness.'

'There's no place for her to go! There's no place for any of them to go. The whites say they're savages and won't let them live the way they used to. Comes Singing and Moon are the best damn farm workers you could hope for, but no one else around here is willing to hire a Sauk. Makwa and Moon and Comes Singing keep the rest of the pack going, with what little money they earn from her. She works hard and she's loyal, and I can't send her away to starvation or worse.'

Jay sighed and nodded, and didn't speak of it again.

Delivery of a letter was a rarity. Almost on occasion. One came for Rob J., sent on by the postmaster at Rock Island, who had held it for five days until Harold Armes, the insurance agent, made a business trip to Holden's Crossing.

Rob opened the envelope eagerly. It was a long letter from Dr Harry Loomis, his friend in Boston. When he finished reading, he went back and read it again, more slowly. And then again.

It had been written on November 20, 1846, and had taken all winter to reach its destination. Harry obviously was on the road to a fine career, a Boston career. He reported that he'd recently been appointed an assistant professor of anatomy at Harvard, and he hinted at impending marriage to a lady named Julia Salmon. But the letter was more medical intelligence than personal report. A discovery now made pain-free surgery a reality, Harry wrote with discernible excitement. It was the gas known as ether, which had been used for years as a solvent in the manufacture of waxes and perfumes. Harry reminded Rob J. of past experiments held in Boston hospitals to assess the painkilling effectiveness of nitrous oxide, known as 'laughing gas'. He added roguishly that Rob might remember recreations with nitrous oxide that were conducted outside of hospitals. Rob did remember, with combined guilt and pleasure, sharing with Meg Holland a flask of laughing gas Harry had given to him for a little party. Perhaps time and distance made the memory better and funnier than it had been.

'On October 5 just past,' Loomis wrote, 'another experiment, this time with ether, was scheduled to take place in the operating dome of the Massachusetts General Hospital. Past attempts to kill pain with nitrous oxide had been complete failures, with galleries of students and doctors jeering and calling out "Humbug! Humbug!" The attempts had taken on a tone of hilarity, and the scheduled operation at the Massachusetts General promised to be more of the same. The surgeon was Dr John Collins Warren. I'm certain you'll remember that Dr Warren is a crusty, hardened cutter, more known for his swiftness with the scalpel than for his patience with fools. So a number of us flocked to the surgical dome that day as if attending an entertainment.

'Picture it, Rob: the man delivering the ether, a dentist named Morton, is late. Warren, vastly annoyed, uses the delay to lecture on how he will proceed to cut a large tumour from the cancerous tongue of a young man named Abbott, who already sits in the red operating chair, half-dead with terror. In fifteen minutes Warren runs out of words and grimly takes out his watch. The gallery already has started to titter, when here arrives the errant dentist. Dr Morton administers the gas and presently announces the patient is ready. Dr Warren nods, still in fury, rolls up his sleeves, and selects his scalpel. Aides pull open Abbott's jaw and grasp his tongue. Other hands pin him to the operating chair so he won't thrash. Warren bends over him and makes the first swift, deep slash, a lightning motion that brings blood trickling from a corner of young Abbott's mouth.

'He doesn't stir.

'There is utter silence in the gallery. The slightest sigh or groan will be heard. Warren bends back to his task. He makes a second incision, and then a third. Carefully, quickly, he excises the tumour, scrapes it, applies stitches, presses a sponge to control bleeding.

'The patient sleeps. The patient sleeps. Warren straightens up.

173

If you can credit it, Rob, the eyes of that caustic autocrat are wet!'
'"Gentlemen," he says, "this is no humbug."'

The discovery of ether as a surgical painkiller has been announced in the medical press of Boston, Harry reported. *'Our Holmes, ever quick off the mark, already has suggested that it be called anaesthesia, from the Greek word for insensibility.'*

Geiger's Pharmacy didn't stock ether.

'But I'm a fair chemist,' Jay said thoughtfully. 'I can make it, probably. I'd have to distill grain alcohol with sulphuric acid. I couldn't use my metal still, because the acid would burn right through it. But I own a glass coil and a big bottle.'

When they searched his shelves, they found lots of alcohol but no sulphuric acid.

'Can you make sulphuric acid?' Rob asked him.

Geiger scratched his chin, clearly enjoying himself. 'For that, I'll need to mix sulphur with oxygen. I've plenty of sulphur, but the chemistry is a mite complicated. Oxidize sulphur once and you get sulphur dioxide. I'll need to oxidize the sulphur dioxide again, to make sulphuric acid. But . . . sure, why not?'

In a few days, Rob J. had a supply of ether. Harry Loomis had explained how to assemble an ether cone out of wire and rags. First Rob tried the gas on a cat who remained insensible for twenty-two minutes. Then he deprived a dog of consciousness for more than an hour, such a long time that it became obvious that ether was dangerous and must be treated with respect. He administered the gas to a male lamb before castration, and the gonads came off without a bleat.

Finally, he instructed Geiger and Sarah in ether's use and they gave it to him. He was unconscious for only a few minutes, because nervousness made them miserly with the dose, but it was a singular experience.

Several days later, Gus Schroeder, already down to eight and one-half fingers, got the index finger of his good hand, the right hand, caught under his stone boat and ground to a pulp. Rob gave him the ether, and Gus woke up with seven and one-half fingers and asked when the operating would begin.

Rob was stunned by possibilities. He felt as though he had been given a glimpse of the limitless stretches beyond the stars, aware at once that ether was more powerful than the Gift. The Gift was shared by only a few members of his family, but every doctor in the world now would be able to operate without causing torturous pain. In the middle of the night Sarah came down to the kitchen and found her husband sitting alone.

'Do you feel all right?'

He was studying the colourless liquid in a glass bottle, as if memorizing it.

'If I'd had this, Sarah, I wouldn't have ever hurt you, those times I operated.'

'You did very well without it. Saved my life, I know.'

'This stuff.' He held up the bottle. To her it looked no different from water. 'It will save lots of lives. It's a sword against the Black Knight.'

Sarah hated when he spoke of death as a person who might open the door and walk into their house at any moment. She hugged her heavy breasts with her white arms and shivered with the night chill. 'Come to bed, Rob J.,' she said.

Next day Rob began to contact doctors in the region, inviting them to a meeting. It was held a few weeks later in a room above the feed store in Rock Island. By that time Rob J. had used ether on three other occasions. Seven doctors and Jason Geiger assembled and listened to what Loomis had written, and Rob's report of his own cases.

Reactions ranged from great interest to open scepticism. Two of those present ordered ether and ether cones from Jay. 'It's a passing fad,' Thomas Beckermann said, 'like all that nonsense about hand-washing.' Several of the doctors smiled, because everyone was aware of Rob Cole's eccentric use of soap and water. 'Maybe metropolitan hospitals can spend time on such things. But no bunch of doctors in Boston should try to tell us how to practice medicine on the western frontier.'

175

The other doctors were more discreet than Beckermann. Tobias Barr said he liked the experience of meeting with other physicians to share ideas, and he suggested that they form the Rock Island County Medical Society, which they proceeded to do. Dr Barr was elected president. Rob J. was elected corresponding secretary, an honour he couldn't refuse, because everyone present was given an office or the chairmanship of a committee that Tobias Barr described as being of genuine importance.

That was a bad year. On a hot, sticky afternoon towards the end of summer, when the crops were reaching ripeness, very quickly the sky became heavy and black. Thunder rumbled and lightning cleaved the roiling clouds. Weeding her garden, Sarah saw that far out on the prairie a slim funnel extended earthward from the cloud mass. It twisted like a giant snake and emitted a serpentine hissing that became a loud roar as its mouth reached the prairie and began to suck up dirt and debris.

It was moving away from her, but still Sarah ran to find her children and bring them down into the cellar.

Eight miles away, Rob J. had watched the tornado from afar, too. It was gone in a few minutes, but when he rode up to Hans Buckman's farm he saw that forty acres of prime corn had been levelled. 'As if Satan wielded a great big scythe,' Buckman observed bitterly. Some farmers lost both corn and wheat. The Muellers' old white mare was sucked up into the vortex and spat out lifeless in an adjoining pasture a hundred feet away. But no human lives had been lost, and everyone knew that Holden's Crossing had been lucky.

People were still congratulating themselves when epidemic broke out in the autumn. It was the season when the cool crispness of the air was supposed to guarantee vigour and good health. The first week of October, eight families came down with a malady Rob J. couldn't put a name to. It was a fever accompanied by some of the bilious symptoms of typhoid, yet he suspected it wasn't typhoid. When he began to hear of at least one new case every day, he knew they were in for it.

He had started toward the longhouse to tell Makwa-ikwa to prepare to ride out with him, but he changed directions and walked to the kitchen of his own house.

'People are beginning to get a nasty fever, and it'll spread, for certain. I may be out there for weeks.'

Sarah was nodding gravely, to show she understood. When he asked if she wanted to come with him, her face came alive in a way that dispelled his doubts.

'You'll be away from the boys,' he cautioned.

'Makwa will care for them while we're gone. Makwa's really good with them,' she said.

They left that afternoon. This early in an epidemic, it was Rob's way to ride to any house where he heard the disease was present, trying to put out the fire before it became a conflagration. He saw that each case started the same way, with sudden high temperature or with inflamed throat followed by the fever. Usually there was diarrhoea early, with lots of yellow-green bile. In every patient the mouth became covered with small papillae, regardless of whether the tongue was dry or moist, blackish or whitish.

Within a week Rob J. knew that if the patient had no additional symptoms, death was coming. If the early symptoms were followed by chills and pain in the extremities, often severe, the patient probably would recover. Boils and other abscesses, erupting at the end of the fever, were favourable signs. He had no idea how to treat the disease. Since the early diarrhoea often broke the high fever, he sometimes tried to encourage its onset by administering physic. When the patients shook with chills, he gave them Makwa-ikwa's green tonic doctored with a little alcohol, to induce sweating, and blistered them with mustard plasters. Soon after the epidemic began, he and Sarah met Tom Beckermann riding out to fever victims.

'Typhoid, for sure,' Beckermann said. Rob didn't think so. There were no red spots on the abdomen, and no one was haemorrhaging from the anus. But he didn't argue. Whatever was striking people down, calling it by one name or another wouldn't make it any less scary. Beckermann told them two of his patients had died the previous day, following copious bleeding and cupping. Rob did his best to argue against bleeding a patient to fight fever, but Beckermann was the kind of physician unlikely to follow any treatment recommended by the only other doctor in town. They didn't spend more than a few minutes with Dr Beckermann before saying good bye. Nothing bothered Rob J. more than a bad physician.

At first it felt strange to have Sarah with him instead of Makwa-ikwa. Sarah couldn't have tried harder, hastening to do whatever he asked. The difference was that he had to ask and he had to teach, whereas Makwa had come to know what was needed without his telling her. In front of patients or riding between houses, he and Makwa had maintained long and comfortable silences; at first Sarah talked and talked, happy for a chance to be with him, but as they treated more patients and exhaustion became the rule, she turned quieter.

The disease spread quickly. Usually, if someone in a household became sick, all the other family members caught it. Yet Rob J. and Sarah went from house to house and didn't come down with anything, as if they wore invisible armour. Every three of four days they tried to return home for a bath, a change of clothing, a few hours of sleep. The house was warm and clean, full of the smell of the hot food Makwa prepared for them. They held their sons for a little while, then packed the green tonic Makwa had brewed while they were gone and had mixed with a little wine at Rob's instruction, and they rode out again. In between visits home, they slept huddled together wherever they could drop, usually in haylofts or on the floor in front of somebody's fire.

One morning a farmer named Benjamin Haskell walked into his barn and became pop-eyed at the sight of the doctor with his arm up his woman's skirt. That was the closest they came to making love during the entire epidemic, six weeks. The leaves had been turning colour when it began, and there was a dusting of snow on the ground when it ended.

The day they came home and realized it was unnecessary for them to ride out again, Sarah sent the children in the buckboard with Makwa to Mueller's farm to fetch baskets of winter apples for making sauce. She took a long soak in front of the fire and then boiled more water and prepared Rob's bath, and when he was in the tin tub she came back and washed him very slowly and gently, the way they had washed patients, yet very different from that, using her hand instead of a washcloth. Damp and shivering, he hastened after her through the chill house, up the stairs, under the warm bedcovers, where they stayed for hours, until Makwa was back with the boys.

Sarah was briefly with child a few months later, but she miscarried early, frightening Rob because her blood splashed, fairly leaping out of her before the haemorrhages finally ceased. He realized it would be dangerous for her to conceive again, and after that he took precautions. He watched anxiously for signs of black shadows settling over her, as often happened after a woman aborted a foetus, but aside from a pale pensiveness that manifested itself in long periods of thought with her violet eyes closed, she appeared to recover as quickly as could be hoped.

24
Spring Music

So, often and for long periods, the Cole boys were left in the care of the Sauk woman. Shaman became as accustomed to Makwa-ikwa's crushed-berries smell as he was to the white odour of his natural mother, as accustomed to her darkness as to Sarah's milky blondeness. And then, more accustomed. If Sarah walked away from mothering, Makwa accepted the opportunity eagerly, holding the man-child, the son of *Cawso wabeskiou*, to the warmth of her bosom and finding a fulfilment she hadn't experienced since she had held her own infant brother, He-Who-Owns-Land. She cast a love spell over the little white boy. Sometimes she sang to him:

> *Ni-na ne-gi-se ke-wi-to-se-me-ne ni-na,*
> *Ni-na ne-gi-se ke-wi-to-se-me-ne ni-na,*
> *Wi-a-ya-ni,*
> *Ni-na ne-gi-se ke-wi-to-se-me-ne ni-na,*
> *I walk with you, my son,*
> *I walk with you, my son,*
> *Wherever you are going,*
> *I walk with you, my son.*

Sometimes she sang to protect him:

> *Tti-la-ye ke-wi-ta-mo-ne i-no-ki,*

Tti-la-ye ke-wi-ta-mo-ne i-no-ki-i-i.
Me-ma-ko-te-si-ta
Ki-ma-ma-to-me-ga.
Ke-te-na-ga-yo-se.
Ghost, I call you today,
Ghost, I speak to you now.
One who is greatly in need
Will worship you.
Send your blessings to me.

Soon these were the songs Shaman hummed as he dogged her steps. Alex followed along glumbly, watching as still another adult claimed part of his brother. He obeyed Makwa, but she recognized that the suspicion and dislike she sometimes saw in his young eyes were a son's reflections of Sarah Cole's feelings toward her. It didn't matter to her much. Alex was a child, and she would work to win his trust. As for Sarah – so long as Makwa could remember, Sauks had had enemies.

Jay Geiger, busy with his pharmacy, had hired Mort London to plough the first section of his farm, a slow and brutal task. It had taken Mort from April to the end of July to break the deep, tough sod, a process made more expensive by the fact that the turned-over clods had to be allowed to rot for two or three years before the field was fit to be reploughed and planted, and because Mort had caught the Illinois mange, which afflected most men who ripped open the prairie. Some thought the rotting sod released a miasma that carried the illness to the farmer, while others said the sickness came from the bites of tiny insects disturbed by the ploughshare. The ailment was unpleasant, the skin breaking out in little sores that itched. Treated with sulphur, it could be contained as an annoyance, but if it was neglected it could develop into a fatal fever such as the one that had killed Alexander Bledsoe, Sarah's first husband.

Jay insisted that even the corners of his field should be carefully ploughed and sown. In accordance with ancient Jewish law, at harvest time he left the corners unreaped, to be gleaned by the poor. When Jay's first section started producing good crops of corn, he was ready to prepare the second section to plant wheat. But by that time Mort London was sheriff, and none of the other homesteaders was willing to work for wages. It was a time when Chinese coolies didn't dare quit the railroad gangs because they were likely to be stoned if they made it to the nearest town. Occasionally an Irishman or the rare Italian, escaping from the near-slavery of digging the Illinois and Michigan Canal, wandered into Holden's Crossing, but papists were viewed with alarm by a majority of the population, and these interlopers were hurried on their way. Jay had developed a passing acquaintance with some of the Sauks because they were the poor whom he had invited to glean his corn. Finally he bought four bullocks and steel plough and hired two of the warriors, Little Horn and Stone Dog, to break the prairie for him.

The Indians knew secrets about slicing the plains and turning it over to expose its flesh and blood, the black earth. As they worked they apologized to the earth for cutting it, and they sang songs in order to imprecate the proper ghosts. They knew the white man ploughed too deep. When they set the ploughshare for shallow cultivation, the root mass below the ploughed earth actually rotted away faster, and they cultivated two and one-quarter acres a day instead of a single acre. And neither Little Horn nor Stone Dog caught the mange.

Marvelling, Jay tried to share their method with all his neighbours, but he found no willing listeners.

'It's because the ignorant bastards consider me a foreigner, even though I was born in South Carolina and some of them were born in Europe,' he complained hotly to Rob J. 'They don't trust me. They hate the Irish and the Jews and the Chinese and the Italians, and God knows who all, for coming to America too late. They hate the French and the Mormons on general principles. And they hate the Indians for being in America too early. Who the hell *do* they like?'

Rob grinned at him. 'Why, Jay . . . they like *themselves*! They think they are just right, having had the sensibility to arrive at exactly the correct time,' he said.

In Holden's Crossing, being liked was one thing, being accepted was another. Rob J. Cole and Jay Geiger gained grudging acceptance because their professions were needed. As they became prominent patches in the community quilt, the two families continued to be close, drawing support and stimulation from one another. The children became accustomed to the works of great composers, lying in bed of an evening and listening to music that rose and fell with the beauty of stringed instruments played with love and passion by their fathers.

The year Shaman was five years old, the major spring illness was measles. The invisible armour protecting Sarah and Rob disappeared, and so did the luck that had kept them unscathed. Sarah brought the disease home and became mildly ill, as did Shaman. Rob J. thought anyone was lucky to catch a light dose, because in his experience measles didn't strike twice in one lifetime; but Alex caught the disease in all its terrible power. Whereas his mother and brother had been feverish, he burned. While they had itched, his body ran bloody from frenzied scratching, and Rob J. wrapped him in wilted cabbage leaves and bound his hands for his own protection.

The spring after that, the prevailing illness was scarletina. The Sauk band caught it, and Makwa-ikwa from them, so that Sarah had to stay home full of resentment and nurse the Indian woman instead of riding out as her husband's assistant. Then both boys came down. This time Alex drew the gentler version of the disease, while Shaman burned, vomited, screamed with the earache, and suffered a rash so damaging that in places his skin peeled off like a snake's.

When the disease had run its course, Sarah opened the house to the warm May air and declared that the family needed a holiday. She roasted a goose and let the Geigers know their presence would be appreciated, and that evening, music reigned where it hadn't been heard for weeks.

The Geiger children were put to bed on pallets next to the bunks in the Cole boys' room. Lillian Geiger slipped into the room and gave each child a hug and a kiss. At the door she paused and wished them goodnight. Alex wished her goodnight in return, as did her own children, Rachel, Davey, Herm, and Cubby, who was too young to be saddled with his real name, which was Lionel. She noticed that one child hadn't answered. 'Good night, Rob J.,' she said. There was no reply, and Lillian saw that the child looked straight ahead, as if lost in thought.

'Shaman? My dear?' In a moment, when there was no reply, she clapped her hands sharply. Five faces looked toward her, but one did not.

In the other room, the musicians were doing the Mozart duet, the piece they played together best, the one that made them shine. Rob J. was amazed when Lillian stood before his viola and put her hand out, stopping his bow during a phrase he especially loved.

'Your son,' she said. 'The little one. He doesn't hear.'

25
The Quiet Child

All his life Rob J., struggling to salvage people from the afflictions that bring about physical and mental failures, was surprised at how much it hurt him when the patient was someone he loved. He cherished all those he treated, even the ones made mean by their sickness, even the ones he knew had been mean before they'd become sick, because by seeking his help, somehow they became his. As a young physician in Scotland he'd seen his mother fail and move toward death, and it had been a special, bitter lesson in his ultimate powerlessness as a doctor. And now he felt a raw hurt because of what had befallen the strong, chucky little boy, large for his age, who had come from his own seed and soul.

Shaman appeared dazed as his father clapped his hands, dropped heavy books to the floor, stood before him shouting.

'CAN... YOU... HEAR... ANYTHING? SON?' Rob yelled, pointing to his own ears, but the little boy only stared in puzzlement. Shaman was profoundly deaf.

'Will it go away?' Sarah asked her husband.

'Perhaps,' Rob said, but he was more frightened than she, because he knew more, had seen tragedies whose possibilities she only sensed.

'You'll make it go away.' She had absolute faith in him.

As once he had saved her, now he would save their child.

He didn't know how, but he tried. He poured warm oil into Shaman's ears. He soaked him in hot baths, he applied compresses. Sarah prayed to Jesus. The Geigers prayed to Jehovah. Makwa-ikwa tapped her water drum and sang to the *manitous* and the ghosts. No god or spirit paid attention.

In the beginning, Shaman was too baffled to be frightened. But within hours he began to whimper and scream. He shook his head and clawed at his ears. Sarah thought the terrible earache had returned, but Rob soon felt it wasn't that, because he had witnessed this before. 'He's hearing noises we can't hear. Inside his head.'

Sarah blanched. 'There is something in his head?'

'No, no.' He could tell her what the condition was called – tinnitus – but he couldn't tell her what was causing the sounds that were so private to Shaman.

Shaman didn't stop crying. His father and mother and Makwa took turns lying on the bed hugging him. Later Rob would learn that his son heard a variety of din, sounds of crackling, rings, thunderous roaring, hissing. All of it was very loud, and Shaman was continually terrified.

The internal barrage disappeared after three days. Shaman's relief was profound and the returned silence was comforting, but the adults who loved him were tortured by the desperation in the small white face.

That night Rob wrote to Oliver Wendell Holmes in Boston, asking for advice about how to treat the deafness. He also asked Holmes, in case nothing could be done regarding the condition, to forward information that would instruct him how to raise a deaf son.

None of them knew how to treat Shaman. While Rob J. cast about for a physician's solutions, it was Alex who assumed responsibility. Although stunned and frightened by what had happened to his brother, Alex adapted swiftly. He took Shaman's hand and didn't let go. Where the older boy walked, the younger followed. When their fingers cramped, Alex crossed to his brother's other side and switched hands.

Shaman quickly became accustomed to the security of Bigger's sweaty, often dirty grasp.

Alex guarded him closely. 'He wants more,' he would remark at the table during meals, taking Shaman's empty bowl and holding it out to his mother so it could be refilled.

Sarah watched her two sons, observing how each of them suffered. Shaman stopped talking, and Alex chose to join him in his muteness, speaking hardly at all, communicating with Shaman in a series of exaggerated gestures while the two sets of young eyes locked with one another earnestly.

She tortured herself with imagined situations in which Shaman faced a variety of terrible fates because he couldn't hear her agonized screams of warning. She made the boys stay close to the house. They grew bored and sat on the ground and played stupid games with nuts and pebbles, drawing pictures in the dirt with sticks. Incredibly, at times she heard them laughing. Not being able to hear his own voice, Shaman was apt to speak too softly, so they'd have to ask him to repeat what he mumbled, and he wouldn't understand them. He took to grunting instead of speaking. When Alex became exasperated, he forgot about reality. 'What?' he shouted. 'What, Shaman!' And then he remembered the deafness and resorted to gestures again. He developed an unfortunate habit of grunting like Shaman to emphasize something he was trying to explain with his hands. Sarah couldn't stand the growling-snorting sound, which made her sons seem like animals to her.

She fell into an unfortunate habit of her own, testing the deafness too often by coming up behind them and clapping her hands, or snapping her fingers, or saying their names. Inside the house, if she stamped her foot the vibrations in the floor caused Shaman to turn his head. At all times, only Alex's scowl noted her interruption.

She had been an on-again, off-again mother, choosing to ride out with Rob J. at every opportunity instead of taking care of her children. She admitted to herself that her husband was the most important thing in her life, just as she acknowledged that medicine was the prime force in his life, even more important that his love for her; that's just the way things were. She'd never felt for Alexander Bledsoe, or for any man, what she felt for Rob J. Cole. Now that one of her sons was threatened, she turned her love back to her boys full force, but it was too late. Alex wouldn't relinquish any part of his brother, and Shaman had become accustomed to depending on Makwa-ikwa.

Makwa didn't discourage the dependence; she took Shaman into the *hedonoso-te* for long periods of time, and she watched his every move. Once Sarah saw her hurry to where the boy had passed water against a tree and scoop some of the wet earth from the ground and take it away in a little cup, as if she was collecting the relic of a saint. Sarah thought the woman was a succubus who tried to claim the part of her husband he valued most about himself, and who now claimed her child. She knew Makwa was casting spells, singing, performing savage rituals whose very thought made her skin crawl, but she dared not object. As desperately as she wanted someone – anyone, anything – to succour her child, she couldn't resist a feeling of self-righteous vindication, an affirmation in the one true faith, when day after day passed and the heathen nonsense brought no improvement to her son's condition.

At night Sarah lay awake, tormented by thoughts of deaf mutes she'd known, remembering in particular a feeble-minded and slovenly woman whom she and her friends had followed through the streets of their Virginia village, taunting the poor creature for her obesity and her deafness. Bessie, her name, Bessie Turner. They'd thrown sticks and pebbles, hilarious to see Bessie respond to physical insults after being able to ignore the horrible things they had shouted. She wondered if cruel children would follow Shaman through the streets.

Slowly it dawned upon her that Rob – even Rob! – didn't know how to help Shaman. He left every morning and rode out on his house calls, absorbed with other people's ills. He wasn't abandoning his own family. It only seemed that way to her sometimes because she remained with her sons day after day, witness to their struggle.

The Geigers, seeking to be supportive, issued several invitations for the kind of evening the families had shared so often, but Rob J. declined. He no longer played his viola da gamba; Sarah believed he couldn't stand to make music that Shaman wouldn't hear.

She threw herself into the work of the farm. Alden Kimball double-dug a new plot for her and she undertook her most ambitious vegetable garden. She foraged the riverbank for miles to find lemon day lilies and transfer them to a bed at the front of the house. She helped Alden and Moon herd small groups of blatting sheep onto a raft and take them out into the middle of the river and push them off so they had to swim ashore, cleansing their wool before the shearing. After castrating the spring lambs, Alden looked askance when she claimed the bucket of prairie oysters, his favourite delicacy. Sarah stripped them of their stringy wrapping, wondering if that's how a man's gonads were under the wrinkled skin. Then she cut the tender little balls in half and fried them in bacon grease along with wild onion and a sliced puffball mushroom. Alden ate his share eagerly, declared it prime, and stopped moping.

She could almost have been content. Except.

Rob J. came home one day and told her he had conferred with Tobias Barr about Shaman. 'A school for the deaf was recently established in Jacksonville, but Barr knows little about it. I could travel there and look it over. But . . . Shaman is so young.'

'Jacksonville is one hundred and fifty miles away. We would scarcely ever see him.'

He told her that the Rock Island physician had confessed to an ignorance about how to treat deafness in children. In fact, some years before, he had given up on a case involving an eight-year-old girl and her six-year-old brother. Ultimately the children had been sent away as wards of the state, to the Illinois Asylum in Springfield.

'Rob J.,' she said. Through the open window came the guttural grunting of her sons, a mad sound, and she had a sudden mental picture of Bessie Turner's vacant eyes. 'To send a deaf child to be shut up with crazy people . . . that is wicked.' The thought of wickedness chilled her, as usual. 'Do you think,' she whispered, 'that Shaman is being punished for my sins?'

He took her in his arms and she drew on his strength the way she always did.

'No,' he said. He held her a long time. 'Oh, my Sarah. You must never think it.' But he didn't tell her what they could do.

One morning while the two boys sat in front of the *hedonosote* with Little Dog and Bird Woman, stripping willow withes of bark Makwa would boil to make her medicine, a strange Indian rode a bony horse out of the riverbank woods. He was an apparition of a Sioux, no longer young, as skinny as his horse, as shabby and tattered. His feet were bare and dirty. He wore leggings and a loincloth of deerskin and a tattered fragment of a buffalo skin around the upper part of his body like a shawl, held in place by a knotted rag belt. His long greying hair had been carelessly tended, with a short braid at the back and two longer braids at the sides of his head, wrapped with strips of otter skin.

A few years earlier, a Sauk would have greeted a Sioux with a weapon, but now each of them knew they were surrounded by a common enemy, and when the horseman greeted her in the sign language used by the Plains tribes whose native tongues are dissimilar, she returned the greeting with her fingers.

She guessed he had ridden through the Ouisconsin, following the fringe of forest along *Masesibowi*. His signs told her he came in peace and followed the setting sun to the Seven Nations. He asked her for food.

The four children were fascinated. They giggled and mimicked the *eat* sign with their small hands.

He was a Sioux, so she couldn't simply give him anything. He traded a plaited rope for a plate of squirrel stew and a big piece of corncake, and a small bag of dried beans for the trail. The stew was cold but he dismounted and ate it with obvious hunger.

190

He saw the water drum and asked if she was a ghost-keeper, and looked uneasy when she indicated it was so. They didn't give each other the power of learning their names. When he'd eaten, she warned him not to hunt the sheep or the white men would kill him, and he got back on the skinny horse and rode away.

The children were still playing at the game with their fingers, making signs that didn't mean anything; except that Alex was making the *eat* sign. She broke off a piece of corncake and gave it to him, and then showed the others how to make the sign, rewarding them with nibbles of cake when they had got it right. The intertribal language was something the Sauk children should be taught, so she gave them the signs for *willow*, including the white brothers as a kindness until she saw that Shaman seemed to pick up the signs easily, and she was struck by an exciting thought that caused her to concentrate on him more than the others.

In addition to *eat* and *willow*, she taught them the signs for *girl*, for *boy*, for *wash*, and for *dress*. That was enough for the first day, she thought, but she set them to practicing them again and again, a new game, until the children knew the signs perfectly.

That afternoon, when Rob J. came home, she brought the children to him and demonstrated what they had learned.

Rob J. watched his deaf son thoughtfully. He saw that Makwa's eyes gleamed with accomplishment, and he praised them all and thanked Makwa, who promised to continue to teach them the signs.

'What earthly good is it?' Sarah asked him bitterly when they were alone. 'Why would we want our son to be able to talk with his fingers so only a bunch of Indians will understand him?'

'There's a sign language like that for the deaf,' Rob J. said thoughtfully. 'Invented by the French, I think. When I was in medical school, I myself saw two deaf people conversing with one another easily, using their hands instead of their voices. If I send for a book of these signs, and we learn it with him, we can talk to Shaman and he can talk to us.'

Reluctantly she agreed it was worth a try. In the mean-

191

time, Rob J. decided that learning the Indian signs would do the boy no harm.

A long letter came from Oliver Wendell Holmes. With typical thoroughness he had searched the literature at the Harvard Medical School library and had interviewed a number of authorities, giving them the details Rob J. had supplied concerning Shaman's case.

He held out very little hope for a reversal of Shaman's condition. *'Sometimes,'* he wrote, *'hearing will return to a patient in whom total deafness has occurred as an aftermath of a disease such as measles, scarlet fever, or meningitis. But often, massive infection during illness scars and damages tissues, destroying sensitive and delicate processes that cannot be restored by healing.*

'You write that you inspected both external auditory canals visually, using a speculum, and I commend your ingenuity in focusing the light of a candle into the ears by means of a hand mirror. Almost certainly the damage occurred deeper than you were able to examine. Having dissected, you and I are aware of the delicacy and complexity of the middle and inner ear. Whether young Robert's problem lies in the eardrums, the auditory ossicles, the mallei, the incudes, the stapes, or perhaps the cochleae, doubtless we shall never know. What we do know, my dear friend, is that if you son is still deaf by the time you read this, in all likelihood he will be deaf for the remainder of his life.

'The problem to be considered, then, is how best to raise him.'

Holmes had consulted with Dr Samuel G. Howe of Boston, who had worked with two deaf, mute, and blind pupils, teaching them to communicate with others by fingerspelling the alphabet. Three years before Dr Howe had toured Europe and had seen deaf children who were taught to talk clearly and effectively.

'But no school for the deaf in America teaches children to speak,' Holmes wrote, *'instead instructing every pupil in the language of signs. If your son is taught the language of signs, he will be able to communicate only with other deaf persons. If he can learn to speak and, by watching the lips of others, to read what they are saying, there is no reason why he can't live his life among people*

192

in general society.

'Therefore, Dr Howe recommends that your son be kept at home and educated by you, and I concur.'

The consultants had reported that unless Shaman was able to talk, gradually he would go dumb through lack of use of the organs of speech. But Holmes warned that if speech was to be accomplished, the Cole family must use no formal signs to young Robert, and they must never accept a single sign from him.

26
The Binding

At first, Makwa-ikwa didn't understand when *Cawso wabes-kiou* told her to stop teaching the signs of the nations to the children. But Rob J. explained to her why the signs were bad medicine for Shaman. The boy already had learned nineteen signs. He knew the gesture with which to indicate hunger, he could ask for water, he could indicate cold, heat, illness, health, could signify appreciation or displeasure, could greet and bid farewell, describe size, comment on wisdom or stupidity. For the other children, the Indian signing was a new game. To Shaman, cut off from communication in the most puzzling way, it was renewed contact with the world.

His fingers continued to speak.

Rob J. forbade the others to participate, but they were only children, and when Shaman flashed a sign, sometimes the impulse to respond was irresistible.

After he witnessed several instances of signing Rob J. unwound a soft rag strip Sarah had rolled for bandages. He lashed Shaman's wrists together, and then tied his hands to his belt.

Shaman screamed and wept.

'You treat our son . . . like an animal,' Sarah whispered.

'It may already be too late for him. This may be his only chance.' Rob took his wife's hands in his and tried to comfort her. But no amount of pleading changed his mind, and his

194

son's hands remained trussed, as if the child were a small prisoner.

Alex remembered how he had felt when he had the terrible itch from the measles and Rob J. had tied his hands so he couldn't scratch. He forgot how his body had bled and remembered only the unrequited itching and the terrors of being bound. At first opportunity he found the sickle in the barn and cut his brother's bonds.

When Rob J. confined him to the house, Alex disobeyed. He took a kitchen knife and went out and freed Shaman again, then took his brother's hand and led him away.

It was midday when their absence was noted, and everybody on the farm stopped all work and joined in the search, spreading out into the woods and over the prairie pastures and along the riverbanks, calling the names only one of the boys would be able to hear. Nobody mentioned the river, but that spring two Frenchmen from Nauvoo had been in a canoe that overturned when the water was at crest. Both men had drowned, and now the menace of the river was very much on everyone's mind.

There was no evidence of the boys until, as light was beginning to fade at day's end, Jay Geiger rode up to the Cole place, Shaman in front of him in the saddle, Alex riding behind. He told Rob J. he'd found them in the middle of his cornfield, sitting on the ground between rows, still holding hands and all cried out.

'If I hadn't gone in to check for weeds, they'd be sitting there still,' Jay said.

Rob J. waited until the tearstained faces were washed and the boys fed. Then he walked Alex out along the river path. The current rippled and sang over the stones along the shore, the water darker than the air, reflecting the coming night. Swallows soared and swooped, sometimes touching the surface. High up, a crane ploughed along as purposefully as a packet boat.

'You know why I've brought you out here?'

'Gonna whup me.'

'Never whipped you yet, have I? Not going to start now.

195

No, I want to consult with you.'

The boy's eyes regarded him with alarm, uncertain if being consulted was any better than being whipped. 'What's that?'

'You know what it is to swap?'

Alex nodded. 'Sure. I've swapped things, lots of times.'

'Well, I want to swap ideas with you. About your brother. Shaman's lucky to have a big brother like you, someone who takes care of him. Your mother and I . . . we're proud of you. We thank you.'

'. . . You treat him mean, Pa, tying his hands and all.'

'Alex, if you do any more signs with him, he's not going to need to speak. Pretty soon he won't remember how to speak, and you'll never hear his voice. Ever again. You believe me?'

The boy's eyes were large, full of burden. He nodded.

'I want you to leave his hands tied. I'm asking you never to use signs with him again. When you talk to him, first point to your mouth, so he looks at it. Then speak slowly and distinctly. Repeat what you're saying to him, so he'll begin to read your lips.' Rob J. looked at him. 'You understand, son? Will you help us teach him to talk?'

Alex nodded. Rob J. pulled him into his chest and hugged him. He stank like a ten-year-old boy who had sat all day in a manured cornfield, sweating and crying. As soon as they got home, Rob J. would help him carry water for baths.

'I love you, Alex.'

'. . . you, Pa,' Alex whispered.

Everybody was given the same message.

Get Shaman's attention. Point to your lips. Speak to him slowly and distinctly. Speak to his eyes instead of to his ears.

In the morning as soon as they were up, Rob J. tied his son's hands. At mealtimes Alex untied Shaman so he could eat. Then he tied his brother's hands again. Alex saw to it that none of the other children signed.

But Shaman's eyes grew more harried in a face that was pinched and closed off to the rest of them. He wasn't able

196

to understand. And he didn't speak at all.

If Rob J. had heard of someone else who kept his boy's hands tied, he'd have done everything in his power to rescue the child. Cruelty wasn't one of his talents, and he saw the effect of Shaman's suffering on the others in his household. It was an escape for him to take his bag and ride out to do his doctoring.

The world beyond his farm went on, unaffected by the Cole family's troubles. Three other families were building new wood-frame homes to replace sod houses in Holden's Crossing that summer. There was a lot of interest in putting up a schoolhouse and hiring a teacher, and both Rob J. and Jason Geiger supported the idea strongly. Each taught his own children at home, sometimes filling in for one another during an emergency, but they agreed it would be better for the children to go to a regular school.

When Rob J. stopped at the apothecary, Jay was bursting with a piece of news. Finally he blurted out the fact that Lillian's Babcock piano had been sent for. Crated in Colombus, it had been carried more than a thousand miles by raft and riverboat. 'Down the Scioto River to the Ohio, down the Ohio to the Mississippi, and up the goldurned Mississippi to the pier of the Great Southern Transport Company in Rock Island, where it now awaits my buckboard and oxen!'

Alden Kimball had asked Rob to treat one of his friends who was sick in the abandoned Mormon town of Nauvoo.

Alden came with him as guide. They bought a ride for themselves and their horses on a flatboat, getting downriver the easy way. Nauvoo was a spooky, largely deserted town, a gridwork of wide streets laid out on a pretty bend in the river, with handsome, substantial houses, and in the middle, the stone ruins of a great temple that looked as if it had been built by King Solomon. Only a handful of Mormons still lived there, Alden told him, old folks and rebels who had broken with the leadership when the Latter-Day Saints had moved to Utah. It was a place that attracted independent thinkers; one corner of the town had been rented to a small colony of Frenchmen who called themselves Icarians and lived cooperatively. Alden led Rob J. right through the French quarter, disdain in the erectness with which he sat his saddle, and eventually to a house of weathered red brick by the side of a pleasant lane.

An unsmiling middle-aged woman answered his knock and nodded in greeting. She nodded also to Rob J. when Alden introduced her as Mrs Bidamon. A dozen people sat or stood in the parlour, but Mrs Bidamon led Rob up the stairs to where a sullen boy of about sixteen lay abed with the measles. It wasn't a severe case. Rob gave his mother ground mustard seed and directions about how to mix it into the boy's bath water, and a packet of dried elderberry blossoms to be used as tea. 'I don't think you'll need me again,' he said. 'But I want you to send for me at once if it causes him an infection of the ears.'

She preceded him downstairs and must have said a reassuring word to the people in her parlour. As Rob J. walked through to the door, they were waiting with gifts, a jar of honey, three jars of preserves, a bottle of wine. And a babble of gratitude. Outside the house, he stood, his arms full, staring at Alden in bewilderment.

'They're grateful to you for treating the boy,' Alden said. 'Mrs Bidamon, she was the widow of Joseph Smith, the Prophet of the Latter-Day Saints, the man who founded the religion. The boy is his son, also named Joseph Smith. They believe the youngling's a prophet too.'

As they rode away, Alden regarded the town of Nauvoo and sighed. 'This was a right good place to live. All ruint because Joseph Smith couldn't keep his pecker in his pants. Him and his polygamy. Called 'em spiritual wives. Nothin' spiritual about it, he just liked poontang.'

Rob J. knew the Saints had been driven from Ohio, Missouri, and finally Illinois, because rumours of their plural marriages had inflamed local populaces. He had never intruded upon Alden with questions of his former life, but now he couldn't resist. 'You had more than one wife yourself?'

'Three. When I broke with the Church, they were parcelled out to other Saints, along with their young uns.'

Rob didn't dare ask how many children. But a demon drove his tongue to one more question. 'Did that bother you?'

Alden considered, and then he spat. 'The variety was right interestin', I shan't deny it. But without 'em, the peace is wonderful,' he said.

That week Rob went from treating a young prophet to treating an old congressman. He was summoned to Rock Island to examine US Representative Samuel T. Singleton, who'd been taken by spells while returning to Illinois from Washington.

As he entered Singleton's home, Thomas Beckermann was leaving; Beckermann told him that Tobias Barr also had examined Congressman Singleton. 'He needs a whole lot of medical opinions, don't he?' Beckermann said sourly.

It indicated the extent of Sammil Singleton's fear, and as Rob J. examined the congressman, he realized the fear was well-founded. Singleton was seventy-nine, a short man, almost entirely bald, with flabby flesh and a huge assault of stomach. Rob J. listened to his heart wheeze and gurgle and sputter, struggling to beat.

He took the old man's hands in his own and looked into the eyes of the Black Knight.

Singleton's assistant, a man named Stephen Hume, and his secretary, Billy Rogers, sat at the foot of the bed. 'We've been in Washington all year. He has speeches to make. Fences to mend. He's got piss-all to do, Doc,' Hume said accusingly, as if it were Rob J.'s fault Singleton was indisposed. Hume was a Scots name, but Rob J. didn't warm up to him.

'You're to stay in bed,' he told Singleton bluntly. 'Forget about speeches and fences. Go on a light diet. Drink alcohol sparingly.'

Rogers glared. 'That's not what the other two doctors told us. Dr Barr said anyone would be worn out after travellin' from Washington. That other fella from your town, Dr

Beckermann, he agreed with Barr, said all the Congressman needs is home cookin' and prairie air.'

'We thought it'd be a good idea to call in several of you fellas,' Hume said, 'in case there was difference of opinion. Which is what we've got, ain't we. And the other docs disagree with you, two to one.'

'Democratic. But this isn't an election.' Rob J. turned to Singleton. 'For your own survival, I hope you do what I advise.'

The old, cold eyes were amused. 'You're a friend of State Senator Holden's. His business partner in several ventures, if I have it right.'

Hume chortled. 'Nick's a little impatient for the congressman to retire.'

'I'm a doctor. I don't give a damn about politics. *You* sent for *me*, Congressman.'

Singleton nodded, shot a messaged glance at the other two men. Billy Rogers led Rob out of the room. When he tried to emphasize the gravity of Singleton's condition, he got a secretary's nod, a politician's oily sentence of thanks. Rogers paid his fee as if tipping a stableboy, and he was quickly and smoothly eased outside the front door.

A couple of hours later, riding Vicky down Main Street in Holden's Crossing, he saw that Nick Holden's intelligence system was working. Nick waited on the porch of Haskins' Store, his chair tipped back against the wall, one boot up on the porch rail. When he spotted Rob J. he gestured him to the hitching post.

Nick led him quickly into the store's back room and made no attempt to hide his excitement.

'Well?'

'Well, what?'

'I know you've just come from Sammil Singleton.'

'I talk about my patients with my patients. Or sometimes with their loved ones. You one of Singleton's loved ones?'

Holden smiled. 'I like him a whole lot.'

'Liking him doesn't do it, Nick.'

'Don't play games, Rob J. I only have to know one thing. Will he have to retire?'

'You want to know, you ask him.'

'Jesus Christ,' Holden said bitterly.

Rob J. stepped carefully around a baited mousetrap as he left the storeroom. Nick's rage followed after him along with the odour of leather harness and rotting seed potatoes. 'Your trouble, Cole, is you're too dumb to know who your goddam real friends are!'

Probably Haskins had to be careful at day's end to tuck away the cheese, cover the cracker barrel, things like that. Mice could play havoc with food merchandise at night, he reflected as he walked through the front of the store; and no way you could avoid having mice when you were this close to the prairie.

Four days later, Samuel T. Singleton was seated at a table with two selectmen from Rock Island and three selectmen from Davenport, Iowa, explaining the tax position of the Chicago and Rock Island Railroad, which was proposing to build a railroad bridge across the Mississippi between their two towns. He was discussing rights of way when he gave a small sigh, as if in exasperation, and slumped where he sat. By the time Dr. Tobias had been sent for and arrived in the saloon, everyone in the neighbourhood knew Sammil Singleton had died.

It took the governor a week to appoint his successor. Immediately following the funeral, Nick Holden had left for Springfield to try to snare the appointment. Rob could imagine the arm-twisting in which he engaged, and no doubt there was effort expended by Nick's sometime drinking friend, the Kentucky-born lieutenant governor. But evidently the Singleton organization had drinking friends of its own, and the governor appointed Singleton's aide, Stephen Hume, to fill the unexpired eighteen months of the term.

'Nick's goose is cooked,' Jay Geiger observed. 'Between now and the end of the term, Hume will dig in. He'll run next time as the incumbent, and he'll be next to impossible for Nick to beat.'

Rob J. didn't care. He was engrossed with what was happening within the walls of his own home.

After two weeks he stopped tying his son's hands. Shaman no longer attempted to sign, but he didn't speak either. There was something dead and grey in the little boy's eyes. They hugged him a lot, but the boy was only momentarily comforted. Whenever Rob looked at his child, he felt self-doubt and helplessness.

Meanwhile, all those around him followed his directions as though he were infallible in the treatment of deafness. When they talked to Shaman, they spoke slowly and enunciated distinctly, first pointing to their mouths when they had gained his attention, encouraging him to read their lips.

It was Makwa-ikwa who thought of a new approach to the problem. She told Rob how she and the other Sauk girls had been taught to speak English so quickly and effectively at the Evangelical School for Indian Girls: they had not been passed anything at mealtimes unless it was requested in English.

Sarah exploded with anger when Rob discussed it with her. 'It was one thing to truss him like a slave. Now you will starve him too!'

But Rob J. didn't have many things to try, and he was growing desperate. He talked long and earnestly to Alex, who agreed to cooperate, and he asked his wife to make a special meal. Shaman had a passion for sweet-and-sour, and Sarah prepared stewed chicken with dumplings, and hot rhubarb pie for dessert.

That evening, when the family was seated around the table and she brought in the first course, the sequence was much as it had been for several weeks. Rob lifted the cover from a steaming bowl and let the mouthwatering scent of the chicken, dumplings, and vegetables waft across the table.

He served Sarah first, and then Alex. He waved his hand until he had gained Shaman's attention, and then he pointed to his own mouth. 'Chicken,' he said, holding up the serving bowl. 'Dumplings.'

Shaman stared at him silently.

Rob J. placed food in his own plate, and sat.

Shaman watched his parents and his brother eating busily, and he lifted his empty plate and grunted in annoyance.

Rob pointed to his own mouth and lifted the serving bowl. 'Chicken.'

Shaman held out his plate.

'Chicken,' Rob J. said again. When his son remained silent, he set down the bowl and resumed eating.

Shaman began to sob. He looked at his mother, who, forcing herself to eat, had just finished her portion. She pointed to her mouth and held out her plate to Rob. 'Chicken, please,' she said, and he served her.

Alex, too, asked for a second helping and was given it. Shaman sat and shook with grief, his face screwed up against this fresh assault, this new terror, deprivation of his food.

The chicken and dumplings eaten, the plates were removed, and then Sarah carried in the dessert, hot from the oven, and a pitcher of milk. Sarah was proud of her rhubarb pie, made from an old Virginia recipe, lots of maple sugar bubbling together with the tart juices of the rhubarb to caramelize on top as a hint of the pleasure contained under the crust.

'Pie,' Rob said, and the word was repeated by Sarah and Alex.

'Pie,' he said to Shaman.

It hadn't worked. His heart was breaking. He could not, after all, permit his son to starve, he told himself; better a mute child than a dead child.

Morosely he cut himself a piece.

'Pie!'

It was a howl of outrage, a blow against all the injustices of the world. The voice was familiar and beloved, a voice he hadn't heard for a while. Still, he sat for a moment stupidly, trying to make certain it hadn't been Alex who had shouted.

'Pie! Pie! Pie!' Shaman screamed. 'PIE!'

The small body shook with fury and frustration. Shaman's face was wet with tears. He pulled away from his mother's attempt to wipe his nose.

Niceties didn't matter at this moment, Rob J. thought; 'please' and 'thank you' could come later too. He pointed to his own mouth.

'Yes,' he told his son, nodding and cutting a huge piece at the same time. 'Yes, Shaman! Pie.'

27
Politics

The flat, tall-grass section of land south of Jay Geiger's farm had been bought from the government by a Swedish immigrant named August Lund. Lund spent three years breaking thick sod, but in the spring of his fourth year his young wife sickened and died quickly of cholera, and her loss poisoned the place for him and brought on a darkness of spirit. Jay bought his cow and Rob J. bought his harnesses and some tools, both of them overpaying because they knew how desperately Lund wanted to get away from there. He returned to Sweden, and for two seasons his newly broken fields remained bleak as a deserted female, struggling to return to what they once were. Then the property was sold by a land broker in Springfield, and several months later a two-wagon caravan arrived bringing a man and five women to live on the land.

Had they been a pimp and his whores they would have caused less excitement in Holden's Crossing. They were a priest and nuns of the Roman Catholic Order of Saint Francis Xavier of Assisi, and word sped throughout Rock Island County that they'd come to open a parochial school and lure young children into popery. Holden's Crossing needed both a school and a church. Each project most likely would have remained in the talking stages for years, but the arrival of the Franciscans stirred up a frenzy. After a series of 'social

205

evenings' in farmhouse parlours, a building committee was named to raise funds for a church structure, but Sarah was irked.

'They simply can't agree, like squabbling children. Some want just a log cabin, to be economical. Others want wood frame, or brick, or stone.' She favoured a stone building herself, with a bell tower, a steeple, and stained-glass windows – a real church. All through the summer, fall, and winter there were arguments, but by March, faced with the knowledge that the townspeople also had to pay for a schoolhouse, the building committee decided on a simple wooden church, the walls planked up and down instead of clapboarded, and painted white. The controversy over the architecture paled next to the cold-eyed debate regarding affiliation with a denomination, but there were more Baptists in Holden's Crossing than any other group, and the majority prevailed. The committee contacted the congregation of the First Baptist Church of Rock Island, which helped with advice and a little seed cash in order to get a new sister church off to a start.

Money was subscribed, and Nick Holden dazzled everyone with the largest gift, five hundred dollars. 'It'll take more than philanthropy to get him elected to Congress,' Rob J. told Jay. 'Hume has worked hard and has the nomination of the Democratic party sewed up.'

Evidently Holden thought so too, for soon it became general knowledge that Nick had broken with the Democrats. Some expected him to seek the support of the Whigs, but instead he declared himself a member of the American party.

'American party. That's a new one on me,' Jay said.

Rob enlightened him, remembering the anti-Irish sermons and articles he'd seen everywhere in Boston. 'It's a party that glorifies the native-born white American and stands for suppression of Catholics and the foreign-born.'

'Nick plays to whatever passions and fears he can find,' Jay said. 'The other evening, on the porch of the general store, he was warning folks about Makwa's little group of Sauks as though they were Black Hawk's band. Got some of the men all worked up. Said that if we don't watch out there's going to be bloodshed, farmers with their throats cut.' He made a face. 'Our Nick. Ever the statesman.'

One day a letter came for Rob J. from his brother, Herbert,
in Scotland. It was an answer to a letter sent by Rob eight
months before, describing his family, his practice, the farm.
His letter had painted a realistic picture of his life in
Holden's Crossing, and in return he had asked Herbert to
send him news of those he loved in the old country. Now
his brother's letter conveyed dread information that wasn't
unexpected, for when Rob had fled Scotland he'd known his
mother's life was winding down. She had died three months
after his departure, Herbert wrote, and was buried next to
their father in the mossy 'new yard' of the kirk in
Kilmarnock. Their father's brother, Ranald, had died the
following year.

Herbert wrote that he'd expanded the flock and built a
new barn, using stone hauled from the base of the cliff. He
mentioned these things gingerly, obviously pleased to let
Rob know he was doing well with the land but carefully
avoiding any discussion of prosperity. There must be times
when Herbert feared his return to Scotland, Rob realized.
The land had been Rob J.'s birthright as the elder son; the
night before he left Scotland he had dazed Herbert, who
passionately loved sheep farming, by signing the holding
over to the younger brother.

Herbert wrote that he'd married Alice Broome, daughter
of John Broome, who judged at the Kilmarnock Lamb Show,
and his wife, Elsa, who had been a McLarkin. Rob
remembered Alice Broome vaguely, a thin mouse-haired
girl who had kept one hand covering her uncertain smile
because her teeth were long. She and Herbert had three
children, all daughters, but Alice was bearing again and this
time Herbert hoped for a son, for the sheep croft was
growing and he needed help.

*The political situation having quieted, will you be thinking of
coming home?*

Rob could sense the tension of the question in Herbert's
cramped writing, the shame over the sweat and apprehension. He sat at once and composed a letter to erase his

brother's fears. He wouldn't return to Scotland, he wrote, unless in a healthy and prosperous retirement some day he might visit. He sent his love to his sister-in-law and his nieces, and commended Herbert for the success he was making; it was clear, he wrote, that the Cole farm was in proper ownership.

When he finished the letter, he went for a walk along the river path, all the way to the stone pile marking the end of his land and the beginning of Jay's. He knew he wouldn't leave here. Illinois had captured him, despite its blizzards and destructive tornadoes, and its wild extremes of temperature, high and low. Or maybe *because* of those things, and a lot more.

This Cole farm was better land than the keeping in Kilmarnock, deeper loam, more water, fatter grass. Already he felt responsible for it. He had memorized its smells and sounds, loving the way it was in the hot, lemony mornings of summer when the wind made the tall grasses whisper, and in the brutal, cold embrace of deep-drifted winter. It was his land, for a fact.

A couple of days later, in Rock Island to attend a meeting of the Medical Society, he dropped by the courthouse and filled out a document declaring his desire for naturalization.

Roger Murray, the Court Clerk, read the application fussily. 'A three-year delay, you know, Doctor, before you can become a citizen.'

Rob J. nodded. 'I can wait. Not going anywhere,' he said.

The more Tom Beckermann drank, the more lopsided the practice of medicine became in Holden's Crossing, the load falling on Rob J., who cursed Beckermann's alcoholism and wished a third doctor would move to town. Steve Hume and Billy Rogers added to his problem by whispering far and wide that Doc Cole had been the only medico to warn Sammil Singleton about how sick he really was. If Sammil had only listened to Cole, they said, he might be here today. Rob J.'s legend grew, and new patients sought him out.

He worked hard at reserving time to be with Sarah and the boys. Shaman amazed him; it was as if a plant organism

208

had been interrupted and endangered but then had responded with a burst of growth, green tendrils everywhere. He developed before their eyes. Sarah, Alex, the Sauks, Alden, everyone who lived on the Cole place practised lip-reading with him long and faithfully – indeed, almost hysterically, so great was their relief at the end of his silence – and once the boy began to speak, he talked and talked. He had learned to read a year before the onset of his deafness, and now they were hard-pressed to keep him in books.

Sarah taught her sons what she was able, but she'd finished only a six-grade rural school and was aware of her limitations. Rob J. drilled them in Latin and arithmetic. Alex did well; he was bright and worked hard. But it was Shaman who stunned with his quickness. Something in Rob ached when he observed the boy's natural intelligence.

'He'd have been *some* doctor, I know it,' he told Jay regretfully one hot afternoon as they sat on the shady side of the Geiger house and drank ginger-water. He admitted to Jay that it was built into a Cole to hope that his man-child would grow to be a physician.

Jay nodded sympathetically. 'Well, there's Alex. He's a likely lad.'

Rob J. shook his head. 'It's the damnedest thing – Shaman, the one who won't ever be a doctor because he can't hear, is the one who's keen to go on house calls with me. Alex, who can be anything when he grows up, chooses to follow Alden Kimball around the farm like a shadow. He'd rather watch the hired man put in a fencepost or slice off some feisty lamb's balls than anything I can do.'

Jay grinned. 'And wouldn't you, at their age? Well, maybe the brothers will farm together. They're both fine boys.'

Inside the house, Lillian was practising Mozart's Twenty-third Piano Concerto. She was very serious about her fingering and it was excruciating to hear her play the same phrase until it had exactly the right colour and expression; but when she was satisfied and let the notes run, it was music. The Babcock piano had arrived perfect in function, but a long, shallow scrape, origin unknown, marred the oiled perfection of one of the sleek walnut legs. Lillian had wept to see it, but her husband said the scratch would never be repaired, 'so it'll remind our grandchildren how we travelled to get here.'

The First Church of Holden's Crossing was dedicated late enough in June so the celebration spilled over into the Fourth of July. Both Congressman Steven Hume and Nick Holden, a candidate for Hume's office, spoke at the dedication. Rob J. thought Hume seemed relaxed and comfortable, while Nick sounded like a man desperate with the knowledge that he was running far behind.

The Sunday after the holiday, the first of what would be a long series of visiting preachers conducted the sabbath service. Sarah admitted to Rob J. that she felt nervous, and he knew she was remembering the Baptist preacher at the Great Awakening who had called down hellfire upon women who bore children out of wedlock. She would have preferred a gentler shepherd, like Mr Arthur Johnson, the Methodist minister who had married her to Rob J., but the choice of a clergyman would be made by the entire congregation. So all summer long, preachers of every type came to Holden's Crossing. Rob went to several services to offer his wife support, but mostly he stayed away.

In August a printed flyer tacked up outside the general store proclaimed the coming visit of one Ellwood R. Patterson, who would deliver a lecture entitled 'The Tide That Threatens Christendom' at the church on Saturday, September 2, at seven p.m., and then would conduct the service and preach on Sunday morning.

On that Saturday morning a man appeared at Rob J.'s dispensary. He sat patiently in the small parlour that served as waiting room while Rob dealt with the middle finger of Charley Haskins' right hand, which had been pinched between two logs. The son of the storekeeper, twenty-year-old Charley was a woodcutter by trade. He was in pain and annoyed at himself for the carelessness that had led to the accident, but he had a brashly uninhibited mouth and irrepressible good humour.

'Well, Doc. This going to keep me from getting married?'

'You'll use the finger as well as ever, eventually,' Rob said dryly. 'You're going to lose the nail, but it'll grow back. Now, get out of here. And return in three days so I can change the dressing.'

Still grinning, he brought in the man from the waiting room, who introduced himself as Ellwood Patterson. The visiting preacher, Rob realized, remembering the name from the flyers. He noted a male of perhaps forty years, overweight but erect, with a large arrogant face, black hair cut long, a florid complexion, and small but prominent blue veins on his nose and cheeks.

Mr Patterson said he suffered from boils. When he removed the clothing from the upper part of his body, Rob J. saw on his skin the pigmented spots of healed areas interspersed with a dozen open sores, pustular eruptions, scabby and granulated vesicles, and soft gummy tumours.

He looked at the man with sympathy. 'You know you have a disease?'

'I'm told it's syphilis. Someone at the saloon said you're a special doctor. I thought I'd see if there wasn't something you could do.'

Three years ago, a whore in Springfield had done him the French way and subsequently he'd developed a hard chancre and a swelling behind the balls, he told Rob. 'I went back to see her. She won't be giving a dose to anyone else.'

A couple of months later he was plagued by fever and copper-coloured body sores, as well as severe pains in his joints and in his head. Every symptom went away on its own and he thought he was all right, but then these sores and lumps appeared.

Rob wrote his name on a record sheet, and next to it, Tertiary Syphilis. 'Where are you from, sir?'

'. . . Chicago.' But his patient had hesitated just long enough for Rob J. to suspect he was lying. It didn't matter.

'There's no cure, Mr Patterson.'

'Yeah . . . what happens to me now?'

It wouldn't serve him to dissemble. 'If it infects your heart, you'll die. If it goes to your brain, you'll go insane. If it enters your bones or your joints, you'll be crippled. But often none of these awful things happens. Sometimes the symptoms just go away and don't come back. What you have to do is hope and believe you're one of the lucky ones.'

Patterson grimaced. 'So far the sores haven't been visible when I'm dressed. Can you give me something to keep them off my face and neck? I lead a public life.'

'I can sell you some salve. I don't know as it'll work on this kind of sore,' Rob said gently, and Mr Patterson nodded and reached for his shirt.

Next morning a boy in bare feet and ragged pants came on a mule just after dawn and said: Please, suh, but his mammy was doin' poorly and could the doctor kindly come? He was Malcolm Howard, eldest son of a family that had come up from Louisiana only a few months ago and settled in bottomland six miles downriver. Rob saddled Vicky and followed the mule over rough trails until they came to a cabin that was only slightly better shelter than the chicken coop leaning against it. Inside he found Mollie Howard with her husband, Julian, and their brood gathered about her bed. The woman was deep in the throes of malaria but he saw that she wasn't badly off, and a few cheerful words and a good dose of quinine eased the patient's concern, and the family's.

Julian Howard made no move toward payment, nor did Rob J. ask for it, seeing how little the family had. Howard followed him outside and engaged him in conversation about the latest action by their US senator, Stephen A. Douglas, who had just successfully pushed through Congress the Kansas-Nebraska Act, which established two new territories in the West. Douglas' bill called for allowing the territorial legislatures to decide whether the areas should have slavery, and for that reason public opinion in the North was running strongly against the bill.

'Them goddamn northerners, what do they know about nigras? Some of us farmers is gettin' together a little organization to see that Illinois smartens up and allows a man to own slaves. Mebbe you'd like to join with us? Them

212

dark-skinned people was meant to work a white man's fields. I see you all got you a coupla red nigras workin' your place.'

'They're Sauks, not slaves. They work for wages. I don't believe in slavery myself.'

They looked at one another. Howard reddened. He was silent, doubtless constrained from setting Rob straight by the fact that the uppity doctor hadn't charged for his services. For his part, Rob was happy to turn away.

He left more quinine and was able to ride back home without delay, but when he got there he found Gus Schroeder waiting in a panic because Alma, in cleaning out the stall, had foolishly got in between the wall and the big brindle bull they were so proud of. The bull had nudged her and knocked her down just as Gus entered the barn. 'Then the Gott-dam thing won't move! Just stants over her, dropping his horns, until I had to take the hayfork and jap him to get him away. She says she's not bad hurt, but you know Alma.'

So, still without breakfast, he went to the Schroeders'. Alma was all right, if pale and shaken. She winced when he pressed the fifth and sixth ribs on her left side, and he didn't dare take a chance on not binding her up. He knew it mortified her to undress in front of him, and he asked Gus to tend to his horse so her husband wouldn't witness her humiliation. He had her hold up her own floppy blue-veined breasts and touched her fat white flesh as little as possible while he bound her, keeping up a steady conversation about sheep and wheat and his wife and children. When it was over, she managed to smile at him and went into the kitchen to make a fresh pot, and then the three of them sat over cups of coffee.

Gus told him that Ellwood Patterson's Saturday 'lecture' had been an ill-disguised campaign speech for Nick Holden and the American party. 'Folks figger Nick arranged for him to come.'

The 'Tide That Threatens Christendom,' according to Patterson, was the immigration of Catholics into the United States. The Schroeders had skipped church that morning

213

for the first time; both Alma and Gus had been raised Lutherans, but they had had enough of Patterson at the lecture; he had said that the foreign-born – and that meant the Schroeders – were stealing the bread of American workmen. He had called for the waiting period for naturalization as a citizen to be changed from three years to twenty-one years.

Rob J. grimaced. 'I wouldn't want to wait that long,' he said. But all three of them had work to do that Sunday, and he thanked Alma for the coffee and went on his way. He had to ride five miles upriver to the homestead of John Ashe Gilbert, whose elderly father-in-law, Fletcher White, was down with a bad cold. White was eighty-three and a tough old bird; he'd weathered bronchial problems before, and Rob J. was confident he would again. He had told Fletcher's daughter Suzy to pour hot drinks down the old man's throat and boil kettle after kettle so Fletcher could breathe in the steam. Rob J. checked on him more often than was necessary, probably, but he especially valued the aged patients, because there were few of them. Pioneers were likely to be strong young folks who left the old folks behind them when they travelled west, and old men who made the trip were rare.

He found Fletcher much improved. Suzy Gilbert gave him a lunch of fried quail and potato pancakes and asked him to stop at the house of her near neighbours, the Bakers, where one of the sons had an infected toe that needed to be opened. He found Donny Baker, age nineteen, very badly off, feverish, in intense pain from a terrible infection. Half the sole of the boy's right foot was blackened. Rob amputated two toes and opened the foot and inserted a wick, but he had real doubts about whether the foot could be saved, and he had seen numerous cases in which this kind of infection couldn't be stopped with only the amputation of a foot.

It was late afternoon when he headed home. He was halfway there when he heard a halloo on the trail and pulled up Vicky so Mort London could catch up to him on his big chestnut gelding. 'Sheriff.'

'Doc, I . . .' Mort took off his hat and irritably whacked at

214

a buzzing fly. He sighed. 'Damnedest thing. Afraid we got need of a coroner.'

Rob J. felt irritable too. Suzy Gilbert's potato pancakes sat heavy in his stomach. If Calvin Baker had got word to him a week earlier, he could have taken care of Donny Baker's toe with little trouble. Now there was going to be big trouble, and perhaps tragedy. He was wondering how many of his patients out there were in harm's way without letting him know it, and he determined to try to check up on at least three of them before nightfall. 'You'd better get Beckermann,' he said. 'I have lots to do today.'

The sheriff turned the brim of his hat in his hands. 'Uh. You might want to do this yourself, Dr Cole.'

'One of my patients?' He started to run down the list of possibilities.

'It's that Sauk female.'

Rob J. looked at him.

'Indian woman been workin' for you,' London said.

28
The Arrest

He told himself it was Moon. It wasn't that Moon was expendable, that he didn't like her and value her, but only two Sauk women worked for him, and if it wasn't Moon, the alternative was unthinkable.

But, 'The one helps you with your doctorin',' Mort London said. 'Stabbed,' he said, 'lots of times. Whoever did it beat her up some, before. Clothes ripped off. I believe she was raped.'

For a few minutes they travelled in silence. 'Might have been a few fellas gave it to her. A shitload of hoof marks in the clearing where she was found,' the sheriff said. Then he was quiet and they just rode.

When they got to the farm, Makwa already had been brought into the shed. Outside, a small group had gathered between the dispensary and the barn: Sarah, Alex, Shaman, Jay Geiger, Moon and Comes Singing and their children. The Indians weren't mourning aloud but their eyes betrayed their grief and futility, their knowledge that life was bad. Sarah was weeping quietly and Rob J. went to her and kissed her.

Jay Geiger walked him away from the others. 'I found her.' He shook his head as if to drive away an insect. 'Lillian had sent me riding over to your place with some peach preserves for Sarah? Next thing I knew, I saw Shaman

216

sleeping under a tree.'

That shocked Rob J. 'Shaman was there? Did he see Makwa?'

'No, he didn't. Sarah says Makwa took him out this morning to collect herbs in the river woods, the way she sometimes did. When he wore out, she just let him take a nap in the cool shade. And you know that no noises, shouts or screams or whatever, would disturb Shaman. I figured he wasn't out there alone, so I just let him sleep and rode on a bit, into that clearing. And I found her . . .

'She's very bad to see, Rob. It took me a few minutes to get hold of myself. I went back and woke up the boy. But he didn't see anything. I brought him here with me, and then I rode over to get London.'

'It seems you're forever bringing my boys home.'

Jay peered at him. 'You going to be all right?'

Rob nodded.

Jay, on the other hand, looked pale and miserable. He grimaced. 'I guess you have work to do. The Sauks are going to want to clean her up and bury her.'

'Keep everybody away for a while,' Rob J. said, and then he went into the shed alone and closed the door behind him.

She was covered with a sheet. It wasn't Jay or any of the Sauks who had brought her in. More likely a couple of London's deputies, because they had dropped her almost carelessly onto the dissecting table, on her side, like some inanimate object of little worth, a log or a dead Indian woman. What he saw at first glance when he threw back the sheet was the rear of her head and her naked back, buttocks, and legs.

The lividity showed she'd been on her back when she'd died; her back and flattened buttocks were purpled with pooled capillary blood. But in the violated crena ani he saw a crust of redness and a dried white smear that had been stained scarlet where it had met bleeding.

Gently he turned her on her back again.

There were scratches on her cheeks made by twigs when her face had been pushed into the forest floor.

217

Rob J. had great tenderness for the female hind. His wife had discovered that early. Sarah loved to offer herself up to him, her eyes pressed into the pillow, her breasts mashed against the sheet, her slender, elegantly arched feet splayed, the split, pear-shaped menisci riding white and pink above the golden fleece. An uncomfortable position, but one she took at times because his sexual excitement set off her own passion. Rob J. believed in coition as a form of love and not merely as a vehicle for procreation, therefore he didn't hold a single orifice to be sacred as a sexual vessel. But as a physician he had observed that it was possible for the anal sphincter to lose elasticity if abused, and it was easy, when he made love to Sarah, to choose acts that would do no harm.

Some person had shown no such consideration for Makwa.

She had had the work-honed body of a woman a dozen years younger than what her age must have been. Years before, he and Makwa had come to terms with their physical attraction for one another, always held carefully in check. But there had been times when he had thought of her body, imagined what it would be like to make love to her. Now death had already begun its ruin. Her abdomen was swollen, her breasts flattened by the breakdown of tissue. There was considerable muscular stiffening, and he straightened her legs at the knees while it still was possible. Her pubes were like black wire wool, quite bloodied; perhaps it was a mercy she hadn't lived, because her medicine would have been gone.

'Basta-a-a-rds! Ye dirty bastards!'

He wiped his eyes, realizing suddenly that those outside would have heard him screaming, knowing he was alone with Makwa-ikwa. Her upper torso was a mass of bruises and wounds, and her lower lip had been pulped, probably by a large fist.

On the floor next to the examining table was the evidence gathered by the sheriff: her torn and bloodstained dress (an old gingham dress Sarah had given her); the basket more than half-full of mints, cress, and some kind of tree leaves,

218

he thought black cherry; and one deerskin shoe. One shoe? He looked for the other and couldn't find it. Her square, brown feet were bare; they were tough, hard-used feet, the second toe of her left foot misshapen from an old fracture. He had seen her barefoot often and had wondered how she had broken that toe, but he hadn't ever asked her.

He looked up at her face and saw his good friend. Her eyes were open but the vitreum had lost pressure and dried and they were the deadest thing about her. He closed them quickly and weighted the lids with pennies, but felt as if she still stared at him. In death her nose was more pronounced, uglier. She wouldn't have been pretty as she aged, but her face already had great dignity. He shuddered and clasped his hands together tightly, like a child at prayer.

'I am so sorry, Makwa-ikwa.' He had no illusion that she heard, but he drew comfort from speaking to her. He got pen and ink and paper and copied the rune-like embossings on her breasts, sensing they were important. He didn't know if anyone would understand them, because she hadn't trained someone to succeed her as ghostkeeper of the Sauks, believing she had many years. He suspected she had hoped one of the children of Moon and Comes Singing would come to be a suitable apprentice.

Quickly he sketched her face, the way it had been.

Something terrible had happened to him as well as to her. Just as he would always have dreams of the medical-student-cum-executioner holding aloft the severed head of his friend Andrew Gerould of Lanark, he would dream of this death. He didn't fully understand what made for friendship, any more than he knew what made for love, but somehow this Indian woman and he had become true friends and her death was his loss. For a moment he forgot his vow of nonviolence; if those who had done this were in his power, he could have squashed them like bugs.

The moment passed. He tried a bandanna to cover his nose and mouth against the odour. Taking up a scalpel, he made quick slashes, opening her in a great U from shoulder to shoulder and then cutting between her breasts in a straight line that ran down to her navel, trisecting to form a

219

bloodless Y. His fingers were without sensation and obeyed his mind clumsily; it was good he wasn't cutting a living patient. Until he peeled back the three flaps, the grisly body was Makwa. But when he reached for the rib cutters to free the sternum, he forced himself into a different level of consciousness that drove everything from his mind but specific tasks, and he fell into the familiar routine and began to do the things that had to be done.

REPORT OF VIOLENT DEATH

Subject: Makwa-ikwa
Address: Cole Sheep Farm, Holden's Crossing, Illinois
Occupation: Assistant, dispensary of Dr Robert J. Cole
Age: Approximately 29 years
Height: 1.752 meters
Weight: Approximately 63 kilograms
Circumstances: Body of the subject, a woman of the Sauk tribe, was discovered in a wooded section of the Cole Sheep Farm by a passerby, midafternoon on September 3, 1851. There were eleven stab wounds, running in irregular line from the jugular notch down the sternum to a position approximately two centimetres inferior to the xiphoid process. The wounds were .947 to .952 centimetres in width. They were made by a pointed instrument, probably a metal blade, triangular in shape, all three edges ground to cutting sharpness.

Subject, who had been a virgin, was raped. Remains of the hymen indicate it was *imperforatus*, the membrane thick and grown inflexible. Probably the rapist(s) could not accomplish penetration by penis; defloration was completed by means of a blunt instrument with rough or jagged small projections, inflicting massive damage to the vulva, including deep scratches in the perineum and the labia majora and tearing and gouging in the labia minora and the vestibule of the vagina. Either before or after this bloody deflowering, subject was turned facedown. Bruises on her thighs suggest that she was held in position while sodomized, indicating that her attackers included at least two individuals, and probably more. Damage of the sodomy included the stretching and tearing of the anal canal. A quantity of sperm was present in the rectum, and marked haemorrhaging was present in the descending colon. Other contusions elsewhere on the body and on the face suggest subject was beaten extensively, probably by men's fists.

There is evidence that subject resisted the attack. Under the nails of the second, third, and fourth fingers of her right hand were shreds of skin and two black hairs, perhaps from a beard.

The stabbings were done with sufficient force to chip the third rib and penetrate the sternum repeatedly. The left lung was penetrated twice and the right lung three times, tearing the pleura and lacerating the inner lung tissue; both lungs would have collapsed at once. Three of the thrusts entered the heart, two of them leaving wounds in the region of the right atrium, .887 centremetres and .799 centimetres in width, respectively. The third wound, in the right ventricle, was .803 centimetres in width. Blood from the lacerated heart had pooled extensively in the abdominal cavity.

Organs were remarkable except for trauma. Weighed, the heart was found to be 263 grams; the brain, 1.43 kilograms; the liver, 1.62 kilograms; the spleen, 199 grams. *Conclusions:* Homicide following sexual assault, by a party or parties unknown.

(signed)   Robert Judson Cole, MD
Associate Coroner
County of Rock Island
State of Illinois

Rob J. stayed up late that night, copying the report for filing with the county clerk and then making another copy to give to Mort London. In the morning, the Sauks came to the farm and they buried Makwa-ikwa on the bluff near the *hedonoso-te*, overlooking the river. Rob had offered the burial site without consulting Sarah.

She was angry when she heard. 'On our land? Whatever were you thinking of? A grave is forever, she'll be here for all time. We'll never be rid of her!' she said wildly.

'Hold your tongue, woman,' Rob J. said quietly, and she turned and went away from him.

Moon washed Makwa and dressed her in her deerskin shaman's dress. Alden offered to make her a pine box, but Moon said it was their way to bury their dead just in their best blanket. So Alden helped Comes Singing dig the grave, instead. Moon had them dig it early in the morning. That was how it was done, she said: grave dug early in the morning, burial early in the afternoon. Moon said Makwa's feet had to point toward the west, and she sent to the Sauk camp for the tail of a female buffalo to be placed in the grave. This would help Makwa-ikwa cross safely over the river of foam that separates the land of the living from the Land in the West, she explained to Rob J.

The funeral was a meagre rite. The Indians and the Coles and Jay Geiger gathered about the grave and Rob J. waited for someone to begin, but there was no one. They had no shaman. To his dismay, he saw that the Sauks were looking at him. If she had been a Christian he might have been weak enough to say some things he didn't believe. As it was, he was totally inadequate. From somewhere, he remembered words:

> *The barge she sat in, like a burnish'd throne,*
> *Burn'd on the water; the poop was beaten gold,*
> *Purple the sails, and so perfumed that the winds*
> *Were lovesick with them; the oars were silver,*
> *Which to the tune of flutes kept stroke, and made*
> *The water which they beat to follow faster,*
> *As amorous of their strokes. For her own person,*
> *It beggar'd all description.*

Jay Geiger stared at him as if he were mad. Cleopatra? But he realized that to him she had had a kind of dusky majesty, a royal-holy glow, a special sort of beauty. She was better than Cleopatra; Cleopatra hadn't known all about personal sacrifice, and faithfulness, and herbs. He would never meet her like again, and John Donne gave him other words to throw at the Old Black Knight:

> Death be not proud, though some have called thee
> Mighty and dreadful, for thou art not so,
> For those whom thou think'st thou dost overthrow,
> Die not, poor Death, nor yet canst thou kill me.

When it became obvious it was all he was going to say, Jay cleared his throat and uttered a few sentences in what Rob J. supposed was Hebrew. For a moment he was afraid Sarah was going to bring Jesus into it, but she was too shy. Makwa had taught the Sauks some prayer chants, and now they sang one of them raggedly but together.

> Tti-la-ye ke-wi-ta-mo-ne i-no-ki,
> Tti-la-ye ke-wi-tap-mopne i-no-ki-i-i.
> Me-ma-ko-te-si-ta
> Ke-te-ma-ga-yo-se.

It was a song Makwa often had sung to Shaman, and Rob J. saw that while Shaman didn't sing, his lips moved along with the words. When the song was over, so was the funeral; that was all.

Afterwards he went to the clearing in the woods where it had happened. It was a mass of hoofprints. He had asked Moon if any of the Sauks were trackers, but she said the good trackers were dead. Anyway, by that time a number of London's people had been out there, and the ground was well-trampled by horses and men. Rob J. knew what he was searching for. He found the stick in the brush, where it had been flung. It looked like any other stick except for the rusty colour on one end. Her other shoe had been thrown into the woods at the other end of the clearing, by someone with a good arm. There was nothing else that he could see, and he wrapped the two items in a cloth and rode over to the sheriff's office.

223

Mort London accepted the paperwork and the evidence without comment. He was cool and a bit short, perhaps because his people had missed the stick and the shoe when they had done their own search. Rob J. didn't linger.

Next door to the sheriff's office, on the porch of the general store, he was hailed by Julian Howard. 'Got somethin' for you,' Howard said. He rummaged in his pocket and Rob J. heard the heavy clinking of large coins. Howard handed him a silver dollar.

'No hurry, Mr Howard.'

But Howard gestured toward him with the coin. 'Pay my debts,' he said balefully, and Rob took the coin, making no mention that payment was fifty cents short, counting the medicine he had left. Howard already had turned away rudely. 'How's your wife?' Rob asked.

'Much improved. You're not needed by her.'

That was good news, saving Rob a long and difficult ride. He went instead to the Schroeders' farmhouse, where Alma was getting an early start on the autumn housecleaning; it was obvious that none of her ribs was broken. When he called next on Donny Baker he saw that the boy still was feverish, and the angry flesh of his foot looked as though it could go either way. Rob could do nothing but change the dressing and give him some laudanum for the pain.

From then on, a grim and unhappy morning went downhill. His last call was at the Gilbert homestead, where he found Fletcher White in deep trouble, his eyes dull and unseeing, his thin old body racked by coughing, every breath a painful labour. 'He was better,' Suzy Gilbert whispered.

Rob J. knew that Suzy had a houseful of children and unending chores; she had stopped the steaming and the hot drinks too soon, and Rob wanted to curse and shake her. But when he took Fletcher's hands he knew the old man had little time left, and the last thing he wanted was to fill Suzy with the idea that her neglect had killed her father. He left them some of Makwa's strong tonic to ease Fletcher. He realized he had little of her tonic left. He had seen her brew it numerous times and believed he knew its few simple

224

herbal ingredients. He would have to start trying to make it himself.

He was scheduled to hold afternoon hours in the dispensary, but when he returned to the farm the world was in chaos. Sarah was white-faced. Moon, who had remained tearless at Makwa's death, was weeping bitterly, and all the children were terrorized. Mort London and Fritz Graham, his regular deputy, and Otto Pfersick, deputized just for the occasion, had come while Rob J. was gone. They had pointed rifles at Comes Singing. Mort had placed him under arrest. Then they had tied his hands behind his back and put him on a rope and pulled him away behind their horses, like a tethered ox.

29

The Last Indians in Illinois

'You've made a mistake, Mort,' Rob J. said.

Mort London looked uncomfortable, but he shook his head. 'No. We think the big sonofabitch most likely killed her.'

When Rob J. had been in the sheriff's office only a few hours earlier, London had said nothing about planning to go to his farm and arrest one of his employees. Something was amiss; Comes Singing's trouble was like a disease with no apparent etiology. He took note of the 'we.' He knew who 'we' was, and he perceived that somehow Nick Holden hoped to make political capital of Makwa's death. But Rob handled his own anger gingerly.

'A bad mistake, Mort.'

'There's a witness saw the big Indian in the very clearing where she was found, a short time before it happened.'

Not surprising, Rob J. told him, seeing that Comes Singing was one of his hired men, and the river woods were part of his farm. 'I want to put up the bail.'

'Can't set bail. We have to wait for a circuit judge to come out from Rock Island.'

'How long will that take?'

London shrugged.

'One of the good things to come from the English was due process of law. We're supposed to have that here.'

'Can't hurry a circuit judge for one Indian. Five, six days. Mebbe a week or so.'

'I want to see Comes Singing.'

London rose and led the way into the two-cell lockup that adjoined the sheriff's office. The deputies sat in the dim corridor between the cells, rifles in their laps. Fritz Graham looked as if he was enjoying himself. Otto Pfersick looked as though he wished he were back in his gristmill, making flour. One of the cells was empty. The other cell was full of Comes Singing.

'Untie him,' Rob J. said thinly.

London hesitated. They were afraid to approach their prisoner, Rob J. recognized. Comes Singing somehow had sustained an angry bruise over his right eye (from a gun barrel?). His very size was intimidating.

'Let me in there. I'll untie him myself.'

London unlocked the cell and Rob J. went in alone. 'Pyawanegawa,' he said, placing his hand on Comes Singing's shoulder, calling him by his proper name.

He went behind Comes Singing and began to pick at the knotted rope that bound him, but the knot was cruelly tight. 'It needs cutting,' he said to London. 'Hand me a knife.'

'Like hell.'

'Pair of scissors, in my medical bag.'

'That ain't hardly less a weapon,' London grumbled, but he allowed Graham to fetch the scissors, and Rob J. was able to get the rope cut. He chafed Comes Singing's wrists between both his hands, looking into his eyes, talking as though to his own deaf son. '*Cawso wabeskiou* will help Pyawanegawa. We are brothers of the same Half, the Long Hairs, the *Keeso-qui*.'

He ignored the amused surprise and contempt in the eyes of the listening whites on the other side of the bars. He didn't know how much of what he had said was understood by Comes Singing. The Sauk's eyes were dark and sullen, but as Rob J. searched them he saw a change there, the leap of something he couldn't be certain of, that may have been fury or just may have been the tiny rebirth of hope.

That afternoon he brought Moon to her husband. She interpreted while London questioned him.

Comes Singing appeared baffled by the interrogation.

He admitted at once that he'd been in the clearing that morning. Time to get in wood for the winter, he said, looking at the man who paid him to do that. And he was hunting sugar maples, marking them in his memory for tapping when spring came.

He lived in the same longhouse as the dead woman, London observed.

Yes.

Did he ever engage in sex with her?

Moon hesitated before translating. Rob J. looked hard at London but touched her arm and nodded, and she asked her husband the question. Comes Singing answered at once and without apparent anger.

No, never.

Rob J. followed Mort London back to his office when the questioning was over. 'Can you tell me why you arrested this man?'

'I told you. A witness saw him at that clearing just before the woman was killed.'

'Who *is* your witness?'

'. . . Julian Howard.'

Rob asked himself what Julian Howard had been doing on his land. He remembered the clink of dollar coins when Howard had settled up with him for the house call. 'You paid him for his testimony,' he said, as if he knew it for a fact.

'I didn't. No,' London said, flushing, but he was an amateur bad man, clumsy at summoning spuriously righteous anger.

It was Nick who would have done the rewarding, along with a liberal dose of flattery and assurances to Julian that he was a saintly fellow, just doing his duty.

'Comes Singing was where he should have been, working on my property. You might just as well arrest me for owning the land Makwa was killed on, or Jay Geiger for finding her.'

228

'If the Indian didn't do it, it'll come out during a fair trial. He lived with the woman –'

'She was his shaman. Same as being his minister. The fact that they lived in the same longhouse made sex between them forbidden, as if they were brother and sister.'

'People have killed their own ministers. And fucked their own sisters, for that matter.'

Rob J. started away in disgust, but he turned back. 'It isn't too late to set this straight, Mort. Being sheriff is only a damn job, if you lose it you'll survive. I believe you're a pretty good man. But you do something like this once, it's going to be easy to do it again and again.'

It was a mistake. Mort could live with the knowledge that the whole town knew he was in Nick Holden's pocket, so long as no one threw it up to his face.

'I read that piece of shit you called an autopsy report, Dr Cole. You'd have a hard time makin' a judge and a jury of six good white men believe that female was a virgin. Good-lookin' Indian female her age, and everyone in the county knowin' she was your woman. You got a nerve, preachin'. Now, you get yourself the fuck out of here. And don't you consider comin' back unless you have to bother me with something that best be official.'

Moon said Comes Singing was afraid.

'I don't believe they'll hurt him,' Rob J. said.

She said he wasn't afraid of being hurt. 'He knows that sometimes white men hang people. If a Sauk is strangled to death, he can't get across the river of foam, can't ever get into the Land in the West.'

'Nobody's going to hang Comes Singing,' Rob J. said irritably. 'They have no evidence he's done anything. It's a political thing, and in a few days they're going to let him go.'

But her fear was contagious. The only lawyer in Holden's Crossing was Nick Holden. There were several lawyers in Rock Island, but Rob J. didn't know them personally. Next morning he took care of the patients who needed immediate attention and then rode into the county seat. There were even more people in Congressman Stephen Hume's waiting room than he usually saw in his own, and he had to wait almost ninety minutes before his turn came.

Hume listened to him attentively. 'Why'd you come to me?' he asked finally.

'Because you're running for re-election and your opponent is Nick Holden. For some reason I haven't figured out, Nick is causing as much trouble as he can for the Sauks in general and Comes Singing in particular.'

Hume sighed. 'Nick's in with a rough bunch, and I can't take his candidacy lightly. The American party's filling the native-born working man with hatred and fear of immigrants and Catholics. They've a secret lodge in every town with a peephole in the door so they can keep out non-members. They're called the Know Nothing party, because if you ask any member about their activities, he's trained to say he knows nothing about it. They promote and use violence against the foreign-born, and I'm ashamed to say they're sweeping the country, politically. Immigrants are flooding in, but at this moment seventy percent of the people of Illinois are native-born, and of the other thirty percent, most aren't citizens and don't vote. Last year the Know Nothings almost elected a governor in New York and did elect forty-nine legislators. A Know Nothing–Whig alliance easily carried the elections in Pennsylvania and Delaware, and Cincinnati went Know Nothing after a bitter fight.'

'But why is Nick after the Sauks? They're not foreign-born!'

Hume grimaced. 'His political instincts probably are very sound. Only nineteen years ago white folks were being massacred by Indians around here, and doing plenty of massacring on their own. A lot of people died during Black Hawk's war. Nineteen years is a mighty short time. Boys who survived Indian raids and a lot of Indian scares are voters now, and they still hate and fear Indians. So my worthy opponent is fanning the flames. The other night in Rock Island he passed out plenty of whisky and then gave a rehash of the Indian wars, not leaving out a single scalping

230

or alleged depravity. Then he told them about the last bloodthirsty Indians in Illinois being coddled out there in your town, and he pledged that when he's elected United States representative, he'll see that they're returned to their reservation in Kansas, where they belong.'

'Can you take steps to help the Sauks?'

'Take steps?' Hume sighed. 'Dr Cole, I'm a politician. Indians don't vote, so I'm not about to take a public stand in their individual or collective favour. But as a political matter it will help me if we can defuse this thing, because my opponent is trying to use it to win my seat.

'The two justices for the Circuit Court in this district are the Honorable Daniel P. Allen and the Honorable Edwin Jordan. Judge Jordan has a mean streak and he's a Whig. Dan Allan is a pretty good judge and an even better Democrat. I've known him and worked with him for a long time, and if he sits on this case he won't let Nick's people turn it into a carnival to convict your Sauk friend on flimsy nonevidence and help Nick win the election. There's no way of knowing whether he or Jordan will get the case. If it's Allan, he'll be no more than fair, but he'll be fair.

'None of the lawyers in town is going to want to defend an Indian, and that's the truth. The best attorney here is a young fella name of John Kurland. You let me have a talk with him, see if we can't twist his arm some.'

'I'm grateful to you, Congressman.'

'Well, you can show it by voting.'

'I'm one of the thirty percent. I've applied for naturalization, but there's a three-year waiting period . . .'

'That'll allow you to vote next time I run for re-election,' Hume said practically. He grinned as they shook hands. 'Meantime, tell your friends.'

The town wasn't going to stay excited too long because of a dead Indian. More interesting was contemplation of the opening of the Holden's Crossing Academy. Everyone in town would have been willing to give a small piece of land as the school site, thus ensuring easy access for their own children, but it was agreed that the institution should be in

231

a central place, and finally the town meeting had accepted three acres from Nick Holden, which satisfied Nick, because the lot was precisely shown as the school site on his early 'dream maps' of Holden's Crossing.

A one-room log schoolhouse had been built cooperatively. Once work had begun, the project caught fire. Instead of puncheon floors, the men hauled logs six miles to be sawed for construction of a plank floor. A long shelf was built along one wall to serve as a collective desk, and a long bench was placed in front of the shelf, so pupils could face the wall while writing and swing around to face the teacher while reciting. A square iron wood stove was set in the middle of the room. It was determined that school would begin each year after harvest and would run for three twelve-week terms, the teacher to be paid nineteen dollars a term plus room and board. State law held that a teacher had to be qualified in reading, writing, and arithmetic, and knowledgeable about either geography, or grammar, or history. There were not many candidates for the job because the pay was small and the aggravations were many, but finally the town hired Marshall Byers, a first cousin of Paul Williams, the blacksmith.

Mr Byers was a slim, pop-eyed youth of twenty-one who had taught in Indiana before coming to Illinois, and therefore knew what to expect from 'boarding around', living for a week at a time with the family of a different pupil. He told Sarah he was glad to stay at a sheep farm because he liked lamb and carrots better than pork and potatoes. 'Everywhere else, when they serve meat, it's pork and potatoes, pork and potatoes,' he said. Rob J. grinned at him. 'You'll love the Geigers,' he said.

Rob J. wasn't taken with the teacher. There was something nasty about the way Mr Byers grabbed covert glances at Moon and Sarah, and stared at Shaman as though the boy were a freak.

'I'm looking forward to having Alexander in my school,' Mr Byers said.

'Shaman is looking forward to school too,' Rob J. said quietly.

232

'Oh, but surely that is impossible. The boy doesn't speak normally. And how can a child who doesn't hear a word hope to learn anything in school?'

'He reads lips. He learns easily, Mr Byers.'

Mr Byers frowned. He looked ready to protest further, but when he glanced at Rob J.'s face he changed his mind. 'Of course, Dr Cole,' he said stiffly. 'Of course.'

Next morning,, before breakfast, Alden Kimball knocked at the back door. He had been to the feed store early and was bursting with news.

'Them damnfool Indians! They done it now,' he said. 'Got drunk last night and burned down the barn out at that popist nuns' place.'

Moon denied it at once when Rob spoke to her. 'I was at the Sauk camp last night with my friends, talking about Comes Singing. It's a lie, what Alden was told.'

'Perhaps they started drinking after you left.'

'No. It's a lie.' She sounded calm but her trembling fingers were already removing her apron. 'I'll go see the People.'

Rob sighed. He decided he'd better visit the Catholics.

He'd heard them described as 'them damn brown beetles'. He understood why when he saw them, because they wore brown wool habits that looked too warm for autumn and must have been a torture in the heat of summer. Four of them were working in the ruins of the fine little Swedish barn August Lund and his wife had built with such fierce young hope. They appeared to be searching the charred remains, still smoking in one corner, for anything worth salvaging.

'Good morning,' he called.

They'd been oblivious of his approach. They had tucked the hems of their long habits into their belts to allow freedom and comfort while they worked, and now they hastened to hide four sturdy pairs of sooty white-stockinged limbs as they pulled their skirts free.

'I'm Dr Cole,' he said, dismounting. 'Your far neighbour.' They stared without speaking, and it occurred to him that perhaps they didn't understand the language. 'May I speak to the person in charge?'

'That would be the mother superior,' one of them said, her voice scarcely more than a whisper.

She made a small motion and went to the house, Rob following. Near a new lean-to shack at the side of the house, an old man dressed in black spaded a frost-killed vegetable garden. The old man showed no interest in Rob. The nun knocked twice, quiet little rappings that went with her voice.

'You may enter.'

The brown habit preceded him and curtsied. 'This gentleman to see you, your Reverence. A doctor and a neighbour,' the whispery-voiced nun said, and curtsied again before fleeing.

The mother superior sat in a wooden chair behind a small table. The face within the veil was large, the nose wide and generous, the quizzical eyes a penetrating blue, lighter than Sarah's eyes and challenging instead of lovely.

He introduced himself and said he was sorry about the fire. 'Is there anything we can do to help?'

'I am confident the Lord will help.' Her English was educated; he thought the accent was German, although her accent and the Schroeders' were dissimilar. Perhaps they were from different regions of Germany.

'Please be seated,' she said, indicating the only comfortable chair in the room, large as a throne, upholstered in leather.

'You carried this all the way in a wagon?'

'Yes. When the bishop visits us, he will have a decent place to sit,' she said, her face serious. The men had come during Night Song, she said. The community had been busy at worship and didn't hear the first rowdy sounds and the crackling, but soon they had smelled the smoke.

'I'm told they were Indians.'

'The kind of Indians who attended that tea party in Boston,' she said dryly.

'You're certain?'

She smiled without humour. 'They were drunken white

234

men, spewing drunken white men's filth.'

'There's a lodge of the American party here.'

She nodded. 'The Know Nothings. Ten years ago I was at the Franciscan community in Philadelphia, newly arrived from my native Württemberg. The Know Nothings treated me to a week of rioting in which two churches were attacked, twelve Catholics were beaten to death, and dozens of Catholic-owned homes were burned. It took me a while to realize they are not all of America.'

He nodded. He noted that they had adapted one of the two rooms in August Lund's soddy into a Spartan dormitory. The room formerly had been Lund's granary. Now sleeping pallets were stacked in a corner. Besides her desktable and its chair, and the bishop's chair, the only furniture was a large and handsome refectory table and benches of new wood, and he commented on the joinery. 'Were they made by your priest?'

She smiled and rose. 'Father Russell is our chaplain. Sister Mary Peter Celestine is our carpenter. Would you like to see our chapel?'

He followed her into the room where the Lunds had eaten and slept and made love and where Greta Lund had died. It had been whitewashed. Against the wall was a wooden altar, and in front of it a prie-dieu for kneeling. Before the crucifix on the altar, a large tabernacle candle in a red glass was flanked by smaller candles. There were four plaster statues that seemed to be segregated by sex. He recognized the Virgin on the right. The mother superior said that next to Mary was Saint Clare, who had founded their order of nuns, and on the opposite side of the altar were Saint Francis and Saint Joseph.

'I'm told you plan to open a school.'

'You are wrongly told.'

He smiled. 'And that you intend to steal children into popery.'

Well, that is not so wrong,' she said seriously. 'We always hope to save a soul through Christ, child or woman or man. We always strive to make friends, draw Catholics from the community. But ours is a nursing order.'

'A nursing order! And where will you nurse? Will you build a hospital here?'

'Ah,' she said regretfully. 'There is no money. Holy Mother Church has bought this property and sent us to this place. And now we must make our way. We are certain the Lord will provide.'

He was less certain. 'May I summon your nurses if they're needed by the sick?'

'To go into their houses? No, that would never do,' she said severely.

He was uncomfortable in the chapel and started to withdraw.

'I think you are not a Catholic yourself, Dr Cole.'

He shook his head. He was struck by a sudden thought. 'If it's necessary to help the Sauks, would you testify that the men who burned your barn were white?'

'Of course,' she said coldly. 'Since it is simple truth, no?'

He realized that her novitiates must live in constant terror of her. 'Thank you . . .' He hesitated, unable to bow to this haughty woman and call her 'Your Reverence'. 'What is your name, Mother?'

'I am Mother Miriam Ferocia.'

He had been a Latinist in school, slaving to translate Cicero and accompanying Caesar through his Gallic Wars, and he retained enough to know that the name meant Mary the Courageous. But ever after, when he thought of this woman – to himself and to himself only – he would call her Ferocious Miriam.

He made the long ride to Rock Island to see Stephen Hume and was immediately rewarded, because the congressman had good news. Daniel P. Allan would preside at the trial. Because of the lack of evidence, Judge Allan saw no problem with releasing Comes Singing on bail. 'Capital crime, though – he couldn't set bail at less than two hundred dollars. For a bondsman you'll have to go to Rockford or Springfield.'

'I'll put up the money. Comes Singing's not going to run out on me,' Rob J. said.

236

'Good. Young Kurland has agreed to represent. Best for you not to go near the jail, under the circumstances. Attorney Kurland will meet you in two hours at your bank. That's the one in Holden's Crossing?'

'Yes.'

'Draw a bank draft made out to Rock Island County, sign it, and give it to Kurland. He'll handle the rest.' Hume grinned. 'The case will be heard within weeks. Between Dan Allan and John Kurland, they'll see to it that if Nick tries to make anything much of this case, he's gonna end up looking mighty foolish.' His handshake was firm and congratulatory.

Rob J. went home and hitched up the buckboard, because he felt that Moon had to have a place in the reception committee. She sat erect in the buckboard, wearing her regular housedress and a bonnet that had belonged to Makwa, unusually silent even for her. He could tell she was very nervous. He hitched the horse in front of the bank and she waited in the wagon while he took care of getting the draft and handing it over to John Kurland, a serious young man who acknowledged his introduction to Moon with politeness but no warmth.

When the lawyer left them, Rob J. got back up into the buckboard seat next to Moon. He left the horse hitched right where it was, and they sat there and peered down the street at the door to Mort London's office. The sun was hot for September.

They sat for what seemed to be an inordinately long time. Then Moon touched his arm, because the door had opened and Comes Singing emerged, stooping so he could get through. Kurland came right after.

They saw Moon and Rob J. at once and started toward them. Either Comes Singing reacted in joy because of his freedom and couldn't resist running or something instinctual made him want to get away from there, but he had taken only a couple of loping strides when something barked from above and to the right, and then from another rooftop across the street there were two more reports.

Pyawanegawa the hunter, the leader, the hero of the ball-

and-stick, should have gone down with majesty, like a giant tree, but he fell clumsily like other men, and his face went into the dirt.

Rob J. was out of the buckboard and to him at once, but Moon was unable to move. When he reached Comes Singing and turned him, he saw what Moon knew. One bullet had struck precisely in the nape of the neck. The other two were chest wounds in a pattern little more than an inch apart, and likely both had caused death by finding the heart.

Kurland reached them and stood in helpless horror. It took another minute for London and Holden to come from the sheriff's office. Mort listened to Kurland's explanation of what had happened and began to shout orders, checking the roofs on one side of the street and then on the other. Nobody seemed terribly surprised to find the roofs deserted.

Rob J. had remained on his knees next to Comes Singing, but now he stood and faced Nick. Holden was white-faced but relaxed, as if ready for anything. Incongruously, Rob was struck anew by his male beauty. He was wearing a revolver in a holster, Rob J. noted, and he knew his words to Nick might place him in danger, must be chosen with the greatest of care, yet needed to be spoken.

'I never want to have anything to do with you again. Not as long as I live,' he said.

Comes Singing was brought to the shed at the sheep farm and Rob J. left him there with his family. At dusk he went out to bring Moon and her children into the house for food and found they were gone, and so was Comes Singing's body. Late that evening Jay Geiger discovered the Coles' buckboard and horse tied to a post in front of his barn, and he brought Rob's property to the sheep farm. He said Little Horn and Stone Dog were gone from the Geiger farm. Moon and her children didn't return. That night Rob J. lay sleepless, thinking about Comes Singing probably in an unmarked grave somewhere in river woods. On somebody else's land that once had belonged to the Sauks.

Rob J. didn't get the news until midmorning next day, when Jay rode over again to tell him that Nick Holden's enormous stock barn had been burned to the ground during the night. 'No doubt about it, this time it was the Sauks. They've all run off. Nick spent most of the night keeping the flames away from his house and promising to call out the militia and the US army. He's already lit out after them with almost forty men, the sorriest Indian fighters anyone could think of – Mort London, Dr Beckermann, Julian Howard, Fritz Graham, most of the regulars from Nelson's bar – half the *shickers* in this part of the county, and all of them thinking they're going after Black Hawk. They're lucky if they don't shoot each other in the foot.'

That afternoon Rob J. rode out to the Sauk camp. The place told him they had left for good. The buffalo robes had been taken down from the doorways of the *hedonoso-tes*, which gaped like missing teeth. The junk of camp life littered the ground. He picked up a tin can, the raggedness of its lid telling him it had been sawed open with a knife or a bayonet. The label revealed it had contained cling peach halves from the state of Georgia. He'd never been able to make the Sauks see any value in dug latrines, and now he was kept from sentimentalizing their departure by the faint smell of human ordure that drifted to him when the wind blew in from the camp outskirts, a last shitty clue that something of value had disappeared from that place and wouldn't be brought back by spells or politics.

Nick Holden and his group chased the Sauks for four days. They never really got close. The Indians stayed in the woodlands along the Mississippi, always heading north. They weren't as good in the wilderness as many of the People who were now dead, but even the poorest of them was better in the woods than the white men, and they doubled back and twisted, laying false trails the whites obligingly followed.

The white men stuck to the pursuit until they were deep into Wisconsin. It would have been better if they could have returned with trophies, a few scalps and ears, but they told

239

each other they'd scored a great victory. They paused at Prairie du Chien and took on a lot of whisky and Fritzie Graham got into a fight with a trooper and ended up in jail, but Nick got him out, convincing the sheriff that a little professional courtesy was called for toward a visiting deputy. When they got back, thirty-eight disciples went forth and spread the gospel that Nick Holden had saved the state from the redskin menace and was a fine fellow to boot.

It was a soft autumn that year, better than summer because all the bugs were killed off by early frosts. A golden time, the leaves along the river coloured by the cold nights but the days mild and pleasurable. In October the church called to its pulpit Reverend Joseph Hills Perkins. He had asked for a parsonage as well as salary, so after harvest a small log house was built and the minister moved into it with his wife, Elizabeth. There were no children. Sarah busied herself as a member of the welcoming committee.

Rob J. found gone-by lilies along the river and planted their roots at the foot of Makwa's grave. It wasn't Sauk custom to mark graves with stone, but he asked Alden to plane a slab of black locust, which wouldn't rot. It didn't seem fitting to memorialize her with English words, but he had Alden carve into the wood the rune-like symbols she had worn on her body, to mark it as her place. He had a single unsatisfactory conference with Mort London in an attempt to get the sheriff to investigate both her death and Comes Singing's, but London said he was satisfied her killer had been shot dead, probably by other Indians.

In November, all over the United States, male citizens over twenty-one went to the polls. Countrywide, working-men reacted to the competition of immigrants for their jobs. Rhode Island, Connecticut, New Hampshire, Massachusetts, and Kentucky elected Know Nothing governors. Know Nothing legislatures were elected in eight states. In Wisconsin, Know Nothings helped elect Republican lawyers who proceeded to abolish the state immigration agencies. Know Nothings carried Texas, Tennessee, California, and Maryland, and ran strongly in most of the Southern states.

In Illinois they won a majority of the votes in Chicago and

in the southern portion of the state. In Rock Island County, incumbent US Congressman Stephen Hume lost his seat by one hundred and eighty-three votes to the Indian fighter Nicholas Holden, who left almost immediately after the election to represent his district in Washington, DC.

IV
THE DEAF BOY
October 12, 1851

30
Lessons

The railroad began in Chicago. Recent arrivals from Germany, Ireland, and Scandinavia found employment pushing the shining rails across the mostly flat land, finally reaching the east bank of the Mississippi at Rock Island. At the same time, on the other side of the river the Mississippi and Missouri Railroad Company was building a railroad across Iowa from Davenport to Council Bluffs, and the Mississippi River Bridge Company had been formed to connect the two railroads via a bridge across the great river.

In the deep mysteries of the flowing waters shortly after dusk on a mild evening, millions of wriggling aquatic larvae were transformed into caddis flies. Each of the dragonflylike insects fluttered out of the river on four silver wings, crowding and jostling, falling on Davenport in a blizzard of shimmering snowflakes that coated windows, got into the eyes and ears and mouths of people and animals, and were a terrible nuisance to anyone who ventured out-of-doors.

The caddis flies lived only one night. Their short onslaught was a phenomenon that occurred once or twice a year, and folks along the Mississippi took them in stride. By dawn the invasion was over, the flies were dead. At eight a.m. four men sat on benches along the waterfront in the thin fall sunlight, smoking and watching work crews sweep the insect corpses into drifts that were shovelled into wagons,

245

from which they were dumped back into the river. Soon another man came on horseback, leading four other horses, and the men left the benches and mounted up.

It was a Thursday morning. Payday. On Second Street, in the office of the Chicago and Rock Island Railroad, the paymaster and two clerks were making up the payroll of the crew constructing the new bridge.

At 8:19 the five men rode up to the office. Four of them dismounted and went inside, leaving one man with the horses. They weren't masked, and they looked like ordinary farmers except that each of them was armed. When they stated their purpose quietly and politely, one of the clerks was foolish enough to try to get a pistol from a nearby shelf and he was shot as dead as the caddis flies, a single pistol bullet to the head. No further resistance was shown, and the four holdup men calmly collected the entire payroll of $1,106.37 into a soiled linen sack before leaving. The paymaster later told authorities he was certain the bandit giving the orders was a man named Frank Mosby, who for several years had farmed land on the other side of the river to the south, beyond Holden's Crossing.

Sarah's timing was unfortunate. That Sunday morning she waited in church until Reverend Perkins asked worshippers to bear witness. Then, fathering her courage, she rose and went forward. In a low voice she told her minister and the congregation that after she had been widowed as a young woman she had had congress outside the bounds of holy matrimony, resulting in the birth of a child. Now, she told them, she sought through public confession to rid herself of sin through the cleansing grace of Jesus Christ.

When she was through, she lifted her white face and gazed into Reverend Perkins' brimming eyes. 'Praise the Lord,' he whispered. His long narrow fingers gripped her head and forced her to her knees. 'God!' he ordered sternly. 'Absolve this good woman of her transgression, for she has unburdened herself here in your house this day, has washed the scarlet from her soul, made it white as the rose, pure as first snow.'

246

The murmurings of the congregation swelled into shouts and ejaculations.

'Praise God!'

'Amen!'

'Hallelujah!'

'Amen, amen.'

Sarah actually felt her soul lighten. She thought she could float to Paradise right at this moment, as the Lord's strength coursed into her body through Mr Perkins' five digging fingertips.

The congregation was abrim with excitement. Every person was aware of the holdup in the railroad office, and that the outlaw leader had been identified as Frank Mosby, whose deceased brother, Will, it was widely whispered, had sired Sarah Cole's first son. So the people in church were caught up in the drama of the confession, studying Sarah Cole's face and body and imagining a variety of lascivious scenes they would pass on in shocked whispers to their friends and neighbours as probable history.

When finally Mr Perkins allowed Sarah to return to her pew, eager hands reached out to hers, and many voices murmured words of joy and congratulation. It was the glowing realization of a dream that had tormented her for years. It was proof that God was good, that Christian forgiveness made new hope possible, and that she had been accepted into a world where love and charity ruled. It was the happiest moment of her life.

Next morning was the opening of the academy, first day of school. Shaman enjoyed the company of eighteen children of varying sizes, the sharp new-wood smell of the building and furniture, his slate and slate pencils, and his copy of *McGuffey's Fourth Eclectic Reader*, battered and used because the school in Rock Island had purchased the newer *McGuffey's Fifth Eclectic Reader* for its pupils and the Holden's Crossing Academy had bought their old books. But almost immediately he was beset by problems.

Mr Byers seated his pupils alphabetically, in four groups according to age, so Shaman sat at one end of the long communal desk-shelf and Alex sat too far away to help him with anything. The teacher spoke with nervous swiftness and Shaman had trouble reading his lips. The pupils were ordered to draw pictures of their homes on their slates and then write their names, their ages, and their fathers' names and occupations. With the enthusiasm of first-day scholars, they turned to the shelf and soon were busily at work.

Shaman's first clue that something was wrong was when the wooden pointer rapped his shoulder.

Mr Byers had ordered his class to stop work and face him again. All had obeyed except the deaf boy, who hadn't heard. When Shaman wheeled in fright, he saw that the other children were laughing at him.

'We shall now read aloud the words on our slates when called upon, and show our pictures to the class. We'll begin with you,' and the pointer rapped him again.

Shaman read, stammering over some of the words. When he had shown his picture and was finished, Mr Byers called on Rachel Geiger, at the other end of the room. Though Shaman leaned as far forward in his seat as he was able, he couldn't see her face or read her lips. He raised his hand.

'What?'

'Please,' he said, addressing the teacher as his mother had sternly instructed. 'I can't see their faces from here. Couldn't I stand in front of them?'

At his last appointment Marshall Byers had had disciplinary problems, sometimes so severe he had dreaded entering the classroom. This new school was a fresh chance, and he was determined to keep a tight rein on the young savages. He had decided that one of the ways to do this was by controlling the seating. Alphabetically. In four small groups, according to age. Everyone in his or her place.

He knew it wouldn't do to have this boy standing in front of the pupils as they recited, gazing at their mouths, perhaps making faces behind his back, inspiring them to laugh and play rowdy tricks. 'No, you may not.'

Much of that morning Shaman simply sat, unable to comprehend what was going on. At lunchtime the children went outside and played tag. He enjoyed that until the biggest boy in the school, Lucas Stebbins, slammed Alex to make him 'it', sending him sprawling. When Alex scrambled to his feet, fists clenched, Stebbins went close to him. 'Wanna fight, yuh shit? We shouldn't let you play with us. You're a bastid. My paw says.'

'What's a bastid?' Davey Geiger asked.

'Don't you know?' Luke Stebbins said. 'It means somebody besides his paw, some dirty outlaw crook named Will Mosby, put his dingus up Mrs Cole's pee-hole.'

When Alex threw himself at the bigger boy, he received a stinging blow to his nose that brought blood dripping forth and sent him to the ground. Shaman ran at his brother's tormentor and received such a boxing about the ears that some of the other children, thoroughly frightened of Luke, turned away.

'You stop that. You'll hurt him,' Rachel Geiger shouted, glowering.

Ordinarily, Luke listened to her, dazzled by the fact that at twelve she already had breasts, but this time he just grinned. 'He's already deaf. Can't do his ears any more harm. Dummies sure do talk funny,' he said cheerfully, giving Shaman a final whack before walking away. If Shaman had allowed it, Rachel would have put her arms around him and comforted him. He and Alex, to their subsequent horror, sat on the ground and wept together while their schoolmates watched.

After lunch, there was music. This consisted of the pupils learning the tunes and words of hymns and anthems, a popular lesson because it was a relief from book-learning. During music, Mr Byers assigned the deaf boy to empty the pail of yesterday's ashes that stood next to the wood stove, and to fill the woodbox by carrying in heavy chunks. Shaman decided he hated school.

It was Alma Schroeder who made admiring reference to Rob J. about the confession in church, believing he knew of it. Once he possessed the details, he and Sarah quarrelled. He had felt her torment and now felt her release, but he was stunned and distressed that she would offer to strangers intimate details of her life, painful or otherwise.

Not strangers, she corrected him. 'Brethren in grace, sisters in Christ, who shared my shriving.' Mr Perkins had told them that anyone wishing to be baptized this coming spring must be shriven, she explained. It baffled her that Rob J. had trouble understanding; it was so clear to her.

When the boys began to come home from school with signs they'd been fighting, Rob J. suspected that at least some of her brethren in grace and sisters in Christ weren't above sharing with others the shrivings they observed in church. His sons were closemouthed about their bruises. He was unable to discuss their mother with them, other than to speak of her with admiration and love whenever it was possible. But he talked to them about fighting. 'It just isn't worth it to hit someone when you're mad. Things can get out of hand fast, even lead to death. Nothing justifies killing.'

The boys were puzzled. They were talking about schoolyard fistfights, not killing. 'How can you help hitting back when somebody hits you first, Pa?' Shaman asked.

Rob J. nodded in sympathy. 'I know it's a problem. You have to use your brain instead of your fists.'

Alden Kimball had overheard. A while later, he looked at the brothers and spat in horror. 'Drat! *Drat!* Your paw has to be one of the smartest men ever drew breath, but I guess he can be wrong. I tell you, somebody hits you, you gotta nail the sumbitch, else he's just gonna keep hittin'.'

'Luke's awful big, Alden,' Shaman said. It was what his big brother was thinking.

'Luke? Is it that ox of a Stebbins kid? Luke Stebbins?' Alden said, and spat again when they nodded miserably.

'When I was a young feller, I was a fair fighter. Know what this is?'

'A fighter who's pretty good?' Alex said.

'Pretty good! I was better than pretty good. Used to box at fairs. Carnivals and such? Fought three minutes with anybody'd come up with four bits. If they whupped me, they'd get three dollars. And don't you think a lot of strong men didn't try for that three dollars, neither.'

'Did you make a lot of money, Alden?' Alex asked.

Alden's face darkened. 'Naw. There was a manager, he made a lot of money. I did it for two years, summer and fall. Then I got beat. Manager paid three dollars to the feller beat me, and hired him to take my place.' He faced them. 'Point is, I can teach you how to fight, you want me to.'

Two young faces looked up at him. Then two heads were nodding.

'Stop that. Just say yes, can't you?' Alden said irritably. 'Look like a couple of damn sheep.'

'Little fear's a good thing,' he told them. 'Gets your blood to flowin'. But you let yourself be too scared, you can't do anythin' but lose. And you don't want to let yourself get too angry, neither. A fighter who's mad starts swingin' wild, leaves himself open to be hit.'

Shaman and Alex grinned self-consciously, but Alden was very serious when he showed them how to hold their hands, left one at eye level to protect the head, right one lower to protect the trunk. He was fussy about the way they made a fist, insisting they clench their curled fingers tight, hardening their knuckles so it would be like hitting their opponents with a rock in each hand.

'Fightin' is just four blows,' Alden said, 'left jab, left hook, right cross, straight right. Jab bites like a snake. Gotta sting a little, but it don't hurt the other fella much, just keep him off-balance, opens him up for something more serious. Left hook don't travel far, but it does a job – you turn left, put your weight on your right leg, swing *hard* at his head. Right cross, now, you put your weight on the other leg, get your power from a quick turn at the waist, like this. My favourite, straight right to the body, I call it the Stick. You turn low to the left, put your weight over your left leg, and drive that right fist straight into his belly as if your whole arm was a spear.'

He gave the punches to them again one at a time, so as not to confuse. The first day he had them jab the air for two hours, getting the strangeness out of throwing a punch, becoming familiar with the muscular rhythm. Next after-

251

noon they were back in the little clearing behind Alden's cabin, where they were unlikely to be disturbed, and every afternoon after that. They practised each punch over and over again before he let them box with one another. Alex was three-and-a-half years older, but because Shaman was so large, it was as if the difference was a single year. They were very careful of one another. Finally Alden had each boy take turns facing him and urged them to hit as hard as they would in a real fight. To their amazement, he twisted and sideslipped, or he blocked each blow with a forearm or parried it with his fist. 'See, what I'm teachin' you ain't no big secret. Others are goin' to know how to throw a punch. You gotta learn to defend.' He insisted that each of them drop his chin until it was guarded tightly against his breastbone. He showed them how to tie up an opponent in a clinch, but he cautioned Alex to avoid a clinch against Luke at all costs. 'Fella that much bigger than you, stay away from him, don't let him rassle you to the ground.'

It was unlikely Alex could whip a boy that big, Alden thought privately, but maybe Alex could punish Luke enough to make him leave them alone. He didn't try to make fair fighters out of the two Cole boys. He just wanted them able to protect themselves, and he taught them only the basics because he knew just enough to teach kids how to fistfight. He didn't try to tell them what to do with their feet. Years later he'd tell Shaman that if he himself had known a little something about what to do with his feet, probably he never would have been beaten by that three-dollar fighter.

Half a dozen times Alex thought he was ready to try Luke, but Alden said he would tell them when Alex was ready, and it wasn't now. So each day Shaman and Alex went to school and knew that the recess period would be a very bad time. Luke had become accustomed to the Cole brothers as game. He punched and insulted them at will, calling them only Dummy and Bastid. He struck them viciously at tag, and when he wrestled them he pushed their faces into the ground.

For Shaman, Luke wasn't his only problem at the

252

academy. He could see only a small portion of what was said during the school day, and from the start he was hopelessly behind. Marshall Byers wasn't dissatisfied to see that happen; he'd tried to tell the boy's father that a regular school wasn't any place for a deaf boy. But the teacher played it cautiously, knowing that when the subject came up again, he had best have his evidence ready. He maintained a careful list of Robert J. Cole's failing marks, and he kept the boy after school regularly for extra work assignments that didn't appear to raise his grades any.

Sometimes Mr Byers also kept Rachel Geiger after school, to Shaman's surprise, since Rachel was regarded as the smartest pupil in the school. When this happened, they trudged home together. On one of these afternoons, a grey day when the first snow of the year had just begun to fall, she frightened him by bursting into tears as they walked.

He could only stare at her in dismay.

She stopped and looked at him, so he could see her lips. 'That Mr Byers! Whenever he can, he stands . . . too close. And he's always touching me.'

'Touching?'

'Here,' she said, placing her hand on the upper front of her blue coat. Shaman was at a loss about the proper reaction to such a disclosure, since it was very far beyond his experience. 'What can we do?' he asked, more of himself than of her.

'I don't know. I don't know.' To his horror, Rachel began to sob again.

'I'll have to kill him,' he decided quietly.

It drew her complete attention, and she stopped crying. 'That's silly.'

'No. I'm going to do it.'

The snow was falling harder. It collected on her hat and hair. Her brown eyes, their thick black lashes still blinking back tears, were wondering. A large white flake melted on a smooth cheek that was darker than his, somewhere in between his mother's fairness and the swarthiness that had been Makwa's. 'You would do that for me?'

He tried to consider it fairly. It would be nice to get rid

of Mr Byers for himself, but her problems with the teacher were a weight that tipped the balance, and he could nod with conviction. Her smile, Shaman discovered, made him feel very good in a new way.

She touched his chest solemnly, in the very area she had declared forbidden to Mr Byers on her own person. 'You're my steadfast friend, and I am yours,' she said, and he realized it was so. When they resumed walking he was amazed when the girl's mittened hand found its way into his. Like her blue mittens, his red ones had been made by her mother, who always made mittens to give to Coles on their birthdays. Through the wool her hand sent an amazing amount of warmth halfway up his arm. But presently she stopped again and faced him.

'How will you . . . you know . . . do it?'

He waited before retrieving out of the cold air an expression he had heard his father use on numerous occasions. 'That will take considerable thought,' he said.

31
Schooldays

Rob J. enjoyed the meetings of the Medical Society. Sometimes they were educational. More often they offered an evening in the company of other men who had shared similar experiences and with whom he spoke a common language. At the November meeting Julius Barton, a young practitioner from the north county, reported on snakebites and then reminisced about some bizarre animal bites he had treated, including a case in which a woman had been bitten on her plump buttock with sufficient force to draw blood. 'Her husband said it was the dog, which made it an especially rare case, because it was apparent from the bite that their dog had human teeth!'

Not to be outdone, Tom Beckermann told of a cat lover with clawed testicles that may or may not have been the work of a cat. Tobias Barr said that sort of thing wasn't uncommon. Just a couple of months back he had treated a man for a ruined face. 'He said he'd been clawed by a cat too, but if so, that cat had only three claws and they were broad as a human pussy's.' Dr Barr said, provoking more laughter.

He started at once on another anecdote, and he was annoyed when Rob Cole interrupted to ask if he could remember exactly when he had treated the patient with the clawed face.

'Nop,' he said, and went back to his story.

Rob J. cornered Dr Barr after the meeting. 'Tobias, that patient with the scratched face. Could you have treated him on Sunday, September 3?'

'Don't rightly know. Didn't write it down.' Dr Barr was defensive about not keeping records, aware that Dr Cole practised a more scientific sort of medicine. 'No need to record every freakin' little thing, is there, for God's sake? Especially with a patient like this, travelling preacher from out-of-county, just passing through. Probably I'll never see him again, much less have to treat him.'

'Preacher? Remember his name?'

Dr Barr wrinkled his forehead, thought hard, shook his head.

'Patterson, perhaps,' Rob J. said. 'Ellwood R. Patterson?'

Dr Barr stared.

The patient hadn't left an exact address, to Dr Barr's recollection. 'I believe he said he was from Springfield.'

'He told me Chicago.'

'Came to you about his syphilis?'

'Tertiary stage.'

'Yes, tertiary syphilis,' Dr Barr said. 'He asked me about that after I dressed his face. The kind of man who wants as much as he can get for his dollar. If he'd had a corn on his toe, would have asked me to remove it for him so long as he was in the office. I sold him some salve for the syphilis.'

'So did I,' Rob J. said, and they both smiled.

Dr Barr looked puzzled. 'He skipped out owing you money, did he? That why you're looking for him?'

'No. I did an autopsy on a woman who was murdered the day you examined him. She'd been raped by several men. There was skin under three of her fingernails, probably from where she'd scratched one of them.'

Dr Barr grunted.

'I remember that two men waited for him outside my office. Got off their horses and sat on my front steps. One of them was big, built like a bear before hibernation, a good layer of fat. The other was kind of skinny, younger. Port-wine stain on his cheek, under his eye. I think the right eye.

256

I never heard their names, and I don't recall much else about them.'

The Medical Society president was inclined to professional jealousies and could be pompous on occasion, but Rob J. always had liked him. He thanked Tobias Barr and took his leave.

Mort London had calmed down since their last meeting, perhaps because he felt insecure with Nick Holden off in Washington, or maybe he'd realized it didn't pay for an elected official to be unable to bridle his tongue. The sheriff listened to Rob J., took notes regarding the physical descriptions of Ellwood Patterson and the other two men, and silkily promised to make inquiries. Rob had the distinct impression that the notes would go into the wastebasket just as soon as he left London's office. Given a choice between Mort angry or smoothly diplomatic, Rob preferred him angry.

So he made his own inquiries. Carroll Wilkenson, the real-estate and insurance agent, was chairman of the church's pastoral committee, and he had arranged for all the guest preachers before the church had called Mr Perkins to its pulpit. A good businessman, Wilkenson kept files on everything. 'Here it is,' he said, pulling out a folded flyer. 'Picked it up at an insurance meeting in Galesburg.' The flyer offered Christian churches a visit from a preacher who would deliver a guest sermon on God's plans for the Mississippi River Valley. The offer was made at no cost to the accepting church, and all expenses of the preacher would be borne by the Stars and Stripes Religious Institute, 282 Palmer Avenue, Chicago.

'I wrote a letter and gave them three open Sunday dates. They sent word back that Ellwood Patterson would preach September 3. They took care of everything.' He acknowledged that Patterson's sermon hadn't been wildly popular. 'Mostly it was warning us against the Catholics.' He smiled. 'Nobody minded that very much, you want the truth. But then he got onto folks who came to the Mississippi Valley from other countries. Said they were stealing jobs from the native-born. People who hadn't been born here were sore as a boil.' He had no forwarding address for Patterson. 'Nobody gave a thought to asking him back. Last thing a new church like ours needs is a preacher bent on dividing the congregation one against t'other.'

Ike Nelson, the saloonkeeper, remembered Ellwood Patterson. 'They's here late into Saturday night. He's a bad drunk, that Patterson, and so were them other two fellas he had with him. Easy with the money, but more trouble than they was worth. The big one, Hank, kept yellin' at me to go out and bring back some whores, but right away he got drunk, forgot all about women.'

'What was his last name, this Hank?'

'Funny name. Not Sneeze . . . Cough! Hank Cough. The other fella, the little skinny younger one, they called him Len. Sometimes Lenny. Never heard his last name that I remember. He had this purple mark on his face. Walked with a limp, like one leg mebbe was shorter than the other one.'

Toby Barr hadn't mentioned a limp; probably he hadn't seen the man walk, Rob realized. 'Which leg did he limp on?' he said, but the question only brought a puzzled stare from the barkeep.

'Did he walk like this?' Rob said, favouring the right leg. 'Or like this?' favouring the left.

'Less of a limp, his was barely noticeable. I don't know which side. All I know, they all three had hollow legs. Patterson popped a good-sized roll of money on the bar, told me to keep pourin' and help myself. End of the evenin' I had to send for Mort London and Fritzie Graham, give them a few dollars off the roll to bring them three back to Anna Wiley's boardinghouse and pour them into bed. But I'm told that next day in church Patterson was cool and holy as anyone might want.' Ike beamed. 'That's my kind of a preacher!'

Eight days before Christmas, Alex Cole came to school with Alden's permission to fight.

At recess Shaman watched his brother walking across the schoolyard. To his horror, he could see that Bigger's legs were shaking.

Alex walked directly to where Luke Stebbins stood with a cluster of boys who were practising running broad jumps into the soft snow of the unshovelled portion of the yard. Fortune shone upon him, for Luke already had made two lumbering runs that had ended in barely creditable jumps, and to gain an advantage had taken off his heavy cowskin jacket. Had he kept the jacket on, to have punched it would have been like slamming a fist into wood.

Luke thought Alex wanted to join the jumping game, and he prepared to have a little bullying fun. But Alex walked up and looped a right into his grin.

It was a mistake, the beginning of a clumsy contest. Alden had given careful instructions. The first surprise blow was to have been to the stomach, hopefully to knock out Luke's wind, but terror drove reason from Alex's mind. The punch pulped Luke's lower lip, and he came after Alex in a fury. Luke charging was a sight that would have frozen Alex with fear two months before, but he'd become accustomed to Alden rushing at him, and now he got out of the way. As Luke went by, he delivered a stinging left jab to the already insulted mouth. Then, as the larger boy checked his momentum, before he could get set, Alex delivered two more jabs to the same hurtful place.

Shaman had begun to cheer at the first blow, and pupils quickly ran towards the fighters from all corners of the yard. Alex's second major error was to glance toward Shaman's voice. Luke's large fist caught him just below the right eye and sent him careening to the ground. But Alden had done his job well, and even as Alex went down he began his scramble and was quickly on his feet and facing Luke, who rushed in again heedlessly.

Alex's face felt numb and his right eye immediately began to swell and close, but amazingly, his legs steadied. He gathered his wits and settled into what had become routine during his daily training. His left eye was all right, and he kept it pinned where Alden had instructed, right on Luke's chest, so he could see which way his body was turning, which hand he was going to throw. He tried to block only

259

one flailing punch, which numbed his entire arm; Luke was too strong. Alex was tiring, but he bobbed and weaved, ignoring the damage Luke could do if one of his punches landed again. His own left hand flicked out, punishing Luke's mouth and face. The strong initial punch that had opened the fight had loosened one of Luke's front teeth, and the steady tattoo of jabs finished the job. To Shaman's awe, Luke gave a furious headshake and spat the tooth into the snow.

Alex celebrated by jabbing again with the left and then throwing a clumsy right cross that landed smack on Luke's nose, bringing more blood. Luke raised his hands to his face in bewilderment.

'The Stick, Bigger!' Shaman screamed. 'The Stick!' Alex heard his brother, and he drove his right hand into Luke's stomach as hard as he was able, bending Luke over and making him gasp. It was the end of the fight, because the watching children were already scattering before the wrath of the teacher. Fingers of steel twisted Alex's ear, and Mr Byers was suddenly glaring down at them and declaring recess at an end.

Inside the school, both Luke and Alex were exhibited before the other pupils as very bad examples – beneath the big sign reading 'PEACE ON EARTH'. 'I will not have fighting in my school,' Mr Byers said coldly. He took the rod he used as a pointer and punished both fighters with five enthusiastic stripes upon the open hand. Luke blubbered. Alex's lower lip trembled when he received his own punishment. His swollen eye already was the colour of an old eggplant and his right hand was tormented on both sides, the knuckles skinned from fighting, the palm red and swollen from Mr Byers' switching. But when he glanced at Shaman, the brothers were suffused with an inner fulfillment.

When school let out and the children left the building and began to walk away, a group clustered about Alex, laughing and asking admiring questions. Luke Stebbins walked alone, morose and still stunned. When Shaman Cole ran at him, Luke thought wildly that the younger brother now was going to take his turn, and he raised his hands, the left a fist, the right open almost in supplication.

Shaman spoke to him kindly but firmly. 'You call my brother Alexander. And you call me Robert,' he said.

Rob J. wrote to the Stars and Stripes Religious Institute and told them he would like to contact Reverend Ellwood Patterson about an ecclesiastic question, requesting that the institute forward Mr Patterson's address.

It would take weeks for a reply to reach him, even if they answered. Meanwhile, he told nobody of what he had learned or of his suspicions, until one evening when he and the Geigers had finished playing 'Eine Kleine Nachtmusik'. Sarah and Lillian were chatting in the kitchen, preparing tea and slicing pound cake, and Rob J. unburdened himself to Jay. 'What shall I do, if I should find this preacher with the scratched face? I know Mort London won't go out of his way to bring him to justice.'

'Then you must make a noise and a smell that will be noticed in Springfield,' Jay said. 'And if the state authorities won't help, you've got to appeal to Washington.'

'Nobody in power has been willing to exert any effort because of one dead Indian woman.'

'In that case,' Jay said, 'if there's evidence of guilt, we'll have to gather about us some righteous men who know how to use guns.'

'You'd do that?'

Jay looked at him in astonishment. 'Of course. Wouldn't you?'

Rob told Jay of his vow of nonviolence.

'I have no such scruples, my friend. If bad people threaten, I'm free to respond.'

'Your Bible says, "Thou shalt not kill".'

'Hah! It also says, "Eye for eye, tooth for tooth". And, "He that smites a man, so that he die, shall be surely put to death".'

'"Whosoever shall smite thee on thy right cheek, turn to him the other also".'

'That isn't from my Bible,' Geiger said.

'Ah, Jay, that's the trouble, too damn many Bibles and

261

they each claim to hold the key.'

Geiger smiled sympathetically. 'Rob J., I would never try to dissuade you from being a freethinker. But I leave you with one more thought. "The fear of the Lord is the beginning of wisdom".' And the conversation turned to other things as their women carried in the tea.

In the time that followed, Rob J. thought often of his friend, sometimes resentfully. It was easy for Jay. Several times a day he wrapped himself in his fringed prayer shawl and it covered him with security and reassurance about yesterday and tomorrow. All was prescribed: these things are allowed, these things are forbidden, directions clearly marked. Jay believed in the laws of Jehovah and of man, and he had only to follow ancient edicts and the statutes of the Illinois General Assembly. Rob J.'s revelation was science, a faith less comfortable and far less comforting. Truth was its deity, proof was its state of grace, doubt was its liturgy. It held as many mysteries as other religions and was beset with shadowy trails that led to profound dangers, terrifying cliffs, and the deepest pits. No higher power shed a light to illuminate the dark and murky way, and he had only his own frail judgment with which to choose the paths to safety.

On the seasonably frigid fourth day of the new year of 1852, violence came to the schoolhouse again.

That morning of intense cold, Rachel was late for school. When she arrived, she slipped silently into her place on the bench without smiling at Shaman and mouthing a greeting, as was her custom. He saw with surprise that her father had followed her into the schoolhouse. Jason Geiger walked up to the desk and looked at Mr Byers.

'Why, Mr Geiger. A pleasure, sir. What can I do for you?'

Mr Byers' pointer lay on the desk and Jay Geiger picked it up and whacked the teacher across the face.

Mr Byers jumped to his feet, overturning his chair. He was a head taller than Jay but ordinary of build. Ever after it would be remembered as comical, the short fat man going after the tall younger man with the teacher's own rod, his arm rising and falling, and the disbelief on Mr Byers' face.

But that morning nobody laughed at Jay Geiger. The pupils sat straight scarcely breathing. They couldn't credit the event any more than Mr Byers could; it was even more unbelievable than Alex's fight with Luke. Shaman mostly watched Rachel, noting that her face had been dark with embarrassment but had become very pale. He had the feeling she was trying to make herself as deaf as he was, and blind as well, to everything that was going on around them.

'What the hell are you doing?' Mr Byers held his arms up to protect his face and squealed in pain as the pointed landed on his ribs. He took a threatening step toward Jay. 'You damn idiot! You crazy little Jew!'

Jay kept hitting the teacher and backing him toward the door until Mr Byers bolted through and slammed it. Jay took Mr Byers' coat and flung it through the door onto the snow, and then he came back, breathing hard. He sat in the teacher's chair.

'School is dismissed for the day,' he said finally, then collected Rachel and took her home on his horse, leaving his sons to walk home with the Cole boys.

It was really cold outside. Shaman wore two scarves, one around his head and under his chin, the other around his mouth and nose, but still his nostrils frosted closed for a moment every time he breathed.

When they got home Alex ran inside to tell their mother what had happened in school, but Shaman walked past the house, down to the river, where he saw that the ice had cracked in the cold, which must make a wonderful sound. The cold had split a big cottonwood tree too, not far from Makwa's snow-covered *hedonoso-te*; it looked as though it had been exploded by lightning.

He was glad Rachel had told Jay. He was relieved that he didn't have to murder Mr Byers and that now most likely he wouldn't ever have to be hanged. But something pestered at him like a rash that wouldn't go away: if Alden thought it was all right to fight when you had to, and if Jay thought it was all right to fight to protect his daughter, what was wrong with his father?

263

32
Night Doctoring

Within hours after Marshall Byers had fled Holden's Crossing, a hiring committee was appointed to find a new teacher. Paul Williams was named to it, to demonstrate that nobody blamed the blacksmith because his cousin, Mr Byers, had turned out to be a bad apple. Jason Geiger was named to it, to show that folks trusted he had behaved correctly in driving Mr Byers away. Carroll Wilkenson was named to it, which was fortunate, because the insurance agent had just paid off a small life-insurance policy that John Meredith, a storekeeper over in Rock Island, had had on his father. Meredith had mentioned to Carroll how grateful he was to his niece, Dorothy Burnham, for leaving her schoolteaching job in order to nurse his father through his last days. When the hiring committee interviewed Dorothy Burnham, Wilkenson liked her for her homely face and the fact that she was an unmarried spinster in her late twenties, and so was unlikely to be taken from the school by marriage. Paul Williams endorsed her because the sooner they hired someone, the quicker people were going to forget his damned cousin Marshall. Jay was drawn to her because she spoke of teaching with a quiet confidence, and with a warmth that indicating a calling. They hired her for $17.50 a term, $1.50 less than Mr Byers because she was a woman.

Eight days after Mr Byers ran from the schoolhouse, Miss

264

Burnham was the teacher. She kept to Mr Byers' seating arrangement because the children were accustomed to it. She'd taught at two previous schools, one in the village of Bloom that was a smaller school than this one, and the other a larger school in Chicago. The only handicap she'd encountered previously in a child was lameness, and she was keenly interested that there was a deaf boy in her charge.

In her first conversation with young Robert Cole she was intrigued that he could read her lips. To her annoyance, it took her almost half a day to comprehend that from his seat on the bench he couldn't see what most of the other children were saying. There was one chair in the schoolhouse for visiting adults, and Miss Burnham now made that Shaman's, placing it in front of the bench and off to the side so he could see her lips as well as his schoolmates'.

The other big change for Shaman occurred when it was time for music. As had become his custom, he started to take out the stove ashes and bring in the firewood, but this time Miss Burnham stopped him and told him to resume his seat.

Dorothy Burnham gave her pupils the pitch by breathing into a small round tone pipe, and then taught them to put words to the ascending scale: 'Our-school-is-a-pre-cious-ha-ven!', and to the descending scale: 'And-we-learn-to-think-and-grow-here!' By the middle of the first song it was clear she hadn't done the deaf boy a good turn by including him, for young Cole simply sat and watched, and soon he eyes were dulled by a patience she found unendurable. He should be given an instrument through whose vibrations he might 'hear' the rhythm of the music, she decided. Perhaps a drum? But the noise of a drum would destroy the music made by the hearing children.

She gave the problem some thought and then she went to Haskins' General Store and begged a cigar box, placing into it six red marbles, the kind used by boys to play knuckles-down in the spring. The marbles made too much noise when their container was shaken, but when she glued soft blue cloth from a discarded chemise to the inside of the box, the results were satisfactory.

265

Next morning during music, while Shaman held the box, she shook it to keep time with each note as the pupils sang 'America'. He caught on, reading the teacher's lips to time his box-shaking. He couldn't sing, but he became acquainted with rhythm and timing, mouthing the lyrics of each song as sung by his classmates, who soon were accustomed to the soft thudding of 'Robert's box'. Shaman loved the cigar box. Its label bore a picture of a dark-haired queen with a prominent chiffon-covered bosom and the words *Panatellas de la Jardines de la Reina*, and the imprint of the Gottlieb Tobacco Importing Company of New York City. When he lifted the box to his nose he could smell aromatic cedar and the faint odours of Cuban leaf.

Miss Burnham soon had every boy take turns coming to school early to take out the ashes and bring in the firewood. Although Shaman never thought about it in those terms, his life had been dramatically changed because Marshall Byers had been unable to refrain from stroking adolescent breasts.

At the frigid beginning of March, with the prairie still frozen hard as flint, patients crowded Rob J.'s waiting room at the house every morning, and when his office hours were over he pushed himself to make as many calls as possible, because in a few weeks the mud would make travel torturous. When Shaman wasn't in school, his father allowed him to make home visits with him, because the boy looked after the horse and allowed the doctor to hurry inside to his patient.

Late one leaden afternoon they were on the river road, having just been to see Freddy Wall, who had the pleurisy. Rob J. was debating whether to go on to visit Anne Frazier, who had been poorly all winter, or to let it go until the next day, when three horsemen moved their mounts out of the trees. They were bundled in clothing and tie-cloths against the cold, as were the two Coles, but Rob J. didn't miss the fact that each of them wore a sidearm, two of the guns in belts worn outside their bulky coats, the third in a holster attached to the front of a saddle.

'You the doc, ain'tcha.'

Rob J. nodded. 'Who are you?'

'We got a friend needs doctorin' bad. Little accident.'

'What kind of accident? Break any bones, you think?'

'No. Well, don't know for certain. Mebbe. Shot. Up here,' he said, stroking his left arm near the shoulder.

'Losing much blood, is he?'

'No.'

'Well, I'll come, but I'll drop the boy at home first.'

'No,' the man said again, and Rob J. looked at him. 'We know where you live, other side of the township. We got a long ride to our friend, this direction.'

'How long a ride?'

'Most of an hour.'

Rob J. sighed. 'Lead away,' he said.

The man who had done the talking did the leading. It wasn't lost to Rob J. that the other two men waited until he had followed and then rode well behind, boxing in the doctor's horse.

In the beginning they rode northwest, Rob J. was certain of that. He was aware they doubled back and twisted against their own route from time to time, the way a hounded fox is supposed to. The stratagem worked, for he was soon confused and lost. In half an hour or so they came to a stretch of wooded hills that rose between the river and the prairie. Between the hills were sloughs; frozen passable now, they would be impregnable mud moats when the melt came.

The leader stopped. 'Gotta blindfold you.'

Rob J. knew better than to protest. 'Just a moment,' he said, and turned to face Shaman. 'They'll cover your eyes, but don't you be afraid,' he said, and was gratified when Shaman nodded. The bandanna that blinded Rob J. was none too clean and he hoped Shaman's luck was better, hating the thought of a stranger's sweat and dried snot against his son's skin.

They put Rob J.'s horse on a lead. It seemed a long while that they rode on between the hills, but probably time passed more slowly for him while blindfolded. At length he felt the horse beneath him begin to climb one of the slopes, and presently they drew up and came to a halt. When the blindfold was removed he saw they were in front of a small structure, more shack than cabin, beneath large trees. Daylight was fading, and their eyes quickly adjusted. He saw his child blinking. 'You doing fine, Shaman?'

'Just fine, Pa.'

He knew that face. Searching it, he saw Shaman was sensible enough to be quite scared. But as they stamped their feet to bring back their circulation and then entered the shack, Rob J. was half-amused to see that Shaman's eyes gleamed with interest as well as fear, and he was furious at himself because he hadn't somehow found a way to leave the boy behind, out of harm's way.

Inside, there were red coals in the fireplace and the air was warm but very bad. There was no furniture. A fat man lay on the floor propped against a saddle, and by the firelight Shaman could see he was bald but had as much coarse black hair on his face as most men have on their heads. Rumpled blankets on the floor indicated where others had slept.

'Took you long enough,' the fat man said. He was holding a black jug, and he took a swallow from it and coughed.

'Didn't tarry any,' the man who had ridden the lead horse said sullenly. When he took off the scarf that had protected his face, Shaman saw he had a small white beard and looked older than the others. He put his hand on Shaman's shoulder and pushed. 'Sit,' he said as if talking to a dog. Shaman squatted not far from the fire. He was content to stay there because he had a good view of the wounded man's mouth, and his father's.

The older man took his pistol from its holster and pointed it at Shaman. 'You better fix up our friend *real good*, Doc.' Shaman was very frightened. The hole at the end of the barrel looked like an unblinking round eye that stared directly at him.

'I don't do anything while somebody holds a gun,' his father said to the man on the floor.

The fat man appeared to consider. 'You get out,' he told

his men.

'Before you go,' Shaman's father told them, 'bring in wood and build up the fire. Put water on to boil. You have another lamp?'

'Lantern,' the old man said.

'Get it.' Shaman's father put his hand on the fat man's forehead. He unbuttoned the man's shirt and drew it aside. 'When did this happen?'

'Yesterday morning.' The man looked at Shaman out of hooded eyes. 'This is your boy.'

'My younger son.'

'The deef one.'

'. . . Appears you know a few things about my family . . .'

The man nodded. 'It's the older one some say is my brother Will's get. Anything like my Willy, he's already a damn hellion. You know who I am?'

'I can make a good guess.' Now Shaman saw his father lean forward just an inch or two and fix the other man with his eyes. 'They're both my boys. If you're talking of my elder son – he's *my* elder son. And you're going to stay away from him in the future, just as you have in the past.'

The man on the floor smiled. 'Now, why shouldn't I claim him?'

'Most important reason is he's a fine, straight boy with every chance for a decent life. And if he *was* your brother's, you don't ever want to see him where you are right now, lying like some hurt and hunted animal in the dirt of a stinking little hideout pigsty.'

They looked at one another for a long moment. Then the man moved and grimaced, and Shaman's father began to doctor him. He took away the jug, got the man's shirt off.

'No exit wound.'

'Oh, the bastard's in there, coulda told you that. Gonna hurt like hell when you probe, I reckon. Can I have another jolt or two?'

'No, I'll give you something, put you to sleep.'

The man glared. 'I ain't goin' to sleep so you can do whichever the hell you want, and me helpless.'

'Your decision,' Shaman's father said. He gave the jug

269

back and let the man drink while he waited for the water to finish heating. Then with brown soap and a clean rag from his medical bag he washed the area around the wound, which Shaman couldn't see clearly. Dr Cole took a thin steel probe and slipped it into the bullet hole, and the fat man froze and opened his jaw and stuck out his big red tongue as far as it would go.

'. . . It's in there almost at the bone, but there's no fracture. Bullet must have been nearly spent when it hit.'

'Lucky shot,' said the man. 'Sumbitch was a good distance away.' His beard was matted with sweat and his skin was grey.

Shaman's father took a foreign-body forceps from his bag. 'This is what I'll use to remove it. It's a lot thicker than the probe. It's going to hurt a lot more.

'Best trust me,' he said simply.

The patient turned his head and Shaman couldn't see what he said, but he must have asked for something stronger than the whisky. His father took an ether cone from his bag and motioned to Shaman, who had watched ether being administered several times but never before had helped. Now he held the cone carefully over the fat man's mouth and nose while his father dripped the ether. The bullet hole was larger than Shaman had expected, with a purple rim. When the ether had taken, his father worked the forceps in very carefully, a little bit at a time. A bright red drop appeared at the edge of the hole and spilled over to run down the man's arm. But when the forceps were withdrawn, they gripped a lead slug.

His father rinsed it clean and dropped it on the blanket for the man to find when he came around.

When his father called the men in out of the cold, they brought in a pot of white beans they'd been keeping frozen on the roof. After they thawed it on the fire, they gave some to Shaman and his father. It had bits of something in it that maybe was rabbit, and Shaman thought it would have profited from molasses, but he ate it hungrily.

After supper his father heated more water and commenced to wash clean his patient's entire body, which the

270

other men at first regarded with suspicion and then with boredom. They lay down and one by one drifted off, but Shaman stayed awake. Soon he was watching the patient's awful retching.

'Whisky and ether don't mix happily,' his father said. 'You go to sleep. I'll tend to it.'

Shaman did, and grey light was coming through the cracks in the walls when his father shook him awake and told him to put on his outside clothes. The fat man was lying there watching them.

'It will give you a fair amount of pain for two, three weeks,' his father said. 'I'm leaving you some morphine, not much, but all I have with me. Most important thing is to keep it clean. If it begins to mortify, you call me and I'll come back right away.'

The man snorted. 'Hell, we're gonna be long gone from this place afore you can come back.'

'Well, if you have trouble, you send for me. I'll come to wherever you are.'

The man nodded. 'You pay him good,' he told the man with the white beard, who took a wad of bills from a pack and handed them over. Shaman's father peeled off two singles and dropped the rest on the blanket. 'Dollar and a half for the night home visit, fifty cents for the ether.' He started to leave but turned back. 'You fellas know anything of a man named Ellwood Patterson? Sometimes travels with a man named Hank Cough and a younger man named Lenny?'

Their faces looked at him blankly. The man on the floor shook his head. Shaman's father nodded, and they went out, into air that smelled of nothing but trees.

This time only the man who had ridden lead came with them. He waited until they were mounted before he fixed the neckerchiefs over their eyes again. Rob J. could hear his son's breathing become faster and wished he had spoken to the boy while Shaman could see his lips.

His own ears were working overtime. Their horse was being led; he could hear the hooves ahead of him. There

271

were no hooves behind. Still, it would be easy for them to have someone waiting on the trail. All he would have to do was let them ride past, lean forward, place a gun only a few inches from a blindfolded head, and pull the trigger.

It was a long ride. When finally they stopped, he knew if a bullet was going to come, it would be now. But their blindfolds were pulled off.

'You just keep riding that way, hear? Presently you'll come to landmarks you know.'

Blinking, Rob J. nodded, not telling him he already recognized where they were. They rode off in one direction, the gunman in another.

Eventually Rob J. stopped in a copse so they could relieve themselves and stretch their legs.

'Shaman,' he said. 'Yesterday. Did you watch my conversation with that fellow who was shot?'

The boy nodded, looking at him.

'Son. Did you understand what we were talking about?'

Nodded again.

Rob J. believed him. 'Now, how come you understood talk like that? Has somebody been saying things to you about . . .' he couldn't say your mother. '. . . your brother?'

'Some boys in school . . .'

Rob J. sighed. An old man's eyes in such a young face, he thought. 'Well, Shaman, here's the thing. I think what happened – our being with those people, treating that man who was shot, and especially what he and I talked about – I think those things should be our secret. Yours and mine. Because to tell your brother and your mother about it, that could hurt. Cause them anxiety.'

'Yes, Pa.'

They got back on the horse. A warm breeze had started to blow. The spring thaw was coming at last, he thought. Streams would be running in a day or two. In a little while he was startled by Shaman's wooden voice.

'I want to be just like you, Pa. Wanna be a good doctor.'

Rob J.'s eyes prickled. It was the wrong time, facing away from Shaman in the saddle, with the boy cold, hungry, and tired, to try to explain to him that some dreams were impossible to realize if you were deaf. He had to content himself with stretching his long arms behind him and pulling his son forward, close to him. He could feel Shaman's forehead pressed into his back and he just stopped tormenting himself and for a while let himself nibble at sleep like a starving man afraid to gulp a plateful of fudge, as the horse plodded along and took them home.

33

Robert J. Cole, M.D.
Holden's Cross

Dear Dr Cole:

We have received your inquiry concerning the whereabouts and address of the Reverend Ellwood Patterson. We are sorry, but we cannot be of service to you in this matter.

As you may be aware, our institute serves both the Churches and the American Workingmen of Illinois, bringing God's Christian Message to the honest Native-Born Mechanics of this state. Last year Mr Patterson contacted us and volunteered to help in our ministry, which resulted in his visit to your community and its fine church. But he has since moved from Chicago and we do not have any information regarding his whereabouts.

Rest assured that if such information should find its way to us, we shall send it to you. In the meantime, if there is some matter with which you may be helped by any of the other fine Ministers of God who are our associates – or some Theological Matter with which I may personally assist you, do not hesitate to contact me.

I am yours in Christ,
(signed)
Oliver G. Prescott, DD, Director
Stars and Stripes Religious Institute

The answer was more or less what Rob J. had expected. He sat down next and wrote, in the form of a letter, a factual account of the murder of Makwa-ikwa. In the letter he reported the presence of the three strangers in Holden's Crossing. He wrote of his finding samples of human skin under three of Makwa's fingernails during the autopsy, and of Dr Barr's having treated the Reverend Ellwood R. Patterson, on the afternoon of the killing, for three severe tearings on his face.

He dispatched identical letters to the governor of Illinois in Springfield and to both his senators in Washington. Then he forced himself to send a third copy to his congressman, addressing Nick Holden formally. He asked the authorities to use their offices to locate Patterson and his two companions and investigate any connection between them and the death of the Bear Woman.

There was a guest at the June meeting of the Medical Society, a doctor named Naismith visiting from Hannibal, Missouri. In the convivial period before the business meeting, he told of a legal suit that had been levied in Missouri by a slave suing to become a free man.

'Before Black Hawk's War, Dr John Emerson was posted as surgeon here in Illinois, at Fort Armstrong. He had a Negro man named Dred Scott, and when the government opened up the former Indian lands for settlement, he claimed a section in what was then called Stephenson and is now Rock Island. The slave built a shack on the land and lived there several years in order that his master could qualify as a settler.

'Dred Scott went to Wisconsin with Emerson when the surgeon was transferred, and then returned with him to Missouri, where the doctor died. The Negro tried to purchase his freedom from the widow, and that of his wife and two daughters. For her own good reasons, Mrs Emerson refused to sell. Thereupon the nervy black rascal petitioned for his freedom in the courts, claiming that for years he'd been a free man in Illinois and Wisconsin.'

Tom Beckermann guffawed. 'A suing blackamoor!'

'Well,' Julius Barton said, 'seems to me his claim has merit. Slavery is illegal in both Illinois and Wisconsin.'

Dr Naismith continued to smile. 'Ah, but of course he'd been sold and bought in Missouri, a slave state, and he had returned there.'

Tobias Barr looked thoughtful. 'What's your opinion on the slavery matter, Dr Cole?'

'I think,' Rob J. said deliberately, 'that it's all right for a man to own a beast if he cares for it and provides sufficient feed and water. But I don't believe it's all right for a human being to own another human being.'

Dr Naismith did his best to remain genial. 'I'm happy you're my medical colleagues, sirs, and not attorneys or the justices of the courts.'

Dr Barr nodded in the face of the man's obvious unwillingness to engage in unpleasant argument. 'Have you folks seen much cholera in Missouri this year, Dr Naismith?'

'Not much cholera, but we've had a lot of what some have called the cold plague,' Dr Naismith said. He went on to describe the apparent etiology of the disease, and the rest of the meeting was occupied with a discussion of materia medica.

Several afternoons later Rob J. was riding past the convent of the Sisters of Saint Francis Xavier of Assisi, and without any decision aforethought, he turned his horse into their lane.

This time his approach was spotted well in advance, a young nun scuttling out of the garden and hurrying inside. Mother Miriam Ferocia offered him the bishop's chair with a quiet smile. 'We have coffee,' she said in a way that told him this wasn't always so. 'Will you have a cup?'

He had no desire to use up their supplies, but something in her face caused him to accept the offer with thanks. The coffee arrived black and hot. It was very strong and tasted old to him, like their religion.

'No milk,' Mother Miriam Ferocia said cheerfully. 'God has yet to send us a cow.'

When he asked how the convent fared, she replied

somewhat stiffly that they were surviving very well, indeed.

'There's a way to bring money into your convent.'

'It is always wise to listen when someone speaks of money,' she said calmly.

'You're a nursing order without a place in which to nurse. I doctor patients who need nursing. Some of them can pay.'

But he didn't get a better reaction than he had the first time he'd raised the subject. The mother superior made a face. 'We are sisters of charity.'

'Some of the patients can pay nothing. Nurse them and you will be charitable. Others can pay. Nurse them and support your convent.'

'When the Lord provides us with a hospital in which to nurse, we shall nurse.'

He was frustrated. 'Can you tell me why you won't allow your nuns to nurse patients in their homes?'

'No. You would not understand.'

'Try me.'

But she merely scowled icily, Mary the Ferocious.

Rob J. sighed, and slurped her bitter brew. 'There's another matter.' He told her the few facts he had learned to date, and of his efforts to trace Ellwood Patterson's whereabouts. 'I wonder if you have learned anything about this man.'

'Not about Mr Patterson. But I have learned about the Stars and Stripes Religious Institute. An anti-Catholic organization backed by a secret action society supporting the American party. It is called the Supreme Order of the Star-Spangled Banner.'

'How did you learn about this . . . Supreme . . .?'

'Order of the Star-Spangled Banner. They call it the SSSB.' She looked at him keenly. 'Mother Church is a vast organization. She has ways of gaining intelligence. We turn the other cheek, but it would be foolish not to learn from which direction the next blow is likely to come.'

'Perhaps the Church can help me find this Patterson.'

'I sense it is important to you.'

'I believe he killed a friend of mine. He shouldn't be allowed to kill others.'

277

'You cannot leave him to God?' she asked quietly.

'No.'

She sighed. 'It is unlikely that you will find him through me. Sometimes an inquiry travels only a link or two in the Church's infinite chain. Often one asks, and never hears again. But I shall make inquiries.'

When he left the convent, he rode to Daniel Rayner's farm to deal unsuccessfully with Lydia-Belle Rayner's sprung back, then proceeded to Lester Shedd's goat farm. Shedd had almost died of an inflammation of the chest and was a prime example of why the nursing of the nuns would have been invaluable. But Rob J. had called upon Lester as often as possible through some of the winter and all of the spring, and with the hard work of Mrs Shedd had eased him back into health.

When Rob J. announced that no more visits were necessary, Shedd was relieved, but he broached the subject of the doctor's bill uneasily.

'Would you happen to have a good nanny in milk?' Rob J. asked. He heard himself almost in astonishment.

'Not giving milk now. But I've a little beauty, just a bit young for freshening. In a couple of months I'll throw in a proved service by one of my billies. Five months later – plenty of milk!'

Rob J. led the protesting animal away on a rope behind his horse, just as far as the convent.

Mother Miriam thanked him properly enough, neverthe-less observing tartly that when he visited seven months hence he would have cream in his coffee, as though accusing him of making the gift out of his own selfish desires.

But he observed that her eyes twinkled. When she smiled it lent warmth and easiness to the strong and forbidding face, so he was able to ride home in the belief his day had been spent well.

Dorothy Burnham never had seen young Robert Cole as anything but an eager and intelligent pupil. At first she was puzzled by the record of low grades she discovered beside his name in Mr Byers' marking book, and then angered, because the boy had an exceptionally good mind and it was obvious he had been treated badly.

She had absolutely no experience with deafness, but she was a teacher who gloried in an opportunity.

When next she came to the Coles' house to board for two weeks, she waited for the proper moment to speak with Dr Cole in privacy. 'It is about Robert's speech,' she said, and saw as he nodded that she had his undivided attention. 'We're fortunate because he speaks clearly. But as you know, there are other problems.'

Rob J. nodded again. 'His speech is wooden and flat. I've suggested that he vary his tones, but . . .' He shook his head.

'I believe he speaks in a monotone because more and more he's forgotten how the human voice sounds, how it rises and dips. I think we may be able to remind him,' she said.

Two days later, with Lillian Geiger's permission, the teacher brought Shaman to the Geiger house after school. She stood him next to the piano with his hand on the wooden case, palm down. Striking the first key in the bass as hard as she was able, and keeping the key depressed so it would vibrate through the soundboard and case and into the boy's hand, she looked at him and said, 'Our!' Her own right hand, palm up, remained on the piano top.

She struck the next key. 'School!' Now her right hand was raised slightly.

The next key. 'Is!' And her hand went slightly higher.

Note by note, she went up the ascending scale, with each note pronouncing part of the litany to which he'd become accustomed in class: 'Our-school-is-a-pre-cious-ha-ven!' And then she went down the descending scale: 'And-we-learn-to-think-and-grow-here!'

She played the scales again and again, allowing him to become thoroughly accustomed to the differences in the vibrations that reached his hand, and making certain that he saw the gradual rising and descent of her hand with each note.

Then she told him to sing the words she had put to the

scales, not by mouthing them silently as was his custom in school, but aloud. The results were far less than musical, but Miss Burnham wasn't looking for music. She wanted Shaman to show some control over the pitch of his voice, and after a number of tries, in response to her hand pumping frantically into the air, his voice did rise. It went up more than a single note, however, and Shaman stared transfixed as his teacher's thumb and forefinger held a tiny measured distance before his eyes.

Thus she pushed and bullied, and Shaman disliked it. Miss Burnham's left hand marched across the piano, banging keys, doggedly climbing up and down the scales. Her right hand lifted one note at a time and then descended the same way. Shaman croaked out his love for his school again and again. Sometimes his face was sullen, and twice his eyes filled with tears, but Miss Burnham didn't seem to notice.

Finally the teacher stopped playing. She opened her arms and gathered young Robert Cole into them, holding him for a long moment and twice stroking the thick hair at the back of his head before releasing him.

'Go home,' she said, but stopped him as he turned away. 'We'll do this again tomorrow, after school.'

His face fell. 'Yes, Miss Burnham,' he said. His voice was without inflection, but she was undismayed. She sat at the keyboard after he was gone, and played the scales one more time.

'Yes,' she said.

There had been a quick spring that year – a very small period of comfortable warmth, and then a blanket of oppressive heat that fell over the plains. On a torrid Friday morning in mid-June, Rob J. was stopped on Main Street in Rock Island by George Cliburne, a Quaker farmer turned grain broker. 'Would thee have just a moment, Doctor?' Cliburne said politely, and by common unspoken consent they moved together out of the sun glare and into the almost sensual coolness of a hickory tree's shade.

'I'm told thee have a sympathy for men who are enslaved.'

Rob J. was nonplussed by the observation. He knew the grain broker only by sight. George Cliburne had a reputation as a good businessman, said to be shrewd but fair.

'My personal views aren't of interest to anyone. Who could have told you that?'

'Dr Barr.'

He remembered their conversation with Dr Naismith at the Medical Society meeting. He saw Cliburne glance about to make certain they continued to have privacy.

'Although our state has barred slavery, Illinois law officers recognize the right of those in other states to own slaves. Therefore, slaves who have run away from Southern states are apprehended here and returned to their masters. They are treated cruelly. I have seen with my own eyes a large house in Springfield which has been filled with tiny cells, each containing heavy manacles and leg irons attached to the walls.

'Some of us . . . people of like mind, who agree on the evils of slavery, are working to assist those who have run away to seek liberty. We invite thee to join us in God's work.'

Rob J. was waiting for Cliburne to say more, and finally he realized some kind of offer had been made.

'Assist them . . . how?'

'We don't know where they come from. We don't know where they go from here. They are brought to us and taken away only on moonless nights. Thee need to prepare a safe hiding place large enough for one man. A root cellar, a cranny, a hole in the ground. Sufficient food for three or four days.'

Rob J. took no time to consider. He shook his head. 'I'm sorry.'

The expression on Cliburne's face contained neither surprise nor resentment, yet was somehow familiar. 'Will thee keep the confidence of our talk?'

'Yes. Yes, of course.'

Cliburne breathed and nodded. 'May God walk with thee,' he said, and they braced against the heat and stepped out of the shade.

Two days later the Geigers came to the Cole house for Sunday dinner. The Cole boys loved it when they came, because then dinner was lavish. At first Sarah had resented it when she had noted that whenever the Geigers dined with her they had refused her roasts, protecting their *kashruth*. But she had come to understand, and to compensate. When they came to dinner she always offered extras, a meatless soup, additional puddings and vegetables, and several desserts.

Jay brought with him a copy of the Rock Island *Weekly Guardian* that contained a story about the Dred Scott legal case, and he commented that the slave's lawsuit had little or no chance of success.

'Malcolm Howard says that back in Louisiana, everybody owns slaves,' Alex said, and his mother smiled.

'Not everybody,' she said thinly. 'I doubt if Malcolm Howard's poppa ever owned slaves or much of anything else.'

'Did your poppa own slaves back in Virginia?' Shaman asked.

'My poppa only had a small lumber mill,' Sarah said. 'He had three slaves, but then times got hard and he had to sell the slaves and the mill both, and go to work for *his* poppa, who had a big farm with more'n forty slaves to work it.'

'How about my poppa's family in Virginia?' Alex said.

'My first husband's family were storekeepers,' Sarah said. 'They didn't keep slaves.'

'Why would someone want to be a slave, anyway?' Shaman asked.

'They don't want to be,' Rob J. told his son. 'They're just poor unfortunate people caught in a bad situation.'

Jay took a drink of well water and pursed his lips. 'See, Shaman, it's just the way things are, the way they've been in the South for two hundred years. There are radicals who write that black folks should be set free. But if a state like South Carolina turned 'em all loose, how would they live? See, now they work for the white folks, and the white folks care for 'em. A few years back, Lillian's cousin, Judah

282

Benjamin, had a hundred and forty slaves on his sugar plantation in Louisiana. And he looked after them real well. My father in Charleston has two house nigras. He's owned 'em most of my life. He treats those two so kindly, I know they wouldn't leave him even if they were driven away.'

'Exactly,' Sarah said. Rob J. opened his mouth, then closed it again and passed the peas and carrots to Rachel. Sarah went out to the kitchen and came back bearing a gigantic potato pudding baked to Lillian Geiger's recipe, and Jay groaned that he was full, but passed his plate anyway.

When the Geigers took their children home, Jay urged Rob J. to come also, so Lillian could join them in playing trios. But he told Jay he was tired.

The truth was, he was feeling unsociable, snappish. To shake the mood, he stalked down to the river for the breeze. At Makwa's grave he noted weeds and made short work of them, pulling savagely until they were gone.

He realized why the expression on George Cliburne's face had been familiar. It was identical to the expression that had been on Andrew Gerould's face the first time he had asked Rob to write the broadside against the English administration and had been refused. The features of both men had been captive to a mixture of feelings – fatalism, stubborn strength, and the uneasiness of knowing that they had made themselves vulnerable to his character and his continued silence.

34
The Return

On a morning when the dawn mist hung like heavy steam over the river and clung to the strip of woodland, Shaman wandered out of the house and bypassed the outhouse to piss languidly into the larger flow. An orange disk was burning through the upper reaches of the fog and turning the lower layers into pale dazzle. The world was new and cool and smelled good, and what he was able to see of the river and woods matched the permanent peace in his ears. If fishing was going to be done that day, it would have to be early, he told himself.

The boy turned from the river. Between him and the house was the grave, and when he saw the figure through the tatters of fog he felt no fear, only a quick struggle between disbelief and an overwhelming rush of the sweetest kind of happiness and thanksgiving. *Ghost, I call you today. Ghost, I speak to you now.* 'Makwa!' he called joyfully, and moved forward.

'Shaman?'

When he reached her, his first crushing realization was that it wasn't Makwa.

'Moon?' he said, the name a question because she looked so bad.

Behind Moon, then, he saw two other figures, two men. One was an Indian he didn't know, and the other was Stone

Dog, who had worked for Jay Geiger. Stone Dog was bare-chested and wore deerskin pants. The stranger wore home-spun pants and a ragged shirt. Both men had on moccasins, but Moon wore white man's work boots and an old and dirty blue dress, torn at the right shoulder. The men were carrying things Shaman recognized, a cloth of cheese, a smoked ham, an uncooked leg of mutton, and he realized they had broken into the springhouse.

'Get whisky?' Stone Dog said, motioning toward the house, and Moon said something sharply in Sauk and then sagged.

'Moon, you all right?' Shaman asked.

'Shaman. So big.' She looked at him with wonder.

He knelt by her. 'Where you been? Are the others here too?'

'No . . . others in Kansas. Reservation. Left children there, but . . .' She closed her eyes.

'I'm going to get my father,' he said, and the eyes opened.

'They did us so bad, Shaman,' she whispered. Her hands scrabbled for his, hung on tight.

Shaman felt something pass from her body into his mind. As if he could hear again and thunder had clapped, and he knew – somehow, *knew* – what was going to happen to her. His hands tingled. He opened his mouth but couldn't yell, couldn't warn her. He was frozen by a fear that was entirely new to him, more savage than the terror of new deafness, far worse than anything he had experienced in his life.

Finally he was able to thrust her hands away.

He fled toward the house as if it was his only chance.

'*Pa!*' he screamed.

Rob J. was accustomed to being awakened to deal with emergency, but not by his son's hysteria. Shaman kept babbling that Moon was back and she was dying. It took several minutes to comprehend his story and to persuade him to focus on their mouths so his parents could ask him questions. When they understood that Moon actually had returned and was very sick, lying on the ground down by the river, they hurried out of the house.

285

The mist was disappearing fast. There was more visibility, and they could see very clearly that now no one was there. His parents questioned Shaman closely and repeatedly. Moon and Stone Dog and another Sauk had been there, he insisted. He went over what they were wearing, what they had said, how they looked.

Sarah hurried away when she heard what the Indians were carrying, and she came back angry because the springhouse had been violated and certain hard-earned foodstuffs were missing. 'Robert Cole,' she said crankily, 'did you take those things yourself because of some mischief, and then make up that story about the Sauks being back?'

Rob J. walked up the riverbank and then downstream, calling Moon's name, but nobody answered.

Shaman was weeping uncontrollably. 'She's dying, Pa.'

'Well, how can you know that?'

'She was holdin' onto my hands, and she . . .' The boy shuddered.

Rob J. stared at his son and sighed. He nodded. He went to Shaman and put his arms around him and hugged him hard. 'Don't you be frightened. It's not your fault, what happened to Moon. I'm going to talk to you about this, and try to explain. First, though, I think I'd better try to find her,' he said.

He searched on horseback. All morning he concentrated on the thick fringe of forest along the riverbanks, because if he were fleeing and wanted to hide, the woods were where he'd have gone. He rode north first, toward Wisconsin, and then came back and rode south. Every little while he'd call her name, but he never heard an answering shout.

It was possible he came close to them as he searched. The three Sauks could have waited in nearby undergrowth, letting Rob J. ride by, perhaps several times. In the early afternoon he admitted to himself that he didn't know how fugitive Sauks would think, because he wasn't a fugitive Sauk. Perhaps they'd left the river right away. There was summer's-end growth on the prairie, tall grasses that would

286

mask the progress of three people, and cornfields where the crops were grown a foot taller than a man's head, providing perfect cover.

When finally he gave it up, he went home and found Shaman, whose disappointment was evident when he learned his father's search had been fruitless.

He sat alone with the boy under a riverside tree and told him about the Gift, how it had come to some in the Cole family for as long as anyone remembered.

'Not to everybody. Sometimes it'll skip a generation. My father had it, but not my brother or my uncle. It comes to some Coles when they're really young.'

'Do you have it, Pa?'

'Yes I do.'

'How old were you, when . . .'

'It didn't come to me until I was almost five years older than you are now.'

'What *is* it?' the boy said faintly.

'Well, Shaman . . . I don't really know. I know there's nothing magical about it. I believe it's a kind of sense, like seeing or hearing or smelling. Some of us are able to hold a person's hands and be able to tell if they're dying. I think it's just an extra sensitivity, like being able to feel the pulse when you touch different parts of the body. Sometimes . . .' He shrugged. 'Sometimes it's a knack that comes in handy, if you're a doctor.'

Shaman nodded shakily. 'I guess it'll come in handy when I become a doctor myself.'

Rob J. faced the fact that if the boy was old enough to learn of the Gift, he was mature enough to face other things. 'You're not going to be a doctor, Shaman,' he said gently. 'A doctor has to be able to hear. I use my hearing every day in treating patients. I listen to their chests, I listen to their breathing, I listen to the quality of their voices. A doctor has to be able to hear a call for help. A doctor simply needs all five senses.'

He hated the way his son looked at him.

'Then what will I do when I'm a man?'

'This is a good farm. You can farm it with Bigger,' Rob J.

287

said, but the boy shook his head.

'Well, then, you can become some kind of businessman, maybe work in a store. Miss Burnham says you're about the brightest pupil she's ever taught. You might want to teach school yourself.'

'No, I don't want to teach school.'

'Shaman, you're still a boy. There are several years before you have to decide. Meantime, keep your eyes peeled. Study different men, their occupations. There are lots of ways to earn a living. You can choose anything.'

'Except,' Shaman said.

Rob J. wouldn't allow himself to open the boy to unnecessary heartache by holding out the possibility of a dream he truly didn't believe could be realized.

'Yes. Except,' he said firmly.

It had been a sorry day that had left Rob J. with an anger at life's unfairness. He hated to kill his child's bright and good dream. It was as bad as telling someone who loves life that there is no use making long-term plans.

He wandered about the farm. Near the river the mosquitoes were bad, contesting him for the shade of trees, and winning.

He knew he'd never see Moon again. He wished he could have said goodbye. He'd have asked her where Comes Singing had been buried. He would have wanted to bury them both properly, but by now Moon, too, perhaps had been abandoned in an unmarked grave. Like burying dogshit.

It made him savage to think about it, and guilty, because he was part of their problems and so was this farm. Once the Sauks had had rich farms, and Villages of the Dead in which the graves were marked.

They did us so bad, she had told Shaman.

There was a good Constitution in America, and he had read it carefully. It gave liberty, but he recognized that it worked only for people in skins whose colour ran from pink to tan. People with darker skins might as well have fur or feathers.

288

All the time he wandered around the farm, he was searching. He didn't know it at first, and then when he recognized what he was doing, he felt a wee bit better, but not very much. The place he wanted should not be located in the fields or woods where Alden or one of the boys, or even a poaching hunter, could stumble on it. The house itself was unsuitable because he'd need to maintain secrecy from the others in the family, something that bothered him greatly. His dispensary was sometimes deserted, but when it was in use it was crowded with patients. The barn was frequented, too. But . . .

At the back of the barn, separated from the milking parlour by a closed wall, was a long narrow shed. Rob J.'s shed. It was the place where he stored drugs, tonics, and other medicinals. Along with all the hung herbs and shelves full of bottles and jars, he kept a wooden table here, and an extra set of drainage pans, because when he was called upon to autopsy, he did the dissecting in the shed, which had a stout wooden door and a strong lock.

The narrow north wall of the shed, like the entire north wall of the barn proper, was built into a ridge. In the shed, part of the wall was ledge, but a section was earthen.

The following day was used up by a crowded dispensary and too many home visits, but the morning after that Rob J. was able to break free of his practice. It proved a fortuitous day, because both Shaman and Alden were repairing fence and building a lean-to feeding station in the far section, and Sarah was working on a project at the church. Only Kate Stryker, whom Sarah had hired as part-time house help after Moon had left, was in the house, and Kate wouldn't disturb him.

He carried in a pick and shovel as soon as the others had departed the area, and went right to work. It had been a little time since he had done extended physical labour, and he paced himself. The soil had rocks in it and was as heavy as most of the other soil on the farm, but he was strong and the pick loosened it with no difficulty. He shovelled it into a barrow from time to time and wheeled it a good distance from the barn, into a small gully. He had guessed that perhaps the digging would take several days, but by early afternoon he ran into ledge. The rocky wall jogged off to the north, so the excavation that resulted was only three feet deep at one end and more than five feet deep at the other, and less than five feet wide. The resultant space was scarcely large enough to lie down in, especially if food and other supplies were stored there, but Rob J. knew it would serve. He covered the opening with one-inch vertical planks that had been stacked outside for almost a year, so they appeared as old as the rest of the barn. He used an awl to make some of the nail holes a little too large, and he oiled the nails that fitted into the holes, so that several of the planks could be removed and replaced easily and without noise.

He was very careful, taking the barrow into the woods and digging leaf mold that he spread in the gully to disguise the new earth.

Then, next morning, he rode into Rock Island and had a brief but meaningful talk with George Cliburne.

35
The Secret Room

That fall the world began to change for Shaman, not an abrupt and startling alteration such as had occurred with the disappearance of his hearing, but a complex shifting of poles that was no less transforming for its gradualness. Alex and Mal Howard had become closest friends, and their laughing, boisterous companionship shut Shaman out much of the time. Rob J. and Sarah frowned on the friendship; they knew that Mollie Howard was a whining slattern and her husband, Julian, was shiftless, and they hated their son to be spending time at the crowded, messy Howard cabin, to which a good portion of the local population made its way to buy the home concoction Julian double-distilled from corn mash with great seriousness in a hidden evaporator with a rusty cover.

Their feelings of unease were given focus that Halloween when Alex and Mal sampled some of the whisky that Mal thoughtfully had misplaced while jugging his father's production. Thus inspired, they proceeded to create a path of pushed-over outhouses that extended through half the township before Alma Schroeder crawled out of her tipped privy, screaming, and Gus Schroeder ended their wet-cheeked hilarity by appearing with his buffalo gun.

The incident set off a series of grim conversations between Alex and his parents that Shaman did his best to wish away, because after watching the initial exchanges he couldn't bring himself to read their lips. A meeting of the boys, their fathers, and Sheriff London, was even more unpleasant.

Julian Howard spat and said it was 'a lot of fuss over a couple of young'uns raisin' a little hell on Halloween.'

Rob J. tried to forget his antipathy for Howard, whom he would have bet was a member of the Supreme Order of the Star-Spangled Banner if there was one in Holden's Crossing, and capable of raising a good deal of trouble on his own. He agreed with Howard that the boys weren't murderers or thugs, but because his work treated human digestion seriously he was inclined not to share the general point of view that anything and everything involved with shit was funny, including the destruction of outhouses. He knew Sheriff London came armed with half a dozen complaints against the boys and would act on them because he didn't like either of their fathers. Rob J. suggested that Alex and Mal be made responsible for setting things right. Three of the outhouses had splintered or come apart. Two shouldn't be set over the same holes, which were full. To make amends, the boys should dig holes and repair privies. If new lumber was needed, Rob J. would pay for it and Shaman and Mal could work off their debt to him on the farm. And if they failed to live up to the bargain, Sheriff London could take action.

Mort London reluctantly admitted he could find nothing wrong with the plan. Julian Howard was against it until he learned that both his son and the Cole boy would also be responsible for their usual chores, and then he agreed. Neither Alex nor Mal was given an opportunity to refuse, so over the next month they became expert in the rehabilitation of latrines, doing the digging first, before deep winter froze the ground, and performing the carpentry with hands that were numb with cold. They built well; all of 'their' privies would last for years, except the one behind the Humphrey's house that was splintered by the twister that levelled the house and barn too in the summer of '63, killing Irving and Letty Humphrey in the bargain.

Alex was irrepressible. Late one night he came into the bedroom he shared with Shaman, carrying the oil lamp, and announced with deep contentment that he'd done it.

'Done what?' Shaman said, blinking the sleep from his eyes so he could see his brother.

'You know. I've done it. With Pattie Drucker.'

Shaman was awake. 'You never. You damn liar, Bigger.'

'No, I did, with Pattie Drucker. Right there in her father's house, with her family off to her uncle's.'

Shaman gazed at him in delighted agony, unable to believe, yet excruciatingly tempted to do so. 'If you did, what was it like?'

Alex smiled at him smugly and addressed himself to the question. 'When you push your dingus in past the hair and everythin', it's warm and cozy. Very warm and cozy. But then it makes you all excited, somehow, and you move back and forth because you're so happy. Back and forth, just like the ram does the ewe.'

'Does the girl move back and forth too?'

'No,' Alex said. 'The girl lies there real happy, lets you do the movin'.'

'Then what happens?'

'Well, your eyes cross. The gizzum shoots outta your dick like a bullet.'

'Wow, like a bullet! Does it hurt the girl?'

'No, you fool, I meant fast like a bullet, not hard like a bullet. It's softer than puddin', just like when you pull your own. Anyway, by then things are pretty much over.'

Shaman had been convinced by a plethora of detail such as he'd never encountered. 'Does this mean Patty Drucker's your girl?'

'No!' Alex said.

'You sure?' Shaman said anxiously. Pattie Drucker already was almost as large as her pasty-faced mother and had a laugh like a bray.

'Too young to understand,' Alex muttered, worried and disgruntled, and blew out the lamp to cut the conversation short.

293

Shaman lay in the dark and thought about what Alex had said, equally excited and worried. He didn't like the eye-crossing part. Luke Stebbins had told him that if you played with yourself, you could go blind. Deaf was enough, he didn't want to lose any more of his senses. He could already have started to go blind, he told himself, and next morning he walked around in extreme anxiety, testing his vision on objects near and far.

The less time Bigger spent with him, the more time Shaman spent with books. He ran through books quickly and begged them shamelessly. The Geigers had a good library and allowed him to borrow. Books were what he received on his birthday and Christmas, fuel for the fire he burned against the cold of loneliness. Miss Burnham said she never had seen such a reader.

She worked him mercilessly to improve his speech. During school holidays she received free room and board at the Cole house, and Rob J. saw to it that her efforts on behalf of his son were rewarded, but she didn't work with Shaman for personal gain. His clear speech had become her personal goal. The drills with his hand on the piano went on and on. She was fascinated to see that from the beginning he was sensitive to the difference between the vibrations, and before long he was able to identify the notes as soon as she struck them.

Shaman's vocabulary grew because of the reading, but he had trouble with pronunciation, being unable to learn correct usage by listening to other voices. For example, he pronounced 'cathedral' as 'cath-a-*dral*', and she realized that part of his difficulty was ignorance of where to place emphasis. She used a rubber ball to demonstrate the problem to him, bouncing it softly to show ordinary stress and harder to demonstrate emphasis. Even that took time, for the ordinary activity of catching a bounced ball gave him great difficulty. Miss Burnham realized that she was pre-pared to catch the ball by the sound it made as it struck the floor. Shaman had no such preparation, and so had to learn to catch by memorizing the exact amount of time it took the ball to reach the floor and rebound to his hand when thrown with a given force.

Once he had come to identify the bouncing ball as representing emphasis, she worked out a series of drills with slate and chalk, printing words and then drawing small balls over syllables that received ordinary vocal stress, and larger balls over syllables to be accented:

Cath-e-dral. Good morn-ing. Pic-ture. Par-ty. A moun-tain.

Rob J. joined the effort by teaching Shaman to juggle, with Alex and Mal Howard often joining in the lessons. Rob had sometimes juggled for their entertainment, and they were amused and interested, but the skill came hard. Nevertheless, he encouraged them to keep at it. 'In Kilmarnock, all the Cole children are taught to juggle. It's an old family custom. If they can learn it, so can you,' he said, and they found he was right. To his disappointment, the Howard boy turned out to be the best juggler of the three, soon able to handle four balls. But Shaman was close behind, and Alex stuck to his practising doggedly until he could keep three balls aloft with aplomb. The purpose was not to produce a performer but to give Shaman a sense of varying rhythms, and it worked.

One afteroon, while Miss Burnham was at Lillian Geiger's piano with the boy, she took his hand from the piano box and placed it on her own throat. 'As I speak,' she said, 'the cords in my larynx vibrate, like the wire strings of the piano. Do you feel the vibrations, how they change with different words?'

He nodded raptly and they smiled at one another. 'Oh, Shaman,' Dorothy Burnham said, taking his hand from her throat and holding it in hers. 'You're making such fine progress! But you need constant drilling, more than I can afford to give when school's in session. Is there anyone who might be able to help?'

Shaman knew his father was busy with his practice. His mother occupied herself with her church work, and he sensed a reluctance on her part to deal with his deafness, puzzling to him but not imagined. And Alex was off with

Mal whenever freed from his chores.

Dorothy sighed. 'Whom can we find who is able to work with you regularly?'

'I'll gladly help,' a voice said at once. It came from a large horsehair wing chair that sat with its back to the piano, and to Dorothy's astonishment, she saw Rachel Geiger rise quickly from the chair and approach them.

How often, she wondered, had the girl sat undetected and listened to them at their drills and exercises?

'I know I can do it, Miss Burnham,' Rachel said somewhat breathlessly.

Shaman appeared to be pleased.

Dorothy smiled at Rachel and squeezed her hand. 'I'm certain you will do splendidly, my dear,' she said.

Rob J. had heard not a word from any of the letters he had sent out regarding Makwa's death. One night he sat down and transferred his frustration to paper, another letter with a sharper tone, trying to stir up the sticky mud.

'. . . *The crimes of rape and murder have been easily ignored by representatives of government and the law, a fact that raises the question of whether the State of Illinois – indeed, of whether the United States of America – is a realm of true civilization or a place where men are allowed to behave like the lowest beasts with perfect impunity.*' He mailed the letters to the same authorities he had already contacted, hoping that the new sharpness of tone would bring some results.

Nobody communicated to him about anything, he thought sulkily. He had dug the room off the shed almost in a frenzy, but now that it waited, he heard nothing from George Cliburne. At first, as days turned into weeks, he spent times pondering how word would be sent to him, then began to wonder why he was being ignored. He put the secret room out of his mind and gave himself up to the familiar shortening of the days, the sight of a long V of geese knifing southward through the blue air, the rushing sound of the river turning crystalline as the water grew colder. One morning he rode into the village and Carroll Wilkenson left a chair on the general-store porch and ambled to where Rob

296

J. was dismounting from a small droop-necked pinto.

'New horse, Doc?'

'Just trying her out. Our Vicky is almost blind now. Fine for riding children in the pasture, but . . . This girl belongs to Tom Beckermann.' He shook his head. Dr Beckermann had told him the pinto was five years old, but her bottom incisors were worn down so far he knew she was more than twice that age, and she shied at every insect and shadow.

'Partial to mares?'

'Not necessarily. Though they're steadier than stallions, for my money.'

'Think you're dead right. Dead right . . . I ran into George Cliburne yesterday. He said tell you he's got some new books out at his place, and you might be interested to take a look at them.'

It was the signal, and it took him by surprise. 'Thank you, Carroll. George has a wonderful library,' he said, hoping his voice was steady.

'Yes, he has.' Wilkenson lifted his hand in farewell. 'Well, I'll spread the word you're looking to buy a horse.'

'I'll be obliged,' Rob J. said.

After supper he memorized the sky until he ascertained there would be no moon. Thick, greasy clouds had scudded in all afternoon. The air felt like a laundry after a two-day washing, and promised rain before morning.

He went to bed early and managed a few hours of sleep, but he had the physician's ability to catnap briefly and by one o'clock he lay awake and alert. He gave himself leeway, pulling away from Sarah's warmth well before two o'clock. He'd gone to bed in his underwear, and he gathered his clothing quietly in the dark bedroom and carried it downstairs. Sarah was accustomed to his going forth to deal with patients at any and every hour, and she slept on undisturbed.

His boots were on the floor beneath his coat in the front hall. In the barn he saddled Queen Victoria, because he was riding only as far as the place where the Coles' house track met the public road, and Vicky knew the way so well she had no need for good sight. In his nervousness he left himself too much time, and for ten minutes after he had arrived at the road he sat and stroked the horse's neck while a light rain began to fall. He strained his ears to catch imagined noises, but at last sounds reached him that weren't imagined, the creak and jingle of harness, the hoof-falls of a plodding workhorse. In a little while the wagon took shape, heavy with loaded hay. 'Is it thee, then?' George Cliburne said calmly.

Rob J. fought the impulse to deny it was himself, and sat while Cliburne rummaged in the hay and a second human form emerged. Cliburne obviously had given the former slave prior instructions, because without conversation the man grasped the back of Vicky's saddle and heaved himself up behind Rob J.

'May thee go with God,' Cliburne said cheerfully, snapping his reins and starting the wagon on its way. At some past moment – perhaps several – the Negro had lost control of his bladder. Rob's experienced nose told him the urine had dried, probably days before, but he inched his body away from the ammoniac stink behind him. When they rode past the house, all was dark. He had intended to place the man in the dugout quickly, see to the horse, and re-enter his own warm bed. But once inside the shed, the process became more complicated.

When he lighted the lamp he saw a black male, perhaps between thirty and forty. With the fearful, wary eyes of an animal in a corner, a big beak of nose, uncombed hair like a black ram's wool. Wearing stout shoes, an adequate shirt, and pants so ragged and holey that more cloth was gone than remained.

Rob J. wanted to ask his name, where he'd run from, but Cliburne had cautioned: No questions, against the rules. He lifted off the boards, explained the contents of the burrow: covered pan for nature's needs, newspaper for wiping, jug of drinking water, bag of crackers. The Negro said nothing; he stopped and entered, Rob replaced the boards.

There was a pan of water on the cold stove. Rob J. laid and lit a fire. Hanging on a nail in the barn he found his oldest work trousers, which were too long and too large, and a pair of once-red braces now grey with dust, the kind of suspenders Alden called galluses. Rolled-up trousers could be dangerous if the wearer had to run, and he cut eight inches off both legs with his surgical scissors. By the time he'd seen to the horse, the water on the stovetop had warmed. He took off the boards again and transferred water, rags, soap, and trousers to the hole, and then replaced the boards, saw to the stove, blew out the lamp.

He hesitated before leaving. 'Goodnight,' he said to the boards. There was a rustling, the sound of a bear in a den, as the man washed. 'Thankeesuh,' the hoarse whisper came finally, as if somebody was talking in church.

The first guest at the inn, Rob J. thought of him. He stayed seventy-three hours. George Cliburne, his greeting relaxed and cheerful, his manner so polite it was almost formal, picked him up in the middle of another night and took him away. Although it was so dark Rob J. couldn't see details, he was certain the Quaker's hair was combed neatly across his bald pate and his pink jowls were as closely shaved as it if were noon.

About a week later, Rob J. was frightened that he, Cliburne, Dr Barr, and Carroll Wilkenson were all going to be arrested for abetting the theft of personal property, because he heard that an escaped slave had been apprehended by Mort London. But it turned out the man wasn't 'his' Negro, but a slave who'd escaped from Louisiana and hidden himself on a river barge without anyone's knowledge or help.

It was a good week for Mort London. A few days after he received a cash award for returning the slave, Nick Holden rewarded his longtime loyalty by getting him appointed a deputy United States marshal in Rock Island. London resigned as sheriff at once, and at his recommendation Mayor Anderson appointed his only deputy, Fritzie Graham, to fill the office until the next election. Rob J. wasn't fond of Graham, but the first time they ran into one another, the new acting sheriff wasted no time in indicating that he wasn't interested in carrying on Mort London's squabbles.

'Certainly hope you'll become active again as a coroner, Doc. Real active.'

'I'll be glad to,' Rob J. said. It was the truth, because he'd sorely missed the opportunities to keep his surgical techniques honed by doing the dissections.

Thus encouraged, he couldn't resist asking Graham to reopen the case of Makwa's murder, but gained only a look of such wary disbelief that he knew the answer, even though Fritzie promised to 'do whatever I can, you may be sure of that, sir.'

Thick, milky cataracts filled Queen Victoria's eyes, and the gentle old mare could no longer see at all. If she were younger he would have operated to remove the cataracts, but her work-strength was gone and he saw no reason to inflict pain. Nor would he put her down, because she seemed content to remain in pasture, where everyone on the farm sooner or later stopped by to feed her an apple or a carrot.

The family had to have a horse to use when he was away. The other mare, Bess, was older than Vicky and would have to be replaced soon too, and he continued to keep his eyes open for likely horseflesh. He was a creature of habit and hated to depend on a new animal, but finally in November he bought a general-use horse from the Schroeders, a small bay mare neither young nor old, for a price reasonable enough so that he wouldn't feel the loss if she wasn't what they wanted. The Schroeders had called her Trude, and he and Sarah saw no need to change her name. He took short rides on her, waiting for her to disappoint, but deep down he knew Alma and Gus wouldn't have sold him a bad horse.

On a crisp afternoon he rode her on his rounds, house calls that took them all over the township and beyond. She was smaller than either Vicky or Bess and seemed bonier under his saddle, but she responded well and wasn't a nervous animal. By the time they came home in the dusk of early evening, he knew she would do very well, and he took his time rubbing her down and giving her water and feed.

The Schroeders had spoken only German to her. Rob J. had talked to her in English all day, but now he patted her flank and grinned. *'Gute Nacht, meine gnadige Liebchen,'* he said, recklessly expending his German vocabulary all at once.

He took the lantern and started to leave the barn, but as he was framed by the door there was a loud report. He hesitated, trying to identify it, striving to believe that any other sound could be similar to a rifle shot, but immediately after the powder clap there was a simultaneous thud and a snicking as a hickory silver was knocked from the barn-door lintel by the slug, not eight inches above his head.

Returned to his senses, he stepped quickly back inside and blew out the lantern.

He heard the back door of the house open and slam, heard feet running. 'Pa? You all right?' Alex called.

'Yes. Get back in the house.'

'What –'

'*Now!*'

Steps retreated, the door opened and slammed. Peering out at the gloom, he took note of his trembling. The three horses moved restlessly in their stalls, and Vicky whickered. Time froze.

'Dr Cole?' Alden's voice approached. 'You fire a shot?'

'No, somebody fired and hit the barn. Damn near hit me.'

'You stay in there,' Alden called crisply.

Rob J. knew the way the hired man's mind worked. It would take him too long to get to the goose gun in his own cabin; instead, he'd fetch the hunting rifle from the Cole house. Rob heard his steps, his cautionary, 'It's only me,' and the door opening and closing.

. . . And opening again. He heard Alden walking away, and then nothing. A century passed in maybe seven minutes, and footsteps came back to the barn.

'Nobody out there now that I can see, Dr Cole, and I looked pretty good. Whereabouts did it hit?' When Rob J. pointed out the slivered lintel, Alden had to stand on tiptoe to touch it. Neither of them lit the lantern to see it better. 'What in the world?' Alden said shakily, his face pale in the gathering darkness. 'Never mind that he was poachin' on

301

your land. To hunt that close to the house, and without proper daylight. If I ever find that fool, he'll be a sorry marksman!'

'No harm done. I'm glad you were here,' Rob J. said, touching his shoulder. They went into the house together to soothe the family and to put the near-accident behind them. Rob J. poured Alden a brandy and joined him, a rare happening.

Sarah had made a supper he loved, green peppers and young squash, both stuffed with spiced ground meat and stewed with potatoes and carrots. He ate with appetite and complimented his wife's cooking, but afterwards he sought solitude in a chair on the porch.

It wasn't any hunter, he knew, to be so careless near a house, and to hunt in poor visibility at the end of the day.

He considered a possible connection between the incident and the dugout room, and concluded there was none; anyone who wanted to make trouble because he helped escaped slaves would wait until the next Negro arrived. Then they'd have foolish Dr Cole arrested and collect bounty money on the slave.

Yet Rob couldn't escape a growing awareness that the shot had been a warning somebody wanted him to think about.

There was a high moon: a bright darkness, not a night to be moving hunted people. Sitting and staring out, studying the sudden leaping moon shadows of wind-tossed trees, he acknowledged his certain intuition that at last he'd been sent an answer to his letters.

302

36
The First Jew

Rachel feared the Day of Atonement but loved Passover because the eight days of Pesach more than made up for the fact that other people had Christmas. On Passover the Geigers remained in their own home, which seemed to her to be a haven filled with a warm light. It was a holiday of music and singing and games, of frightening biblical stories with happy endings, and of special food at the Seder, with matzos shipped in from Chicago and her mother baked a series of sponge cakes so tall and light that as a child she believed her father when he told her to watch hard and she would see them float away.

In contrast, for Rosh Hashana and Yom Kippur, every autumn the family packed up, after weeks of planning and preparation, and travelled for most of a day, by wagon to Galesburg, then by train to a wharf on the Illinois River, and down the Illinois by steamboat to Peoria, where there was a Jewish community and a synagogue. Though they came to Peoria only for the two holy weeks out of the year, they were dues-paying members of the congregation, with seats reserved in their names. During the High Holidays, the Geigers always boarded at the home of Morris Goldwasser, a textile merchant who was a prominent member of the *shul*. Everything about Mr Goldwasser was large and expansive, including his body, his family, and his house. He wouldn't accept payment from Jason, pointing out that it was a *mitzvah* to make it possible for another Jew to worship God, and insisting that if the Geigers paid for his hospitality they would deprive him of a blessing. So each year Lillian and Jason worried for weeks about a suitable gift that would demonstrate their appreciation.

Rachel hated the entire production that blighted each autumn – the preparation, the worry about the selection of the gift, the exhausting journey, the ordeal of surviving two weeks of each year in the home of strangers, the pain and light-headedness of the twenty-four-hour Yom Kippur fast.

For her parents, each visit to Peoria was an opportunity to renew their Jewishness. They were sought after socially, because Lillian's cousin, Judah Benjamin, had been elected United States senator from Louisiana – the first Jewish member of the Senate – and everyone wanted to discuss him with the Geigers. They went to synagogue at every opportunity. Lillian exchanged recipes, caught up on gossip. Jay talked politics with the men, drank a convivial *schnapps* or two, exchanged cigars. He spoke to them of Holden's Crossing in glowing terms and admitted he was trying to attract other Jews there, so eventually there would be a *minyan* of ten men, allowing him access to group worship. The other men treated him with warm understanding. Of them all, only Jay and Ralph Seixas, who was born in Newport, Rhode Island, were native Americans. The others had come from abroad and knew what it was to be pioneers. It was hard, they agreed, for a man to be the first Jew to settle anywhere.

The Goldwassers had two plump daughters, Rose, who was a year older than Rachel, and Clara, who was three years older. When Rachel was a little girl she had enjoyed playing games (House, School, and Grown-up) with the Goldwasser girls, but the year Rachel turned twelve, Clara married Harold Green, a hatmaker. The couple lived with Clara's parents, and that year when the Geigers came for the High Holidays, Rachel found changes. Clara no longer would play Grown-up, because she had become a real grown-up, a Married Woman. She talked softly and condescendingly to

304

her sister and Rachel, she waited upon her husband with sweet constancy, and she was allowed to say the blessings over the Sabbath candles, an honour reserved for the matron of the home. But one night when the three girls were alone in the big house, they drank grape wine in Rose's room and fifteen-year-old Clara Goldwasser Green forgot she was a matron. She told Rachel and her sister all about what it was like to be married. She divulged for them the most sacred secrets of the adult sorority, dwelling with delicious detail on the physiology and habits of the Jewish male.

Both Rose and Rachel had seen the penis, but always in miniature, attached to infant brothers or young cousins, babies in the bath – a soft, pink appendage ending in a circumcised knob of smooth flesh dotted with a single hole so the pee could come out.

But Clara, draining the wine with her eyes closed, wickedly outlined the differences between Jewish babies and Jewish men. And, finding the last drops on the outside of the cup with her tongue, she described the transformation of sweet and inoffensive flesh when a Jewish man lay down next to his wife, and what subsequently occurred.

Nobody screamed in terror, but Rose had taken her pillow and was pressing it into her face with both hands. 'This happens often?' her muffled voice asked.

Very often, Clara affirmed, and without fail on the Sabbath and religious holidays, God having informed the Jewish male that it was a blessing. 'Except, of course, during the bleeding.'

Rachel knew about the bleeding. It was the only secret her mother had told her; it hadn't happened to her yet, a fact she didn't share with the sisters. But she was troubled by something else, a matter of the mechanics of measurement, of common sense, and she had been visualizing a disturbing diagram in her mind. Unconsciously she protected her lap with her hand. 'Surely,' she said palely, 'it is not possible to do that.'

Sometimes, Clara informed them loftily, her Harold employed pure kosher butter.

Rose Goldwasser removed the pillow from her face and

305

stared, her face alight with revelation. 'That is why we are always running out of butter?' she cried.

The days that followed were particularly difficult for Rachel. She and Rose, given the choice of regarding Clara's disclosures as horrifying or comical, in self-defence opted for comedy. During breakfast and lunch, which usually were dairy meals, they had only to meet each other's gaze to engender explosions of mirth so witless that on several occasions they were sent from the table in disgrace. At dinner, when the two families were joined by their men, it was worse for her, for she couldn't sit across the table and two chairs down from Harold Green, and look at him, and make conversation, without thinking of him buttered.

On the following year when the Geigers visited Peoria, Rachel was disappointed to learn that neither Clara nor Rose lived in their parents' home any longer. Clara and Harold had become parents of a baby boy and had moved into a small house of their own on the river bluff; when they came to the Goldwasser's, Clara busied herself with her son and paid little attention to Rachel. Rose had been married the previous July, to a man named Samuel Bielfield, who had taken her to live in St Louis.

That Yom Kippur, standing outside the synagogue, Rachel and her parents were approached by an elderly man named Benjamin Schoenberg. Mr Schoenberg wore a stovepipe hat of beaver felt, a ruffled white cotton shirt, and a black string tie. He chatted with Jay about the state of the pharmaceuticals business and then began to question Rachel pleasantly about her schooling and the extent to which she helped run her mother's household.

Lillian Geiger smiled at the old man and shook her head enigmatically. 'It is too soon,' she said, and Mr Schoenberg smiled back and nodded, and went away after a few more pleasantries.

That evening Rachel overheard snatches of conversation between her mother and Mrs Goldwasser which revealed that Benjamin Schoenberg was a *shadchen*, a marriage broker. Indeed, Mr Schoenberg had arranged the matches of both Clara and Rose. She felt terrible fear, but it was relieved by the memory of what her mother had told the matchmaker. She was too young for marriage, as her parents fully realized, she told herself, disregarding the fact that Rose Goldwasser Bielfield was only eight months older.

All that autumn, including the two weeks she spent in Peoria, Rachel's body was changing. When her breasts developed, they were womanly from the start, throwing her thin body out of balance, so she had to learn about support garments, and muscle fatigue and back pains. That was the year when Mr Byers touched her and made her life ugly before her father set things right. When Rachel examined herself in her mother's looking glass she was reassured that no man would want a girl with straight black hair, narrow shoulders, a neck that was too long, breasts that were too heavy, skin unfashionably sallow, and undistinguished brown cow's eyes.

Then it occurred to her that any man who would accept such a girl would be ugly himself, and stupid, and very poor, and she knew that every day brought her closer to a future she didn't wish to contemplate. She resented her brothers and treated them spitefully because they didn't know what gifts and privileges they had been given with their masculinity, the right to live in the warm safety of their parents' home as long as they wanted, the right to go to school and learn without limits.

Her menstruation came late. Her mother had asked her casual questions from time to time, revealing her concern that it hadn't happened yet; and then one afternoon while Rachel was in the kitchen helping to make wild-strawberry jam, with no warning, cramps made her double over. Her mother told her to look, and the blood was there. Her heart had pounded, but it wasn't unexpected, nor had it happened while she was off alone somewhere. Her mother was with her and spoke soothingly, and showed her what to do. Everything was all right until her mother kissed her cheek and told her that now she was a woman.

Rachel began to cry. She couldn't stop. She wept for hours

and was inconsolable. Jay Geiger came into his daughter's room and lay down on her bed with her as he hadn't done since she was little.

He stroked her head and asked what was the matter. Her shoulders shook in a way that broke his heart, and he had to ask her again and again.

Finally she whispered, 'Poppa. I don't want to be married. I don't want to leave you, or my home.'

Jay kissed her cheek and went to talk with his wife. Lillian was very troubled. Many girls were married at thirteen, and she thought it would be better for her daughter if they arranged her life through a good Jewish union than if they indulged her foolish terror. But her husband pointed out that when he had been matched with Lillian she had been past her sixteenth birthday, not a young girl. What was good for the mother would be good for the daughter, who needed a chance to grow up and become accustomed to the thought of marriage.

So Rachel had a long reprieve. At once, her life was better. Miss Burnham reported to her father that she was a natural student and would benefit greatly from continuing her education. Her parents decided that she should stay in the academy instead of working full-time in the house and on the farm, as might have been expected, and they were gratified by her pleasure, and by the way life returned to her eyes.

She had an instinctive kindness that was part of her nature, but her own unhappiness had made her particularly sensitive to those trapped by circumstances. She had always been as close to the Coles as if they were related by blood. When Shaman was a toddler, once he had been placed in her bed and had lost control of his bladder, and it had been Rachel who had comforted him and eased his embarrassment, and protected him from the teasing of the other children. The illness that had stolen his hearing had unsettled her, because it was the first incident in her life that indicated to her the presence of unknown and unsuspected dangers. She had watched Shaman's struggles with the frustration of someone who wanted to make things better but was powerless to do so, and she witnessed each improvement that he achieved with as much pride and gladness as if he were her brother. During the period of her own development she'd seen Shaman change from a little boy to a large youth, easily outstripping his brother, Alex, in size. Because his body matured early, in the first years of growth he was often clumsy and bumbling, like a puppy with new growth, and she regarded him with a special tenderness.

She had sat undetected in the wing chair several times and marvelled at Shaman's courage and tenaciousness, listening in fascination to Dorothy Burnham's skill as a teacher. When Miss Burnham had wondered who could help him, Rachel had reacted instinctively, eager for the chance. Dr Cole and his wife had been grateful for her willingness to work with Shaman, and her own family had been pleased by what they considered a generous gesture. But she understood that, at least in part, she wanted to help him because he was her steadfast friend, because once, in perfect seriousness, a little boy had offered to kill a man who was doing her harm.

The basis of Shaman's remedial work was long hours piled upon long hours, in which weariness had to be disregarded, and he was quick to test Rachel's authority in ways he wouldn't have tried with Miss Burnham. 'No more today. I'm too tired now,' he said the second time they met alone, after Miss Burnham had accompanied Rachel through Shaman's drills half a dozen times.

'No, Shaman,' Rachel had said firmly. 'We're not nearly finished.' But he had escaped.

The second time it happened, she'd given in to anger that had merely made him smile, and reverted to their playmate days, calling him names. But when it happened again the next day, tears sprang into her eyes and he was undone.

'Let's try it again, then,' he'd told her reluctantly.

Rachel was grateful, but she never yielded to the temptation of controlling him in that way, sensing he would benefit more from a steelier approach. After a while, the

309

long hours became routine for them both. As the months passed and Shaman's capabilities were expanded, she adapted Miss Burnham's drills and they went beyond them.

They spent a long time practising how meaning could be changed by accenting different words in an otherwise unchanged sentence:

The child is sick.

The child is sick.

The child is sick.

Sometimes Rachel held his hand and squeezed it to show him where emphasis belonged, and he enjoyed that. He'd come to dislike the piano exercise in which he identified the note by the vibrations he felt in his hand, because his mother had seized upon it as a a parlour trick and sometimes called upon him to perform. But Rachel continued to work with him at the piano, and she was fascinated when she played the scale in a different key and he was able to detect even that subtle change.

Slowly he graduated from feeling the notes of the piano to discerning the other vibrations in the world around him. Soon he could detect somebody knocking at the door, although he didn't hear the knocking. He was able to feel the footsteps of someone mounting a stairway, although they were unnoticed by hearing people nearby.

One day, as Dorothy Burnham had done, Rachel took his large hand and placed it at her throat. At first she spoke to him loudly. Then she moderated the sonority of her voice and dropped it into a whisper. 'Do you feel the difference?'

Her flesh was warm and very smooth, delicate yet strong. Shaman could feel muscles and cords. He thought of a swan, and then of a tinier bird as the beat of her pulse fluttered against his hand in a way that hadn't happened when he'd held Miss Burnham's thicker, shorter neck.

He smiled at her. 'I do,' he said.

37
Water Marks

Nobody else shot at Rob J. If the incident at the barn had been a message that he should stop pressuring for an investigation of Makwa's death, whoever had pulled the trigger had reason to believe the warning was heeded. He did nothing else because he knew of nothing else he could do. Eventually polite letters came from Congressman Nick Holden and from the governor of Illinois. They were the only officials to answer him, and their replies were bland dismissals. He brooded, but he addressed himself to more immediate problems.

In the beginning, he was called upon only infrequently to offer the hospitality of his dugout room, but after he'd been helping slaves to run away for several years the trickle grew to a freshet, and there were times when new occupants came to the secret room often and regularly.

There was general and controversial interest in Negroes. Dred Scott had won his plea for freedom in a Missouri lower court, but the State Supreme Court declared him still a slave, and his abolitionist attorneys appealed the case to the Supreme Court of the United States. Meanwhile, writers and preachers thundered, and journalists and politicians fulminated on both sides of the slavery issue. The first thing Fritz Graham did after he was elected to a regular five-year term as sheriff was buy a pack of 'nigger hounds', because bounties had become a lucrative sideline. Rewards for the return of runaways had increased in size, and penalties for helping fugitive slaves had grown more severe. Rob J. continued to be frightened when he thought of what could happen to him if he were caught, but mostly he didn't allow himself to think of it.

George Cliburne greeted him with sleepy politeness whenever they encountered one another by chance, as though they weren't meeting under different circumstances in the dark of night. A by-product of the association was Rob J.'s access to Cliburne's extensive library, and he availed himself of volumes that he regularly carried home for Shaman, and sometimes read himself. The grain broker's book collection was heavy in philosophy and religion but light in science, which was how Rob J. found its owner.

When he'd been a Negro-smuggler for about a year, Cliburne invited him to attend a Quaker meeting and was diffident and accepting when he refused. 'I thought thee might find it helpful. Since thee does the work of the Lord.'

It was on Rob's lips to correct him, to say he did the work of man and not of God; but the thought was pompous enough without putting it to voice, and he merely smiled and shook his head.

He realized his hiding was only one link in what doubtless was a large chain, but he had no knowledge of the rest of the system. He and Dr Barr never referred to the fact that the other physician's recommendation had led him to become a lawbreaker. His only clandestine contacts were with Cliburne and with Carroll Wilkenson, who told him whenever the Quaker had 'an interesting new book.' Rob J. was certain that when the runaways left him they were taken north, through Wisconsin and into Canada. Probably by boat across Lake Superior. That's the way he would route the escapes if he were doing the planning.

Once in a while Cliburne would bring a female, but most of the fugitives were men. They came in infinite variety, dressed in ragged tow cloth. Some had skins of such negritude it seemed to him the very definition of blackness, the shiny purple of ripe plums, the jet of burnt bone, the

312

dense darkness of ravens' wings. The complexions of others showed a dilution with the paleness of their oppressors, resulting in shades that ranged from café au lait to the colour of toasted bread. Most of them were large men with hard, muscular bodies, but one was a slender young man, almost white, who wore metal-rimmed spectacles. He said he was the son of a house nigger and a plantation owner in a place called Shreve's Landing, in Louisiana. He could read and was grateful when Rob J. gave him candles and matches and back copies of Rock Island newspapers.

Rob J. felt thwarted as a physician because he kept the fugitives too short a time to treat their physical problems. He could tell that the lenses of the light-skinned Negro's spectacles were far too powerful for him. Weeks after the youth had left him, Rob J. found a pair of eyeglasses he thought might be better. Next time he was in Rock Island he went to see Cliburne and asked if he could somehow arrange to forward the glasses, but Cliburne only stared at the spectacles and shook his head. 'Thee must have better sense, Dr Cole,' he said, and walked away without saying good day.

On another occasion a large man with very black skin stayed in the secret room for three days, more than long enough for Rob to observe that he was nervous and suffered from abdominal discomfort. Sometimes his face was grey and sick-looking, and his appetite was irregular. Rob was certain he had a tapeworm. He gave him a bottle of specific but told him not to take it until he arrived wherever he was going. 'Otherwise you'll be too weak to travel, and you'll leave a trail of loose stool that every sheriff in the country can follow!'

He would remember each of them as long as he lived. He felt an immediate sympathy for their fears and their feelings, and it was more than the fact that once he'd been a fugitive himself; he realized that an important ingredient of his concern was his family and their plight, because he had witnessed the afflictions of the Sauks.

He had long since ignored Cliburne's orders that they weren't to be questioned. Some were loquacious and some

313

tight-lipped. At the very least, he tried to get their names. Although the youth with the glasses had been named Nero, most of the names were Judeo-Christian: Moses, Abraham, Isaac, Aaron, Peter, Paul, Joseph. He heard the same names again and again, reminding him of the stories Makwa had told him about the biblical names at the Christian school for Indian girls.

He spent as much time with the talkative ones as safety would allow. One man from Kentucky had escaped once before and had been caught. He showed Rob J. the scarred stripes on his back. Another, from Tennessee, said he hadn't been treated badly by his master. Rob J. asked why he had run in that case, and the man pursed his lips and squinted, as if searching for the answer.

'Cudden wait for Jubilee,' he said.

Rob asked Jay about Jubilee. In ancient Palestine, every seventh year agricultural land was allowed to lie fallow and replenish itself, in accordance with the dictates of the Bible. After seven sabbatical years, the fiftyith year was declared a year of jubilee, and slaves were given a gift and set free.

Rob J. suggested Jubilee was better than keeping humans in perpetual servitude but hardly the ultimate kindness, since in most case fifty years of slavery was more than a lifetime.

He and Jay circulated each other warily on the topic, having learned long ago the depth of their differences.

'Do you know how many slaves there are in the Southern states? Four million. That's one black skin for every two white skins. Free them, and the farms and plantations that feed a lot of abolitionists up North will have to close. And then what would we do with those four million black folks? How would they live? What would they become?'

'Eventually they'd live same as anybody. If they got some education, they could become anything. Pharmacists, for instance,' he said, unable to resist.

Jay shook his head. 'You simply don't understand. The South's very existence depends on slavery. That's why even nonslave states make it a crime to aid runaways.'

314

Jay had struck a nerve. 'Don't talk to me about crime! The African slave trade's been outlawed since 1808, but African people are still being taken at gunpoint and stuffed into ships and carried to every Southern state and sold on the block.'

'Well, that's national law you're talking about. Each state makes its own laws. Those are the laws that count.'

Rob J. snorted, and that was the end of that conversation.

He and Jay remained close and mutually supportive in all other things, but the slavery question raised a barrier between them that they both regretted. Rob was a man who valued a quiet talk with a friend, and he began to turn Trude into the path leading to the Convent of St Francis whenever he was in that neighbourhood.

It was hard for him to pinpoint just when he became Mother Miriam Ferocia's friend. Sarah gave him physical passion that was unwavering and as important to him as meat and drink, but she spent more time talking with her pastor than with her husband. Rob had discovered in his relationship with Makwa that it was possible for him to be close to a woman without sexuality. Now he proved it again with this sister of the Order of St Francis, a female fifteen years older than he, with stern eyes in a strong cowl-framed face.

He'd seen her only infrequently until that spring. The winter had been mild and strange, with heavy rains. The water table rose unnoticed until the streams and creeks suddenly were hard to cross, and by March the township paid for being on land between two rivers, because the situation already had become the Flood of '57. Rob watched the river come over the banks on the Cole place. It swirled inland, washing away Makwa's sweat lodge and her woman's lodge. Her *hedonoso-te* was spared because she had built it cleverly on a knoll. The Cole house was higher than the flood reached too. But soon after the waters receded, Rob was summoned to treat the first case of virulent fever. And then another person came down sick. And another.

Sarah was pressed into service as a nurse, but she and

315

Rob and Tom Beckermann were swiftly overwhelmed. Then one morning Rob came to the Haskell farm and found a feverish Ben Haskell already sponge-bathed and comforted by two Sisters of St Francis. All of 'the brown beetles' were out and nursing. He saw at once and with a great thankfulness that they were excellent nurses. Each time he met them they were in pairs. Even their prioress nursed with a partner. When Rob protested to her, thinking it was a quirk in their training, Miriam Ferocia responded with cold vehemence, making it clear his objections were useless.

It came to him that they worked in pairs so they could guard one another from lapses of faith and flesh. A few evenings later, ending the day with a cup of coffee at the convent, he put it to her that she was afraid to allow her sisters to be alone in a Protestant house. He confessed it was a puzzle to him. 'Is your faith weak, then?'

'Our faith is strong! But we like warmth and comfort as well as the next. The life we've chosen is bleak. And cruel enough without the added curse of temptations.'

He understood. He was happy to accept the sisters under Miriam Ferocia's terms, and their nursing made all the difference.

The prioress' typical comment to him dripped with scorn. 'Have you no other medical bag, Dr Cole, than that shabby leather thing decorated with porky quills?'

'It's my *Mee-shome*, my Sauk medicine bundle. The straps are made of Izze cloths. When I wear them, no bullets can harm me.'

She looked at him wide-eyed. 'You don't have the faith in Our Saviour, but you accept protection from Sauk Indian heathenry?'

'Ah, but it works.' He told her of the shot that had been fired at him outside his barn.

'You must use extreme caution,' she admonished, pouring him coffee. The nanny goat he'd donated had dropped kids twice, supplying two males. Miriam Ferocia had traded one of the bucks and somehow had acquired three more does, dreaming of a cheese industry; but still whenever Rob J. came to the convent he had no milk for his coffee, because every nanny always seemed to be pregnant or nursing. He did without, like the nuns, and learned to love his coffee black.

Their talk turned sober. He was disappointed that her churchly inquiry had thrown no light on Ellwood Patterson. He had been considering a plan, he confided. 'What if we were able to place a man within the Supreme Order of the Star-Spangled Banner? It might be possible to learn of their mischief early enough to stop it.'

'How would you do that?'

He had given it a good deal of thought. It required a native-born American who was both completely trustworthy and close to Rob J. Jay Geiger wouldn't do, because SSSB probably would reject a Jew. 'There's my hired man, Alden Kimball. Born in Vermont. A very good person.'

She shook her head in concern. 'That he's a good person would make it worse, because you might very well sacrifice him, and yourself, with such a scheme. These are extremely dangerous men.'

He had to face the wisdom of what she said. And the fact that Alden had been showing his age. Not failing yet, but showing his age.

And he drank a lot.

'You must be patient,' she said gently. 'I shall make my inquiries again. Meanwhile, you must wait.'

She removed his cup and he knew it was time to rise from the bishop's chair and leave, so she could prepare for Night Song. He collected his quilled bullet shield and smiled at the competitive glare she directed at the *Mee-shome*. 'Thank you, Reverend Mother,' he said.

317

38
Hearing the Music

The educational pattern in Holden's Crossing was for a family to send children to the academy for a semester or two of schooling, so they could read a little and do simple sums and write a painstaking hand. Then the schooling was over, and the children began their lives as full-fledged farm workers. When Alex was sixteen he said he'd had enough school. Despite Rob J.'s offer to finance higher education, he went to work with Alden full-time on the sheep farm, and Shaman and Rachel were left as the oldest pupils in the academy.

Shaman was willing to keep on learning, and Rachel was thankful to drift along in the even flow of her days, clutching her unchanging existence as if it were a lifeline. Dorothy Burnham was aware of her good fortune in having even one pupil come into a teacher's life. She treated the pair like treasures, lavishing everything she knew on them and pushing herself to keep them challenged. The girl was older than Shaman by three years and had more schooling, but soon Miss Burnham was teaching them as a class of two. It was natural for them to spend a good deal of time studying together.

Whenever their schoolwork was done, Rachel went directly to Shaman's speech training. Twice a month the two young people met with Miss Burnham and Shaman ran through his routine for the teacher. Sometimes Miss Burnham suggested a change or a new exercise. She was delighted with his progress, and happy that Rachel Geiger had been able to do him so much good.

As their friendship ripened, sometimes Rachel or Shaman would allow the other some small inner glimpse. Rachel told him how she dreaded having to go to Peoria every year for the Jewish High Holidays. He awoke her tenderness by revealing to her, without putting it into so many words, his anguish that his mother treated him coldly. ('Makwa was more of a mother to me than she is, and she knows it. It gripes her, but it's plain truth.') Rachel had noticed that Mrs Cole never referred to her son as Shaman, the way everyone else did; Sarah called him Robert – almost formally, the way Miss Burnham did in school. Rachel wondered if it was because Mrs Cole didn't like Indian words. She'd heard Sarah telling her mother that she was glad the Sauks were gone forever.

Shaman and Rachel worked on his vocal exercises anywhere they happened to be, floating in Alden's flatboat or sitting on the riverbank while fishing, picking watercress, hiking across the prairie, or peeling fruit or vegetables for Lillian on the Geigers' Southern-style veranda. Several times a week they found their way to Lillian's piano. He could experience her vocal tonality if he touched her head or her back, but he especially liked to place his hand on the smooth warm flesh of her throat while she talked. He knew she must be able to feel his fingers trembling.

'I wish I could remember the sound of your voice.'

'Do you remember music?'

'I don't really remember it . . . I heard music the day after Christmas, last year.'

She stared at him, puzzled.

'Dreamed it.'

'And you *heard* the music in the dream?'

He nodded. 'All I could see was a man's feet and legs. I think they must have belonged to my father. You remember how sometimes our parents would put us to sleep on the floor while they played? I didn't see your mother and father, but I heard their violin and piano. I don't remember what they played. I just remember . . . music!'

She had trouble speaking. 'They like Mozart, maybe it was this,' she said, and played something on the piano.

But after a while he shook his head. 'It's just vibrations, to me. The other was real music. I've been trying ever since to dream of it again, but I can't.'

He noticed that her eyes glittered, and to his amazement she leaned forward and kissed him full on the mouth. He kissed her back, something new, very much like a different kind of music, he thought. Somehow his hand held her breast, and when they stopped kissing, it stayed there. Perhaps everything would have been all right if he'd taken his hand away at once. But, like the vibration of a musical note, he was able to sense the firming, and the small movement of her hardened bud. He pressed, and she drew back her hand and smashed him on the mouth.

Her second blow landed below his right eye. He sat dumbly and made no attempt to defend himself. She could have killed him if she'd wanted to, but she only hit him once more. She'd grown up doing farmwork and was strong, and she struck out with her closed fist. His upper lip was mashed and blood was trickling from his nose. He saw her crying raggedly as she sprang away.

He trailed after her into the front hall; it was fortunate no one was home. 'Rachel,' he called once, but he couldn't tell if she answered, and he didn't dare follow her upstairs.

He let himself out of her door and walked to the sheep farm, snuffling to keep the blood out of his handkerchief. As he moved toward the house he met Alden coming out of the barn.

'Weeping Christ. Who happened to you?'

'. . . In a fight.'

'Well, I can see. What a relief. I'se beginning to think Alex is the only Cole boy has any spunk. What's t'other scoundrel look like?'

'Terrible. Much worse than this.'

'Oh. That's good, then,' Alden said cheerfully, and departed.

320

At supper Shaman had to endure several long lectures against brawling.

In the morning the younger children studied his battle wounds with respect, while they were pointedly ignored by Miss Burnham. He and Rachel barely spoke to one another during the day, but to his surprise, when school let out she waited for him outside as usual, and they walked together in glum silence toward her house.

'You tell your father I touched you?'

'No!' she said sharply.

'That's good. I wouldn't want him to horsewhip me,' he said, and meant it. He had to watch her to talk with her, so he was able to observe how she looked with colour rising, but to his confusion he also saw that she was laughing.

'Oh, Shaman! Your poor face. I'm really sorry,' she said, and squeezed his hand.

'Me too,' he said, although he wasn't quite certain what he was apologizing for.

At her house, her mother gave them ginger cake. When they'd eaten it, they sat across the table from one another and did their schoolwork. Then they went into the parlour again. He shared the piano bench with her but took care not to sit too close. What had happened the previous day had changed things, as he'd feared, but to his surprise, it wasn't a bad feeling. It simply rested warmly between them as something private to them alone, like a shared cup.

A legal paper summoned Rob J. to the courthouse in Rock Island 'on the twenty-first day of June, in the year of Our Lord one thousand, eight hundred, fifty and seven, for the purpose of naturalization.'

The day was clear and warm, but the windows in the courtroom were closed because the Honourable Daniel P. Allan was on the bench and didn't appreciate flies. The legal traffic was light, and Rob J. had every reason to believe he'd be out of there swiftly, until Judge Allan started to administer the oath.

'Now, then. Do you pledge that you hereby renounce all foreign titles and allegiances to any other country?'

321

'I do,' Rob J. said.

'And do you pledge to support and defend the Constitution, and to bear arms on behalf of the United States of America?'

'Well, no sir, your Honour, I do not,' Rob J. said firmly.

Startled out of his torpor, Judge Allan stared.

'I don't believe in killing, your Honour, so I won't ever practise war.'

Judge Allan appeared annoyed. At the clerk's table next to the bench, Roger Murray cleared his throat. 'Law says, Judge, cases like this, candidate has to prove he's a conscientious objector whose beliefs prevent him from bearing arms. Means he has to belong to some group like the Quakers, that make it generally known they won't fight.'

'I know the law and what it means,' the judge said acidly, furious that Murray couldn't ever seem to find a less public way to instruct him. He peered over his spectacles. 'You Quaker, Dr Cole?'

'No, your Honour.'

'Well, what the hell are you, then?'

'Not affiliated with any religion,' Rob J. said, and saw that the judge looked as if he'd been personally insulted.

'Your Honour, may I approach the bench?' someone said from the back of the court. Rob J. saw it was Stephen Hume, who'd been a railroad lawyer ever since Nick Holden had won his seat in the Congress. Judge Allan signalled him to approach. 'Congressman.'

'Judge,' Hume said with a smile. 'Like to personally vouch for Dr Cole? One of the most distinguished gentlemen in Illinois, serves the people night and day as a physician? Everybody knows his word is gold. If he says he can't fight in a war because of his beliefs, that's all the proof a reasonable man should need.'

Judge Allan frowned, uncertain whether or not a politically connected lawyer before his bench had just called him unreasonable, and decided the safest thing was to glare at Roger Murray. 'We'll proceed with the naturalization,' he said, and without any more fuss, Rob J. became a citizen.

On the ride back to Holden's Crossing he had a few

322

strange, regretful memories of the Scots homeland he'd just renounced, but it felt good to be an American. Except that the country had more than its share of troubles. The US Supreme Court had just decided for good and all that Dred Scott was a slave because it wasn't legal for Congress to exclude slavery from the territories. At first Southerners rejoiced, but already they were furious again, because the Republican party leaders said they wouldn't accept the court decision as binding.

Neither would Rob J., even though his wife and his elder son had become hot-blooded Southern sympathizers. He'd sent dozens of runaway slaves through the secret room to Canada, and in the process had had several close calls. Alex told him one day that he'd met George Cliburne the night before on the road about a mile from the sheep farm. 'There he was, sitting on top of a wagonload of hay at three o'clock in the morning! Now, what do you make of that?'

'I guess you have to work hard to get up earlier than an industrious Quaker. But what were you doing coming home at three in the morning?' Rob J. said, and Alex was so busy getting away from the subject of his late-night drinking and tomcatting with Mal Howard that George Cliburne's strange work ethic wasn't brought up again.

In the middle of another night Rob J. was closing the padlock on the shed door when Alden had come along. 'Couldn't sleep. Ran outta varmint juice, and remembered I had this stashed in the barn.' He lifted the jug and proffered it. Though Rob J. seldom craved a drink and knew alcohol diminished the Gift, he wanted to share something with Alden. He uncorked the jug, took a swallow, and coughed. Alden grinned.

Rod would have liked to move the hired man away from the shed. In the dugout room on the other side of the door was a middle-aged Negro with a slight asthmatic wheeze when he breathed. Rob J. suspected that at times the wheeze became pronounced, and he wasn't certain the sound couldn't be heard from where he and Alden were talking. But Alden wasn't going anywhere; he hunkered down on his heels and showed how a champion drank whisky, finger

323

through the handle, jug swung onto his elbow, elbow raised just high enough to send the proper amount of raw liquor into his mouth.

'Trouble sleeping nowadays?'

Alden shrugged. 'Most nights I go right off, tired from work. When I don't, little drink helps me sleep.'

Alden had looked a lot more worn ever since Comes Singing had died. 'Ought to get another man to help you work the farm,' Rob J. said, for perhaps the twentieth time.

'Hard to find good white man willin' to hire out. Wouldn't work with a nigger,' Alden said, and Rob J. wondered how well sound travelled in the other direction, into the shed. 'Besides, got Alex workin' with me now, and he's doin' real good.'

'Is he?'

Alden stood erect, somewhat shakily; he must have had a lot of varmint juice before he'd run out. 'Damn,' he said deliberately. 'Doc, you never do give them pore young boogers their due.' Holding his jug carefully, he made his way back toward his own cabin.

One day near the end of that summer a middle-aged Chinese, name unknown, drifted into Holden's Crossing. Refused service in Nelson's Saloon, he hired a prostitute named Penny Davis to buy a bottle of whisky and take him to her shack, where next morning he died in her bed. Sheriff Graham said he didn't want any whore in his town who'd share her chink with a Chink and then peddle it to white men, and he personally arranged for Penny Davis to leave Holden's Crossing. Then he had the corpus put in the back of a wagon and delivered to the nearest coroner.

That afternoon, Shaman was waiting for his father when Rob J. approached his shed.

'Never seen an Oriental.'

'This one happens to be dead. You know that, don't you, Shaman?'

'Yes, Pa.'

Rob J. nodded and unlocked the shed door.

There was a sheet covering the body, and he folded it and

placed it on the old wooden chair. His son was pale but composed, intently studying the figure on the table. The Chinese was a small man, thin but muscular. his eyes had been closed. His skin colour fell somewhere between the paleness of whites and the redness of Indians. His toenails, horny and yellow, needed cutting; seeing them through his son's eyes, Rob was moved.

'Have to do my work now, Shaman.'

'Can I watch?'

'You're sure you want to?'

'Yes, Pa.'

Rob took his scalpel and opened the chest. Oliver Wendell Holmes had a flamboyant style of introducing death: Rob's own way was to be simple. He warned that the insides of a man stank worse than any hunting prey the boy had dressed, and advised Shaman to breathe through his mouth. Then he noted that the cold tissue was no longer a person. 'Whatever it was that made this man alive – some call it his soul – has left his body.'

Shaman's face was pallid but his eyes were alert. 'Is that the part goes to heaven?'

'I don't know where it goes,' Rob said gently. As he weighed the organs, he allowed Shaman to record the weight, a help to him. 'William Fergusson, who was my mentor, used to say that the spirit leaves the body behind like a house that's been emptied, so we have to treat it carefully and with dignity, out of respect for the man who used to live here.

'This is the heart, and here's what killed him.' He removed the organ and placed it in Shaman's hands so he could study the darkened dead circle of tissue that ballooned out from the muscle wall.

'Why'd that happen to him, Pa?'

'I don't know, Shaman.'

He replaced the organs and closed the incisions, and by the time they washed up together, colour had returned to Shaman's face.

Rob J. was impressed by how well the boy had done. 'I've been thinking,' he said. 'Would you like to study with me out here, from time to time?'

'I would, Pa!' Shaman said, his face alight.

'Because it occurs to me you might want to get a degree in science. You could earn your living teaching, maybe even in a college. Think you'd like that, son?'

Shaman looked at him soberly, his face burdened again as he considered the question. He shrugged.

'Maybe,' he said.

39
Teachers

That January Rob J. put extra blankets in the dugout room because runaways from the deep South suffered grievously from the cold. There was less snow than usual, but enough to cover the cultivated fields and make them look like prairie in winter. Sometimes as he travelled home from a house call in the middle of the night he would pretend that at any moment he'd be able to look up and see a long file of red men riding good horses across the white glitter of unbroken plains, following their shaman and chiefs; or massive humpbacked creatures moving out of the darkness at him, hoarfrost clinging to their shaggy brown fur and the moon gleaming on curved horns with wicked silvered tips. But he never saw anything, because he believed in ghosts even less than he believed in God.

When spring came, the runoff was light and the rivers and streams kept to their banks. Maybe that had something to do with the fact that he treated less fever that season; but for some reason, more of the people who came down with fever died. One of the patients he lost was Matilda Cowan, whose husband, Simeon, raised half a section of corn in the northern township, very good land even if slightly dry. They had three small daughters. When a young woman died leaving children, it was expected her husband would remarry quickly, but when Cowan proposed to Dorothy

Burnham, the schoolteacher, it surprised a lot of people. He was accepted at once.

At the breakfast table one morning, Rob J. chuckled as he told Sarah that the school board was upset. 'We thought we could count on Dorothy being a spinster forever. Cowan's smart. She'll be a good wife.'

'She's a fortunate woman,' Sarah said dryly. 'Considerably older than he is.'

'Oh, Simeon Cowan's but three or four years younger than Dorothy,' Rob J. said, buttering a biscuit. 'That's not such a difference.' And he grinned in astonishment to see his son Shaman nodding in agreement, joining in on the gossip about his teacher.

On Miss Burnham's last day at the academy, Shaman lingered until the others had left for the day and then went to say goodbye.

'I guess I'll be seeing you around the town. I'm glad you didn't decide to go to some other place to get married.'

'I'm glad too, that I'll be living in Holden's Crossing, Robert.'

'Want to thank you,' he said clumsily. He knew what this warm and homely woman had meant to his life.

'You're welcome, my dear.' She had informed his parents that she wouldn't be working on his speech anymore, what with the farm and a new husband and three children to see for. 'I'm sure you and Rachel will be able to do wonderfully without me. Besides, you've reached the point where voice drills might be dispensed with.'

'You think I sound like other people when I talk?'

'Well . . .' She treated the question seriously. 'Not exactly. When you're tired, you're still guttural. You have become very aware of how words should sound, so you don't slur your speech as much as some people. So there's a slight difference.' She saw that this troubled him, and she took his hand and squeezed it. 'It is a very charming difference,' she said, and was happy to see his face clear.

He'd bought her a small gift in Rock Island with his own money, handkerchiefs edged in pale blue lace. 'I have something for you too,' she said, and gave him a volume of Shakespeare's sonnets. 'When you read them, you are to think of me,' she ordered. 'Except for the romantic ones, of course!' she added daringly, and then laughed with him in the freedom of knowing that Mrs Cowan would be able to do and say things that poor Miss Burnham the schoolteacher wouldn't have dreamed of.

With all the spring river traffic, there were drownings up and down the Mississippi. A young crewman fell from a barge and was lost upstream, his body snatched deep by the currents and not given up until he was in the jurisdiction of Holden's Crossing. The bargemen didn't know where he had come from or anything else save that his name had been Billy, and Sheriff Graham delivered him to Rob J.

Shaman watched his second autopsy and recorded organ weights again in his father's notebook, and learned what happened to the lungs when somebody drowned. This time it was harder for him to watch. The Chinese man had been separated from him by age and exotic origins, but this was a youth only a few years older than his brother, Bigger, a death that spoke to Shaman of his own mortality. Still, he managed to put all that out of his mind, well enough to observe and learn.

When they were through with the autopsy, Rob J. began to dissect below Billy's right wrist. 'Most surgeons live in horror of the hand,' he confided to Shaman. 'It's because they never spent enough time studying it. If you become a teacher of anatomy or physiology, you must know the hand.'

Shaman could understand why they would fear to cut the hand, because it was all muscles and tendons and hinged joints, and he was amazed and terrified when they completed the dissection of the right hand and his father told him to dissect the left hand by himself.

His father smiled at him, seeming to know exactly what he was feeling. 'Don't worry. Nothing you can do will hurt him.'

So Shaman spent much of that day cutting and probing

and witnessing, memorizing the names of all the tiny bones, learning how the joints were enabled to move in the hands of the living.

Several weeks later the sheriff brought Rob J. the body of an old woman who had died in the county's poor farm. Shaman was eager to resume his lessons, but his father barred his way into the shed.

'Shaman, have you ever seen a woman without her clothes on?'

'. . . Saw Makwa once. She took me into the sweat lodge with her, sang songs to try to get my hearing back.'

His father stared in amazement, and then felt constrained to explain. 'The first time you saw a woman's body, I didn't think she should be old and ugly and dead.'

He nodded, feeling the heat in his face. 'It's not the first time, Pa. Makwa wasn't old or ugly.'

'No, she was not,' his father said. He patted Shaman on the shoulder, and they both went into the shed and shut the door.

In July the school committee offered Rachel Geiger the position of teacher at the academy. It wasn't unusual for one of the older pupils to be given an opportunity to teach at a school when a faculty opening existed, and the girl had been enthusiastically recommended by Dorothy Burnham in her resignation letter. Besides, as Carroll Wilkenson pointed out, they could get her for a beginner's salary and she already lived at home so she wouldn't have to be boarded.

The offer created anguished indecision in the Geiger household, and earnest, low-toned conversations between Lillian and Jay. 'We've already put things off too long,' Jay said.

'But a year as a teacher would be a genuine asset for her, help her to make a finer match. A teacher is such an *American* thing to be!'

Jason sighed. He cherished his three sons, Davey, Herm, and Cubby. Good, loving boys. All three played the piano like their mother, with varying degrees of skill, and Dave and Herm wanted to learn wind instruments, if ever they could find a teacher. Rachel was his only daughter and his firstborn, the child he had taught to play the violin. He knew the day would come when she would have to go out of his home, to live for him mostly in rare letters, to be seen only briefly in infrequent visits from or to a faraway place.

He decided to be selfish and keep her in the bosom of the family awhile longer. 'All right, let her be a teacher,' he told Lillian.

It had been several years since the floods had washed away Makwa's sweat lodge. All that remained were two stone walls, six feet long, three feet high, and two and one-half feet apart. In August Shaman began to build a hemisphere of bent saplings over the walls. He worked slowly and clumsily, weaving green willow withes between the saplings. When his father saw what he was doing he asked if he could help, and the two of them, working for almost two weeks in their spare time, managed to approximate what the sweat lodge had looked like when Makwa had built it in a few hours with the help of Moon and Comes Singing.

Using more saplings and withes, they built a man-size basket crib and set it inside the lodge, across the tops of the stone walls.

Rob J. owned a tattered buffalo robe and a single deerskin. When they stretched the skins over the framework, a big section remained uncovered.

'Mebbe a blanket?' Shaman suggested.

'Better use two, a double layer, or it won't hold steam.'

They tried out the lodge on the first frosty day in September. Makwa's sweatbath stones were right where she'd left them, and they built a wood fire and set the stones in it to become very hot. Shaman entered the lodge wearing only a blanket that he dropped outside; shivering, he lay down in the basket crib. Rob J. brought in the hot stones, using forked sticks to handle them, and placed them below the crib, then doused them with pails of cold water and tightly closed the lodge. Shaman lay in the rising steam, feeling the moisture bloom, remembering how frightened he'd been the first time, how he had burrowed into Makwa's arms against the heat and the murk. He recollected the strange marks on her breasts, how the scars had felt against his cheek. Rachel was thinner and taller than Makwa, and had heavier breasts. Thinking about Rachel made him hard and he became anxious lest his father come back and see him. He forced himself to think of Makwa again, remembering the quiet affection she had exuded, as comforting as the first warmth of the steam. It was strange to be in the lodge where she had been so many times. Her memory grew more indistinct with every year, and he wondered why anyone would kill her, why there were bad people. Almost without knowing it, he began singing one of the songs she had taught him, 'Wi-a-ya-ni, Ni-na ne-gi-seke-wi-to-seme-ne ni-na . . .' Wherever you are going, I walk with you, my son.

In a little while his father brought more hot rocks and doused them with cold water, and the steam absolutely filled the lodge. He endured it as long as he could, until he lay gasping and in a profuse sweat, then jumped from the crib and ran out through the chill air to plunge into the cold river. For a moment he thought he had died a very clean death, but as he splashed and swam the blood beat through his body, and he yipped like a Sauk as he left the water and ran to the barn, where he briskly rubbed himself dry and dressed in warm clothes.

Obviously he had revealed too much enjoyment, because when he came out of the barn his father was waiting to try the sweat lodge, and it was Shaman's turn to heat and carry the stones and pour the water to make steam.

They finally reached the house glowing and grinning, to find they'd sweated right through suppertime. Shaman's mother, greatly put out, had left their plates on the table, and the food was cold. He and his father went without soup and had to scrape congealed fat off the mutton, but they agreed it was worth it. Makwa really had known how to take a bath.

When school opened, Rachel found it not at all difficult to become the teacher. The routine was so familiar: the lessons, the classwork, the songs, the home assignments. Shaman was better than she at mathematics and she asked him to give the classes in arithmetic. Although he got no pay, Rachel praised him to parents and the school board, and he enjoyed working with her in planning the lessons.

Neither of them mentioned Miss Burnham's opinion that perhaps his vocal exercises no longer were necessary. Now that Rachel was teacher, they did his drills at the academy after the children left for the day, except for the exercises that needed her mother's piano. Shaman liked sitting close to her on the piano bench, but enjoyed more being alone with her in the schoolhouse, the intimacy.

The pupils had always laughed over the fact that Miss Burnham never seemed to need to pee, and now Rachel exercised the same discipline, but as soon as the others were gone, she couldn't wait to rush out to the privy. Waiting for her to come back, he did a good deal of speculation about what she wore under her skirts. Bigger had told Shaman that when he did it with Pattie Drucker he had to help her out of an old, holey suit of her father's underwear, but Shaman knew most women either wore whalebone crinolines or horsehair shifts that were itchy but warmer. Rachel wasn't partial to the cold. When she came back inside she'd hang her cloak on its peg and then hurry to the stove to toast first her front side and then her back.

She'd been a teacher only a month when she had to go to Peoria with her family for the Jewish holidays, and Shaman was substitute teacher for half of October, for which he was paid. The pupils already were accustomed to his teaching them arithmetic. They knew he had to see their lips to understand them, and on the first morning Randy Williams, the blacksmith's youngest son, said something smart when his back was turned to the teacher. Shaman nodded easily when the children laughed, and asked Randy if he wanted to be held by his heels for a little bit. He was bigger than most of the men they knew, and the smiles disappeared as Randy said somewhat shakily that no, he didn't want that to happen. For the rest of the two weeks, teaching them wasn't hard.

The first day Rachel was back in school, she was subdued. That afternoon, when the children were gone, she came back from the outhouse shivering and crying.

Shaman came and put his arms around her. She made no protest, just stood between him and the stove with her eyes closed. 'I loathe Peoria,' she said quietly. 'Hateful, meeting so many people. My mother and father . . . they placed me on display.'

It seemed reasonable to him that they were proud of her. Besides, she wouldn't have to go to Peoria again for a whole year. He said nothing. He didn't even dream of kissing her, happy just to stand in contact with her softness, certain that nothing a man and a woman did together could be better than this. In the briefest of moments she pulled back and considered him gravely through wet eyes. 'My steadfast friend.'

'Yes,' he said.

Two incidents brought revelation to Rob J. On a sharp November morning, Shaman stopped his father on the way to the barn.

'I visited Miss Burnham – that is, Mrs Cowan – yesterday. She asked me to give you and Mother her best regards.'

Rob J. smiled. 'Oh? That's fine. I suppose she's becoming accustomed to life on the Cowan farm?'

'Yes. The little girls seem to like her. Of course, there's a lot of work, only the two of them.' He glanced at his father. 'Pa? Are there lots of marriages like theirs? That is, with the woman older than the man?'

'Why, Shaman, it's usually the other way around, but not always. I suppose there are a good many.' He waited for the conversation to go somewhere, but his son merely nodded and wandered off to the academy, and he went in and saddled his horse.

A few days later he and the boy were working together in the house. Sarah had seen some floor coverings in several homes in Rock Island, and she had begged Rob J. until he agreed she could have three floor coverings of her own. They were made by sizing canvas cloth with resin and then applying five coats of paint. The result was mudproof, waterproof, and decorative. She had employed Alex and Alden to apply the resin and the first four layers of paint, but had drafted her husband to supply the finish.

Rob J. had mixed the paint for all five coats, using buttermilk, store-bought oil, and finely ground brown eggshells to make a good paint that was the colour of new wheat. He and Shaman had applied the final surface together, and now, on a sunny Sunday morning, they were painstakingly adding a thin black border around the outside edges of each floor covering, trying to finish the job before Sarah came home from church.

Shaman was being patient. Rob J. knew that Rachel waited for him in their kitchen, but he saw that the boy didn't try to hurry their work as they applied the decorative border to the last of their three projects. 'Pa?' Shaman said. 'Does it take a lot of money to be married?'

'Hmm. Considerable.' He wiped his small paintbrush on a rag. 'Well, it varies, of course. Some couples live with her family, or his, until they can make it on their own.' He had made a stencil of thin wood in order to make his work easier, and now Shaman moved it along the painted surface and he applied the black paint, bringing their work to an end.

They cleaned up the brushes, put things away in the barn. Before he turned back to the house, Shaman nodded. 'I can see that it would vary.'

'What would vary?' Rob J. asked absently, his mind already dwelling on exactly how he was going to drain the fluid from Harold Hayse's grossly swollen knee.

'The money you would need to get married. It would depend on how much you made from your work, how soon a baby would come, things like that.'

'Exactly,' Rob J. said. He was mystified, puzzled by a feeling that he'd missed a vital part of their conversation.

But a few minutes later Shaman and Rachel Geiger walked past the barn toward the house road. Shaman's eyes were on Rachel so he could see what she was saying, but watching his son's face, Rob J. understood at once what it

335

revealed.

As certain things fell into place, he grimaced.

Before he tended to Harold Hayse's knee, he rode to the Geiger farm. His friend was in his toolshed, sharpening a pair of scythes, and smiled a welcome without stopping the sweeping rasp of the stone against the blade.

'Rob J.'

'Jason.'

There was another whetstone and Rob J. picked it up and began to work on the second scythe.

'I have to talk with you about a problem,' he said.

336

40
Growing Up

Winter's last diehard layer of snow still dominated the fields like a thin frosting when Rob J. set into motion the spring activities on the sheep farm, and Shaman was startled but pleased to be included in the work plans for the first time. Always before, he'd done only occasional chores and had been left to pursue his studies and his voice therapy. 'This year we sorely need your help,' his father told him. 'Alden and Alex won't admit it, but no three men, together or alone, can do the work Comes Singing used to, all by himself.' Besides, he said, every year the flock grew and they enclosed more pasture. 'I've talked with both Dorothy Cowan and Rachel. They both feel you've learned everything you can at the academy. They tell me you don't need the voice exercises anymore, either, and' – he grinned at Shaman – 'I must say I agree with them. You sound fine to me!'

Rob J. was careful to tell Shaman the arrangement wouldn't be permanent. 'I know you don't want to farm. But you help us out now, and we can be thinking about what you want to do next.'

Alden and Alex took care of the slaughtering of lambs. Shaman was set to work planting brush borders as soon as the ground could be penetrated. Split-rail fences were no good when you had sheep, because the animals had little trouble escaping between the rails, which also admitted

337

predators. To mark off a new pasture, Shaman ploughed a single strip around the perimeter, then he planted Osage orange close enough to form a thick barrier. He sowed carefully, because the seed cost five dollars a pound. The orange trees grew strong and brushy, with long wicked thorns that combined to keep sheep in and coyotes and wolves out. It took three years for Osage orange to make a hedge that would protect a field, but Rob J. had been growing thorn barriers from the start of the farm, and when Shaman had finished planting new hedges he spent days on a ladder, cutting back established ones. When the trimming was done, there were field stones to be coaxed from the ground, firewood to be worked up, posts to be made, stumps to be worried from the earth at the edge of the woods.

His hands and arms were scratched by the thorns, his palms became callused, his muscles ached and then toughened. At night he had sexual dreams. Sometimes he couldn't recollect the dreams or identify the women in them, but several times he had clear memories of Rachel. At least once, he knew the woman had been Makwa, which confused and frightened him. He did his futile best to remove the evidence before his bedsheet was added to the laundry for boiling.

For years he'd seen Rachel every day, and now he seldom saw her. On a Sunday afternoon he walked to her house and her mother answered his knock. 'Rachel is occupied and can't see you now. I shall give her your best, Rob J.,' Lillian said, not unkindly. On an occasional Saturday evening, when their families joined for music and fellowship, he managed to sit with Rachel and talk about the school. He missed teaching the children arithmetic, and asked her about them, and helped her plan future lessons. But she seemed strangely ill-at-ease. Something he loved about her, a kind of warmth and light, had been dampened, like a fire with too much wood. When he suggested they go for a walk, it was as if the adults in the room waited for her reply and didn't relax until she said no, she didn't care to walk right now, but thank you, Shaman.

Her mother and her father had explained the situation to Rachel, speaking understandingly about a young boy's infatuation and stating plainly that it was her responsibility to guard against showing him any kind of encouragement. It was very hard. Shaman was her friend and she missed his company. She worried about his future, but she was poised over a personal abyss, and trying to see into its murky depths claimed most of her anxiety and fear.

She should have realized that Shaman's infatuation would be the precipitating force for change, but so strong was her denial of her future that when Johann C. Regensberg came to spend the weekend at her parents' home, she accepted him at once as a friend of her father's. He was an affable, slightly plump man in his late thirties, who respectfully referred to his host as Mr Geiger but asked Jason to call him Joe. Of medium height, he had lively, slightly squinting blue eyes that peered thoughtfully at the world from behind metal-framed spectacles. His pleasant face was balanced nicely between a short beard and a head of shrinking brown hair that rode atop his scalp. Later, Lillian would describe him to friends as having 'a high forehead'.

Joe Regensberg appeared at the farm on a Friday, well in time for the *Shabbat* dinner. That evening and the next day he spent in leisure with the Geiger family. On Saturday morning he and Jason read the Scriptures and studied the Book of Leviticus. After a cold lunch he inspected the barn and the apothecary shop and then, bundled against an overcast day, walked along the road with them to see the fields that would be planted in the spring.

The Geigers ended the Sabbath with a supper of *cholent*, a dish containing beans, meat, pearl barley, and prunes, that had been cooking slowly in hot coals since the previous afternoon, because Jews were enjoined from kindling a fire during the *Shabbat*. Afterward there was music, with Jason playing part of a Beethoven violin sonata and then deferring to Rachel, who enjoyed finishing it while the stranger watched with evident pleasure. At the end of the evening Joe Regensberg went to his huge tapestry suitcase and drew presents from it, a nest of bread pans for Lillian, made in the tinware factory he owned in Chicago; a bottle of fine aged brandy for Jay; and for Rachel, a book, *The Pickwick Papers*.

She observed that there were no gifts for her brothers. At once she knew the significance of his visit and was overtaken by terror and confusion. Through lips that felt stiff and numb she thanked him, telling him she liked the writing of Mr Dickens but thus far had read only *Nicholas Nickleby*.

'*The Pickwick Papers* is a particular favourite of mine,' he said. 'We must discuss it after you read it.'

He could not be described as handsome by anyone honest, but he had an intelligent face. A book, she thought hopefully, was a first gift an exceptional man would give a woman in these circumstances.

'I thought it a suitable gift for a teacher,' he said, as if he could read her mind. His clothes fitted better than the clothes of the men she knew; probably his were better made. When he smiled, there were humour wrinkles in the corners of his eyes.

Jason had written to Benjamin Schoenberg, the *shadchen* in Peoria, and for insurance had sent another letter to a marriage broker named Solomon Rosen in Chicago, where there was a growing Jewish population. Schoenberg had replied with a flowery letter, stating he had a number of young men who would make wonderful bridegrooms, and the Geigers could meet them when the family came to Peoria for the high holidays. But Solomon Rosen had acted. One of his best potential grooms was Johann Regensberg. When Regensberg mentioned he was about to travel to western Illinois to call upon outlets that carried his tinware, including several stores in Rock Island and Davenport, Solomon Rosen arranged the introduction.

Several weeks after the visit, another letter arrived from Mr Rosen. Johann Regensberg had been very favourably impressed by Rachel. Mr Rosen informed them that the Regensberg family had *yiches*, the true family distinction

340

that comes·from many generations of community service. The letter said that among Mr Regensberg's ancestors were teachers and biblical scholars, back to the fourteenth century.

But as Jay continued to read, his face darkened with insult. Johann's parents, Leon and Golda Regensberg, were dead. They were represented in this matter by Mrs Harriet Ferber, sister of the late Leon Regensberg. In an attempt to follow the tradition of her family, Mrs Feber had requested that testimony or other proofs be furnished regarding the virginity of the prospective bride.

'This is not Europe. And they are not buying a cow,' Jason said thinly.

His cool note of refusal was answered at once by a conciliatory letter from Mr Rosen, withdrawing the request and asking instead if Johann's aunt could be invited to visit the Geigers. So a few weeks later Mrs Ferber came to Holden's Crossing, a small, erect woman with gleaming white hair pulled back against her skull and woven into a knot. Accompanied by a hamper containing candied fruits, brandied cakes, and a dozen bottles of kosher wines, she, too, arrived in time for the *Shabbat*. She took pleasure in Lillian's cooking and in the musical accomplishment of the family, but it was Rachel she watched, and conversed with about education and children, and obviously doted upon from the start.

She was not nearly as forbidding as they had feared. Late in the evening, while Rachel cleared the kitchen, Mrs Ferber sat with Jay and Lillian, and they acquainted one another with their respective families.

Lillian's ancestors were Spanish Jews who had fled the Inquisition, first to Holland, then to England. In America they had a political heritage. On her father's side she was related to Francis Salvador, who had been elected by his Christian neighbours to the Provincial Congress of South Carolina, and who, while serving with patriot militia only a few weeks after the adoption of the Declaration of Independence, became the first Jew to die for the United

341

States, ambushed and scalped by Tories and Indians. On her mother's side she was a Mendes, cousin to Judah Benjamin, the United States senator from Louisiana. Jason's family, established pharmaceutical manufacturers in Germany, had come to Charleston in 1819, fleeing the riots in which crowds had coursed the streets looking for Jews and shouting 'Hep! Hep! Hep!', a cry that went back to the Crusaders, formed by the initials of *Hierosolyma est perdiat*, Jerusalem is lost.

The Regensbergs had left Germany a decade before the Hep riots, Mrs Ferber disclosed. They had vineyards in the Rhineland. The didn't have great wealth but enjoyed financial comfort, and Joe Regensberg's tinware business was prosperous. He was a member of the tribe of *Kohane*, the blood of high priests in Solomon's Temple flowed in his veins. If there was a marriage, she indicated delicately to Lillian and Jay, their grandchildren would be descended from two chief rabbis of Jerusalem. The three of them sat and contemplated one another with pleasure, drinking a good English tea that had come out of Mrs Ferber's opulent hamper. 'My mother's sister was named Harriet,' Lillian said. 'We called her Hattie.' No one called *her* anything but Harriet, Mrs Ferber said, but with such warm good humour that they found it easy to accept when she invited them to Chicago.

A few weeks later, on a Wednesday, all six members of the Geiger family boarded a locomotive coach at Rock Island for a direct five-hour trail trip, without changing trains. Chicago was large, sprawling, dirty, crowded, shabby, noisy, and, to Rachel, very exciting. Her family had rooms on the fourth floor of Palmer's Illinois House Hotel. On Thursday and Friday, during two dinners at Harriet's home on South Wabash Avenue, they met other relatives, and on Saturday morning they attended worship services at the Regensbergs' family synagogue, Congregation *Kehilath Anshe Maarib*, where Jason was honoured to be called to the Torah to chant a blessing. That evening they went to a hall where a touring opera company was presenting *Der Freischütz*, by Carl Maria von Weber. Rachel had never before attended an opera, and the soaring, romantic arias transported her. At the first interval between acts, Joe Regensberg led her outside and asked her to be his wife, and she accepted him. It was accomplished with little trauma, because the real proposal and acceptance had been accomplished by their elders. From his pocket he took a ring that had been his mother's. The diamond, the first Rachel had ever seen, was modest but was set beautifully. The ring was a bit large, and she kept her fist clenched so it wouldn't fall off her finger and be lost. When they slipped back into their seats the opera was resuming. Sitting in the dark next to Lillian, Rachel took her mother's hand and placed it on the ring, and smiled broadly at the instantaneous gasp. As she allowed the music to carry her gloriously back into the German forest, she realized that the event she had feared for so long might actually be a door to freedom and a very pleasant kind of power.

The hot May morning she came to the sheep farm, Shaman had worked up a heavy sweat mowing with a scythe for several hours and then had begun to rake, so he was covered with dust and chaff. Rachel wore a familiar old grey dress with dark heat moisture already beginning to show under her arms, a wide grey bonnet he hadn't seen before, and white cotton gloves. When she asked if he could walk her home, he dropped the rake gladly.

For a while they talked of the academy, but almost at once she began to tell him of herself, of what was happening in her life.

Smiling at him, Rachel took off the left glove and showed him the ring, and he understood she was to marry.

'You'll move away from here, then?'

She took his hand. Years later, thinking of the scene again and again, Shaman was ashamed he hadn't talked to her. Wished her a good life, said what she had meant to him, thanked her.

Said goodbye.

But he couldn't look at her, so he didn't know what she was saying. He became like a stone, and her words rolled off like rain.

When they reached her lane and he turned away and started back, his hand ached because she'd held it so tightly.

The day after the Geigers went to Chicago, where she was to be married under a canopy in a synagogue, Rob J. came home and was met by Alex, who said he'd take care of the horse. 'You better go see. Something's the matter with Shaman.'

In the house, Rob J. stood outside Shaman's room and listened to hoarse, guttural sobbing. When he had been just Shaman's age he had wept like this because his bitch dog had turned savage and biting and his mother had given her away to a crofter who lived off by himself in the hills. But he knew his son was grieving for a human being and not for an animal.

He went in and sat down on the bed. 'There are some things you should know. There are very few Jews, and they're mostly surrounded by very many of the rest of us. So they feel that unless they marry their own kind, they won't survive.

'But that didn't apply to you. You never, ever had a chance.' He reached over and brushed back his son's damp hair with his hand, then rested his hand on Shaman's head. 'Because she's a woman,' he said. 'And you're a boy.'

During the summer the school committee, sniffing after a good teacher who could be paid a small salary because of youth, offered the job at the academy to Shaman, but he said no.

'Then what do you want to do?' his father asked.

'I don't know.'

'There's a higher school over in Galesburg. Knox College,' Rob J. said. 'It's supposed to be a very good place. Would you like more education? And a change of scene?'

His son nodded. 'I believe I would,' he said.

So two months after his fifteenth birthday, Shaman left home.

41
Winners and Losers

In September of 1858 the Reverend Joseph Hills Perkins was called to the pulpit of the largest Baptist church in Springfield. His prosperous new flock included the governor and a number of state legislators, and Mr Perkins was only slightly more dazzled by his good fortune than were the members of his church in Holden's Crossing, who saw in his success clear evidence of their intelligence in having chosen him. For a time, Sarah was occupied by a series of farewell dinners and parties; then, when the Perkinses had left, the search for a clergyman began again, and there was a whole new series of guest preachers to feed and board, and new wrangling and debate about the relative desirability of the candidates.

For a time they favoured a man from Northern Illinois who was a fiery denouncer of sin, but to the relief of several who didn't care for his style, Sarah among them, he was taken out of consideration by the fact that he had six children, with another on the way, and the parsonage was small. They decided finally on Mr Lucian Blackmer, a red-cheeked, barrel-chested man newly come West. 'From the State of Rhode Island, to the State of Grace,' was the way Carroll Wilkenson put it when he introduced the new minister to Rob J. Mr Blackmer seemed a pleasant man, but Rob J. was depressed to meet his wife, because Julia Blackmer was thin and anxious, with the pallor and cough of advanced lung sickness. While he bade her welcome he could feel her husband's gaze, as if Blackmer waited for reassurances that Dr Cole could offer new hope and a certain cure.

Holden's Crossing, Illinois
October 12, 1858

My dear Shaman,

I was pleased to learn from your letter that you have settled into life in Galesburg and are enjoying your studies in good health. All are well here. Alden and Alex have finished slaughtering the pigs and we are luxuriating in new bacon, ribs, shoulders, hams (boiled, smoked, and pickled), souse, head cheese, and lard.

Reports indicate that the new minister is an interesting fellow once he climbs into a pulpit. To give him his due, he is a man of courage, because his first sermon was on certain moral questions raised by slavery, and while it seems to have met with the approval of a majority of those in attendance, a strong and vocal minority (including your mother) offered disagreement with him after the church had been departed.

I was excited to hear that Abraham Lincoln of Springfield and Senator Douglas were scheduled to debate at Knox College on October 7, and I hope you had an opportunity to attend. Their race for the Senate ends with my first vote as a citizen, and I scarcely know which of the candidates will be a worse choice. Douglas thunders against the ignorant bigotry of the Know Nothings, but he placates the slave owners. Lincoln fulminates against slavery but accepts – indeed, woos – the support of Know Nothings. Both of them annoy me very much. Politicians!

Your courses sound challenging. Keep in mind that along with botany and astronomy and physiology, there are secrets to be learned from poetry.

Perhaps the enclosed will make it easier for you to buy Christmas presents. I do look forward to seeing you during the holiday!

Your loving
Father

He missed Shaman. His relationship with Alex was more wary than warm. Sarah was always preoccupied with her church work. He enjoyed occasional musical evenings with the Geigers, but when the playing ended they were confronted with their political differences. More and more, in the late afternoons after his house calls were done, he guided his horse to the Convent of Saint Francis of Assisi. With every passing year he had a clearer understanding that Mother Miriam was more courageous than ferocious, more valuable than forbidding.

'I have something for you,' she told him one afternoon, and handed him a sheaf of brown papers covered with small, cramped handwriting in watery black ink. He read it as he sat in the leather chair and drank his coffee, and saw it was a description of the inner workings of the Order of the Star-Spangled Banner, and that it could have been written only by someone who was a member.

It began with an outline of the national structure of the political secret society. Its base was composed of district councils, each of which chose its own officers, enacted its own bylaws, and initiated its own members. Above them were county councils, made up of a single delegate from each of the district councils. The county councils supervised the political activities of the district councils and selected local political candidates worthy of the order's support.

All units in a state were controlled by a grand council, composed of three delegates from every district council, and governed by a grand-president and other elected officials. At the top of the elaborate structure was a national council that decided all national political matters, including the selection of the order's candidates for the presidency and the vice-presidency of the United States. The national council decided the punishment for dereliction of duty by members, and it fixed the order's extensive rituals.

There were two degrees of membership. To attain the first, a candidate had to be an adult male born in the United States of Protestant parents, who was not married to a Catholic woman.

Each prospective member was asked a blunt question:

'Are you willing to use your influence and vote only for native-born American citizens for all offices of honour, trust, or profit in the gift of the people, the exclusion of all foreigners and Roman Catholics in particular, and without regard to party predilections?'

A man who so swore was required to renounce all other party allegiance, to support the political will of the order, and to work to change the naturalization laws. He was then entrusted with secrets, carefully described in the report – the sign of recognition, the handshake grip, the challenges, and the warnings.

To attain the second degree of membership, a candidate had to be a trusted veteran. Only second-degree members were eligible to hold office in the order, to engage in its clandestine activities, and to have its support in attaining office in local and national politics. When elected or appointed to power, they were ordered to remove all foreigners, aliens, or Roman Catholics working under them, and in no case 'to appoint such to any office in your gift'.

Rob J. stared at Miriam Ferocia. 'How many are they?'

She shrugged. 'We don't believe there are great numbers of men in the secret order. Perhaps a thousand. But they are the steel in the backbone of the American party.

'I give these pages to you because you oppose this group that seeks to harm my Mother Church, and because you should know the nature of those who do us evil, and for whose souls we pray to God.' She regarded him soberly. 'But you must promise not to use any of this information to approach a suspected member of the order in Illinois, for to do so might place the man who wrote this report in terrible danger.'

Rob J. nodded. He folded the pages and offered them back to her, but she shook her head. 'It is for you,' she said. 'Along with my prayers.'

'You mustn't pray for me!' It made him uncomfortable to talk with her regarding matters of faith.

'You cannot stop me. You deserve prayers, and I speak of you often to the Lord.'

'Just as you pray for our enemies,' he pointed out

grumpily, but she was undisturbed.

Later, at home, he read the report again, scrutinizing the spidery penmanship. Someone had written it (perhaps a priest?) who was living a sham, pretending to be what he was not, risking his safety, perhaps his life. Rob J. wished he could sit and talk with that man.

Nick Holden had easily won re-election twice on his reputation as an Indian fighter, but now he was running for a fourth term and his opponent was John Kurland, the Rock Island attorney. Kurland was highly regarded by Democrats and others, and perhaps Holden's Know Nothing support was flagging. Some people were saying the congressman might be turned out of office, and Rob J. was waiting for Nick to make a spectacular gesture designed to win votes. So he was only slightly surprised when he came home one afternoon to hear that Congressman Holden and Sheriff Graham were gathering another volunteer posse.

'Sheriff says Frank Mosby, that outlaw, is holed up in the north country,' Alden said. 'Nick's got folks so stirred up, they're more in a mood to lynch than to arrest, you ask me. Graham is deputizin' people right and left. Alex left here all excited. He took the goose gun and rode Vicky to town.' He frowned apologetically. 'Tried to talk him out of it, but . . .' He shrugged.

Trude hadn't had a chance to cool, but Rob J. threw the saddle back on and rode to town himself.

Men were clustered in the street in small groups. There was loud laughter on the porch of the store, where Nick and the sheriff were holding sway, but he ignored them. Alex was standing with Mal Howard and two other youths, all of them holding firearms, their eyes bright with importance. His face fell when he saw Rob J.

'Like to talk to you, Alex,' Rob said, leading him away from the others.

'I want you to come home,' he said when they were out of earshot.

'No, Pa.'

Alex was eighteen years old, and volatile. If he felt

349

pushed, he might just say go to hell and walk away from home for good. 'I don't want you to go. I have good reason.'

'I've been hearing about that good reason all my life,' Alex said bitterly. 'I once asked Ma outright, is Frank Mosby my uncle? And she said he isn't.'

'You're a fool, to put your mother through that. It doesn't matter if you go up there and shoot Mosby all by yourself, don't you know that? Some people are still going to talk. What they say doesn't matter at all.

'I could tell you to come home because it's my gun, and because it's my poor blind horse. But the real reason you can't go is that you're my boy, and I won't let you do something that'll eat at you the rest of your life.'

Alex shot a desperate glance to where Mal and the others were watching curiously.

'You tell them I said you had too much work waiting at the farm. And then you go get Vicky from wherever you tied her, and you come home.'

He went back and mounted Trude and rode up Main Street. Men were roughhousing in front of the church, and he could see that already there had been some drinking.

He didn't turn around for half a mile, but when he did, he saw the horse with the prissy, uncertain trot she had developed with her bad vision, and the figure bent over her neck like a man riding against a strong wind, the little bird gun held with its muzzle high, the way he'd taught his sons.

The next few weeks, Alex stayed out of his way, not so much angry at him as avoiding his authority. The posse stayed away two days. They found their quarry in a crumbling sod house, taking elaborate precautions before sneaking up on him, but he was asleep and unheeding. And he wasn't Frank Mosby. He was a man named Buren Harrison who had stuck up a storekeeper in Geneseo and robbed him of fourteen dollars, and Nick Holden and his lawmen escorted him triumphantly and drunkenly to justice. Subsequently it was learned that Frank Mosby had drowned in Iowa two years before, while trying to ride his horse across the Cedar River during floodwater.

In November, Rob J. voted to send John Kurland to Congress and to return Stephen A. Douglas to the Senate. The following evening he joined the crowd of men who waited for election news in Haskins' store, and in a display case he saw a pair of marvellous pocket knives. Each had a big blade, two smaller blades, and a little scissors, all of tempered steel, a case of polished tortoiseshell, and caps of gleaming silver on both ends. They were knives for men who weren't afraid to whittle life with thick shavings, and he bought them to give to his sons at Christmas.

Just after dark, Harold Ames rode in from Rock Island with the election returns. It had been a day for incumbents. Nick Holden, Indian fighter and upholder of the law, had narrowly defeated John Kurland, and Senator Douglas also would be going back to Washington.

'That'll teach Abraham Lincoln not to tell people they can't keep slaves,' Julian Howard chortled, shaking his fist in triumph. 'That's the last we'll hear from *that* son of a bitch!'

42
The Collegian

Inasmuch as Holden's Crossing wasn't on the railroad, Shaman's father drove him the thirty-two miles to Galesburg in the buckboard, with his trunk in back. The town and the college had been planned a quarter-century before in New York State, by Presbyterians and Congregationalists who came and built houses on streets laid out in a precise checkerboard pattern around a public square. At the college, the dean of students, Charles Hammond, said that since Shaman was younger than most of the others enrolled, he should not live in the dormitory. The dean and his wife took a few boarders into their white frame house on Cherry Street, and it was there, in a room at the rear of the second floor, that Shaman was housed.

Outside his room, stairs went down to a door that led to the backyard pump and the privy. In the room on his right were a pair of pale Congregational divinity students who preferred to talk only with one another. In the two rooms across the hall lived the short, dignified college librarian and a senior student named Ralph Brooke, who had a freckled, cheerful face, and eyes that always seemed slightly amazed. Brooke was a student of Latin. At breakfast the first morning, Shaman saw that he carried a volume of Cicero. Shaman's father had schooled him well in Latin. '*Iucundi acti labores,*' he said: Accomplished labours are pleasant.

Brooke's face lighted like a lamp. *'Ita vivam, ut scio'*: As I live, I know. Brooke became the only person in the house whom Shaman regularly talked to, with the exception of the dean and his skinny white-haired wife, who tried to mutter a few dutiful words daily.

'Ave!' Brooke greeted him each day. *'Quomodo te habes hodie, iuvenis?'* How are you on this morning, young fellow?

'Tam bene quam fieri possit talibus in rebus, Caesar.' As well as can be expected, under these circumstances, O Caesar, Shaman always said. Every morning. Their little joke.

At breakfast Brooke stole biscuits and was continually yawning. Only Shaman knew why. Brooke had a woman in the town and he stayed out very late, and very often. Two days after Shaman moved in, the Latinist convinced him to steal down the stairs and unlock the back door after all the others were abed, so Brooke could sneak in undetected. It was a service Brooke frequently would call upon.

Classes began each day at eight. Shaman took physiology, English composition and literature, and astronomy. To Brooke's awe, he passed an examination in Latin. Forced to study an additional language, he chose Hebrew over Greek, for reasons he wouldn't contemplate. His first Sunday in Galesburg, Dean and Mrs Hammond took him to the Presbyterian church, but after that he told the Hammonds he was a Congregationalist and he told the divinity students he was a Presbyterian, and every Sunday morning he was free to walk about the town.

The railroad had reached Galesburg six years before Shaman did, and had brought prosperity and a boomtime mixture of people. In addition, a cooperative colony of Swedes had failed at nearby Mission Hill, and a lot of its members had come to Galesburg to live. He loved to watch the Swedish women and girls, with their light yellow hair and lovely skin. When he took steps to make certain he didn't stain Mrs Hammond's sheets at night, his fantasy females were Swedish. Once on South Street he was stopped short by the sight of a darker head of female hair he was certain he knew, and for a moment he was unable to breathe. But it turned out that the woman was a stranger.

353

She smiled at him quickly when she saw him staring, but he put down his head and hurried away. She looked to be at least twenty. He didn't want to get to know any older women.

He was homesick and lovesick, but both maladies soon diminished to become bearable pains, like toothaches that were not excruciating. He made no friends, perhaps because of his youth and his deafness, which resulted in good scholarship because mostly he studied. His favourite courses were astronomy and physiology, although physiology was a disappointment, being a mere listing of body parts and components. The closest Mr Rowells, the instructor, came to discussing processes was a lecture on digestion and the importance of regularity. But in the physiology classroom was a wired-together skeleton suspended from a screw in the top of the skull, and Shaman spent hours alone with it, memorizing the name, shape, and function of each of the old bleached bones.

Galesburg was a pretty town, its streets lined with elm, maple, and walnut trees that had been planted by the first settlers. Its inhabitants were proud of three things. Harvey Henry May had invented a steel self-scouring plough there. A Galesburger named Olmsted Ferris had developed good popcorn; he had gone to England and popped it in front of Queen Victoria. And Senator Douglas and his opponent, Lincoln, debated at the college on October 7, 1859.

Shaman went to the debate that night, but when he arrived at Main Hall there already was a crowd, and he realized that from the best seat available he wouldn't be able to read the candidates' lips. He left the hall and climbed the stairs until he reached the door to the roof, where Professor Gardner, his astronomy teacher, maintained a small observatory at which each student in his class was required to study the heavens for several hours each month. Tonight Shaman was alone, and he peered into the ocular of Professor Gardner's pride and love, a five-inch Alvan Clark refracting telescope. He adjusted the knob, shortening the distance between the eyepiece and the convex front lens, and the stars sprang straight at him, two hundred times larger than a moment before. A cold night, clear enough to reveal two of the rings of Saturn. He studied the nebulae of Orion and Andromeda, then began moving the telescope on its tripod, searching the heavens. Professor Gardner called this 'sweeping the sky', and said a woman named Maria Mitchell had been sweeping the sky and had won lasting fame by discovering a comet.

Shaman discovered no comets. He watched until the stars seemed to wheel, enormous and glittering. What had formed them up there, out there? And the stars beyond? And *beyond*?

He felt that each star and planet was part of a complicated system, like a bone in a skeleton or a drop of blood in the body. So much of nature seemed organized, thought out – so orderly, yet so complicated. What had made it so? Mr Gardner had told Shaman that all anyone needed to become an astronomer were good eyes and mathematical ability. For a few days he'd considered making astronomy his life's work, but then he changed his mind. The stars were magical, but all you could do was watch them. If a heavenly body went awry, you couldn't ever hope to make it well again.

When he went home for Christmas, somehow Holden's Crossing was different than it had been before, lonelier than his room in the dean's house, and at the end of the holiday he returned to the college almost willingly. He was delighted with the knife his father had given him, and he bought a small whetstone and a tiny vial of oil and sharpened each blade until it could cut a single hair.

Second semester, he took chemistry instead of astronomy. He found composition difficult. You have told me BEFORE, his English professor scribbled crankily, that Beethoven wrote much of his music while deaf. Professor Gardner encouraged him to use the telescope whenever he pleased, but the night before a chemistry examination in February he sat on the roof and swept the sky instead of learning Berzelius' table of atomic weights, and he received a poor grade. After that, he managed less star-watching but he did

355

very well in chemistry. When he went back to Holden's Crossing again for the Easter holiday, the Geigers invited the Coles to dinner, and Jason's interest in chemistry made the ordeal less awkward for Shaman because Jay kept asking him questions about the course.

His answers must have been satisfactory. 'What do you plan to do with your life, old Shaman?' Jay asked.

'I don't know yet. I've thought . . . perhaps I can work in one of the sciences.'

'If you'd like pharmacy, I'd be honoured to apprentice you.'

He could see on his parents' faces that the offer pleased them, and he thanked Jay clumsily and said he'd certainly like to think about that; but he knew he didn't want to be a pharmacist. He kept his eyes on his plate for a few minutes and missed some of the conversation, but when he looked up again he saw that Lillian's face was shadowed with grief. She was telling his mother that Rachel's child would have been born in five months, and for a while thereafter they talked about losing babies.

That summer Shaman worked with the sheep and read philosophy books borrowed from George Cliburne. When he returned to college, Dean Hammond allowed him to escape from Hebrew, and he elected to study Shakespeare's plays, advanced mathematics, botany, and zoology. Only one of the divinity students had come back to Knox for another year, but so had Brooke, with whom Shaman continued to converse like a Roman, keeping his Latin fresh. His favourite teacher, Professor Gardner, taught the zoology course but was a better astronomer than a biologist. They dissected only frogs and mice and little fishes, making a lot of diagrams. Shaman didn't have his father's artistic talent, but being a child around Makwa had given him a head start in botany; he wrote his first project on the anatomy of flowers.

That year the debate about slavery waxed hot at the college. Along with other students and faculty members, he joined the Society for the Abolition of Slavery, but there were many at the college and in Galesburg who identified with the Southern states, and at times the debate became ugly.

Mostly, people left him alone. The townspeople and students had become accustomed to him, but to the ignorant and superstitious he had become a mystery, a local legend. They didn't understand about deafness, and about how deaf people could develop compensating sensitivities. They had quickly established that he was tone deaf, but some thought he had occult powers, because if he was studying alone and someone came in quietly behind him, he always detected a presence. They said he had 'eyes in the back of his head'. They didn't comprehend that he was reached by the vibrations of approaching steps, that he could feel the coolness from the opened door, or see the flicker of air movement in the paper he held in his hand. He was happy none of them would ever witness his ability to identify notes played on a piano.

He knew they referred to him sometimes as 'that *strange* deaf boy'.

On a soft early-May afternoon he had been walking about the town, observing the progress of the flowers in the yards, and at South Street and Cedar a railroad lorry pulled by four horses came around the corner too fast. Though he was spared the thunder of hooves and the yipping, he saw the small furry shape narrowly miss disaster from the front end, only to be caught by the right rear wheel that carried the dog around through almost a full rotation before finally it was flung clear. The lorry lumbered away, leaving the dog flopping in the dust of the street, and Shaman hurried closer.

The critter was a nondescript yellow female with stubby legs and a white-tipped tail. Shaman thought there was some terrier in her. She was writhing on her back, and a thin trickle of red ran from the corner of her mouth.

A couple who had been walking nearby came and stared.

'Disgraceful,' the man said. 'Mad drivers. It could as easily have been one of us.' He held out a warning hand as he saw

357

that Shaman was about to kneel. 'I wouldn't. It's sure to bite you in its pain.'

'Do you know who owns her?' Shaman asked.

'No,' the woman said.

'Just a street cur, this one,' the man said, and he and the woman walked away.

Shaman knelt and patted the dog warily, but the animal licked his hand. He felt all four limbs, and they didn't appear broken, fortunately. After a moment he took his jacket off and wrapped it around the dog. Holding her in his arms like an infant or a bundle of laundry, he carried her back to the house. No one looked out of the side windows and noticed him bearing his burden into the back yard. He met nobody on the back stairs. In his room he put the dog on the floor and then took his underwear and stockings out of the bottom drawer of his bureau. From the hall cupboard he helped himself to some of the rags Mrs Hammond kept for housecleaning. They made a kind of nest in the drawer, and he put the dog there. When he inspected his jacket, he saw there was only a little blood on it. Besides, it was on the inside.

The dog lay in the drawer, panting, and regarded him.

When it was time for supper, Shaman went out. In the corridor, Brooke watched in astonishment as he locked the door to his room, something nobody did who was going to be elsewhere in the house. '*Quid vis?*' Brooke said.

'*Condo parvam catulam in meo cubiculo.*'

Brooke's eyebrows rose in astonishment. 'You have . . .' He didn't trust his own Latin. '. . . Hidden a little bitch in your room?'

'*Sic est.*'

'Haw!' Brooke said in disbelief, and slapped Shaman on the back. In the dining room, it being Monday, there was leftover Sunday roast. Shaman slipped several small pieces from his plate and into his pocket, Brooke observing with interest. When Mrs Hammond went into the pantry to see about the dessert, he took half a cup of milk and left the table while the dean was engrossed in conversation about the book budget with the librarian.

The dog wasn't the least bit interested in the meat, nor would she lap the milk. Shaman took some milk on his fingers and put it on her tongue, as if she were feeding a motherless lamb, and that way he got a little nourishment into her.

For several hours he studied. At the end of the evening he stroked and petted the listless dog. Her nose was hot and dry. 'Go to sleep, there's a girl,' he said, and blew out the lamp. It was strange having another living creature in the room, but he liked it.

In the morning he went straight to the dog and found that her nose was cool. In fact, her whole body was cool, and stiff.

'Damnation,' Shaman said bitterly.

Now he would have to think of how to get rid of her. Meantime, he washed and dressed and went to breakfast, locking his room again. Brooke was waiting for him in the hall.

'I thought you were joking,' he said fiercely. 'But I could hear her crying and whimpering half the night.'

'Sorry,' Shaman said. 'You won't be bothered again.'

After breakfast, he went up and sat on his bed and looked at the dog. There was a flea on the lip of the drawer, and he tried to crush it but kept missing. He would have to wait until everyone left for the morning, and carry the dog out then, he thought. There must be a shovel in the cellar. It would mean he would miss his first class.

But he realized eventually that this was an opportunity to do a postmortem investigation.

The possibility intrigued him, but presented problems. Blood, for one. From helping his father during autopsy he knew that blood coagulated somewhat after death, but there would still be bleeding . . .

He waited until almost everyone had left the house, then went to where the large metal bathtub hung from a nail on the wall of the back hall. He carried it to his room and set it by the window, where the light was good. When he put the dog in the tub on her back, with her paws in the air, she looked as though she was waiting to have her tummy rubbed. Her toenails were long, like a neglected person's, and one was broken. She had four claws on her hind feet and an extra, smaller claw above each of her front feet, like thumbs that somehow had wandered upward. He wanted to see how the joints of the limbs compared to human joints. He snapped up the small blade of the pocketknife his father had given him. The dog had loose long hairs and thicker short hairs, but the fur on the underside didn't impede at all, and the flesh parted easily as the knife opened her.

He didn't go to classes or stop for lunch. All day he dissected and made notes and rough diagrams. Late in the afternoon, he'd finished with the internal organs and several of the joints. He still wanted to study and draw the spine, but he returned the dog to the bureau and closed the drawer. Then he poured water into his washbasin and scrubbed long and hard, using lots of brown soap, and emptied the basin into the tub. Before going down to supper, he put on fresh clothing from the skin out.

Still, they were scarcely on soup when Dean Hammond wrinkled his fleshy nose.

'What?' asked his wife.

'Something,' the dean said. 'Cabbage?'

'No,' she said.

Shaman was happy to escape when the meal was over. He sat in his room in a sweat, dreading lest someone should decide to take a bath.

No one did. Too nervous to be sleepy, he waited an exceptionally long time, until it was so late that everyone else would have gone to bed. Then he carried the tub from his room, down the stairs, and out into the soft air of the backyard, and emptied the bloody slops into the lawn. The pump seemed especially noisy as he worked the handle, and there was always the danger that someone would come out to use the privy, but they didn't. He scrubbed the tub with soap several times and rinsed it well, then took it back inside and hung it on the wall.

In the morning he faced the fact that he wouldn't be able

to dissect the spine, because the room had grown warmer and the scent was heavy. He kept the drawer closed and piled his pillow and bedclothes around it, hoping to seal in the smell. But when he went down to breakfast, the faces around the table were grim.

'A mouse, dead in the walls, I expect,' the librarian said. 'Or perhaps a rat.'

'No,' Mrs Hammond said. 'We found the source of the stench this morning. It seems to be coming from the ground around the pump.'

The dean sighed. 'I hope we shall not have to dig a new well.'

Brooke looked as if he had gone sleepless. He kept looking nervously away.

Numb, Shaman hurried off to his chemistry class, to give them a chance to clear out of the house. When chemistry was over, instead of going to Shakespeare he hastened home, eager to take care of things. But when he climbed the back stairs he found Brooke and Mrs Hammond and one of the town's two policemen standing in front of his door. She held her key.

They all looked at Shaman. 'Something is dead in there?' the policeman asked.

Shaman found he couldn't answer.

'He told me he hid a woman in there,' Brooke said.

Shaman found his voice. 'No,' he said, but the policeman had taken the key from Mrs Hammond and unlocked the door.

Inside, Brooke started to look under the bed, but the policeman saw the pillow and the bedding and went directly to open the drawer. 'A dog,' he said. 'All cut up, like.'

'Not a woman?' Brooke said. He looked at Shaman. 'You said a bitch.'

'You said a bitch. I said *catulam*,' Shaman told him. 'Dog, feminine gender.'

'I don't suppose, sir,' the policeman said, 'that there is anything else dead and hidden here? On your honour, now?'

361

'No,' Shaman said. Mrs Hammond looked at him but didn't say a word. She hurried out and down the stairs, and at once they heard the front door open and slam.

The policeman sighed. 'She'll be going straight to her husband's office. I expect that is where we should go too.'

Shaman nodded and followed him out past Brooke, whose eyes were regretful above the handkerchief held against his mouth and nose.

'*Vale*', Shaman said.

He was evicted. Less than three weeks remained of the semester, and Professor Gardner allowed him to sleep on a cot in his garden shed. Shaman spaded the garden and planted thirty-two feet of potatoes out of appreciation. A snake that lived under some pots gave him a start, but when he ascertained that it was only a small milk snake, they got on well.

He received excellent grades, but he was given a sealed letter to deliver to his father. When he reached home, he sat in the study and waited while his father read it. Shaman pretty much knew what it said. Dean Hammond had told him he'd earned two years of college credits but was suspended for a year, to allow him to mature sufficiently to fit into an academic community. When he returned, he would have to find other lodging.

His father finished reading the letter and regarded him. 'Did you learn anything from this little adventure?'

'Yes, Pa,' he said. 'A dog is surprisingly similar to a human being, inside. The heart is much smaller, of course, less than half the size, but it looked very much like the human hearts I've seen you remove and weigh. The same mahogany colour.'

'Not quite mahogany . . .'

'Well . . . reddish.'

'Yes, reddish.'

'The lungs and intestinal tract are similar too. But not the spleen. Instead of being round and compact, the spleen was like a big tongue, a foot long, two inches wide, an inch thick.

'The aorta was ruptured. That's what killed her. I guess

she haemorrhaged most of her blood. A whole lot was pooled in the cavity.'

His father regarded him.

'I took notes. If you'd be interested in reading them.'

'I would be very interested,' his father said thoughtfully.

43
The Applicant

At night Shaman lay in the bed with the rope springs that needed tightening, staring at walls so familiar that from the variations of the sunrise light on them he could tell the season of the year. His father had suggested that he spend the time of his suspension at home. 'Now that you've learned some physiology, you can be more useful to me when I do an autopsy. And you're an extra pair of steady hands on a house call. In between,' Rob J. said, 'you can help with the farm.'

Soon it seemed as if Shaman never had left at all. But for the first time in his life, the silence that enwrapped him was acutely lonely.

That year, with the bodies of suicides and derelicts and kinless indigents as his textbooks, he learned the art of dissection. In the homes of the ill and the injured, he prepared instruments and dressings and watched how his father rose to meet the demands of each new situation. He knew his father was watching him too, and he worked hard at staying alert, learning the names of the instruments and splints and dressings so he could have them ready even before Rob J. asked for them.

One morning when they'd stopped the buggy by the river woods to relieve their bladders, he told his father he intended to study medicine instead of going back to Knox

364

College when his year of suspension was over.

'The hell,' Rob J. said, and Shaman felt the sour lurch of disappointment, because he could see in the face before him that nothing had altered his father's mind.

'Don't you understand, boy? I'm trying to save you from hurt. It's clear you have a real talent for science. Finish college, and I'll pay for the best graduate education you can find, anywhere in the world. You can teach, do research. I believe you have it in you to do great things.'

Shaman shook his head. 'I don't mind hurting. Once you tied my hands and wouldn't give me food until I used my voice. You were trying to make me the best I could be, not protecting me from pain.'

Rob J. sighed and then nodded. 'Very well. If your mind's made up to try medicine, you can apprentice with me.'

But Shaman shook his head. 'You'd be doing your deaf son a charity. Trying to make something of value out of inferior goods, against your better judgement.'

'Shaman . . .' his father said heavily.

'I intend to study the way you did, at a medical school.'

'That's an especially bad idea. I don't imagine a good school will take you. All kinds of shoddy medical schools are springing up everywhere, and they'll accept you. They accept anyone with funds. But it would be a sad mistake to try to learn medicine at one of those places.'

'I don't intend to.' Shaman asked his father to give him a list of the best medical schools within decent travelling distance of the Mississippi Valley.

Rob J. went to his study as soon as they got home and made out the list, handing it over before supper, as if wanting to erase the subject from his mind. Shaman put fresh oil in the lamp and sat at the small table in his room until well past midnight, writing letters. He took pains to make it clear that the applicant was a deaf man, not wishing any unpleasant surprises.

The horse called Bess, the former Monica Grenville, had been skinny after carrying Rob J. halfway across the continent, but now she was plump and pleasant in her

365

workless old age. But for poor blind Vicky, the horse that had been bought as Bess' replacement, the world had turned bad. Late in the fall Rob J. rode home one afternoon and saw Vicky trembling in the pasture. Her head drooped, her skinny legs were slightly splayed, and she was as oblivious of her surroundings as any human who had ever passed, addled and weak, into sick old age.

Next morning he went to Geiger's and asked Jay if he had a supply of morphine.

'How much do you want?'

'Enough to kill a horse,' Rob J. said.

He led Vicky out into the middle of the pasture and fed her two carrots and an apple. He injected the drug into her right jugular vein, talking to her softly and stroking her neck while she chomped the last sweet meal. Almost at once she sank to her knees and rolled over. Rob J. stayed there until she was gone, then sighed and told his sons to take care of her, and went off to make his calls.

Shaman and Alex started digging right next to her back. It took them a long time, because the hole had to be deep and wide. When it was ready, they stood and looked at the horse. 'Odd, the way her incisors angle out like that,' Shaman said.

'It's the way horses show their age, in the teeth,' Alex said.

'I can remember when her teeth were as straight as yours or mine. . . . She was a good old girl.'

'She farted a lot,' Alex said, and they both smiled. Still, after they tipped her into the hole, they shovelled the dirt in quickly, unable to look at her. They were sweating despite the cool day. Alex led Shaman into the barn and showed him where Alden had hidden whisky under some sacking, and he took a long pull from the jug and Shaman took a little one.

'I've got to get out of here,' Alex said.

'Thought you liked working the farm.'

'. . . Can't get along with Pa.'

Shaman hesitated. 'He cares about us, Alex.'

'Sure, he does. He's been good to me. But . . . I have

questions about my natural father. Nobody answers them, and I go out and raise some more hell because it makes me feel like a sure-enough bastard.'

It hurt Shaman. 'You've got a ma and a pa. And a brother,' he said sharply. 'That should be enough for anybody who isn't a damn fool.'

'Old Shaman, always there with the common sense.' He flashed his grin. 'Tell you what, let's you and me just . . . go away. To Californ-i-ay. There must be some gold left out there. We can have a high old time, get rich, come back, and buy the damn town from Nick Holden.'

It was an appealing prospect, to be footloose with Alex, and the offer was more than half-serious. 'Got me some other plans, Bigger. And don't you go running off, because if you weren't here, who'd shovel the sheep shit?'

Alex smacked into him, bore him to the ground. Whooping and grunting, each of them strained for a wrestling hold. Alden's jug went flying, to empty gurgling and unheeded as they rolled over and over on the hay-littered barn floor. Alex was hardened by continuous labour, and strong, but Shaman was larger and stronger, and soon he had his brother in a headlock. After a while it occurred to him that Alex was trying to say something, and he held his left arm around Alex's neck while his right hand pulled his brother's head back to see his face.

'Give up, and I'll let you go,' Alex managed to croak, and Shaman collapsed back into the hay, laughing.

Alex crawled to the toppled jug and looked at it mournfully. 'Alden will be fit to be tied.'

'Tell him I drank it.'

'Naw. Who'd believe a thing like that?' Alex said, putting the jug to his lips and salvaging the last drops.

That fall it rained a lot, well into the season when usually there was snow. The rains fell in hard silver sheets, but intermittently, with several days of grace between storms, so that the rivers became giants that roared with fast water but kept to their banks. In the pasture the dirt on Vicky's grave, which had been mounded high, settled until soon it was impossible to locate.

Rob J. bought a rawboned grey gelding for Sarah. They called him Boss, though when Sarah was in the saddle it was she who did the bossing.

Rod J. said he'd keep his eyes open for a likely horse for Alex. Alex was properly grateful because he wasn't strong on thrift to begin with, and whatever money he could put by was earmarked for the purchase of a breech-loading hunting rifle.

'Seems like I'm forever looking for a horse,' Rob J. said, but he didn't suggest he'd look for a horse for Shaman.

The mail sack came to Holden's Crossing from Rock Island every Tuesday and Friday afternoon. Starting around Christmastime Shaman began to anticipate each mail delivery, but it wasn't until the third week in February that the first letters came. That Tuesday he received two short, almost curt letters of rejection, one from the Medical College of Wisconsin and the other from the Medical Department of the University of Louisiana. On Friday another letter informed him his training and background appeared to be excellent, but 'the Rush Medical College of Chicago has no facilities for persons who are deaf'.

Facilities? Did they think he needed to be caged?

His father knew the letters had arrived, and he understood from Shaman's controlled demeanour that they'd been refusals. Shaman would have hated it if Rob J. had treated him gingerly or with sympathy, but that didn't happen. The rejections smarted; no other letters appeared for the next seven weeks, and that was all right with him.

Rob J. had read the notes Shaman had made while dissecting the dog, and he found them promising, if unsophisticated. He suggested that his own files might teach Shaman about anatomical records, and Shaman studied them whenever he had time to spare. Thus it was by accident that he came upon the autopsy report on Makwa-ikwa. He felt strange as he read it, knowing that while the terrible things described in the report were happening, he'd been a little boy, asleep in the woods only a short distance away.

'She was raped! I knew she was murdered, but –'

'Raped and sodomized. It's not the kind of thing you tell a child,' his father said.

He read the report again and again, mesmerized.

Eleven stab wounds, running in irregular line from the jugular notch down the sternum to a position approximately two centimetres inferior to the xiphoid process.

Triangular wounds, .947 to .952 centimetres in width. Three of them reaching the heart, .887 centimetres, .799 centimetres, .803 centimetres.

'Why do the wounds have different widths?'

'It means the weapon was pointed, becoming progressively wider down the blade. The more force to the thrust, the wider the wound.'

'Do you think they'll ever get whoever did this?'

'No, I don't,' his father said. 'There were three of them, most likely. For a long time I had people looking hard and wide for an Ellwood R. Patterson. But there isn't a trace of him. Probably it was a false name. There was a man with him named Cough. I've never run across or even heard of a man of that name. And a young fellow with a port-wine stain on his face, and a limp. I used to tense up anytime I saw someone with a facial stain or a gimpy leg. But always, either they'd have the mark or the limp. Never both.'

'The authorities never cared to find them, and now . . .' He shrugged. 'Too much time has passed, too many years.' Shaman recognized sadness in his father's voice, but he saw that most of the anger and passion long since had been burned away.

One day in April, as Shaman and his father were riding past the Catholic convent, Rob J. turned Trude into the lane and Shaman followed on Boss.

Inside the convent house, Shaman noted that several of the nuns greeted his father by name and didn't seem surprised to see him. His father introduced him to Mother Miriam Ferocia, who appeared to be the leader. She seated

369

them, his father in a great leather throne and Shaman in a straight wooden chair beneath a wall crucifix from which hung a sad-eyed wooden Jesus, and one of the other nuns served them with good coffee and hot bread.

'I'll have to bring the boy again,' his father told the mother superior. 'Usually I don't get bread with my coffee.' Shaman realized Rob J. was a man of surprising parts, and that probably he never would understand his father.

Shaman had seen nuns nursing his father's patients from time to time, always in pairs. Rob J. and the nun talked briefly about several cases, but soon they turned to politics, and it was obvious that the visit was a social one. Rob J. glanced at the crucifix. 'Ralph Waldo Emerson is quoted in the Chicago *Tribune* as saying that John Brown made his gallows as glorious as a cross,' he said.

Miriam Ferocia observed that Brown, an abolitionist zealot who'd been hanged for seizing a United States armoury in western Virginia, was fast becoming a martyr in the eyes of those who opposed slavery. 'Yet slavery isn't the real cause of the trouble between the regions. It is economics. The South sells its cotton and sugar to England and Europe, and buys manufactured goods from those places instead of from the industrial North. The South has decided it has no need for the rest of the United States of America. Despite Mr Lincoln's speeches against slavery, that is the sore that festers.'

'I don't know economics,' Shaman said thoughtfully. 'I was to study it this year if I had returned to college.'

When the nun asked why he hadn't returned, his father revealed he was suspended for dissecting a dog.

'Oh, dear! And was it dead at the time?' she asked.

Assured that it was, she nodded. '*Ja*, that is all right, then. I never studied economics either. But it is in my blood. My father started life as a carpenter who repaired hay wagons. Now he owns a wagonworks in Frankfurt and a carriage factory in München.' She smiled. 'My father's name is Brotknecht. It means breadmaker, because in the Middle Ages my family were bakers. Yet in Baden, where I was a novice, there was a baker named Wagenknecht!'

370

'What was your name before you became a nun?' Shaman asked. He saw her hesitation and his father's frown and realized the question was rude, but Miriam Ferocia answered him. 'When I was of the world, I was Andrea.' She rose from her chair and went to a shelf to take down a book. 'It may interest you to borrow this,' she said. 'It is by David Ricardo, an English economist.'

Shaman stayed up late that night and read the book. Some of it was hard to understand, but he saw that Ricardo argued for free trade among the nations, which was what the South was insisting upon.

When finally he fell asleep, he witnessed Christ on the cross. As he dreamed, he saw the long aquiline nose become shorter and broader. The skin darkened and reddened, the hair turned black. Female breasts developed, dark-dugged, marked by runic signs. The stigmata appeared. In his sleep, without counting, Shaman knew there were eleven wounds, and as he watched, blood welled to trickle down the body and drip from Makwa's feet.

Forty-nine lambs were born to Cole ewes in the spring of 1860, and the entire family helped with the problem births and the castrating. 'The flock's growin' bigger every spring,' Alden told Rob J. with worried pride. 'You're goin to have to tell me what you want done with this bunch.'

Rob J.'s choices were limited. They could butcher only a few. Little demand for bought meat existed among their neighbours, who raised animals of their own, and of course the meat would spoil before it could be carried to the city for sale. Live animals could be transported and sold, but that was complicated and required time, effort, and money. 'Fleeces are very valuable in proportion to their bulk,' Rob J. said. 'The best plan is to keep building the flock and make our money from the sale of wool, the way my family's always done in Scotland.'

'Yuh. Well, then, they's goin' to be more work than ever. That's goin' to require hirin' another pair of hands,' Alden said uneasily, and Shaman wondered if Alex had said anything to the hired man about wanting to run off. 'Doug Penfield's willin' to work for you part-time. Told me so.'

'You think he's a good man?'

'Sure he is, comes from New Hampshire. That's not same's comin' from Vermont, but it's close.'

Rob J. agreed with him that it was, and Doug Penfield

was hired.

That spring, Shaman made connection with Lucille Williams, daughter of Paul Williams, the farrier. For several years Lucille had attended the Academy, where Shaman had taught her mathematics. Now Lucille was a young woman. If her blonde hair, which she wore in a great knot, was more ashen than that of the yellow-maned Swedish girls of his dreams, she had a quick smile and a sweet face. Whenever he met her in the village he stopped to pass the time of day as an old friend, and to inquire about her work, which was split between her father's stables and Roberta's Women's Wear, her mother's Main Street shop. The arrangement allowed her flexibility and a certain freedom, for her parents always took her absence without question, each assuming she had gone to attend some duty for the other. Therefore, when Lucille asked Shaman if he couldn't bring her some farm butter, to be delivered at her house at two in the afternoon next day, he was nervously excited.

She was careful to explain to him that he must tie his horse on Main Street in front of the stores, then walk around the block to Illinois Avenue, cut through the Reimers' property behind the row of tall lilac bushes and out of sight of the house, climb over the picket fence into the Williams' backyard, and tap at her back door.

'So it won't look . . . you know, misleading for the neighbours,' she said, dropping her eyes. He wasn't surprised, because Alex had delivered butter to her fully a year earlier, with reports, but Shaman was apprehensive: he wasn't Alex.

Next day, the Reimers' lilacs were in full bloom. The fence was easy to scale, and the back door opened at once to his knock. Lucille was effusive in her appreciation of how nicely the butter was wrapped in towels, which she folded and left on the kitchen table with the dish when she brought the butter to the cold cellar. On her return she took his hand and led him into a room off the kitchen that obviously was Roberta Williams' fitting room. Half a bolt of gingham cloth leaned against one corner, and remnants of silk and satin

373

and drill and cotton goods were folded neatly on a long shelf. Alongside a great horsehair sofa was a dressmaker's form of wire and cloth, and to Shaman's fascination, it had ivory buttocks.

She offered her face for a single long kiss, and then each of them was undressing with dispatch and neatness, leaving their clothes in two fussy, well-matched little piles, their stockings in their shoes. He observed clinically that her body was out-of-balance; her shoulders were narrow and sloping, her breasts like slightly raised pancakes, each centred with a small pool of syrup and adorned with a brownish berry, while her bottom half was heavier, with wide hips and thick legs. When she turned to throw a greyish sheet across the couch ('The horsehair scratches!'), he saw that the dressmaker's form was not for her skirts, which would be more ample.

She didn't let down her hair. 'It takes so long to put it back up,' she said apologetically, and he assured her almost formally it was quite all right.

In the doing, it was easy. She made it so, and he'd listened to the boasting stories of Alex and others for so long that, if he had never been down the trail himself, he had a good idea of the landmarks. The day before, he wouldn't have dreamed of touching the ivory buttocks of the dressmaker's dummy, but now he dealt with warm, living flesh, and he licked the syrup and tasted the berries. Very quickly, and with great relief, he laid down the burden of chastity with a shuddering climax. Lacking the ability to hear what she panted in his ears, he utilized each of his other senses to the utmost, and she obliged by assuming any and all positions for his close inspection, until he was able to repeat the earlier experience, taking somewhat longer. He was ready to keep on, on and on, but soon Lucille glanced at the clock and bounded off the couch, saying she had to have supper ready when her mother and father came home. As they dressed, they planned for the future. She (and this empty house!) were readily available during the day. Alas, that was when Shaman worked. They agreed she would try to be at home each Tuesday at two p.m., in case he could make it to

374

town. That way, he explained practically, he could pick up the mail.

She was just as practical, revealing as she kissed him goodbye that she loved rock candy, the pink sugary kind, not the greenish variety that was flavoured with mint. He assured her he understood the difference. On the other side of the fence, walking with an unfamiliar lightness, he went back down the long line of blossom-laden lilacs, through the heavy purple scent that for the rest of his life would be a highly erotic smell.

Lucille liked the smoothness of his hands, not knowing they were soft because much of the time they were covered with lanolin-rich yolk from the fleeces. The farm took wool well into May, Shaman, Alex, and Alden doing most of the shearing, with Doug Penfield eager to learn but clumsy with the clippers. Mostly they put Doug to work picking and scouring the fleeces. He brought them news of the outside world when he came, including the intelligence that the Republicans had chosen Abraham Lincoln as their presidential nominee. By the time all the fleeces were rolled up, tied, and packed in bales, they had also heard that the Democrats had met in Baltimore and had chosen Douglas after acrimonious debate. Within weeks, Southern Democrats had called a second Democratic convention in the same city, and nominated Vice-President John C. Breckinridge to run for president, calling for the protection of their right to own slaves.

Locally, the Democrats were more united, and had once again chosen John Kurland, the Rock Island attorney, to challenge Nick Holden for his congressional seat. Nick was running as the nominee of both the American party and the Republicans, and he was stumping hard for Lincoln, hoping to ride in on the presidential bandwagon. Lincoln had welcomed Know Nothing support, and it was why Rob J. declared that he couldn't vote for the man.

Shaman found it hard to concentrate on politics. In July he heard from the Cleveland Medical College, another refusal, and by summer's end he'd also been rejected by the

375

Ohio College of Medicine and the University of Louisville. He told himself he needed only one acceptance. The first week in September, on a Tuesday when Lucille waited in vain, his father rode home with the mail and handed him a long brown envelope whose return address said it came from the Kentucky School of Medicine. He took it out to the barn before he ripped it open. He was glad to be alone, because it was another failed application, and he lay back in the hay and tried not to succumb to panic.

There was still time to go to Galesburg and enroll in Knox College as a third-year student. It would be safe, a return to a routine in which he'd survived, in which he'd done well. Once he had his baccalaureate degree, life could even be exciting, because he could go east to study science. Maybe even go to Europe.

If he didn't go back to Knox, and he couldn't enter medical school, what would his life be?

But he made no move to go to his father and ask to be returned to college. He lay in the hay a long time, and when he got up, he took a shovel and the barrow and began to muck out the barn, an act that in itself was a kind of answer.

Politics were impossible to avoid. In November Shaman's father freely admitted that when he went to the polls he'd voted for Douglas, but it was Lincoln's year, because the Northern and Southern Democrats split the party with their separate candidates, and Lincoln won easily. It was small consolation that Nick Holden finally had been turned out of office. 'At least Kurland will make us a good congressman,' Rob J. said. In the general store, folks wondered if Nick would come back to Holden's Crossing now, and resume the practice of law.

The question was put to rest within a few weeks, when Abraham Lincoln began to announce some of the upcoming appointments that would be made under the new administration. The Honourable Congressman Nicholas Holden, hero of the Sauk wars and ardent supporter of Mr Lincoln's candidacy, had been named United States Commissioner of Indian Affairs. He was charged with the task of completing treaties with the Western tribes, and furnishing them with suitable reservations in return for peaceful conduct and forfeit of all other Indian land and territories.

Rob J. was cranky and depressed for weeks.

It was a tense and unhappy time for Shaman personally, and a tense and unhappy time for the nation, but much later Shaman would look back at that winter with nostalgia, remembering it as a precious country scene carved by skilled and patient hands and then frozen in a crystal: the house, the barn. Icy river, snowy fields. The sheep and horses and milch cows. Each individual person. All of them safe and together in their proper place.

But the crystal had been knocked from the table and already was falling.

Within days of the election of a President who had run on the premise that they shouldn't own slaves, the Southern states began moving toward secession. South Carolina was hotly first, and United States Army forces that had occupied two forts in Charleston harbour moved into the larger of the two, Fort Sumter. At once they were under siege. In quick succession, state militias in Georgia, Alabama, Florida, Louisiana, and Mississippi seized United States installations from outnumbered peacetime federal forces, sometimes after fighting.

Dear Ma and Pa;

I'm going off with Mal Howard to join up with the South. We don't know exactly what state we'll enlist in. Mal kind of would like to go to Tennessee, to serve with his kinfolk. It don't matter much to me, unless I can get to Virginia and say hello to our own kin.

Mr Howard says it's important for the South to field a whopper army to show Lincoln they won't be trifled with. He says there's not to be a war, it's just a family quarrel. So I'll be back in plenty time for spring lambing.

Meantime, Pa, maybe I'll be given a horse and gun of my own!

377

Your loving son,
Alexander Bledsoe Cole

Shaman found another note in his room, scrawled on a torn piece of brown wrapping paper and weighted down on his pillow with the mate to the pocket knife his father had given him:

Little Brother,

Take care of this for me. I wouldn't want to lose it. See you directly.

Bigger

Rob J. went at once to Julian Howard, who admitted in uneasy defiance that he'd driven the boys to Rock Island in his buckboard the previous evening, right after chores. 'No need to get all riled, for goodness' sake! They're grown-up lads, and it's just a small adventure.'

Rob J. asked him at what river wharf he had left them. Howard saw how Rob J. Cole stood close to him at his full bulky height, and felt the chill and contempt in the uppity doctor's voice, and he stammered out that he had left them off near the Three-Star Freight Transport pier.

Rob J. rode straight there, against the slim chance he could bring them home. If there had been the low temperatures of some other winters, perhaps he'd have had more luck, but the river wasn't icebound and traffic was heavy. The manager of the freight company looked at him in amazement when he asked if the man had noticed two youths looking to work on one of the flatboats or rafts heading downstream.

'Mister, we had seventy-two craft off-load or take on cargo at this pier yesterday, and that's in slow season, and we're just one Mississippi freight company of many. And most of those boats hire young men who walked away from a family somewheres, so I don't hardly take notice of any of 'em,' he said, not unkindly.

Shaman thought the Southern states seceded like corn popping in a hot skillet. His red-eyed mother spent her time praying, and his father went on his home visits without smiling. In Rock Island one of the feed stores moved as much stock as possible into the back room and rented half its space to an army recruiter. Shaman drifted into the place once himself, thinking that perhaps if all else failed in his life, he could be a stretcher-bearer, because he was big and strong. But the corporal who was signing up men raised his eyebrows comically as soon as he learned Shaman was deaf, and told him to go home.

He felt that with so much of the world going to hell, he didn't have much right to be troubled about the confusion in his own life. The second Tuesday in January his father brought home a letter, and then another one that Friday. His father surprised him, because Rob J. knew he'd recommended nine schools, and he had kept track of the nine answering letters. 'That's the last of them, isn't it?' he said to Shaman after supper that night.

'Yes. From Missouri Medical College. A rejection,' Shaman said, and his father nodded without surprise.

'But this is the letter that came on Tuesday,' Shaman said, and he took it from his pocket and unfolded it. It was from Dean Lester Nash Berwyn, MD, of the Cincinnati Polyclinic Medical School. It accepted him as a student on the condition that he successfully complete the initial term of study as a trial period. The school, affiliated with the Southwestern Ohio Hospital of Cincinnati, offered a two-year programme of study leading to the degree of Doctor of Medicine, four terms in each year. The next term was to begin on January 24.

Shaman should have felt the joy of victory, but he knew his father was seeing the words 'on condition' and 'trial period', and he prepared himself for an argument. With Alex gone, he was needed on the farm, but he was determined to escape, to grasp his chance. For many reasons, some of them selfish, he was angry that his father had allowed Alex to run away. While he was about it, he was angry at his father for being so damned certain there

379

wasn't a God, and for not realizing that most people just weren't strong enough to be pacifists.

But when Rob J. looked up from the letter, Shaman saw his eyes and his mouth. The knowledge that Dr Rob J. Cole wasn't invulnerable entered him like an arrow.

'Alex won't be hurt. He's going to be all right!' Shaman cried, but he knew it wasn't the honest assessment of a responsible person, of a man. Despite the existence of the room with the ivory-assed dummy, and the arrival of the letter from Cincinnati, he understood it was only the worthless promise of a desperate boy.

V
A FAMILY QUARREL
January 24, 1861

45
At the Polyclinic

Cincinnati sprawled larger than Shaman had expected, the streets teeming with traffic, the Ohio River ice-free and busy with boats. The intimidating smoke of factories rose from tall chimneys. Everywhere, there were people; he could imagine their noise.

A horse-car trolley took him from the riverside railroad depot straight to the promised land on Ninth Street. The Southwestern Ohio Hospital was composed of a pair of red-brick buildings, each three storeys high, and a two-storey wood-frame pesthouse. Across the street, in another brick building surmounted by a cupola with glass sides, was the Cincinnati Polyclinic Medical School. Inside the school building Shaman saw shabby classrooms and lecture halls. He asked a student for the dean's office and was directed up an oak staircase to the second floor. Dr Berwyn was a hearty middle-aged man with white moustaches and a hairless head that gleamed in the soft light of the high and grimy windows.

'Ah, so you are Cole.'

He motioned Shaman into a seat. There followed a short talk on the history of the medical school, the responsibilities of good doctors, and the necessity of rigorous study habits. Shaman knew instinctively that the greeting was a set piece, recited for every new student, but this time there was a finish just for him. 'You must not allow yourself to be intimidated by your conditional status,' Dr Berwyn said carefully. 'In a sense, every student here is on trial and must prove himself a worthy candidate.'

In a sense. Shaman would have wagered that not every student had been informed of his conditional status by letter. Still, he thanked the dean politely. Dr Berwyn directed him to the dormitory, which proved to be a three-storey wood-frame tenement building hiding behind the medical school. A dormitory roster tacked to the hallway wall informed him that Cole, Robert J., was billeted in room Two-B, along with Cooke, Paul P.; Torrington, Ruel; and Henried, William.

Two-B was a small room entirely filled by two double bunks, two bureaus, and a table with four chairs, one of which was occupied by a plump youth who stopped writing in a notebook when Shaman came in. 'Halloo! I'm P.P. Cooke, from Xenia. Bill Henried's gone to get his books. So you must be either Torrington from Kentucky, or the deaf fellow.'

Shaman laughed, suddenly very relaxed. 'I'm the deaf fellow,' he said. 'Do you mind if I call you Paul?'

That evening they watched one another, drawing conclusions. Cooke was the son of a feed merchant, and prosperous, judging from his clothing and belongings. Shaman could see he was accustomed to playing the fool, perhaps because of his portliness, but there was shrewd intelligence in his brown eyes, which missed little. Billy Henried was slight and quiet. He told them he'd grown up on a farm outside of Columbus and had attended a seminary for two years before deciding he wasn't cut out for the priesthood. Ruel Torrington, who didn't arrive until after supper, was a surprise. He was twice as old as his roommates, and already a veteran medical practitioner. Apprenticed to a physician at a young age, he had decided to attend medical school to legitimize his title of *Doctor*.

The other three students in Two-B were cheered by his background, at first believing it would be an advantage to study alongside an experienced physician, but Torrington

384

arrived in a bad mood that never changed as long as they knew him. The only bed that was unclaimed when he arrived was the top bunk against the wall, which he didn't fancy. He made it obvious that he scorned Cooke because he was fat, Shaman because he was deaf, and Henried because he was a Catholic. His animosity welded the other three into an early alliance, and they didn't waste much time on him.

Cooke had been there several days and had gathered intelligence which he shared with the others. The school had a faculty of generally high repute, but two of its stars shone more brightly than any others. One was the professor of surgery, Dr Berwyn, who also served as dean. The other was Dr Barnett A. McGowan, a pathologist who taught the dreaded course known as 'A&P' – anatomy and physiology. 'They call him Barney behind his back,' Cooke confided. 'They say he's responsible for failing more medical students than the rest of the faculty put together.'

The next morning Shaman went to a savings bank and deposited most of the money he'd brought with him. He and his father had planned his financial needs carefully. Tuition was sixty dollars per year, fifty dollars if paid in advance. They had added money for room and meals, books, transportation, and other expenses. Rob J. had been happy to pay whatever was necessary, but Shaman stubbornly had held the idea that since his medical education was his own plan, he should pay for it. In the end they agreed that he would sign a note to his father, promising to repay every dollar following his graduation.

After leaving the bank, his next errand was to find the school's bursar and pay his tuition. It didn't help his spirits when that official explained that if Shaman should be dismissed for academic or health reasons, his tuition money could be only partially refunded.

The first class he attended as a medical student was a one-hour lecture on the diseases of women. Shaman had learned in college that it was essential to reach every class as early as possible, in order to sit close enough to lip-read with a high degree of accuracy. He showed up early enough to gain a place in the front row, which was fortunate, because Professor Harold Meigs lectured rapidly. Shaman had learned to take notes while watching the lecturer's mouth instead of the paper. He wrote carefully, aware Rob J. would ask to read his notes to learn what was happening in medical education.

His next class, chemistry, revealed that he had sufficient laboratory background for medical school; this cheered him and stimulated his appetite for food as well as for work. He went to the hospital dining room for a hasty lunch of crackers and meat soup, less than wonderful. Then he hurried to Cruikshank's Bookstore, which serviced the medical school, where he rented a microscope and bought his books from the required list: Dunglison's *General Therapeutics and Materia Medica*, McGowan's *Human Physiology*, Quain's *Anatomical Plates*, Berwyn's *Operative Surgery*, Fowne's *Chemistry*, and two books by Meigs, *Woman, Her Diseases and Their Remedies* and *Diseases of Children*.

As the eldely clerk was totting up his bill, Shaman glanced away to see Dr Berwyn in conversation with a short glowering man whose neat beard was sprinkled with grey, like his mane of hair. He was as hirsute as Berwyn was bald. They were obviously deeply engaged in argument, although evidently they kept their voices low, because none of the people nearby paid them attention. Dr Berwyn was half-turned from Shaman's sight, but the other man faced him squarely, and Shaman read his lips more by reflex than out of any desire to eavesdrop.

. . . know that this country is going to war. I am well aware, sir, that this incoming class is forty-two students instead of the usual sixty, and I know well that some of these will run off to battle when the study of medicine gets too tough. Especially at such a time we must guard against lowering our standards. Harold Meigs says you have accepted some students whom last year you'd have rejected. I am told that among them there is even a deaf mute . . .

Mercifully, at that point the clerk touched Shaman's arm and showed him the amount due.

'Who is the gentleman talking with Dr Berwyn?' Shaman

asked, the mute finding his voice.

'That is Dr McGowan, sir,' the clerk said, and Shaman nodded, gathered up his books, and fled.

Several hours later, Professor Barnett Alan McGowan sat at his desk in the dissection laboratory of the medical school and transcribed notes into permanent records. All the records dealt with death, since Dr McGowan seldom had anything to do with a living patient. Because some people looked upon death as a less-than-happy environment, he'd grown accustomed to being assigned working places that were out of the public's eye. In the hospital, where Dr McGowan was chief pathologist, the dissection room was in the basement of the main building. Although it was convenient to the brick-lined tunnel that ran under the street between the hospital and the medical school, it was a drab place notable for the pipes that crisscrossed its low ceilings.

The medical-school anatomy laboratory was in the rear of its building on the second floor. It was reached from both the corridor and a separate stairway of its own. One tall window, curtainless, let leaden winter light into the long narrow room. At one end of the splintery floor, facing the professor's desk, was a small amphitheatre, its rising tiers of seats placed too close for comfort but not for concentration. At the other end stood a triple row of students' dissecting tables. In the centre of the room was a large brine tank full of human parts and a table bearing rows of dissecting instruments. The body of a young woman, completely covered by a clean white sheet, lay on a board placed out of the way on sawhorses. It was the facts concerning this body that the professor was entering into the records.

At twenty minutes before the hour, a lone student came into the laboratory. Professor McGowan didn't look up or greet the large young man; he dipped his steel pen into the ink and continued to write as the student went directly to the middle seat in the front row and claimed it with his notebook. He didn't take the seat, but instead strolled through the laboratory on an inspection tour.

Stopping before the brine tank, to Dr McGowan's amazement he picked up the wooden staff with the iron hook at the end of it, and began fishing among the body parts in the saline solution, like a small boy playing in a pond. In the nineteen years Dr McGowan had taught first lessons in anatomy, no one ever had behaved in such a fashion. New students came to anatomy class for the first time with portentous dignity. Usually they walked slowly, often with dread.

'Here, now! Stop that at once. Put the hook down,' McGowan commanded.

The young man gave no sign he had heard, even when the professor clapped his hands sharply, and McGowan knew suddenly whom he was dealing with. He started to rise, but then sank back, curious to see where this might lead.

The young man moved the hook selectively among the items in the brine. Most of them were old, and many had been cut upon by other classes of students. Their general condition of mutilation and decomposition was the key element in the shock of a first anatomy class. McGowan saw the youth bring a wrist and hand to the surface, a tattered leg. Then he brought up a lower arm and hand that evidently was in better shape that most of the anatomical pieces. McGowan watched as he used the hook to bring the desired specimen into the top-right corner of the tank and then covered it with several disreputable objects. Hiding it!

At once the youth placed the hooked stick where he had found it and moved to the table, where he proceeded to inspect the scalpels for sharpness. When he found one he liked, he moved it slightly above the others on the table and returned to the amphitheatre to take his seat.

Dr McGowan chose to disregard him, and for the next ten minutes continued to work with the records. Eventually students began to drift into the laboratory. They took seats at once. Many were already pale, for there were odours in the room that gave flight to their fantasies and fears.

Precisely on the hour, Dr McGowan put down his pen and moved in front of the desk, 'Gentlemen,' he said.

When they had fallen silent, he introduced himself. 'In

388

this course we study the dead in order that we may learn about, and help, the living. The first records of such studies were made by early Egyptians, who dissected the bodies of poor wretches they killed as human sacrifices. The ancient Greeks are the true fathers of physiological investigation. There was a great medical school in Alexandria, where Herophilus of Chalcedon studied the human organs and viscera. He named the calamus scriptorius and the duodenum.'

Dr McGowan was aware that the eyes of the young man in the centre seat of the first row never left the professor's mouth. They literally hung on to his every word.

Gracefully he traced the disappearance of anatomical study into the superstitious void of the Dark Ages, and its renaissance after AD 1300.

The final portion of his lecture concerned the fact that after the living spirit has left, researchers must treat the body without fear but with deference. 'In my student days in Scotland, my professor likened the body after death to a house whose owner had moved. He said the corpus must be treated with careful dignity, out of respect for the soul who had lived there,' Dr McGowan said, and was annoyed to see that the youth in the front row was smiling.

He told them each to take a specimen from the brine tank and a knife, and to dissect their anatomical object and make a drawing of what they saw, to be turned in before they left the class. Always at the first class there was a moment's hesitation, a reluctance to begin. During this hanging-back, the youth who had arrived early was first again, for he'd risen at once and gone to the tank to collect the specimen he'd stashed, and then the sharp scalpel. While the others began to mill about the tank, he was already setting up shop at the dissection table with the most favourable light.

Dr McGowan was acutely aware of the pressures of the first anatomy class. He was accustomed to the sweetish stink that rose from the brine tank, but he knew of its effect on the uninitiated. He'd given some of the students an unfair task, because many of the specimens were in such poor condition it would be impossible to dissect them well and

389

draw them accurately, and he took that into account. The exercise was a discipline, the first blooding of green troops. It was a challenge to their ability to face unpleasantness and adversity, and a harsh but necessary message that the practice of medicine consisted of more than collecting fees and enjoying a respected place in the community.

Within minutes several people had left the room, one of them a young man who departed in a great hurry. To Dr McGowan's satisfaction, at length each of them returned. For almost an hour he strolled among the dissection tables, checking on their progress. The class contained several mature men who had practiced medicine after apprentice-ships. They were spared the nausea of some of the other students. Dr McGowan knew from experience that some would be excellent doctors; but he watched one of them, a man named Ruel Torrington, slashing away at a shoulder, and he sighed, thinking of the terrible surgery this man must have left behind him.

He paused a fraction longer at the last table, where a fat youth with a sweating face struggled to work on a head that was mostly skull.

Across from the fat youth, the deaf boy worked. He was experienced and had used the scalpel well to open the arm in layers. The fact that he'd known to do this revealed a prior knowledge of anatomy that both pleased and surprised McGowan, who noted that joints, muscles, nerves, and blood vessels were neatly depicted in the drawing, and labelled. As he watched, the young man printed his name on the drawing and handed it to him. Cole, Robert J.

'Yes. Ah. Cole, in the future, you must make your printed letters a bit larger.'

'Yes, sir,' Cole said quite distinctly. 'Will there be anything else?'

'No. You may return your specimen to the tank and clean up after you. Then you may go.'

The dismissal brought half a dozen other drawings to Dr McGowan, but each of the students was turned back with a suggestion for revision of the drawing or several ways to improve the dissection.

While he conferred with the students, he watched Cole return the specimen to the tank. He saw him wash and wipe the scalpel before replacing it on the table. He observed that Cole carried water to the dissection table and scrubbed the side of it he'd used, and then took brown soap and clean water and washed his own hands and arms carefully before rolling down his sleeves.

Cole paused by the chubby youth on the way out and examined his drawing. Dr McGowan saw him lean over and whisper. Some of the desperation left the other boy's face, and he nodded as Cole patted his shoulder. Then the fat one went back to work, and the deaf one left the classroom.

46
Heart Sounds

It was as if the medical school were a remote foreign land in which Shaman occasionally heard fearsome rumours of impending war in the United States. He learned of a Peace Convention in Washington, DC, attended by one hundred and thirty-one delegates from twenty-one states. But the morning the Peace Convention opened in the capital, the Provisional Congress of the Confederate States of America convened in Montgomery, Alabama. A few days later the Confederacy voted to secede from the United States, and everyone was sickeningly aware there would be no peace.

Still, Shaman was able to give the nation's problems only passing attention. He was fighting his own war for survival. Fortunately, he was a good student. He pored over his books at night until he couldn't see any longer, and most mornings he managed several hours of study before breakfast. Classes were held Monday through Saturday, from ten to one and from two to five. Often a lecture was delivered before or during one of the six clinics that gave the medical school its name: Tuesday afternoons, diseases of the chest; Thursday evenings, the ailments of females; Saturday mornings, surgical clinic; and Saturday afternoons, medical clinic. Sunday afternoons, students observed the staff physicians in the wards.

It was on Shaman's sixth Saturday at the Polyclinic that

392

Dr Meigs lectured about the stethoscope. Meigs had studied in France under doctors who had been taught by the instrument's inventor. He told the students that one day in 1816 a physician named René Laënnec, reluctant to place his ear against the chest of a bosomy and embarrassed female patient, had rolled up some paper and tied the resultant tube with a piece of string. When Laënnec had placed one end of the tube to the patient's chest and listened at the other end, he was surprised to note that, instead of being a less efficient way to listen, the method amplified the chest sounds.

Meigs said that until recently stethoscopes had been simple wooden tubes listened to by doctors who used one ear. He had a more modern version of the instrument, in which the tube was of woven silk, leading to ivory earpieces that fitted into both ears. During the medical clinic that followed the class, Dr Meigs used an ebony stethoscope with a second outlet to which a tube was attached, so both the professor and a student could listen to a patient's chest sounds at the same time. Each student was given an opportunity to listen, but when it was Shaman's turn he told the professor of medicine it was no use. 'I wouldn't be able to hear anything.'

Dr Meigs pursed his lips. 'You must at least try.' He was careful to show Shaman precisely how to hold the instrument to his ear. But Shaman could only shake his head.

'I am sorry,' Professor Meigs said.

There was to be an examination in clinical practice. Each student was to examine a patient, using the stethoscope, and make a report. It was clear to Shaman that he was going to be failed.

On a cold morning he bundled himself in his coat and gloves, tied a muffler around his neck, and hiked away from the school. A boy on a corner was hawking newspapers that told about Lincoln's inauguration. Shaman walked down to the riverfront and along the wharves, deep in thought.

When he returned, he went into the hospital and walked through the wards, studying the orderlies and nurses. Most were men, and many were drunkards who had gravitated to hospital work because the standards were low. He observed those who seemed sober and intelligent, and finally determined that a man named Jim Halleck would serve his purpose. He waited until the orderly had carried in an armload of wood and dumped it on the floor near the potbellied stove, then approached him.

'I've a proposition for you, Mr Halleck.'

The afternoon of the examination, both Dr McGowan and Dr Berwyn showed up at the medical clinic, heightening Shaman's nervousness. Dr Meigs tested the class alphabetically. Shaman was third, after Allard and Bronson. Israel Allard had an easy time of it; his patient was a young woman with a strained back, whose heart sounds were strong, regular, and uncomplicated. Clark Bronson was assigned to examine an asthmatic man, no longer young. He stumblingly described the sound of rales in the chest. Meigs had to ask him several leading questions to get the information he needed, but evidently he was satisfied in the end.

'Mr Cole?'

It was evident that he expected Shaman to decline to participate. But Shaman came forward and accepted the monaural wooden stethoscope. When he looked to where Jim Halleck was sitting, the orderly rose and joined him. The patient was a sixteen-year-old male, of husky build, who had cut his hand in a carpentry shop. Halleck held one end of the stethoscope to the boy's chest and placed his ear on the other end. Shaman took the patient's wrist and felt the push of the boy's pulse against his fingers.

'The patient's heartbeat is normal and regular. At a rate of seventy-eight times per minute,' he said at length. He glanced inquiringly at the orderly, who shook his head slightly. 'There are no rales,' Shaman said.

'What is the meaning of this . . . theatre?' Dr Meigs said. 'What is Jim Halleck doing here?'

'Mr Halleck is serving as my ears, sir,' Shaman said, and was unfortunate enough to note broad grins on the faces of several of the students.

Dr Meigs did not smile. 'I see. As your ears. And would you marry Mr Halleck, Mr Cole? And take him with you wherever you would practice medicine? For the rest of your life?'

'No, sir.'

'Then, will you ask other folks to be your ears?'

'Perhaps I shall, at times.'

'And if you're a physician who comes on someone in need of your help, and you are alone, just you and the patient?'

'I can get the heart rate from the pulse.' Shaman touched two fingers to the carotid artery in the patient's throat. 'And feel whether it is normal, or bounding, or weak.' He spread his fingers and placed his palm on the boy's chest. 'I can feel the rate of respirations. And see the skin, and touch it to learn whether it is feverish or cool, moist or dry. I can see the eyes. If the patient is awake, I can talk with him, and conscious or not, I can observe the consistency of his sputum and see the colour of his urine and smell it, even taste it if I have to.' Looking at his professor's face, he anticipated the objection before Dr Meigs could make it.

'But I'll never be able to hear rales in the chest.'

'No, you will not.'

'For me, rales will not be warnings of trouble. When I see the early stages of croupy breathing, I will know that if I could hear them, the rales in his chest doubtless would be crackling. If my patient becomes markedly croupy, I will know that there are bubbling rales in the chest. If there is asthma or an infection of the bronchia, I'll know there are sibilant rales. But I won't be able to confirm that knowledge.' He paused and looked directly at Dr Meigs. 'I can't do anything about my deafness. Nature has robbed me of a valuable diagnostic tool, but I have other tools. And in an emergency, I would care for my patient, using my eyes and my nose and my mouth and my fingers and my brain.'

It wasn't the deferent answer Dr Meigs would have appreciated from a first-year student, and his face showed annoyance. Dr McGowan came to him and leaned over his chair, speaking into his ear.

Soon Dr. Meigs looked back at Shaman. 'It is suggested that we take you at your word, and give you a patient to diagnose without using the stethoscope. I am ready to do so, if you agree.'

Shaman nodded, although his stomach lurched.

The medical professor led them into the nearest ward, where he paused before a patient whose card at the foot of his bed revealed he was Arthur Herrenshaw. 'You may examine this patient, Mr Cole.'

Shaman saw at once from Arthur Herrenshaw's eyes that the man was in terrible trouble.

He pulled back the sheet and blanket and raised the gown. The patient's body looked extremely fat, but when Shaman placed his hand on Mr Herrenshaw's flesh, it was like touching raised dough. From his neck, where the veins were distended and pulsating, to his shapeless ankles, the swollen tissues were laden with fluid. He heaved with the effort of breathing.

'How are you today, Mr Herrenshaw?'

He had to ask again, in a loud voice, before the patient responded with a slight shake of his head.

'How old are you, sir?'

'... I ... fift ... two.' He gasped profusely between syllables, like a man who has run a long way.

'Do you have pain, Mr Herrenshaw? . . . Sir? Do you have pain?'

'Oh . . .' he said, his hand on his sternum. Shaman noted he seemed to be straining upward.

'You wish to sit up?' He helped him to do so, supporting his back with pillows. Mr Herrenshaw was sweating profusely, but he also shivered. The only heat in the ward came from a thick black stovepipe that bisected the ceiling as it ran from the wood-burning stove, and Shaman pulled the blanket up over Mr Herrenshaw's shoulders. He took out his watch. When he checked Mr Herrenshaw's pulse, it was as if the second hand suddenly slowed. The pulse was light and thready and incredibly fast, like the desperate skittering footsteps of a small animal fleeing a predator. Shaman had trouble counting fast enough. The animal

396

slowed, stopped, took a couple of slow hops. Began to scurry again.

He was aware that now was the time Dr Meigs would have used the stethoscope. He could imagine the interesting, tragic sounds he could have reported, the noises of a man drowning in his own juices.

He held both of Mr Herrenshaw's hands in his own and was chilled and saddened by their message. Without knowing he did it, he touched the bowed shoulder before he turned away.

They went back to the clinic room for Shaman's report. 'I don't know what caused the fluids to collect in his tissues. I don't have the experience to understand that. But the patient's pulse was light and thready. Irregular. His heart is in failure, beating one hundred and ninety-two times a minute when racing.' He looked at Meigs. 'In the last several years I helped my father to autopsy two males and a female whose hearts failed. In each, a small portion of the heart wall was dead. The tissue appeared burnt, as if it had been touched by a live coal.'

'What would you do for him?'

'I would keep him warm. I would give him soporifics. He'll die in a few hours, so we should ease his pain.' At once, he knew he had said too much, but the words couldn't be recalled.

Meigs pounced. 'How do you know he will die?'

'I sensed it,' Shaman said in a low voice.

'What? Speak up, Mr Cole, so the class may hear.'

'I sensed it, sir.'

'You do not have enough experience to know about body fluids, but you are able to sense impending death,' the professor said cuttingly. He looked at his class. 'The lesson here is clear, gentlemen. While there is life in a patient, we never – you shall *never*! – consign them to death. We struggle to give them renewed life until they are gone. Do you understand that, Mr Cole?'

'Yes, sir,' Shaman said miserably.

'Then you may sit down.'

397

He took Jim Halleck to supper at a riverside saloon with sawdust on the floor, where they ate boiled beef and cabbage and each had three schooners of bitter dark beer. It wasn't a victory meal. Neither of them felt good about what had occurred. Besides agreeing that Meigs was a real misery, they had little to say to one another, and when they had eaten, Shaman thanked Halleck and paid him for his help, allowing him to go home to his wife and four children several dollars less poor than he had left them that morning.

Shaman stayed there and drank more beer. He didn't allow himself to worry about the effect of the alcohol on the Gift. He didn't imagine that he would be in a position very much longer in which the Gift could be important to his life.

He walked back to the dormitory carefully, not allowing himself to think of very much except the necessity of placing each foot just so as he progressed, and climbed up into his bunk fully dressed as soon as he had arrived. In the morning he knew another good reason to avoid strong drink, because his head and his facial bones ached, fitting punishment. He took a long time to wash and to change his clothing, and he was slowly heading to a late breakfast when another first-year student named Rogers hurried into the hospital dining room. 'Dr McGowan says you are to come at once to his hospital lab.'

When he reached the low-ceilinged dissection room in the basement, Dr Berwyn was there with Dr McGowan. The body of Arthur Herrenshaw lay on the table.

'We've been waiting for you,' Dr McGowan said irritably, as though Shaman were late for a preordained appointment.

'Yes, sir,' he managed, not knowing what else he could say.

'Would you care to open?' Dr McGowan said.

Shaman had never. But he had seen his father do it often enough, and Dr McGowan handed him a scalpel when he nodded. He was aware of the two physicians watching closely as he incised the chest. Dr McGowan used the rib cutters himself, and when he had removed the sternum the pathologist bent over the heart and then reached in and lifted it slightly so Dr Berwyn and Shaman could see the

roundish burned-looking damage that had been done to the
wall of Mr Herrenshaw's heart muscle.

'Something you should know,' Dr Berwyn told Shaman.
'Sometimes the failure occurs inside the heart, so that it
can't be seen in the heart wall.'

Shaman nodded, to show he understood.

McGowan turned to Dr Berwyn and said something, and
Dr Berwyn laughed. Dr McGowan looked at Shaman. His
face was like seamed leather, and this was the first time
Shaman had seen it lit by a smile.

'I told him, "Go out and get me more of them that are
deaf,"' Dr McGowan said.

47
Cincinnati Days

Every day during that slate-grey spring of national torment, anxious crowds gathered outside the offices of the Cincinnati *Commercial* to read new bulletins of the war, written in chalk on a blackboard. President Lincoln had ordered a blockade of all Confederate ports by the federal Department of the Navy, and asked men in all the Northern states to answer the call to the colours. Everywhere there was talk of the war, speculation aplenty. General Winfield Scott, general in chief of the Union Army, was a Southerner who supported the United States, but he was a tired old man; a patient on the medical ward shared with Shaman the rumour that Lincoln had approached Colonel Robert E. Lee and asked him to take command of the Union Army. But a few days later there were newspaper reports that Lee had resigned his federal commission, preferring to fight on the side of the South.

Before that semester was over at the Polyclinic Medical School, more than a dozen students, most of them in academic trouble, had quit to join one army or the other. Among them was Ruel Torrington, who left two empty bureau drawers that retained the smell of unwashed clothing. Other students spoke of finishing the semester and then joining up. In May Dr Berwyn called a meeting of the student body and explained that the faculty had considered closing the medical school during the military emergency, but after much soul-searching they had decided to continue to teach. He urged each student to stay in school. 'Very soon doctors will be needed as never before, both in the army and to care for civilians.'

But Dr Berwyn had bad news. Because the faculty was paid from tuition receipts, and because enrolment had decreased, tuition fees had to be raised sharply. For Shaman, this meant he would have to come up with funds he hadn't planned for. But if he wouldn't allow deafness to stand in his way, he was determined that a little thing like money wouldn't stop him from becoming a doctor.

He and Paul Cooke became friends. In matters of school and medicine, Shaman was the adviser and the guide, while in other matters Cooke did the leading. Paul introduced him to restaurant dining and the theatre. In awe, they went to Pike's Opera house to see Edwin Thomas Booth as Richard III. The opera house had three tiers of balconies, three thousand seats, and standing room for another thousand. Even the eighth-row seats Cooke had wangled from the box office wouldn't have allowed Shaman full comprehension of the play, but he had read all of Shakespeare at College, and he reread this play before the performance. Being familiar with the story and the speeches made all the difference, and he enjoyed the experience tremendously.

On another Saturday evening Cooke took him to a whorehouse, where Shaman followed a taciturn woman to her room and received a fast servicing. The woman never lost her fixed smile and said almost nothing. Shaman didn't ever feel impelled to go there again, but at times, because he was normal and healthy, sexual desire presented a problem. On a day when it was his duty to drive a hospital ambulance, he went to the P. L. Trent Candle Company, which employed women and children, and treated a thirteen-year-old boy for leg burns suffered from a splash of boiling wax. They took the boy back to the ward, accompanied by a peach-skinned young woman with black hair who gave up her own hourly wages to go to the hospital with the patient, her cousin. Shaman saw her again that Thursday evening during the weekly visiting hour in the charity wards. Other relatives waited to see the burned boy, so her visit was short, and he had a chance to talk with her. Her name was Hazel Melville. Although he couldn't afford it, he asked her to have supper with him on the following Sunday; she tried to appear shocked, but instead she smiled in satisfaction and nodded.

She lived within walking distance of the hospital, on the third floor of a tenement building very similar to the medical-school dormitory. Her mother was dead. Shaman was very conscious of his guttural speech as her red-faced father, a bailiff at the Cincinnati Municipal Courthouse, regarded him with cool suspicion, not certain what was different about Hazel's caller.

If the day had been warmer, he might have taken her boating on the river. There was a wind from the water, but they wore coats and it was comfortable to walk. They looked in the windows of shops by the waning light. She was very pretty, he decided, except for her lips, which were thin and severe, etching tiny lines of habitual discontent into the corners of her mouth. She was shocked to learn of his deafness. While he explained about lip-reading, she wore an uncertain smile.

Still, it was pleasant to talk to a female who wasn't ill or hurt. She said she'd been dipping candles for a year; she hated it, but there were few jobs for females. She told him resentfully that she had two older male cousins who had gone to work for good money at Wells & Company. 'Wells & Company has received an order from the Indiana State Militia to cast ten thousand barrels of minié musket balls. I do so wish they would employ women!'

They had supper in a small restaurant Cooke had helped him choose, selected because it was both inexpensive and well-lit, so he could see what she was saying. She appeared to enjoy it, though she sent the rolls back because they weren't hot, speaking sharply to the waiter. When they returned to her flat her father wasn't at home. She made it easy for Shaman to kiss her, responding so completely that

402

it was a natural progression for him to touch her through her clothing and eventually to make love to her on the discomfort of the fringed settee. Lest her father return, she kept the lamp on and wouldn't remove her clothing, pulling her skirts and shift back above her waist. Her womanly odour was overlaid with the smell of bayberry from the paraffin into which she dipped her wicks six days a week. Shaman took her hard and fast and without any semblance of enjoyment, conscious of possible enraged interruption by the bailiff, sharing no more human contact with her than he had experienced with the woman in the bordello.

He didn't even think of her for seven weeks.

But one afternoon, impelled by a familiar longing, he walked to the Trent Candle factory and sought her out. The air in the interior of the candle works was hot with grease and heavy with the concentrated scent of bayberry. Hazel Melville was annoyed when she saw him. 'Mustn't have visitors, want me discharged?' But before he left, she said hurriedly that it wouldn't be possible to see him again, because during the weeks of his neglect she had become promised to another man, someone she'd known a long time. He was a professional person, a company bookkeeper, she told Shaman, making no attempt to disguise her satisfaction.

The truth was, Shaman had less physical distraction than he would have expected. He turned everything – all yearning and desire, every hope and expectation of pleasure, his energies and his imagination – into the study of medicine. Cooke said with frank envy that Robert J. Cole had been designed to become a medical student, and Shaman felt it was so; all his life he'd been waiting for something that he had found in Cincinnati.

Midway in the term he began dropping into the dissection laboratory whenever he had a free hour, sometimes alone but more often with Cooke or Billy Henried, to help them develop their techiques with the instruments or to drive home a fine point made by their textbook or in a lecture. Early in the P&A course, Dr McGowan had begun

403

asking him to help students who were having difficulty. Shaman knew his grades in his other courses were excellent, and even Dr Meigs had been known to nod pleasantly at him when encountered in the corridor. People had become accustomed to his differentness. Sometimes, concentrating hard during a lecture or a laboratory class, he fell into his old bad habit of making humming sounds without realizing it. Once Dr Berwyn had paused during a lecture and said, 'Stop humming, Mr Cole.' In the beginning, other students would titter, but they soon learned to touch him on the arm and give him a look that told him to be quiet. It didn't bother him. He was confident.

He enjoyed wandering alone through the wards. One day a patient complained that he had walked past her bed unheeding although she had called his name repeatedly. After that, to prove to himself that his deafness need not hurt his patients, he developed the habit of stopping briefly at every bed, holding the patient's hands in his own, and speaking briefly and quietly to each person.

The spectre of conditional status was well behind him one day when Dr McGowan offered him a job in the hospital during July and August, when the medical school would be on holiday. McGowan told him frankly that both he and Dr Berwyn had considered competing for Shaman's services, but had decided to share him. 'You'd spend the summer working for us both, doing dirty work for Berwyn in the operating theatre every morning, and helping me autopsy his mistakes every afternoon.'

It was a wonderful opportunity, Shaman realized, and the small salary would allow him to meet the rise in tuition. 'I would like it,' he told Dr McGowan. 'But my father is expecting me home to help work the farm this summer. I'll have to write and ask his permission to stay on here.'

Barney McGowan smiled. 'Ah, the farm,' he said, dismissing it. 'I predict that you are done with farming, young man. Your father is a country physician in Illinois, I believe? I have been meaning to inquire. There was a man several years ahead of me at University College Hospital in Edinburgh. Same name as yourself.'

'Yes. That was my father. He tells the identical anecdotes you told our anatomy class, about Sir William Fergusson's description of a corpse as a home from which the owner has moved.'

'I recall that you smiled when I told that story. And now I understand why.' McGowan gazed contemplatively, through narrowed eyes. 'Do you know why . . . ah . . . your father left Scotland?'

Shaman saw that McGowan was trying to be discreet. 'Yes. He's told me. He got into political trouble. He was almost transported to Australia.'

'I remember.' McGowan shook his head. 'He was held up to us as a warning. Everyone at University College Hospital knew of him. He was Sir William Fergusson's protégé, with an unlimited future. And now he's a country doctor. What a pity!'

'There is no need for pity.' Shaman wrestled with anger and ended up smiling. 'My father is a great man,' he said, and with surprise he recognized that it was true. He began telling Barney McGowan about Rob J., about how he'd worked with Oliver Wendell Holmes in Boston, about his trek across the country in lumber camps and as a railroad doctor. He described a day when his father had had to swim his horse across two rivers and a stream to reach the sod house where he delivered a woman of twins. He described the prairie kitchens in which his father had operated, and told of times when Rob J. Cole had performed surgery on a table moved from a dirty house into the clean sunshine. He told of his father being kidnapped by outlaws who had held a gun on him and ordered him to remove a bullet from a man who had been shot. He told of his father riding home on a night when the temperature on the plains was thirty degrees below zero, and saving his own life by slipping from his horse and clutching the horse's tail, running behind Boss in order to force his blood back into circulation.

Barney McGowan smiled. 'You're right,' he said. 'Your father *is* a great man. And he is a fortunate father.'

'Thank you, sir.' Shaman started to move away, but then he stopped. 'Dr McGowan. In one of my father's autopsies, a woman had been killed by eleven stab wounds to the chest, approximately .95 centimetres in width. Made by a pointed instrument, triangular in shape, all three edges ground to sharpness. Do you have any idea what instrument would make that sort of wound?'

The pathologist considered, interested. 'It could have been a medical instrument. There is Beer's knife, a three-sided scalpel used to operate for cataracts and to cut out defects of the cornea. But the wounds you describe were too large to have been made by Beer's knife. Perhaps they were made by some kind of bistoury. Were the cutting edges of uniform breadth?'

'No. The instrument, whatever it was, was tapered.'

'I know of no such bistoury. Probably the wounds were not made by a medical instrument.'

Shaman hesitated. 'Could they have been made by an object commonly used by a woman?'

'Knitting needle or some such? It's possible, of course, but neither can I think of a housewife's object that would make such a wound.' McGowan smiled. 'Let me consider the problem for a time, and we'll discuss it again.

'When you write to your father,' he said, 'you must give him the best regards of one who came to William Fergusson a few years after he did.'

Shaman promised he would do so.

His father's reply didn't arrive in Cincinnati until eight days before the end of the semester, but it came in time to allow Shaman to accept the summer hospital job.

His father didn't remember Dr McGowan at all but expressed pleasure that Shaman was studying pathology under another Scot who had learned the art and science of dissection from William Fergusson. He asked his son to extend his respects to the professor, as well as his permission for Shaman to work in the hospital.

The letter was warm but brief, and from its lack of chattiness Shaman knew that his father's mood was melancholy. There had been no word of the whereabouts or safety of Alex, and his father revealed that with each new round of fighting, Shaman's mother became more fearful.

48
The Boat Ride

It wasn't lost on Rob J. that both Jefferson Davis and Abraham Lincoln had emerged into leadership by helping to destroy the Sauk nation in Black Hawk's War. As a young army lieutenant Davis personally had taken Black Hawk and the medicine man White Cloud down the Mississippi from Fort Crawford to Jefferson Barracks, where they were imprisoned in balls and chains. Lincoln had fought the Sauks with the militia, both as a private and as a captain. Now each of these men answered when addressed as *Mr President*, and each was leading one half of the American nation against the other half.

Rob J. wanted to be left alone by the gibbering world, but it was too much to expect. The war was six weeks old when Stephen Hume rode to Holden's Crossing to see him. The former congressman was frank to say he had used influence to gain a commission as colonel in the US Army. He had taken leave as the railroad's legal counsel in Rock Island in order to organize the Illinois 102nd Volunteer Regiment, and he'd come to offer Dr Cole a job as regimental surgeon.

'It's not for me, Stephen.'

'Doc, it's all right to object to the idea of war in the abstract. But now we're down to cases, there are good reasons why this war should be fought.'

'. . . I don't think killing a lot of people is going to change anybody's mind about slavery or free trade. Besides, you want someone younger and meaner. I'm a forty-four-year-old man with a thick waist.' He *had* put on weight. Back when escaped slaves came to the secret room, Rob J. had become accustomed to putting food in his pocket as he walked through the kitchen – a baked yam, a piece of fried chicken, a couple of sweet rolls – to help feed the fugitives. Now he continued to take the food, but he ate it himself in the saddle, for comfort.

'Oh, I want you, all right, fat or thin, mean or sweet,' Hume said. 'What's more, at this moment there are only ninety medical officers in the whole damn army. There's going to be great opportunity. You'll go in as captain, be major before you know it. Doctor like you, bound to move way up.'

Rob J. shook his head. But he liked Stephen Hume and held out his hand. 'I wish you a safe return, Colonel.'

Hume smiled wryly and shook his hand. A few days later Rob J. heard at the general store that Tom Beckermann had been appointed surgeon of the 102nd.

For three months both sides had been playing at war, but by July it was obvious that a large-scale confrontation was shaping up. Many people were still convinced that the trouble would be over quickly, but that first battle was an epiphany for the nation. Rob J. read the newspaper reports as avidly as any war lover.

More than thirty thousand Union soldiers under General Irvin McDowell faced twenty thousand Confederates under General Pierre G. T. Beauregard at Manassas, Virginia, twenty-five miles south of Washington. About eleven thousand additional Confederates were in the Shenandoah Valley under General Joseph E. Johnston, squared off before another Union force of fourteen thousand, led by General Robert Patterson. Expecting Patterson to keep Johnston occupied, on July 21 McDowell led his army against the Southerners near Sudley Ford on Bull Run Creek.

It was scarcely a surprise attack.

Just before McDowell charged, Johnston slipped away

from Patterson and joined his forces with Beauregard's. The Northern battle plan was so widely known that congressmen and civil servants had streamed out of Washington, carrying their wives and children in traps and buggies to Manassas, where they ate elaborate picnic meals and prepared to watch the spectacle as though it were a celebrated footrace. Dozens of civilian drivers had been hired by the army to stand by with teams and buckboards to be used as ambulances in case there were wounded. Many of the ambulance drivers brought their own whisky to the picnic.

While this audience gazed in fascinated pleasure, McDowell's soldiers flung themselves at the combined Confederate force. Most of the men on both sides were untrained new troops, fighting with more zeal than art. The Confederate citizen-soldiers gave a few miles and then held fast, allowing the Northerners to use themselves up in several frenzied assaults. Then Beauregard ordered a counterattack. The exhausted Union troops gave way, and turned. Presently their retreat became a rout.

The battle wasn't what the audience had expected; the combined sounds of the rifle fire and artillery and human noise were terrible, the sights, worse. Instead of athletics, they witnessed the transformation of living men into the disemboweled, the headless, the limbless. The myriad dead. Some of the civilians fainted, others wept. All tried to flee, but a shell blew up a wagon and killed a horse, blocking the main road of retreat. Most of the terrorized civilian ambulance drivers, the drunk and the sober, had driven off with empty buckboards. The few who tried to collect wounded found themselves marooned in a sea of civilian vehicles and rearing horses. The sorely hurt lay on the battlefield where they screamed until they died. It took some of the ambulatory wounded several days to make it into Washington.

In Holden's Crossing the Confederate victory gave new life to Southern sympathizers. Rob J. was more depressed about the criminal neglect of the casualties than about the defeat. By early autumn it became known that Bull Run had produced almost five thousand dead, wounded, or missing, and many lives had been thrown away through lack of care.

One evening, seated in the Coles' kitchen, he and Jay Geiger avoided conversation of the battle. They spoke awkwardly of the news that Lillian Geiger's cousin Judah P. Benjamin had been appointed Secretary of War for the Confederacy. But they were in complete agreement about the cruel idiocy of armies that didn't salvage their own wounded.

'As difficult as it is,' Jay said, 'we mustn't allow this war to end our friendship.'

'No. Of course not!' It might not end it, Rob J. thought, but their friendship already had been strained and spoiled. He was startled when Geiger, departing for home, embraced him like a lover. 'I look upon your loved ones as my own,' Jay said. 'There's nothing I wouldn't do to ensure their happiness.'

Next day Rob J. understood Jay's farewell mood when Lillian, sitting dry-eyed in the Coles' kitchen, told them her husband had left for the South at daybreak, to volunteer his services to the forces of the Confederacy.

It seemed to Rob J. the whole world had turned as sombre as Confederate grey. Despite all he could do, Julia Blackmer, the minister's wife, coughed herself to death just before the winter air turned thin and cold. In the churchyard the minister wept as he recited the prayers of interment, and as the first shovelful of dirt and stone fell with a thump on Julia's pine box, Sarah squeezed Rob J.'s hand so hard it hurt. The members of Blackmer's flock gathered to support their clergyman in the days that followed, and Sarah organized the women so that Mr Blackmer never lacked for sympathetic company or a prepared meal. It appeared to Rob J. that the minister should have a little privacy in his grief, but Mr Blackmer appeared grateful for the good works.

Before Christmas, Mother Miriam Ferocia confided to Rob J. that she'd received a letter from a firm of Frankfurt solicitors, telling her of the death of Ernst Brotknecht, her father. His will had arranged for the sale of the Frankfurt wagonworks and the carriage factory in München, and the letter said that a considerable sum of money was waiting for his daughter, known in her former life as Andrea Brotknecht.

Rob J. expressed his regrets about her father, whom she hadn't seen in years. Then, 'Good grief. Mother Miriam, you're rich!'

'No,' she said calmly. She had promised to turn all worldly goods over to Holy Mother Church when she took the habit. She had already signed papers giving the inheritance into the jurisdiction of her archbishop.

Rob J. was irked. Over the years, hating to see the nuns suffer, he had made a series of small gifts to their community. He had observed the rigour of their lives, the severe rationing and the lack of anything that might be considered a luxury. 'A little money would make such a difference to the sisters of your community. If you couldn't accept for yourself, you might have thought of your nuns.'

But she wouldn't allow him to draw her into his anger. 'Poverty is an essential part of their lives,' she said, and nodded with infuriating Christian forbearance when he said goodbye too abruptly and rode away.

With Jason gone, a lot of warmth went out of Rob's life. He might have continued to make music with Lillian, but the piano and the viola da gamba sounded strangely unsubstantial without the melodious cement of Jay's violin, and they found excuses to avoid playing alone.

The first week of 1862, at a moment when Rob J. felt particularly discontented, he was happy to receive a letter from Harry Loomis in Boston, accompanied by the translation of a paper published in Vienna several years before by a Hungarian doctor named Ignaz Semmelweis. Semmelweis' work, entitled *The Etiology, Concept, and Prophylaxis of Childbirth Fever*, essentially buttressed the work done in America by Oliver Wendell Holmes. At the Vienna General Hospital, Semmelweis had concluded that childbed fever, which killed twelve mothers out of one hundred, was contagious. Just as Holmes had done decades earlier, he had discovered that doctors themselves spread the disease by

411

not cleaning their hands.

Harry Loomis wrote that he was becoming increasingly interested in ways of preventing infection in wounds and surgical incisions. He wondered whether Rob J. was aware of the research of Dr Milton Akerson, who worked on these problems at the Hospital of the Mississippi Valley in Cairo, Illinois, which Harry believed was not too far distant from Holden's Crossing.

Rob J. hadn't heard of Dr Akerson's work, but at once he knew he wanted to visit Cairo and observe it. Opportunity didn't arrive for several months. He rode through the snow and made his calls, but at last things turned quiet, just as the spring rains came. Mother Miriam assured him that she and her sisters would keep an eye on his patients, and Rob J. announced he was going to Cairo for a brief vacation. On April 9, a Wednesday, he plodded Boss through the rich gumbo on the roads as far as Rock Island, where he boarded the horse in the stable; then, at dusk, he caught a ride on a log raft down the Mississippi. Throughout the night he floated downriver, reasonably snug under the roof of the raft shack, sleeping on the logs next to the cookstove. When he left the raft at Cairo next morning, he was stiff and it was still raining.

Cairo was in awful shape, fields flooded and many of the streets under water. He made a careful toilet at an inn that also sold him a poor breakfast, then found the hospital. Dr Akerson was a swarthy, bespectacled little man whose heavy moustache continued across his cheeks to join his hair at his ears, after the regrettable fashion made popular by Ambrose Burnside, whose brigade had made the first attack against the Confederates at Bull Run.

Dr Akerson greeted Rob politely and was detectably pleased to hear that his work had gained the attention of colleagues as far away as Boston. The air in his wards was sharp with the odour of hydrochloric acid, which was the agent he believed could fight the infections that so often brought death to the wounded. Rob J. noted that the smell of what Akerson called the 'disinfectant' masked some of the disagreeable odours of the ward, but he found it irritating to his nose and his eyes.

He soon saw that the Cairo surgeon had no miraculous cure.

'At times, there definitely seems to be a benefit from treating the wounds with hydrochloric acid. At other times . . .' Dr Akerson shrugged. 'Nothing seems to work.'

He had experimented with spraying hydrochloric acid into the air of the operating room and the wards, he told Rob, but had discontinued that practice because the fumes made it difficult to see and breathe. Now he contented himself with saturating dressings in the acid and placing them directly on the wounds. He said he believed that gangrene and other infections were caused by pus corpuscles floating in the air as dust, and that the acid-soaked dressings kept these contaminants from the wounds.

An orderly came by bearing a tray laden with the dressings, and one fell from the tray onto the floor. Dr Akerson picked it up, brushed some dirt from it with his hand, and showed it to Rob. It was an ordinary dressing, made from a cotton rag soaked with hydrochloric. When Rob returned it to Dr Akerson, the surgeon sighed and put it back on the tray to be used. 'A pity we can't determine why sometimes it works and sometimes it doesn't,' Akerson said.

Their visit was interrupted by a young physician who informed Dr Akerson that Mr Robert Francis, a representative of the United States Sanitary Commission, had asked to see him on 'most urgent business'.

As Akerson walked Rob J. to the door, they found Mr Francis waiting anxiously in the corridor. Rob J. knew and approved of the Sanitary Commission, a civilian organization established to raise funds and recruit personnel to care for the wounded. Now, speaking hurriedly, Mr Francis told them there had been a desperate two-day battle at Pittsburgh Landing, Tennessee, thirty miles north of Corinth, Mississippi. 'There are terrible casualties, many times worse than Bull Run. We've gathered volunteers to serve as nurses, but we're frantically short of physicians.'

Dr Akerson looked pained. 'The war has taken most of our

413

doctors. There is no one who could leave here.'

Rob J. spoke at once. 'I'm a physician, Mr Francis. I'm able to go.'

With three other physicians gathered from nearby towns, and fifteen assorted civilians who never had nursed anyone before, Rob J. boarded the river packet *City of Louisiana* at noon and steamed to the wet murk that covered the Ohio River. At five p.m. they reached Paducah, Kentucky, and entered the Tennessee River. It was a long two hundred and thirty miles the Tennessee. In the dark of night, unseen and unseeing, they passed Fort Henry, which Ulysses S. Grant had captured only a month before. All the next day they chugged past river towns, laden wharves, more flooded fields. It was almost dark again when they reached Pittsburgh Landing at five p.m.

Rob J. counted twenty-four steamships there, including two gunboats. When the medical party disembarked, they found the bank and the bluffs had been trodden into mud by a Yankee retreat on Sunday, and they sank halfway to their knees. Rob J. was detailed to go onto the *War Hawk*, a ship that was laden with four hundred and six wounded soldiers. They were almost finished loading when he boarded, and they got under way without delay. A grim first officer told Rob J. quietly that the enormously high battle casualties had taxed the hospital facilities in communities throughout Tennessee. The *War Hawk* would have to carry its passengers six hundred and fifty-eight miles up the Tennessee River to the Ohio, and up the Ohio River to Cincinnati.

Wounded men had been set down on every surface – below, in the officers' and passengers' cabins, and all over the open decks under the unceasing rain. Rob J. and an army medical officer from Pennsylvania named Jim Sprague were the only doctors. All the supplies had been dumped in one of the staterooms, and the voyage wasn't two hours old when Rob J. saw that medicinal brandy was being stolen. The military commander of the ship was a young first lieutenant named

Crittendon, his eyes still dazed from combat. Rob convinced him that the supplies needed an armed guard, which began at once.

Rob J. hadn't brought his own medical bag with him from Holden's Crossing. There was a surgical kit with the supplies, and he asked that the engineering officer sharpen several of the instruments. He had no desire to use them. 'Travel's a rough shock to wounded men,' he told Sprague. 'I think whenever it's possible, we should postpone surgery until we can get these people to hospitals.'

Sprague agreed. 'I'm not much for cutting,' he said. He hung back, letting Rob J. make the decisions. Rob decided Sprague wasn't much for doctoring either, but he put him in charge of dressing wounds and seeing that the patients received soup and bread.

Rob saw almost at once that some of the men had been badly mangled and required amputation without delay.

The volunteer nurses were eager but green – bookkeepers, teachers, liverymen – all facing blood and pain and kinds of tragedy they had never imagined. Rob gathered several around him to help with the amputations and set the rest to work under Dr Sprague, bandaging wounds, changing dressings, bringing water to the thirsty, and sheltering those on deck from the chill rain with whatever blankets and coats could be found.

Rob J. would have liked to go to each of the wounded men in turn, but there wasn't opportunity to do that. Instead, he went to a patient whenever a nurse told him there was a man who was 'bad.' In theory, none of those who'd been placed on the *War Hawk* should have been so 'bad' that they couldn't survive the trip, but several died almost at once.

Rob J. ordered everyone removed from the second mate's cabin and began to amputate there by the light of four lanterns. That night he took fourteen limbs. Many on board had been amputated before they were placed on the boat, and he examined some of these men, saddened by the poor quality of some of the surgery. A man named Peters, nineteen years old, had lost his right leg at the knee, his left leg at the hip, and all of his right arm. Sometime during the night be began to bleed from his left leg stump, or perhaps he'd been bleeding when brought aboard. He was the first to be discovered dead.

'Poppa, I tried,' wept a soldier with long yellow hair and a hole in his back in which his spine gleamed, white as a trout's bones. 'I tried hard.'

'Yes, you did. You're a good son,' Rob J. told him, stroking his head.

Some screamed, some wrapped themselves in silence like armour, some wept and babbled. Slowly Rob J. puzzled the battle out of small pieces of their individual pain. Grant had been at Pittsburgh Landing with forty-two thousand troops, waiting for General Don Carlos Buell's forces to join up with him. Beauregard and Albert Johnston decided they could defeat Grant before Buell got there and forty thousand Confederates fell on the bivouacked Union troops. Grant's line was pushed back on both the left and the right, but the centre, manned by soldiers from Iowa and Illinois, held through the most savage kind of fighting.

The rebels had taken many prisoners on Sunday. The bulk of the Union force was driven back all the way to the river, into the very water, their backs to the bluff that prevented them from further retreat. But Monday morning, when the Confederates would have mopped up, boats emerged from the morning mist, carrying twenty thousand reinforcements from Buell, and the battle was turned. At the end of that savage day of fighting, the Southerners retreated to Corinth. By nightfall, as far as the eye could see from the Shiloh Church on the battlefield, dead bodies covered the ground. And some of the injured were picked up and placed aboard boats.

In the morning the *War Hawk* slipped past forests bright with new leaves and thick with mistletoe, and greening fields, and now and then a peach orchard alight with blossom, but Rob J. didn't notice.

The boat captain's plan had been to pull into a river town morning and evening in order to take on wood. At the same time, the volunteers were to go ashore and forage whatever water and food they could obtain for their patients. But Rob J. and Dr Sprague had prevailed upon the boat captain to make a stop each noon as well, and sometimes in the middle of the afternoon, because they found it was easy to run out of water. The afflicted thirsted.

To Rob J.'s despair, the volunteers couldn't begin to maintain hygiene. Many of the soldiers had had dysentery before being hurt. Men defecated and urinated where they lay, and it was impossible to clean them. There were no changes of clothing, and their wastes caked on their bodies as they lay in the cold rain. The nurses spent most of their time distributing hot soup. On the second afternoon, when the rain stopped and a strong sun came out, Rob J. greeted the warmth with great relief. But with the steam that rose from the decks and the people came a magnification of the enormous smell that gripped the *War Hawk*. The stench became almost palpable. Sometimes when the boat stopped, patriotic civilians came aboard with blankets, water, and food. They blinked, their eyes watered, and they always hurried away without delay. Rob J. found himself wishing that he had a supply of Dr Akerson's hydrochloric acid.

Men died and were sewn into the dirtiest sheets. He amputated half a dozen times more, the worst cases, and among the thirty-eight dead when they reached their destination were eight of his twenty amputees. They reached Cincinnati early on Tuesday morning. He had been without sleep, and almost without food, for three and one-half days. Suddenly no longer responsible, he stood on the pier and watched stupidly as others divided the patients into batches that were sent off to the various hospitals. When a dray was laden with men for the Southwestern Ohio Hospital, Rob J. climbed in and sat on the floor between two stretchers.

When they unloaded the patients, he wandered through the hospital, moving very slowly because the air in Cincinnati seemed thick as pudding. Members of the staff looked askance at the middle-aged, unshaven giant who stank. When an orderly asked him sharply what it was he wanted, he said Shaman's name.

Eventually he was brought to a little balcony overlooking the surgical theatre. They had already started operating on the patients from the *War Hawk*. Four men stood around a table, and he saw that one of them was Shaman. For a brief time he watched them operate, but too soon the warm tide of sleep rose above his head and he drowned in it with perfect ease and eagerness.

He didn't remember being led from the hospital to Shaman's room, or being undressed. The rest of the day and all that night he slept all unknowing in his son's bed. When he awoke it was Wednesday morning, brilliant sunshine outside. While he shaved and took a bath, Shaman's friend, a helpful young man named Cooke, picked up Rob J.'s clothing from the hospital laundry, where it had been boiled and ironed, and went to fetch Shaman.

Shaman was thinner but seemed healthy. 'Have you heard anything of Alex?' he asked at once.

'No.'

Shaman nodded. He led Rob J. to a restaurant away from the hospital, for privacy. They had a solid meal of eggs and potatoes and side meat, and poor coffee that was mostly parched chicory. Shaman allowed him to take the first hot, sourish swallow of coffee before he began to ask questions, and he absorbed the story of the *War Hawk*'s trip with great attention.

Rob J. asked questions about the medical school, and said how proud he was of Shaman.

'At home,' he said, 'you know that old blue steel scalpel of mine?'

'The antique, the one you call Rob J.'s knife? Supposed to have been in the family for centuries?'

'That's the one. It *has* been in the family for centuries. It goes to the first son to become a doctor. It's yours.'

Shaman smiled. 'Hadn't you best wait until December, when I graduate?'

'I don't know that I'll be able to be here for your graduation. I'm going to become an army doctor.'

Shaman's eyes widened. 'But you're a pacifist! You *hate* war.'

'I am, and I do,' he said in a voice more bitter than the drink. 'But you see what they do to one another.'

They sat long, sipping renewed cups of bad coffee they didn't want, two large men looking intently into one another's eyes, speaking slowly and quietly, as if they had plenty of time to be together.

But by eleven a.m. they were back in the operating theatre. The onslaught of wounded from the *War Hawk* had taxed the hospital's facilities and surgical staff. Some surgeons had worked all through the night and the morning, and now Robert Jefferson Cole was operating on a young man from Ohio whose skull, shoulders, back, buttocks, and legs had taken a shower of small Confederate shrapnel. The procedure was long and painstaking, because each piece of metal had to be dug from the flesh with a minimum of damage to the tissues, and the suturing was equally delicate in order that muscles might hopefully grow together. The small gallery was filled with medical students and several faculty members, observing the kinds of terrible cases doctors must expect from the war. Seated in the front row, Dr Harold Meigs poked Dr Barney McGowan and with a motion of his chin indicated a man who stood to one side on the operating floor below, far enough removed so he wasn't in the way, but able to witness. A large, paunchy man with greying hair, he stood with his arms folded and his eyes fixed on the operating table, oblivious of everything else around him. As he observed the steady competence and confidence of the surgeon, he nodded in unconscious approval, and the two professors looked at one another and smiled.

Rob J. went back by train, arriving at the Rock Island depot nine days after he had left Holden's Crossing. In the street beyond the railroad station he met Paul and Roberta Williams, in Rock Island to shop.

'Hey, Doc. You just get off that train?' Williams said. 'Heard you been away, little vacation?'

'Yes,' Rob J. said.

'Well, you have a good time?'

Rob J. opened his mouth, then closed it again. 'Very pleasant, thank you, Paul,' he said quietly. Then he went to the stable to get Boss and go home.

49
The Contract Surgeon

It took Rob J. most of the summer to plan. His first thought had been to make it financially attractive for another doctor to take over in Holden's Crossing, but after a time he had to face the fact that this was impossible, because the war had created an acute shortage of physicians. The best he could do was arrange for Tobias Barr to come to the Cole dispensary every Wednesday, and for emergencies. For less serious matters the people of Holden's Crossing would make the trip to Dr Barr's office in Rock Island or consult the nursing nuns.

Sarah raged – as much because Rob J. was joining 'the wrong side' as because he was going off, it seemed to him sometimes. She prayed and consulted with Blackmer. She would be defenceless without him, she insisted. 'Before you go, you must write to the Union Army,' she said, 'and ask them if they have records to show that Alex is their prisoner or a casualty.' Rob J. had done this months before, but he agreed it was time to write again, and he took care of it.

Sarah and Lillian had become closer than ever. Jay had worked out a successful system of sending mail and Confederate news through the lines to Lillian, probably with river smugglers. Before the Illinois newspapers published the story, Lillian told them Judah P. Benjamin had been promoted from the Confederacy's secretary of war to

421

its secretary of state. Once Sarah and Rob J. had dined with the Geigers and Benjamin when Lillian's cousin had come to Rock Island to confer with Hume about a railroad lawsuit. Benjamin had seemed intelligent and modest, not the kind of man to seek out an opportunity to lead a new nation.

As for Jay, Lillian said her husband was safe. He had the rank of warrant officer and was assigned as steward, or administrator, of a military hospital somewhere in Virginia.

When she heard Rob J. was going to the Northern army, she nodded carefully. 'I pray you and Jay will never meet while we're at war.'

'I think it highly unlikely,' he said, and patted her hand.

He said goodbye to people with as little fuss as possible. Mother Miriam Ferocia listened to him with almost stony resignation. It was part of a nun's discipline, he thought, to say farewell to those who had become part of their lives. They went where their Lord ordered; in that respect, they were like soldiers.

He was wearing the *Mee-shome* and carrying one small suitcase on the morning of August 12, 1862, when Sarah saw him off at the steamboat dock in Rock Island. She was crying, and she kissed him on the lips again and again, almost wildly, oblivious of the stares of the other people on the dock.

'You are my own dear girl,' he told her gently.

He hated to leave her that way, yet it was a relief to board the boat, and to wave goodbye as the craft tooted two short signals and a long one and moved into the pull of midstream, and away.

He stayed out on deck most of the trip downriver. He loved the Mississippi and enjoyed watching the traffic in its busiest season. To date, the South had had fighting men with more recklessness and dash, and far better generals than the North. But when the federals had taken New Orleans that spring, they had linked the Union's supremacy over the lower and upper sections of the Mississippi. Along with the Tennessee and other lesser rivers, it gave federal forces a navigable route straight at the vulnerable belly of the South.

One of the military jumping-off centres along that water road was Cairo, where Rob J. had started his voyage on the *War Hawk*, and it was here that he disembarked now. There were no floods in Cairo in late August, but that was scant improvement, for thousands of troops were camped on the outskirts, and the detritus of concentrated humanity had spilled over into the town, with garbage, dead dogs, and other rotting offal piled in the muddy streets in front of fine homes. Rob J. followed the military traffic to the encampment, where he was challenged by a sentry. He identified himself and asked to be taken to the commanding officer, and soon was led to a colonel named Sibley, of the 67th Pennsylvania Volunteers. The 67th Pennsylvania already had the two surgeons allowed it by the army's table of organization, Colonel Sibley said. He said there were three other regiments in the encampment, the 42nd Kansas, the 106th Kansas, and the 23rd Ohio. He volunteered that the 106th Kansas had an opening for an assistant surgeon, and it was there Rob J. went next.

The commanding officer of the 106th was a colonel named Frederick Hilton, whom Rob J. found in front of his tent, chewing tobacco and writing at a small table. Hilton was eager to have him. He spoke of a lieutenancy ('Captain, soon as possible') and a year's enlistment as assistant medical officer, but Rob J. had done a good deal of investigation and thinking before leaving home. If he had chosen to take the surgeon general's examination, he would have qualified for a majority, a generous quarters allowance, and posting as a medical staff officer or as a surgeon at a general hospital. But he knew what he wanted. 'No enlistment. No commission. The army employs temporary civilian doctors, and I'll work for you on a three-month contract.'

Hilton shrugged. 'I'll draw up the papers for acting assistant surgeon. You come back here after supper, sign 'em. Eight dollars a month, you supply your own horse. I can send you to a uniform tailor in town.'

'I won't be wearing a uniform.'

The colonel appraised him. 'You'd be advised to. These

men are soldiers. They're not going to jump at orders from a civilian.'

'Nevertheless.'

Colonel Hilton nodded blandly, spat tobacco juice. He called for a sergeant and instructed the man to show Dr Cole to the medical officers' tent.

They hadn't gone far down the company street before the first bugle notes signaled retreat, the ceremony for lowering the colours at sundown. All sound and motion ceased as men faced the flag and snapped into salute.

It was his first retreat, and Rob J. found it strangely moving, for he sensed it was akin to a religious communion among all these men who held the salute until the last quavering note of the far-off bugle had fallen away. Then the activity of the camp resumed.

Most of the shelters were pup tents, but the sergeant led the way into an area of conical tents that reminded Rob J. of *tipis*, and stopped in front of one of these. 'Home, sir.'

'Thank you.'

Inside, it was just two sleeping places on the ground, under cloth. A man, doubtless the regimental surgeon, lay in sodden sleep, giving off sour body odour and the heavy smell of rum.

Rob J. put his bag on the ground and sat next to it. He'd made many mistakes and had played the fool more than some and less than others, he thought. He could but wonder if perhaps now he wasn't taking one of the most foolish steps of his life.

The surgeon was Major G. H. Woffenden. Rob J. quickly learned that he'd never attended medical school, but had apprenticed for a while 'under ole Doc Cowan' and then struck out on his own. That he'd been commissioned by Colonel Hilton in Topeka. That a major's pay was the best regular money he'd ever earned. And that he was content to devote himself to serious drinking and let the acting assistant surgeon handle daily sick call.

Sick call took almost the entire day, every day, because the line of patients seemed unending. The regiment had two battalions. The first was up to strength, five companies. The second battalion had only three companies. The regiment was less than four months old, and had been formed when the fittest men already were in the army. The 106th had taken what was left, and the second battalion had taken the dregs of Kansas. Many of the men who waited to see Rob J. were too old to be soldiers, and many were too young, including half a dozen who seemed barely into their teens. All of them were in extremely poor condition. The most prevalent complaints were of diarrhoea and dysentery, but Rob J. saw a variety of fevers, heavy colds involving the chest and lungs, syphilis and gonorrhea, delirium tremens and other signs of alcoholism, hernias, and lots of scurvy.

There was a dispensary tent containing a US Army medicine pannier, a large wicker-and-canvas chest containing a variety of medical supplies. According to its inventory list, it should also have contained black tea, white sugar, coffee extract, beef extract, condensed milk, and alcohol. When Rob J. asked Woffenden about these items, the surgeon appeared to be offended. 'Stolen, I suppose,' he snapped, too defensively.

After the first few meals, Rob J. could see the reason for so many stomach problems. He sought out the commissary officer, a harried second lieutenant named Zearing, and learned that the army gave the regiment eighteen cents a day to feed each man. The result was a daily ration of twelve ounces of fat salt pork, two and one-half ounces of navy beans or peas, and either eighteen ounces of flour or twelve ounces of hardtack. The meat was liable to be black on the outside and yellow with putrefaction when cut, and the soldiers called the hardtack 'worm castles' because the large thick crackers, often mouldy, were frequently tenanted by maggots or weevils.

Each soldier received his ration uncooked and prepared it himself over the flame of a small campfire, usually boiling the beans and frying both the meat and the crumbled hardtack – even frying flour – in pork fat. Combined with disease, the diet spelled disaster for thousands of stomachs, and there were no latrines. The men defecated anywhere they chose, usually behind their tents, although many with loose bowels made it only as far as the space between their tent and their neighbours'. About the camp was an effluvia reminiscent of the *War Hawk*, and Rob J. decided the entire army stank of faeces.

He realized he could do nothing about the diet, at least at once, but he was determined to improve conditions. Next afternoon, after sick call, he walked to where a sergeant from Company C, First Battalion, was drilling half a dozen men in the use of the bayonet. 'Sergeant, do you know where there are some shovels?'

'Shovels? Why, yes, I do,' the sergeant said warily.

'Well, I want you to get one for each of these men, and I want them to dig a ditch,' Rob J. said.

'A ditch, sir?' The sergeant stared at the curious figure in the baggy black suit, the wrinkled shirt, the string tie, and the wide-brimmed black civilian hat.

'Yes, a ditch,' Rob J. said. 'Right over here. Ten feet long, three feet wide, six feet deep.'

This civilian doctor was a large man. He appeared very determined. And the sergeant knew he had simulated rank of first lieutenant.

The six men were digging industriously a short time later, while Rob J. and the sergeant watched, when Colonel Hilton and Captain Irvine of Company C, First Battalion, came down the company street.

'What the hell is this?' Colonel Hilton said to the sergeant, who opened his mouth and looked at Rob J.

'They're digging a sink, Colonel,' Rob J. said.

'A *sink*?'

'Yes, sir, a latrine.'

'I know what a sink is. Their time is better spent at bayonet practice. Very soon these men will be in battle. We're showing them how to kill rebels. This regiment is going to shoot Confederates, and bayonet them, and stab them, and if it's necessary, we will shit and piss them to death. But we will not dig latrines.'

From one of the men with shovels came a guffaw. The sergeant was grinning, watching Rob J.

'Is that clearly understood, Acting Assistant Surgeon?'

Rob J. did not smile. 'Yes, Colonel.'

That was on his fourth day with the 106th. After that, there were eighty-six more days, and they passed very slowly and were counted very carefully.

50

A Son's Letter

Cincinnati, Ohio
January 12, 1863

Dear Pa,

Well, I claim Rob J.'s scalpel!

Colonel Peter Brandon, a principal aide to Surgeon General William A. Hammond, delivered the commencement address. There were those who said it was a fine talk, but I was disappointed. Dr Brandon told us that doctors have tended to the medical needs of their armies all through history. He gave a lot of examples, the Hebrews of the Bible, the Greeks, the Romans, etc, etc. Then he told all about the splendid opportunities the wartime United States Army offers a doctor, the salaries, the gratification one receives when serving his country. We yearned to be reminded of the healing glories of our new profession – Plato and Galen, Hippocrites and Andreas Vesalius – and he gave us a recruitment speech. Moreover, it was unnecessary. Seventeen of my class of thirty-six new physicians already had arranged to enter the Medical Department of the Army.

I know you will understand when I write that although I would dearly have loved to see Ma, I was relieved by her decision not to attempt the trip to Cincinnati. Trains, hotels, etc, are so crowded and dirty nowadays that a woman travelling alone would have to suffer discomfort, or worse. I especially missed

*your presence, which gives me another reason to hate the war.
Paul Cooke's father, who sells feed and grain in Xenia, came to
commencement and afterward took the two of us for a grand feed,
with wine toasts and nice compliments: Paul is one of those
going directly into the army. He's deceptive because he's so full
of fun, but he was the brightest in our class and was awarded his
degree* summa cum laude. *I was of help to him in the
laboratory work, and he helped me earn* magna cum laude,
*because whenever we finished a reading assignment he asked me
questions that were a lot fiercer than any our professors ever
asked.*

*After dinner, he and his father went to Pike's Opera House to
hear Adelina Patti in concert, and I went back to the Polyclinic. I
knew precisely what I wanted to do. There is a brick-lined tunnel
that runs under Ninth Street between the medical school and the
main hospital building. It is for the use of physicians only. In
order that it is clear during emergencies, it is off-limits to medical
students, who must cross the street aboveground, no matter how
inclement the weather. I went into the basement of the medical
school, very much still the student, and entered the lamplit
tunnel. Somehow, when I walked through on the other side into
the hospital, for the first time I felt like a doctor!*

*Pa, I've accepted a two-year appointment as a house officer of
the Southwestern Ohio Hospital. It pays only three hundred
dollars per annum, but Dr Berwyn said it will lead to a good
income as a surgeon. 'Never downplay the importance of income,'
he told me. 'You must remember that the person who complains
bitterly about a doctor's earnings usually is not a doctor.'*

*Embarrassingly, and to my wonderful fortune, both Berwyn
and McGowan squabble about which of them shall take me under
his wing. The other day, Barney McGowan outlined this plan for
my future: I shall work with him for a few years as a junior
associate, then he will arrange an appointment for me as associate
professor of anatomy. Thus, he said, when he retires, I'll be ready
to take over the mantle as professor of pathology.*

*It was too much, they both set my head to spinning, because
my own dream always has been simply to become a doctor. In the
end, they worked out a programme that is advantageous to me.
Just as I did during my summer employment, I'll spend*

429

mornings in the operating theatre with Berwyn and afternoons on pathology with McGowan, only instead of doing dirty work as a student, I'll function as a doctor. Despite their kindness, I don't know whether I'll ever want to settle in Cincinnati. I miss living in a small place where I know the people.

Cincinnati is more Southern in feeling and sentiment than Holden's Crossing. Billy Henried confided to a few trusted friends that he would join the Confederate Army as a surgeon after graduation. Two nights ago I went to a farewell dinner with Henried and Cooke. It was strange and sad, each of them aware of where the other was going.

News that President Lincoln has signed a proclamation granting liberty to the slaves has caused lots of anger. I know you don't care for the President because of his part in destroying the Sauks, but I admire him for freeing the slaves, whatever his political reasons. Northerners hereabouts seem able to make any sacrifice when they tell themselves it is to save the Union, but they don't want the goal of the war to become the abolition of slavery. They seem unprepared to pay this terrible blood-price if the purpose of the fighting is to free the Negroes. The losses have been terrifying at battles like Second Bull Run and Antietam. Now there is news of slaughter at Fredericksburg, where almost thirteen thousand soldiers were mowed down while trying to take high ground from the South. It has produced despair in many of the people with whom I have talked.

I worry constantly about you and Alex. It may irk you to know I've begun to pray, although I don't know to whom or what, and I ask regularly only that both of you will come home.

Please do your best to care for your own health as well as that of others, and remember that there are those who anchor their lives on your strength and goodness.

Your loving son,
Shaman
(Dr! Robert Jefferson Cole)

430

51
The Horn Player

It wasn't as hard as Rob J. feared to live in a tent, to sleep on the ground again. What was more difficult was dealing with questions that haunted him: why in the world he was there, and what the outcome of this terrible civil war would be. Events continued to go badly for the cause of the North. 'We can't seem to win for losing,' Major G. H. Woffenden observed in one of his less drunken moments.

Most of the troops Rob J. lived among drank hard when off-duty, especially following payday. They drank to forget, to remember, to celebrate, to commiserate with one another. The dirty and often drunken young men were like pit dogs on a leash, apparently oblivious to impending mortality, straining to get at their natural enemy, other Americans who doubtless were just as dirty and just as often drunken.

Why were they so eager to kill Confederates? Very few of them really knew. Rob J. saw that the war had taken on substance and meaning for them that went far beyond reasons and causes. They thirsted to fight because the war existed, and because it had been officially declared admirable and patriotic to kill. That was enough.

He wanted to howl and scream at them, to lock the generals and politicians in a dark room like errant, foolish children, to take them by the scruff of their collective necks and shake them and demand: *What is the matter with you?*

What is the matter with you?

But instead, he went to sick call every day and doled out the ipecac and the quinine and the paregoric, and he was careful to look at the ground wherever he walked, like a man who made his home in a giant kennel.

On his final day with the 106th Kansas, Rob J. sought out the paymaster and collected his eighty dollars and then went to the conical tent and slung his *Mee-shome* over his shoulder and picked up his suitcase. Major G. H. Woffenden, curled up in his rubber poncho, didn't open his eyes or mutter goodbye.

Five days before, the men of the 67th Pennsylvania had marched raggedly onto steamboats and were carried southward toward combat in Mississippi, according to rumour. Now other boats had disgorged the 131st Indiana, which was raising its tents where the Pennsylvanians lately had lived. When Rob J. sought out the commanding officer, he found a baby-faced colonel still in his twenties, Alonzo Symonds. Colonel Symonds said he had his eye out for a doctor. His surgeon had concluded a three-month enlistment and had gone back to Indiana, and he never had had an assistant surgeon. He questioned Dr Cole closely and seemed impressed by what he learned, but when Rob J. began to indicate that certain conditions had to be met before he could sign on, Colonel Symonds' face showed doubt.

Rob J. had kept careful records of his sick calls for the 106th. 'On almost any given day, thirty-six percent of the men were on their backs or in my sick line. Some days the percentage was higher. How does that compare with your daily sick list?'

'We've had a lot of them sick,' Symonds conceded.

'I can give you more healthy men, Colonel, if you will help me.'

Symonds had been a colonel only four months. His family owned a factory in Fort Wayne where glass lamp chimneys were made, and he knew how ruinous sick workers could be. The 131st Indiana had been formed four months before, raw troops, and within days had been thrown into picket

432

duty in Tennessee. He considered himself fortunate that they'd had only two skirmishes serious enough to be called contact with the enemy. He had lost two killed and one wounded, but on any given day he had had so many down with fever that the Confederates could have waltzed through his regiment without trouble, had they known.

'What do I have to do?'

'Your troops are raising their tents on the shitpiles of the Pennsylvania 67th. And the water's bad here, they drink river water that's spoiled by their own runoff. There's an unused site less than a mile on the other side of the encampment, with clean springs that should give good water through the winter, if you drive pipes into them.'

'God Almighty. A mile's a long way to go to confer with the other regiments. Or to expect their officers to come if they want to see me.'

They studied one another, and Colonel Symonds made up his mind. He went to his sergeant major. 'Order the tents to be struck, Douglass. The regiment's going to move.'

Then he came back and talked business with this difficult doctor.

Again Rob J. turned down a chance to be commissioned. He asked to be hired as acting assistant surgeon, on a three-month contract.

'That way, you don't get what you want, you can leave,' the young colonel observed astutely. The middle-aged doctor didn't deny it, and Colonel Symonds considered him. 'What else do you want?'

'Latrines,' Rob J. said.

The ground was firm but not yet frozen. In a single morning the sinks were dug and logs were fixed on one-foot posts at the edge of the trenches. When the order was read to all companies that defecating or urinating any place but in designated sinks would result in swift and severe punishment, there was resentment. The men needed something to hate and ridicule, and Rob J. realized he had filled that need. When he passed among them, they nudged one another, their eyes raked him, they grinned cruelly at the ridiculous

433

figure he made in his ever-shabbier civilian suit.

Colonel Symonds didn't give them a chance to spend much time thinking about grievances. He invested four days in labour details that built a series of spare, half-excavated huts of logs and sod. They were damp and poorly ventilated, but they gave considerably more shelter than tents, and a small fire made it possible for the men to sleep through a winter's night.

Symonds was a good commander and had attracted decent officers. The regiment's commissary officer was a captain named Mason, and Rob J. didn't find it difficult to explain the dietary causes of scurvy, because he could point out examples of the disease's effects among the troops. The two of them took a buckboard into Cairo and bought barrels of cabbages and carrots, which were made part of the ration. Scurvy was even more prevalent among some of the other units in the encampment, but when Rob J. tried to confer with the physicians of the other regiments, he met with little success. They seemed more conscious of their roles as army officers than as doctors. All were uniformed, two sported swords like line officers, and the surgeon of the Ohio regiment wore custom fringed epaulets like those in a picture Rob J. once had seen of a pompous French general.

In contrast, he embraced his civilian self. When a supply sergeant, grateful for banished stomach cramps, issued him a blue woollen overcoat, he welcomed it but took it to town and had it dyed black and given plain bone buttons. He liked to pretend he was still a country doctor who had moved temporarily to another town.

In many respects, the camp *was* like a small town, albeit exclusively male. The regiment had its own post office, with a corporal named Amasa Decker as postmaster and mail-man. On Wednesday evenings the band gave concerts on the drill field, and sometimes, when they played a popular song like 'Listen to the Mockingbird', or 'Come Where My Love Lies Dreaming', or 'The Girl I Left Behind Me', the men sang along. Sutlers brought a variety of goods into the camp. Out of thirteen dollars per month, the average soldier couldn't afford much cheese at fifty cents a pound, or condensed milk at seventy-five cents a can, but they bought the sutlers' liquor. Rob J. indulged himself several times a week in molasses cookies, six for a quarter. A photographer had set up shop in a large wall tent, in which one day Rob paid a dollar for a ferrotype photograph of himself, stiff and unsmiling, that he sent off to Sarah at once as proof that her husband was still alive and well and loved her dearly.

Having taken raw troops into disputed territory once, Colonel Symonds was determined that they would never be unprepared for combat again. Through the winter, he worked his soldiers hard. There were training hikes of thirty miles that produced new patients for Rob J., because some of the men suffered strained muscles from carrying a full field pack and heavy rifled musket. Others developed hernias from wearing belts hung with heavy cartridge boxes. Squads constantly trained in bayonet warfare, and Symonds forced them to practise the laborious loading of their muskets again and again: 'Bite off the end of the paper-wrapped cartridge like you're mad at it. Pour the powder down the barrel, insert the minié bullet and then the paper wrapping for a wad, and ram the whole damn mess home. Take a percussion cap from your pouch, place it on the nipple in the breech. Aim that beautiful thing and *fire!*'

They did it again and again, repeatedly, unendingly. Symonds told Rob J. he wanted them to be able to load and fire when awakened from a sound sleep, when numb with panic, when their hands were shaking with excitement or fright.

In the same way, so they would learn to take orders without hesitation instead of cussing out or challenging their officers, the colonel marched them incessantly in close-order drill. Several mornings when the landscape was covered with snow, Symonds borrowed huge wooden rollers from the Cairo road department, and teams of army horses pulled them around the parade ground until it was flat and hard enough for the companies to drill some more, while the regimental band played marches and quicksteps.

It was on a bright winter's day, while passing the

perimeter of the parade ground filled with squads of drilling men, that Rob J. glanced at the seated band and noted that one of the horn players had a port-wine stain on his face. The man's heavy brass instrument rested on his left shoulder, the long throat and the bell flashing golden behind him in the winter sun, while as he blew into the mouthpiece – they were playing 'Hail, Columbia' – his cheeks ballooned enormously and then relaxed, again and again. Each time the man's cheeks filled with air, the purple mark under his right eye darkened, like a signal.

For the eleven long years Rob J. had tensed whenever he met a man with a stain mark on his face, but now he simply proceeded to sick call, automatically walking to the beat of the insistent music all the way to the dispensary tent.

The next morning, when he saw the band marching on the parade ground to play for a First Battalion review, he looked for the horn player with the marked face, but the man wasn't there.

Rob J. walked to the row of huts where the band lived, and at once he came upon the man taking frozen garments off the washline. 'Stiffer than a dead man's dick', the man said to him in disgust. 'It don't make sense to have inspections in dead of winter.'

Hypocritically, Rob J. agreed, although the inspections had been his suggestion, to force the men to wash at least some of their clothing. 'Got the day off, have you?'

The man gave him a surly look. 'I don't march. I'm spavined.'

As he walked away with his armload of frozen clothes, Rob J. saw he was. The horn player would destroy the symmetry of a military-band formation. His right leg seemed slightly shorter than the left, and he walked with a decided limp.

Rob J. went into his own hut and sat on his poncho in the cold gloom with his blanket around his shoulders.

Eleven years. He remembered the day precisely. He recalled each of the individual house calls he had made while Makwa-ikwa was being violated and murdered.

436

He thought of the three men who had come to Holden's Crossing just prior to the murder and then had disappeared. In eleven years he'd managed to learn nothing about them, save that they were 'bad drunks'.

A spurious preacher, the Reverend Ellwood Patterson, whom he had treated for syphilis.

A burly, physically powerful fat man named Hank Cough.

A skinny young man they'd called Len. Sometimes Lenny. With a port-wine stain on his face under his right eye. And a limp.

Not so skinny anymore, if this was the man. But then, not so young anymore either.

This probably wasn't the one he was looking for, he told himself. It was probable that there was more than one man in America with a facial stain and a gimpy leg.

He didn't want this to be the man, he realized. He faced the fact that he no longer really wanted to find them. What would he do if the horn player was Lenny? Slit his throat?

Helplessness gripped him.

Makwa's death was something he had managed to put away in a separate compartment of his mind. Now that compartment had been reopened, Pandora's box, and he felt an almost-forgotten iciness begin to grow deep inside him, a coldness that had nothing to do with the temperature in the small hut.

He went outside and walked to the tent that served as the regimental office. The sergeant major's name was Stephen Douglass, spelled with one more S than the senator's. He'd grown accustomed to the doctor's working with personnel files. He had told Rob J. he'd never seen an army surgeon so driven to keep complete medical records. 'More paper-work, Doc?'

'A little.'

'Help yourself. The orderly's gone out for a pitcher of hot coffee. Welcome to some of it when it comes. Just don't drip any on my damn records, please.'

Rob J. promised he wouldn't.

The band was attached to Headquarters Company. Sergeant Douglass kept each company's records neatly in a separate grey box. Rob J. found Headquarters Company's box, and inside it was a group of records tied with cord as a discrete bundle marked *Indiana 131st Regimental Band*.

He leafed through the records, one by one. There was nobody in the band whose first name was Leonard, but when Rob J. found the card, he knew at once and without uncertainty that this was the right man, the way he sometimes knew if somebody would live or die.

ORDWAY, LANNING A., private. Residence, Vincennes, Indiana. One-year enlistment, July 28, 1862. Enlistment credit, Fort Wayne. Born, Vincennes, Indiana, November 11, 1836. Height, 5' 8". Complexion, fair. Eyes, grey. Hair, brown. Enlisted for limited duty as musician (E-flat bass cornet) and general labourer, due to disability.

52
Troop Movements

It was weeks after Rob's contract ran out before Colonel Symonds came to him to discuss its renewal. By that time the spring fevers had begun to rage through the other regiments, but not in the Indiana 131st. The men of the 131st had colds from the damp ground and runny bowels from the ration, but Rob J.'s sick-call lines were the shortest he'd seen since he'd begun working for the army. Colonel Symonds knew that three regiments were tormented with fever and ague, and his own was relatively sound. Some of the oldest men, who shouldn't have been there in the first place, had been sent home. Most of the others had lice, and filthy feet and necks, and itchy loins, and they drank too much whisky. But they were lean and hard from the long marches, keen from the constant drilling, and bright-eyed and eager because somehow Acting Assistant Surgeon Cole had gotten them through the winter fit for duty, as he had promised. Out of six hundred men in the regiment, seven had died during the winter, a mortality rate of twelve per thousand. In comparison, fifty-eight men per thousand had died in the other three regiments, and now that the fevers had come, that percentage was certain to rise.

So the colonel came to his doctor ready to be reasonable, and Rob J. signed the contract for another three months of employment with no hesitation. He could tell when he was

439

in a good position.

What they had to do now, he told Symonds, was set up an ambulance to serve the regiment in battle.

The civilian Sanitary Commission had lobbied the secretary of war until finally ambulances and stretcher-bearers were part of the Army of the Potomac, but the reform movement had stopped there, without providing similar care for the wounded of the units in the Western sector. 'We're going to have to take care of ourselves,' Rob J. said.

He and Symonds sat cozily in front of the dispensary tent and smoked cigars, the smoke drifting into the warming spring air as he told the colonel of his trip to Cincinnati on the *War Hawk*. 'I talked to men who just lay there on the battlefield for two days after they were hit. It was a mercy it rained because they were without water. One man told me that during the night, pigs came close to where he lay and began to eat the bodies. Some of them weren't dead yet.'

Symonds nodded. He was familiar with all the terrible details. 'What do you need?'

'Four men from each company.'

'You want an entire platoon to carry stretchers,' Symonds said, shocked. 'This regiment is markedly under strength. To win battles I need fighters, not stretcher-bearers.' He considered the tip of his cigar. 'Too many still are old and disabled, shouldn't have enlisted. Take some of those.'

'No. We need men strong enough to get to others under fire and bring them to safety. It isn't a job that can be done by sickly old men.' Rob J. studied the troubled face of this young man he'd come to admire and pity. Symonds loved his troops and wanted to protect them, yet the colonel owned the unenviable job of having to expend human lives as if they were bullets or rations or chunks of firewood. 'Suppose I use men from the regimental band,' Rob J. said. 'They can tootle most of the time, and after a fight they can carry stretchers.'

Colonel Symonds nodded, relieved. 'Very good. See if the bandmaster can give you some men.'

Bandmaster Warren Fitts had been a shoemaker for sixteen years when he was recruited in Fort Wayne. He had had rigorous musical training and as a young man had tried for several years to establish a music school in South Bend. When he left that town owing money, he'd turned with bitter relief to shoemaking, his father's trade. His father had taught him well, and he was a good shoemaker. He'd earned a modest but comfortable living, and on the side gave music lessons, teaching both piano and the brass instruments. The war had refurbished dreams for him that he had thought worn out and discarded. At the age of forty he had been given a chance to recruit a military band and mould it as he wished. He had had to scour the musical talent of the Fort Wayne area to find enough musicians for the band, and now he listened with astonishment as the surgeon proposed to take some of his men for stretcher-bearers.

'Never!'

'They'd only have to be with me part of the time,' Rob J. said. 'The rest of the time they would be with you.'

Fitts tried to hide his contempt. 'Each musician has to give the band his undivided attention. When he's not playing, he must practice and rehearse.'

From his own experience with the viola da gamba, Rob J. knew this was true. 'Are there instruments in the band for which you have extra players?' he asked patiently.

The question struck a responsive chord in Fitts. His position as bandmaster was the closest he would ever come to being a conductor, and he was careful to see that his own appearance, and that of the band, was worthy of their roles as artists. Fitts had a full head of greying hair. His face was clean-shaven save for moustaches that he kept clipped; he dressed the ends with wax and twirled them into points. His uniform was carefully maintained, and the musicians knew they had to keep their brasses polished, their uniforms clean, and their boots blacked and buffed. And they had to march smartly, because when the bandmaster strutted out, wielding his baton, he wanted to be followed by a band that reflected his standards. But there were a few who marred this image . . .

441

'Wilcox, Abner,' he said. 'Bugler.' Wilcox was decidedly walleyed. Fitts liked musicians to have physical beauty as well as talent. He couldn't bear to see any sort of defect spoiling the crisp perfection of his ensemble, and he had assigned Wilcox to spare duties as a regimental bugler.

'Lawrence, Oscar. A drummer.' A clumsy sixteen-year-old boy whose lack of coordination not only made him a poor drummer but too often caused him to lose step when the band marched, so that his head sometimes bobbed out of rhythm with the heads of the other marchers.

'Ordway, Lanning,' Fitts said, and the surgeon gave a funny little nod. 'E-flat bass cornet.' A mediocre musician and driver of one of the band's wagons, who sometimes worked as a labourer. Adequate to play bass horn when they were providing music for the troops on Wednesday evenings or when they were practising while seated in chairs on the drill field, but his limp made it impossible for him to march without destroying the military effect.

'Perry, Addison. Piccolo and fife.' A bad musician, and slovenly of person and dress. Fitts was happy to get rid of such dead wood.

'Robinson, Lewis. E-flat sopranino cornet.' A capable musician, Fitts had to admit to himself. But a source of extreme irritation, a smartass with aspirations. On several occasions Robinson had shown Fitts pieces he had said were original compositions, and had asked if perhaps the band could play them. He claimed to have had experience conducting a community philharmonic in Colombus, Ohio. Fitts didn't need anyone looking over his shoulder or breathing down his neck.

'. . . And?' the surgeon asked him.

'And nobody else,' the bandmaster said with satisfaction.

All through the winter, Rob J. had watched Ordway from afar. He was nervous, because although Ordway's enlistment had a long way to run, it wasn't hard for a man to desert and disappear. But whatever kept the majority of them in the army also worked on Ordway, and he was one of the five privates who reported to Rob J., not an

442

unpleasant-looking man for a suspected murderer, except for watery, anxious eyes.

None of the five was pleased to hear of his new assignment. Lewis Robinson reacted with panic. 'I must play my music! I'm a musician, not a doctor.'

Rob J. corrected him. 'Stretcher-bearer. For the time being, you're a stretcher-bearer,' he said, and the others knew he was speaking to each of them.

He made the best of a bad bargain by asking the bandmaster to give up any demands on their time, and won that concession with suspicious ease. To train them, he began at the beginning, teaching them to roll bandages and form dressings, and then simulating various types of wounds and teaching them to apply the dressing needed. He taught them how to move and carry the wounded, and furnished each man with a small rucksack that contained dressings, bandages, a container of fresh water, and opium and morphine in powder and pills.

Several splints came with the Army's medical pannier, but Rob J. didn't like them, and he requisitioned lumber that allowed the stretcher-bearers to make their own splints under his fussy direction. Abner Wilcox turned out to be an adequate carpenter, and innovative. He fashioned a number of excellent lightweight litters by stretching canvas between two poles. The supply officer offered a two-wheeled trap to be designated as an ambulance, but Rob J. had had years of answering house calls over bad roads, and knew that for evacuating wounded men over rough terrain he needed the security of four wheels. He found a sound buckboard and Wilcox built sides and a roof to enclose it. They painted it black, and Ordway very cleverly duplicated the medical caduceus that was printed on the pannier, painting one in silver on each side of the ambulance. From the remount officer Rob J. wheedled a pair of ugly but strong work horses, castoffs like the rest of the rescue corps.

The five men were beginning to feel an unwilling group pride, but Robinson worried openly about the increased risks of their new assignment. 'Of course there will be danger,' Rob J. said. 'The infantry on the line faces danger too, and there's danger in a cavalry charge, or there wouldn't be need for litter-bearers.'

He'd always known that war corrupted, but he saw now that it had corrupted him as much as everyone else. He'd arranged the lives of these five young men so that now they were expected to go after the wounded again and again, as if they could shed musket rounds and shake off artillery, and he was trying to avert their enraged awareness by pointing out to them that they were members of the death generation. His specious words and attitude sought to disclaim his responsibility, as he tried desperately to believe with them that they were no worse off now than when their lives were complicated only by Fitts' foolish temperament, and by how much expression they achieved in the playing of their waltzes and schottisches and quickstep marches.

He split them into litter teams: Perry and Lawrence. Wilcox and Robinson.

'What about me?' Ordway said.

'You will stick close to me,' Rob J. said.

Corporal Amasa Decker, the mailman, had come to know Rob J. because he delivered a steady stream of mail from Sarah, who wrote long and passionate letters. The fact that his wife was so physical had always been one of her charms for Rob J., and sometimes he lay in his hut and read letter after letter, transported so by desire that he imagined he could smell her scent. Though there were females in abundance in Cairo, ranging from the hired to the patriotic, he had made no attempt to approach a woman. He was afflicted with the curse of faithfulness.

He spent much of his free time writing tender, supportive letters as counterpoint to Sarah's anguished heat. Sometimes he wrote to Shaman, and he wrote constantly in his journal. Other times he lay on his poncho and pondered how he could learn from Ordway what happened the day Makwa-ikwa was killed. He knew that somehow he had to gain Ordway's confidence.

He thought of the report Ferocious Miriam had given him on the Know-Nothings and their Order of the Star-Spangled

Banner. Whoever had written that report – he'd always fancied it had been a spying priest – had passed himself off as a Protestant anti-Catholic. Could the same tactic be successful again? The report was in Holden's Crossing with the rest of his papers. But he had read it so often and so intently that he found he remembered the signs and signals, the code words and the passwords – an entire panoply of secret communication that could have been invented by a dramatic boy with an overactive imagination.

Rob J. ran exercises with the stretcher-bearers, one of them playing wounded victim, and discovered that while two men could put a man into a litter and lift him into an ambulance, those same two men would quickly tire, and might collapse, if they had to carry the litter an appreciable distance. 'We need a bearer in each corner,' Perry said, and Rob J. knew he was right. But that left him with only one manned litter, which clearly wasn't adequate if the regiment ran into any sort of trouble at all.

He took his problem to the colonel. 'What do you want to do about it?' Symonds asked.

'Use the entire band. Make my five trained stretcher-bearers corporals. Each of them can captain a litter in situations where we have lots of wounded, with three other musicians assigned to each corporal. If the soldiers have to choose between musicians who play wonderfully during a fight and musicians who will save their lives if they're shot, I know how they'll vote.'

'They won't vote,' Symonds said drily. 'I do all the voting around here.' But he voted correctly. The five bearers sewed stripes on their sleeves, and whenever Fitts happened to pass Rob J., the bandmaster didn't say hello.

In mid-May the weather turned hot. The encampment was located between the conjoining Ohio and Mississippi rivers, both befouled by runoff from the camp. But Rob J. issued half a bar of brown soap to each man in the regiment and the companies were marched, one at a time, to a clean place upstream on the Ohio, where the men were ordered to disrobe and bathe. At first they entered the water with

445

curses and groans, but most of them were country-raised and couldn't resist a swimming hole, and the bath deteriorated into splashing and horseplay. When they emerged they were inspected by their sergeants, with special emphasis on their heads and their feet, and to the jeers of their comrades, some were sent back for rewashing.

Some of the uniforms were ragged and motley, woven of inferior cloth. But Colonel Symonds had acquired a number of new uniforms, and when they were distributed the men correctly assumed they were to ship out. Both of the Kansas regiments had been taken down the Mississippi by steamboat. The conventional wisdom was that they'd gone to help Grant's army take Vicksburg, and that the Indiana 131st would follow.

But on the afternoon of the 27th May, with Warren Fitts' band making a number of discernible nervous errors but playing lustily, the regiment was marched to the railroad yard instead of to the river. The men and the animals were loaded into boxcars, and there was a two-hour wait while wagons were lashed to flatcars, and then at dusk the 131st said goodbye to Cairo, Illinois.

The doctor and the stretcher-bearers rode in a hospital car. It was otherwise empty when they left Cairo, but within an hour a young private had fainted in one of the boxcars, and when he was brought to the hospital car, Rob J. found that he was burning with fever, and incoherent. He gave the boy alcohol sponge baths and made up his mind to offload him to a civilian hospital at the earliest opportunity.

Rob J. admired the hospital car, which would have been invaluable if they had been returning from battle instead of riding toward it. On side of the aisle a triple tier of litters ran the length of the car. Each litter was cleverly suspended by means of India-rubber loops connecting its four corners to hooks set in the walls and posts, so that the stretching and contracting of the rubber absorbed much of the train's jostle and sway. In the absence of patients, the five new corporals each had chosen a litter and agreed they couldn't ride in greater comfort if they were generals. Addison Perry, who had proved he could doze anywhere, day or night, already was asleep, and so was the youngster, Lawrence. Lewis Robinson had taken a litter apart from the others, under the lantern, and was making little black pencil marks on a piece of paper, composing music.

They had no idea where they were going. When Rob J. walked to the end of the car and opened the door, the noise was loud and rackety, but he looked up between the swaying cars at the points of light in the sky and found the Big Dipper. He followed the two pointer stars at the end of the bowl and there was the North Star.

'We're travelling East,' he said, back in the car.

'Shit,' Abner Wilcox said. 'They're sending us to the Army of the Potomac.'

Lew Robinson stopped making his little black marks. 'What's wrong with that?'

'Potomac Army ain't done nothin good, ever. All it does is wait around. When it fights, once in a blue moon, those fartheads always manage to lose to the rebels. I wanted to go to Grant. That man's a general.'

'You don't get killed waiting around,' Robinson said.

'I hate to go East,' Ordway said. 'Whole damn East is full of Irishers, Roman Catholic scum. Filthy buggers.'

'Nobody performed better at Fredericksburg than the Irish Brigade. Most of them died,' Robinson said thinly.

It didn't require much thought on Rob J.'s part, just an instant decision. He placed his fingertip under his right eye and slid it slowly down the side of his nose, the signal from one member of the order to another that he was saying too much.

Did it work, or was it coincidence? Lanning Ordway stared at him for a moment, then stopped talking and went to sleep.

At three o'clock in the morning there was a long stop at Louisville, where an artillery battery joined the troop train. The night air was heavier than in Illinois, and softer. Those who were awake left the train to stretch their legs, and Rob J. arranged for the sick corporal to be taken to the local hospital. When he was finished, he walked down the track, past two pissing men. 'No time to dig sinks here, sir,' one of them said, and they both laughed. The civilian doctor was still a joke.

He went to where the battery's great ten-pound Parrotts and twelve-pound howitzers were being secured to flatcars with heavy chains. The cannons were being loaded in the yellow light of large calcium lamps that sputtered and flickered, throwing shadows that appeared to move with a life of their own.

'Doctor,' someone said softly.

The man stepped out of the darkness next to him and took his hand, making the signal of recognition. Too nervous even to feel absurd, Rob J. endeavoured to perform the countersign as though he had done it many times before.

Ordway looked at him. 'Well,' he said.

53
The Long Grey Line

They came to hate the troop train. It crept so slowly across the length of Kentucky and wound so tiredly between the hills, a snake-shaped, boring jail. When the train entered Virginia the news travelled from car to car. The soldiers peered from the windows, expecting at once to witness the face of the enemy, but all they saw was a country of mountains and woods. When they stopped for fuel and water in small towns, the people were as friendly as they'd been in Kentucky, because the western section of Virginia supported the Union. They could tell when they reached the other parts of Virginia. There were no women at the stations with drinks of cool mountain water or lemonade, and the men had bland, blank faces, and watchful, heavy-lidded eyes.

The 131st Indiana detrained at a place called Winchester, an occupied town, blue uniforms everywhere. While the horses and equipment were unloaded, Colonel Symonds disappeared inside a headquarters building near the railroad station, and when he emerged the troops and the wagons were arrayed in marching order, and they set out southward.

When Rob J. had signed on, he'd been told he had to buy his own horse, but there had been no urgent need for him to have a horse in Cairo, because he didn't wear a uniform

449

or take part in parades. Besides, horses were scarce wherever the army was located, because the cavalry claimed every remount in sight, whether the animal ran races or pulled a plough. So now, horseless, he rode in the ambulance on the seat next to Corporal Ordway, who drove the team. Rob J. was still tense in Lanning Ordway's presence, but Ordway's only question had been to wonder warily why a member of the OSSB should 'speak with a foreigner's tongue', referring to the trace of Scots burr that on occasion still crept into Rob J.'s speech. Rob had said he'd been born in Boston and taken to Edinburgh as a youth to be educated, and Ordway appeared satisfied. He was now cheerful and friendly, obviously pleased to be working for a man who had a political reason for taking good care of him.

They passed a marker on the dusty road that indicated it was the route to Fredericksburg. 'God Almighty,' Ordway said. 'I hope nobody's got it in mind to send a second group of Yankees up against those rebel gunners on the heights at Fredericksburg.'

Rob J. could only agree.

Several hours before dusk the 131st came to the banks of the Rappahannock River, and Symonds halted them and ordered a camp. He called a meeting of all officers in front of his tent, and Rob J. stood on the fringes of the uniform and listened.

'Gentlemen, for half a day we have been members of the Federal Army of the Potomac, under the command of General Joseph Hooker,' Symonds said.

He told them Hooker had gathered a force of about one hundred and twenty-two thousand men, spread out over a long perimeter. Robert E. Lee had about ninety thousand Confederates and was at Fredericksburg. Hooker's cavalry had scouted Lee's army for a long time and they were convinced Lee was getting ready to invade the North in an attempt to draw Union forces away from the siege at Vicksburg, but no one knew where or when the invasion would take place. 'The people in Washington are understandably nervous, with the Confederate Army only a couple of hours away from the White House door. The 131st is travelling to join other units near Fredericksburg.'

The officers took the news soberly. They laid out several layers of pickets, far and near, and the camp settled down for the night. When Rob J. had eaten his pork and beans, he lay back and looked up at the fat summer stars of evening. It was too much for him to contemplate contending forces that were so enormous. About ninety thousand Confederate men! About one hundred and twenty-two thousand Union men! And all of them doing their best to kill one another.

A limpid night. The six hundred and fourteen soldiers of the Indiana 131st lay on the warm bare ground without bothering to raise tents. Most of them still had northern colds, and the sound of their coughing was enough to warn any nearby enemy of their existence. Rob J. had a brief doctor's nightmare, wondering about the sound of one hundred and twenty-two thousand men all coughing at the same time. The acting assistant surgeon clasped his arms about his body, chilled. He knew that if two such giant armies were to meet and fight, it would take more than the men of the band to carry the wounded away.

It took them two and one half days to march to Fredericksburg. On the way they almost succumbed to Virginia's secret weapon, the chigger. The tiny red mite fell on them when they passed under overhanging trees and became attached to them as they walked through grass. If it clung to their clothing, it migrated until it reached bare skin, where it burrowed its entire body into human flesh to feed. Soon men had chigger rashes between their fingers and toes, in their buttocks and on their penises. The mite had a two-part body; if a soldier saw one working its way into his flesh and tried to pull it out, the chigger broke at its narrow waist, and the portion that was embedded did as much damage as a whole chigger would have. By the third day most of the soldiers were scratching and swearing, and some of the wounds already had begun to fester in the moist heat. Rob J. could no nothing more than sprinkle sulphur on the embedded insects, but a few of the men had had experience

451

with chiggers, and they taught the rest that the only remedy was to hold the glowing end of a stick or a lighted cigar just off the skin until the chigger started to back up, drawn to the heat. Then it could be seized and pulled out slowly and carefully, so it wouldn't break. All over the camp, men removed chiggers from one another, reminding Rob J. of the monkeys he used to watch grooming each other for lice in the Edinburgh Zoo.

Chigger misery didn't eradicate terror. Their apprehension grew as they approached Fredericksburg, which had been the scene of such Yankee slaughter at the earlier battle. But when they arrived they saw only Union blue, because Robert E. Lee had adroitly and quietly pulled out his troops several nights earlier under cover of darkness, and his Army of Northern Virginia was heading north. The Union cavalry was scouting Lee's progress but the Army of the Potomac wasn't in pursuit, for reasons only General Hooker knew.

They camped at Fredericksburg for six days, resting, tending to blisters on their feet, removing chiggers, cleaning and oiling weapons. When they were off-duty, in small groups they climbed the ridge where only six months before almost thirteen thousand Union men had been killed or wounded. Looking down at the easy targets their comrades made struggling to climb after them, they were glad Lee had left before they got there.

When Symonds got new orders, they had to move north again. They were on the march along a dusty road when they heard the news that Winchester, where they had disembarked from their troop train, had been hit hard by Confederates under General Richard S. Ewell. It was another rebel victory – ninety-five Union men had been killed, three hundred and forty-eight wounded, and more than four thousand were missing or taken prisoner.

Riding uncomfortably in the ambulance along that peaceful country lane, Rob J. didn't allow himself to believe in combat, just as when he had been a young boy he hadn't allowed himself to believe in death. Why should people die? It made no sense, since it was more pleasant to live. And why should people actually fight during a war? It was more pleasant to proceed sleepily down this curving, sun-baked road than to engage in the business of killing.

But just as Rob J.'s childhood disbelief in mortality had been ended by his father's death, the reality of the present was brought home to him when they came to Fairfax Courthouse and he saw what the Bible meant when it described an enormous army as a host.

They camped on a farm in six fields amid artillery and cavalry and other infantry. Everywhere Rob J. looked there were Union soldiers. The army was in flux, troops coming and leaving. The day after the 131st arrived they learned that Lee's Army of Northern Virginia already had invaded the North, crossing the Potomac River into Maryland. Once Lee had committed himself, so did Hooker, tardily sending the first units of his army north, trying to stay between Lee and Washington. It was forty more hours before the 131st fell in and resumed its northward march.

Each army was too large and diffuse to be relocated swiftly and completely. Part of Lee's force still was in Virginia, moving to cross the river and join its commander. The two armies were shapeless, pulsating monsters, spreading and contracting, always on the move, sometimes alongside one another. When their edges happened to touch there were skirmishes like bursts of sparks – at Upperville, at Haymarket, at Aldie, and a dozen other places. The Indiana 131st had no concrete evidence of the fighting except in the middle of one night when the outer line of pickets exchanged brief and ineffectual fire with horsemen who hurried away.

The men of the 131st crossed the Potomac in small boats at night, on the 27th June. The next morning they resumed their march north, and Fitts' band struck up 'Maryland, My Maryland'. Sometimes when they came to people, somebody would wave, but the Maryland civilians they passed seemed unimpressed, because for days they had been witnessing troops marching through. Rob J. and the soldiers soon grew heartily sick of the Maryland state anthem, but the band still was playing it on the morning when they

453

made their way through good rolling farmland and into a neat central village.

'What part of Maryland is this?' Ordway asked Rob J.

'I don't know.' They were passing a bench on which an old man sat and watched the military. 'Mister,' Rob J. called, 'what's the name of this pretty place?'

The compliment seemed to disconcert the old man. 'Our town? This town is Gettysburg, Pennsylvania.'

Although the men of the 131st Indiana didn't know it, the day they passed into Pennsylvania they had had a new commanding general for twenty-four hours. General George Meade had been named to replace General Joe Hooker, who paid the price for his tardy pursuit of the Confederates.

They went through the little town and marched along the Taneytown Road. The Union Army was massed south of Gettysburg, and Symonds called a halt at an enormous rolling meadow where they could camp. The air was heavy and hot and full of moisture and fearful bravado. The men of 131st talked about the rebel yell. They hadn't heard it when they were in Tennessee, but they had heard a lot about it, and listened to a lot of imitations. They wondered if they were going to hear the real thing in the next few days.

Colonel Symonds knew work was the best thing for nerves, so he got up labour parties and had them dig shallow firing positions behind piles of boulders that could be used as sangars. That night they went to sleep to birdsong and katydid shrill, and next morning awoke to more hot and heavy air and the sound of frequent firing several miles to the northwest, towards the Chambersburg Pike.

About eleven a.m. Colonel Symonds received new orders, and the 131st was marched half a mile over a wooded ridge to a meadow on high ground east of the Emmitsburg Road. Evidence that the new position was closer to the enemy was the grim discovery of six Union soldiers who seemed to be sprawled asleep on the mowing. All the dead pickets were barefoot, the poorly shod Southerners having stolen their shoes.

454

Symonds ordered new breastworks dug, and he placed living pickets. At Rob J.'s request, a long narrow log framework like a grape arbor was put up at the edge of the woods and roofed over with leafy branches to provide shade for the wounded, and outside this shelter Rob J. placed his operating table.

They learned from dispatch riders that the first gunfire had been a clash between cavalry. As the day progressed, the sounds of battle grew to the north of the 131st, a steady, hoarse noise of rifled muskets like the barking of thousands of deadly dogs, and a great ragged, unending cannon thunder. Each slight movement of the heavy air seemed to smite their faces.

Early in the afternoon the 131st was moved a third time that day and marched toward the town and the sound of the fighting, toward the flash of cannon fire and clouds of white-grey smoke. Rob J. had come to know the soldiers and was aware that most of them yearned for a minor wound, no more than a scratch, but one that would leave a mark when it quickly healed, so the folks back home could see how they had suffered for a valorous victory. But now they were moving toward where men were dying. They marched through the town and presently, as they climbed a hill, they were surrounded by the sounds they had earlier heard from afar. Several times artillery rounds whooshed overhead, and they passed dug-in infantry and four batteries of cannon being fired. At the top, where they were told to settle in, they found they'd been placed in the middle of a burial ground that gave the place its name, Cemetery Hill.

Rob J. was setting up his medical station behind an imposing mausoleum that offered both protection and a little shade, when a heavily perspiring colonel came up and asked for the medical officer. He identified himself as Colonel Martin Nichols of the Medical Department, and said he was the organizer of medical services. 'Are you experienced at surgery?' he asked.

It didn't seem the time for modesty. 'Yes, I am. Quite experienced,' Rob J. said.

'Then I need you at a hospital where serious cases are

being sent for surgery.'

'If you don't mind, Colonel, I want to remain with this regiment.'

'I do mind, Doctor, I do. I have some good surgeons, but also some young and inexperienced physicians performing vital surgery and making a damn mess of it. They're amputating limbs without leaving flaps, and several are making stumps that have several inches of exposed bone. They're trying strange experimental operations that experienced surgeons wouldn't – resection of the head of the humerus, disarticulation of the hip joint, disarticulation of the shoulder joint. Making unnecessary cripples and patients who are going to wake up crying with terrible pain every morning for the rest of their lives. You'll relieve one of those so-called surgeons, and I'll send him up here to slap dressings onto the wounded.'

Rob J. nodded. He told Ordway he was in charge of the medical station until another doctor got there, and he followed Colonel Nichols down the hill.

The hospital was in town, in the Catholic church, which he saw was named for Saint Francis; he would have to remember to tell that to Ferocious Miriam. There was an operating table placed in the entry, with the double doors wide open to give the surgeon maximum light. The pews had been covered with boards spread with straw and blankets to make beds for the wounded. In a small, damp room in the cellar, illuminated by lamps that gave off a yellow light, there were two more surgical tables, and Rob J. took over one of these. He removed his coat and rolled up his sleeves as far as they would go, while a corporal of the First Cavalry Division administered chloroform to a soldier whose hand had been carried off by a cannonball. As soon as the boy was anaesthetized, Rob J. took the arm off above the wrist, leaving a good flap for the stump.

'Next!' he called. Another patient was carried in, and Rob J. gave himself up to the work.

The basement was about twenty by forty feet. There was another surgeon at a table across the room, but he and Rob seldom looked at one another and had little to say. In the course of the afternoon Rob J. noted that the other man did good work, and received a similar appraisal, and each of them focused on his own table. Rob J. probed for bullets and metal, replaced eviscerated intestines and sewed up the wounds, and amputated. And amputated some more. The minié ball was a slow-moving projectile, especially damaging when it hit bone. When it carried away or destroyed bone in large pieces, the only thing the surgeons could do was take the limb. On the dirt floor between Rob J. and the other surgeon there rose a pile of arms and legs. From time to time, men came in and took the severed limbs away.

After four or five hours, another colonel, this one in a grey uniform, came into the basement room and told the two doctors they were prisoners. 'We're better soldiers than you folks, we've taken the whole town. Your troops have been pushed to the north, and we've captured four thousand of you.' There wasn't much to say. The other surgeon looked at Rob J. and shrugged. Rob J. was operating and told the colonel he was in the way of the light.

Whenever there was a brief lull, he tried to doze for a few minutes, on his feet. But there were few lulls. The warring armies slept at night, but the doctors worked steadily, trying to save the men the armies had torn apart. There was no window in the basement room, and the lamps were kept turned up. Soon Rob J. lost all comprehension of the time of day.

'Next,' he called.

Next! Next! Next!

It was the equivalent of having to clean out the Augean stables, because as soon as he finished with one patient, they carried in another. Some wore bloodstained and ragged grey uniforms and some wore bloodstained and ragged blue, but he soon understood they were available in inexhaustible supply.

Other things weren't inexhaustible. The church hospital soon ran out of dressings; they had no food. The colonel who had told him the South had better soldiers, now told him the South had neither chloroform nor ether.

'You can't put shoes on their feet or give them anaesthesia for their pain. That's why you'll lose in the end,' Rob J. said without satisfaction, and asked the officer to round up a supply of liquor. The colonel went away, but sent someone with whisky for the patients and hot pigeon soup for the doctors, which Rob J. drank down without tasting.

Without anaesthesia, he got several strong men to hold the patients and he operated the way he had when he was younger, cutting, sawing, sewing, fast and expertly, the way William Fergusson had taught him. His victims screamed and thrashed. He didn't yarn, and although he blinked a lot, his eyes stayed open. He was aware that his feet and ankles were becoming painfully swollen, and sometimes as they carried out one patient and carried in another, he stood and rubbed his right hand with his left. Every case was different, but there are only so many ways to destroy human beings and soon they were all the same, all duplicates, even the ones with their mouths destroyed, or their genitals shot off, or their eyes shot out.

The hours passed, one by one.

He came to feel he had spent most of his life in the small damp room cutting up human beings, and that he was damned to be there forever. But eventually there was change in the noises that reached them. The people in the church had grown accustomed to groans and cries, the cannon and musket sounds, the crumping of the mortars, and even the shuddering concussion of near-hits. But the firing and bombardment reached a new crescendo, a sustained frenzy of bursting sound that lasted for several hours, and then there was a relative silence in which those in the church suddenly could hear what they said to one another. Then there came a new sound, a roar that lifted and went on and on like the ocean, and when Rob J. sent a Confederate orderly to find out what it was, the man came back and muttered brokenly that it was the goddamn mizzable fuckin' Yankees cheerin', that's what it was.

Lanning Ordway came a few hours later and found him still standing in the little room.

'Doc. My God, Doc, you come with me.'

Ordway told him he'd been there the better part of two days, and told him where the 131st was bivouacked. And Rob J. allowed Mine Good Comrade and Mine Terrible Enemy to lead him away into a safe and untenanted storage room where a soft bed of clean hay could be prepared, and he lay down and he slept.

It was late the next afternoon when he was awakened by the groaning and screams of the wounded they had placed all around him on the storeroom floor. Other surgeons were at the tables, doing fine without him. There was no point in trying to use the church's latrine, which long since had been overtaxed. He went outside into a hard, driving rain, and in the healing wet he emptied his bladder behind some lilac bushes that the Union owned again.

The Union owned all of Gettysburg again. Rob J. walked through the rain, taking in the sights. He forgot where Ordway had said the 131st was camped, and he asked everyone he met. Finally he found them spread out over several farm fields south of the town, hunkered inside their tents.

Wilcox and Ordway greeted him with warmth that moved him. They had eggs! While Lanning Ordway crushed hardtack and fried the crumbs and the eggs in pork grease for the doctor's breakfast, they filled him in on what had happened, the bad first. The band's best bass horn player, Thad Bushman, had been killed. 'One tiny little hole in his chest, Doc,' Wilcox said. 'Must of hit just the right spot.'

Of the litter-bearers, Lew Robinson was the first to get shot. 'He got hit in the foot right after you left us,' Ordway said. 'Oscar Lawrence got near cut in two by artillery yesterday.'

Ordway finished scrambling the eggs and set the pan before Rob J., who was thinking with genuine sorrow about the clumsy young drummer. But to his shame he couldn't resist the food, wolfing it down.

'Oscar was too young. He should of been home with his momma,' Wilcox said bitterly.

Rob J. burned his mouth on the black coffee, which was terrible but tasted fine. 'We all should have been home with our mommas,' he said, and belched. He finished the rest of the eggs slowly and had another cup of coffee while they told him what had happened while he was in the church cellar.

'That first day, they pushed us back to the high ground north of the town,' Ordway said. 'That was the luckiest thing could of happened to us.

'The next day we was on Cemetery Ridge in a long skirmish line that run between two pairs of hills, Cemetery Hill and Culp's Hill on the north, closest to the town, and Round Top and Little Round Top a couple of miles to the south. The fightin' was terrible, terrible. A lot was killed. We kept busy haulin' the wounded.'

'We did all right, too,' Wilcox said. 'Just like you showed us.'

'I bet you did.'

'Next day the 131st was moved out onto Cemetery Ridge, to reinforce Howard's Corps. Around noon we took a hell of a beatin' from the Confederate cannon,' Ordway said. 'Our forward pickets could see that while they was shellin' us, a whole lot of Confederate troops was movin' well below us, into the woods other side of the Emmitsburg Road. We could see metal, shiny here and there among the trees. They kept up the shellin' for a hour or more, and they scored a good many hits too, but all the time we was gettin' ready, because we knew they was goin' to attack.

'Midafternoon, their cannon stopped, and so did ours. And then somebody yelled, 'They're comin'!' and fifteen thousand rebel bastards in grey uniforms stepped outta those woods. Those boys of Lee's moved toward us shoulder to shoulder, line after line. Their bayonets was like a long curvin' fence of steel pickets above their heads, with the sun bright and hard on it. They didn't yell, didn't say a word, just come toward us at a fast, steady walk.

'I tell you, Doc,' Ordway said, 'Robert E. Lee whipped our arse lots of times and I know he's a mean, smart sonofabitch, but he wasn't smart here in Gettysburg. We couldn't believe

460

it, watchin' them rebels come at us like that across open fields, with us on high, protected ground. We knew they was dead men, and they must of knew it too. We watched them come most a mile. Colonel Symonds and other officers up and down the line was yellin', Hold your fire! Let 'em get close. Hold your fire!' They must of been able to hear that too.

'When they was close enough for us to make out their faces, our artillery from Little Round Top and Cemetery Ridge opened up, and a lot of them just disappeared. Those that was left came at us through the smoke, and Symonds finally yelled 'Fire!' and everybody shot hisself a rebel. Somebody yelled, 'Fredericksburg! Fredericksburg!' and shootin' and reloadin', and shootin' and reloadin', and shootin' . . .

'They reached the stone wall at the bottom of our ridge only at one place. Them that did fought like doomed men, but they was all killed or captured,' Ordway said, and Rob J. nodded. That, he knew, was when he had heard the cheering.

Wilcox and Ordway had worked all night carrying wounded, and now they were going back. Rob J. went with them, through the downpour. As they approached the place of the battle, he saw the rain was a blessing, because it kept down the smell of death, which already was terrible nonetheless. Swelling bodies lay everywhere. Amid the wreckage and carnage of war, rescuers searched to glean the living.

For the rest of the morning Rob J. worked in the rain, dressing wounds and carrying one corner of a litter. When he brought the wounded to the hospitals, he saw why his boys had had eggs. Wagons were being unloaded everywhere. There was plenty of medicine and anaesthesia, plenty of dressings, plenty of food. Surgeons were three deep at every operating table. A grateful United States had heard that at last they had a victory, paid for at a terrible price, and they had determined nothing should be spared those who had survived.

Near the railroad depot he was approached by a civilian man about his own age, who asked him politely if he knew where it might be possible to get a soldier embalmed, as if asking him for the time of day or the directions to the town building. The man said he was Winfield S. Walker, Jr, a farmer from Havre de Grace, Maryland. When he'd heard of the battle, something had told him to come and see his son Peter, and he had found him among the dead. 'Now I would like to have the body embalmed so I can take him home, don't you know.'

Rob J. did. 'I've heard they are embalming at the Washington House Hotel, sir.'

'Yessir. But they told me where they have an exceedingly long list, many before me. I thought to look elsewhere.' His son's body was at the Harold farm, a farmhouse-hospital off the Emmitsburg Road.

'I'm a physician. I can do it for you,' Rob J. said.

He had the necessary items in the medical pannier back at the 131st, and he went and collected them and then met Mr Walker at the farmhouse. Rob J. had to tell him as delicately as possible to go get an army coffin that was zinc-lined, because there would be leakage. While the father was off on that sorry errand, he tended to the son, in a bedroom where six other dead men were stored. Peter Walker was a beautiful young man, perhaps twenty years old, with his father's chiselled features and thick dark hair. He was unmarked save that a shell had torn off his left leg at the thigh. He had bled to death, and his body had the whiteness of a marble statue.

Rob J. mixed an ounce of chloride of zinc salts into two quarts of alcohol and water. He tied off the artery in the severed leg so the fluid would be retained, then slit the femoral artery of the uninjured leg and injected the embalming fluid into it with a syringe.

Mr Walker had no trouble getting a casket from the army. He tried to pay for the embalming, but Rob J. shook his head. 'One father helping another,' he said.

The rain continued. It was a beastly rain. In the first savage downpour, it had brought some small streams over

462

their banks and drowned some of the severely wounded. Now it fell more gently, and he went back to the battlefield and looked for wounded until dusk. He stopped then, because younger and stronger men had appeared with lamps and torches to search the battlefield, and because he was bone tired.

The Sanitary Commission had set up a kitchen in a warehouse near the centre of Gettysburg, and Rob J. went there and had soup containing the first beef he had had in months. He had three bowls, and six slices of white bread.

After he had eaten, he went into the Presbyterian church and went along the pews, stopping at each improvised bed to try to do some homely thing that might help – give water, wipe a sweaty face. Whenever the patient was a Confederate, he always asked the same question. 'Son, have you ever run across, in your army, a twenty-three-year old yellow-haired man from Holden's Crossing, Illinois, name of Alexander Cole?'

But nobody he talked to ever had.

54

Skirmishing

As rain fell again in sheets, General Robert E. Lee picked up his bloodied army and limped slowly back into Maryland. Meade didn't have to let him get away. The Army of the Potomac was hurt badly too, with more than twenty-three thousand casualties, including some eight thousand dead or missing, but the Northerners were flushed with victory and far stronger than Lee's men, who were slowed and hampered by a wagon train of wounded stretching behind them fully seventeen miles. But just as Hooker had failed to act in Virginia, now Meade failed to act in Pennsylvania, and there was no pursuit.

'Where does Mr Lincoln find his generals?' Symonds muttered to Rob J. in disgust. But if the delay frustrated colonels, the enlisted men were content to rest and recover, and perhaps write home the extraordinary news that they were still alive.

Ordway found Lewis Robinson in one of the farmhouse hospitals. His right foot had been amputated four inches above the ankle. He was thin and pale but otherwise appeared in good health. Rob J. examined the stump and told Robinson it was healing well, and that the man who had cut off his foot had known his job. Clearly, Robinson was happy to be out of the war; there was a sense of relief in his eyes that was so profound it was almost palpable. Rob

J. felt that Robinson had been bound to be hit, because he had feared the possibility so. He brought Robinson his sopranino cornet and some pencils and paper and knew he would be all right, because you didn't need two feet to compose music or play the horn.

Both Ordway and Wilcox were promoted to sergeant. A number of the men had been promoted, Symonds filling the regimental table of organization with the survivors, handing out the ratings and ranks that had belonged to the fallen. The 131st Indiana had received eighteen percent casualties, which was light compared to many regiments. A regiment from Minnesota had lost eighty-six percent of its men. That regiment and several others were wiped out, in effect. Symonds and his staff officers spent several days recruiting survivors of the ruined regiments, with success, bringing the 131st strength up to seven hundred and seventy-one men. With some embarrassment, the colonel told Rob J. he'd found a regimental surgeon. Dr Gardner Coppersmith had been with one of the disbanded Pennsylvania units as a captain, and Symonds had lured him with promotion. A graduate of a Philadelphia medical school, he'd had two years of combat experience. 'I'd make you regimental surgeon in a minute if you weren't a civilian, Doc Cole,' Symonds said. 'But the slot calls for an officer. You understand that Major Coppersmith will be your superior, that he'll run things?'

Rob J. assured him that he understood.

For Rob J. it was a complicated war, fought by a complicated nation. In the newspaper he read that there had been a race riot in New York because of resentment over the first drawing of names for the military draft. A mob of fifty thousand, most of them Irish Catholic working men, set fire to the draft office, the offices of the New York *Tribune*, and a Negro orphanage, fortunately empty of children at the time. Apparently blaming Negroes for the war, they swarmed through the streets, beating and robbing every black person they could find, murdering and lynching Negroes for several days before the riot was put down by federal troops

465

freshly returned from fighting Southerners at Gettysburg.

The story wounded Rob J.'s spirit. Native-born Protestants loathed and oppressed Catholics and immigrants, and Catholics and immigrants scorned and murdered Negroes, as if each group fed off its hate, needing the nourishment provided by the bone marrow of someone weaker.

When Rob J. had prepared for citizenship he'd studied the United States Constitution and marvelled at its provisions. Now he saw that the genius of those who had written the Constitution was that it foresaw man's weakness of character and the continuing presence of evil in the world, and sought to make individual freedom the legal reality to which the country had to return again and again.

He was fascinated by what made men hate one another, and studied Lanning Ordway as if the lame sergeant were a bug under his microscope. If Ordway didn't spew hatred every now and then, like a kettle running over, and if Rob J. didn't know that a terrible unpunished crime had been committed a decade before in his own Illinois woods, he would have found Ordway among the more likeable young men in the regiment. Now he was watching the litter-bearer grow and blossom, probably because the experiences Ordway had had in the army represented more success than he had ever before achieved.

There was a spirit of success in the entire regiment. The Indiana 131st Regimental Band showed dash and elan as it went from hospital to hospital, giving concerts for the wounded. The new tuba player wasn't as good as Thad Bushman had been, but the musicians played with pride, because they'd shown they were valuable during battle.

'We been through the worst together,' Wilcox announced solemnly one night when he had had too much to drink, fixing Rob J. with his ferocious, walleyed squint. 'We strolled in and out of the jaws of death, sashayed on through the Valley of the Shadow. We stared right into the damned eyes of the terrible critter. We heered the rebel yell and hollered back.'

The men treated one another with great tenderness. Sergeant Ordway and Sergeant Wilcox and even sloppy

Corporal Perry were honoured because they'd led their fellow musicians to pluck up wounded soldiers and carry them back under fire. The story of Rob J.'s two-day marathon with the scalpel was repeated in all the tents, and the men knew he was responsible for the ambulance service in their regiment. They smiled warmly to see him now, and nobody mentioned latrines.

His new popularity pleased him inordinately. One of the soldiers of B Company, Second Brigade, a man named Lyon, even brought him a horse. 'Just found him walking riderless by the side of the road, I thunk of you right away, Doc,' Lyon said, handing him the reins.

Rob J. was embarrassed but elated by this evidence of affection. True, the mud-coloured horse wasn't much, a skinny and swaybacked gelding. Probably he'd belonged to a slain or wounded rebel soldier, because both the animal and the bloodstained saddle bore the CSA brand. The horse's head and his tail drooped, his eyes were dull, and his mane and tail were full of burrs. He looked like a horse that had worms. But, 'Why soldier, he's beautiful!' Rob J. said. 'I don't know how to thank you.'

'I figger forty-two dollars would be fair,' Lyon said.

Rob J. laughed, more tickled by his own foolish yearning for love than by the situation. When the dickering was over, the horse was his in exchange for $4.85 and the promise that he wouldn't bring Lyon up on charges as a battlefield looter.

He gave the animal a good feed, patiently picked the burrs from his mane and tail, washed the blood off the saddle and rubbed oil on the horse where the leather had chafed, and brushed the gelding's coat. When all that was done, it was still an extremely sorry-looking horse, so Rob J. named him Pretty Boy, on the outside chance that perhaps such a name would give the ugly animal a modicum of pleasure and self-respect.

He was riding the horse when the Indiana 131st marched out of Pennsylvania on August 17. Pretty Boy's head and tail still drooped, but he moved along with the loose, steady gait of a beast that was accustomed to the long ride. If anybody in the regiment didn't know for certain which direction they were heading, all doubt disappeared when Bandmaster Warren Fitts blew his whistle, lifted his chin and his baton, and the band began to play 'Maryland, My Maryland'.

The 131st recrossed the Potomac six weeks after Lee's troops and a full month after the first units of their own army. They followed the late summer south, and the mild and seductive autumn didn't catch up with them until they were well into Virginia. They were veterans, chigger-wise and battle-tested, but most of the action of the war at that moment was in the western theatre, and for the 131st Indiana, things were quiet. Lee's army moved along the Shenandoah Valley, where Union scouts spied on it and said it was in good condition except for an obvious shortage of supplies, especially decent shoes.

The Virginia skies were dark with fall rains when they came to the Rappahannock and found evidence that the Confederates had camped there in the not-distant past. Over Rob J.'s objections, they raised their tents right on the former Rebel campsite. Major Coppersmith was a well-educated and competent doctor, but he didn't hold with worrying about a little shit, and he never bothered anybody about digging latrines. He wasn't subtle about informing Rob J. that the time was over when an acting assistant surgeon could make medical policy for the regiment. The major liked to run his own sick call, unassisted, except on days when he might be feeling poorly, which wasn't often. And he said that unless an engagement turned into another Gettysburg, he thought that he and one enlisted man were enough to apply dressings at a medical station.

Rob smiled at him. 'What does that leave for me?'

Major Coppersmith frowned and smoothed his moustaches with a forefinger. 'Well, I'd like you to handle the litter-bearers, Dr Cole,' he said.

So Rob J. found himself caught by the monster he had created, trapped in the web of his own spinning. He had no desire to join the litter men, but once they became his main task, it seemed foolish to think that he would simply send the teams out and watch to see what happened to them. He

468

recruited his own team: two musicians – the new bass horn player, name of Alan Johnson, and a fifer named Lucius Wagner – and for the fourth man, he drafted Corporal Amasa Decker, the regimental postmaster. The litter teams took turns going out. He told the new men, as he had told the first five litter-bearers (one now dead and one now an amputee), that going after wounded involved no more danger than anything else connected with war. He assured himself that everything would be all right, and he placed his litter team in the rotation schedule.

The 131st and a lot of other units of the Army of the Potomac followed the trail of the Confederates along the Rappahannock River to its chief tributary, the Rapidan, moving along water that reflected the grey of the skies, day after day. Lee was outnumbered and outsupplied and kept ahead of the federals. Things didn't heat up in Virginia until the war in the western theatre turned very sour for the Union. General Braxton Bragg's Confederates struck a terrible blow against General William S. Rosecrans' Union forces on Chicamauga Creek, outside of Chattanooga, with more than sixteen thousand federal casualties. Lincoln and his cabinet held an emergency meeting and decided to detach Hooker's two corps from the Army of the Potomac in Virginia and send them to Alabama by rail, to support Rosecrans.

With Meade's army deprived of two corps, Lee stopped running. He split his army in two and tried to flank Meade, moving west and north, toward Manassas and Washington. So skirmishing began.

Meade was careful to keep between Lee and Washington, and the Union Army fell back a mile or two at a time, until they had given up forty miles to the Southern assault, with sporadic fighting.

Rob J. observed that each of the litter-bearers approached his task differently. Wilcox went after a wounded man with dogged determination, while Ordway showed an uncaring bravery, scuttling out like a great fast crab with his uneven gait, and carrying the victim back carefully, holding his end of the stretcher high and steady, taking the strain on his muscular arms to compensate for his limp. Rob J. had several weeks to think about his first pickup before it occurred. His trouble was, he had as much imagination as Robinson, and maybe more. He could think about getting hit in any number of ways and circumstances. In his tent and by lamplight he did a series of drawings for his journal, showing Wilcox's team running out, three men bent against a possible headwind of lead, the fourth carrying the stretcher in front of him as he ran, a flimsy shield. He showed Ordway coming back, carrying the right-rear corner of the stretcher, the other three bearers with tight, scared faces, and Ordway's thin lips bent into a rictus that was half-smile, half-snarl, a largely no-account man who had finally found something he was very good at. What would Ordway do, Rob J. wondered, when the war ended and he couldn't go after wounded men under fire?

Rob J. drew no pictures of his own team. They hadn't gone out yet.

Their first time was on November 7. The Indiana 131st was sent across the Rappahannock near a place called Kelly's Ford. The regiment crossed the river at midmorning but soon was bogged down by intense enemy fire, and within ten minutes word came to the ambulance corps that somebody had been hit. Rob J. and his three bearers went forward to a riverside hay field where half a dozen men huddled behind an ivy-covered stone wall, firing into the woods. All the way up to the wall, Rob J. expected the bite of a projectile into his flesh. The air felt too thick to suck up into his nostrils. It was as if he had to force his way through it by brute strength, and his limbs seemed to work slowly.

The soldier had been hit in the shoulder. The ball was in the flesh and needed to be probed for, but not under fire. Rob J. took a dressing from his *Mee-shome* and bandaged the wound, making certain that the bleeding was controlled. Then they put the soldier on the litter and started back at a good pace. Rob J. was aware of the broad target his exposed back presented at the rear of the litter. He could hear every shot that was fired, and the sounds of bullets passing, tearing through the tall grass, thunking solidly into the earth near them.

Amasa Decker grunted on the other side of the litter.

'You hit?' Rob J. gasped.

'Naw.'

Feet thudding, they half ran with their burden, sliding after an eternity into the shallow defilade in which Major Coppersmith had set up his medical station.

When they had given over the patient to the surgeon, the four bearers lay on the soft grass like fresh-caught trout.

'They sounded like bees, those minies,' Lucius Wagner said.

'I thought we was shit dead,' Amasa Decker said. 'Didn't you, Doc?'

'I was scared, but I figured I had some protection.' Rob J. showed them the *Mee-shome*, and told them its strap of cords, the *Izze* cloths, would protect him from being hurt by bullets, according to the Sauk promise. Decker and Wagner listened seriously, Wagner with a small smile.

That afternoon, firing almost ceased. The sides were at stalemate until around dusk, when two entire Union brigades crossed the river and swept past the 131st's position in the only bayonet charge Rob J. would see in the war. The 131st infantry fixed its own bayonets and joined the attack, whose surprise and ferocity allowed the Union to overrun the enemy, killing or capturing several thousand Confederates. Union losses were light, but Rob J. and his bearers went out half a dozen more times for wounded men as evening fell. The three soldiers had become convinced that Doc Cole and his Injun medicine bag made them a lucky crew, and by the time they had come back safely for the seventh time, Rob J. believed in the power of his *Mee-shome* as strongly as any of them.

That night in their tent, after the wounded had been tended to, Gardner Coppersmith looked at him with shining eyes. 'Glorious bayonet charge, wasn't it, Cole?'

He treated the question seriously. 'More butchery,' he said, very tired.

The regimental surgeon regarded him with disgust. 'If

471

you feel that way, why the hell are you here?'

'Because this is where the patients are,' Rob J. said.

Still, by the end of the year he had decided he would leave the Indiana 131st. It *was* where the patients were; he'd come to the army to give good medical care to soldiers, and Major Coppersmith wouldn't allow him to do that. He saw that it was a waste of an experienced physician for him to do little more than carry a stretcher, and it made no sense for an atheist to live as if he were seeking martyrdom or sainthood. It was in his mind to go back home when his contract ran out, the first week of 1864.

Christmas Eve was a strange affair, sorry and touching at the same time. There were services of worship before the tents. On one side of the Rappahannock the musicians of the 131st Indiana played 'Adeste Fidelis'. When they were done, a Confederate band on the far bank played 'God Rest Ye Merry, Gentlemen', the music floating eerily over the dark waters, and then started right in on 'Silent Night'. Bandmaster Fitts raised his baton and the Union band and the Confederate musicians played together, the soldiers of both sides singing along. They could see each other's fires.

As it turned out, it was a silent night, no gunfire. For supper there had been no festive birds, but the army had provided a very acceptable soup with something in it that may have been beef, and each soldier of the regiment was given a tot of holiday whisky. That may have been a mistake, for it whetted thirsts for more of the same. After the concert, Rob J. met Wilcox and Ordway, weaving in from where they had killed a jug of sutler's rotgut at the edge of the river. Wilcox was supporting Ordway, but he was unsteady himself.

'You go on to sleep, Abner,' Rob J. told him. 'I'll see this one into his tent.' Wilcox nodded and walked away, but Rob J. didn't do as he had promised. Instead, he helped Ordway away from the tents and sat him against a boulder.

'Lanny,' he said. 'Lan, boy. Let us talk, you and I.'

Ordway considered him with half-closed drunkard's eyes.

'. . . Merry Christmas, Doc.'

472

'Merry Christmas, Lanny. Let's talk about the Order of the Star-Spangled Banner,' Rob J. said.

So he decided that whisky was a key that would unlock everything Lanning Ordway knew.

On January 3, when Colonel Symonds came to him with another contract, he was watching Ordway carefully filling his knapsack with fresh dressings and morphia pills. Rob J. hesitated only a moment, never taking his eyes off Ordway. Then he scribbled his signature and signed on for another three months.

55

'When Did You Meet Ellwood R. Patterson?'

Rob J. thought he'd been very subtle, very circumspect, in the way he had questioned the drunken Ordway on Christmas Eve. The interrogation had confirmed his picture of the man, and of the OSSB.

Sitting against the tent post, with his journal against his drawn-up knees, he wrote the following:

Lanning Ordway began going to meetings of the American party in Vincennes, Indiana, 'five years before I was old enough to vote'. (He asked me where I had joined, and I said, 'Boston'.)

He was taken to the meetings by his father, 'because he wanted me to be a good American.' His father was Nathanael Ordway, an employed broom maker. The meetings were on the second floor over a tavern. They would go through the tavern, out the back door, up a flight of stairs. His father rapped the signal on the door. He remembers that his father was always proud when 'the Guardian of the Gate' (!) looked out at them through a peekhole and let them come in 'because we were good people'.

Within a year or so, when his father was drunk or sick, Lanning sometimes went to the meetings alone. When Nathanael Ordway died ('of drink and pleurisy'), Lanning went to Chicago to work in a saloon off the railroad yards on Galena Street, where a cousin of his father dispensed whisky. He cleaned up after sick drunkards, spread fresh sawdust every morning, washed the long mirrors, polished the brass rail – whatever had to be done.

It was natural for him to search out a Know Nothing chapter in Chicago, like making contact with family, because he had more in common with the American party regulars than with his father's cousin. The party worked to elect only public officials who would hire American-born workers in preference to immigrants. Despite his lameness (from talking to him and observing him, I believe he was born with a hip socket that is too shallow), the regulars learned to call on him when they needed somebody young enough to do important errands and old enough to keep his mouth closed.

It was a source of pride to him when, after only a couple of years, at the age of seventeen, he was brought into the secret Order of the Star-Spangled Banner. He intimated it was a source of hope too, because he felt that a poor and crippled American-born youth needed the connections of a powerful organization if he was going to amount to anything, 'with foreign Roman Catholics willing to work every American job for almost no money at all'.

The order 'did things the party couldn't do'. When I asked Ordway what he did for the order, he said, 'This and that. Travelled about, here and there.'

I asked if he had ever run across a man named Hank Cough, and he blinked. 'Of course I know him. And you know that man too? Imagine that. Yes. Hank!'

I asked where Cough was, and he looked at me strangely. 'Why, he's in the army.'

But when I asked what work they had done together, he put his forefinger under his eye and ran it down his nose. And he staggered to his feet, and the interview was over.

Next morning, Ordway gave no sign that he recalled the questioning. Rob J. was careful to stay away for a few days. In fact several weeks passed before another such opportunity presented itself, because the sutlers' supplies of whisky had been bought out by the troops during the holiday season, and the Northern merchants who travelled with the Union forces were afraid to replenish their whisky in Virginia, for fear that the product might be poisoned.

But an acting assistant surgeon had a supply of government-issued whisky for medicinal purposes. Rob J.

gave the jug to Wilcox, knowing he would share it with Ordway. That night he waited and watched for them, and when finally they arrived, Wilcox merry, Ordway morose, he said goodnight to Wilcox and took charge of Ordway as he had done before. They went to the same boulders, away from the tents.

'Well, Lanny,' Rob J. said. 'Let us have another talk.'

'About what Doc?'

'When did you meet Ellwood R. Patterson?'

The man's eyes were like icy pins. 'Who are you?' Ordway said, and his voice was completely sober.

Rob J. was ready for hard truth. He had waited a long time. 'Who do you think I am?'

'I think you're a goddamned Catholic spy, askin' all those questions.'

'I have more questions. I have questions about the Indian woman you killed.'

'What Indian woman?' Ordway asked in genuine horror.

'How many Indian women have you killed? Do you know where I'm from, Lanny?'

'You said Boston,' Ordway said sullenly.

'That was before. I've lived in Illinois for years. A little town called Holden's Crossing.'

Ordway looked at him and said nothing.

'The Indian woman who was killed, Lanny. She was my friend, she worked for me. Her name was Makwa-ikwa, in case you never knew. She was raped and murdered in my woods, on my farm.'

'The Indian woman? My God. Get away from me, you crazy misery, I don't know what you're talkin' about. I warn you. If you're a smart person – if you know what's good for your welfare at all, you son of a prick-bastard spy – you'll forget anythin' and everythin' you may think you know about Ellwood R. Patterson,' Ordway said. Lurching past Rob J., he walked unevenly into the darkness, moving as fast as if he were being fired upon

Rob J. kept one eye on him all the next day without seeming to watch him. He saw him drill his team of bearers, saw him inspect their knapsacks, listened to him warn them they must be very chary of using morphine pills, because the regiment was just about out, until the army came up with more. Lanning Ordway, he had to acknowledge, had turned into a good and efficient sergeant of the Ambulance Corps.

In the afternoon he saw Ordway in his tent labouring over a paper, pencil in hand. It took him long hours.

After retreat, Ordway brought an envelope to the postal tent.

Rob J. made a stop and then went to the post office himself. 'I found a sutler this morning with some real cheese,' he told Amasa Decker. 'I left a hunk of it in your tent.'

'Why, Doc, that was kind,' Decker said, very pleased.

'I have to take care of my litter-bearers, don't I? You'd best go and eat it before someone else finds it. I'll be happy to play postmaster while you're gone.'

That was all it took. Directly after Decker hurried off, Rob J. went to the box of outgoing mail. It took him only a few minutes to find the envelope and slip it into his *Mee-shome*.

It wasn't until he was alone in the privacy of his own tent that he took out the letter and opened it. It was addressed to *Rev David Goodnow, 237 Bridgeton Street, Chicago, Illnois*.

Dere Mr Goodnow, Lanning Ordway. Im in the Indiana 131st, you recawl. Ther is a man here, askin kwestians. Doctur, name of Robit Col. He wants to no abowt Henry. He talks funny, I bin wachin him. He wants to no abowt L. wood Padson. Tole me we rapt and kilt that injun gurl, that time in Illnois. I kin tak kare a him, lots a ways. But I yuse my head an let you no so you kin fine owt how he fine owt abowt us. Im a sgt. Wen the war ends Ile werk for the Odder agin. Lanning Ordway.

56
Across the Rappahannock

Rob J. was painfully aware that in the midst of a war, with weapons at every hand and on every person, and with wholesale murder unremarkable, there would be many ways and many opportunities available for an experienced killer who was determined to 'tak kare' of him.

For four days he tried to be aware of what was behind his back, and for five nights he slept lightly or not at all.

He lay awake wondering how Ordway would attempt it. He decided that in Ordway's place and temperament, he would wait until both of them were participants in a noisy skirmish, with lots of firing. On the other hand, he had no idea whether Ordway might be a knife fighter. If Rob J. were found stabbed, or with his throat cut, after a long dark night when every jittery picket had speculated that each moon-shadow was a Confederate infiltrator, there would be little surprise or investigation of his death.

This situation was changed on January 19, when Company B of the Second Brigade was sent across the Rappahannock on what was supposed to be a quick intelligence probe and then a swift withdrawl, but didn't work out that way. Instead, the light company of infantry found Confederate positions in strength where they hadn't expected Confederates to be, and they were pinned down by enemy fire in an exposed place.

It was a repeat of the situation in which the entire regiment had found itself some weeks earlier, but instead of some seven hundred men with fixed bayonets surging across the river to mend the situation, there was no support from the army of the Potomac. The one hundred and seven men stayed where they were and took the fire, all returning it as best they could. When darkness fell, they fled back across the river, bringing along four dead bodies and seven wounded men.

The first person they carried into the hospital tent was Lanning Ordway.

Ordway's crewman said he'd been hit just before nightfall. He had reached into his jacket pocket for the paper-wrapped hard biscuit and piece of fried pork he had placed there that morning, when two minié balls struck him in swift succession. One of the balls had taken a chunk from his abdomen wall, and a loop of greyish abdomen now protruded. Rob J. started to push it back inside, thinking to close the wound, but he saw several other things quickly, and he recognized that he couldn't do anything to save Ordway.

The second wound was perforating, and too much damage had been done internally, to the bowel or stomach, or perhaps both. He knew if he opened the belly he'd find the body's haemorrhaged blood pooled in the abdominal cavity. Ordway's drained face was white as milk.

'Is there anything you want, Lanny?' he asked gently.

Ordway's lips worked. His eyes locked with Rob J.'s, and a certain calmness Rob J. had seen before in the dying revealed that he was aware. 'Water.'

It was the worst thing to give a man who was gut-shot, but Rob J. knew it didn't matter. He took two opium pills from his *Mee-shome* and gave them to Ordway with a long drink. Almost at once Ordway vomited redly.

'Do you want a minister?' Rob J. asked as he worked to make things right. But Ordway made no reply, only kept looking at him.

'Maybe you want to tell me exactly what happened to Makwa-ikwa that day in my woods. Or tell me about

479

anything else, anything at all.'

'You . . . hell,' Ordway managed.

Rob J. didn't believe that he ever would go to hell. He didn't believe Ordway or anyone else would go there, either, but it wasn't a time for debate. 'I thought it might help you to talk just now. If you have anything to get off your mind.'

Ordway closed his eyes and Rob J. knew he had to leave him in peace.

He always hated to lose somebody to death, but he especially hated the loss of this man who'd been prepared to kill him, because locked in Ordway's brain was information he had yearned after for years, and when the man's brain died like a turned-off lamp, the information would be gone.

He knew, too, that in spite of everything, something within him had responded to the strange, complicated young man who had been caught in the grinder. What would it have been like to have known an Ordway who had been delivered of his mother without injury, who had had some schooling instead of illiteracy, some care instead of hunger, and a different birthright from his drinking father?

He knew the futility of such speculation, and when he glanced at the still figure he saw that Ordway was beyond any consideration.

For a time he handled the ether cone while Gardner Coppersmith removed a minié ball, not unskilfully, from the meaty part of a boy's left buttock. Then he returned to Ordway and tied up his jaw and weighted his eyelids with pennies, and they laid him on the ground next to the four others Company B had brought back.

480

57
The Full Circle

On February 12, 1864, Rob J. wrote in his journal:

Two rivers back home, the great Mississippi and the modest Rock, have placed their mark on my life, and now in Virginia I've come to know another mismatched pair of rivers too well, witnessing repeated slaughter along the Rappahannock and the Rapidan. Both the Army of the Potomac and the Army of Northern Virginia have sent small groups of infantry and cavalry across the Rapidan to have at one another all through the late winter and into early spring. As casually as I crossed the Rock in former times to visit an ailing neighbour or catch an emerging child, now I accompany troops across the Rapidan in dozens of places, seated on Pretty Boy or splashing on foot over shallow fords, or riding over deep water in boats or on rafts. This winter there was no big battle that killed thousands, but I've become accustomed to seeing a dozen bodies, or one. There's something infinitely more tragic about a single dead man than there is about a field full of corpses. I've learned somehow not to see the hale and the dead, but to focus on the wounded, going out and fetching young damned fools, more often than not under fire from other young damned fools . . . .

The soldiers on both sides had taken to pinning to their clothing slips of paper bearing their names and addresses, in the hope that their loved ones would be notified if they became casualties. Neither Rob J. nor the three stretcher-bearers on his team bothered with the identification labels. They went out now without thought or fear, because Amasa Decker, Alan Johnson, and Lucius Wagner had become convinced that Makwa-ikwa's medicine truly was protecting them, and Rob J. had allowed himself to be infected by their conviction. It was as if the *Mee-shome* somehow generated a force that deflected all bullets, making their bodies inviolable.

Sometimes it seemed there had always been the war, and that it would exist forever. Yet Rob J. could see changes. One day he read in a tattered copy of the *Baltimore American* that all white Southern males between seventeen and fifty had been conscripted for service in the Confederate Army. It meant that from then on, whenever a Confederate became a casualty he would be irreplaceable, and his army would grow smaller. Rob J. saw with his own eyes that the Confederate soldiers who were taken or killed all wore ragged uniforms and sorry shoes. He wondered desperately whether Alex was alive, and fed, and clothed, and shod. Colonel Symonds announced that soon the 131st Indiana would receive a quantity of Sharps carbines equipped with priming magazines that would allow rapid fire. And that summed up where the war seemed to be heading, with the North manufacturing better guns, ammunition, and ships, and the South struggling with dwindling manpower and a dearth of anything that had to be made in a factory.

The problem was, the Confederates didn't seem to realize that they laboured under a terrible industrial disadvantage, and they fought with a fierceness that promised the war wouldn't soon end.

One day late in February the four litter-bearers were summoned to where a captain named Taney, the commander of Company A of the First Brigade, lay stoically smoking a cigar after a ball had chopped through his shin. Rob J. saw there was no point in applying a splint because several inches of the tibia and the fibula had been carried away, and the leg would have to be amputated halfway between the ankle and the knee. When he reached to take a dressing out of the *Mee-shome*, the medicine bag wasn't there.

With a sick lurch of his stomach, he knew exactly where he had left it, on the grass outside the hospital tent.

The others knew too.

He took the leather belt from around Alan Johnson's waist and used it as a tourniquet; then they loaded the captain onto the litter and carried him away almost drunkenly.

'Dear God,' Lucius Wagner said. He always said that, in an accusing tone, when he was very scared. Now he whispered it over and over until it was an annoyance, but nobody complained or told him to shut up, being too busy anticipating the painful impact of the bullets into their bodies, which were so cruelly and suddenly naked of magic.

The carry was slower and more agonized than their very first. There were bursts of shooting, but nothing happened to the bearers. Finally they were back at the hospital tent, and when they had turned the patient over to Coppersmith, Amasa Decker picked the *Mee-shome* from the grass and thrust it into Rob J.'s hands. 'Put it on. Quick,' he said, and Rob J. did so.

The three bearers consulted sombrely, weak with relief, and agreed to share the responsibility of seeing that Acting Assistant Surgeon Cole put on the medicine bag first thing every morning.

Rob J. was glad he was wearing the *Mee-shome* two mornings later when the 131st Indiana, half a mile from the point where the Rapidan met the larger river, came around a curve in the road and literally stared into the startled faces of a brigade of men in grey uniforms.

Men on both sides began to fire at once, some of them at very close range. The air was filled with curses and shouts, the reports of muskets, the screaming of those who were struck, and then the front ranks closed with one another, officers hacking with swords or firing small arms, soldiers swinging their rifles as clubs or using fists and fingernails and teeth, there being no time to reload.

On one side of the road was an oak wood, and on the

other was a manured field that looked soft as velvet, ploughed and ready for seed. A few men in each force took shelter behind roadside trees, but the main strength of both forces spread out to mar the perfection of the dirt field. They fired at each other from a rough, ragged skirmish line.

Ordinarily Rob J. would be in the rear during a skirmish, waiting to be sent for as needed, but in the confusion of the melée he found himself struggling with his terrified horse in the very midst of the savagery. The gelding shied and half-reared, and then seemed to fold beneath him. Rob J. managed to leap clear as the horse crashed to the ground and lay twitching and thrashing. There was a bloodless hole the size of a nickel in Pretty Boy's mid-coloured throat, but a double rivulet of red already coursed from the horse's nostrils as he struggled to breathe, kicking spasmodically in his agony.

The medicine bag contained a hypodermic syringe with a brass needle, and morphine, but opiates still were in short supply and couldn't be used for a horse. Thirty feet away a young Confederate lieutenant lay dead, and Rob J. went to him and slid a heavy black revolver from the boy's holster. Then he went back to the ugly horse and placed the muzzle of the gun under Pretty Boy's ear and pulled the trigger.

He'd taken no more than half a dozen steps away when there was a fiery pain in the upper part of his left arm, as though he'd been stung by a foot-long bee. He took three more steps, then the umber, manure-sweet earth seemed to rise in order to receive him. He was thinking clearly. He knew he had fainted and presently would regain his strength, and he lay and looked up with a painter's appreciation at the raw ochre sun in a madder-blue sky, the sounds around him diminishing as if someone had thrown a blanket over the rest of the world. How long he lay like that, he didn't know. He became aware he was losing blood from the injury in his arm, and he fumbled to take a wad of dressings from the medicine bag and press it hard into the wound to stop the bleeding. Looking down, he saw blood on the *Mee-shome* and found the irony irresistible, so that soon he was laughing at the notion of the atheist who had tried to create a god out of an old quill bag and a couple of straps of cured leather.

Eventually, here came Wilcox's crew to pick him up. The sergeant – as ugly as Pretty Boy, his wall eyes full of love and concern – said the kinds of bluff meaningless things Rob J. had said a thousand times to patients in vain attempts to comfort. The Southerners, seeing they were vastly outnumbered, had already pulled back. There was a litter of dead men and horses and broken wagons and strewn equipment, and Wilcox remarked to Rob J. mournfully that the farmer was going to have a hell of a time getting that good-looking field reploughed.

He knew he was fortunate the wound wasn't worse, but it was more than a scratch. The ball had missed the bone but had taken flesh and muscle. Coppersmith had sewn the wound partially and dressed it with care, seeming to gain a good deal of satisfaction from the task.

Rob J. was taken with thirty-six other wounded to a sector hospital in Fredericksburg, where he stayed for ten days. It was a former warehouse and wasn't as clean as it might have been, but the medical officer in charge, a major named Sparrow who had practiced in Hartford, Connecticut, before the war, was a decent sort. Rob J. remembered Dr Milton Akerson's experiments with hydrochloric acid in Illinois, and Dr Sparrow agreed to allow him to wash his own wound with a mild hydrochloric-acid solution from time to time. It stung, but the wound began to crystallize beautifully and without infection, and they agreed that probably it would be fruitful to try it on other patients. Rob J. was able to flex the fingers and move his left hand, though it hurt to do so. He agreed with Dr Sparrow that it was too soon to tell how much strength and usefulness would return to the wounded arm.

Colonel Symonds came to see him when he'd been there a week. 'Go home, Dr Cole. When you've recovered, if you want to return to us, you'll be welcome,' he said, although they both knew he wouldn't be back. Symonds thanked him clumsily. 'If I survive, and someday you may find yourself in Fort Wayne, Indiana, you must come to me at the Symonds Lamp Chimney Factory, and we will eat too much wonderful food and drink too well and talk too long of bad old times,' he said, and they shook hands hard before the young colonel walked away.

It took him three and one-half days to get home, over five different railroad systems, starting with the Baltimore & Ohio Railway. All of the trains were behind schedule, dirty, and crammed with out-of-sorts travellers. His arm was in a sling but he was just another middle-aged civilian and on several occasions he stood in a swaying car for fifty miles or more. In Canton, Ohio, he waited half a day to change trains, and then he shared a double seat with a drummer named Harrison who worked for a large firm of sutlers that sold ink powders to the army. The man had been within hearing distance of firing several times, he confided. He was full of improbable war stories, peppered with the names of important military and political figures, but Rob J. didn't mind, for the stories made the miles go faster.

The hot, crowded cars ran out of water. Like others, Rob J. drank what was in his canteen and then thirsted. Finally the train stopped at a way station next to an army encampment outside of Marion, Ohio, to renew its fuel and take on water from a small stream, and the passengers boiled out of the cars to fill their containers.

Rob J. was among them, but as he knelt with his canteen, something caught his eye on the other side of the stream, and with disgust he recognized at once what it was. He went up close to confirm that somebody had dumped used dressings, bloody bandages, and other hospital offal into the steam, and when a short walk revealed other nearby dumping sites, he replaced the lid on his canteen and advised the other passengers to do the same.

The conductor said there would be good water in Lima, down the line a bit, and he returned to his seat; by the time the train had resumed its way he had fallen asleep despite the rocking of the car.

When he awoke, he learned the train had just left Lima

behind. 'I had wanted to get water,' he said, irritated.

'Not to worry,' Harrison said. 'I have plenty now,' and passed over his flask, from which Rob J. drank deeply and gratefully.

'Was there a large crowd waiting for water in Lima?' he asked, returning the flask.

'Oh, I didn't get it in Lima. I filled my container back at Marion, when we stopped for fuel,' the salesman said.

The man paled when Rob J. told him what he had seen in the stream at Marion. 'Shall we get sick, then?'

'Can't tell.' After Gettysburg Rob J. had seen an entire company drink four days out of a well that turned out to contain two dead Confederates, without much subsequent disconfort. He shrugged. 'I wouldn't be surprised if we both get some real diarrhoea in a few days.'

'Can't we take something?'

'Whisky might help, had we any.'

'You leave that to me,' Harrison said, and hurried off in search of the conductor. When he returned, doubtless with a lighter purse, it was with a large bottle, two-thirds full. The whisky was raw enough to do the job, Rob J. said upon sampling it. By the time they parted woozily in South Bend, Indiana, each was convinced the other was a fine fellow, and they shook hands with great warmth. Rob was in Gary before he realized he hadn't learned Harrison's first name.

He came to Rock Island in the freshness of early morning, the wind blowing in from the river. He left the train gratefully and walked through the town carrying his suitcase in his good hand. He intended to rent a horse and trap, but straightway he met George Cliburne on the street, and the feed merchant pumped his hand and clapped him on the back and insisted on driving him to Holden's Crossing himself, in his buggy.

When Rob J. walked through the farmhouse door, Sarah was just sitting down to her breakfast egg and yesterday's biscuit, and she looked at him without saying a word and started to cry. They just held each other.

'Are you bad hurt?'

He assured her he wasn't.

'You turned skinny.' She said she'd make him some breakfast, but he said he'd eat afterwards. He started kissing her and he was urgent as a boy, he wanted her on the table or on the floor, but she told him it was about time he came back to his own bed, and he followed close behind her up the stairs. In the bedroom she made him wait until everything was all off. 'I need a good bath,' he said nervously, but she whispered he could bathe afterwards too. All the years, and his heavy fatigue, and the pain of his wound, fell away with their clothing. They kissed and explored one another more eagerly than they had in the farmer's barn after they were married at the Great Awakening, because now they knew what they'd been missing. His good hand found her and his fingers spoke. After a while her legs wouldn't support her, and he winced in pain when she sagged against him. She looked at the wound without blanching, but helped him return his arm to the sling and made him lie back on the bed while she took charge of everything, and when they made love Rob J. cried out loud several times, once because his arm hurt.

There was joy, not only in returning to his wife but also in going to the barn to feed dried apples to the horses and noting that they remembered him; and in coming up to Alden, who was mending fences, and seeing terrible gladness in the old man's face; and in walking the Short Path through the woods to the river and stopping to pull weeds from Makwa's grave; and in just sitting with his back against a tree near where the *hedonoso-te* had been, and watching the peaceable water gliding by, with nobody coming from the other bank to scream like animals and shoot at him.

Late that afternoon he and Sarah walked the Long Path between their house and the Geigers'. Lillian, too, wept to see him, and kissed him on the mouth. Jason was alive and well when last she had heard, she said, and was steward of a large hospital on the James River.

'I was very near to him,' Rob J. said. 'Only a couple of

488

hours away.'

Lillian nodded. 'God willing, he'll be home soon too,' she said dryly, and couldn't keep from looking at Rob J.'s arm.

Sarah wouldn't stay there for supper, wanting him all to herself.

She was able to keep him alone with her for only two days, because by the third morning word had spread that he was back and people began to come, a few just to welcome him home, but several more to turn the conversation casually to a boil on the leg, or a heavy cough, or a pain in the stomach that wouldn't go away. On the third day Sarah capitulated. Alden saddled Boss for him and Rob J. rode to half a dozen places, dropping in on old patients.

Tobias Barr had held a clinic in Holden's Crossing almost every Wednesday, but people had tended to go to it only for the most acute situations, and Rob J. found the same kind of problems he had discovered when first he had come to Holden's Crossing: neglected hernias, rotted teeth, chronic coughs. When he went to the Schroeders' he told them he was relieved to see Gustav hadn't lost any more fingers in farm accidents, which was true even if he said it as a joke. Alma gave him chicory coffee and *mandelbrot*, and caught him up on the local news, some of which saddened him. Hans Grueber had dropped dead in his wheat field last August. 'His heart, I suppose,' Gus said. And Suzy Gilbert, who had always insisted that Rob J. stay for heavy potato pancakes, had died in the childbed, a month ago.

There were new people in town, families from New England and from New York State. And three families of Catholics, new immigrants from Ireland. 'Can't even speak der langvich,' Gus said, and Rob J. lost the fight to keep from smiling.

In the afternoon he rode into the lane of the Convent of St Francis Xavier of Assisi, past what was now a respectable herd of goats.

Miriam the Ferocious beamed to greet him. He sat in the bishop's chair and told her what had happened to him. She was keenly interested to hear of Lanning Ordway and of Ordway's letter to the Reverend David Goodnow

489

in Chicago.

She asked his permission to copy Goodnow's name and address. 'There are those who will be anxious to receive this information,' she said.

In turn she told him of her world. The convent prospered. She had four new nuns and a pair of novitiates. Lay people came to the convent now for Sunday worship. If settlers continued to come, soon there would be a Catholic church.

He suspected she had expected a visit, for he'd been there only a while before Sister Mary Peter Celestine served a platter of fresh-baked crackers and very good goat cheese. And real coffee, the first he'd tasted in more than a year, with creamy goat's milk to lighten it.

'The fatted calf, Reverend Mother?'

'It is good you're home,' she said.

Each day he felt stronger. He didn't overdo, sleeping late, eating good food with pleasure, walking about the farm. He saw a few patients every afternoon.

Still, he had to become reaccustomed to the good life. On the seventh day he was home, his arms and legs ached and his back hurt. He laughed, and told Sarah he wasn't used to sleeping in a bed.

He was lying in the bed in the early hours of the morning when he felt the flutter in his stomach and tried to ignore it, because he didn't want to get up. Finally he knew he had to, and he was halfway down the stairs when he began to lurch and run, and Sarah awoke.

He didn't make it to the outhouse, but stepped off the path and squatted in the weeds like a drunken soldier, grunting and sobbing as it burst out of him.

She had followed him downstairs and out, and he hated it that she came upon him like that. 'What?' she said.

'Water . . . on the train,' Rob J. gasped.

He had three more episodes during the night. In the morning he dosed himself with castor oil to clean the illness from his system, and when the malady was still on him that evening, he took Epsom salts. The following day he began to burn with fever, and terrible headaches started, and he knew what ailed him even before Sarah stripped him to bathe him that evening and they saw the red spots on his abdomen.

She was resolute when he told her. 'Well, we've nursed people with typhoid before and pulled them through. Tell me of the diet.'

It made him nauseous to think of food, but he told her. 'Meat broths, cooked with vegetables, if you can get some. Fruit juices. But this time of year . . .'

There were still some apples in a barrel in the cellar, and Alden would crush them, she said.

She kept herself busy, preferring to work so she wouldn't worry, but in another twenty-four hours she knew she needed help, because she had been able to sleep only a little, what with bedpans, and constantly changing him and bathing him to fight the fever, and boiling fresh laundry. She sent Alden to the Catholic convent to request the help of the nursing nuns. A pair of them came – she had heard they always worked in pairs – a young babyfaced nun by the name of Sister Mary Benedicta and an older woman, tall and long-nosed, who said she was Mother Miriam Ferocia. Rob J. opened his eyes and saw them and smiled, and Sarah went to the boys' room and slept for six hours.

The sick chamber was kept orderly and sweet-smelling. The nuns were good nurses. When they had been there three days, Rob J.'s temperature dropped. At first the three women rejoiced, but it was the older one who showed Sarah when the stools began to get bloody, and she sent Alden riding to Rock Island for Dr Barr.

By the time Dr Barr arrived, the stools were almost wholly composed of blood, and Rob J. was very pale. It was eight days since the first crampy onset.

'It moved very quickly,' Dr Barr said to him, as if they were at a meeting of the Medical Society.

'It does that at times,' Rob J. said.

'Perhaps quinine, or calomel?' Dr Barr said. 'Some believe it's malarial.'

Rob J. indicated that quinine and calomel were useless. 'Typhoid fever isn't malarial,' he said with effort.

Tobias Barr hadn't done as much anatomy work as Rob J., but they both knew the severe haemorrhaging meant the bowels were riddled with perforations caused by the typhoid, and the ulcers would become more pronounced, not better. It wouldn't take many haemorrhages.

'I could leave some Dover's powders,' Dr Barr said. Dover's powder was a mixture of ipecac and opium. Rob J. shook his head, and Dr Barr understood that he wanted to be conscious as long as possible, in his own room, in his own house.

It was easier for Tobias Barr when the patient knew nothing, and he could leave hope in a bottle, with instructions about when to take it. He patted Rob J.'s shoulder and allowed his hand to stay there for a few moments. 'I'll come by tomorrow,' he said, his face composed; he had been through this so many times before. But his eyes were heavy with regret.

'Can we not help you in some other way?' Miriam Ferocia asked Sarah. Sarah said she was a Baptist, but the three women knelt for a time in the hallway outside the bedchamber and prayed together. That evening, Sarah thanked the nuns and sent them away.

Rob J. rested quietly until sometime before midnight, when he had a small bloody flow. He had forbidden her to allow the minister to visit, but now she asked him again if he would like to talk to the Reverend Blackmer.

'No, I can do it as well as Ordway,' he said clearly.

'Who is Ordway?' she asked, but Rob J. seemed too tired to answer.

She sat by his bed. Soon he reached out his hand and she took it, and both of them fell into a light sleep. Just before two a.m. she awoke and at once was aware of the coolness of his hand.

For a time she sat with him, and then she made herself get up. She turned up the lamps and then washed him for a final time, rinsing away the last haemorrhage that had taken his life. She shaved his face and did the things he had shown her how to do for others down through the years, and then she dressed him in his best suit. Now it was too large, but she knew it didn't matter.

A good physician's wife, she collected the linens that were too bloody for boiling and placed them in a sheet, to be burned. Then she heated water and prepared a bath in which she scrubbed herself with brown soap while she wept. By the time day broke, she was dressed in good clothes and seated in a chair by the kitchen door. As soon as she heard Alden pushing open the barn door, she went out to him and told him her husband was gone, and gave him the message to take to the telegraph office, asking her son to come home.

VI
THE COUNTRY DOCTOR
May 2, 1864

58
Advisers

It was remarkable that when Shaman awoke he was assailed by two such contradictory emotions: the quick and bitter flood of reality that Pa was gone, and the familiar security of home, as if every part of his body and mind had been milled with this place in mind and easily slipped into its vacancy and filled it in perfect comfort. The shuddering of the house before a sudden wind from the plains was a sensation he knew, the feel of the pillow and rough sheets on his skin, the breakfast scents that drifted up the stairway and lured him down, even the familiar glitter of the hot yellow sun in the dew of the backyard grass. When he left the privy he was tempted by the path to the river, but it would be several weeks yet before it was warm enough to swim.

As he returned to the house, Alden came out of the barn and motioned for him to stop. 'How long will you be staying, Shaman?'

'I'm not certain, Alden.'

'Well, thing is. There's a heap of pasture barriers to be planted. Doug Penfield already ploughed the strips, but we're late dealin' with the spring lambs and a dozen other things, what with everythin' that's happened. I could use a hand from you plantin' the Osage orange. Mebbe it'll take you four days.'

Shaman shook his head. 'No, Alden, I can't.'

When he saw the look of annoyance on the old man's face he felt a guilty need to explain, but he resisted it. Alden still regarded him as the boss' younger boy to be told what to do, the deaf one who wasn't quite as good a farm worker as Alex. The refusal constituted a change in their status, and he tried to soften it. 'Maybe I can do some work on the farm in a couple of days. But if not, you and Doug are going to have to manage by yourselves,' he said, and Alden turned away with a sour look.

Shaman and his mother exchanged guarded smiles as he slid into his chair.

They had learned to talk safely of unimportant things. He complimented her on the farm sausage and eggs, cooked perfectly, a breakfast he hadn't had since he'd left home.

She remarked that she'd seen three blue herons yesterday on her way to town. 'I believe they're more numerous this year than ever. I think perhaps they've been frightened away from some other places by the war,' Sarah said.

He had been up late with his father's journal. There were questions he would have liked to ask her, and he knew it was sad that he couldn't.

After breakfast he spent time with his father's patient records. Nobody had kept better medical records than Robert Judson Cole. Bone weary or not, his father always had completed his records before going to bed, and now Shaman was able to make a careful list of all the people his father had treated in the few days after his return.

He asked his mother if he could have the use of Boss and the trap for the day. 'I want to call on the people Pa visited. Typhoid fever is such a spreadable disease.' She nodded. 'It's a good idea to take the horse and buggy. What of your lunch?' she asked.

'I'll just wrap a couple of your biscuits and carry them in my pocket.'

'He often did that,' she said in a low voice.

'I know he did.'

'I'll pack you a lunch.'

'If you want to, Ma, that'll be good.'

He went to her and kissed her on the forehead. Sarah sat without moving, but she took her son's hand and held it tightly. When finally she let go, Shaman was struck again by how beautiful she was.

The first place he stopped was at a farm owned by William Bemis who had injured his back delivering a calf. Bemis was limping about with a wry neck but said his back was better. 'I'm about out of the stinky liniment your daddy left me, though.'

'You been having any fever, Mr Bemis?'

'Hell, no. Just hurt my back, why would I have a fever?' He frowned at Shaman. 'You chargin' me for this visit? I didn't send for no doctor.'

'No sir, no charge. Glad you're feeling better,' Shaman said, and threw in a refill of the stinky liniment so he could leave the patient happy.

He tried to include stops he knew his father would make just to say hello to old friends. He reached the Schroeder place a little bit after noon. 'In time for dinner,' Alma told him cheerfully, and pursed her lips in disdain when he told her he was carrying a lunch.

'Well, you just bring it in, eat it while we have ours,' she said, and he did, happy for the company. Sarah had given him cold sliced lamb, and a baked sweet potato, and three biscuits sliced open and spread with honey. Alma brought out a platter of fried quail and peach turnovers. 'You're not gonna pass up the turnovers I made with the last of my preserves,' she said, and he had two, and a helping of the quail.

'Your pa knew better than to carry in a lunch when he came to my house, dinnertime,' Alma told him scornfully. She looked him full in the eyes. 'You gonna stay in Holden's Crossing now, do our doctoring for us?'

It made him blink. It was a natural question, a question he should have been asking himself, the one he'd been avoiding. 'Why, Alma . . . I haven't given it much thought,' he said lamely.

Gus Schroeder leaned forward and whispered to him, as

499

though conveying a secret, 'Why don't you tink about it?'

Midafternoon, Rob J. was at the Snow place. Edwin Snow raised wheat on a farm on the northern edge of the township, about as far as one could get from the Cole farm and still be in Holden's Crossing. He was one of those who'd sent for Doc Cole when word got out he was back, because Ed had had a badly infected toe. Shaman found him walking around, no trace of a limp. 'Oh, the foot's fine,' he said cheerfully. 'Your father had Tilda hold it while he slit it open with his little knife in his good hand, steady as a rock. I soaked it in salts like he said to, to draw out the stuff. Funny thing you should come by today, though. Tilda's feelin' poorly.'

They found Mrs Snow feeding the chickens, looking as though she didn't have the strength to throw the corn. She was a big heavyset woman with a flushed face, and she admitted to being 'a mite warm'. Shaman saw at once that she had a high fever, and he sensed her relief at being ordered to bed, although she protested all the way back to the house that it wasn't necessary.

She told him she had had a dull pain in her back for a day or so, and her appetite was off.

Shaman was apprehensive, but he forced himself to speak easily, telling her to get some rest, that Mr Snow could care for the chickens and the rest of the critters. He left them a bottle of tonic and said he'd drop in on them next day. Snow tried to argue when he refused payment, but Shaman was firm. 'No charge. It's not as though I'm your regular doctor. I'm just passing through,' he said, unable to accept money to treat an illness she might have caught from his father.

He made the Convent of Saint Francis Xavier of Assisi his last stop for the day.

Mother Miriam seemed genuinely happy to see him. When she asked him to sit, he chose the straight-backed wooden chair he'd sat on the few times he'd come to the convent with his father.

'So,' she said. 'You are looking about your old home?'

'I'm doing more than that today. I'm trying to see if my

father may have given typhoid fever to anyone else in Holden's Crossing. Have you or Sister Mary Benedicta displayed any symptoms?'

Mother Miriam shook her head. 'No. Nor do I expect that we shall. We're accustomed to nursing people with all kinds of disease, as your father was. Probably you are the same way now, *Ja?*'

'Yes, I think I am.'

'I believe the Lord looks after people like us.'

Shaman smiled. 'I hope you're right.'

'Have you treated a good deal of typhoid in your hospital?'

'We've seen our share of it. We keep people with transmissible diseases in a separate building, away from the others.'

'*Ja,* that is sensible,' she said. 'Tell me about your hospital.'

So he told her about the Southwestern Ohio Hospital, beginning with the nursing staff because she would be interested in that, and then moving into the medical and surgical staff, and pathology. She asked good questions that drew him out. He told her of his work in surgery with Dr Berwyn, and in pathology with Barney McGowan.

'So you have had good training, and good experience. And now what? Will you stay in Cincinnati?'

Shaman found himself telling her what Alma Schroeder had asked him, and how unprepared he'd been to answer the question.

Mother Miriam looked at him with interest. 'And why do you find it so hard to answer?'

'When I lived here, I always felt incomplete, a deaf boy growing up among people who could hear. I loved and admired my father and wanted to be like him. I yearned to be a doctor, worked and struggled, although everyone – even my father – said I couldn't achieve it.

'The dream always was to become a doctor. I'm already beyond where the dream ended. I'm no longer incomplete, and I'm back in the place that I love. To me, this place always will belong to the real doctor, my father.'

Mother Miriam nodded. 'But he is gone, Shaman.'

Shaman said nothing. He could feel the thudding of his heart, as if he were receiving the news for the first time.

'I want you to do something for me,' she said. She pointed to the leather chair. 'Sit over there, where he always sat.'

Reluctantly, almost stiffly, he rose from the wooden chair and sat in the upholstered one. She waited a moment. 'It is not so uncomfortable, I think?'

'It's quite comfortable,' he said steadily.

'And you fill it very well.' She smiled slightly and then gave him advice that was almost identical to what Gus Schroeder had told to him. 'You must think about it,' she said.

On the way home he stopped by the Howard place and bought a jug of whisky. 'Sorry about your pa,' Julian Howard muttered uncomfortably, and Shaman nodded, aware that neither man had had any use for the other. Mollie Howard said she figured that Mal and Alex had made it into the Confederate Army, because the Howards hadn't heard a single thing from Mal since the boys had run off. 'I figger if they was anywhere this side of the war line, one or the other would of sent word home,' she said, and Shaman told her he thought she was right.

After supper he brought the jug to Alden's cabin, a peace offering. He even poured a little for himself into one of the jelly glasses, knowing Alden didn't like to drink alone when somebody was with him. He waited until Alden had had several drinks before deliverately turning the conversation to the farm. 'Why is it you and Doug Penfield are having such a hard time keeping up with the work this year?'

The words sprang forth. 'This has been building up for a long time! We hardly ever sell a critter, except a spring lamb or two to a neighbour for Easter dinner. So every year the flock grows, and there are more animals to dip and shear and provide closed-off pasture for. I tried to get your pa to look at things straight before he went to the army, but I never could.'

'Well, let's you and me talk about it right now. What are

we getting per pound of fleece?' he asked, taking his notebook and pencil out of his pocket.

For almost an hour they sat and talked of wool grades and prices, and what the market was likely to be after the war, and the estimated area of range needed per sheep, and days of labour, and costs per day. When they finished, Shaman had a notebook full of scribbles.

Alden was mollified. 'Now, if you can tell me Alex will be back soon, it would change the picture, because that boy is a worker. But the truth is, he may be dead someplace down there in the hot country, and you know that's right, Shaman.'

'Yeah, it's right. But unless I hear differently, I'm thinking of him as alive.'

'Well, God, yes. But you'd best not figger him in when you're doin' your plannin', is all.'

Shaman sighed, and stood to go. 'Tell you what, Alden. I have to ride out again tomorrow afternoon, but I'll spend the morning on the Osage orange,' he said.

Next morning he was out in the fields early, in work clothes. It was a good day to work outside, dry and breezy, with a big sky full of rainless clouds. He hadn't done physical labour for a long time, and he could feel his muscles knotting tight before he finished digging the first hole.

He had set only three plants when his mother came riding out onto the prairie on Boss, followed by a Swedish beet farmer named Par Swanson, whom Shaman knew slightly.

'It's my daughter,' the man yelled before he had reached Shaman. 'I think she's broken her neck.'

Shaman took the horse from his mother and followed after the farmer. It was a ride of about twelve minutes to the Swanson house. From the brief description, he dreaded what he would find, but when they arrived he soon established that the girl was alive, and in a lot of pain.

Selma Swanson was a little towhead, less than three years old. She liked to ride the manure-spreader with her father. That morning her father's team had startled a big hawk that was feeding on a mouse in the field. The hawk flew up

503

suddenly, terrifying the horses. As they jolted forward, Selma had lost her balance and fallen off. Fighting to control the animals, Par saw that his daughter had been struck by the corner of the spreader as she fell. 'Looked to me, it got her in the neck,' he said.

The little girl was holding her left arm against her chest with her right hand. Her left shoulder was pushed forward. 'No,' Shaman said after he'd examined her. 'It's her collarbone.'

'Broken?' her mother said.

'Well, bent some, and maybe a little cracked. Don't you worry. It'd be serious if it were you or her father. But at her age bones bend like green twigs and they heal really fast.' The clavicle was injured not far from where it joined the scapula and the sternum. With rags supplied by Mrs Swanson he fashioned a small sling for Selma's left arm and then tied the slinged arm to her body with another rag, to keep the clavicle from moving.

The child had quieted by the time he finished the coffee Mrs Swanson had hot on her stove. He was a short ride from several of the people he had to see that day, and it made no sense for him to ride all the way home and then ride out again, so he just started out on his calls.

A woman named Royce, the wife of one of the new settlers, gave him meat pie for lunch. It was late afternoon before he got back to the sheep farm. As he rode past the field where he had started to work that morning, he saw that Alden had put Doug Penfield on the barrier planting, and a long, admonishing line of green Osage orange shoots already stretched out into the prairie.

59
The Secret Father

'God forbid,' Lillian whispered.

None of the Geigers showed any sign of having contracted typhoid fever, she said. Shaman thought Lillian's face showed the strain of running her farm and household and family without her husband. While the apothecary business had suffered, she even continued some aspects of Jason's pharmaceutical trade, importing drugs for Tobias Barr and Julius Barton.

'The problem is, Jay used to get so much material from his family's pharmaceutical company in Charleston. And of course, South Carolina is shut off from us now by the war,' she told Shaman, pouring his tea.

'Have you heard from Jason lately?'

'Not lately.'

She seemed ill-at-ease whenever he asked questions about Jason, but he could understand that she would be reluctant to speak too much about her husband lest she reveal something that could hurt Jason, or reveal military information, or endanger her family. It was difficult for a woman to live in a Union state while her husband worked in Virginia with the Confederates.

Lillian was more at ease when they discussed Shaman's medical career. She was familiar with his progress at the hospital and with the promises that had been made to him there. Obviously Shaman's mother shared the news that came in his letters.

'Cincinnati is such a cosmopolitan place,' Lillian said. It will be wonderful for you to establish your career there, to teach in the medical school, and to have a fine practice. Jay and I are extremely proud of you.' She cut thin, unbroken slices of coffee cake, and kept his plate filled. 'Do you have any idea when you will be returning there?'

'I'm not certain.'

'Shaman.' She placed her hand over his and leaned forward. 'You came back when your father died, and you have taken care of things very well. Now you must begin thinking of yourself, and of your career. Do you know what your father would want you to do?'

'What is that, Aunt Lillian?'

'Your father would want you to return to Cincinnati and pick up your career. You must return there as soon as possible!' she said solemnly.

He knew she was right. If he was going to go, it would be best if he went without delay. Every day he was summoned to different houses as people reached out, responding to the fact that there was a doctor in Holden's Crossing again. Each time he treated someone, it was as if he were bound by another gossamer thread. It was true that such threads could be broken; when he left, Dr Barr could take over the treatment of anyone who still required medical help. But the patients added to his feeling that there were things he didn't want to leave unfinished here.

His father had kept a list of names and addresses, and Shaman went through it carefully. He wrote of his father's death to Oliver Wendell Holmes in Boston, and to the uncle Herbert he'd never seen, and who wouldn't have to worry ever again that his older brother would return to Scotland to reclaim his land.

Every free moment Shaman spent reading the journals, captivated by glimpses of his father that were exciting and unfamiliar. Rob J. Cole had written of his son's deafness with anguish and tenderness, and Shaman felt the warmth of his love as he read. His father's pain in describing Makwa-ikwa's death, and the subsequent deaths of Comes Singing and Moon, reawoke deep-buried feelings. Shaman reread his father's report of Makwa-ikwa's autopsy, asking himself if he had missed something in previous readings, and then trying to determine whether his father had missed anything during his examination, and whether he would have done anything differently if he had been conducting the autopsy himself.

When he reached the volume that covered 1853, he was astounded. In his father's desk drawer he found the key to the locked shed behind the barn, and he took the key to the barn and opened the big lock and went inside. It was just the shed, a place he had been hundreds of times before. Wall shelves held stores of drugs, tonics and medicinals, and bunches of dried herbs hung from the rafters, Makwa's legacy. There was the old wood stove, not far from the wooden autopsy table where he had assisted his father so many times. Drainage pans and pails hung from nails in the walls. From another nail in a tree-trunk post, his father's old brown sweater still drooped.

The shed hadn't been dusted or swept out for several years. There were spiderwebs everywhere, but Shaman ignored them. He went to the place in the wall that he thought was about right, but when he tugged at the board, it held firm. There was a pry bar in the front part of the barn, but it wasn't necessary to get it, because when he tried the next board it pulled out easily, and so did several others.

It was like looking into the mouth of a cave. It was too dark in the shed, there was grey natural light only from one small, dusty window. First he opened the shed door wide, but the light was still poor, and he took down the lantern, which still contained a little oil, and lit it.

When he held it to the opening, it threw flickering shadows into the secret room.

Shaman crawled inside. His father had left it clean. It still contained a bowl, a cup, and an old neatly folded blanket Shaman recognized as one they had had for a long time. It was a small space, and Shaman was a big man, as large as

507

his father had been.

Certainly some of the runaway slaves had been large men too.

He blew out the lantern, and it was dark in the secret space. He tried to imagine that the entrance was boarded up and that the world outside was a baying hound hunting him. That the choice was between being a work animal or a hunted animal.

When he crawled out in a little while, he took the old brown sweater from the nail and put it on, although the day already was warm. It had his father's smell.

All that time, he thought, all through the years when he and Alex had lived in the house and had quarrelled and been boisterous, and caught up in their own needs and wants, his father had carried this enormous secret, had lived this experience alone. Now Shaman felt an overwhelming need to talk with Rob J., to share the experience, to ask him questions, to convey his love and admiration. In his room at the hospital he had wept briefly when he had received the telegraph message about his father. But he had been stolid on the train and stalwart during and after the funeral, for his mother's sake. Now he leaned back against the barn wall next to the secret room and slid down until he was seated on the dirt floor like a child, and like a child calling for his father, he gave himself up to grief in the knowledge that his silence was always going to be lonelier than it had been before.

508

60

A Child with the Croup

They were blessed. There was no additional typhoid fever in Holden's Crossing. Two weeks had gone by, yet no rash had appeared on Tilda Snow's body. Her fever had broken early, without haemorrhage or even sign of bloody flux, and one afternoon Shaman came to the Snow farm and she was out swilling the pigs. 'It was a bad grippe, but she's over it,' he told her husband. If Snow had wanted to pay him for his services then, he'd have accepted money, but instead the farmer gave him a brace of fine geese he had killed, hung, cleaned, and plucked just for Shaman.

'I've an old hernia givin' me trouble,' Snow said.

'Well, let me take a look at it.'

'Don't want to start with it while I'm gettin' in the first cut of hay.'

'When will you be done? Six weeks?'

'Thereabouts.'

'Come see me then, at the dispensary.'

'What, you'll still be here?'

'Yes,' he said, and grinned at Snow, and that was how he decided to stay for good, quietly and without anguish, without even knowing he had made up his mind.

He gave his mother the geese and suggested they invite Lillian Geiger and her sons to dinner. But Sarah said it

509

wasn't a convenient time for Lillian to come to dinner just then, and she thought it would be good if they ate the birds alone, just the two of them and the two hired men.

That night Shaman wrote separate letters to Barney McGowan and Lester Berwyn, expressing appreciation for what they'd done for him at medical school and in the hospital, and explaining that he was resigning his position at the hospital in order to take over his father's practice in Holden's Crossing. He also wrote to Tobias Barr in Rock Island, thanking him for contributing his Wednesdays to Holden's Crossing. Shaman wrote that he would be in Holden's Crossing full-time from now on, and he asked Dr Barr to sponsor his application to the Rock Island County Medical Society.

He told his mother as soon as he had written the letters, and he saw her pleasure and relief that she wouldn't be alone. She went to him quickly and kissed him on the cheek. 'I'll tell the women of the church,' she said, and Shaman smiled, knowing there was no practical need for any other kind of announcement.

They sat and talked and planned. He would use the dispensary and the barn shed just as his father had, keeping morning hours in the dispensary and making house calls every afternoon. He would retain the same schedule of fees his father had used, because it wasn't excessive, yet it always had kept them in comfort.

He had given thought to the problems of the farm, and Sarah listened as he outlined his suggestions to her; then she nodded in agreement.

Next morning, he sat in Alden's cabin and drank terrible coffee while he explained that they had decided to reduce the size of the farm's flock.

Alden listened intently, his eyes on Shaman while he sucked at and relit his pipe. 'You understand what you're sayin', do you? You know the price of wool is goin' to stay high as long as the war goes on? And that a reduced flock will give you fewer profits than you now enjoy?'

Shaman nodded. 'My mother and I understand that our only other choice is to have a larger business requiring more

510

help and more management, and neither of us wants that. My business is doctoring, not sheep farming. But we don't ever want to see the Cole farm without sheep, either. So we'd like you to go through the flock and separate out the best fleece producers, and we'll keep those, and breed them. We'll cull the flock every year to produce better and better wool, and that will ensure that we continue to get good prices. We'll keep just the number of sheep you and Doug Penfield are able to take care of.'

Alden's eyes gleamed. 'Now, that's what I call a wonderful decision,' he said, and refilled Shaman's mug with the vile coffee.

Sometimes it was very hard for Shaman to read the journal, too painful to creep into his father's brain and emotions. There were times when he pushed it away for as long as a week, but always he returned to it, needing to read the next pages because he knew they would be his last contact with his father. When the journal was completely read, he'd have no new information about Rob J. Cole, only memories.

It was a rainy June and a queer summer, with everything early, crops as well as fruit trees, and plants in the woodlands. The population of rabbits and hares exploded, and the ubiquitous animals nibbled grass close to the house and ate the lettuce and flowers of Sarah Cole's garden. The wet made haying difficult, with whole fields of fodder rotting on the ground, unable to dry, and it ensured a bountiful crop of insects that bit Shaman and sucked his blood as he rode on his calls. Despite that, he found it wonderful to be the physician of Holden's Crossing. He had enjoyed being a doctor at the hospital in Cincinnati; if he had needed help or reassurance from an older physician, the entire staff had been right there at his beck and call. Here he was all alone and had no idea from day to day what he was going to confront. It was the essence of the practice of medicine, and he loved it.

Tobias Barr told him the County Medical Society was defunct because most of its members were off to the war. He suggested that in its absence he and Shaman and Julius

Barton should meet one evening a month for dinner and professional talk, and they had the first such evening with mutual enjoyment, the main topic of discussion being measles, which had begun to break out in Rock Island but not in Holden's Crossing. They agreed that it should be stressed to both young and old patients that the pustules mustn't be scratched and broken, no matter how irritating, and that treatment should consist of soothing salves, cooling drinks, and Seidlitz powders. The other two men were interested when Shaman told them that at the Cincinnati hospital, treatment had included alum gargles whenever there was respiratory involvement.

Over dessert the talk turned to politics. Dr Barr was one of many Republicans who felt that Lincoln's approach to the South was too soft. He applauded the Wade-Davis Reconstruction Bill, which called for severe punitive measures against the South when the war ended, and which the House of Representatives had passed despite Lincoln's objections. Encouraged by Horace Greeley, dissident Republicans had gathered in Cleveland and agreed to nominate their own presidential candidate, General John Charles Frémont.

'Do you think the general could possibly beat Mr Lincoln?' Shaman asked.

Dr Barr shook his head gloomily. 'Not if there is still a war. There is nothing like a war to get a president re-elected.'

In July the rains finally stopped but the sun was like brass, and the prairie steamed and toasted and turned brown. The measles finally reached Holden's Crossing, and Shaman began to be called out of bed to attend some of its victims, although it wasn't as violent an outbreak as had occurred in Rock Island. His mother told him that measles had swept through Holden's Crossing the previous year, killing half a dozen people, including several children. Shaman thought that perhaps a severe onslaught of the disease somehow served to produce partial immunity in subsequent years. He thought of writing to Dr Harold Meigs, his former professor of medicine in Cincinnati, and asking if there could be value in the theory.

On a still, sultry evening that ended in a thunderstorm,

Shaman went to bed feeling the vibrations of an occasional thunderclap of heroic proportions, and opening his eyes whenever the room was transformed by the white illumination of lightning. Finally his weariness transcended the natural disturbances and he slept, so deeply that when his mother shook his shoulder it took him several seconds to realize what was happening.

Sarah held her lamp to her face so he could see her lips. 'You must get up.'

'Someone with measles?' he asked, already pulling on his outer clothing.

'No. Lionel Geiger is here to fetch you.'

By that time he had slid into his shoes and was outside. 'What is it, Lionel?'

'My sister's little boy. Choking. Tries to suck up air, makes a bad sound, like a pump can't send up water.'

It would have taken too long to run over the Long Path through the woods, too long to hitch the buggy or saddle one of his own animals. 'I'll take your horse,' he told Lionel, and did so, galloping the animal down their lane, up the quarter of a mile of road, and then up the Geigers' lane, clutching the medical bag so he wouldn't lose it.

Lillian Geiger waited by the front door. 'In here.'

Rachel. Seated on the bed in her old room, with a child in her lap. The little boy was very blue. He kept weakly trying to bring in air.

'Do something. He's going to die.'

In fact, Shaman believed the boy was close to death. He opened the child's mouth and stuck his first and second fingers into the small throat. The back of the child's mouth and the opening of his larynx were covered by a nasty mucous membrane, a killing membrane, thick and grey. Shaman stripped it away with his fingers.

At once the child pulled great shuddering breaths into his body.

His mother held him and wept. 'Oh, God. Joshua, are you all right?' Her night-breath was strong, her hair was dishevelled.

Yet, incredibly, it was Rachel. An older Rachel, more

513

womanly. Who had eyes only for the child.

The little boy already looked better, less blue, his normal colour flooding back as oxygen reached his lungs. Shaman placed his hand on the child's chest and held it there to feel the strength of the heartbeat; then he took the rate of the pulse and for a few moments held a small hand in each of his own large ones. The little boy had started to cough.

Lillian took a step into the room, and it was to her that Shaman spoke.

'What does the cough sound like?'

'Hollow, like a . . . barking.'

'Is there a wheeze?'

'Yes, at the end of each cough, almost a whistle.'

Shaman nodded. 'He has a catarrhal croup. You must start boiling water and give him warm baths for the rest of the night, to relax the respiratory muscles of his chest. And he has to breathe steam.' He took one of Makwa's medicines from his bag, a tea of black snakeroot and marigold. 'Brew this and let him drink it sweetened and as hot as possible. It will keep his larynx open, and help with the cough.'

'Thank you, Shaman,' Lillian said, pressing his hand. Rachel didn't appear to see him at all. Her bloodshot eyes looked crazed. Her gown was smeared with the child's snot.

As he let himself out of the house, his mother and Lionel came walking down the Long Path, Lionel carrying a lantern that had attracted an enormous swarm of mosquitoes and moths. Lionel's lips were moving, and Shaman could guess what he was asking.

'I think he will be all right,' he said. 'Blow out the lantern and make sure the bugs are gone before you go into the house.'

He went up the Long Path himself, a route he had taken so many times the dark wasn't a problem. Now and then the last of the lightning flickered and the black woods on both side of the path sprang at him in the brightness.

When he was back in his room, he undressed like a sleepwalker. But when he lay on his bed, he was unable to sleep. Numb and confused, he stared up at the murky ceiling or at the black walls, and wherever he looked, he saw the same face.

61
A Frank Discussion

When he went to the Geigers' house next morning, she answered the door wearing a new-looking blue housedress. Her hair was neatly combed. He smelled her light, spicy fragrance as she took his hands.

'Hello, Rachel.'

'. . . Thank you, Shaman.'

Her eyes were unchanged, wonderful and deep, but he noticed they were still raw with fatigue. 'How is my patient?'

'He appears to be better. His cough isn't as frightening as before.' She led him up the stairs. Lillian sat next to her grandson's bed with a pencil and some sheets of brown paper, entertaining him by drawing stick figures and telling stories. The patient, whom Shaman had seen only as an afflicted human being the night before, this morning was a small dark-eyed boy with brown hair and freckles that stood out in his pale face. He looked about two years old. A girl, several years older but with a remarkable resemblance to her brother, sat at the foot of his bed.

'These are my children,' Rachel said, 'Joshua and Hattie Regensberg. And this is Dr Cole.'

'How do you do,' Shaman said.

'Ha do.' The boy regarded him warily.

'How do you do,' Hattie Regensberg said. 'Mama says you don't hear us, and we must look at you when we speak, and say our words 'stinctly.'

'Yes, that's true.'

'Why don't you hear us?'

'I'm deaf because I was sick when I was a little boy,' Shaman said easily.

'Is Joshua going to be deaf?'

'No. Joshua definitely isn't going to be deaf.'

In a few minutes he was able to assure them that Joshua was much better. The baths and steam had broken his fever, his pulse was strong and steady, and when Shaman positioned the stethoscope bell and told Rachel what to listen for, she could hear no rales. Shaman placed the ear pieces in Joshua's ears and let him hear his own heart beating, and then Hattie took a turn with the stethoscope and placed the bell on her brother's stomach, announcing that all she heard was 'guggles'.

'That's because he's hungry,' Shaman said, and advised Rachel to put the boy on a light but nourishing diet for a day or two.

He told Joshua and Hattie their mother knew some very good fishing spots along the river, and he invited them to visit the Cole farm and play with the lambs. Then he said goodbye to them, and to their grandmother. Rachel walked him to the door.

'You have beautiful children.'

'They *are*, aren't they!'

'I'm sorry about your husband, Rachel.'

'Thank you, Shaman.'

'And I wish you good luck in your impending marriage.'

Rachel appeared startled. 'What impending marriage?' she asked, just as her mother came down the stairway.

Lillian passed through the foyer quietly, but the high colour in her face was like an advertisement.

'You have been misinformed, I have no marriage plans,' Rachel said crisply, loud enough for her mother to hear, and her face was pale when she said goodbye to Shaman.

That afternoon as he was riding Boss toward home, he overtook a solitary female figure trudging along, and when he drew closer he recognized the blue housedress. Rachel wore stout walking shoes and an old bonnet to guard her face from the sun. He called out to her, and she turned and greeted him quietly.

'May I walk along with you?'

'Please do.'

So he swung down from the saddle and led the horse.

'I don't know what got into my mother, to tell you I was to be married. Joe's cousin has shown some interest, but we won't marry. I think my mother is pushing me toward him because she's so anxious for the children to have a proper father again.'

'There seems to be a conspiracy of mothers. Mine neglected to tell me you were back, purposely, I'm sure.'

'It's so insulting of them,' she said, and he saw tears in her eyes. 'They assume that we're fools. I'm aware I have a son and a daughter who need a Jewish father. And certainly the last thing you're interested in is a Jewish woman who has two children, and is in mourning.'

He smiled at her. 'They're very nice children. With a very nice mother. But it's true, I'm not an infatuated fifteen-year-old anymore.'

'I thought of you often, after I was married. I so regretted that you'd been hurt.'

'I got over it very quickly.'

'We were children, thrown together during difficult times. I dreaded marriage so, and you were such a good friend.' She smiled at him. 'When you were a little boy you said you'd kill to protect me. And now we're adults, and you've saved my son.' She placed her hand on his arm. 'I hope we'll remain steadfast friends forever. As long as we live, Shaman.'

He cleared his throat. 'Oh, I know we will,' he said awkwardly. For a moment they walked in silence, and then Shaman asked if she would like to ride the horse.

'No, I prefer to continue my walk.'

'Well, then, I'll ride him myself, because I have a good deal to do before I can eat my supper. Good afternoon, Rachel.'

'Good afternoon, Shaman,' she said, and he remounted and rode away, leaving her walking purposefully down the road behind him.

He told himself she was a strong and practical woman who had the courage to face things as they were, and he determined to learn from her. He needed the company of a woman. He made a house call to Roberta Williams, who was suffering from 'women's troubles' and had begun to drink to excess. Averting his eyes from the dressmaker's dummy with the ivory buttocks, he asked after her daughter and was told that Lucille had married a postal worker three years before, and lived in Davenport. 'Has a youngun every year. Never comes to see me unless she needs money, that one,' Roberta told him. Shaman left her a bottle of tonic.

At just the moment of his deepest discontent, he was hailed on Main Street by Tobias Barr, who sat in his buggy with two women. One of them was his dimunitive blonde wife, Frances, and the other was Frances' niece, who was visiting from St. Louis. Evelyn Flagg was eighteen years old, taller than Frances Barr but blonde like her, and she had the most perfect female profile Shaman had ever seen.

'We're showing Evie about, thought she'd like to see Holden's Crossing,' Dr Barr said. 'Have you read *Romeo and Juliet*, Shaman?'

'Why yes, yes, I have.'

'Well, you've mentioned that when you know a play, you enjoy attending a performance. A touring company is in Rock Island this week, and we're getting up a theatre party. Will you join us?'

'I would like that,' Shaman said, and smiled at Evelyn, whose answering smile was dazzling.

'A light supper at our house first, then, at five o'clock,' Frances Barr said.

He bought a new white shirt and a black string tie, and reread the play. The Barrs also had invited Julius Barton and his wife Rose. Evelyn wore a blue gown that suited her blondeness. For a few moments Shaman struggled, trying to

518

remember where he'd seen that shade of blue recently, and then he realized it had been in Rachel Geiger's housedress.

Frances Barr's idea of a light supper was six courses. Shaman found it difficult to carry on a conversation with Evelyn. When he asked her a question, she was inclined to answer with a quick, nervous smile and a nod or a shake of her head. She spoke twice of her own volition, once to tell her aunt that the roast was excellent, and a second time during dessert, to confide in Shaman that she doted on both peaches and pears and was very grateful they ripened in different seasons so she wasn't forced to choose between them.

The theatre was crowded, and the evening was hot as only the end of summer can be. They arrived just before the curtain rose, because the six courses had taken time. Tobias Barr had bought the tickets with Shaman in mind. They sat in the centre section of the third row, and they were scarcely settled before the actors were speaking their lines. Shaman watched the play through opera glasses that allowed him to lip-read quite well, and he enjoyed it. During the first intermission he accompanied Dr Barr and Dr Barton outside, and while waiting in line to use the privy behind the theatre, they agreed the production was interesting. Dr Barton thought that perhaps the actress playing Juliet was pregnant. Dr Barr said Romeo was wearing a truss beneath his tights.

Shaman had been concentrating on their mouths, but during Act Two he studied Juliet and saw no basis for Dr Barton's supposition. There was no doubt about the fact that Romeo wore a truss, however.

At the end of Act Two the doors were opened to a welcome breeze, and the lamps were lit. He and Evelyn remained in their seats and tried to talk. She said she often went to the theatre in St. Louis. 'I find it inspiring to attend the plays, don't you?'

'Yes. But I seldom go,' he said absently. Curiously, Shaman felt he was being watched. With his opera glasses he studied the people in the balconies on the left side of the stage, and then on the right. In the second balcony, on the right, he saw Lillian Geiger and Rachel. Lillian wore a brown linen dress with great bell-like sleeves of lace. Rachel sat just beneath a lamp, which caused her to brush at the moths that swooped about the light, but it gave Shaman a chance to examine her closely. Her hair was carefully done, brushed up behind her in a gleaming knot. She wore a black dress that appeared to be made of silk; he wondered when she would stop wearing mourning in public. The dress was collarless against the heat, with short puff sleeves. He studied her round arms and full bosom, and always came back to her face. While he was still looking, she turned from her mother and glanced down at where he was sitting. For a full moment she observed him looking up at her through his glasses, and then she glanced away as ushers turned down the lamps.

Act Three seemed unending. Just as Romeo said to Mercutio, *Courage, man. The hurt cannot be much*, he became aware that Evelyn Flagg was trying to say something to him. He felt her slight warm breath on his ear as she whispered, while Mecutio replied, *No, 'tis not so deep as a well, nor so wide as a church door; 'tis enough, 'twill serve.*

He took the glasses from his eyes and turned towards the girl who sat next to him in the dark, mystified because small children like Joshua and Hattie Regensberg could remember the principles of lip-reading, while she wasn't able to.

'I cannot hear you.'

He was unaccustomed to whispering. Doubtless his voice was too loud, because the man directly in front of him in the second row turned and stared.

'I beg your pardon,' Shaman whispered. It was his earnest hope that his words were softer this time, and he put the glasses back up to his eyes.

62
Fishing

Shaman was curious about what allowed men like his father and George Cliburne to turn their backs on violence, when others couldn't. Only a few days after the theatre party he found himself riding to Rock Island again, this time to speak with Cliburne about pacifism. He could hardly credit the journal's revelation that Cliburne was the cool and courageous person who had brought runaway slaves to his father and then picked them up to take them to their next station of hiding. The plump, balding feed merchant didn't look heroic or appear the kind of person who would risk everything for a principle in defiance of the law. Shaman was filled with admiration for the steely secret man who inhabited Cliburne's soft storekeeper body.

Cliburne nodded when he made his request at the feed store. 'Well, thee can ask thy questions about pacifism and we shall talk, but I expect it will be good if thee begins by reading about the subject,' he said, and told his clerk he'd be back presently. Shaman rode after him to his house, and soon Cliburne had selected several books and a tract from the library. 'Thee might wish to attend Friends' Meeting sometime.'

Privately Shaman doubted he would, but he thanked Cliburne and rode home with his books. They turned out to be something of a disappointment, being mostly about

Quakerism. The Society of Friends apparently was started in England in the 1600's, by a man named George Fox, who believed 'the Inner Light of the Lord' dwelt in the hearts of quite ordinary people. According to Cliburne's books, Quakers supported one another in simple lives of love and friendship. They weren't comfortable with creeds or dogmas, they regarded all life as sacramental, and observed no special liturgy. They had no clergy, but believed that laymen were capable of receiving the Holy Spirit, and it was basic to their religion that they rejected war and worked toward peace.

The Friends were persecuted in England, and their name originally was an insult. Hauled before a judge, Fox told him to 'tremble at the Word of the Lord', and the judge called him 'a quaker'. William Penn founded his colony in Pennsylvania as a haven for persecuted English Friends, and for three quarters of a century Pennsylvania had no militia and only a few policemen.

Shaman wondered how they had managed to handle the drunkards. When he put Cliburne's books away, he had neither learned much about pacifism nor been touched by the Inner Light.

September came warmly but was clear and fresh, and he chose to follow river roads whenever he could while making his calls, enjoying the glitter of the sun on the moving water, and the stilt-legged beauty of the wading birds, fewer now because many already were flying south.

He was riding slowly on his way home one afternoon when he saw three familiar figures under a tree on the riverbank. Rachel was removing the hook from a catch while her son held the fishpole, and when she dropped the flapping fish back into the water, Shaman could see from Hattie's stance and expression that she was angry about something. He turned Boss off the road, toward them.

'Hello, there.'

'Hello!' Hattie said.

'She doesn't let us keep any of the fish,' Joshua said.

'I'll bet they were all catfish,' Shaman said, and grinned.

Rachel hadn't ever been allowed to bring catfish home because they weren't kosher, lacking scales. He knew that for a child the best part of fishing was watching your family eat the fish you caught. 'I've been going up to Jack Damon's every day, because he's poorly. Well, you know that spot where the river turns sharply at his place?'

Rachel smiled at him. 'That bend where there are lots of rocks?'

'That's the spot. I saw some boys taking very nice small bass beyond the rocks the other day.'

'I'm obliged. I'll bring them there tomorrow.'

He observed that the little girl's smile was very much like hers. 'Well, nice seeing you.'

'Nice seeing you!' Hattie said.

He tipped his hat at them and turned the horse.

'Shaman.' Rachel took a step toward the horse, looking up at him. 'If you're going up to Jack Damon's tomorrow around midday, come share our picnic lunch with us.'

'Well, I might just try to do that, if I'm able,' he said.

Next day when he fled Jack Damon's laborious breathing and rode to the bend in the river, he saw her mother's brown buggy right away, the grey mare tethered in the shade and cropping sweet grass.

Rachel and the children had been fishing off the rocks, and Joshua took Shaman's hand and pulled him to where six black bass, just the right size for eating, were swimming on their sides in a shaded shallow, with a fishline threaded through their gills and tied to a tree branch.

Rachel had taken a piece of soap as soon as she saw him, and was scrubbing her hands. 'Lunch is apt to taste fishy,' she said cheerfully.

'I won't mind a bit,' he said, and didn't. They had deviled eggs and pickled cucumbers, and lemonade with molasses cookies. After lunch Hattie announced seriously that it was sleepy time, and she and her brother lay on a blanket nearby and took their nap.

Rachel cleaned up after the meal, placing things into a carpet bag. 'You can use one of the poles and fish a bit, if you're inclined.'

'No,' he said, preferring to watch what she was saying instead of tending a fishline.

She nodded and looked out over the river. Upstream, a large flock of swallows, probably passing through from far north, wheeled and glided as if they were one bird, and kissed the water before darting away. 'Isn't it extraordinary, Shaman. Isn't it fine to be home?'

'Yes, it is, Rachel.'

They talked for a time about life in the cities. He told her about Cincinnati and answered her questions about the medical school and the hospital. 'And you, did you like Chicago?'

'I liked having theatres nearby, and concerts. I played my violin in a quartet every Thursday. Joe wasn't musical, but he indulged me. He was a very kind man,' she said. 'He was very careful with me when I lost a child, the first year we were married.'

Shaman nodded.

'Well, but then Hattie came, and the war. The war took whatever time my family didn't need. We had less than a thousand Jews in Chicago. Eighty-four young men joined a Jewish company and we raised funds and completely outfitted them. They became Company C of the 82nd Illinois Infantry. They have served with distinction at Gettysburg and other places, and I was part of that.'

'But you're Judah P. Benjamin's cousin, and your father's a fervent Southerner!'

'I know. But Joe wasn't, and neither am I. The day my mother's letter arrived that told me he'd gone to the Confederates, I had a kitchen full of the Hebrew Ladies Soldier Aid Society rolling bandages for the Union.' She shrugged.

'And then Joshua came. And then Joe died. And that's my story.'

'Up to now,' Shaman said, and she looked at him. He'd forgotten the vulnerable curve of her smooth cheek beneath the high facial bones, the soft fullness of her lower lip, and how the darkness of her brown eyes contained lights and

524

shadows. He didn't mean to ask the next question, but it was wrenched from him somehow. 'So you were happy in your marriage?'

She studied the river. For a moment he thought he had missed her answer, but then she looked back at him. 'I would like to say satisfied. Truth is, I was resigned.'

'I've never been satisfied or resigned,' he said wonderingly.

'You don't give in, you keep struggling, that's why you're Shaman. You must promise you'll never allow yourself to become resigned.'

Hattie woke up and left her brother sleeping on the blanket. She came to her mother and snuggled into her lap.

'Promise me,' Rachel said.

Shaman smiled. 'I promise.'

'Why do you talk funny?' Hattie asked.

'Do I talk funny?' he asked, more of Rachel than of the child.

'Yes!' Hattie said.

'You're more guttural than you were before I left,' Rachel said carefully. 'And you seem less in control of your voice.'

He nodded, and told her of his difficulty when he'd tried to whisper during the performance at the theatre.

'Have you been keeping up your exercises?' Rachel asked.

She looked stricken when he admitted he hadn't given much thought to his speech since leaving Holden's Crossing for medical school.

'I had no time for speech drills. I was too busy trying to become a doctor.'

'But now you mustn't be comfortable! You must go back to your exercises. If you don't do them from time to time, you'll forget how you're supposed to speak. I'll work with you on your speech, if you'd like, the way we used to do.' Her eyes were earnest as she sat and looked at him, the river breeze ruffling her loose hair, and the little girl with her eyes and her smile leaning into her breasts. Her head was high, and her taut and lovely neck reminded Shaman of pictures he'd seen of a lioness.

I know I can do it, Miss Burnham.

525

He remembered the young girl who had volunteered to help a small deaf boy speak, and he recalled how much he had loved her.

'I'd be grateful, Rachel,' Shaman said steadily, careful to emphasize the first syllable in grateful and to drop his voice at the end of the sentence.

They had decided to meet at a central point on the Long Path between their homes. He felt certain she hadn't told Lillian she'd be working with him again, and he saw no reason to mention it to his own mother. The first day, Rachel appeared at the appointed hour of three o'clock accompanied by both children, whom she set to gathering hazelnuts along the path.

Rachel sat on a small blanket she had carried with her, her back against an oak tree, and he sat dutifully facing her. The drill she chose was to speak a sentence to Shaman, who would read her lips and repeat it with the proper intonation and emphasis. To help, she held his fingers and squeezed them to show where a word should be stressed or a syllable accented. Her hand was warm and dry and as businesslike as if she held a pressing iron or laundry that had to be washed. His own hand felt hot and sweaty to him, but he lost self-consciousness when he turned his attention to the tasks she set him. His speech had developed even more problems than he had feared, and contending with them was no pleasure. He was relieved when finally the children came, struggling with a bucket almost half filled with hazelnuts. Rachel said they'd crack them with a hammer when they got home and take out the meats, and then they'd bake a nut bread to share with Shaman.

He was due to meet with her the following day for more speech exercises, but next morning when he finished at the dispensary and rode out on his calls, he found that Jack Damon was finally caving in to the consumption. He stayed by the dying man, trying to ease him. When the end came, it was too late to get back in time to meet Rachel, and he rode home moodily.

The day after that was Saturday. In the Geiger home a

strict Sabbath was observed and there would be no meeting with Rachel that day, but after Shaman had finished in the dispensary, he ran through the vocal exercises by himself.

He felt rootless, and somehow, in a way that had nothing to do with his work, he was dissatisfied with his life.

That afternoon he went back to Cliburne's books and read more about pacifism as a Quaker movement, and on Sunday morning he rose early and rode to Rock Island. The feed merchant was just finishing breakfast when he got to the Cliburne place. George accepted back the books and served him a cup of coffee, and nodded without surprise when Shaman asked if he could go along to the Quaker meeting.

George Cliburne was a widower. He employed a house-keeper, but she had Sundays off, and he was a neat man. Shaman waited while he washed his own breakfast dishes, and he allowed Shaman to wipe. They left Boss in the barn and he rode with Cliburne in his buggy, and on the way George told him a few things about meeting.

'We enter the meeting house without speaking and take a seat, men on one side, women on the other. That's so there'll be fewer distractions, I guess. People sit in silence until the Lord lays on someone the burden of the world's suffering, and then that person just gets up and speaks.'

Cliburne tactfully advised Shaman to sit in the middle or the rear of the meeting house. They wouldn't sit together. 'It's custom for the elders, who've done the society's work for many, many years, to sit up front.' He leaned forward confidentially. 'There are Quakers who call us Weighty Friends,' he said, and grinned.

The meeting house was small and plain, a white frame structure without a steeple. Inside were white walls, a grey floor. Dark-stained benches were arranged against three walls to form a square, shallow U that would enable everyone to face one another. Four men already were seated. Shaman took a place on a rear bench, close to the door, like someone testing deep waters by putting a toe in the shallowest shallows. Opposite him sat half a dozen women, and there were eight children. All the elders were elderly; George and five of his Weighty Friends sat on a bench atop a little platform, a foot high, in the front of the room.

There was a repose to match the silence in Shaman's world.

From time to time, people came and took bench seats without speaking. Eventually, no one else came, and there were eleven men, fourteen women, and twelve children, by Shaman's count.

In silence.

It was restful.

He thought of his father and hoped he was at peace.

He thought of Alex.

Please, he sent into the perfect silence he now shared with others. Out of the hundreds of thousands of the dead, please spare my brother. Please bring my crazy, lovable, runaway brother home.

He thought of Rachel, but he didn't dare pray.

He thought of Hattie, who had her mother's smile and her eyes, and who talked a lot.

He thought of Joshua, who said little but who always seemed to be looking at him.

A middle-aged man arose from a bench only a few feet away. He was thin and fragile, and he began to speak. 'This terrible war is finally beginning to wind down. It's happening very, very slowly, but now we perceive it can't go on forever. Many of our newspapers are calling for the election of General Fremont as President. They say President Lincoln will be too easy on the South when peace comes. They say it isn't a time for forgiveness, but a time for vengeance upon the people of the Southern states.

'Jesus said, "Father, forgive them, for they know not what they do." And he said, "If thine enemy hunger, feed him, and if he thirst, give him drink."

'We must forgive the sins committed by both sides in this terrible war, and pray that soon the words of the psalm will be true, that mercy and truth are met together, and righteousness and peace have kissed each other.

'"Blessed are they that mourn, for they shall be comforted."

' "Blessed are the meek, for they shall inherit the earth." '

' "Blessed are they which do hunger and thirst after righteousness, for they shall be filled." '

' "Blessed are the merciful, for they shall obtain mercy." '

' "Blessed are the peacemakers, for they shall be called the children of God." '

He sat, and then there was more white silence.

A woman arose almost directly opposite Shaman. She said she was seeking to grant forgiveness to a person who had done her family a grievous wrong. She desired her heart to be free of hatred and wished to show forebearance and merciful love, but she was engaged in a struggle with herself, for she didn't wish to forgive. She asked her friends to pray that she be given strength.

She sat, and another woman stood, this time in the far corner, so Shaman couldn't see her mouth well enough to have any idea what she spoke about. After a while she sat, and people were silent until a man stood at a bench near the window. He was a man in his twenties, with an earnest face. He said he had to make an important decision that would affect the rest of his life. 'I need the Lord's help, and thy prayers,' he said, and he sat.

After that, no one spoke. Time drifted on, and then Shaman saw George Cliburne turn to the man next to him and shake his hand. It was the signal for the breaking of the meeting. Several people near Shaman shook his hand, and there was a general movement to the doors.

It was the strangest church service Shaman ever had attended. On the way back to Cliburne's house, he was thoughtful. 'Is a Quaker expected to show forgiveness, then, for every crime? What about the satisfaction when justice prevails over evil?'

'Oh, we believe in justice,' Cliburne said. 'We just don't believe in revenge, or in violence.'

Shaman knew his father had longed to avenge Makwa's death, and he certainly yearned to do so himself. 'Would you be violent if you witnessed someone about to shoot your mother?' he asked, and was put out when George

Cliburne chuckled.

'Sooner or later, that question is asked by anyone who thinks about pacifism. My mother's long gone, but if I ever get in that kind of situation, I trust that the Lord will point out the right thing for me to do.

'See here, Shaman. Thee's not going to reject violence because of anything I say to thee. It's not going to come from here,' he said, touching his lips. 'And it's not going to come from here.' He touched Shaman's forehead.

'If it happens, it must come from here.' He tapped Shaman's chest. 'So until then, thee must continue to strap on thy sword,' he said, as if Shaman were a Roman or a Visigoth instead of a deaf man who had been refused for military service. 'When and if thee unbuckles the sword and casts it from thee, it will be because thee has no other choice,' Cliburne said, and his tongue made a clucking motion as he shook the reins to make the horse go faster.

63
The End of the Journal

'We are invited to have tea this afternoon at the Geigers',' Shaman's mother told him. 'Rachel says we must come. Something to do with the children, and filberts?'

So that afternoon they walked the Long Path and sat in the Geigers' dining room. Rachel brought in a new fall cloak of soft forest-green wool to show Sarah. 'Spun from Cole fleeces!' Her mother had made it for her because her year of mourning was over, she said, and everyone complimented Lillian for fashioning a lovely garment.

Rachel observed that she would wear it the following Monday on a trip to Chicago.

'Will you be there long?' Sarah asked, and she said no, she would be gone only a few days.

'Business,' Lillian said in a tone that spoke volumes of disapproval.

When Sarah remarked hurriedly on the fulsome flavour of the English tea, Lillian sighed and said she felt fortunate to have it. 'There's almost no coffee in the entire South, and no decent tea. Jay says either coffee or tea sells for fifty dolars a pound in Virginia.'

'Then you've heard from him again?' Sarah asked.

Lillian nodded. 'He reports he is well, thank God.'

Hattie's face beamed when her mother carried in the bread, still warm from the oven. 'We made it!' she announced. 'Momma put in the things and stirred them up, and Joshua and me poured in the nuts!'

'Joshua and I,' her grandmother said.

'*Bubbie*, you weren't even in the kitchen!'

'The nuts are simply delicious,' Sarah told the little girl.

'Me and Hattie got them,' Joshua said proudly.

'Hattie and I,' Lillian said.

'No, *Bubbie*, you weren't there, it was on the Long Path and me and Hattie picked up the nuts while Momma and Shaman sat on the blanket and held hands.'

There was a moment of silence.

'Shaman has been having small difficulties with his speech,' Rachel said. 'He just needs some practice. I'm helping him again, the way I used to. We met on the wood path so the children could play nearby, but he'll be coming to the house so we can use the piano in the exercises.'

Sarah nodded. 'It will be a good thing for Robert to work on his speech.'

Lillian nodded too, but stiffly. 'Yes, how fortunate you are home, Rachel,' she said, and took Shaman's cup and refilled it with the English tea.

The next day, although he'd made no appointment with Rachel, when he returned from his home visits, he walked out on the Long Path and met her walking the other way.

'Where are my friends?'

'They were helping with fall house cleaning and missed sleepy time, so they're having late naps.'

He turned and walked along with her. The woods were full of birds, and he saw, in a nearby tree, a cardinal issuing an imperious, silent challenge.

'I've been quarrelling with my mother. She wanted us to go to Peoria for the High Holidays, and I refused to go there and be placed on display for the eligible bachelors and widowers. So we'll spend the holidays at home.'

'Good,' he said quietly, and she smiled. The other quarrel, she told him, was brought on because Joe Regensberg's cousin was marrying someone else, and had made an offer to buy the Regensberg Tinware Company, since he hadn't

532

been able to acquire it through marriage. That was why she was going to Chicago, she confided – to sell the company.

'Your mother will calm down. She loves you.'

'I know she does. Would you like to do some exercises?'

'Why not?' He extended his hand.

This time he could detect a slight trembling of her hand as it held his. Perhaps the exertion of the house cleaning had exhausted her, or the quarreling. But he dared to hope it was more than that, and he recognized a current of awareness pass between their fingers, so that his hand involuntarily moved in hers.

They were working on the breath control necessary to adequately manage the small explosions of the letter p, and he was unsmilingly repeating a nonsense sentence about a perfect possum pursuing a perturbed partridge, when she shook her head.

'No, feel how I do it,' she said, and placed his hand on her throat.

But all he could feel beneath his fingers was Rachel's warm flesh.

It wasn't something he had planned; if he had thought about it, he wouldn't have done it. He slid his hand up to cup her face gently and bent to her. The kiss was infinitely sweet, the dreamed-about and yearned-for kiss of a fifteen-year-old boy and the girl with whom he was hopelessly in love. But they soon became a man and a woman kissing, and the mutual hunger was so shocking to him, so contradictory to the determined control of the everlasting friendship she had offered him, that he was afraid to credit it.

'Rachel . . .' he said when they broke apart.

'No. Oh, God.'

But when they came together again she planted little kisses all over his face like hot rain. He kissed her eyes, missed the centre of her mouth and kissed its corner, and her nose. He could feel her body straining against him.

Rachel was struggling with shocks of her own. She placed a tremulous hand on his cheek and he moved his head until his lips pressed into her palm.

He saw her say words familiar from long ago, that

Dorothy Burnham had used to signify the end of each school day. 'I think that is all for today,' she said breathlessly. She turned from him, and Shaman stood and watched her walk quickly away until she disappeared around a curve in the Long Path.

That evening he began reading the last portion of his father's journal, observing with dread and a great sadness the dwindling of Robert Judson Cole's existence and caught up in the terrible war along the Rappahannock as his father had recorded it in his large clear hand.

When Shaman came to Rob J.'s discovery of Lanning Ordway, he sat for a time without reading. It was difficult for him to accept that, after so many years of trying, his father had made contact with one of the men who had caused Makwa's death.

He sat up through the night, hunching over to make use of the light of the lamp in order to read on and on.

He went over Ordway's letter to Goodnow several times.

Just before dawn he came to the end of the journal – and the end of his father. He lay on his bed fully clothed for a lonely hour. When he sensed his mother in the kitchen, he went down to the barn and asked Alden to come inside. He showed both of them Ordway's letter and told them how he had found it.

'In his journal? You read his journal?' his mother said.

'Yes. Would you like to read it?'

She shook her head. 'I don't need that, I was his wife. I knew him.'

They both saw that Alden was hungover and poorly, and she poured coffee for the three of them.

'I don't know what to do about the letter.'

Shaman let each of them read it slowly.

'Well, what *can* you do?' Alden said irritably. Alden was getting old fast, Shaman realized. Either he was drinking more or finding it harder to handle whisky. His trembling hands spilled sugar as he spooned it into his cup. 'Your pa tried every way to get the law to act on what happened to that Sauk female. You think they're gonna be any more

534

interested now, becaue you have somebody's name in a dead man's letter?'

'Robert, when is this going to end?' his mother said bitterly. 'That woman's bones have been lying out there in our land all these years, and the two of you, your father and now you, haven't been able to allow her to rest in peace, or any of us either. Can't you just tear up the letter and forget all that old pain, and let the dead lie?'

But Alden shook his head. 'Meanin' no disrespect, Miz Cole. But this man isn't about to listen to good sense or reason about them Indians, any more than his father could.' He blew on his coffee, held it to his face with both hands, and took a swallow that must have burned his mouth. 'No, he'll just worry this to death like a dog chokin' on a bone, the way his pa used to do.' He looked at Shaman. 'If my advice means anythin', which it probably don't, you ought to go to Chicago sometime when you're able, and look up this Goodnow, see if he can tell you somethin'. Otherwise, you're goin' to work yourself into a frazzle, and us too in the bargain.'

Mother Miriam Ferocia didn't agree. When Shaman rode to the convent that afternoon and showed her the letter, she nodded. 'Your father told me about David Goodnow,' she said calmly.

'If the Reverend Goodnow was indeed the Reverend Patterson, he should be made accountable for Makwa's death.'

Mother Miriam sighed. 'Shaman, you are a doctor, not a policeman. Can you not leave this man's judgement to God? it is as a doctor that we need you desperately.' She leaned forward and fixed him with her eyes. 'I have momentous news. Our bishop has sent word that he will send us funds to establish a hospital here.'

'Reverend Mother, that is wonderful news!'

'Yes, wonderful.'

Her smile illuminated her face, Shaman thought. He recalled from his father's journal that she had received a legacy after her father's death and had turned it over to the

535

Church; he wondered if it was her own inheritance the bishop would send her, or part of it. But her joy wouldn't tolerate the existence of cynicism.

'The people of this area will have a hospital,' she said, beaming. 'The nursing nuns of this convent will nurse at the hospital of Saint Francis Xavier of Assisi.'

'And I shall have a hospital to care for my patients.'

'Actually, we hope you will have more than that. The sisters are agreed. We wish you to be the hospital's medical director.'

It silenced him for a moment. 'You honour me, your Reverence,' he said finally. 'But I would suggest as medical director a doctor with more experience, someone older. And you're aware I'm not a Catholic.'

'Once, when I dared dream of this, I hoped your father would be our medical director. God sent your father to us to be our friend and physician, but your father is gone. Now God has sent you to us. You have education and skill, and already you have fine experience. You are the physician of Holden's Crossing, and you should head its hospital.'

She smiled. 'As for your lack of old age, we believe that you are the oldest young man we ever have met. It will be a small hospital, of only twenty-five beds, and we shall all grow with it.

'I should like to presume to give you some advice. Do not be reluctant to value yourself highly, for others do so. Nor should you hesitate to aspire to any goal, because God has been lavish in his gifts to you.'

Shaman was embarrassed, but he smiled with the assurance of a doctor who had just been promised a hospital. 'It is always my pleasure to believe you, Reverend Mother,' he said.

64
Chicago

Shaman confided his conversation with the prioress only to his mother, and Sarah surprised and warmed him with the intensity of her pride. 'How good it will be to have a hospital here, and for you to direct it. How happy it would have made your father!'

He cautioned her that construction funds wouldn't be forthcoming from the Catholic archdiocese until plans for the hospital had been made and approved. 'Meanwhile, Miriam Ferocia has asked me to visit several hospitals and study their departments,' he told her.

He knew at once where he would go and what train he would take.

On Monday he rode to Moline and arranged to stable Boss for a few days. The train for Chicago stopped in Moline at 3:20 p.m., only long enough to load the freight being shipped by the John Deere plough factory, and by 2:45 Shaman was waiting on the wooden platform.

When it arrived, he boarded at the last car and began to walk forward. He knew Rachel had taken the train in Rock Island only minutes before, and he found her three cars down, seated alone. He'd been prepared to greet her lightheartedly, to make a joke of their 'chance' encounter, but the blood drained from her face when she saw him.

'Shaman . . . something wrong with the children?'

'No, no, not at all. I'm going to Chicago on business of my own,' he said, annoyed at himself for not realizing this would be the result of his surprise. 'May I sit with you?'

'Of course.'

But when he'd placed his suitcase next to hers on the shelf and taken the aisle seat, they were constrained.

'About the other day on the wood path, Shaman . . .'

'I enjoyed it very much,' he said firmly.

'I can't allow you to get the wrong idea.'

Again, he thought in despair. 'I believed you enjoyed it very much too,' he said, and colour flooded her face.

'That isn't the point. We mustn't indulge ourselves with the kind of . . . enjoyment that only serves to make reality more cruel.'

'What *is* reality?'

'I'm a Jewish widow with two children.'

'And?'

'I've sworn never again to allow my parents to pick a husband for me, but that doesn't mean I won't be sensible in my own choice.'

It stung. But this time he wouldn't be deterred with things left unsaid. 'I've loved you most of my life. I've never met a woman whose appearance or mind I've found more beautiful. There's a goodness in you I need.'

'Shaman. Please.' She turned away from him and stared out the window, but he went on.

'You've made me promise never to be resigned or passive to life. I won't be resigned to losing you again. I want to marry you and to be a father to Hattie and Joshua.'

She remained turned from him, watching the fields that rolled by, and the farms.

He had said what he wanted to say, and he took a medical journal from his pocket and began to read about the etiology and treatment of whooping cough. Presently Rachel removed her knitting bag from under the seat and took out her knitting. He saw she was making a small sweater of dark blue wool.

'For Hattie?'

'For Joshua.' They looked at one another for a long

moment, then she smiled slightly and resumed her knitting.

The light failed before they had travelled fifty miles, and the conductor came in and lit the lamps. It was scarcely five o'clock when they became too hungry to wait any longer to eat. Shaman had brought a supper package containing fried chicken and apple pie, and Rachel had brought bread, cheese, hard-boiled eggs, and four small sugar pears. They divided his pie and her eggs and fruit. He had well water in a flask.

After the train stopped at Joliet, the conductor turned down the lamps, and Rachel fell asleep for a time. When she awoke, her head was on Shaman's shoulder and he was holding her hand. She reclaimed her hand but let her head stay on his shoulder for a few seconds. When the train slid from the prairie darkness into a sea of lights, she was sitting up fixing her hair, holding a hairpin clenched in her strong white teeth. When she was finished, she told him they were in Chicago.

They took a carriage from the station to Palmer's Illinois House Hotel, where Rachel's attorney had reserved a room for her. Shaman registered there too, and was assigned a room on the fifth floor, 508. He saw her up to Room 306 and tipped the bellman.

'Would you like anything else. Some coffee, perhaps?'

'I don't think so, Shaman. It's getting late, and I've a lot to attend to tomorrow.' Nor did she want to join him for breakfast. 'Why don't we meet back here at three o'clock, and I'll show you Chicago before dinner?'

So he told her that sounded fine, and he left her. He went up to 508, got his own things unpacked into the bureau drawers and hung up in the closet, and then walked down the five flights again to use the privy behind the hotel, which was encouragingly clean and well-tended.

On the way back up he paused for a moment on the third landing and looked down the corridor toward her room, then climbed the other two flights of stairs.

In the morning, directly after breakfast, he sought out

Bridgeton Street, which turned out to be a workingman's neighbourhood of attached wooden houses. At number 237 the tired-looking young woman who answered his knock was holding an infant, while a small boy clutched her skirts.

She shook her head when Shaman asked for the Reverend David Goodnow. 'Mr Goodnow's not lived here for over a year. He's very ill, I'm told.'

'Do you know where he's gone?'

'Yes, he's in a . . . kind of a hospital. We never have met him. We send our rent to the hospital every month. That's the arrangement his lawyer made.'

'Could I have the name of the hospital? It's important that I see him.'

She nodded. 'I have it written down in the kitchen.' She left, but she was back in a moment, trailing her son and holding a slip of paper.

'It's the Dearborn Asylum,' she said. 'On Sable Street.'

The sign was modest and dignified, a bronze tablet set in the central column rising above a low wall of red brick:

> *Dearborn Asylum*
> *For Inebriates*
> *And the Insane*

The building was a three-storey mansion of red brick, and the heavy iron gridwork on the windows matched the ironwork pickets that topped the brick wall.

Inside the mahogany door was a lightless entry containing a pair of horsehair chairs. In a small office off the entry, a middle-aged man sat at a desk, making entries in a large bookkeeping ledger. He nodded when Shaman made his request.

'Mr Goodnow hasn't had a visitor since Lord knows when. Don't know as he's ever had one. You just sign the guest book, and I'll go ask Dr Burgess.'

Dr Burgess appeared a few minutes later, a short man with black hair and thin, fussy moustaches. 'Are you family, or a friend of Mr Goodnow's, Dr Cole? Or is your visit professional?'

'I know people who know Mr Goodnow,' Shaman said carefully. 'I'm in Chicago only briefly, and I thought to visit him.'

Dr Burgess nodded. 'Visiting hours are in the afternoon, but for a busy physician we can make an exception. You will follow me, please.'

They climbed a flight of stairs, and Dr Burgess knocked at a locked door, which was opened by a large attendant. The burly man led them down a long corridor, where pale women sat against both walls, talking to themselves or staring at nothing. They stepped around a pool of urine, and Shaman saw smeared faeces. In some of the rooms off the corridor, women were chained to the wall. Shaman had spent four sad weeks working in the Ohio State Asylum for the Insane when he was in medical school, and he wasn't surprised at the sights or the smells. He was glad he couldn't hear the sounds.

The attendant unlocked another door and led them down a corridor in the men's ward, no better than the women's. Finally Shaman was conducted into a small room containing a table and some wooden chairs, and instructed to wait.

Presently the doctor and the attendant returned, leading an elderly man dressed in work trousers with buttons missing from the flies, and a filthy suit jacket worn over his underwear. He needed a haircut and his grey facial hair was wild and untrimmed. There was a small smile on his lips, but his eyes were elsewhere. 'Here is Mr Goodnow,' Dr Burgess said.

'Mr Goodnow, I'm Dr Robert Cole.'

The smile remained the same. The eyes didn't see him.

'He can't speak,' Dr Burgess said.

Nevertheless, Shaman got up from his chair and moved close to the man.

'Mr Goodnow, were you Ellwood Patterson?'

'He hasn't spoken in more than a year,' Dr Burgess said patiently.

'Mr Goodnow, did you kill the Indian woman you raped in Holden's Crossing? When you went there for the Order

541

of the Star-Spangled Banner?'

Dr Burgess and the attendant stared at Shaman.

'Do you know where I can find Hank Cough?'

But there was no answer.

And again, sharply, 'Where can I look for Hank Cough?'

'He's syphilitic. Part of his brain has been destroyed by paresis,' Dr Burgess said.

'How do you know he's not pretending?'

'We see him all the time, and we know. Why would someone pretend in order to live like this?'

'Years ago, this man took part in an inhuman, terrible crime. I hate to see him escape punishment,' Shaman said bitterly.

David Goodnow had begun to dribble from the mouth. Dr Burgess looked at him and shook his head. 'I don't think he has escaped punishment,' he said.

Shaman was led back through the wards and to the front door, where Dr Burgess tendered him a polite good bye and mentioned that the asylum welcomed referrals from physicians in western Illinois. He went away from that place, blinking in the bright sunlight. The stinks of the city were good smells, by contrast. His head swam, and he walked several blocks deeply lost in thought.

It felt to him like the end of a trail. One of the men who had destroyed Makwa-ikwa was dead. Another, as he had just witnessed, was caught in a living hell, and the whereabouts of the third man were unknown.

Miriam Ferocia was right, he decided. It was time for him to leave Makwa's killers to God's justice and to concentrate on medicine and his own life.

He took a horse trolley to the centre of Chicago, and another horse trolley to the Chicago Hospital, which reminded him at once of his hospital in Cincinnati. It was a good hospital, and large, with almost five hundred beds. When he asked for an interview with the medical director and explained his errand, he was treated with pleasant courtesy.

The physician-in-chief brought him to a senior surgeon,

and the two men gave him their opinion about the equipment and supplies that a small hospital would need. The hospital purchasing agent recommended supply houses that could offer ongoing service and reasonable deliveries. And Shaman spoke to the head housekeeper about the number of linens needed to keep each bed in clean sheets. He wrote busily in his notebook.

Just before three o'clock, when he returned to Palmer's Illinois House Hotel, Rachel was seated in the lobby, waiting for him. The moment he saw her face, he knew her day had gone well.

'It's over, the company is no longer my responsibility,' she said. She told him the lawyer had done an excellent job of preparing the necessary documents, and most of the receipts of the sale already had been placed in trust for Hattie and Joshua.

'Well, we must celebrate,' he said, and the grey mood that had been established by his morning activities was banished.

They took the first hansom carriage in the line at the curb in front of the hotel. Shaman didn't want to see the concert hall or the new stockyards. Only one thing about Chicago interested him. 'Show me the places you knew when you lived here,' he said.

'But that will be so dull!'

'Please.'

So Rachel leaned forward and gave directions to the driver, and the horse moved off.

At first she was embarrassed, as she pointed out the instrument shop where she had bought strings and a new bow for her violin, and had had the pegs repaired. But she began to enjoy herself as she identified the shops where she had bought her shoes and her hats, and the shirtmaker's where she had ordered some dress shirts for her father's birthday present. They rode for twenty blocks, until she showed him an imposing edifice and told him it was the Sinai Congregation. 'This is where I played with my quartet on Thursdays, and where we came to services Friday evenings. It isn't where Joe and I were married. That was the *Kehilath Anshe Maarib* synagogue, where Joe's aunt,

543

Harriet Ferber, was a prominent member.

'Four years ago, Joe and a number of others broke away from the synagogue and founded Sinai, a congregation of Reform Judaism. They did away with a good deal of ritual and tradition, and it created an enormous scandal here. Aunt Harriet was furious, but it didn't cause a lasting rift, and we remained close. When she died a year later, we named Harriet after her.'

She directed the driver next to a neighbourhood of small but comfortable homes, and on Tyler Street she pointed out a house of brown shingles.

'There is where we lived.'

Shaman remembered how she'd looked then, and he leaned forward, trying to fit the girl of his memory into this house.

Five blocks away there was a cluster of stores. 'Oh, we must stop!' Rachel said. They left the carriage and went into a grocery that smelled of spices and salt, where a ruddy-faced white-bearded old man, fully as large as Shaman, came toward them, beaming as he wiped his hands on his grocer's apron.

'Mrs Regensberg, how good to see you again!'

'Thank you, Mr Freudenthal. It's good to see you too. I want to get some things to carry back home to my mother.'

She bought several varieties of smoked fish, black olives, and a large square of almond paste. The grocer cast a keen glance over Shaman.

'Ehr is nit ah Yiddisheh,' he observed to her.

'Nein,' she said. Then, as if an explanation were called for, 'Ehr is ein guteh freind.'

Shaman didn't have to understand the language to realize what had been said. He felt a flash of resentment, but almost as quickly he realized that the old man's question was part of the reality that came along with her, like Hattie and Joshua. When he and Rachel had been children in a more innocent world there had been few dissimilarities to deal with, but now they were adults, and the differences had to be faced.

So when he accepted her packages from the grocer, he

544

smiled at the old man. 'Good day to you, Mr Freudenthal,' he said, and followed Rachel out of the store.

They brought the packages back to the hotel. It was time for dinner, and Shaman would have settled for the hotel dining room, but Rachel said she knew a better place. She took him to the Parkman Café, a small restaurant within walking distance of the hotel. It was unostentatious and moderately priced, but the food and service were good. After dinner, when he asked her what she would like to do next, she said she wanted to walk along the lake.

The breeze blew in from the water, but there was a reversion to summer warmth in the air. The sky held bright stars and the last phase of the harvest moon, but it was too dark for him to see her mouth, and they didn't talk. With another woman this would have made him anxious, but he knew Rachel took his silence for granted in the absence of visibility.

They walked along on the lake causeway until she paused beneath a street lamp and pointed ahead at a pool of yellow light. 'I hear wonderfully bad music, lots of cymbals!'

When they reached the lighted place they saw a curious sight, a round platform, large as a milking parlour in a barn, on which painted wooden animals were fixed. A thin man with a seamed and weathered face turned a great crank.

'Is it a music box?' Rachel said.

'*Non*, it is *un carrousel*. One chooses an animal and rides upon it, *très drole, très plaisant*,' the man said. 'Each ride twenty cents, mistaire.'

Rob sat on a brown bear. Rachel rode a horse painted an improbable red. The Frenchman grunted, turning the crank, and at once they began to whirl.

In the centre of the *carrousel* a brass ring hung from a pole, beneath a sign that said that a free ride would be awarded to anyone able to seize the ring while seated on a steed. Doubtless it was well out of the reach of most riders, but Shaman stretched his long body. When the Frenchman saw Shaman trying for the ring, he turned the crank faster and the *carrousel* speeded up, but Shaman snatched the ring on

545

his second try.

He earned several free rides for Rachel, but soon the proprietor called a halt in order to rest his arm, and Shaman got off his brown bear and took over the turning of the crank. He cranked faster and faster, and the red horse went from a canter to a gallop. Rachel threw her head back and screamed with laughter like a child as she passed him, her white teeth flashing. There was nothing childlike about her attraction. It wasn't only Shaman who was spellbound; the Frenchman stole fascinated peeks as he busied himself, preparing to close down. 'You are the last customair of 1864,' he told Shaman. 'It is *finis* for the season. Soon will come the ice.' Rachel stayed on for eleven rides. It was obvious that they'd kept the proprietor late; Shaman tipped him when he paid, and the man presented Rachel with a white glass mug on which a cluster of roses had been painted.

They got back to the hotel windblown and smiling.

'I had such a good time,' she said at the door of Room 306.

'So did I.' Before he could do or say anything else, she had kissed him lightly on the cheek and her door had opened and closed.

In his own room he lay on his bed for an hour, fully clothed. Finally he got up and walked down the two flights of stairs. It took her a little while to respond to his knock. He almost lost his courage and turned away, but at last the door opened, and she was there in her robe.

They stood and looked at one another. 'Shall you come in, or shall I come out?' she said. He saw she was nervous.

He went into her room and closed the door.

'Rachel –' he said, but she covered his mouth with her hand. 'When I was a young girl, I used to walk down the Long Path and stop at a certain perfect place where the woods dipped away to the river, just on my father's side of the boundary between our lands. I told myself you were going to grow older quickly and build a house there and save me from having to marry an old man with bad teeth. I pictured our children, a son like you and three daughters to whom you'd be loving and patient, allowing them to go to school and live in their home until they were ready to leave.'

'I've loved you all my life.'

'I know,' she said, and as he kissed her, her fingers worked on the buttons of his shirt.

They left the lamp on, so she could talk to him, and to see one another.

After making love she fell asleep as easily as a cat taking a nap, and he lay there and studied her breathing. At length she woke and her eyes widened to see him.

'Even after I was Joe's wife . . . even after I was a mother, I dreamed of you.'

'I somehow knew. That's what made it so bad.'

'I'm afraid, Shaman!'

'Of what, Rachel?'

'For years I've buried any hope of this . . . Do you know what an observant family does when someone marries out of the faith? They cover the mirrors with cloths and go into mourning. They say the prayer for the dead.'

'Don't be afraid. We'll talk to them until they understand.'

'And if they never understand?'

He felt a stab of fear, but the question had to be faced. 'If they don't, you'll have to make a decision,' he said.

They looked at one another.

'No more resignation to life, for either of us,' Rachel said. 'Correct?'

'Correct.'

They understood a commitment had been made, more serious than any vow, and they came together and clung as if each was a life raft.

The next day, on the train travelling west, they talked.

'I'll need time,' Rachel said.

When he asked how much time, she said she wanted to tell her father in person, not in a smuggled letter. 'It shouldn't be long. Everyone feels the war is almost over.'

'I've waited for you a long time. I can wait longer, I guess,' he said. 'But I won't meet you in secret. I want to call for you at your home, and take you out with me. And I want

547

to spend time with Hattie and Joshua, so we can come to really know each other.'

Rachel smiled and nodded. 'Yes,' she said, and took his hand.

She was being met in Rock Island by Lillian. Shaman left the train in Moline and went to the stable and claimed his horse. He rode upriver thirty miles and took the ferry across the Mississippi to Clinton, Iowa. That night he stayed at the Randall Hotel, in a good room with a marble mantel and hot and cold running water. The hotel had a marvellous five-storey brick privy, accessible from all floors. But next day the purpose of his visit was a disappointment, when he went to inspect the Inman Hospital. It was small, like the hospital that was planned for Holden's Crossing, but it was filthy and badly run, a lesson in what not to do. Shaman escaped as soon as possible and paid money to the captain of a flatboat to take him and Boss downriver to Rock Island.

A cold rain began to fall during his ride to Holden's Crossing, but he kept warm by thinking of Rachel and the future.

When finally he was home and had seen to his horse, he let himself into the kitchen to find his mother sitting very straight at the edge of her chair. Obviously she had been waiting eagerly for him to come back, because the words spilled from her as soon as he entered the door.

'Your brother is alive. He is a prisoner of war,' Sarah said.

65
A Telegraph Message

A letter from her husband had been delivered to Lillian Geiger the day before. Jason wrote that he'd seen the name of Corporal Alexander Bledsoe on a list of Confederate prisoners of war. Alex had been taken by Union forces on November 11, 1862, at Perryville, Kentucky.

'That's why Washington hasn't answered our letters asking if they had a prisoner named Alexander Cole,' Sarah said. 'He used my first husband's name.'

Shaman was exultant. 'At least he may still be alive! I'll write straight off, to try to find out where he's being held.'

'That would take months. If he's still living, he's been a prisoner almost three years. Jason writes that conditions are terrible in prison camps on both sides of the war. He says we should try to get to Alex right away.'

'Then I'll go to Washington myself.'

But his mother shook her head. 'I read in the newspaper that Nick Holden is coming to Rock Island and Holden's Crossing, to speak in favour of Lincoln's re-election. You go to him, and ask his help in finding your brother.'

Shaman was puzzled. 'Why should we go to Nick Holden instead of to our congressman or senator? Pa despised Holden for helping destroy the Sauks.'

'Nick Holden probably is Alex's father,' she said quietly.

For a moment Shaman was struck dumb.

'. . . I always thought . . That is, Alex believes his natural father is someone named Will Mosby.'

His mother looked at him. She was very pale, but her eyes were dry. 'I was seventeen years old when my first husband died. I was all alone in a cabin in the middle of the prairie, on what is now the Schroeder farm. I tried to keep on homesteading by myself, but I didn't have the strength. The land broke me quickly. I had no money. There were no jobs, and very few people hereabouts, then. First Will Mosby found me. He was a criminal, he'd be gone for long periods, but when he came back, he always had plenty of money. Then Nick started coming around.

'They were both handsome, charming men. At first I thought neither one knew about the other, but when I got pregnant, it turned out both of them knew, and each claimed the other was the father.'

Shaman found it difficult to speak. 'They furnished you no help at all?'

She gave him a bitter smile. 'Not so you'd notice. I think Will Mosby loved me and would have married me, finally, but he led a dangerous, reckless life, and he chose that moment to get killed. Nick stayed away, although I've always thought he was Alex's father. Alma and Gus had come and taken the land, and I suppose he knew the Schroeders would feed me.

'When I gave birth, Alma was there, but the poor thing gets addled in an emergency, and mostly I had to tell her what to do. After Alex came, for a few years life was very bad. First my nerves went, and then my stomach, and that brought on kidney stones.' She shook her head. 'Your father saved my life. Until he came along, I didn't believe there was such a thing in the world as a kind and gentle man.

'The thing is, I had sinned. When you lost your hearing, I knew I was being punished and it was my fault, and I couldn't hardly go near you. I loved you so much, and my conscience hurt me so bad.' She reached out and touched his face. 'I'm sorry you've had such a weak and sinful mother.'

Shaman took her hand. 'No, you're not weak and sinful.

you're a strong woman who needed real courage just to survive. For that matter, it took courage to tell me this story. My deafness isn't your fault, Ma. God doesn't want to punish you. I've never been so proud of you, nor loved you more.'

'Thank you, Shaman,' she said, and now when he kissed her, her cheek was wet.

Five days before Nick Holden was due to speak in Rock Island, Shaman left a note for him with the chairman of the County Republican Committee. It said that Dr Robert Jefferson Cole would deeply appreciate an opportunity to talk with Commissioner Holden about a matter of great and urgent importance.

On the day of the first political rally, Shaman went to Nick's large frame house in Holden's Crossing, where a secretary nodded when he gave his name.

'The commissioner's expecting you,' the man said, and showed Shaman into the office.

Holden had changed since Shaman had seen him last. He was stout, his grey hair was thinning, and webs of veins had appeared in the corners of his nose, but he still was a fine-looking man, and he wore assurance like a well-tailored suit of clothes.

'Well, by God, you're the little one, the youngest one, ain't you? And now you're a doctor? I'm certainly glad to see you. Tell you what, I need me a good country meal, you come along to Anna Wiley's Dining Room and let me buy you a Holden's Crossing dinner.'

Shaman had read his father's journal recently enough so that he still saw Nick through Rob J. Cole's eyes and pen, and the last thing he wanted was to break bread with him. But he knew why he was there, so he suffered being driven to the boardinghouse dining room on Main Street in Nick's carriage. Of course, they had to get out at the general store first, where he waited while Nick shook hands with each man on the porch, like a good politician, and made certain everyone there was acquainted with 'my good friend, our doctor'.

In the dining room Anna Wiley made a fuss over them, and Shaman got to eat her pot roast, which was good, and her apple pie, which was ordinary. And finally he got to tell Nick Holden about Alex.

Holden listened without interruption, then nodded. 'Been a prisoner three years, has he?'

'Yes sir. If he's still alive.'

Nick took a cigar from his inside breast pocket and offered it. When it was refused, he bit off the end and lighted it for himself, blowing thoughtful little puffs of smoke toward Shaman. 'Why'd you come to me?'

'My mother thought you'd be interested,' Shaman said.

Holden glanced at him and nodded. He smiled. 'Your father and I . . . You know, when we were young men, we were great friends. Had some high old times together.'

'I know,' Shaman said drily. Something in his tone must have warned Nick away from that topic. He nodded again. 'Well, you give your mother my warmest regards. And tell her I'll take a personal interest in this matter.'

Rob thanked him. Just the same, when he got home he wrote to his congressman and his senator, asking their help in locating Alex.

A few days after their return from Chicago, both Shaman and Rachel told their mothers they had decided to keep company.

Sarah's lips thinned when she heard, but she nodded without surprise. 'You'll be very good with her children, of course, the way your pa was good with Alex. If you have children of your own, will they be baptized?'

'I don't know, Ma. We haven't got that far yet.'

'I would talk about it, were I you two.' It was all she had to say to him about the matter.

Rachel wasn't that fortunate. She and her mother quarrelled often. Lillian was polite to Shaman when he came to her house, but showed him no warmth. He took Rachel and the two children out with him in the buggy whenever possible, but nature conspired against him, for the weather turned mean. Just as summer had come early and hot with almost no spring, so winter fell upon the plains prematurely that year. October was frigid. Shaman found his father's skates in the barn; he bought the children 'double runners' at Haskins' store and took them skating on the frozen buffalo slough, but it was too cold for long enjoyment. There was snow by election day, when Lincoln was easily re-elected, and on the eighteenth of the month a blizzard struck Holden's Crossing, and the ground had a white cover that would last until spring.

'Have you taken note of Alden's palsy?' his mother said to Shaman one morning.

As a matter of fact, he had been watching Alden for some time. 'He has Parkinson's disease, Ma.'

'What on earth is that?'

'I don't know what causes the trembling, but the disease affects the way he controls his muscles.'

'Is it going to kill him?'

'Sometimes it causes death, but not often. Most likely, it will slowly keep getting worse. Maybe cripple him.'

Sarah nodded. 'Well, poor soul's getting too old and sick to run this farm. We'll have to think about putting Doug Penfield in charge, and hire someone to help him. Can we afford it?'

They were paying Alden twenty-two dollars a month and Doug Penfield ten dollars. Shaman did some rapid calculations and finally nodded.

'And then what will become of Alden?'

'Well, he'll stay on in his cabin and we'll take good care of him, of course. But it's going to be hard to convince him to stop doing the hard work.'

'The best thing might be to ask him to do a lot of jobs that don't require great exertion,' she said shrewdly, and Shaman nodded.

'I think I've got one of those for him right now,' he said.

That evening he brought 'Rob J.'s scalpel' up to Alden's cabin.

'Needs sharpenin', does it?' Alden said, taking it from him.

Shaman smiled. 'No, Alden, I keep it sharp myself. It's a

surgical knife that's been in my family for hundreds of years. My father told me that in his mother's house it was kept in a glass-enclosed frame and hung on the wall. I wondered if you could make a frame for me.'

'I don't know why not.' Alden turned the scalpel in his fingers. 'Good piece of steel, here.'

'It is. It takes a wonderful edge.'

'I could make you a knife like this, should you want another.'

Shaman was intrigued. 'Would you try? Could you make one with a blade longer than this one, and narrower?'

'Shouldn't be a problem,' Alden said, and Shaman tried not to notice how his hand shook as he handed back the scalpel.

It was very hard, being so close to Rachel, and yet so far from her. There was no place where they could make love. They trudged in deep snow into the woods, where they bundled into each other's arms like bears and exchanged icy kisses and well-padded caresses. Shaman grew short-tempered and morose, and he noticed that Rachel was developing dark circles beneath her eyes.

When he left her, Shaman took vigorous walks. One day he trudged down the Short Path and noticed that the portion of Makwa-ikwa's wooden grave marker that stood above the snow was cracked. The weather had almost obliterated the runelike markings that his father had had Alden carve into the wood.

He felt Makwa's furious will rise through the earth, through the snow. How much of it was his imagination, how much his conscience?

I've done what I can. What more can I do? There's more to my life than the fact that you can't rest, he told her crankily, and he turned around and clumped through the snow, back to the house.

That afternoon he went to the home of Betty Cummings, who had severe rheumatism in both shoulders. He tied up his horse and was going to the back door when he saw, just beyond the barn, a double track and a series of curious markings.

He waded through a drift and knelt to examine them.

The marks in the snow were triangular in shape. They sank into the surface six inches or so, and they varied slightly in size, according to their depth.

These triangular wounds in the white were bloodless, and there were many more than eleven of them.

He remained kneeling, staring at them.

'Dr Cole?'

Mrs Cummings had come out and leaned over him, her face concerned.

She said the holes were made by her son's ski poles. He had fashioned the skis and the poles from hickory, whittling the ends into points.

They were too large.

'Is everything all right, Dr Cole?' She shivered and clutched her shawl closer, and he was suddenly ashamed for keeping a rheumatic old woman out in the cold.

'Everything's perfectly all right, Mrs Cummings,' he said, and he stood and followed her into her warm kitchen.

Alden had done a beautiful job on the frame for Rob J.'s scalpel. He had made it of quartered oak and had got a small remnant of light blue velvet from Sarah to mount the scalpel on. 'Couldn't find a piece of used glass, though. Had to buy the glass new from Haskins'. Hope that's all right.'

'It's more than all right.' Shaman was very pleased. 'I'll hang it in the front hall of the house,' he said.

He was even more pleased to see the scalpel Alden had made to his specifications.

'I forged it from an old brandin' iron. There's enough good steel left over for two or three more of these knives, should you want them.'

Shaman sat down with pencil and paper and drew a probing knife and an amputation fork. 'Do you think you could make these?'

'Don't doubt that I can.'

Shaman regarded him thoughtfully. 'We're going to have

a hospital here soon, Alden. That means we're going to need instruments, beds, chairs – all sorts of things. How would it be if you got somebody to help you make some of those things for us?'

'Well, it would be pleasant, but . . . Don't believe I can spare the time for all that.'

'Yes, I can see that. But suppose we hired somebody to work the farm with Doug Penfield, and they just met with you a couple of times a week so you would tell them what to do.'

Alden considered, then nodded. 'That might be fine.'

Shaman hesitated. 'Alden . . . how's your memory?'

'Good as the next person's, I suppose.'

'Near as you can remember, tell me where everybody was the day Makwa-ikwa was killed.'

Alden sighed heavily and lifted his eyes heavenward. 'Still at it, I see.' But with a little persuasion, he cooperated. 'Well, to begin with you. You was asleep in the woods, I'm told. Your pa was out callin' on his patients. I was over to Hans Grueber's, helpin' him butcher in exchange for your pa's gettin' the use of his bullocks to pull the manure spreader in our pastures . . . Let's see, who's left?'

'Alex. My mother. Moon and Comes Singing.'

'Well, Alex was off someplace, fishin', playin', I dunno. Your mother and Moon . . . I remember, they was cleanin' out the springhouse, gettin' it ready to hang meat in when we done our own butcherin'. The big Indian was workin' with the stock, and then later, workin' in the woods.' He beamed at Shaman. 'How's that for memory?'

'It was Jason who found Makwa. How had Jay spent his day?'

Alden was indignant. 'Now, how the hell am I supposed to know? You want to know about Geiger, talk to his wife.'

Shaman nodded. 'I think I'll do that,' he said.

But when he returned to the house, all other thoughts were driven from his mind, because his mother told him that Carroll Wilkenson had ridden over with a message for him. It had come to the telegraph office in Rock Island.

His fingers trembled as badly as Alden's while he tore at

556

the envelope.

The message was concise and businesslike:

Corporal Alexander Bledsoe, 38th Louisiana Mounted Rifles, presently incarcerated as prisoner of war, Elmira Prison Camp, Elmira, New York. Please call upon me if any other way I can be of service. Good luck. Nicholas Holden, US Cmsr., Indian Affairs.

66

The Elmira Camp

In the president's office at the bank, Charlie Andreson
looked at the amount on the withdrawal form and pursed
his lips.

Although it was Shaman's money to withdraw, without
hesitation he told Andreson the reason he was taking it,
because he knew the banker could be trusted with confiden-
tial business. 'I'll need funds to help him.'

Andreson nodded, and left his office. When he returned,
he carried a stack of currency in a small cloth basket. He also
had a money belt that he handed to Shaman. 'A little gift
from the bank to a valued patron. Along with our heartfelt
best wishes and some advice, if you don't mind. Keep the
money in the belt and wear it next to your skin, under your
clothing. Do you own a pistol?'

'No.'

'Well, you should buy one. You're going a distance, and
there are dangerous men out there who would kill without
thought to get hold of this much money.'

Shaman thanked the banker and placed the currency and
the belt into a small tapestry bag he'd brought with him. He
was riding down Main Street when he realized he *did* have
a gun, the Colt .44 his father had taken from a dead
Confederate in order to kill a horse, and had brought back
from the war. Ordinarily it wouldn't have occurred to

Shaman to travel armed, but he couldn't afford to let anything get in the way of his finding and helping Alex, and he turned the horse and rode back to Haskins' store, where he bought a box of ammunition for the .44. The bullets and the revolver were heavy and took up room in the single valise that he carried, along with his medical bag, when he left Holden's Crossing the next morning.

He took a steamer downriver to Cairo and then rode east by rail. Three times, there were long delays as his trains were held up in order to allow troop trains to go through. It was four days and nights of hard travel. The snow disappeared when he left Illinois, but not the winter, and the hard cold that dominated the rocking railroad cars crept into Shaman's bones. When finally he reached Elmira he was travel-weary, but he made no attempt to bathe or change his clothing before trying to see Alex, because he had an irresistible urge to make certain his brother was alive.

Outside the station, he walked past a hansom cab and took a buggy instead so he could sit next to the driver and see what he was saying. The driver said proudly that the town's population had reached fifteen thousand. They travelled through a pleasant town of small homes to a neighbourhood on the outskirts of Elmira, and down Water Street, along what the man said was the Chemung River. Soon a wooden fence delineated the prison.

The driver was proud of the local embellishment and practised in his delivery of facts. He told Shaman the fence was built twelve feet high of 'native boards', and enclosed twenty eight acres on which more than ten thousand captured Confederates lived. 'Been up to twelve thousand rebels in there, at times,' he said.

He pointed out that four feet from the top of the fence and on the outside was a catwalk on which armed sentries patrolled.

They drove down West Water Street, where entrepreneurs had made the camp a human zoo. A three-storey-high wooden tower, complete with stairs that led to a railed platform, allowed anyone with fifteen cents to look down on the milling men within the walls.

'Used to be two towers here. And a whole bunch of refreshment stands. Sold cakes, crackers, peanuts, lemonade, and beer to them watchin' the prisoners. But the damn army closed 'em down.'

'Pity.'

'Yeah. You wanna stop and go up, have yourself a look?'

Shaman shook his head. 'Just let me out at the main gate to the camp, please.'

There was a very military coloured sentry at the gate. It appeared that most of the sentries were Negroes. Shaman followed a private to a headquarters orderly room, where he identified himself to a sergeant and requested permission to see the prisoner called Alexander Bledsoe.

The sergeant conferred with a lieutenant who sat behind a desk in a tiny office, and then emerged to mutter that there'd been a message from Washington on Dr Cole's behalf, which made Shaman think more kindly of Nicholas Holden.

'Visits are no more than ninety minutes.' He was told that the private would take him to his brother at tent Eight-C, and he followed the Negro over frozen ruts, deep into the camp. Everywhere he looked, there were prisoners, listless, miserable, ill-clothed. He understood at once that they were half-starved. He saw two men standing at an overturned barrel on which they were skinning a rat.

They bypassed a number of low wooden barracks. Beyond the barracks were rows of tents, and beyond the tents a long narrow pond that obviously was used as an open sewer, because the closer Shaman drew to it, the stronger its stink became.

Finally the Negro soldier stopped in front of one of the tents. 'This is Eight-C, suh,' he said, and Shaman thanked him.

Inside, he found four men whose faces were pinched with cold. He didn't know them, and his first thought was that one of them was a man who shared Alex's name, and he had come all this way because of a case of mistaken identity.

560

'I'm looking for Corporal Alexander Bledsoe.'

One of the prisoners, a man-boy whose dark moustaches were far too large for his bony face, motioned at what had seemed to be a pile of rags. Shaman approached it cautiously, as if a feral animal waited beneath the dirty cloths – two feed bags, a piece of carpeting, something that may once have been a coat. 'We keep his face covered against the cold,' the dark moustaches said, and reached down and removed a feed sack.

It was his brother, yet not so much his brother. Shaman might have passed him in the street without recognition, because Alex was vastly changed. He was very thin, and age had been etched into him by experiences Shaman didn't want to consider. Shaman took his hand. Eventually Alex opened his eyes and stared up at him without recognition.

'Bigger,' Shaman said, but couldn't go on.

Alex blinked up at him in bewilderment. Then realization crept into his mind like a tide slowly taking possession of a battered shore, and he began to cry.

'Ma and Pa?'

They were the first words Alex spoke to him, and Shaman lied instantly and instinctively. 'They're both well.'

The brothers sat and held each other's hands. There was so much to say, so much to ask and to tell, that they were at first struck dumb. Soon the words began to come to Shaman, but Alex wasn't up to it. Despite his excitement, he began to drift back into sleep, and it told Shaman how sick he was.

He introduced himself to the other four men, and learned their names. Berry Womack of Spartanburg, South Carolina, short and intense, with long dirty blond hair. Fox J. Byrd of Charlottesville, Virginia, who had a sleepy face and slack skin, as if once he'd been fat. James Joseph Waldron of Van Buren, Arkansas, stocky, swarthy, and the youngest there, no more than seventeen, Shaman guessed. And Barton O. Westmoreland of Richmond, Virginia, the boy with the large moustaches, who shook hands fiercely and told Shaman to call him Buttons.

While Alex slept, Shaman examined him.

His left foot was gone.

'. . . Was he shot?'

'No, sir,' Buttons said. 'I was with him. A whole bunch of us were bein' transferred here by train from the prison camp at Point Lookout, Maryland, last July 16 . . . Well, there was a terrible train wreck in Pennsylvania . . . Sholola, Pennsylvania. Forty-eight prisoners of war and seventeen federal guards, killed. They just buried 'em in a field close to the tracks, like after a battle.

'Eighty-five of us were hurt. Alex's foot was crushed so bad, they just cut it off. I was real lucky, only had a sprained shoulder.'

'Your brother did right well for a while,' Berry Womack said. 'Jimmie-Joe made him a crutch and he was right nimble with it. He was the sick-sergeant in this tent and took care of us all. Said he learned a little doctorin' from watchin' your daddy.'

'We call him Doc,' Jimmie-Joe Waldron said.

When Shaman lifted Alex's leg, he saw it was the source of his brother's troubles. The amputation had been done badly. The leg wasn't yet gangrenous, but half the ragged stump was unhealed, and beneath the scar tissue in the healed portion there was pus.

'You a sure-enough doctor?' Waldron said when he saw the stethoscope. Shaman said he was. He positioned the bell on Alex's chest for Jimmie-Joe, and he was elated to conclude from the Waldron's reports that the lungs were blessedly clear. But Alex was feverish, and his pulse was light and thready.

'There is pestilence, sir, all through the camp,' Buttons said. 'Smallpox. Any number of fevers. Malaria, many varieties of agues. What do you reckon is wrong with him?'

'His leg is mortified,' Shaman said heavily. It was obvious that Alex also suffered from malnutrition and exposure to the cold, as did the other men in the tent. They told Shaman that some tents had tin stoves and some had a few blankets, but most had neither.

'What do you eat?'

'In the morning each man gets a piece of bread and a small

piece of bad meat. In the evening each man gets a piece of bread and a cup of what they call soup, the water the bad meat was boiled in,' Buttons Westmoreland said.

'No vegetables?'

They shook their heads, but he already knew the answer. Signs of scurvy had greeted him as soon as he'd entered the camp.

'When we came here, there were ten thousand of us,' Buttons said. 'They keep adding prisoners, but only five thousand of the original ten thousand are left. They have a busy dead house, and a big cemetery just beyond the camp. About twenty-five men die here every day.'

Shaman sat on the cold ground and held Alex's hands, watching his face. Alex slumbered on, too deeply.

Presently the guard stuck his head through the flap and told him it was time.

In the headquarters orderly room, the sergeant listened impassively as Shaman identified himself as a physician and described his brother's symptoms. 'I'd like to be allowed to take him home. I know if he remains imprisoned, he'll die.'

The sergeant rummaged in a file and came up with a card, which he studied. 'Your brother isn't eligible for parole. He's been an engineer here. That's what we call a prisoner who's tried to tunnel out.'

'Tunnel!' Shaman said wonderingly. 'How could he dig? He has only one foot.'

'He has two hands. And before he came here, he escaped from another camp and was recaptured.'

Shaman tried to use reason. 'Isn't it what you'd have done? What any honourable man might do?'

But the sergeant shook his head. 'We got our rules.'

'May I bring him a few things?'

'Nothing sharp or made of metal.'

'Is there a boardinghouse nearby?'

'There's a place, eighth of a mile west of the main gate. They rent out rooms,' the sergeant said, and Shaman thanked him and picked up his bags.

563

As soon as Shaman was in his rented room and rid of his landlord, he removed one hundred and fifty dollars from his money belt and placed the bills in his coat pocket. There was a handyman who was happy to drive the new boarder to town for a fee. At the telegraph office Shaman sent a message to Nick Holden in Washington: *Alex is gravely ill. Must secure his release or he will die. Please help.*

There was a large stable and livery, where he rented a horse and a flatbed wagon.

'By the day or the week?' the stableman asked. Shaman rented by the week, and paid in advance.

The general store was larger than Haskins', and he filled his rented wagon with things for the men in Alex's tent: firewood, blankets, a dressed chicken, a side of sound bacon, six loaves of bread, two bushels of potatoes, a sack of onions, a crate of cabbages.

The sergeant's eyes widened when he saw the 'few things' Shaman had brought for his brother. 'You've already used today's ninety minutes. Just unload that plunder and get out.'

At the tent, Alex was still sleeping. But for the others, it was like Christmas in good times. They called in their neighbours. Men from a dozen tents came in and got wood and vegetables. Shaman had meant the things to make a real difference to the men of tent Eight-C, but they had chosen to share most of the things he had brought.

'Do you have a pot?' he asked Buttons.

'Yessir!' Buttons produced a very large and battered tin can.

'Cook a soup of chicken meat, onions, cabbage, potatoes, and some of the bread. I'm counting on you to get as much hot soup into him as possible.'

'Yessir, we will,' Buttons said.

Shaman hesitated. An alarming amount of food already had disappeared. 'I'll bring more tomorrow. You must try to keep some of it for those in this tent.'

Westmoreland nodded somberly. They both knew the unspoken condition that had been laid down and accepted: above all, Alex must be fed.

564

His landlord kept Shaman's water pitcher filled and urged him to drink, with as much pleasure in his voice as if he were offering wine. The water was pleasant-tasting but unremarkable so far as Shaman could tell.

'Even the wells in the prison camp have excellent water. That is no small thing. Was your brother perhaps in Point Lookout, as so many others in this camp were?'

Shaman nodded.

'They will tell you the water at Point Lookout was poison.'

Shaman couldn't resist pointing out that despite the wonderful water, a large number of prisoners of war died in the Elmira camp.

The landlord nodded. 'Water alone cannot provide health. The government's first interest is in waging the war, and not in nurturing prisoners.' He sighed, and confided it was common knowledge that the surgeon in the camp was a sorry example of Dr Cole's profession, and possessed by demons that caused him to consume many of the drugs the government furnished for his patients. 'You must attempt to get your brother released as early as possible.'

When he went to the camp the next morning, Alex was asleep, and Jimmie-Joe was watching him. Jimmie-Joe said he had taken a good amount of soup.

When Shaman adjusted the blankets, Alex awoke with a start, and Shaman patted his shoulder. 'It's all right, Bigger. It's only your brother.' Alex closed his eyes again, but in a moment he spoke. 'Is old Alden still alive?'

'Yes, he is.'

'Good . . .' Alex opened his eyes and caught sight of the stethoscope peeping out of the medical bag. 'What you doin' with Pa's bag?'

'. . . I borrowed it,' Shaman said hoarsely. 'I'm a doctor now myself.'

'You're never!' Alex said, as if they were children telling whoppers.

'Yes, I am,' he said, and they smiled at one another before Alex fell back into a sound sleep. He took Alex's pulse and didn't care for it one bit, but there was nothing he could do about it just then. Alex's unwashed body stank generally, but when Shaman uncovered the stump and bent to sniff it, his heart sank. Long exposure to his father and then to Lester Berwyn and Barney McGowan had given him the knowledge that there was nothing good about what less-enlightened surgeons welcomed as 'laudable pus'. Shaman knew that pus in an incision or wound often meant the onset of blood poisoning, abscesses, or gangrene. He knew what had to be done, and he knew it couldn't be done in the prison camp.

He covered his brother with two of the new blankets and sat there and held his hands and studied his face.

When the soldier kicked him out of the prison camp after an hour and a half, Shaman drove the rented horse and wagon southeast along the road that followed the Chemung River. The country was more hilly than Illinois, and more wooded. About five miles beyond the town line he came to a general store whose sign said it was Barnard's. Inside, he bought some crackers and a piece of cheese for his lunch, and then had two slices of good apple pie and two cups of coffee. When he asked the proprietor about accommodations in the area, the man gave him directions to Mrs Pauline Clay's a mile down the road, outside the village of Wellsburg.

The house proved to be small and unpainted, and surrounded by woods. Four rosebushes were wrapped with flour sacks against the cold, and tied with baling cord. A small sign on the picket fence said ROOMS.

Mrs Clay had an open, friendly face. She sympathized at once when he told her about his brother, and showed him through the place. Her sign should have been singular, he saw at once, because there were only two bedrooms. 'Your brother could have the guest room, and you could have mine. I often sleep on the couch,' she said.

She was clearly taken aback when he said he wanted to rent the entire house.

'Oh, I'm afraid . . .' But her eyes widened when he disclosed what he was willing to pay. She said frankly that

566

a widow who had struggled for years couldn't refuse such generosity, and that she could move into her sister's house in the village while the Cole brothers were in her place.

Shaman went back to Barnard's store and loaded up on foodstuffs and supplies, and while he moved them into the house that afternoon, Mrs Clay was moving out.

The following morning, the sergeant was grumpy and decidedly cool, but obviously the army had heard from Nick Holden, and perhaps from some of his friends.

The sergeant gave Shaman a printed sheet that was a formal parole, promising that, in return for Alex's freedom, 'the undersigned shall not again bear arms against the United States of America.'

'You have your brother sign this, and you can take him.'

Shaman was worried. 'He might not be well enough to sign.'

'Well, the rule is, he has to give his parole or he isn't released. I don't care how sick he is, if he doesn't sign, he doesn't go.'

So Shaman brought ink and a pen to Tent Eight-C, and he had a quiet conversation with Buttons outside the tent. 'Will Alex sign this thing if he's able?'

Westmoreland scratched his chin. 'Well, some are willing to sign it in order to get out of here, and some consider it a disgrace. I don't know how your brother feels.'

The box the cabbages had come in was on the ground near the tent, and Shaman overturned it and placed the paper and the ink on it. Dipping the pen, he quickly wrote on the bottom of the page: *Alexander Bledsoe.*

Buttons nodded in approval. 'That's right, Dr Cole. You get his arse out of this hellish place.'

Shaman told each of Alex's tentmates to write the name and address of one of his loved ones on a piece of paper, and he promised to write and tell them the men were alive.

'You reckon you can get the letters through the lines?' Buttons Westmoreland asked.

'I believe I can, once I get back home.'

Shaman worked fast. He left the parole with the sergeant, and he hurried to the boardinghouse for his suitcase. He paid the handyman to fill the wagon with loose straw, and then he drove back to the camp. A Negro sergeant and a private oversaw the prisoners as they loaded Alex into the wagon and covered him with blankets.

The men of tent Eight-C gripped Shaman's hand and made their goodbyes.

'So long, Doc!'

'Goodbye, ole Bledsoe!'

'Give 'em hell!'

'Get well, now!'

Alex, whose eyes remained closed, gave them no response.

The sergeant waved them off, and the private clambered up and took the reins, driving the horse as far as the main gate of the camp. Shaman studied his dark and serious face and smiled, remembering something from his father's journal.

'Jubilee day,' he said. The soldier looked startled, but then he smiled, showing fine white teeth.

'I believe you right, suh,' he said, and handed over the reins.

The wagon springs were poor; lying in the straw, Alex was jostled. He cried out in pain and then groaned as Shaman drove through the gates and turned onto the road.

The horse moved the wagon past the observation tower, past the end of the wall around the prison. From the catwalk a soldier with a rifle watched them intently as they moved away.

Shaman kept the horse under tight rein. He could make no speed without torturing Alex, but he moved slowly also because he wanted to call no attention to themselves. However irrationally, he felt that at any moment the long arm of the United States Army would reach out and pluck his brother back, and he didn't begin to breathe evenly until the walls of the prison camp were far behind them and they had passed beyond the town line, out of Elmira.

568

67
The House in Wellsburg

Mrs Clay's house felt friendly. It was so small there was very little to learn about it, and it quickly became familiar, as if Shaman had lived in it for many years.

He built a roaring fire in the stove that soon turned the iron of the firebox a fierce cherry red; then he heated water in Mrs Clay's largest cooking pots and filled the bathtub, which he'd placed next to the warmth.

When Alex was set into the water like a babe, his eyes widened with pleasure.

'When's the last time you had a real bath?'

Alex slowly shook his head. Shaman knew it had been so long ago, he couldn't remember. He didn't dare let Alex sit and soak, lest he catch a chill as the water cooled, so he washed him with a soapy rag, trying to ignore the fact that Alex's ribs felt like a washboard beneath the cloth, and taking care to be as gentle as possible with the mortified left leg.

When he took his brother out of the tub, he set him down on a blanket in front of the stove and towelled him dry, then put a flannel nightshirt on him. A few years ago, carrying him upstairs would have been a challenging task, but Alex had lost so much weight it wasn't difficult.

Once Alex had been placed in the bed in the guest room, Shaman went to work. He knew exactly what needed to be done. There was no sense in waiting, and delay might result in a good deal of danger.

He removed everything from the kitchen but the table and one chair, stacking the other chairs and the dry sink in the parlour. Then he scrubbed the walls, the floor, the ceiling, the table, and the chair with hot water and strong soap. He washed the surgical instruments and laid them out on the chair, within easy reach of the table. Finally he trimmed his fingernails short and scrubbed his hands.

When he carried Alex down again and placed him on the table, his brother looked so vulnerable that for a moment Shaman was shaken. He was very certain about what he was doing, except for this part. He had brought chloroform with him, but he wasn't certain how much to use, because the trauma and malnutrition had left Alex so weak.

'What?' Alex complained drowsily, confused by all the carrying.

'Breathe deeply, Bigger.'

He spilled chloroform and held the cone over Alex's face as long as he dared. Please God, he thought.

'Alex! You hear me?' Shaman pinched Alex's arm, slapped him lightly on the cheek, but he slept deeply.

Shaman didn't need to think or plan. He had done his thinking at length, and he had planned carefully. He forced all emotion from his mind and set about to do what was needed.

He wanted to keep as much of the limb as possible, while at the same time taking enough to make certain that the amputated portion would include all the infected bone and tissue.

He made the first circular incision at a place six inches below the insertion of the hamstring muscle, and prepared a good flap for the stump to come, stopping the cutting only to tie off the great and small saphenous veins, the tibial veins, and the peroneal vein. He sawed through the tibia with the same motions as a man cutting kindling. He proceeded to saw through the fibula, and the infected portion of the limb was free – a neat, clean job.

Shaman bandaged tightly with clean dressings, to make a

570

well-shaped stump. With that done, he kissed the still-unconscious Alex and then carried him back to bed.

For a time he sat by the bed and watched his brother, but there was no sign of trouble, no nausea or vomiting, no cries of pain. Alex slumbered like a labourer who deserved his rest.

Eventually Shaman carried the severed piece of leg out of the house in a towel, along with a spade he'd found in the cellar. He went into the woods behind the house and attempted to bury the amputated section of tissue and bone, but the ground was deeply frozen, and the spade skittered along the icy surface. Finally he gathered wood and made a pyre to give the piece of leg a Viking's funeral. He placed the flesh-log on wood and heaped more wood on it, and sprinkled a little lamp oil. When he struck a match, the fire flared. Shaman stood near it with his back against a tree, dry-eyed but filled with terrible emotion, convinced that in the best of worlds, a man shouldn't have to cut off and burn his big brother's leg.

The sergeant in the orderly room at the prison camp was familiar with the non-commissioned hierarchy in his region, and he knew this fat barrel-chested sergeant major wasn't stationed in Elmira. Ordinarily he would ask a soldier coming from elsewhere to identify the unit to which he was attached, but this man's demeanor, and especially his eyes, said clearly that he was looking to garner information, not to give it.

The sergeant knew that sergeant majors weren't deities, but he was acutely aware that they ran the army. The few men who were the army's highest possible non-coms could arrange for someone to get a good assignment or a punishment posting to an isolated fort. They could get a man in or out of military trouble, and they could make or break careers. In the sergeant's real world, a sergeant major was more intimidating than any commissioned officer, and he hastened to be accommodating.

'Yessir, Sarn Majuh,' he said smartly after examining the records. 'You've missed him by little moren' a day. This

571

fella's real sick. Has only the one foot left, you see. His brother's a doctor, name of Cole. Took him away in a wagon just yesterday morning.'

'Which direction they go?'

The sergeant looked at him and shook his head.

The fat man grunted, spat on the clean floor. Leaving the orderly room, he mounted his beautiful brown cavalry mare and rode through the main gate of the prison camp. One day's start was nothing, when the brother was toting an invalid. There was just the one road; they could have taken only one direction or the other. He chose to turn northwest. From time to time, whenever he passed a store, or a farmhouse, or another traveller, he stopped and made inquiry. In that way, he passed through the village of Horseheads, and then through the village of Big Flats. Nobody he talked to had seen the men he was looking for.

The sergeant major was an experienced tracker. He knew that when a trail was this invisible, most likely it was the wrong trail. So he turned his horse and began to ride in the other direction. He rode past the prison camp, and through the town of Elmira. Two miles down the road, a farmer remembered seeing their wagon. A couple of miles past the Wellsburg town line, he came to a general store.

Inside, the proprietor smiled to see the fat soldier crowd close to his stove. 'A cold one, ain't it?' When the sergeant major asked for coffee, black, he nodded and served it.

He nodded again when the man asked his question.

'Oh, certainly. They're boarding at Mrs Clay's, I'll tell you how to find it. Awfully nice feller, Dr Cole. He's been in to buy groceries and such. Friends of yours, are they?'

The sergeant major smiled. 'It will be good to see them,' he said.

The night following the operation, Shaman sat in a chair next to his brother's bed, and kept the lamp burning throughout the long night. Alex slept, but his slumber was pain-ridden and restless.

Toward daybreak, Shaman drifted into sleep for a brief time. When he opened his eyes in the grey light, he saw

572

Alex looking at him.

'Hey, Bigger.'

Alex licked dry lips, and Shaman brought water and supported his head while he drank, allowing him only a few small sips.

'Wondering,' Alex said finally.

'What?'

'How I can ever . . . kick your ass again . . . without falling on my face.'

How good it was for Shaman to see his crooked grin!

'You whittled away more of my leg, didn't you?' Alex's gaze was accusatory, which stung the exhausted Shaman.

'Yes, but I saved something else, I think.'

'What's that?'

'Your life.'

Alex considered, and then he nodded. In a moment he went back to sleep.

That first postoperative day, Shaman changed the dressings twice. Each time, he sniffed the stump and studied it, terrified lest he detect the stink or sight of corruption, because he'd seen many die of infection within a few days of amputation. But there was no smell, and the pink tissue above the stump appeared to be sound.

Alex had almost no fever, but he had little energy, and Shaman had no confidence in his brother's recuperative powers. He began to spend time in Mrs Clay's kitchen. Midmorning he fed Alex a small amount of gruel, and at midday a coddled egg.

Shortly after noon, large white flakes began to fall thickly outside. Snow soon covered the ground, and Shaman took an uneasy account of the supplies he had put in, and decided he would like to take the wagon to the general store once more, in case they should be snowed in. During an interval in which Alex was awake, he explained what he was going to do, and Alex nodded that he understood.

It was pleasant, driving through the silent, snowy world. The real reason he had come was to get a soup fowl; to his disappointment, Barnard hadn't a fowl to sell, but he had

573

some decent beef that would make nourishing soup, and Shaman told him that would have to do.

'Your friend find you all right?' the storekeeper asked, trimming the fat.

'Friend?'

'That soldier. I told him how to ride to Mrs Clay's house from here.'

'Oh? When was that?'

'Yesterday, couple of hours before closing. Heavy man, fat. Black beard. Lots of stripes,' he said, touching his arm. 'He never came?' He looked narrowly at Shaman. 'I suppose it was all right to tell him where you are?'

'Of course, Mr Barnard. Whoever it was, he probably decided he didn't have time for a visit after all, and drove right by.'

What does the army want now? Shaman thought as he left the store.

Halfway home, he was afflicted with the feeling that he was being watched. He resisted the urge to turn in the wagon seat and look back, but in a few minutes he pulled the horse up and descended to fuss with the bridle, as though making an adjustment. At the same time, he took a good look behind him.

It was hard to see through the falling snow, but then the wind brought a high swirl, and Shaman could see there was a rider following, distant.

When he reached the house, he saw that Alex was fine. He unhitched the wagon and settled the horse in the barn, and went back in and put the meat on the stove to simmer in water, along with potatoes, carrots, onions, and turnips.

He was troubled. He debated whether to disclose what he had learned to Alex, and finally he sat by the bed and told him. 'So, we may have a visit from the army,' he concluded.

But Alex shook his head. 'If it was the army, they'd have hammered on our door right away. . . . Somebody like you, come to get a kinsman out of prison, is bound to be carrying money. More likely, he's after that. . . . I don't suppose you own a gun?'

'I do.' He went and dug the Colt from his bag. At Alex's insistence, he cleaned it while his brother watched, and loaded it, making certain a fresh round was in the chamber. When he placed it on the bed table, he was even more troubled than before. 'Why would this man just wait and watch us?'

'Scouting us . . . to make certain we're alone here. To study the lamplight at night and learn which bedroom we're in . . . things like that.'

'I think we're making too much of this,' Shaman said slowly. 'I think probably the man who inquired about us is some kind of army intelligence soldier, making certain we're not planning to help other prisoners get out of the camp. We'll probably never hear of him again.'

Alex shrugged and nodded. But Shaman had a harder time believing his own words. If there was to be trouble, the last circumstance he'd have chosen was to be holed up in this house next to his weak and newly amputated brother.

That afternoon, he gave Alex warm milk sweetened with honey. He wanted to force-feed him with rich puddings, to will flesh back on his ribs, but he knew it would take time. Early in the afternoon Alex slept again, and when he awoke several hours later, he wanted to talk.

Slowly Shaman learned what had happened to him after he had left home.

'Mal Howard and I worked our way down to New Orleans on a flatboat. We had a falling-out over a girl, and he went on alone to Tennessee to enlist.' Alex stopped and looked at his brother. 'Do you know what's happened to Mal?'

'His people haven't heard a word.'

Alex nodded without surprise. 'I almost came home then. I wish I had. But there were Confederate recruiters all over the place, and I enlisted. I thought I could ride and shoot, so I joined the cavalry.'

'Did you see much fighting?'

Alex nodded sombrely. 'Two years' worth. I was so damn mad at myself when I was captured in Kentucky! They kept us in a stockade a baby could have walked away from. I waited my chance, then I skedaddled. I was free for three days, stealing food from gardens and such. Then I stopped at a farmhouse and asked for something to eat. A woman gave me breakfast, and I thanked her like a gentleman, didn't make any improper moves, which was probably my mistake! Half an hour later I heard the pack of dogs they turned out after me. I ran into this enormous cornfield. Tall green stalks, planted stingy close, so I couldn't pass between the rows. I had to break them down as I ran, so it looked like a bear had been in there. I was in that corn most of a morning, running from the dogs. I began thinking I'd never get out. Then I came out on the far side of the planting, and there were these two Yankee soldiers pointing their guns and grinning at me.

'This time, the federals sent me to Point Lookout. That was the worst prison camp! Bad food or none, foul water, and they'd shoot you dead if you came within four paces of the fence. I was surely glad when they shipped me out of there. But then, of course, the train wreck happened.' He shook his head. 'I just remember a big grinding noise and a pain in my foot. I was unconscious awhile, and when I woke up, they had already cut my foot off, and I was on another train heading for Elmira.'

'How did you manage to tunnel after an amputation?'

Alex grinned. 'That was easy. I heard that a bunch was tunnelling out. I was feeling pretty good, those days, and I took a turn digging. We tunnelled two hundred feet, right under the wall. My stump wasn't healed and I kept getting it dirty in the tunnel. Maybe that's why I had trouble with it. I couldn't go out with them, of course, but ten men ran free, and I never heard that any of them got caught. I used to go to sleep happy, thinking about those ten free men.'

Shaman drew a breath. 'Bigger,' he said, 'Pa is dead.'

Alex was silent for a while, then nodded. 'I believe I knew when I saw you had his bag. If he was alive and well, he'd have come for me himself instead of sending you.'

Shaman smiled. 'Yes, that's true.' He told his brother what had happened to Rob J. before he had died. During the telling, Alex began to weep weakly, and he took Shaman's hand. When the narrative was over, they sat silently, hands still clasped. Well after Alex had fallen asleep, Shaman sat there without letting go.

It snowed until late afternoon. After night fell, Shaman went to a window on every side of the house in turn, and peered outside. The moonlight gleamed on unbroken snow, no tracks. By that time he had worked out an explanation. He thought the fat soldier had been sent looking for him because somebody needed a doctor. Perhaps the patient had died or recovered, or maybe the man had found another physician and no longer needed Dr Cole.

It was plausible, and it comforted him.

He gave Alex a bowl of rich broth for supper, with a softened cracker in it. His brother slept fitfully. Shaman had thought to sleep that night in the bed in the other room, but he dozed off in the chair next to Alex's bed.

Early in the morning – he saw by his watch next to the gun on the table that it was 2:43 – he was awakened by Alex. His brother's eyes were wild. Alex had pulled himself half out of the bed.

Someone is breaking a window downstairs, Alex mouthed.

Shaman nodded. He stood and picked up the gun, holding it in his left hand, an unfamiliar tool.

He waited, his eyes on Alex's face.

Had Alex imagined it? Maybe dreamed it? The bedroom door was closed. Perhaps he'd heard the sound of breaking icicles?

But Shaman stood still. His whole body became his hand on the piano sounding board, and he could feel the stealthy steps.

'He is inside,' he whispered.

Now he began to sense the ascent, like the notes on a rising scale.

'He's coming up the stairs. I'm going to blow out the lamp,' He saw that Alex understood. They knew the layout of the bedroom, while the intruder didn't, an advantage in the dark. But Shaman was agonized, because without light

577

he couldn't read Alex's lips.

He took his brother's hand and placed it on his own leg. 'When you hear that he's in the room, squeeze,' he said, and Alex nodded.

Alex's single boot was on the floor. Shaman shifted the gun to his right hand and bent and picked up the boot, then blew out the lamp flame.

It seemed a very long time. There was nothing to do but wait, frozen in darkness.

Finally the cracks around the bedroom door changed from yellow to black. The intruder had reached the lamp in the hallway wall and had snuffed it so he wouldn't be silhouetted in the doorframe.

Trapped in his familiar world of perfect silence, Shaman sensed when the man had opened the door, informed by the flow of frigid air from the opened window.

And Alex's hand squeezing his leg.

He threw the boot across the room, to the far wall.

He saw the twin yellow blossomings, one after the other, and tried to aim the heavy Colt to the right of the spurts of flame. When he pulled the trigger, the revolver bucked savagely in his hand, and he used both hands to hold the gun as he pulled the trigger again and again, feeling the blasts, blinking at each flare, smelling the devil's breath. When the gun was finished, feeling more naked and more vulnerable than ever before, Shaman stood and waited for the smashing bite of return fire.

'You all right, Bigger?' he called at last, like a fool, unable to hear any reply. He fumbled for the matches on the table and finally lighted the lamp with unsteady hands.

'All right?' he said to Alex again, but Alex was stabbing with his finger toward the man on the floor. Shaman was a poor gunfighter. Had the man been able, he might have shot both of them, but he wasn't able. Shaman approached him now as if he were a hunted bear whose mortality was uncertain. His own wild marksmanship was evident, because there were holes in the wall, and a splintered floor. The intruder's shots had missed the shoe but had ruined the upper drawer of Mrs Clay's maple dresser. The man lay on his side as if sleeping, a fat soldier with a black beard, a look of surprise on the dead face. One of the shots had nicked him in the left leg, at just the point where Shaman had cut off Alex's limb. Another had hit him in the chest, directly over his heart. When Shaman palpated his carotid artery, the flesh of this throat was still warm but there was no pulse.

Alex had no resources left, and he quickly fell apart. Shaman sat on the bed and held his brother in his arms, rocking him like a child while he trembled and wept.

Alex was certain that if the death were discovered, he'd go back to prison. He wanted Shaman to take the fat man into the woods and burn him, the way he'd burned Alex's leg.

Shaman comforted him and patted his back, but he was thinking clearly and coldly.

'I killed him, you didn't. If anyone's in trouble, it isn't you. But this man will be missed. The storekeeper knows he was coming here, and maybe so do others. This room is damaged and needs a carpenter, who would talk about it. If I hide or destroy his body, I can hang. We're not going to touch his body again.'

Alex calmed. Shaman sat with him and they talked until the grey light of day came into the room and he was able to extinguish the lamp. He carried his brother downstairs to the parlour and laid him on the sofa under warm blankets. He filled the stove with wood and reloaded the Colt and set it on a chair next to Alex. 'I'll be back with the army. For God's sake, don't shoot anyone until you make certain it isn't us.'

He looked into his brother's eyes. 'They're going to question us, again and again, apart and together. It's important that you tell the exact truth about everything. That way, they can't twist what we tell them. You understand?'

Alex nodded, and Shaman patted him on the cheek and left the house.

The snow was knee-deep and he didn't take the wagon. There was a halter hanging in the barn and he put it on the horse and rode her bareback. Well past Barnard's store, it was slow going over the snowy ground, but after the Elmira line the snow had been packed down by rollers, and he made better time.

He felt numb, and not from the cold. He had lost patients he thought he should have saved, and that always bothered him. But he had never killed a human before.

He reached the telegraph office early and had to wait until it opened at seven a.m. Then he sent a message to Nick Holden:

Have killed soldier in self-defence. Please send civil, military authorities in Elmira your endorsements at once regarding my character and that of Alex Bledsoe Cole. Gratefully, Robert J. Cole.

He went directly to the office of the sheriff of Steuben County and reported a homicide.

68
Struggling in the Web

In a short time, Mrs Clay's little house was crowded. The sheriff, a stocky grey-haired man named Jesse Moore, suffered from morning dyspepsia, and he frowned occasionally and belched often. He was accompanied by two deputies, and his message to the army had quickly summoned five soldiers: a first lieutenant, two sergeants, and a pair of privates. Within half an hour Major Oliver P. Poole arrived, a swarthy bespectacled officer with thin black moustaches. Everyone deferred to him – clearly he was in charge.

At first the soldiers and civilians spent their time viewing the body, going in and out of the house, clumping up and down the stairs in their heavy boots, and conversing privately, with their heads close together. They wasted whatever heat was in the house and tracked in snow and ice that made a disaster of Mrs Clay's waxed wooden floors.

The sheriff and his men were watchful, the military men were very serious, and the major was coldly polite.

Upstairs in the bedroom, Major Poole examined the bullet holes in the floor, the wall, the bureau drawer, and the body of the soldier.

'You can't identify him, Dr Cole?'

'I never saw him before.'

'Do you suppose he wanted to rob you?'

'I don't have the slightest idea. All I know is, I threw that boot at the wall in a dark room, and he shot at the sound, and I shot at him.'

'Have you looked in his pockets?'

'No, sir.'

The major proceeded to do so, placing the contents of the fat soldier's pockets on the blanket at the foot of the bed. There wasn't much: a can of Clock-Time snuff; a bunched-up and snot-encrusted handkerchief; seventeen dollars and thirty-eight cents; and an army furlough that Poole read and then passed to Shaman. 'Does the name mean anything to you?'

The furlough had been made out to Sergeant Major Henry Bowman Korff, Headquarters, US Army Eastern Quartermaster Command, Elizabeth, New Jersey.

Shaman read it and shook his head. 'I never saw or heard that name before,' he could say honestly.

But a few minutes later, as he started to descend the stairway, he realized that the name had produced troublesome echoes in his mind. Halfway down the stairs, he knew why.

Never again would he have to speculate, as his father had until he died, regarding the whereabouts of the third man who had fled Holden's Crossing the morning Makwa-ikwa was raped and killed. He no longer had to search for a fat man named 'Hank Cough'. Hank Cough had found him.

Presently the coroner came to declare the deceased legally dead. His greeting to Shaman was cool. All the men in the house displayed open or reserved antagonism, and Shaman understood its source. Alex was their enemy; he'd fought against them, probably killed Northerners, and until lately had been their prisoner of war. And now Alex's brother had killed a Union soldier in uniform.

Shaman was relieved when they loaded the ponderous dead man onto a litter and laboriously carried him down the stairs and out of the house.

That was when the serious questioning began. The major sat in the bedroom in which the shooting had taken place.

582

Near him, on another kitchen chair, one of the sergeants sat and took notes of the interrogation. Shaman sat on the edge of the bed.

Major Poole asked about his affiliations, and Shaman told him the only two organizations he'd ever joined were the Society for the Abolition of Slavery while he was in college, and the Rock Island County Medical Society.

'Are you a Copperhead, Dr Cole?'

'I am not.'

'You don't have even the slightest sympathy for the South?'

'I don't believe in slavery. I want the war to end without additional general suffering, but I'm not a supporter of the Southern cause.'

'Why did Sergeant Major Korff come to this house?'

'I've no idea.' He had decided almost immediately not to mention the long-ago murder of an Indian woman in Illinois, and the fact that three men and a covert political society had been implicated in her violation and death. It was all too remote, too arcane. He understood that to open it up would be to invite the incredulity of this unpleasant army officer, and a myriad of dangers.

'You're asking us to accept that a sergeant major in the United States Army was killed attempting an armed robbery.'

'No, I'm not asking you to accept anything. Major Poole, do you believe that I issued an invitation to this man to break a window in my rented house, enter it illegally at two o'clock in the morning, and come upstairs and into my brother's sickroom, firing a gun?'

'Then why did he do it?'

'I don't know,' Shaman said, and the major frowned at him.

While Poole questioned Shaman, in the parlour the lieutenant questioned Alex. At the same time, the two privates and the sheriff's deputies were conducting a search of the barn and the house, inspecting Shaman's luggage, emptying bureau drawers and closets.

From time to time there was a break in the questioning while the two officers conferred.

'Why didn't you tell me your mother is a Southerner?' Major Poole asked Shaman after one such pause.

'My mother was born in Virginia but has lived in Illinois more than half her life. I didn't tell you that because you didn't ask me.'

'These were found in your medicine bag. What are they, Dr Cole?' Poole laid out on the bed four pieces of paper. 'Each has a person's name and address. A Southern person.'

'They're the addresses of kinfolk of my brother's tent-mates in the Elmira prison camp. Those men cared for my brother and kept him alive. When the war is over, I'll write to determine whether each of them made it through. And, if so, thank them.'

The questioning droned on and on. Often Poole duplicated questions he'd asked before, and Shaman repeated his former answers.

At midday the men departed to get food at Barnard's store, leaving the two privates and one of the sergeants in the house. Shaman went into the kitchen and cooked a gruel, bringing a bowl to Alex, who looked dangerously exhausted.

Alex said he couldn't eat.

'You must eat, it's your way of continuing to fight!' Shaman told him fiercely, and Alex nodded and began to spoon the pasty stuff into his mouth.

After lunch, the interrogators exchanged places, the major questioning Alex, the lieutenant directing his queries at Shaman. Midafternoon, to the irritation of the officers, Shaman called a halt in the proceedings and took his time changing the dressing on Alex's stump, before an audience.

To Shaman's amazement, Major Poole asked him to accompany three of the soldiers to the place in the woods where he had burned the amputated section of Alex's leg. When he had pointed out the place, they dug away the snow and grubbed in the charcoal remains of the fire until they had recovered some bits of whitened tibia and fibula that they placed into a kerchief and took away. The men departed by late afternoon. The house felt blessedly uncrowded, but insecure and violated. A blanket had been tacked over the broken window. The floors were muddy, and the air retained the odour of their pipes and their bodies.

Shaman heated the meat soup. To his pleasure, Alex suddenly displayed real hunger, and he gave his brother ample portions of beer and vegetables as well as broth. It stimulated his own hunger as well, and following the soup they ate bread and butter with jam, and applesauce, and he brewed fresh coffee.

Shaman carried Alex upstairs and placed him in Mrs Clay's bed. He tended to his brother's needs and sat by his side until late, but finally he went back into the guest room and fell exhausted into the bed, trying to forget that there were bloodstains on the floor. That night, they slept little.

Next morning, neither the sheriff nor his men appeared, but the soldiers were there before Shaman had cleaned up after breakfast.

At first it appeared that the day was to be a repeat of the preceding one, but the morning was still early when a man knocked at the door and announced himself to be George Hamilton Crockett, an assistant United States Commissioner for Indian Affairs, stationed in Albany. He sat with Major Poole and conferred at length, transferring to the officer a sheaf of papers to which they referred several times in the course of their conversation.

Presently the soldiers gathered up their things and put on their coats. Led by the sullen Major Poole, they went away.

Mr Crockett remained for some time, talking with the Cole brothers. He told them they had been the subject of a large number of telegraph messages from Washington to his office.

'The incident is unfortunate. The army finds it hard to swallow the fact that it has lost one of its own, in a Confederate soldier's house. They are accustomed to killing Confederates who kill them.'

'They've made that clear, with their questions and their persistence,' Shaman said.

'You have nothing to fear. The evidence is too obvious. Sergeant Major Korff's horse was tied up in the woods where it was hidden. The sergeant major's footprints in the snow went from the horse to the window at the rear of the house. The glass was broken, the window left open. When they examined his body, he was still holding the gun, which had been fired twice.

'In the heat of wartime passions, an unscrupulous investigation might overlook the strong evidence in such a case, but not when powerful interested parties are scrutinizing it closely.'

Crockett smiled, and extended the warm greetings of the Honorable Nicholas Holden. 'The commissioner has asked me to assure you he'll come to Elmira himself if he's needed. I'm happy to be able to assure him that such a journey won't be necessary.'

The next morning Major Poole sent one of the sergeants with word that the Cole brothers were requested not to leave Elmira until the investigation was formally closed. When the sergeant was asked when that might be, he said, politely enough, that he didn't know.

So they stayed on in the small house. Mrs Clay had heard at once what had happened, and she paid a white-faced visit, peering wordlessly at the broken window and in horror at the bullet holes and the bloodstained floor. Her eyes filled when she saw the ruined bureau drawer. 'That was my mother's.'

'I'll see it's repaired, and the house set to rights,' Shaman said. 'Can you recommend a carpenter?'

She sent someone over that afternoon, a lanky, aging man named Bert Clay, a cousin of her late husband's. He tut-tutted, but went right to work. He brought glass in the proper dimension and repaired the window straightaway. The shambles in the bedroom was more complicated. The splintered floorboards had to be replaced, and the blood-stained section sanded and refinished. Bert said he'd fill the holes in the wall with plaster and paint the room. But he looked at the bureau drawer and shook his head. 'I dunno.

That's bird-eye maple. I might be able to find a piece of that someplace, but it'll be *dear*.'

'Get it,' Shaman said grimly.

It took a week for the repairs to be made. When Bert was finished, Mrs Clay came and inspected everything closely. She nodded and thanked Bert and said it would do, even the bureau drawer. But she was cool to Shaman and he understood that her home would never be the same to her.

Everyone he met was cold. Mr Barnard no longer smiled and chatted when Shaman came into the store, and he saw people look at him in the street and say things to one another. The general animosity got on his nerves. Major Poole had confiscated the Colt when he came to the house, and both Shaman and Alex felt unprotected. Shaman went to bed at night with the fireplace poker and a kitchen knife on the floor next to the bed, and he lay awake as the house shook in the wind, and tried to detect the vibrations of intruders.

At the end of three weeks Alex had gained weight and looked better, but he was chafing to be away from there, and they were relieved and happy when Poole sent word that they could leave. Shaman had bought Alex civilian clothes, and he helped his brother into them, pinning up the left trouser leg so it wouldn't get in his way. Alex tried walking with the aid of his crutch, but he had difficulty. 'I feel lopsided with that much of the leg gone,' he said, and Shaman told him he would get used to it.

Shaman bought a great wheel of cheese at Barnard's and left it on the table for Mrs Clay, a guilt offering. He had arranged to return the horse and wagon to the stableman at the railroad station, and Alex rode to the depot lying on straw, the way he had left the prison camp. When the train arrived, Shaman carried him aboard in his arms and settled him in a window seat while other passengers stared or looked away. They talked little, but as the train lurched out of Elmira, Alex placed his hand on his brother's arm, and the gesture spoke volumes.

They travelled home via a more northerly route than the one

Shaman had used to come to Elmira. Shaman aimed for Chicago instead of Cairo, because he didn't trust the Mississippi to be unfrozen when they reached Illinois. The journey was hard. The lurching of the train brought Alex severe and unremitting pain. There were many transfers along the route, and each time, Alex had to be carried from train to train in his brother's arms. Trains almost never arrived or left on schedule. Numerous times, the train they rode in was shunted to a side track to allow a troop train to go through. Once, for about fifty miles, Shaman managed to get them upholstered chairs in a parlour car, but most of the time they travelled on the hard wooden seats of coaches. By the time they reached Erie, Pennsylvania, there were white patches in the corners of Alex's mouth, and Shaman knew his brother could travel no more.

He took a room in a hotel so Alex could rest for a time in a soft bed. That evening, as he changed the dressing, he began to tell Alex some of the things he'd learned from reading his father's journal.

He told him of the fate of the three men who had raped and murdered Makwa-ikwa. 'I believe it's my fault Henry Korff came after us. When I was at the asylum in Chicago where David Goodnow is being held, I talked too much about the murderers. I asked about the Order of the Star-Spangled Banner, and about Hank Cough, and I left a definite impression that I'd cause them as much trouble as I could. Someone on the staff probably was a member of the order – perhaps everyone running the asylum is! No doubt they got word to Korff, and he decided to come after us.'

Alex was quiet for a moment, but then he looked at his brother in concern. 'But Shaman . . . Korff knew where to look for us. Which means somebody in Holden's Crossing informed him you'd left for Elmira.'

Shaman nodded. 'I have thought about that a great deal,' he said quietly.

They reached Chicago a week after they left Elmira. Shaman sent a telegraph message to his mother, telling her he was bringing Alex home. He disclosed that Alex had lost a leg, and asked her to meet their train.

When the train arrived in Rock Island an hour late, she was on the station platform with Doug Penfield. Shaman carried Alex down the coach steps, and Sarah threw her arms about her son and wept wordlessly.

'Let me put him down, he's heavy,' Shaman complained at last, and he placed Alex on the seat of the buggy. Alex had been crying too. 'You look good, Ma,' he said finally. His mother sat next to him and held his hand. Shaman handled the reins, while Doug rode his horse, which had been tied to the back of the buggy.

'Where's Alden?' Shaman asked.

'He's taken to his bed. He's been failing, Shaman, the palsy is much worse. And he slipped and had a bad fall a few weeks ago, when they were cutting ice on the river,' Sarah said.

Alex watched the countryside hungrily as they travelled. So did Shaman; he felt strange. Just as Mrs Clay's house would always seem different to her, so was his life afflicted. Since his departure from here, he had killed a man. The world seemed awry.

When they reached home at dusk, they placed Alex in his own bed. He lay there with his eyes closed, sheer pleasure in his face.

Sarah cooked for her prodigal son's return. She fed him roasted chicken and potatoes mashed with carrots. No sooner was supper done than Lillian came hurrying down the Long Path carrying a tureen of stew. 'Your days of hunger are over!' she told Alex after she had kissed him and welcomed him home.

She told him Rachel had to stay with her children but would be over to see him in the morning.

Shaman left them talking, his mother and Lillian seated as close to Alex as their chairs would allow. He walked up to Alden's cabin. When he let himself in, Alden was asleep, and the cabin smelled of raw whisky. Shaman let himself out quietly and walked down to the Long Path. The snow on the path had been trampled and then had frozen, and it was slippery in spots. When he reached the Geiger house, through the front window he could see Rachel sitting and reading by the fire. She dropped her book at his rap on the glass.

They kissed as though one of them was dying. She took his hand and led him up the stairs to her room. The children were asleep down the hall, her brother Lionel was mending harness in the barn, and her mother could come home at any time, but they made love on Rachel's bed with their clothes on, sweetly and determinedly, and with a desperate gratitude.

When he walked back over the path, the world was on an even plane again.

69
Alex's Last Name

Shaman's heart sank when he saw Alden making his way about the farm. There was a stiffness to his neck and shoulders that hadn't been there when Shaman had left home, and his face seemed a rigid, patient mask, even when the attacks of palsy were severe. He did everything slowly and deliberately, like a man moving underwater.

But his mind was clear. He found Shaman in the barn shed and delivered the small display case he'd fashioned to house Rob J.'s scalpel, and the new bistoury Shaman had asked him to make. He sat Shaman down and gave him a rundown of how the farm had survived the winter – the number of animals, the amount of fodder consumed, the prospects for spring lambing. 'I'm having Doug move seasoned wood to the sugar house, so we can boil syrup soon as the weather tells the sap to run.'

'Good,' Shaman said. He steeled himself for the unpleasant task, and told Alden casually that he had instructed Doug to find a good worker to help handle the spring chores.

Alden nodded slowly. He harrumphed for a long time to clear his throat, and then carefully spat. 'Ain't as spry as I once was,' he said, as if breaking the news gently.

'Well, let somebody else plough this spring. No need for the farm manager to do the hard work when we can get young fellas to use their muscles,' Shaman said, and Alden nodded again before he moved out of the shed. Shaman saw that it took him a time to begin to walk, like a man who had made up his mind to piss, but couldn't. But then, when he began, it was as if his feet moved steadily in their own small rush, and the rest of Alden just went along for the ride.

It felt good for Shaman to get back to his practice. No matter how carefully the nursing nuns tried to look after his patients, they couldn't substitute for a doctor. For several weeks he worked hard, catching up on postponed surgery and making more home visits every day than had been his custom.

When he stopped at the convent, Mother Miriam Ferocia greeted him warmly and listened to his report of Alex's return with quiet joy. She had news of her own. 'The archdiocese has sent word that our preliminary budget has been authorized, and they ask us to move ahead with the construction of the hospital.'

The bishop had reviewed the plans himself, and had approved them, but had advised against building the hospital on convent grounds. 'He says the convent is too inaccessible, too far from the river and the main roads. So we must search for a site.'

She reached behind her chair and handed Shaman two heavy cream-coloured bricks. 'What do you think of these?'

They were hard and almost rang when he tapped them together. 'I don't know much about brick, but they look wonderful.'

'They will make walls like a fortress,' the prioress said. 'The hospital will be cool in summer, warm in winter. This is vitrified brick, so dense it won't absorb water. And it's available nearby, from a man named Rosswell, who has built a kiln near his clay deposits. He has enough on hand to allow construction to begin, and he is eager to make more. He says if we desire a darker colour, he can smoke the brick.'

Shaman hefted the bricks, which felt solid and real, as though he held the very walls of the hospital in his hands. 'I think this colour is perfect.'

'So do I,' Mother Miriam Ferocia said, and they grinned at one another with pleasure, like children sharing a sweetmeat.

Late at night, Shaman sat in the kitchen and drank coffee with his mother. 'I've told Alex about his . . . relationship to Nick Holden,' she said.

'. . . And how did he take it?'

Sarah shrugged. 'He just . . . accepted it.' She smiled wanly. 'He said he might as well have Nick for a father as a dead outlaw.' She was silent for a moment, but then she turned toward Shaman again, and he saw she was nervous.

'The Reverend Mr Blackmer is leaving Holden's Crossing. The minister of the Baptist church in Davenport has been called to Chicago, and the congregation has offered the pulpit to Lucian.'

'I'm sorry. I know how you value him. And now the church here will have to search for a new clergyman.'

'Shaman,' she said, 'Lucian has asked me to go with him. To marry him.'

He took her hand, which was cold. '. . . And what do you want to do, Mother?'

'We have become . . . very close since his wife died. When I was widowed, he was a tower of strength.' She gripped Shaman's hand tightly. 'I loved your father completely. I'll always love him.'

'I know.'

'In a few weeks, it will be a year since his death. Would you resent me if I remarried?'

He rose and went to her.

'I'm a woman who needs to be a wife.'

'I just want your happiness,' he said, and put his arms around her.

She had to struggle back from the embrace so he could see her lips. 'I told Lucian we can't be married until Alex no longer needs me.'

'Ma, he'll do better when you stop waiting on him hand and foot.'

'Really?'

'Really.'

Her face had become radiant. He had a heart-stopping glimpse of what she had looked like when she was young.

'Thank you, darling Shaman. I'll tell Lucian,' she said.

Alex's stump was healing beautifully. He was fussed over interminably by his mother and by the ladies of the church. Although he gained weight and his bony frame began to fill out, he seldom smiled, and his eyes held shadows.

A man named Wallace was making a reputation and a business in Rock Island as a builder of false limbs, and after much urging, Alex agreed to allow Shaman to take him there. Hanging along the wall of Wallace's workshop was a fascinating array of carved wooden hands, feet, legs, and arms. The limb-maker had the rotund physical makeup that led men to be classified as jolly, but he took himself very seriously. He spent more than an hour measuring while Alex stood, sat, stretched, walked, flexed one knee, flexed both knees, knelt, and lay down as if retiring for the night. Then Wallace told them to call for the false leg in six weeks.

Alex was only one of an army of returned cripples. Shaman saw them whenever he went to town, former soldiers with missing parts, and many of them with maimed spirits. His father's old friend Stephen Hume returned as a one-star general, having won a battlefield promotion to brigadier at Vicksburg three days before taking a bullet just below his right elbow. He hadn't lost the limb, but the wound had destroyed the nerves, so that the appendage was useless, and Hume carried it in a black sling, as if he had a permanent broken arm. Two months before Hume came home, the Honourable Daniel P. Allan, Justice of the Circuit Court of Illinois, had died, and the governor appointed the hero general to take his place. Judge Hume was already hearing cases. Shaman saw that some former soldiers had the ability to return to civilian life without blinking, while others had problems that haunted and disabled them.

He tried to consult with Alex whenever a decision had to be made about the farm. Hired help still was scarce, but Doug Penfield found a man named Billy Edwards who had worked with sheep in Iowa. Shaman spoke with him and saw him to be strong and willing, and he came well-recommended by George Cliburne. Shaman asked Alex if he wanted to interview Edwards.

'No, I don't care to.'

'Wouldn't it be a good idea if you did? After all, the man will be working for you when you go back to farming.'

'Don't believe I'll go back to farming.'

'Oh?'

'Perhaps I'll work with you. I can be your ears, like that fellow you told me about at the Cincinnati hospital.'

Shaman smiled. 'I don't need full-time ears. I can borrow somebody's ears anytime I need them. Seriously, do you have an idea what you'll want to do?'

'. . . I don't rightly know.'

'Well, you have time to decide,' Shaman said, and was happy to let the matter rest.

Billy Edwards was a good worker, but when he stopped work, he was a talker. He talked of soil quality and of sheep breeding, and of crop prices and the difference it made if you had a railroad. But then he talked of the return of the Indians to Iowa, and he had Shaman's attention.

'What do you mean, they came back?'

'A mixed group of Sauk and Mesquakie. They left the reservation in Kansas and came back to Iowa.'

Like Makwa-ikwa's group, Shaman thought. '. . . Are they having any trouble? From the people of the area?'

Edwards scratched his head. 'No. Nobody can rightly make'm any trouble. These are *smart* Indians, who bought their own land, all legal. Paid good American cash.' He grinned. 'Course, the land they bought is most likely the worst in the state, lots of yellow soil. But they got cabins on it, and a few fields in crops. Got a real little town. They call it Tama, after one of their chiefs, I'm told.'

'Where is this Indian town?'

'About a hundred miles west of Davenport. And a little north.'

Shaman knew he wanted to go there.

A few mornings later, he studiously avoided asking the US Commissioner for Indian Affairs about the Sauks and Mesquakies in Iowa. Nick Holden rode to the Cole farm in a splendid new carriage with a driver. When both Sarah and Shaman thanked him for his help, Holden was polite and friendly, but it was clear he'd come to see Alex.

He spent the morning in Alex's room, sitting next to the bed. When Shaman had finished with his duties in the dispensary at midday, he was surprised to see Nick and his driver helping Alex into the carriage.

They were gone all afternoon and part of the evening. When they returned, Nick and the driver assisted Alex into the house, wished everyone a polite good evening, and went away.

Alex didn't speak much about the events of the day. 'We drove around some. We talked.' He smiled. 'That is, mostly he talked and I listened. We had a good dinner at Anna Wiley's dining room.' He shrugged. But he appeared thoughtful, and he went to bed early, fatigued by the activity of the day.

Next morning Nick and the carriage were back. This time, Nick took Alex to Rock Island, and that evening Alex described the fancy dinner and supper they had enjoyed at the hotel.

The third day they went to Davenport. Alex came home earlier than he had on the other two trips, and Shaman heard him wish Nick a pleasant journey back to Washington.

'I'll stay in touch, if I may,' Nick said.

'By all means, sir.'

That night when Shaman came up to bed, Alex called him into his room. 'Nick wants to claim me,' he said.

'Claim you?'

Alex nodded. 'The first day he was here, he told me President Lincoln has asked for his resignation so he can appoint somebody else. Nick says it's time he came back here and settled down. He has no desire to marry, but he'd like a son. Said he's always known he was my father. We spent three days driving all around the area, looking at his

596

properties. He also owns a profitable pencil factory in western Pennsylvania, and who knows what-all. He wants me to become his heir and change my name to Holden.'

Shaman felt a sadness, and an anger. 'Well, you said you didn't want to farm.'

'I told Nick I had no doubt who my father was. My father was the man who took all my hell-raising and youthful shit without blinking, and who gave me discipline and love. I told him my name was Cole.'

Shaman touched his brother's shoulder. He was unable to speak, but he nodded. Then he kissed Alex on the cheek and went to bed.

On the day when the artificial leg had been promised, they returned to the limb shop. Wallace had carved the foot cleverly, so it would take a stocking and a shoe. Alex's stump fitted into the socket, and the limb was fastened to his leg by means of leather straps below and above his knee.

From the first moment Alex put on the limb, he hated it. It gave him terrible pain to wear it.

'It's because your stump is tender,' Wallace said. 'The more you wear the leg, the sooner the stump will develop calluses. Pretty soon it won't hurt you at all.'

They paid for the leg and took it home. But Alex placed it in the hall closet and wouldn't wear it, and when he walked he dragged himself along on the crutch made for him by Jimmie-Joe in the prison camp.

On a morning in mid-March, Billy Edwards was manoeuvering a wagonload of logs around the barnyard, trying to turn the team of oxen rented from young Mueller. Alden was standing behind the wagon, leaning on his cane and shouting instructions to the befuddled Edwards.

'Back 'em up, boy! Back 'em on up!'

Billy obeyed. It was reasonable to assume, since Alden had ordered him to back the wagon, that the older man would step out of the way. A year before, Alden might have done so easily and without incident, but now, although his mind told him to move out of harm's way, his disease wouldn't allow the message to pass swiftly into his legs. A log projecting out of the end of the wagon struck him on the right side of his chest with the force of a battering ram, and he was thrown several feet, to lie limply in the muddy snow.

Billy burst into the dispensary, where Shaman was in the midst of examining a newcomer named Molly Thornwell, whose pregnancy had survived the long trip from Maine. 'It's Alden. I believe I've killed him,' Billy said.

They carried Alden inside and set him on the kitchen table. Shaman cut away his clothing and examined him carefully.

White-faced, Alex had left his room and made his own hopping way down the stairs. He looked at Shaman inquiringly.

'He has several broken ribs. We can't take care of him in his cabin. I'm going to put him in the guest room, and I'll move back into our room with you.'

Alex nodded. He moved to the side and watched as Shaman and Billy brought Alden upstairs and into the bed.

A while later, Alex had an opportunity to be Shaman's ears, after all. He listened intently to Alden's chest and reported what he heard. 'Will he be all right?'

'I don't know,' Shaman said. 'His lungs appear to be undamaged. Broken ribs can be tolerated by a strong and healthy person. But at his age, and with the problems of his disease . . .'

Alex nodded. 'I'll sit by him and nurse him.'

'Are you certain? I can ask Mother Miriam for nurses.'

'Please, I'd like to,' Alex said. 'I have plenty of time.'

So in addition to the patients who placed their faith in Shaman, he had two members of his own household who needed him. Though he was a compassionate physician, he discovered that taking care of loved ones wasn't the same as taking care of other patients. There was a special edge and urgency to the responsibility and the daily concern. As he hurried home at the end of each day, the shadows seemed longer and darker.

Still, there were bright moments. One afternoon, to his delight, Joshua and Hattie came to visit him alone. It was their first unescorted trip down the Long Path, and they were dignified and serious as they asked Shaman if perhaps he could take the time to play. He was pleased and honoured to wander off with them into the woods for an hour, to see the first bluets and the clear tracks of a deer.

Alden was in pain. Shaman gave him morphine, but for Alden the best painkiller was distilled from grain. 'All right, give him whisky,' Shaman told Alex, 'but in moderation. Is that understood?'

Alex nodded, and he was true to his word. The sickroom came to have Alden's characteristic whisky smell, but he was allowed only two ounces at noon and two ounces in the evening.

Sometimes Sarah or Lillian relieved Alex as Alden's nurse. One evening Shaman took over, sitting next to the bed and reading a surgical journal that had arrived from Cincinnati. Alden was restless, slipping in and out of troubled slumber. When he was in a half-sleeping state he muttered and conversed with unseen persons, reliving farm conversations with Doug Penfield, cursing at predators after the lambs. Shaman studied the old seamed face, the tired eyes, the great red nose with its hairy nostrils, thinking of Alden as he had first known him, strong and capable, the former fair fighter who had taught the Cole boys to use their fists.

Alden quieted and slept deeply for a time, and Shaman finished an article on greenstick fractures and was just beginning to read of cataract of the eye when he looked up and saw Alden looking at him calmly, his eyes unpuzzled and hard in a brief moment of clarity.

'I didn't mean for him to try to kill you,' Alden said. 'I just thought he'd scare you off.'

70
A Trip to Nauvoo

Sharing their room once more, sometimes Shaman and Alex felt as if they small boys again. Lying abed sleepless, one morning at daybreak Alex lit the lamp and described for his brother the sounds of the vernal loosening – the lush bursts of birdsong, the tinkling impatience of rivulets beginning their annual rush to the sea, the hurtling roar of the river, the occasional grinding crash as giant ice cakes collided. But Shaman's mind wasn't on the nature of nature. Instead, he pondered the nature of man, and he remembered things, and added the sums of occurrences that suddenly could be connected in meaningful ways. More than once in the middle of the night he rose from bed to pad through the silent house over chill floors in order to consult his father's journals.

And he watched over Alden with special care and a strange kind of fascinated tenderness, a new and cold vigilance. Sometimes he looked at the old hired man as if he were seeing him for the first time.

Alden continued in a restless half-sleep. But one evening when Alex listened through the stethoscope, his eyes widened. 'There's a new sound . . . as if you took two locks of hair and rubbed them together with your fingers.'

Shaman nodded. 'Those sounds are called rales.'

'What do they mean?'

'Something's amiss with his lungs,' Shaman said.

On April 9, Sarah Cole and Lucian Blackmer were married in the First Baptist Church of Holden's Crossing. The ceremony was performed by the Reverend Gregory Bushman, whose pulpit Lucian would be filling in Davenport. Sarah wore her best grey dress, which Lillian had enlivened by adding a collar and cuffs of white lace that Rachel had finished tatting only the day before.

Mr Bushman spoke well, obviously taking pleasure in marrying a fellow minister in Christ. Alex told Shaman that Lucian declared his vows in confident clergyman's tones and that Sarah spoke hers in a soft and trembling voice. When the ceremony was complete and they turned, Shaman saw that his mother was smiling behind her short veil.

After the wedding service the congregation removed to the Cole farmhouse. Most congregants came to the reception with a covered dish, but Sarah and Alma Schroeder had cooked and Lillian had baked all week in preparation. People ate and ate, and Sarah showed her happiness. 'We've depleted the hams and sausages in the springhouse. You'll need a spring butchering this year,' she told Doug Penfield.

'My pleasure, Mrs Blackmer,' Doug said gallantly, the first person to call her by that name.

When the last guest had departed, Sarah took her packed valise and kissed her sons. Lucian drove her in his buggy to the parsonage she would leave within a few days, to move with him to Davenport.

A short time later, Alex went to the hall closet and took out the false leg. He strapped it on without asking for help. Shaman settled down in the study, reading medical journals. Every minute or so, Alex clumped by the open door, traversing the length of the hallway with hesitant steps. Shaman could feel the impact of the false leg being raised too high and then lowered, and he knew the pain that each step brought his brother.

By the time he entered the bedroom, Alex already had escaped into sleep. The stocking and shoe still were on the leg, and the limb stood on the floor next to Alex's right shoe,

601

looking as if it belonged there.

Next morning, Alex wore the limb to church, a wedding present for Sarah. The brothers weren't churchgoers, but their mother had asked them to attend that Sunday as part of her wedding observance, and she didn't take her eyes from her firstborn as he walked down the aisle to the front-row pew that belonged to the minister's family. Alex leaned on an ash walking stick that Rob J. had kept to lend out to patients. Sometimes he dragged his false foot, and sometimes he still lifted it too high. But he didn't lurch or fall, and he made his way steadily until he reached Sarah.

She sat between her sons, watching her new husband lead his congregation in devotions. When it was time for his sermon, he began by expressing gratitude to those who had joined in celebrating his nuptials. He said that God had led him to Holden's Crossing and now God was leading him away, and he thanked those who had made his ministry so meaningful to him.

He was just warming to the task of mentioning by name some of the individuals who had helped him in the Lord's work, when a variety of sounds began to enter the church through the half-open front windows. First there was faint cheering, which quickly became louder. A woman screamed, and there were hoarse shouts. Someone on Main Street fired a shot, and there followed an entire fusillade.

The church door opened suddenly, and Paul Williams came in. He hurried down the aisle and up to the minister, to whom he whispered urgently.

'Brothers and sisters,' Lucian said. He seemed to be having trouble speaking. 'A telegraph message has been received in Rock Island. . . . Robert E. Lee yesterday surrendered his army to General Grant.'

A buzz swept the congregation. Some stood. Shaman saw that his brother leaned back in the pew, his eyes closed.

'What does it mean, Shaman?' his mother asked.

'It means it's finally over and done with, Ma,' Shaman said.

It seemed to Shaman that wherever he went for the next four days, people were drunk with peace and hope. Even the grievously ill smiled and spoke of the better days that had arrived, and there was exhilaration and laughter, as well as sorrow, because everyone knew somebody who had been lost.

When he returned home that Thursday after making his rounds, he found Alex both hopeful and anxious, because Alden was showing signs that puzzled him. Alden's eyes were open and he was aware. But Alex said the rales in his chest sounded heavier. 'And he feels warm to me.'

'Are you hungry, Alden?' Alex asked him. Alden looked at him, but didn't reply. Shaman had Alex prop him up and they fed him some broth, but it was difficult because his palsy was worse. They had fed him only soup or gruel for days, because Shaman had been afraid he would aspirate food into his lungs.

In truth, Shaman had little medicine to give him that would do any good. He poured turpentine into a bucket of boiling water and made a tent with a blanket, enclosing both the bucket and Alden's face. Alden breathed in the fumes for a long time, and ended up coughing so copiously that Shaman removed the bucket and didn't try that particular course of treatment again.

The bittersweet joy of that week turned to horror on Friday afternoon, when Shaman rode down Main Street. At first glance he knew there had been news of a horrible catastrophe. People stood about in small groups and talked. He saw Anna Wiley, leaning against a post on the porch of her boardinghouse, weeping. Simeon Cowan, Dorothy Burnham Cowan's husband, sat on the seat of his buckboard with his eyes half-closed, his mouth pinched between his forefinger and his big chapped thumb.

'What is it?' Shaman asked Simeon. He was certain peace had been called off.

'Abraham Lincoln is dead. Shot last night in a Washington theatre by some damn actor.'

Shaman refused to accept such news, but he dismounted

and received confirmation on all sides. Although everyone lacked details, it was apparent the story was true, and he rode home and shared the terrible facts with Alex.

'The vice-president will take his place,' Alex said.

'No doubt Andrew Johnson's already been sworn.'

They sat in the parlour a long time without speaking.

'Our poor country,' Shaman said finally. It was as if America were a patient who had struggled long and hard to survive the most terrible of plagues, and now had hurtled over a cliff.

A grey time. When he made his house calls, faces were sombre. Each evening, the church bell was rung. Shaman helped Alex up onto Trude, and Alex rode out; it was the first time he'd been on a horse since before his capture. When he came back, he told Shaman the tolling of the bell drifted far out onto the prairie, a sad and lonely sound.

Sitting alone by Alden's bedside after midnight, Shaman looked up from his reading to see the old man's eyes on him.

'You want something, Alden?'

He shook his head, almost imperceptibly.

Shaman leaned over him. 'Alden. You remember that time my father was leaving the barn and somebody took a shot at his head. And you searched the woods and couldn't find anybody?'

Alden's eyes didn't blink.

'It was you fired a rifle at my father.'

Alden licked his lips. '. . . Fired to miss . . . scare him quiet.'

'You want water?'

Alden didn't answer. Then, 'How you come to know?'

'You said something while you were sick that made me understand a lot of things. Like why you urged me to go to Chicago and find David Goodnow. You knew he was hopelessly insane, and mute. That I wouldn't learn a thing.'

'. . . What else you know?'

'I know that you're involved in this thing. Up to your damn neck.'

Again the tiny nod. 'I didn't kill her. I . . .' Alden was

604

gripped by a long and terrible paroxysm of coughing, and Shaman held a basin for him and allowed him to spit out a quantity of grey mucus, pink-tinged. When he stopped coughing he was white and spent, and he closed his eyes.

'Alden. Why did you tell Korff where I'd gone?'

'You wouldn't let it be. Shook 'em bad in Chicago. Korff sent someone to see me, day after you left. I told 'em where you went. I thought he'd just talk to you, scare you. Way he scared me.'

He was panting. Shaman had questions crowding his tongue, but he knew how sick Alden was. He sat and struggled between his anger and the oath he had sworn. In the end he watched, and swallowed his words, while Alden lay with his eyes closed, now and then coughing up a little blood or twitching with the palsy.

Almost half an hour later, Alden started speaking on his own.

'I led the American party here . . .'

'That morning, I helped Grueber . . . butcher. Left early to meet them three. In our woods. I got there, they'd already . . . had the woman. She's just lyin' there, heard them talkin' with me. I started yellin'. Said, how could I stay here now? Told 'em they were leavin', but the Indian'd get me in terrible trouble.

'Korff never said a word. Just grabbed up the blade, killed her.'

Shaman couldn't ask him anything just then. He could feel himself trembling with anger. He wanted to scream like a child.

'They just warned me not to talk, and they rode away. I went home, packed a few things in a box. Figgered I'd have to run . . . didn't know where. But nobody paid me any mind or even asked me any questions after they found her.'

'You even helped bury her, you misery,' Shaman said. He couldn't help himself. Perhaps it was his tone of voice that reached Alden more than his words. Alden's eyes closed, and he began to cough. This time, the coughing wouldn't let up.

605

Shaman went to fetch quinine and some black root tea, but when he tried to give it, Alden choked and sprayed, wetting his nightshirt so it had to be changed.

Several hours later, Shaman sat and remembered the hired man as he'd known him all his life. The artisan who made fishing poles and ice skates, the expert who taught them to hunt and fish. The irascible drunkard.

The liar. The man who had abetted in rape and murder.

He got up and took the lamp and held it over Alden's face. 'Alden. Listen to me. What kind of knife did Korff stab her with? What was the weapon, Alden?'

But the eyelids remained closed. Alden Kimball gave no sign that he heard Shaman's voice.

Toward morning, whenever he touched Alden he felt fever in the upper range. Alden was unconscious. When he coughed, the discharge was foul, and now the sputum was a brighter red. Shaman put his fingers to Alden's wrist and the pulse ran away from him, 108 beats per minute.

He undressed Alden and was sponging him with alcohol when he looked up and saw that daylight had broken. Alex was peering through the door.

'God. He looks awful. Is he in pain?'

'I don't think he can feel anything anymore.'

It was hard for him to tell Alex, and harder for Alex to hear what he was told, but Shaman left nothing out.

Alex had worked closely with Alden a long time, sharing the cruel and dirty daily work of the farm, being instructed in a hundred homely tasks, and depending on the older man for stability during the time when he'd felt like a fatherless bastard and had rebelled against Rob J.'s parental authority. Shaman knew Alex loved Alden.

'Will you report to the authorities?' Alex appeared calm. Only his brother would know the extent to which he was disturbed.

'There's no point. He has pneumonia, and it's moving quickly.'

'He's dying?'

606

Shaman nodded.

'For his sake, I'm glad,' Alex said.

They sat and discussed the chances of notifying survivors. Neither of them knew the whereabouts of the Mormon wife and children the hired man had deserted before he came to work for Rob J.

Shaman asked Alex to search Alden's cabin, and he went to do so. When he returned, he shook his head: 'Three jugs of whisky, two fishing poles, a rifle. Tools. Some harness he was repairing. Dirty laundry. And this.' He held a paper in his hand. 'A list of local men. I think it must be the membership of the American party in this town.'

Shaman didn't take it. 'Best burn it.'

'You're certain?'

He nodded. 'I'm going to spend the rest of my life here, taking care of them. When I go into their homes as their doctor, I don't want to know which of them is a Know Nothing,' he said, and Alex nodded and took the list away.

Shaman sent Billy Edwards to the convent with the names of several patients who needed to be checked at home, and asked Mother Miriam Ferocia to make the house calls for him. He was asleep when Alden died at midmorning. By the time he was awake, Alex already had closed Alden's eyes, and washed him, and dressed him in clean clothing.

When Doug and Billy were told, they came and stood by the side of the bed for a few moments, and then they went to the barn and began to build a box.

'I won't have him buried here, on the farm,' Shaman said.

Alex was silent for a moment, but then he nodded. 'We can take him to Nauvoo. I think he still had friends among the Mormons there,' he said.

The casket was brought to Rock Island in the buckboard, and placed on the deck of a flatboat. The Cole brothers sat nearby on a crate of ploughshares. That day, while a train began to bear the body of Abraham Lincoln on a long, slow journey west, the hired man's body was floated down the Mississippi.

607

At Nauvoo, the coffin was unloaded at the steamboat landing, and Alex waited near it while Shaman went into a warehouse and explained their errand to a clerk named Perley Robinson. 'Alden Kimball? Don't know him. You'll have to get permission from Mrs Bidamon to bury him here. Wait. I'll go ask her.'

He was back presently. The widow of Prophet Joseph Smith had told him she knew Alden Kimball as a Mormon and a former settler in Nauvoo, and that he could be buried in the cemetery.

The small cemetery was inland. The river was out of sight, but there were trees, and someone who knew how to use a scythe kept the grass cut. Two stalwart young men dug the grave, and Perley Robinson, who was an elder, read unendingly from the Book of Mormon while the afternoon shadows lengthened.

Afterwards Shaman settled up. The funeral costs came to seven dollars, including $4.59 for the plot. 'For another twenty dollars I'll see he has a nice stone,' Robinson said.

'All right,' Alex said quickly.

'What year was he born?'

Alex shook his head. 'We don't know. Just have them engrave it, "Alden Kimball, Died 1865."'

'Tell you what. Under that, I can tell them to put "Saint."'

But Shaman looked up at him and shook his head. 'Just the name and the date,' he said.

Perley Robinson said a boat was due. He put out the red flag so it would come in, and soon they were sitting in chairs on the port deck while the sun sank toward Iowa out of a bleeding sky.

'What made him end up with the Know Nothings?' Shaman said finally.

Alex said he wasn't surprised. 'He always knew how to hate. He was bitter about a lot of things. He told me several times that his father had been born in America and died a hired man in Vermont, and he was going to die a hired man too. It used to gall him to see foreigners owning farms.'

'What stopped him? Pa would have helped him get his

608

own place.'

'It was something inside. We thought better of him, all those years, than he thought of himself,' Alex said. 'No wonder he drank. Think of what the poor old bastard had to live with.'

Shaman shook his head. 'When I think of him, I'll remember him laughing secretly at Pa. And telling my whereabouts to a man he knew was a murderer.'

'It didn't stop you from taking good care of him after you knew,' Alex observed.

'Yes, well . . . Shaman said bitterly. 'The truth is, for the second time in my life, I wanted to kill someone.'

'But you didn't. You tried to save him instead,' Alex said. He looked at Shaman. '. . . In the camp at Elmira, I took care of the men in my tent. When they were sick, I tried to think what Pa would have done, and then I did it for them. It made me happy.'

Shaman nodded.

'Do you think I could become a physician?'

The question stunned Shaman. He made himself pause a long moment before he answered. Then he nodded. 'I do, Alex.'

'I'm not nearly the student you are.'

'You're brighter than you're ever willing to admit. You didn't care to study much in school. But if you worked hard now, I believe you could do it. You could apprentice with me.'

'I'd like to work with you as long as it takes to prepare in chemistry and anatomy and whatever else you think I need. But I'd rather go to a medical school, the way you and Pa did. I'd like to go East. Maybe study with Pa's friend Dr Holmes.'

'You have it all planned. You've been thinking about this for a long time.'

'Yeah. And I've never been so scared,' Alex said, and they both smiled for the first time in a number of days.

609

71
Family Gifts

On their way back from Nauvoo, they went to Davenport and found their forlorn mother sitting in the midst of unpacked boxes and crates in the small brick parsonage next to the Baptist church. Lucian already was out on pastoral calls. Shaman saw that Sarah's eyes were reddened.

'Something wrong, Ma?'

'No. Lucian is the kindest man, and we dote on one another. This is where I want to be, but ... it's a real change. It's new and frightening, and I let myself get silly.'

But she was happy to see her sons.

She wept again when they told her about Alden. She couldn't seem to stop. 'I'm crying as much from guilt as for Alden,' she said when they tried to comfort her. 'I never liked Makwa-ikwa, nor was I nice to her. But ...'

'I believe I know the way to cheer you up,' Alex said. He began to unpack her boxes, and so did Shaman. In a few minutes she dried her eyes and joined them. 'You don't know where anything should go!'

While they unpacked, Alex told her of his decision to go into medicine, and Sarah responded with awed pleasure. 'It would have made Rob J. so happy.'

She showed them through the small house. The furniture was in poor shape, and there wasn't enough of it. 'I'm going to ask Lucian to move a few pieces into the barn, and we'll bring some of my things from Holden's Crossing.'

She made coffee and sliced an applesauce cake one of 'her' churchwomen had brought. While they ate it, Shaman scribbled some figures on the back of an old bill.

'What are you doing?' Sarah asked.

'I have an idea.' He looked at them, not knowing how to start, and then simply asked the question. 'How would you feel about donating a quarter-section of our land to the new hospital?'

Alex had been about to eat a forkful of cake, and he stopped the fork in midair and said something. Shaman pushed the fork down with his hand so he could see his brother's mouth.

'One-sixteenth of the entire farm?' Alex said again.

'By my figuring, if we gave the land, the hospital could have thirty beds instead of twenty-five.'

'But, Shaman . . . twenty acres?'

'We've cut the flock. And there would be plenty of land left to farm, even if we should ever want to enlarge the flock again.'

His mother frowned. 'You'd have to be careful not to place the hospital too close to the house.'

Shaman drew a breath. 'The house is in the quarter-section I'd give to the hospital. It could have its own dock on the river, and a right-of-way to the road.'

They simply looked at him.

'You'll be living here now,' he said to his mother. 'I'm going to build Rachel and the children a new house. And', he said to Alex, 'you'll be away for years, studying and training. I'd turn our house into a clinic, a place where patients not sick enough to be hospitalized would come and see a doctor. We'd have additional examining rooms, waiting rooms. Perhaps the hospital office and a pharmacy. We could call it the Robert Judson Cole Memorial Clinic.'

'Oh, I like that,' his mother said, and when he looked into her eyes he knew he had her.

Alex nodded.

'You're certain?'

'Yes,' Alex said.

611

It was late when they left the parsonage and took the ferry across the Mississippi. Night had fallen by the time they collected the horse and buckboard from the stable in Rock Island, but they were intimately familiar with the road and drove home in the dark. When they reached Holden's Crossing, it wasn't an hour when Shaman could think of calling at the Convent of Saint Francis Xavier of Assisi. He knew he wouldn't sleep that night, and that he would go there early next morning. He couldn't wait to tell Mother Miriam Ferocia.

Five days later, four surveyors moved over the quarter-section with their transits and steel measuring tapes. There was no architect in the area between the rivers, but the building contractor with the best reputation was a man named Oscar Ericsson, from Rock Island. Shaman and Mother Miriam Ferocia met with Ericsson and talked at length. The contractor had built a town hall and several churches, but mostly he had raised homes and stores. This was his first opportunity to build a hospital, and he listened closely to what they told him. When they studied his rough sketches, they knew they had found their builder.

Ericsson began by mapping the site and suggesting the routes of driveways and paths. A walk between the clinic and the steamboat landing would go right past Alden's cabin. 'You and Billy had best dismantle it, and cut the logs for firewood,' Shaman told Doug Penfield, and they started on it at once. By the time Ericsson's first labour crew arrived to clear the hospital building site, it was as if the cabin never had existed.

That afternoon Shaman was in the buggy, driving Boss to house calls, when he met the hackney rig from the Rock Island stables, coming the other way. There was a man sitting in the seat with the driver, and Shaman waved at them as they passed. It took him only seconds before it registered in his mind who the passenger was, and he turned Boss in a sweeping U and hurried to overtake them.

When he did, he waved the driver to a stop, and he was out of his buggy in a moment. 'Jay,' he called.

Jason Geiger climbed down too. He had lost weight; it wasn't any wonder he hadn't been recognized at a glance. 'Shaman?' he said. 'My God, it is.'

He had no suitcase, just a cloth bag with a drawstring, which Shaman transferred to his own buggy.

Jay sat back in the seat and seemed to breathe in the scenery. 'I've missed this.' He glanced at the medical bag and nodded. 'Lillian wrote that you're a doctor. I can't tell you how proud I was to hear. Your father must have felt . . .' He didn't go on.

Then he said, 'I was closer to your father than to my brothers.'

'He always felt fortunate you were his friend.'

Geiger nodded.

'Do they expect you?'

'No. I only knew a few days ago. Union troops came to my hospital with their own medical people and just said we could go home. I put on civilian dress and got on a train. When I reached Washington, somebody said Lincoln's body was on the Capitol rotunda, and I went there. You never witnessed such a crowd. I stood in the line all day.'

'You saw his body?'

'For a few moments. He had great dignity. You wanted to pause and say something to him, but they moved you along. It occurred to me that if some of those in the crowd could have seen the grey uniform in my bag, they'd have torn me limb from limb.' He sighed. 'Lincoln would have been a healer. Now I'm afraid those in power will use his killing to grind the South into dust.'

He broke off, because Shaman had turned the horse and buggy into the track leading from the road to the Geiger house. Shaman drove Boss to the side door the family used.

'Will you come in?' Jay asked. Shaman smiled and shook his head. He waited while Jay took his bag from the buggy and walked stiffly up the steps. It was his house and he walked in without knocking, and Shaman clucked softly to Boss and drove away.

Next day, Shaman waited until after he'd finished with the

patients in the dispensary, then walked down the Long Path
to the Geiger house. When he knocked, the front door was
opened by Jason, and Shaman took one look at his face and
understood that Rachel had talked to her father.

'Come in.'

'Thank you, Jay.'

It didn't make things any better that the two children
recognized Shaman's voice from those few words and came
hurtling from the kitchen, Joshua to grasp one of his legs
and Hattie to seize the other. Lillian came rushing after, and
pried them away from him, at the same time nodding hello.
She took them back to the kitchen, while they complained.

Jay led the way into the parlour and pointed to one of the
horsehair chairs, which Shaman took obediently.

'My grandchildren are afraid of me.'

'They don't know you yet. Lillian and Rachel told them
about you all the time. Grandpa this and *Zaydeh* that. As
soon as they link you up with that nice Grandpa, they'll be
fine.' It occurred to him that Jay Geiger might not appreciate
being patronized about his own grandchildren under these
circumstances, and he sought to change the subject.
'Where's Rachel?'

'She went for a walk. She is . . . upset.'

Shaman nodded. 'She told you about me.'

Jason nodded.

'I've loved her all my life. Thank God I'm no longer a
boy . . . Jay, I know what you fear.'

'No, Shaman. With due respect, you will never know.
Those two children have the blood of high priests. They
must be raised as Jews.'

'They will be. We've talked at length. Rachel won't give
up her beliefs. Joshua and Hattie can be taught by you, the
man who taught their mother. I'd like to learn Hebrew with
them. I had a little in college.'

'You'll convert?'

'No . . . actually, I'm thinking of becoming a Quaker.'

Geiger was silent.

'If your family were locked away in a town of your own
people, you might expect the kind of matches you want for

your children. But you led them into the world.'

'Yes, I take responsibility. Now I must lead them back.'

Shaman shook his head. 'They won't go. They can't.'

The expression on Jay's face didn't change.

'Rachel and I will marry. And if you wound her mortally by draping your mirrors and chanting the prayer for the dead, I'll ask her to take the children and go with me, far away from here.'

For a moment he feared the legendary Geiger temper, but Jay nodded. 'She told me this morning she'd go.'

'Yesterday you said my father was closer in your heart than your brothers. I know you love his family. I know you love me. Can't we love each other for what we are?'

Jason was pale. 'It seems we must try,' he said heavily. He stood and held out his hand.

Shaman ignored the hand and swept him up in a great embrace. In a moment he felt Jason's hand rising and falling on his back, bestowing comforting pats.

In the third week of April, winter came back to Illinois. The temperature dropped, and it snowed. Shaman worried about the tiny buds on the peach trees. Work ceased on the building site, but he and Ericsson walked through the Cole house and determined where the contractor would build shelves and instrument cases. Happily they agreed that very little structural work would have to be done to convert the house into a clinic.

When the snow stopped, Doug Penfield took advantage of the cold to do some spring slaughtering, as he had promised Sarah. Shaman passed the outdoor abattoir behind the barn and saw three pigs, tied and hung from a high rail by their rear legs. He realized three were too many; Rachel wouldn't be using hams or smoked shoulder in their house, and he smiled at this evidence of the interesting complexities his life was beginning to assume. The pigs already had been bled, gutted, dipped into vats of boiling water, and scraped. They were pink-white, and as he passed them he was stopped short by three small, identical openings in the large veins of their throats, by which they had been bled.

Triangular wounds, like the holes left in new snow by the tips of ski poles.

Without having to measure them, Shaman knew that these wounds were the right size.

He was standing transfixed by them when Doug came with his meat saw.

'These holes. What did you use to make them?'

'Alden's pig-sticker.' Doug smiled at him. 'That's the funniest thing. I'd been asking Alden to make me one, ever since the first time I butchered here. Asking and asking. He always said he would. He said he knew sticking pigs was better than cutting their throats. Said he used to own a sticker and lost it. But he never made one for me.

'Then we tore down his cabin, and there was his, on a joist under the puncheon floor. He must have set the thing down for a minute while he repaired one of the floorboards, and forgot about it, and put the floorboard right back over it. Didn't even need much of a sharpening.'

In a moment it was in Shaman's hand. It was the instrument whose use had baffled Barney McGowan when he had tried to picture it in the pathology laboratory of the Cincinnati hospital, working from only a description of Makwa's wounds. It was about eighteen inches long. Its handle was round and smooth, easy to hold. As Shaman's father had guessed during the autopsy, the last six inches of the triangular blade tapered, so that the more the blade was pushed into tissue, the larger the wound would be. The three edges gleamed dangerously, and it was obvious that the steel took a fine edge. Alden had always liked to use good steel.

He could see the arm rising and falling. Rising and falling. Eleven times.

She wouldn't have screamed or cried out. He told himself she would have been deep within herself, at the place where there was no pain. He fervently hoped that was true.

Shaman left Doug at his work. He carried the instrument down the Short Path, holding it in front of him carefully, as though it might be transformed into a serpent and rear back to bite him. He went through the trees, passed Makwa's

616

grave and the ruined *hedonoso-te*. On the riverbank he drew back his arm and flung.

The thing turned and turned, swimming through the spring air, glittering all the way in the bright sun, like a thrown sword. But it wasn't Excalibur. No God-sent hand and arm rose out of the depths to catch and brandish it. Instead, it knifed into the current in the deepest water with scarcely a ripple. Shaman knew the river wouldn't give it up, and a weight he'd carried for years – so long a time that he had lost awareness of it – lifted from his shoulders and was gone like a bird.

72
Breaking Ground

By the end of April no snow was to be found, even in the secret nooks where the river woods produced deep shade. The tips of the peach trees had been blasted by frost, but new life struggled beneath the blackened tissue and pushed the green buds toward blossom. On May 13, when there was a formal groundbreaking ceremony at the Cole farm, the weather was mild. Shortly after noon, the Most Reverend James Duggan, Bishop of the Diocese of Chicago, alighted from the train at Rock Island, accompanied by three monsignors.

They were met by Mother Miriam Ferocia and two hired carriages that drove the party to the farm, where people already had assembled. The group included most of the area's doctors; the nursing nuns of the convent and the priest who was their confessor; the town fathers; assorted politicians, including Nick Holden and Congressman John Kurland; and a number of citizens. Mother Miriam's voice was firm as she welcomed them, but her accent was more marked than usual, which happened when she was nervous. She introduced the prelates and asked Bishop Duggan to give the invocation.

Then she introduced Shaman, who led a walking tour of the land. The bishop, a portly man with a ruddy face framed by a great mane of grey hair, clearly was pleased by what he saw. When they reached the site of the hospital building, Congressman Kurland spoke briefly, describing what the presence of a hospital would mean to his constituents. Bishop Duggan was handed a shovel by Mother Miriam and excavated a helping of earth as if he had done it before. Then the prioress used the shovel, and next Shaman, followed by the politicians, and then several other people who would be pleased to be able to tell their children they'd broken the ground for the Hospital of Saint Francis.

Following the groundbreaking, everyone went to a reception at the convent. There were more tours – of the garden, of the flock of sheep and the herd of goats in the fields, of the barn, and finally of the convent house itself.

Miriam Ferocia had had a narrow line to walk, wishing to honour her bishop with fitting hospitality, yet aware that she mustn't appear a spendthrift in his eyes. She had managed admirably, using the products of her convent to bake small cheese pasties that were served warm on trays to accompany tea and coffee. Everything appeared to go very well, but it seemed to Shaman that Miriam Ferocia was growing increasingly anxious. He observed her staring pensively at Nick Holden, who sat in the upholstered chair next to the prioress' table.

When Holden got up and moved away, she seemed to wait expectantly, glancing again and again at Bishop Duggan.

Shaman had met and talked with the bishop at the farm. Now he moved closer, and when the opportunity arose, spoke to him.

'Your Excellency, do you observe, behind me, the large upholstered chair with the carved wooden arms?'

The bishop appeared puzzled. 'Yes, I do.'

'Your Excellency, that chair was carried across the prairie in a wagon by the nuns when they came here. They call it the bishop's chair. It was their dream that someday their bishop might come to visit, and that he would have a fine chair in which to rest.'

Bishop Duggan nodded seriously, but his eyes twinkled. 'Dr Cole, I believe you will go far,' he said. He was a circumspect man. He went first to the congressman and discussed the future of the chaplains of the army now that the war was over. After a few minutes had passed, he approached Miriam Ferocia. 'Come, Mother,' he said. 'Let us have a little talk.' He pulled a straight chair close to the upholstered one, into which he sank with a pleased sigh.

Soon they were engrossed in conversation about the affairs of the convent. Mother Miriam Ferocia sat erect in the straight chair, her eyes taking in the fact that the bishop sat the chair well, almost regally – his back supported, his hands resting comfortably over the ends of the carved arms. Sister Mary Peter Celestine, serving pastries, took note of her prioress' glowing face. She glanced at Sister Mary Benedicta, who was pouring coffee, and they both smiled.

The morning after the reception at the convent, the sheriff and a deputy drove a buckboard to the Cole farm, bearing the body of a plump middle-aged woman with long dirty brown hair. The sheriff didn't know who she was. She had been discovered dead in the back of a closed freight wagon that had brought an order of bagged sugar and flour to Haskins' store.

'We figure she crawled into the back of the wagon in Rock Island, but nobody there knows where she came from, or anything else about her,' the sheriff said. They carried her into the shed and put her on the table, then nodded and drove away.

'Anatomy lesson,' Shaman told Alex.

They undressed her. She wasn't clean, and Alex watched as Shaman combed nits and chaff from her hair. Shaman used the scalpel Alden had made for him, to make the Y incision that opened the chest. He worked the rib-cutter and removed the sternum, explaining what everything was, and what he was doing, and why, and when he glanced up, he saw that Alex was struggling with himself.

'No matter how soiled the human body is, it's a miracle to be marvelled at and treated well. When a person dies, the soul or the spirit – what the Greeks called *anemos* – leaves it. Men have always argued about whether it dies too, or it goes elsewhere.' He smiled, remembering his father and Barney delivering the same message, and inordinately pleased that now he was passing the legacy himself. 'When Pa studied medicine, he had a professor who told him the spirit leaves the body behind the way someone leaves a house he's lived in. Pa said we have to treat a body with dignity, out of respect for the person who used to live in the house.'

Alex nodded. Shaman saw that he leaned over the table with genuine interest, and that colour had begun to return to Bigger's face as he watched his brother's hands.

Jay had volunteered to tutor Alex in chemistry and pharmacology. That afternoon they sat on the porch of the Cole house and reviewed the elements, while Shaman read a journal nearby, and occasionally dozed. They were forced to put away their books, and Shaman to abandon all hope for a nap, by the arrival of Nick Holden. Shaman saw that Alex greeted Nick politely but without warmth.

Nick had come to say goodbye. He was still Commissioner of Indian Affairs, and he was returning to Washington.

'Has President Johnson asked you to stay on, then?' Shaman asked.

'Only for a time. He'll put in his own bunch, never fear,' Nick said, making a face. He told them all Washington was agog with the rumour of a connection between the former vice-president and President Lincoln's assassin. 'They say a note to Johnson has been discovered, bearing the signature of John Wilkes Booth. And that on the afternoon of the shooting, Booth called at Johnson's hotel and asked for him at the desk, only to be told that Johnson wasn't in.'

Shaman wondered whether reputations were assassinated in Washington as well as presidents. 'Has Johnson been asked about these stories?'

'He chooses to ignore them. He merely acts presidential and talks about funding the deficit caused by the war.'

'The greatest deficit caused by the war can't be funded,' Jay said. 'A million men have been killed or wounded. And more will die, because there are pockets of Confederates who still haven't surrendered.'

They contemplated the terrible thought. 'What would have happened to this country had there been no war?' Alex asked suddenly. 'What if Lincoln had allowed the South to go in peace?'

'The Confederacy would have been short-lived,' Jay said. 'Southerners place their faith in their own state and mistrust a central government. There would have been squabbles almost at once. The Confederacy would have fractured into smaller regional groups, and in time these would have broken down into the individual states. I think that all the states, one by one and at their own humiliated and embarrassed request, would have come back into the Union.'

'The Union's changing,' Shaman said. 'The American party had very little effect on the last election. American-born soldiers have seen Irish and German and Scandinavian comrades die in battle, and they're no longer willing to listen to bigoted politicians. The Chicago *Daily Tribune* says the Know Nothings are finished.'

'And good riddance,' Alex said.

'It was just another political party,' Nick said mildly.

'A political party that fanned into life other, more ominous groups,' Jay said. 'But never fear. Three and a half million former slaves are spreading out to seek jobs of work. There will be new terror societies aimed against them, probably with the same names on their membership rolls.'

Nick Holden rose to take his leave. 'By the way, Geiger, has your good wife received any word from her celebrated cousin?'

'If we knew Judah Benjamin's whereabouts, Commissioner, do you believe I would tell you?' Jay said quietly.

Holden smiled his smile.

It was true he had saved Alex's life, and Shaman was grateful. But gratitude never would enable him to like Nick. Deep in his heart he fervently hoped his brother had been fathered by the young outlaw whose name had been Will Mosby.

It didn't enter his mind to invite Holden to the wedding.

Shaman and Rachel were married May 22, 1865, in the parlour of the Geiger house, with only their families attending. It wasn't the wedding their elders would have wanted. Sarah had suggested to her son that since his stepfather was a clergyman, it would be a gesture toward family unity if Lucian were asked to perform the ceremony. Jay offered his daughter the opinion that the only way a Jewish woman could be married was by a rabbi. Neither Rachel nor Shaman argued, but they were married by Judge Stephen Hume. Hume couldn't handle pages or notes with one hand unless he had a lectern, and Shaman had to borrow the one in the church, a task made easier by the fact that a new minister hadn't yet been hired. They stood before the judge with the children. Joshua's sweaty little hand grasped Shaman's index finger. Rachel, in a wedding dress of blue brocade with a wide collar of cream-coloured lace, held Hattie's hand. Hume was a fine man who wished them good things, and that came through. When he pronounced them husband and wife and bade them to 'Go in joy and peace,' Shaman took him literally. The world slowed, and he experienced a rising in his soul such as he'd felt only once before, when he had walked the tunnel between the Cincinnati Polyclinic Medical School and the Southwestern Ohio Hospital for the first time as a physician.

Shaman had expected Rachel to want to go to Chicago or some other city for their wedding trip, but she had heard him say Sauks and Mesquakies had come back to Iowa, and to his pleasure she'd asked if they could visit the Indians.

They needed an animal to pack their supplies and bedding. Paul Williams had a big good-natured grey gelding in his stable, and Shaman rented him for eleven days. Tama, the Indian town, was about one hundred miles away. He figured four days or so travelling time each way, and a couple of days for the visit.

A few hours after they were married they rode away, Rachel on Trude, Shaman on Boss and leading the pack-horse, whose name Williams had said was Ulysses, 'no disrespect to General Grant.'

Shaman would have stopped for the day by the time they

got to Rock Island, but they were dressed for rough travel, not for a hotel, and Rachel wanted to spend the night on the prairie. So they brought the horses across the river by ferry and rode about ten miles beyond Davenport.

They followed a narrow dusty road between great ploughed expanses of black soil, but there were still patches of prairie between the cultivated fields. When they reached a stretch of unbroken grass, and a brook, Rachel rode close and waved her hand to gain his attention. 'Can we stop here?'

'Let's find the farmhouse.'

They had to ride about another mile. Closer to the house, the grass became cultivated field that doubtless would be planted to corn. In the barnyard a yellow dog lunged at the horses, barking. The farmer was putting a new bolt on the share of his plough, and he frowned with suspicion when Shaman asked permission to camp by the brook. But when Shaman offered to pay, he waved his hand. 'Gonna build a fire?'

'I had thought to. Everything's green.'

'Oh, yes, it won't spread. Brook's drinkable. Follow it a ways, there's dead trees where you can get wood.'

So they thanked him and rode back to a good spot. They took off the saddles together and unloaded Ulysses. Then Shaman made four trips to carry wood, while Rachel laid out the camp. She spread an old buffalo robe that her father had bought years ago from Stone Dog. Brown leather showed through where it was missing clumps of fur, but it was just the thing to have between them and the earth. Over the buffalo robe she spread two blankets woven of Cole wool, because summer was a month away.

Shaman piled wood between some rocks and lit a fire. He put brook water and coffee into a pot and set it on to brew. Sitting on the saddles, they ate cold leftovers from their wedding feast – pink sliced spring lamb, brown potatoes, candied carrots. For a sweet they ate white wedding cake with whisky frosting, and then they sat near the fire and drank their coffee black. The stars showed up as night fell, and a quarter-moon lifted itself above the flat land.

624

Presently she set down her mug and found soap, a rag, and a towel, and slipped into the gathering darkness.

It wouldn't be the first time they had made love, and Shaman wondered why he felt so awkward. He undressed and went to another part of the brook to wash hurriedly, and was waiting for her between the blankets and the bison skin when she joined him; their flesh still had the chill of the water, but it warmed. He knew she had picked the location of the fire so their bed would be beyond its light, but he didn't mind. It left only her, and their hands and mouths and bodies. They made love for the first time as man and wife, and then they lay on their backs and held hands.

'I love you, Rachel Cole,' he said. They could see the whole sky like a bowl over the flatness of the earth. The low stars were huge and white.

Soon they made love again. This time when they were through, Rachel got up and ran to the fire. She picked up a branch with an ember on one end and whirled it like a pinwheel until it burst into flame. Then she came back and knelt so close he could see the gooseflesh in the valley of her brown breasts, and the torchlight turning her eyes into gems, and her mouth. 'I love you too, Shaman,' she said.

The next day, the deeper they rode into Iowa, the more space there was between farms. The road moved through a piggery for half a mile, where the stink was so strong they could touch it, but then there was grassland again, and sweet air.

Once Rachel stiffened in the saddle and raised her hand. 'What?'

'Howling. Can it be a wolf?'

He thought it had to be a dog. 'Farmers must have hunted down the wolves, the way they have at home. Wolves have gone the way of the bison and the Indians.'

'Maybe before we get home we'll see one prairie miracle,' she said. 'Perhaps a buffalo, or a wildcat, or the last wolf in Iowa.'

They passed through little towns. At noon they came to a general store and dined on soda crackers and hard cheese and canned peaches.

'Yesterday we heered that soldiers arrested Jefferson Davis. They have him in Fort Monroe, Virginia, in chains,' the storekeeper said. He spat on his own sawdust floor. 'I hope they hang the sonofabitch. Beggin' your pardon, ma'am.'

Rachel nodded. It was hard to be ladylike when she was draining the dregs of the peach juice from the can. 'Did they also capture his secretary of state? Judah P. Benjamin?'

'The Jew? No, they ain't got him yet, far's I know.'

'Good,' Rachel said clearly.

She and Shaman took the empty cans to use on the trail, and moved out to the horses. The grocer stood on his porch and looked after them as they rode down the dusty road.

That afternoon they forded the Cedar River carefully without getting wet, only to be drenched in a sudden spring rain. It was almost dark when they came to a farm and took shelter in a barn. Shaman felt oddly pleased, remembering the description of his parents' wedding night in his father's journal. He braved the wet to seek permission to stay, and it was readily given by the farmer, whose name was Williams but who was unrelated to the stableman in Holden's Crossing. When Shaman returned, Mrs Williams was hard on his heels with half a pot of a hearty milk soup swimming with carrots and potatoes and barley, and fresh bread. She left them so quickly they were sure she knew they were newly married.

The next morning was very clear, and warmer than it had been. In the early afternoon they reached the Iowa River. Billy Edwards had told Shaman that if they followed it northwest, they'd find the Indians. The stretch of river was deserted, and after a time they came to a cove with clear, shallow water and a sand bottom. They stopped and tethered their horses, and Shaman was quickly out of his clothes and splashing in the water. 'Come in!' he urged.

She didn't dare. Yet, the sun was hot, and the river looked as if it never had been seen by other humans. In a few minutes Rachel went into some bushes and took off everything but her cotton shift. In the cold water she squealed, and they played like children. The wet shift clung, and soon he reached for her, but she became frightened. 'Someone's certain to come along!' she said, and ran out of the water.

She put on her dress and hung the shift on a limb to dry. Shaman had fishhooks and line in his pack, and when he was dressed he found some worms under a log and broke a branch for a pole. He walked upriver to a likely pool and in a short time had caught a pair of half-pound spotted bass.

They had eaten hard-boiled eggs at noon from Rachel's copious supply, but the fish would feed them that evening. He cleaned them at once. 'We'd best cook them now so they won't spoil, and wrap them in a cloth and take them with us,' he said, and built a small fire.

While the bass were cooking, he came to her again. This time she lost all caution. It didn't matter to her that scrubbing with river water and sand hadn't taken the fish smell from his hands, or that it was full daylight. He lifted her shiftless dress and they made love in their clothing on the hot, sunny riverbank grass, with the sound of the rushing water in her ears.

A few minutes later, while she was turning the fish so they wouldn't burn, a flatboat came around the bend in the river. In it were three bearded, barefoot men dressed only in ragged trousers. One of them lifted his hand in a lazy wave, and Shaman waved back.

As soon as the boat had gone, she rushed to where her shift was hung like a great white signal flag of what they had done. When he came after her, she turned on him. 'What is the matter with us?' she said. 'What's the matter with *me*? Who am I?'

'You're Rachel,' he told her, wrapping her into his arms. He said it with such satisfaction that when he kissed her, she was smiling.

73
Tama

Early in the morning of the fifth day, they overtook another horseman on the road. When they approached him to ask directions, Shaman saw he was dressed plainly but rode on a good horse and an expensive saddle. His hair was long and black and his skin was the colour of fired clay.

'Can you tell us the way to Tama?' Shaman asked.

'Better than that. Going there myself. Just ride along with me, if you like.'

'Thank you kindly.'

The Indian leaned forward and said something else, but Shaman shook his head. 'Hard for me to talk while we're riding. I have to see your mouth. I'm deaf.'

'Oh.'

'My wife hears fine, though,' Shaman said. He grinned, and the man grinned back and turned to Rachel and tipped his hat. They exchanged a few words, but mostly the three of them just rode along companionably through the warm morning.

When they came to a small pond, though, they stopped to let the horses take a small amount of water and a little grass, while they stretched their legs, and they met properly. The man shook hands and said he was Charles P. Keyser.

'You live in Tama?'

'No, I've got a farm eight miles from here. I was born

628

Potawatomi, but raised by whites when my family all died of the fever. I don't even speak the Indian jabber except for a few words of Kickapoo. I married a woman who was half-Kickapoo, half-French.'

He said he went to Tama every few years and spent a couple of days. 'I don't really know why.' He shrugged and smiled. 'Red skin calling to red skin, I guess.'

Shaman nodded. 'Our animals had enough grass, you suppose?'

'Oh, yes. Don't want them mounts to blow up on us, do we?' Keyser said, and they got back on the horses and resumed the ride.

At midmorning Keyser led them straight into Tama. Long before they reached the group of cabins clustered about in a large circle, they were being followed by brown-eyed children and barking dogs.

Soon Keyser signalled a stop, and they dismounted. 'I'll let the chief know we're here,' he said, and went to a nearby cabin. By the time he reappeared with a wide-built middle-aged redman, a small crowd had gathered.

The stocky man said something Shaman couldn't lip-read. It was in English, but the man took Shaman's hand when it was offered.

'I'm Dr Robert J. Cole of Holden's Crossing, Illinois. This is my wife, Rachel Cole.'

'Dr Cole?' A young man stepped out of the crowd and peered at Shaman. 'No. You're too young.'

'. . . Maybe you knew my father?'

The man's eyes searched him. 'You the deaf boy? . . . That you, Shaman?'

'Yes.'

'I'm Little Dog. Son of Moon and Comes Singing.'

Shaman felt pleasure as they clasped hands, remembering how they had played together as children.

The stocky man said something.

'He is Medi-ke, Snapping Turtle, chief of the town of Tama,' Little Dog said. 'He wants you three to come to his cabin.'

629

Snapping Turtle signalled to Little Dog that he should come too, and to the others that they should leave. His cabin was small and smelled of a recent meal of charred meat. Folded blankets showed where people slept, and a canvas hammock was slung in a corner. The dirt floor was hard and swept, and it was where they sat as Snapping Turtle's wife – Wapansee, Small Light – served them black coffee, very sweet with maple sugar, and altered and changed by other ingredients. It tasted like the coffee Makwa-ikwa had made. After Small Light served it, Snapping Turtle spoke to her, and she left the house.

'You had a sister named Bird Woman,' Shaman said to Little Dog. 'Is she here?'

'Dead, a long time now. I have another sister, Green Willow, the youngest. She's with her husband on the Kansas reservation.' No one else in Tama had been with the group in Holden's Crossing, Little Dog said.

Snapping Turtle said through Little Dog that he was a Mesquakie. And that there were about two hundred Mesquakies and Sauks in Tama. Then he spoke a torrent of words and looked at Little Dog again.

'He says the reservations are very bad, like big cages. We were sick with remembering former days, the old ways. We caught wild horses, broke them, sold them for what we could get. We saved every bit of money.

'Then about a hundred of us came here. We had to forget that Rock Island used to be Sauk-e-nuk, the great town of the Sauks, and that Davenport was Mesquak-e-nuk, the great town of the Mesquakies. The world has changed. We paid white man's money for eighty acres here, and we had the white governor of Iowa sign the deed as witness.'

Shaman nodded. 'That was good,' he said, and Snapping Turtle smiled. Evidently he understood some English, but he continued to speak in his own language, as his face grew stern.

'He says the government always pretends it has bought our vast lands. The White Father grabs our land and offers the tribes small coins instead of big paper money. He even cheats us of the coins, giving cheap goods and ornaments and saying Mesquakies and Sauks are paid an annuity. Many of our people leave the worthless goods to rot on the earth. We tell them to say loudly that they will accept only money, and to come here and buy more land.'

'Is there trouble with white neighbours?' Shaman said.

'No trouble,' Little Dog said, and listened to Snapping Turtle. 'He says we're no threat. Whenever our people go to trade, white men push coins into the bark of trees and tell our men they may keep the coins if they hit them with arrows. Certain of our people say it's an insult, but Snapping Turtle allows it.' Snapping Turtle spoke, and Little Dog smiled. 'He says it keeps some of us good with the bow.'

Small Light came back, bringing a man in a frayed cotton shirt and stained brown wool pants, and with a red kerchief tied about his forehead. He said this was Nepepaqua, Sleep Walker, a Sauk and the medicine man. Sleep Walker wasn't a man to waste time. 'She says you're a doctor.'

'Yes.'

'Good. You will come with me?'

Shaman nodded. He and Rachel left Charles Keyser drinking coffee with Snapping Turtle. They stopped only to get Shaman's bag. Then they followed after the medicine man.

Walking through the village, Shaman sought familiar sights to match his memories. He saw no *tipis*, but there were some *hedonoso-tes* beyond the cabins. The people mostly wore the shabby dress of white folks; moccasins were as he remembered, although many of the Indians wore work boots or army footwear.

Sleep Walker brought them to a cabin on the other side of the village. Inside, a skinny young woman lay and writhed, her hands over her great belly.

She was glassy-eyed and looked out of her mind. She didn't respond when Shaman asked her questions. Her pulse was rapid and bounding. He was fearful, but when he took her hands in his, he felt more vitality than he would have believed.

She was Watwaweiska, Climbing Squirrel, Sleep Walker

631

said. His brother's wife. The time for her first birthing had come on her yesterday morning. Earlier, she'd chosen a soft dry place in the woods, and she went there. The harsh pains came and came, and she had squatted as her mother had taught. When the waters had broken free, her legs and her dress became wet, but nothing else happened. The agony didn't go away, the child didn't come. At nightfall, other women had searched for her and found her, and they had carried her here.

Sleep Walker hadn't been able to help her.

Shaman stripped the sweat-soaked dress away and studied her body. She was very young. Her breasts, although heavy with milk, were small, and her pelvis was narrow. The pudenda gaped, but no small head was revealed. He gently pressed the surface of her belly with his fingers, then took out his stethoscope and placed the earpieces for Rachel. When he held the bell to Climbing Squirrel's stomach in several places, the conclusions he'd reached with his eyes and hands were confirmed by the sounds Rachel described.

'The child is presenting wrong.'

He went outside and asked for clean water, and Sleep Walker led him into the trees, to a brook. The medicine man watched curiously as Shaman lathered with brown soap and scrubbed his hands and arms. 'It's part of the medicine,' Shaman said, and Sleep Walker accepted the soap and imitated him.

When they returned to the cabin, Shaman took out his jar of clean lard and lubricated his hands. He inserted one finger into the birth canal, and then another, like probing a fist. He moved upward slowly. At first he felt nothing, but then the girl went into spasm, and the tight fist was pushed open slightly. An infant foot moved onto his fingers, and around it he felt the wrapped cord. The umbilical cord was tough, but it was stretched, and he didn't attempt to free the foot until the birth spasm had been spent. Then, working carefully with only his two fingers, he unwrapped the cord and drew the foot down.

The other foot was higher, braced against the wall of the canal, and he was able to reach it during the next spasm and

632

lead it down until two tiny red feet extended from the young mother. The feet became legs, and soon they could see it was a man-child. The baby's abdomen emerged, trailing the cord. But all progress stopped when the infant's shoulders and head jammed into the canal like a cork in the neck of a bottle.

Shaman could draw the child no farther, nor could he reach high enough to keep the mother's flesh from sealing the baby's nostrils. He knelt with his hand in the canal and his mind searching for a solution, but he felt that the baby would smother.

Sleep Walker had a bag of his own in a corner of the cabin, and from it he took a four-foot length of vine. The vine ended in what looked remarkably like the flat, ugly head of a pit viper, inset with black beady eyes and fibre fangs. Sleep Walker manipulated the 'serpent' so it appeared to crawl up Climbing Squirrel's body until the head was close to her face, weaving. The medicine man was chanting in his own language, but Shaman wasn't trying to read his lips. He was watching Climbing Squirrel.

Shaman could see the girl's eyes focus on the snake and widen. The medicine man caused the snake to turn and crawl down her body until it was just over the place where the baby rested.

Shaman felt a quivering in the birth canal.

He saw Rachel open her mouth to protest, and he warned her off with his eyes.

The fangs touched Climbing Squirrel's belly. Suddenly Shaman felt a widening. The girl gave a tremendous push, and the child came down so easily it took no effort to draw him out. The baby's lips and cheeks were blue, but at once they began to redden. With a tremulous finger Shaman cleared mucus from the mouth. The small face screwed up in indignation, the mouth opened. Shaman could feel the child's abdomen retract to draw in air, and he knew that the others were hearing a high, thin crying. Maybe it was in D-flat, because the belly vibrated exactly as Lillian's piano did whenever Rachel struck the fifth black key from the end.

He and the medicine man went back to the brook to wash. Sleep Walker looked pleased. Shaman was very thoughtful. Before leaving the cabin, he had examined the vine again to make certain it was only a vine.

'The girl thought the snake would devour her baby, so she bore it to save it?'

'My song said the snake was bad *manitou*. Good *manitou* helped her.'

He realized the lesson was that science can take medicine only so far. Then it is helped tremendously if there is faith or belief in something else. It was an advantage the medicine man had over the medical man, because Sleep Walker was a priest as well as a doctor.

'Are you a shaman?'

'No.' Sleep Walker looked at him. 'You know about the Tents of Wisdom?'

'Makwa told us about seven Tents.'

'Yes, seven. For some things, I am in the fourth Tent. For too many things, I'm in the first tent.'

'Will you become a shaman someday?'

'Who will teach me? Wabokieshiek is dead. Makwa-ikwa is dead. The tribes are scattered, the *Mide'wiwin* is no more. When I was young and knew I wanted to be a ghostkeeper, I heard of an old Sauk, almost a shaman, in Missouri. I found him, spent two years there. But he died of the fevered pox, too soon. Now I seek old people, to learn from them, but they're few, and mostly they don't know. Our children are taught reservation English, and the Seven Tents of Wisdom are gone.'

He was saying he had no medical schools to send letters of application to, Shaman realized. The Sauks and the Mesquakies were a remnant, robbed of their religion, their medicine, and their past.

He had a brief terrifying vision of a green-skinned horde sweeping down on the earth's white race and leaving only a few haunted survivors with nothing but rumours of a former civilization, and the faintest echoes of Hippocrates, and Galen, and Avicenna, and Jehovah, and Apollo, and Jesus.

It seemed as though the entire village heard of the child's birth almost at once. They weren't a demonstrative people, but Shaman was aware of their approval as he walked among them. Charles Keyser came to him and confided that the girl's case was similar to the childbirth that had killed his wife the previous year. 'The doctor didn't get there in time. The only woman there was my mother, and she didn't know any more than I did.'

'You mustn't get to blaming yourself. Sometimes we just can't save somebody. Did the baby die too?'

Keyser nodded.

'You have other children?'

'Two girls and a boy.'

Shaman suspected that one of the reasons Keyser had come to Tama was that he was looking for a wife. The Tama Indians seemed to know and like him. Several times people who passed them greeted him, calling him Charlie Farmer.

'Why do they call you that? Aren't they farmers too?'

Keyser grinned. 'Not my kind. My daddy left me forty acres of the blackest Iowa soil you ever did see. I till eighteen acres and plant most of it in winter wheat.

'When I first came here, I tried to show these people how to plant. Took me a while to understand they don't want a white man's farm. The men who sold them this land must have thought they were cheating them, because the soil's poor. But they pile brush and weeds and garbage on small gardens and let them rot out, sometimes for years. Then they put down seeds, using planting sticks instead of ploughs. The gardens give them plenty of food. The land is full of small game, and the Iowa River gives good fishing.'

'They really have the old-time life they came here looking for,' Shaman said.

Keyser nodded. 'Sleep Walker says he's asked you to do some more doctoring. It would please me to help you, Dr Cole.'

Shaman already had Rachel and Sleep Walker to assist him. But it occurred to him that although Keyser looked like the other inhabitants of Tama, he wasn't fully comfortable, and perhaps needed the company of other outsiders. So he told the farmer he'd appreciate his help.

The four of them made a strange little caravan as they went from cabin to cabin, but soon it was obvious they complemented one another. The medicine man gained them acceptance and chanted his prayers. Rachel carried a bag of boiled sweets and was especially good at gaining the confidence of children, and Charlie Keyser's big hands had the strength and gentleness that enabled him to hold someone still when steadiness was required.

Shaman pulled a number of rotten teeth and was treated to the sight of patients spitting stringy blood, but smiling because a source of ongoing torture was suddenly gone.

He lanced boils, he removed a blackened infected toe, and Rachel was kept busy listening with the stethoscope to the chests of coughers. Some of them he dosed with syrups, but others had consumption, and he was forced to tell Sleep Walker there was nothing that could be done for them. They also saw half a dozen men and several women who were stuporous with alcohol, and Sleep Walker said there were others who would be drunk if they could get the whisky.

Shaman was aware that far more red men had been wiped out by white man's diseases than by bullets. Smallpox, especially, had laid waste to the woodland and plains tribes, and he had brought with him to Tama a small wooden box half-filled with cowpox scabs.

Sleep Walker was plainly interested when Shaman told him he had medicine to prevent smallpox. But Shaman took great pains to explain exactly what was involved. He would scratch their arms and insert tiny pieces of cowpox scab into the wound. A red, itchy blister would develop, the size of a small pea. It would turn into a grey sore shaped like a navel, with a large area around it that was red, hard, and hot. After the inoculations, most of the people would be ill for about three days with cowpox, a far milder and more benign disease than smallpox, but one that would provide immunity from the deadly disease. Those inoculated would most likely have headaches and fevers. After the brief illness, the sore would become larger and darker as it dried, until the scab dropped off at about the twenty-first day, leaving a pink, pitted scar.

Shaman told Sleep Walker to explain this to the people and determine if they wanted to be treated. The medicine man was gone only a short time. Everyone wanted to be protected from smallpox, he reported, and so they settled down to the task of inoculating the entire community.

It was Sleep Walker's job to keep a line of people moving toward the white doctor and to make certain they knew what to expect. Rachel sat on a tree stump and used two scalpels to shave very small pieces from the cowpox scabs in the small wooden box. Whenever a patient reached Shaman, Charlie Keyser would take the person's left hand and raise it, exposing the inner part of the upper arm, the place that was least likely to suffer accidental bumping or scraping. Shaman used a pointed scalpel to make shallow, scarifying cuts in the arm, and then placed a tiny bit of the scabrous material into each cut.

It wasn't complicated, but it had to be done with care, and the line moved slowly. When finally the sun was setting, Shaman called a halt. A quarter of the people of Tama still had to be inoculated, but he told them the doctor's office was closed and to come back in the morning.

Sleep Walker had the instincts of a successful Baptist preacher, and that night he called the people together to honour the visitors. A celebration fire was built and lighted in the clearing, and the people gathered about it, seated on the ground.

Shaman sat on Sleep Walker's right. Little Dog sat between Shaman and Rachel, so he could translate for them. Shaman saw that Charlie was sitting with a slender smiling woman, and Little Dog told him she was a widow who had two small boys.

Sleep Walker asked that Dr Cole tell them about the woman who had been their shaman, Makwa-ikwa.

Shaman was aware that undoubtedly everyone there knew more about the massacre at Bad Axe than he did.

What had happened where the Bad Axe River met the Mississippi must have been described to them around thousands of fires, and would continue to be. But he told them that among those killed by the Long Knives had been a man named Green Buffalo, whose name Sleep Walker translated as Ashtibugwa-gupichee, and a woman named Union-of-Rivers, Matapya. He told how their daughter of ten years, Nishwri Kekawi, Two Skies, had taken her baby brother beyond the fire of the United States Army's rifles and cannon by swimming down *Masesibowi*, while holding the soft flesh of the infant's neck in her teeth to keep him from drowning.

Shaman told how the girl Two Skies had found her sister Tall Woman, and how the three children had hidden in the brush like hares until the soldiers had discovered them. And how a soldier had taken the bleeding baby away and he had never been seen again.

And he told them that the two Sauk girls were carried off to a Christian school in Wisconsin, and that Tall Woman had been impregnated by a missionary and was last seen in 1832, when she was taken to become a servant in a white farm beyond Fort Crawford. And that the girl named Two Skies had escaped from the school and made her way to Prophets-town, where the shaman White Cloud, Wabokieshiek, had taken her into his lodge and guided her through the Seven Tents of Wisdom and given her a new name, Makwa-ikwa, the Bear Woman.

And that Makwa-ikwa had been the shaman of her people until she was raped and murdered by three white men in Illinois, in 1851.

The people listened soberly, but nobody wept. They were accustomed to stories of horror about those they loved.

They passed a water-drum from hand to hand until it reached Sleep Walker. It wasn't Makwa's water drum, which had disappeared when the Sauks had left Illinois, but Shaman saw that it was similar. They had passed a single stick along with the drum, and now Sleep Walker knelt in front of the drum and began to bear it, in bursts of four rhythmic strokes, and to chant.

Ne-nye-ma-wa-wa,
Ne-nye-ma-wa-wa,
Ne-nye-ma-wa-wa.
Ke-ta-ko-ko-na-na.
I beat it four times,
I beat it four times,
I beat it four times,
I beat our drum four times.

Shaman looked around and saw that the people sang with
the medicine man and that many of them were holding
gourds in both hands and shaking them in time to the music,
the way Shaman had shaken the marble-filled cigar box in
music class when he was a boy.

Ke-te-ma-ga-yo-se lye-ya-ya-ni,
Ke-te-ma-ga-yo-se lye-ya-ya-ni,
Me-to-se-ne-ni-o lye-ya-ya-ni,
Ke-te-ma-ga-yo-se lye-ya-ya-ni.
Bless us when you come,
Bless us when you come,
The people, when you come,
Bless us when you come.

Shaman leaned over and placed his hand on the water drum
just below the hide cover. When Sleep Walker struck it, it
was like holding thunder between his palms. He watched
Sleep Walker's mouth and saw with pleasure that the chant
was now one he knew, one of Makwa's songs, and he sang
along with them,

. . . Wi-a-ya-ni,
Ni-na ne-gi-se ke-wi-to-se-me-ne ni-na.
. . . Wherever you are going,
I walk with you, my son.

Someone came with a log and threw it on the fire, sending
a column of yellow sparks swirling into the black sky. The

radiance of the fire mingled with the heat of the night and made him dizzy and faint, ready to see visions. He looked for his wife, concerned for her, and saw that Rachel's mother would have been furious at her appearance. She was bareheaded, her hair was mussed and awry, her face was shiny with sweat, and her eyes were gleaming with delight. She had never seemed more womanly to him, more human, or more desirable. She saw his glance and smiled as she leaned past Little Dog to speak. A hearing person would have lost her words in the booming of the drum and the chanting, but Shaman had no trouble in reading her lips. *It's as good as seeing a buffalo!*

The next morning, Shaman slipped away early without waking his wife and bathed in the Iowa River while swallows swooped to feed and tiny fingerlings with dull gold bodies darted in the water at his feet.

It was a little after sunup. Children already called and hooted to one another in the village, and as he went past the houses he saw barefoot women and a few men planting their garden patches in the morning cool. At the edge of the village he came face-to-face with Sleep Walker and the two of them stood comfortably and conversed like a pair of country squires meeting during their morning constitutionals.

Sleep Walker asked him questions about Makwa's burial and grave. Shaman wasn't comfortable about answering. 'I was only a boy when she died. I don't remember a lot,' he said. But from his reading of the journals he was able to say that Makwa's grave had been dug in the morning, and she'd been buried in the afternoon, in her best blanket. Her feet had pointed west. The tail of a buffalo cow had been buried with her.

Sleep Walker nodded approvingly. 'What is located ten steps northwest of her grave?'

Shaman stared. 'I don't remember. I don't know.'

The medicine man's face was intent. The old man in Missouri, the one who had been almost a shaman, had taught him about the deaths of shamans, he said. He explained that wherever a shaman is buried, four *watawino-nas*, the imps of wickedness, take up residence ten steps northwest of the grave. The *watawinonas* take turns being awake – one imp is always awake while the other three asleep. They can't harm the shaman, Sleep Walker said, but while they are allowed to remain there, she can't use her powers to aid living people who ask for her help.

Shaman stifled a sigh. Perhaps if he'd grown up believing these things, he could summon more tolerance. But during the night he had been awake wondering what was happening to his patients. And now he wanted to finish his work here and start home early enough so they could camp for the night at the good river cove where they had camped on the way up.

'To drive away the *watawinonas*,' Sleep Walker said, 'you have to find their sleeping place and burn it.'

'Yes. I'll do that,' Shaman said shamelessly, and Sleep Walker appeared relieved.

Little Dog came by and asked if he could take Charlie Farmer's place when the arm-scratching resumed. He said Keyser had left Tama the night before, right after the fire had been allowed to die.

Shaman was disappointed Keyser hadn't said goodbye. But he nodded to Little Dog and said that would be fine.

They began early to do the rest of the inoculations. It went a little faster than the day before, because Shaman had grown adept with practice. They were almost finished when a pair of bay horses pulled a farm wagon into the village clearing. Keyser was driving, and there were three children in the back of the wagon, gazing at the Sauks and the Mesquakies with great interest.

'I'd appreciate it if you'd scratch them agains the pox too,' Charlie said, and Shaman said he'd be glad to.

When the rest of the people and the three children had been inoculated, Charlie helped Shaman and Rachel gather up their things.

'I would like to bring my children to visit the shaman's grave sometime,' he said. Shaman told him they'd be welcome.

641

It took little time to pack Ulysses. They received a gift from Climbing Squirrel's husband, Shemago, the Lance, who came with three large whisky jugs full of maple syrup, which they were happy to receive. The jugs were tied together with the same kind of vine that had made Sleep Walker's snake. When Shaman lashed them to Ulysses' pack, it appeared that he and Rachel were on their way to an enormous celebration.

He shook hands with Sleep Walker and told him they'd return the following spring. Then he shook hands with Charlie, and with Snapping Turtle, and with Little Dog.

'Now you are *Cawso wabeskiou*,' Little Dog said.

Cawso Wabeskiou, the White Shaman. It gave Shaman pleasure, because he knew that Little Dog wasn't simply using his nickname.

Many of the people raised their hands, and so did Rachel and Shaman as they and the three horses went down the road along the river, out of Tama.

74

The Early Riser

For four days after they reached home, Shaman paid the price exacted of physicians who have taken a holiday. His dispensary was crowded with patients every morning, and each afternoon and evening he visited the homebound patients who were his responsibility, to return to the Geiger house late at night, and tired.

But by his fifth day home, a Saturday, the tide of patients had ebbed until he was more or less normally busy, and on Sunday morning he awoke in Rachel's room to the delicious realization that he had a breathing space. As usual, he was up before anyone else, and he gathered his clothes and carried them downstairs, where he dressed quietly in the parlour before letting himself out the front door.

He walked down the Long Path, stopping in the woods where Oscar Ericsson's labourers had cleared a site for the new house and barn. It wasn't the spot where Rachel had stood as a girl and yearned; unfortunately, the dreams of young girls don't take drainage into account, and Ericsson had inspected that site and shaken his head. They'd settled on a more suitable place a hundred yards away, which Rachel declared was close enough to her dream. Shaman had asked permission to buy the building lot, and Jay insisted it was a wedding gift. But he and Jay were treating one another with warmth and exquisite consideration these days, and the matter would be settled gently.

When he reached the site of the hospital, he saw that the cellar hole was almost completely dug. Surrounding it, piles of dirt made a landscape of giant anthills. The hole looked smaller than he had imagined the hospital building, but Ericsson had said that the hole always looked smaller. The foundation would be of grey stone quarried beyond Nauvoo, taken up the Mississippi on flatboats, and brought here from Rock Island by oxcart, a dangerous prospect that made Shaman fret, but which the contractor faced with equanimity.

He walked down to the Cole house, which Alex soon would leave. Then he took the Short Path, trying to imagine it being used by patients who would come to the clinic by boat. Certain changes had to be made. He contemplated the sweat lodge, which suddenly was in the wrong place. He decided to make a careful sketch of the placement of each flat rock, and then take up the rocks and rebuild the sweat lodge behind the new barn, so Joshua and Hattie would have the experience of knowing what it was like to sit in the remarkable heat until it was impossible not to run into the redeeming waters of the river.

When he turned to Makwa's grave, he saw that the wooden marker had become so cracked and weather-bleached that the rune-like markings no longer could be detected. The inscriptions were preserved in one of the journals, and he determined to get a more permanent marker and to place some sort of barrier around the grave, so it wouldn't be disturbed.

Spring weeds had made inroads. As he pulled bluestem grass and prairie dock that had worked its way between the clumps of day lilies, he found himself telling Makwa that some of her people were safe in Tama.

The cold anger that he'd felt here, whether or not it had come from deep within himself, was gone. All he could feel now was quietude. But . . .

There was something.

He stood and fought the impulse, for a while. Then he located true northwest and began to walk from the grave,

644

counting his steps.

When he had gone ten paces, he was in the middle of the ruins of the *hedonoso-te*. The longhouse had deteriorated through the years and now was a low, uneven pile of narrow logs and strips of mouldering tree bark, with cordgrass and wild indigo poking through.

It didn't make sense, he told himself, to spruce up the grave, move the sweat lodge, and leave this unsightly heap. He walked down the path to the barn, where there was a large crock of lamp oil. It was almost full, and he carried it back and emptied it. The material in the pile was wet with dew but his sulphur match caught the first time he tried, and the oil ignited and flared.

In a moment, the entire *hedonoso-te* was being consumed by leaping blue and yellow flames, and a column of dark grey smoke rose straight up and then was bent by the breeze and swept out over the river.

An acrid eruption of black smoke spewed like a bursting boil, and the first demon, the one who was awake, surged upward and away. Shaman imagined a lonely furious demonic screaming, a hissing cry. One by one, the other three creatures of wickedness, so rudely awakened, lifted off like hungry birds of prey abandoning delectable flesh, *watawinonas* roiling elsewhere on wings of smoky rage.

From the nearby grave Shaman sensed something like a sigh.

He stood close and felt the lick of the heat, like the fire in a Sauk celebration ceremony, and imagined what this place had been like when young Rob J. Cole saw it for the first time, unbroken prairie running all the way to the woods and the river. And he thought of others who had lived here, Makwa, and Moon, and Comes Singing. And Alden. As the fire burned lower and lower, he sang in his mind, *Tti-la-ye ke-wi-ta-mo-ne i-no-ki-i-i, ke-te-ma-ga-vo-se*. Ghosts, I speak to you now, send your blessings to me.

Soon it was a thin layer of residue from which wisps of smoke rose. He knew the grass would move in, and there would be no trace of where the *hedonoso-te* had been.

When it was safe to leave the fire, he returned the crock

to the barn and started back. On the Long Path he met a grim, small figure looking for him. She was trying to walk away from a little boy who had fallen and scraped his knee. The little boy limped after her doggedly. He was crying, and his nose was running.

Shaman used his handkerchief on Joshua's nose and kissed his knee next to the bloody part. He promised he'd make it better when they got home. He seated Hattie behind his neck with her legs over his shoulders, and he scooped Joshua up and began to walk. These were the only imps in the world that mattered to him, these two good imps who had claimed his soul. Hattie tugged at his ears to make him go faster, and he trotted like Trude. When she yanked his ears so hard they hurt, he pinned Joshua against her legs so she wouldn't fall off, and he began to canter like Boss. And then he was galloping, galloping in time to a perfectly hidden melody – fine and glorious new music that only he was able to hear.

Acknowledgments and Notes

Sauks and Mesquakies still live in Tama, Iowa, on land they own. Their original eighty-acre purchase has been added to considerably. Some five hundred and seventy-five Native Americans now live on three thousand five hundred acres along the Iowa River. In the summer of 1987 I visited the settlement at Tama with my wife, Lorraine. Don Wanatee, then the executive director of the Tribal Council, and Leonard Young Bear, a noted Native American artist, answered my questions patiently. In subsequent conversations, so did Muriel Racehill, current executive director, and Charlie Old Bear.

I have tried to present the events of Black Hawk's War as close to history as possible. The warrior leader known as Black Hawk – the literal translation of his Sauk name, Makataime-shekiakiak, is Black Sparrow Hawk – is a historic figure. The shaman Wabokieshiek, White Cloud, also was a living man. In this book he evolves into a fictional character after he meets the girl who is to become Makwa-ikwa, the Bear Woman.

For much of the Sauk and Mesquakie vocabulary utilized in this novel, I relied heavily on a number of early publications of the Smithsonian Institution's Bureau of American Ethnology.

The early days of the charitable organization known as the

Boston Dispensary were much as I have depicted them. I have exercised an author's licence in the matter of the salaries of the visiting physicians. Although the pay scale is authentic, compensation didn't begin until 1842, several years after Rob J. is shown as salaried to attend the poor. Until 1842, being a physician at the Boston Dispensary was a kind of unpaid internship. Conditions among the impoverished were so difficult, however, that the young doctors rebelled. First they demanded payment, and then they refused to continue visiting patients in the slums. Instead, the Boston Dispensary moved into quarters and became a clinic, the patients coming to the doctors. By the time I covered the Boston Dispensary in the late 1950s and early 1960s as science editor of the old Boston *Herald*, it had grown into an established hospital-clinic and was in a loose administrative association with the Pratt Diagnostic Clinic, the Floating Hospital for Infants and Children, and Tufts Medical School, as the Tufts-New England Medical Center. In 1965 the component hospitals were united and absorbed into the present distinguished institution known as the New England Medical Center Hospitals. David W. Nathan, former archivist at the medical centre, and Kevin Richardson of the medical centre's Department of External Affairs furnished me with information and historical material.

While writing *Shaman*, I found an unexpected load of information and insights right at home, and I am grateful to close friends, neighbours, and fellow townspeople.

Edward Gulick talked with me about pacifism and told me about Elmira, New York. Elizabeth Gulick shared thoughts about the Society of Friends and allowed me to read some of her own writings about Quaker worship. Don Buckloh, a resource conservationist with the US Department of Agriculture, answered questions about early Midwestern farms. His wife, Denise Jane Buckloh, the former Sister Miriam of the Eucharist, OCD, gave me details about Catholicism and the daily life of a convent nun.

Donald Fitzgerald lent me reference books and presented me with a copy of the Civil War diary of his great-grandfather John Fitzgerald, who at sixteen had walked

648

home from Rowe, Massachusetts, to Greenfield, twenty-five miles down the Mohawk Trail, to enlist in the Union Army. John Fitzgerald fought with the 27th Massachusetts Volunteers until captured by Confederates, and he survived several prison camps, including Andersonville.

Theodore Bobetsky, a lifelong farmer whose land abuts ours, gave me information about butchering. Attorney Stewart Eisenberg discussed with me the system of bail utilized by nineteenth-century courts, and Nina Heiser allowed me to borrow her collection of books on Native Americans.

Walter A. Whitney Jr. gave me a copy of a letter written April 22, 1862, by Addison Graves, to his father, Ebenezer Graves Jr., of Ashfield, Massachusetts. The letter is an account of Addison Graves' experience as a volunteer nurse on the hospital ship *War Eagle*, which carried Union wounded from Pittsburgh Landing, Tennessee, to Cincinnati. It was the basis for Chapter 48 in which Rob J. Cole serves as a volunteer surgeon on the hospital ship *War Hawk*.

Beverly Presley, map and geography librarian at Clark University, calculated the distance travelled during the voyages of the historic and fictional hospital ships.

The faculty of the Classics Department at the College of the Holy Cross assisted me with several Latin translations.

Richard M. Jakowski, VMD, associate professor in the Department of Pathology at the Tufts-New England Veterinary Medical Center, in North Grafton, Massachusetts, answered my questions about the anatomy of dogs.

I am grateful to the University of Massachusetts at Amherst for continuing to grant me faculty privileges to all of its libraries, and to Edla Holm of the Interlibrary Loans Office at that university. I thank the American Antiquarian Society, in Worcester, Massachusetts, for giving me access to its collections.

I received help and materials from Richard J. Wolfe, curator of rare books and manuscripts and Joseph Garland Librarian at the Countway Medical Library of Harvard Medical School, and I enjoyed long-term loans from the Lamar Soutter Library of the University of Massachusetts

Medical School, in Worcester. I also thank the reference
staffs of the Boston Public Library and the Boston Athenaeum for their help.

Bernard Wax, of the American Jewish Historical Society at
Brandeis University, supplied me with information and
research regarding Company C of the 82nd Illinois, 'the
Jewish company'.

My resource concerning the Yiddish language was my
mother-in-law, Dorothy Seay.

In the summer of 1989 my wife and I visited several Civil
War battlefields. In Charlottesville, Professor Ervin L. Jordan
Jr, archivist at the Alderman Library of the University of
Virginia, showed me the hospitality of that library and
provided me with information about the hospitals of the
Confederate Army. Civil War medical conditions, battles,
and events in *Shaman* are based on history. The regiments
with which Rob J. Cole served are fictitious.

During much of the writing of this book, Ann N. Lilly was
a staff member at both the Forbes Library in Northampton
and the Western Massachusetts Regional Library System in
Hadley, Massachusetts. She often conducted title searches
for me, and hand-carried books from both institutions to her
Ashfield home. I also thank Barbara Zalenski of the Belding
Memorial Library of Ashfield, and the staff of the Field
Memorial Library of Conway, Massachusetts, for their help
with research.

The Planned Parenthood Federation of America sent me
material about the manufacture and use of condoms during
the 1800s. At the Center for Disease Control, in Atlanta,
Georgia, Robert Cannon, MD, gave me information about
the treatment of syphilis during the period of my story, and
the American Parkinson Disease Association, Inc, furnished
me with information about that disease.

William McDonald, a graduate student in the Department
of Metallurgy at the Massachusetts Institute of Technology,
told me about metals used to make instruments during the
Civil War era.

Jason Geiger's analysis of what would have happened if
Lincoln had allowed the Confederacy to break away from the

Union without war, as expressed in Chapter 72, is based on the opinion of the late psychographer Gamaliel Bradford in his biography of Robert E. Lee (*Lee the American*, Houghton Mifflin, Boston, 1912).

I thank Dennis B. Gjerdingen, president of the Clarke School for the Deaf, in Northampton, Massachusetts, for granting me access to the staff and library of that school. Ana D. Grist, former librarian at the Clarke School, allowed me to borrow books for long periods of time. I am especially grateful to Marjorie E. Magner, who has spent forty-three years teaching deaf children. She provided me with a number of insights and also read the book manuscript to ensure its accuracy about deafness.

Several Massachusetts physicians have been generous in helping me with this book. Albert B. Giknis, MD, the medical examiner of Franklin County, Massachusetts, discussed rape and murder with me at length, and allowed me to borrow his pathology texts. Joel F. Moorhead, MD, outpatient medical director of the Spaulding Hospital and clinical instructor in rehabilitation medicine at Tufts Medical School, answered questions about injury and disease. Wolfgang G. Gilliar, DO, programme director for rehabilitation medicine at the Greenery Rehabilitation Center and instructor in rehabilitation medicine at Tufts Medical School, talked with me about physical medicine. My family internist, Barry E. Poret, MD, gave me information and made available his own medical books. Stuart R. Jaffee, MD, senior urologist at St Vincent Hospital in Worcester, Massachusetts, and assistant professor of urology at the University of Massachusetts Medical School, answered my questions about lithocenosis and read the book manuscript for medical accuracy.

I am grateful to my agent, Eugene H. Winick of McIntosh & Otis, Inc, for his friendship and enthusiasm, and to Dr Karl Blessing, Geschaftsführer at the Droemer Knaur Publishing Company in Munich. *Shaman* is the second book in a projected trilogy about the Cole medical dynasty. Dr Blessing's early faith in the first book of the trilogy, *The Physician*, helped it to become a bestseller in Germany and other countries and greatly encouraged me during the

651

writing of *Shaman*. For their efforts on behalf of this book I thank Peter Mayer, Elaine Koster, and Robert Dressen of Penguin Books USA. Raymond Phillips did a wonderful job of copy-editing.

In many ways, *Shaman* was a family project. My daughter Lise Gordon edited *Shaman* before it reached my publishers. She is meticulous, tough even with her own father, and wonderfully encouraging. My wife, Lorraine, helped me prepare the manuscript and, as usual, gave me her love and total support. My daughter Jamie Beth Gordon, a photographer, eased my fear of the camera during a special and hilarious shoot, when she took my pictures for use on the book's jackets and in publishers' catalogues. She sustained me with her notes and cards. And the frequent long-distance calls from my son, Michael Seay Gordon, invariably came when I needed the lift he always brings.

These four people are the most important part of my life, and they have increased, at least tenfold, my joy in finishing this novel.

Ashfield, Massachusetts
November 20, 1991

652